O SHEPHERD, SPEAK!

THE "LANNY BUDD" NOVELS

IN ORDER OF PUBLICATION

World's End

Between Two Worlds

Dragon's Teeth

Wide Is the Gate

Presidential Agent

Dragon Harvest

A World to Win

Presidential Mission

One Clear Call

O Shepherd, Speak!

O SHEPHERD, SPEAK!

Upton Sinclair

The Viking Press · New York

1949

Acknowledgments

A HISTORICAL novelist who was not at the scene is dependent upon records for his facts. The present writer gratefully acknowledges help from the following worth-while books: *Lucky Forward,* by Robert S. Allen (Vanguard); *Reilly of the White House,* by Michael F. Reilly and William J. Slocum (Simon & Schuster); *Salt Mines and Castles,* by Thomas C. Howe, Jr. (Bobbs-Merrill); *Nuremberg Diary,* by G. M. Gilbert (Farrar, Straus); *Alsos,* by Samuel A. Goudsmit (Shumann); *Roosevelt and Hopkins,* by Robert E. Sherwood (Harper).

Personal thanks are due to some of these authors for personal help. Dr. Goudsmit, Nobel Prize-winning physicist, read and checked every word of this large manuscript; Dr. Howe, director of the Palace of the Legion of Honor, the municipal art museum of San Francisco, read all those pages having to do with his adventures in Europe; Robert Sherwood read the chapter having to do with the death of Roosevelt; Dr. Gilbert read the two chapters having to do with the Nürnberg trials; Colonel Allen answered questions, as did a number of other Army officers who are named in the story, including General Leslie A. Groves, who read and checked the chapter having to do with the New Mexico bomb test.

In this, which I hope will be the last volume of the series, I owe tribute to friends who read every one of its more than three million words and helped me avoid errors. S. K. Ratcliffe, English journalist and lecturer in America, knows his native land and its language better than any other man I know. R. E. Engelsberg, onetime deputy finance minister of Austria and for years a refugee in Pasadena, knows Europe and its major languages. Martin Birnbaum, art expert, and my school-mate and violin teacher, knows all the arts, and consented to play the role of Zoltan in these books. And Ben Huebsch, best publisher any author could have or wish for, read *World's End* in forty-eight hours and accepted it by telegraph; since then he has read three hundred and twenty-one chapters, one by one, and kept up my spirits for ten years. Also, you will find him as a character—has any novelist hitherto used his publisher as a character? (If so, perhaps it was not with praise.)

v

Finally, no *envoi* would be complete without a tribute to my wife, Mary Craig Sinclair. Her health has not permitted her to read three million words; her job has been to keep her husband alive and to exercise supervision by watching the mail and the clippings. By temperament, she agrees with the critics; by love and prayer she has kept the Lanny Budd books in the paths of righteousness. She thinks the author makes too many excuses for his erring characters; but she admits that perhaps the readers require that. Our address is Monrovia, California, and you may write and tell her if the spirit moves you.

Contents

Book One:
The Mighty Scourge of War

Book Two:
Love, and Man's Unconquerable Mind

Book Three:
Come the Three Corners of the World in Arms

Book Four:
Tears from the Depth of Some Divine Despair

Book Five:
Appeal from Tyranny to God

Book Six:
'Tis Excellent to Have a Giant's Strength

Book Seven:
Thy Friends Are Exaltations

Book Eight:
Tell Truth and Shame the Devil

Book Nine:
Truth Crushed to Earth Shall Rise

Book Ten:
He Shall Stand before Kings

Appendix

BOOK ONE

The Mighty Scourge of War

1

Treasures on Earth

I

LANNY BUDD, arriving in Paris in the middle of November 1944, was driven through pelting rain to the Crillon, a sumptuous hotel which was history to him, and also biography from his earliest days. Robbie Budd, then a munitions salesman, had made it his headquarters on his innumerable trips to Europe, and Lanny as a toddler had been brought here to see his father and to learn by example how to be a perfect little gentleman: to walk sedately, to speak quietly, to listen to conversation, learn the meaning of long words in several languages and appreciate the relative importance of numerous titled and wealthy persons. From one of the hotel's broad windows he had watched the beginning of World War I, the troops marching to the railroad stations, cheered and cheering, confident of early victory; from that sight he had turned back to serve as an emergency secretary, fourteen years old, but able to decode cablegrams and to answer the telephone and explain firmly that Budd Gunmakers was booked for two years ahead and had absolutely nothing that it could sell to the most hard-pressed European nation.

Yes, and from another of these windows the mature Lanny had looked out upon what he had believed was the beginning of social revolution in Paris; the organized mobs filling the immense Place de la Concorde and forcing their way across the bridge to the Palais Bourbon, where the Chamber of Deputies was in session. That had been in 1937, and three years later the Nazis had come, and Lanny, posing as a convert to the cause, had met Hitler here in the hour of his greatest glory. Now the wheel of fortune had made another half turn, and the Führer was back in Berlin, cowering in his bomb shelter; the Americans had the Crillon, and the spacious lobby was full of uniforms, male and female. Lanny was wearing one of them, for he was now a colonel in the Army, of what was called an "assimilated rank"; he received the pay of a colonel, the food and shelter of a colonel, but he couldn't give military orders. The Army needed civilians, specialists of many sorts, and this was the method of getting them something to eat and a place to sleep.

Lanny's first thought upon coming down at Orly Airport had been to grab a newspaper and see what this biggest of all American armies was doing now. There was a communiqué—always a couple of days behind the event. General Patton's Third Army had begun an offensive in front of Metz; something that Lanny had been expecting and had helped to prepare. A couple of months ago he had been sent to Nancy, headquarters of the Third, to interview a captured German general and persuade him to reveal the secrets of the fortifications. Now the long-prepared offensive was under way in freezing rain and primordial sticky mud. Lanny, who had left the place with a bad cold, was content to read about it in a Paris newspaper and hear about it from friends in the Crillon.

II

His first thought was of his mail. There were letters, including one in the handwriting of his wife; he opened it, and it drove the war entirely out of his thoughts. Laurel had gone to the Riviera to gather material for a magazine article about the American Army there and how the residents had taken their liberation. Incidentally, she was going to see what had happened to Bienvenu, the villa which belonged to Lanny's mother.

It was about this that Lanny was expecting to read, but there were only two lines on the subject. "The place is dirty and uncared for, but not seriously harmed. I will report later. This is just a hurried line to give you an extraordinary item of news. I got it from Margy, Lady Eversham-Watson, who called me on the telephone soon after I entered—she is living near by. She asked after you, and I told her you were expected back from Washington; then she asked, 'Does he know about Emily Chattersworth's will?' I said I was fairly sure you didn't, and she told me that Emily had left you a good part of her estate, more than a million dollars. She phrased it, 'in trust, to be used in his judgment for the prevention of future wars.' I made Margy repeat the words, and she said, 'What do you suppose Lanny will make of that?' All Cannes is full of gossip about it, and Margy is coming over to collect some from me—on a bicycle, if you can imagine it! There is no other way for even an elderly countess to get about. I had a chance to buy a man's for only three thousand francs, and now I am cutting

up one of the dark blue window curtains from your bedroom to make
a pair of slacks.

"I will do my best to get a copy of the will and send it to you. I
think you had better come down here if it is at all possible. I suppose that a million dollars is important, even though you may not
know what to do with it. That is the case with most of the people we
know who are so fortunate, or unfortunate, as to own that much. I
forgot to mention that Margy was among the British residents interned by the Germans. They let her have small amounts of her
own money to buy her food. She must be close to seventy, and her
hair has turned entirely white."

So there was the son of Budd-Erling, with something to occupy his
spare thoughts for many a day. He had seen enough of large sums of
money to know that whereas you might think you were managing
them, in reality they would be managing you. It was a kind of doom
that his old friend had pronounced upon him. She had threatened it,
and had talked about it; but he had learned that people who possess
great wealth almost invariably use it to buy personal esteem and attention. If they do not get it, they change their minds and their wills.
Lanny had gone off on his mysterious errands, leaving his mother's
closest friend to die alone.

The chatelaine of Sept Chênes, however, had been a person of firm
mind. She had known Lanny since his infancy, and had loved him as
a son. She had left him a million dollars "in trust," and charged him
with the task of ending war all over the world—no less! The trustee
couldn't keep from smiling to himself as he thought of the many
dollars he knew of whose owners were interested in making war, or
at any rate were willing to make war in order to protect themselves
and their privileges. Millions of dollars, yes, and of pounds and francs
and marks, and even roubles, alas! How they would hate anyone who
tried to interfere with them, even by speaking the truth about them!

Lanny thought about this deceased *grande dame*—"good old Emily,"
he had called her, in the informal fashion of his generation. She had
been a sort of godmother to him ever since he was born and before
that. Robbie Budd, European representative of Budd Gunmakers, had
confided to her that he was in love with a painter's model in Paris, an
American girl whom he couldn't marry because some malicious person
had sent his grim old Puritan father a photograph of a painting of this
girl in the nude. Robbie had set her up in a villa on the Cap d'Antibes
and had told everybody there that she was his wife. Emily had agreed
to protect her and had kept the secret. Now, forty-five years later,

Emily was dead, and had handed over to the next generation a burden which she had contemplated but had never had the courage to take upon her shoulders. The rich cling to their wealth, so often their only form of distinction; they part with it only when they set out for an unknown destination, by a train which carries no baggage compartment.

III

Lanny couldn't come to the Riviera. He wrote his wife that he was duty-bound; he couldn't say more, and she wouldn't expect it. He put the exciting thought of the bequest out of his mind and read the rest of his mail. A letter from Beauty, his mother, who was a refugee in Morocco and now wanted to come back to her home. Apparently she had heard nothing about Emily's action; her letter was mostly about the difficulties of getting transportation across the Mediterranean, and complaints concerning this war, so inconsiderate of the comfort and convenience of the leisure class.

There was a letter from Lanny's old friend Raoul Palma; Raoul was in Toulon, where he had been working with the underground, and now had come up to the surface with whoops. He was a lifelong Socialist, and was expecting to make a great French naval base over in the image of his own theories. But, alas, the American Army seemed to have no sympathy with social theories and desired only to get the port in order so that supplies could be brought in and entrained for the front. Most of Raoul's time was being given to hunting down collaborators and getting them into jail; also, to quarreling with the Communists, who would collaborate only on the terms of having their own way. A long letter, and not a very happy one, it gave the impression that postwar France was going on with the same party strife which had laid *la patrie* open to the Nazi-Fascists.

These thoughts Lanny also put out of his mind. All men and women who wore the uniform of the Armed Forces were supposed to have only one thought, to get on with the war. Lanny himself was here with three assignments, one general and two special. The general one was to collect and send to President Roosevelt any information which might be of use to him; the other two were to give advice and assistance to groups working in fields of which Lanny had special knowledge. One of these was the so-called "Roberts Commission," and the other was known by the code name of "Alsos," of which no explanation had been given to the assimilated colonel.

Lanny bummed a ride in the first staff car going out to Versailles, some twelve miles to the northwest. The wide boulevard led through the Bois and past Longchamps, where in happier days the youthful Lanny had attended fashionable horse races. In Versailles was the great palace which the Sun King had erected to his own glory, and facing it were the Grandes Ecuries, tremendous stables in which the divinely appointed ruler had housed his hundreds of horses. Long since, the building had been turned into offices, and on the mezzanine floor were two rooms, labeled on the door: "Monuments, Fine Arts, and Archives Section, Office of Military Government, G-5." To its own members, in a hurry, it was "Monuments."

Americans and British were working together; the Americans were mostly young fellows, graduates of the Fogg Museum and the Fine Arts Department of Harvard University. Lanny Budd, just forty-five, was an elder statesman to them. He had lived most of his life in Europe whereas they knew it only as tourists; he spoke French and German as a native whereas they had learned from books. He had been to every place they mentioned and seemed to know everybody they had ever heard of. Incredibly, he had been a friend of the Nazi lords and masters, and this would have made them suspicious, but for the fact that he carried a letter of credential from the President of the United States. In addition to that, he was good looking, suave, and agreeable; he had made money as an art expert whereas they, alas, had earned only the modest salaries of scholars, and now were on Army pay.

This agreeable gentleman would sit down with a group of them and answer a hundred questions in an evening, with a stenographer taking notes. He had met the heads of the Einsatzstab and many of their subordinates; he had sat in Karinhall and listened to their conversations; he had even bought paintings from them and placed them in America. He knew many of the wealthy art collectors in Paris and its environs, and if they had fled to California or the Argentine, he could suggest someone who would have their addresses. All over the world were plundered persons who hadn't yet learned that the Allies were going to restore their property; they had to be written to and invited to submit their claims.

For example, there was Mme. de Brousailles, née Olivie Hellstein, daughter of the great Jewish banking clan which had branches all over Europe. Emily Chattersworth had arranged for Lanny to be invited to Olivie's home, thinking that he might make the right sort of son-in-law for this family. During the war the clan had been scattered.

some of them murdered and all of them robbed; Olivie had sought refuge in Spain, and now she had come back to her palace. She was happy to receive the son of Budd-Erling and tell him how to reach the surviving members of her family and various other persons who had owned *objets d'art* and lost them. There was a French group co-operating with Monuments, exchanging data and ideas, and Lanny took along a representative of this group.

In Paris is a museum which was once the handball court of the play-ful monarchs, the Musée du Jeu de Paume. The Nazi plunderers had used it as a sort of clearing house, where their trophies were brought and exhibited to the privileged few. Hitler had come now and then; Hermann Göring had come frequently, in spite of his pressing duties as Air Marshal; they had chosen what they wanted and left the rest for the underlings. Lanny had met the heads of this Einsatzstab at Karin-hall and had been offered a million dollars' worth of its treasures in exchange for the small service of bringing to Göring the blueprints of the latest model of the Budd-Erling pursuit plane.

The large staff of the Musée had been mostly German, but several French employees had managed to win favor and be retained. One of these was secretly a member of the Resistance and had made it her business to smuggle out copies of the lists and records of the institu-tion, and even photographs of its employees, so that they could not change their names and hide. Lanny Budd, visiting Paris in his double role of art expert and Nazi sympathizer, had met this gray-haired lady, and each of them had felt a proper secret contempt for the other. Here they met again, and it took some persuading to convince the lady, now an officer in the French Army, that this rich and elegant American was not really a traitor and spy. "*Madame la capitaine,*" he told her, "have you not proved that it could be done?"

IV

Painting was one of Lanny's specialties; the other was science. He didn't really know anything about the latter subject, he would say, but had crammed for examinations, so that on trips into Germany he might try to find out what they were doing in the field of nuclear physics and of jet propulsion, and with the terrible V-2 rocket bombs which were now making life miserable for the people of London. To Paris had recently come a staff of real scientists and their helpers, whose duty it was to follow the Army into enemy territory and ferret out these secrets. Lanny didn't know any Greek, so the name Alsos remained a riddle to him.

The presidential agent had met some of these mystery men at Columbia University and had given them all the information he had. Now they were happy to have him turn up in Paris and reveal that his roving commission included assistance to them. They knew the names of the top atomic men in Germany whom they wished to find and interview; but some of these men might go into hiding and others might refuse to talk. There was another way to get information, and that was through the workers and technicians, without which no project of any size and importance could be carried on. The son of Budd-Erling, a Socialist sympathizer from his youth, had contacts with labor in Germany and might pick up many hints from such sources.

The young scientists of the Alsos mission were in an extremely anxious mood. Only their leader knew how far the Americans had progressed with the atom-splitting project, but they all knew that the Germans had begun their research at least two years ahead of the United States, and they all had a profound respect, even awe, of German scientific ability. It was Otto Hahn who had discovered the principle of atomic fission, and another German had published the first paper on the theory of the chain-reacting pile. The head of the German project was Werner Heisenberg, one of the greatest theoretical physicists in the world; for these reasons Alsos was prepared for any terrifying discovery, even for having an atom bomb dropped on their own heads when they ventured into Naziland.

Lanny did what he could to comfort them. He couldn't say, "I was sent into Germany to find out about their atomic work." He couldn't say, "I was briefed for two months by Professor Einstein." He could only say, vaguely, "I think it extremely unlikely that the Germans could have achieved a chain reaction without my having picked up some hint of it. Both Hitler and Göring are braggarts, and they cannot refrain from telling of the wonders they have up their sleeves. You know how Hitler has told the world about his *Wuwa*; and he told me in detail about his all-destroying 'high-pressure pump.'"

The young scientists knew all about these. *Wuwa* was short for *Wunderwaffe*—the "wonder weapon"—the rocket bombs which were now exploding over London; the Führer had been promising them for a year or two over the radio. As for the "high-pressure pump," that was the code name for an extraordinary concoction of Hitler's own, a huge steel tube like a stovepipe a hundred yards long; it was a gun, and fired a shell, and as the shell went through the barrel there were booster charges all along the way, to send it faster and faster. It was supposed to reach London. But the darn thing never had worked; the charges kept going off at the wrong time and blowing up the gun and the gunners. But Hitler couldn't give up; he so hated England, his thoughts kept going across that narrow body of water and wreaking cataclysms. At the moment there were thousands of laborers, badly needed in the *Armee,* working at underground installations for *Hochdruckpumpen* which would never get a shell across the Channel.

V

Georgie Patton's assault upon Metz had spread up and down the line and become a general winter offensive. Winter fighting is hard upon all armies, but would be harder upon the Germans because they lacked the elaborate equipment of the Americans. What they had was even more urgently needed on the Russian front, where there was a still bigger offensive, and where it never rained, only snowed, and men would freeze in part or in whole if they did not have warm clothing and other protection.

Presently came word that the American Seventh Army had taken Strasbourg, a great French city on the upper reaches of the Rhine. This was of importance to Alsos, for there was a famed university there, and it had a competent physics department—German for the past four years and part of a fifth. Alsos sent a representative, and first he telegraphed that he had been unable to locate any of the physicists; then came a second telegram—the nuclear laboratory had been situated in a wing of the Strasbourg Hospital, and its four physicists had been posing as physicians. Just a little matter of changing two letters in a word!

They were put under arrest—the head physicist in jail, so that he would have no chance to agree upon a story with the others. The Alsos men set out for Strasbourg, full of anticipation, hoping to find clues that would tell them what German science had achieved in one remote and difficult field. Prior to the past five years the nuclear men of all lands had been a tight little group of abstruse thinkers, exchanging reports, meeting in small conventions, having what amounted to a secret code which nobody else could understand. Now there would be a new sort of convention, in which four Germans would do the talking and as many Americans the listening.

Professor Goudsmit, head physicist of Alsos, invited the son of Budd-Erling to go along, and nothing could have pleased Lanny more. The party was flown to Strasbourg in very bad weather—no other sort was available; the operations at the front were semi-amphibious, there being so many swollen rivers and flooded fields to cross. The plane was a bucket-seat job, and you were strapped to a ring in the wall. Fortunately the flight took only a couple of hours, and they were set down safely at an airport with an inch or two of water on its surface. The Germans were just across the river; the great bridge had not been blown up, but was constantly being shelled, and now and then there were hit-and-run air raids—it was the fighting front.

The ancient city of Strasbourg was marked with a red circle on Lanny Budd's mental map, for at this bridge, eleven years ago, the Nazis had turned over to him the broken body of his boyhood friend Freddi Robin. It was in the Hôtel de la Ville-de-Paris that he had sat by the bedside of this young Socialist, weeping for man's cruelty to man, and preparing himself mentally for the role of secret agent against the Nazi beasts. Now the secrecy was over, and here was this swarming brown-clad Army, all over the airport and the city, disciplined, trained, and on its toes to get at the foe.

Lanny knew this part of the Force, the Seventh, for he had ridden with it all the way from St. Raphael on the Riviera by way of Grenoble to Lyon and beyond: a delightful trip along the foothills of the Alpes Basses et Hautes, interviewing German prisoners on the way and making reports on what he had been able to get out of them. It had been a combination of war and picnic, always in sound of the guns yet out of range; a sweet sort of revenge, satisfying yet amiable, for he never carried out any of the dire threats which he made to the enemy, and wouldn't have been permitted to do it even if he had wished to. Poor devils, they knew only what they had been taught— and what a new set of lessons they were learning! First the superiority of American arms, and then the superiority of American food, strangely known as "K-rations"!

VI

Now the presidential agent sat and listened while the American specialists questioned their German colleagues. Some of them had met in earlier days, and then they had been friends; now they were enemies— or were they? You could never be sure how any interview would turn out; some would be cautious and sly, while others would take the position that there had never been any war so far as scientists were concerned and that knowledge was free as it had always been. German scientists had received orders and had had to obey them, and surely nobody could hold them responsible for what use was made of their discoveries! That was up to the government.

The tactics of Alsos were to assent to all this and be friendly and casual. No German was to know that they were seeking knowledge of nuclear fission; the Alsos men were just ordinary scientists, interested in all new ideas and discoveries. The Germans were questioned closely but apparently didn't have much to tell, except the names of their colleagues who had fled: Weizsäcker, a leading theoretical physicist, and Haagen, who was a virus specialist, believed to be preparing dreadful diseases to be turned loose behind the American armies.

The invaders confiscated all the papers in the laboratory, and in Weizsäcker's office at the University. All night they sat studying these, by the light of candles and one compressed gas lamp. Planes flew overhead, and bombs and shells exploded; American mortars roared near by, but the scientists paid no heed, for they had come upon an alarming discovery, an envelope with the imprint: "The Representative of the Reichsmarshall for Nuclear Physics." The implications of this were obvious: a Reichsmarshall is the highest rank in the German military system, and if they had one of these in charge of nuclear physics they must have a colossal establishment, possibly even greater than that of the Americans; they might be producing bombs wholesale!

The son of Budd-Erling pointed out the obscurity in this title; it might just as well mean the Reichsmarshall's Representative for Nuclear Physics, which would mean one of Göring's assistants, and he might be a person of less importance than, for example, the Reichsmarshall's Representative for Stag Hunting. The American scientists drew an audible breath of relief.

They found still greater comfort before this night and early morning had passed, for in the Weizsäcker papers they got the information they were seeking. This Herr Professor Carl Friedrich Freiherr von Weizsäcker was an important person, and not merely in the field of physics; he was a Prussian aristocrat, son of a diplomat who had been Hitler's Undersecretary for Foreign Affairs. The son considered himself a privileged character, and perhaps that was why he had carried on elaborate correspondence with other German physicists concerning their most secret work. It took no skill in divination to know that "*Lieber* Walter" was Professor Gerlach and that "*Lieber* Werner" was Professor Heisenberg. Evidently it had never occurred to "*Lieber Carl Friedrich*" that American physicists might get to Strasbourg, and in his hurry to get out he must have forgotten these papers.

There was another professor, named Fleischmann, who had been even more indiscreet. He was a gossipy person who liked to record interesting events and personalities. He dated everything, which was a great help. He put down names and addresses of the leading physicists of Germany, and even the telephone numbers of secret laboratories. The Americans would have liked to call them up—if the Germans hadn't cut the lines across the river. Professor Fleischmann wrote in shorthand part of the time, but one of the Americans knew the Gabelsberger system, so that was easy. Sometimes he wrote formulas, and if they were wrong, this gave the Americans satisfaction and made up for the strain of reading by candlelight.

Here was the story of what the Germans had done with the *Kern*, as they call the nucleus. They knew a tremendous lot about it, but surely didn't know how to turn it into an explosive. They didn't even know what plutonium was—at any rate, their top men never mentioned it. They thought that a uranium pile in chain reaction would be a bomb! How they expected to transport that enormously heavy mass of metal and heavy water through the air they did not discuss, nor how they were going to keep the bomb from blowing up the laboratory. Now and then they mentioned the American efforts with a patronizing word; their certainty of their own superiority was most comforting to Alsos.

"This settles it," said Professor Goudsmit. "They haven't got the bomb, and won't have it in this war."

"Then perhaps we won't have to use it either," remarked one of the younger scientists wistfully.

Lanny permitted himself an indiscreet reply. "Don't fool yourself. If we get it we will surely use it."

The scientists looked unhappy. They were full of dread at the idea of what they were doing, creating this awful weapon and entrusting it to politicians and military men. They were making for themselves the same excuse the Germans all made.

VII

The party went back to Paris by motorcar, taking the captives along. One of them rode by Lanny's side, and they chatted agreeably—speaking English, because the German was proud of his fluency. They talked about places they had visited, in America as well as on the Continent. They became friendly, and the German made it clear that he was willing to give Lanny's country the benefit of his rare and special knowledge. Lanny was politely sure that his country would treat its scientific guests with all courtesy, and he was careful to give no hint of his belief that America was at least a decade ahead of Germany in nuclear research. Cautiously he ventured to suggest that the Fatherland had injured its cause by the exiling of able Jewish scientists. The German agreed and revealed in confidence that the greatest theoretical physicist in the world—so he called Werner Heisenberg—had ventured to approach no less a person than Reichsminister Himmler on the subject of the ban against the teaching of the Einstein theory of relativity in German universities. Lanny might have made quite a sensation by remarking, "I too have had the honor of meeting Reichsminister Himmler." But he didn't.

Back at the Crillon, Lanny's first duty was to prepare a brief report for his Boss. Roosevelt would get one through the Army, of course, but he would be more interested in the statement of a man whom he knew and trusted. The P.A. had brought along his well-worn little portable, a priceless possession in wartime, and he pecked away diligently on it; he permitted himself to go into some detail, for this was, quite literally, the most important subject in the whole world to the President of the United States. It was by his fiat that the atomic bomb was coming into existence, and it would be by his fiat that it would be used. He would name the time and the place, and would carry the responsibility for the tens or hundreds of thousands of lives it might take.

Lanny Budd didn't actually know that there was going to be this dreadful weapon of war. He knew only that a large share of his country's resources had been mobilized in the effort to create it, spurred by the fear that the Nazis might get it first. He knew that Albert Einstein had written to Roosevelt, pointing out how new discoveries in nuclear physics had made the project a possibility; and this seemed like a bit of irony or Providence or fate, for Einstein was one of those Jewish scientists who had been forced to flee from the Nazis. What the Nazis had lost the Americans had gained.

At present the P.A. knew only a little about the success his own country was having. Two years ago F.D.R. had entrusted him with the secret that the first chain reaction had been achieved, and later on Lanny's friend Professor Alston had whispered that an enormous atom-splitting project was under way. That was enough, and Lanny had never asked questions. But in the last few months he had gathered a hint here and there from the Alsos people and had realized that the bomb might soon be a reality. Professor Goudsmit, Jewish physicist born in Holland, was a top man, co-discoverer of the so-called "spin of the electron." He undoubtedly knew everything, but his younger assistants didn't. They guarded every word, and the soldiers who protected them had no idea what they were looking for; on the first night in Strasbourg the soldiers had sat in the room, playing cards by candlelight, while the scientists were ferreting out secrets which might determine the fate of the American Army, and indeed of civilization for centuries to come.

The ethics of this fearful new weapon Lanny had discussed with Einstein and his assistant, with Alston, and briefly with F. D. R. The country was at war, and this war was not of American making. Not only had Japan attacked America, but Germany had at once declared war on America, a fact which some Americans overlooked in their thinking. It was Japanese and German lives against American lives, and who could measure the value of enemy lives against our own? There could be no comparison; the President would not be justified in sacrificing a single American life in order to spare ten thousand enemy lives. As for the question of bombing civilians, the Nazi-Fascists had set the pattern; they had been the first to bomb—Guernica, Barcelona, Valencia, Madrid; then Warsaw, London, Rotterdam. The Japanese had killed many civilians at Pearl Harbor; and having made the bed, they must lie in it.

But what about the future? Who else would follow this pattern, who else would lie in this bed? Knowledge of nuclear physics being general throughout the scientific world, it would be impossible to keep the secret of the bomb very long. Who else would have the handling of it, who else would have the say as to where it might be used? This was the question which tormented the soul of every scientist who shared the awful knowledge.

Shakespeare had said that it was excellent to have a giant's strength, but it was tyrannous to use it like a giant. Who could guess what tyrannous men might arise in the future world, and what use they might make of the power to destroy whole cities, even whole countries? For no physicist could guess what might be the total consequences of a chain reaction. Suppose that it were to start a fission of light atoms: the whole earth might dissolve into alpha and beta and gamma particles in a fraction of a second. That would make a minor event in the history of a universe in which colossal suns exploded now and then, their light reaching the telescopes of the astronomers some millions of years after the event. Had there been nuclear scientists somewhere in these galactic systems, and had they invented atomic bombs for the overcoming of their own kind of enemies?

VIII

Laurel's next letter contained a copy of Emily Chattersworth's will, and Lanny studied it carefully and made sure that the bequest was a reality. In order to avoid inheritance taxes, a "charitable trust" had been established, the American Peace Foundation, with Lanny as the sole trustee. Emily had had two nieces, whom Lanny had met long ago, with the knowledge that either of them was "eligible." Now the aunt had left money to each, and to a list of pensioners and old servants; she had added the proviso that if anyone should attempt to contest the will, that person would forfeit his or her claim. It was a carefully drawn document, and Lanny could recognize the well-trained mind and pen of old Mr. Satterlee, international lawyer, who had made his home in a villa near Sept Chênes; he had come, bringing his white whiskers and his black leather briefcase, to advise a wealthy widow about her affairs. Mr. Satterlee wouldn't know how to end war in the world and would doubtless consider it a fantastic idea, but he would know how to draw a will so that it would be valid in both Paris and New York.

Once more it became difficult for the son of Budd-Erling to keep his mind upon *objets d'art* and scientific secrets. He had seen a great deal of war, and he disliked it. To know how to end the evil you must know what caused it; and on this you might get a different opinion from every authority you consulted. Modern greeds and ancient prejudices; competition for markets and raw materials; notions of racial superiority; national jealousies, hereditary fears, professional ambitions, religious fanaticism, population pressures—you might accumulate a long list, and each item would have something to do with your problem, adding to its complexity and your own confusion of mind.

Lanny would think of the friends he had, a host of them, and would interview each in his imagination; he knew pretty well what advice they would give. His friend Rick would tell him that it was capitalism, and so would Lanny's half-sister, Bessie Budd Robin; but when they got to discussing the remedy, a war would start right there. Rick was a parliamentary Socialist, while Bess was a party Communist, and before they got through the woman would be calling the man "a Social Fascist" and the man would be calling the woman "a fundamentally reactionary Red imperialist."

Lanny, who really wanted peace in the world and had learned to get along with all sorts of people, suffered in these controversies because he understood so many different points of view and saw so much truth in all of them. He had told himself that the one set of ideas in which there was no good whatever was Nazi-Fascism, and therefore it was necessary to finish this war before you tried to think about anything else. But now he had begun to worry about this too; for he had seen the armies go through North Africa and Italy and leave behind them in both countries an administration that had very little understanding of fundamental democracy and proceeded to put affairs back into the hands of big businessmen, big landlords, and big priestly hierarchs. Names were changed, but realities remained the same. "Get on with the war," the brass would say, and then go to dine and dance in the homes of the local aristocracy.

The presidential agent was pinning his hopes upon the man in the White House. F. D. R. kept telling him to take it easy, that everything was going to work out in the end; the people of North Africa, of Italy, of France, would be given a chance to say what they wanted, and there would be democratic decisions. But Lanny was growing more and more uncomfortable every time he returned to Europe, for he knew that the time to shape iron is while it is hot, and that when it has grown cold it may be steel-hard. The Army didn't know who its true friends were; it considered Socialists to be crackpots, just as they were called in America, and the people who knew how to get things done were the powerful ones at the top—the same who had hired the Nazi-Fascist gangsters to put down labor and keep political control in the hands of the well-born and well-to-do. F. D. R. himself understood this quite clearly; but how many in his administration understood it, and how many in Congress—and how many in AMG—the American Military Government that was being set up in so many strange parts of the world?

2

Chaos Comes Again

I

THE winter battle was continuing, and Alsos had to wait until some other town with a university or a physics laboratory had fallen to Allied arms. Monuments also was waiting—since it was hardly to be assumed that the enemy would leave valuable works of art close to the fighting zone. Lanny was tempted, and yielded; a colonel in uniform, all he had to do was to go to Orly or Le Bourget, stroll among the parked planes, and ask, "Anybody going south?" They would point out a plane, and he would ask the pilot, "Can you make room for a passenger?" The pilot would reply, "If you don't mind being uncomfortable, sir."

So, in a couple of hours, he would exchange rain and penetrating chill for warm sunshine. Some wit had called the Riviera "a sunny place for shady characters," and that had been painfully true, but was less so now. The idle rich and those who preyed upon them had fled from the fighting, and only a few had come back. The famed waterfront of Cannes was hardly to be recognized, the fashionable hotels having been taken over by the Air Force for its overstrained flyers. They were all over the Boulevard de la Croisette in bathing trunks, and they ate in the dining-rooms in their clean white undershirts, a sight contrasting comically with the waiters in proper black ties and tails.

Lanny hadn't notified his wife, for in these days planes were faster than telegrams. At the Cannes airport he strolled again, carrying his bag, his heavy overcoat over his arm. "Anybody going east?" And quickly the driver of a jeep took him in. The little car rolled swiftly along the wide boulevard lined with double rows of palm trees. There were hotels and mansions on one side, and beaches dotted with bright-colored umbrellas on the other. Lanny was happy to see that there had been little destruction; the Americans had landed to the east of Cannes, and the ships had concentrated their fire upon the few military installations. The workshops of Europe were being destroyed, but its playground had survived.

II

Just beyond the town is the Cap d'Antibes, and Juan-les-Pins, in Lanny's boyhood a tiny fishing village, now a tourist resort with its own showy casino and other means of parting you from your money. The road led along the rocky shore and came to the little beach, where Lanny had played with the fisherboys, and the wrought-iron gates of Bienvenu with the spiky agave plants on each side. Lanny said, "Thank you, soldier," and got out. (Tips were not in order.) He opened the gates and went in. There were no dogs to rush and welcome him; he would never know what had become of them and wondered if they had been eaten. The villa of Bienvenu had been occupied by the Vichy militia; the house was dingy and unpainted, the grounds untended, but all that could be remedied as soon as the war was over.

Laurel was living in the villa with one woman servant, whose peasant family lived up in the hills and considered the positions at Bienvenu their hereditary property. When Laurel opened the door and saw her husband she gave a cry, louder than she would have considered proper. But like so many other women in these days, she had a husband who went off to places where bombs were falling and men were being horribly mutilated; so first she exclaimed, and then she fell into his arms and began to weep. She tried to wipe her eyes and said she felt foolish. He told her that this was a stolen leave and that he would soon be recalled. She held him off and looked at him, to be sure he was all there. They were both wearing uniforms and looked strange and a trifle amusing to each other.

She told him the news of the neighborhood, which had been his home ever since he could remember. The Midi, like the rest of France, had withstood a four-year siege of hunger, cold, and terror. The Nazis had wielded this three-thonged whip over them, with the help of renegade Frenchmen, and the rest of the people hated the renegades with a fury beyond description. Laurel had done her best to describe it in the articles she had written for her magazine. She had a carbon copy, and it was a husbandly duty as well as a pleasure to read it at once. She had been out among the people, collecting their stories, the sort which become legends and are told by firesides for generations.

There was a woman known as "Catherine," recuperating here in Cannes, who had become a legend already. She had helped a total of

sixty-eight American and British flyers and secret agents to escape
from the enemy—many of them persons who had been under sentence
of death. The Nazis had known all about her—except who she was.
There were countless people of the underground who lived two lives,
hardworking and respectable by day and criminal by night. There
were fishermen who had carried men out, hidden under their nets, or
even wrapped up in them; there were peddlers of fish or vegetables
who carried in their carts radio sending sets by which messages were
sent and appointments made for meeting such fugitives at sea. The
enemy had detecting devices by which they could instantly locate the
spot from which such messages came, but before they could get to
the spot the cart would have moved and been safely hidden.

But often the plans had gone awry, and there were stories of failure
and martyrdom. Women whose husbands and sons had been tortured
to death hated the *collaborateurs* even more than they hated the Nazis;
they would have torn these wretches limb from limb if the victorious
armies had not intervened. As it was, many had been hunted down and
shot or hanged in the first turbulent days. Now the rest were being
tried, and the trials were public spectacles; the women came and sat
with their knitting, reincarnations of the *tricoteuses* of the Revolution
of a century and a half ago.

III

"What on earth are you going to do with that money?" asked Laurel;
it was a subject that might last them the rest of their lives. Lanny told
the ideas that had been floating through his mind, and Laurel told hers.
They decided that they would have to see the estate of Sept Chênes,
a part of the bequest. There was a caretaker on the place, and Laurel
had talked with him by telephone but had not taken time for the trip.
In France now you did no more traveling than was necessary. There
were busses, but they were dingy and fearfully crowded; they ran on
charcoal, and when they came to a hill the power was apt to give out,
and you had to wait while more was generated.

Lanny walked to the village and succeeded in renting a bicycle for
a week. (The franc, which had been worth twenty cents before
World War I, was now worth only two, and so a dollar would buy
pretty nearly anything in Juan.) The servant put up a lunch for them,
and bright and early next morning they set out, not forgetting to strap
their coats in front, for if clouds came up, or if they stayed until late,
it would be cold on the heights. They rode through Cannes, a half-

get a stenographer and dictate a letter to his father in Newcastle, Connecticut, telling that wise man of affairs the news and charging him to have his law firm in New York make sure that a copy of the will had been duly filed there. Most of the fortune existed in the form of bonds and "blue chip" stocks in the vaults of one of the great Wall Street banks; the heavy steel doors of those vaults moved so easily that a child's finger might open them, but before anything could start them a great quantity of legal red tape would have to be unwound.

All that was duty, and the grown-up playboy did it patiently, thinking all the while how pleasant the world would be when the task was completed and there was no more war. This called for some imagining, now while the greatest war of all history was at its dreadful climax and there was no part of the globe where men were not either fighting or manufacturing war goods and training others for the battlefronts. One front all the way from the North Sea to the Alps, another across Italy, and the longest of all from the White Sea down to the Black, with ten million men in a death struggle in snow and arctic cold. Not to mention all the fronts in China and Burma, and some thousands of islands and millions of square miles of water in the Western Pacific! All that war going on day and night, and you read about it twice a day in the papers, and listened to news about it over the radio when you could get near one; you speculated and discussed, and found it hard indeed to think consecutively about anything else.

Now you were going to end all that cruelty and waste! You were going to find a way to reach people, to persuade them to listen and to act upon what you said. People who spoke a hundred different languages and cherished ten thousand sacred and wholly delusive notions! Free men in the American Army, who had been taught how to handle jeeps and bazookas, radar and jet engines, but who had been taught almost nothing about what they were fighting for. Lanny told his wife of a GI in North Africa who had remarked, "First the Japs attack us and then we attack the Germans; I don't get it." And one in France who had attended Christian Front meetings in New York and who remarked, "We are fighting the wrong guys."

The best of all stories of American military education was one that Laurel had read in Ernie Pyle's newspaper column. A week or so after D-day Ernie had observed an ack-ack gunner sitting on a heap of sand and reading a copy of *Stars and Stripes*, the Army paper. Ernie met all the men he could, so he got up a conversation with this one, and was asked, "Where is this here Normandy beachhead that it talks about here?" The newspaperman looked at the gunner, to make sure

empty city, and along one of the well-paved roads leading into the hills. They pushed their bikes up the slopes, and rested now and then, looking down upon the sights which had been Lanny's joy since childhood: the beautiful estates that were like parks, the tier below tier of red-roofed villas, with orchards of olives, almonds, and oranges, the last now with golden fruit; the white city, with its yacht harbor, all the vessels now gray-painted for war; and beyond that the blue sea in which Lanny Budd had swum and fished from childhood, and over which he had been transported upon many strange errands, all the way from Gibraltar to Palestine, and from Tunis to Toulon.

He would have liked to tell his wife the most recent of these adventures: how he had been secretly landed at night on the shore close to Cannes, in an effort to persuade his friend Charlot de Bruyne, a *capitaine* of the Légion Tricolore, to come over to the Allied side. Laurel had learned of the tragic ending of that effort. She had taken Lanny out behind the garage of Bienvenu and shown him the spot where Charlot had been led by his comrades and shot to death; he had fallen against the wall, and the stains of his blood had not yet been washed away. But Lanny didn't say that he had had any part in that tragedy; he didn't tell how he had climbed to safety in these heights and from them had watched the approach of the huge Allied armada, surely one of the most remarkable spectacles of history. To have told these things would have been only to frighten a sensitive woman and provide her imagination with raw material for future anxiety. Lanny wasn't supposed to go on any more secret missions, but Laurel wouldn't believe that; she would know that if he were sent he would keep the fact from her and lie to her as part of his duty.

IV

They continued climbing. Here and there were the wrecked carcasses of trucks and tanks which had been dumped off the roads; they had been hit by bombs or shells, or had broken down and been shoved out of the way. Trees had been splintered, and some houses showed gaping wounds. Repairs were difficult because materials could not be had.

The travelers came to the gates of the fine estate of Sept Chênes, which means Seven Oaks, but two of them had died of a mysterious disease. Emily Chattersworth had lived here through her last years, having sold her much larger estate northwest of Paris, and later her Paris town house. She had taken the former step partly at Lanny's urging, because he was so sure that a second world war was coming. The Germans had looted Les Forêts in the first war, and repeated the performance as Lanny foretold, but it was a new owner who met the loss and would have the task of collecting indemnity.

Wherever Emily lived she had continued her role of what the French call a *salonnière*, that is, a woman who has not merely wealth but also intelligence, and who makes her home a gathering place for intellectual persons interested in some field—art or literature, science or philosophy, politics or economics, or possibly a little of all these. A *salonnière* is more than a hostess; she is like the conductor of an orchestra, the chairman of an assembly. Distinguished persons come to her home not merely to enjoy good food and drink and elegant surroundings, but because they meet others of their own sort and spend an evening according to long-established rules of social life in France. The hostess tactfully sees to it that everybody has a chance to be heard, that dangerous subjects are dropped, difficult moments safely passed, and courtesy, wit, and *élan* continuously maintained.

This is a difficult art for a foreigner to learn, but Emily had devoted her long widowhood to it. So it had come about that Lanny Budd had a hundred delightful memories of this gracious mansion; from youth on he had sat discreetly, never speaking unless spoken to, listening to Anatole France and Bernard Shaw, Paul Valéry and Romain Rolland, Auguste Rodin and Isadora Duncan, Blasco-Ibáñez and Henri Bergson—an odd assortment, but all of them persons of *esprit*, having something to say and knowing how to say it well. Emily's salon was called "liberal"; she invited the "free thinkers," in the broad sense of that phrase; she did not invite the dull aristocracy or the filthy rich, the reactionaries or the religious with closed minds. These had their own salons and turned up their noses at the American, calling her an interloper and a sensation seeker.

Now she had passed on the torch to her near-foster son. Lanny, who was conscientious, would carry it as best he could, although looking forward to the prospect with dismay. He had several times refused to take a regular job under F. D. R., pleading that he had no training in administration and didn't know how to give orders. Now he would have the spending of a million dollars, and as soon as word got about he would be besieged by people who wanted to take his orders, or perhaps to give orders for him or even to him. There would be publicity, something he had always avoided and which had been poison to a secret agent. He would have to attend committee meetings, read and

sign documents, listen to grievances, and decide who was right and who was wrong in clashes of temperament—oh, dear, oh, dear!

Emily had met Laurel only in the last few years; but she had liked her and approved her as a wife for Lanny. She revealed that in the will, by providing that in the event of Lanny's death, Laurel would carry out the obligation. Now Lanny would lean upon her heavily. So far, they managed to agree in their beliefs; but Lanny couldn't help thinking, suppose they should fail to agree about the best way to end war in the world?

Laurel Creston was the quietest-appearing person you could imagine; she had been brought up on the Eastern Shore of Maryland, very strictly, and her ideas of what was proper conduct for a gentlewoman were fixed; she had never made a scene or raised her voice in public in all her life. She was rather small, had gentle brown eyes, and an appearance of submissiveness that was deceptive; when she walked alongside the tall and handsome Lanny everybody thought her insignificant. She was content to have it that way, for she too had been a secret agent of a sort, writing against the Nazis with a pen full of acid so strong that it withered them up. She had used a nom de plume not merely so that she might gather material, but in order to protect her husband from suspicion and death in a torture dungeon.

When you knew her you were astonished to discover what a dynamo was working inside that small head and what energy was driving it. Laurel Creston had had to make herself a writer, whereas Lanny Budd had just naturally grown up as a playboy, doing whatever he wanted to do, which was to learn something new every day about a strange and fascinating world. Lanny was easygoing, whereas Laurel was developing more and more determination, and especially where war was concerned; she had never hated it more than when she was wearing the uniform of a WAC officer. It was she who generated most of the ideas as to how to slay the monster; it was she who drove Lanny to take various tiresome legal steps—right away, quickly, before he was called to new duties.

V

Old Mr. Satterlee having carried his legal learning across the ocean, Lanny had to go and consult a French *avocat* in Cannes, to make sure that the will had been properly entered for probate. He had to identify himself legally and sign a variety of documents. He had to

that he wasn't spoofing. Then he said, "Why, you're sitting on it." The gunner replied in astonishment, "Well, I'll be damned! I never knowed that."

VI

The Allied armies were carrying on two great offensives, one in the Saar, which had reached the Rhine over a long stretch, and the other in the north, across the River Roer, aimed at Cologne. The latter had not done so well, perhaps because it was facing heavier forces, and also because the weather was so bad that the lighter planes, designed to bomb enemy communications, were grounded most of the time. Studying the map he always carried, Lanny realized that this was one more of those blind slugging matches which comprised a war of attrition. The Americans could stand them because they had more reserves than the enemy.

It was the second week in December, the worst time, when the ground is waterlogged and not yet frozen hard; trucks sank up to their hubcaps when they ventured off the paving. Exhausted men slept where they dropped, with no chance to dry their clothing, and trench feet and frostbite crippled both armies. Lanny had seen these miseries in the field, and Laurel in the hospitals, and each day of the fighting built up their hatred of war. The man was troubled in conscience because he was living in Riviera sunshine and having food brought to him by the peasant family who had performed that service in Bienvenu for forty years and had no idea of letting rationing regulations interfere with their accumulation of dollars.

The expected summons came in the form of a telegram from Monuments: "An interesting project has come up and you can be in on it if you come at once." That was equivalent to a command. The art expert threw his few belongings into a bag, took his overcoat on his arm, and thumbed an Army ride. He didn't have to thumb a plane, for all he had to do was to show his telegram to the airport officer, and he had a seat assigned to him, a cushioned seat this time. As a special favor he was set down at Versailles and made his way to the Grand Monarque's stables just as the sun was going down behind dark rain clouds. There could be meaner weather than Paris in December, but you would have to go to London to find it.

The first person he encountered in the office was Peggy Remsen, niece of Lanny's stepmother, Esther Remsen Budd. Peggy was a lovely young woman with a New England conscience; she had not been content to be a social butterfly but had studied diligently to equip herself to become the curator of a museum. She had never dreamed that it might be her fate to go to Europe and act as a curator of its greatest art treasures. She was in a state of delight, but also of vexation, because of a rule that women would not be permitted close to the fighting front. It was a man's world, scolded this great-granddaughter of the Puritans, and Lanny agreed, adding that the men were making such a mess of it he would be willing to let the women have a try.

The men told him what the situation was. A telegram had come from G-2 of the 28th Infantry Division, stationed in the Ardennes, reporting that a German truck, carrying art treasures from Paris at the time of the evacuation, had broken an axle; the Germans, being desperately short of transportation, were believed to have hidden the art works somewhere on a hunting estate in the forest. Would Monuments care to come and look for them? Monuments surely would, and a dozen volunteered for a job to which only two would be assigned. These happened to be admirers of the son of Budd-Erling and had asked his help.

VII

The expedition set out early next morning in a staff car, Lanny and the two younger art experts riding in the rear seat; a military chauffeur drove them, and another soldier who was to act as general handyman rode beside him. Their baggage was in the trunk, and they were told that further military protection would be assigned them by the unit to which they were traveling. Their route was eastward and somewhat north, through Reims and Sedan, a highway which Lanny had traveled often in times of peace.

In those days he had considered two hundred miles less than a morning's drive, but now the military highway was full of traffic and getting ahead was difficult. They passed through the city with the magnificent cathedral, destroyed by Teutonic fury, restored by French devotion, and now, alas, destroyed again. They passed through the great bastion of the Maginot line, Sedan, with its many scattered forts, once believed to be impregnable. But the Germans had overwhelmed it in 1870 and in 1914 and yet again in 1940; they had turned it around, facing France, and believed that they had made it impregnable again. But the Americans had taken it in this year of 1944, and they hadn't bothered to turn it again, because they subscribed to the well-worn maxim that the best form of defense is attack.

The Army was all over the place; not the show Army you had seen on parade, but the work Army, tired, soiled, and grim, doing its job because it had to and wishing it didn't. There were roadblocks, and you stopped and showed your credentials; there was Army chow, and you were invited to have yours because nobody in uniform ever went hungry if the Army could help it. Officers and men ate much the same food, but they ate it separately. During the meal you gave and received news and opinions; ahead was a quiet sector, but there was a big show going on to the northeast and another to the southeast—you could hear the heavy guns when the wind was right.

The route of the car was northeast, and soon they heard the guns, but they weren't going near enough for trouble. They were in the Ardennes Forest, a vast tract of hills and mountains, rough country with poor communications, easy to defend. Farther to the east of it, close to the Rhine, lay the Eifel hills, and they were one more reason that the Army had halted. The car climbed, and soon there was snow instead of rain, and the ground was frozen hard; a north wind was blowing, and it was colder than any place they had been in for a long time. Throughout the forest the snow was tracked by deer and pig. Lanny said they were wild pig; it was hunting country, and it was a safe guess that the Americans were not always respecting the game ordinances.

They passed through one village after another, most of the houses lined along the road. Presently they crossed the Belgian border, but there was nothing to mark it; the Nazis had made all countries one, wherever they came, and the Americans were leaving things as they found them. Farther on they were in the Grand Duchy of Luxembourg, supposed to be another independent country, but here too there were no customs officials to delay them. In this region Germans, French, Belgians, and Luxembourgers had mixed and mingled freely except when they were fighting one another. The names of the towns were German, French, or halfway between—Diekirch, Clervaux, Oudler, and Weiswampach.

VIII

The car's destination was the town of Wiltz, headquarters of Major General Cota, known as "Dutch." He commanded the 28th Division, which the Germans greatly feared and called the "Bloody Bucket" Division. That was because of the shoulder patch the troops wore, a red keystone, it having been organized from units of the National Guard of Pennsylvania, the "Keystone State." To the Germans the insigne looked like a bucket, and they called it "*Blut-Eimer-Division*" either because of the losses it had suffered or those it had inflicted.

All members of the division were proud of its record, and an aide of its commander occupied suppertime in telling the three visitors about it. At Mortain in Normandy the Germans had launched an offensive intended to take Avranches and cut the American Army in halves. The 28th had stood in their way and they had failed. The division had fought all the way across France, had been the only American division to parade through Paris, also the first to enter German territory in force. As part of the First Army it had helped to clear the Hürtgen Forest in some of the fiercest fighting of the war. This offensive was still going on, but the division's losses had been so heavy that it had been sent to this quiet sector to recuperate; its replacements consisted of green troops who had never fired a shot except in practice.

"Forests appear to be bad luck for us," said the young officer who told this story. "And now we are in another." He knocked on the wooden table for luck as he said it. He was Lieutenant Seemann, a Pennsylvania Dutchman who had left college to enlist in the Army. He had never heard of Monuments, and was naïvely curious about it. The information had come from the 109th Regiment, which was stationed farther up the line.

The art experts were lodged for the night in the home of the town's *Bürgermeister*, who gladly gave up his best bedroom for the distinguished gentlemen—"*die Herrschaften*" they were, a title about equivalent to the English "the quality." "*Was wünschen die Herrschaften?*" The obsequiousness of the family was pitiful; they had expected the worst and were hardly yet used to the idea that it wouldn't develop. Lanny slept near a window which could not be opened; half lost in a soft mattress and under one of those thick German feather quilts which cover the lower half of the body and leave the upper half to shift for itself.

IX

Before full daylight the expedition set out, the guest car preceded by a jeep with four soldiers, and followed by two more jeeploads. All the men carried battle equipment, for their destination was only about five miles behind the front, across a small stream and over another line of forest-clad hills. Both sides sent out scouting parties, and the 28th CP (Command Post) admitted anxiety because of reports of enemy concentrations in front of them. But the enemy was kept so occupied by hard fighting to the north and south of the Ardennes that it was difficult to imagine him making more than a feint through this rough country with few and poor roads.

The expedition came to the regimental headquarters, in another village, and there a guide car was added. This car was also equipped for combat—Bren guns, "burp" guns, bazookas, everything. The chauffeur of Lanny's car remarked, "Enough to hold off a Kraut regiment." The enemy troops in front of them, he had been told, were the last sweepings; the cripples, the graybeards, the tubercular, and those known as *Magenbattalione*, because they had stomach ulcers.

The cortege left the paved highway, and it was rough going, for the ground had frozen into deep ruts; Army men repairing a big bulldozer grinned and promised them better luck on the return trip. A mile or two more, and they halted while the guide made up his mind which of two forest tracks was the right one; the Germans had destroyed all road signs before evacuating the district. After a few kilometers the guide decided he was wrong, and they turned and retraced their steps. At last they came to a handsome group of rustic buildings which had been the hunting lodge of one of the lords of Ruhr steel, those gentry who had put up the campaign funds for Adolf Hitler at a time his fortunes had reached their lowest ebb.

There was a caretaker and his wife, the former so old that he could hardly get about, to say nothing of rendering military service. They were both frightened half out of their wits and took every opportunity to bow to each member of the expedition who approached them. *Herrschaften* was not enough for them—they said "*die gnädigen Herren*," and would have said "*Ihre Hoheiten*" if that would have done any good. They were comically relieved to discover somebody who could speak fluent German and proceeded to pour out a flood of explanations and apologies. They had been sent here just before the German evacuation; they hardly knew the place, they knew nothing about any *Kunstwerke*, the place was at the command of the *Hoheiten*, they would be so good as to condescend to make a search and satisfy their honorable selves?

The search was made, from attic to cellars—the latter full of broken bottles. SS men had been quartered here, and everything had been looted; now the rooms had been scrubbed clean, that being the nature of elderly Germans. There were no concealed art works and nothing else of value. So then began a search of the grounds: the stables, converted to garage purposes, but with no tools and not a drop of gasoline; the storerooms with no stores, the smokehouse with nothing but black stains, the icehouse with nothing but sawdust.

"Must have buried the stuff," said the sergeant who commanded the military group. But somebody discovered a woodroad, and then others leading out into the forest, and the jeeps sped away on these, and presently one of them came back, the driver shouting. One of the soldiers who was a woodsman had noticed a depression in the snow, suggestive of a path, and had followed it to a cabin on a hillside, well hidden by a thicket. There was a padlocked door, and they had jimmied it open, and reported the existence of "a lot of junk."

The cars followed the leader, and the next couple of hours were spent examining the stuff with flashlights—it was packed in so closely that it was difficult to move anything, and they did not want to carry it outside on account of the weather. There were objects screwed up in wooden cases, and others in heavy leather. There were framed paintings tied in burlap, presumably a hasty job. There were rugs rolled up, doubtless old and valuable, but there was no way to tell without unrolling them, and that could not be done in snow-covered underbrush.

In the back part of the little structure were medieval saints, some carved in wood and some in stone, some plain and others multicolored. This obviously was ancient stuff and might have come out of a museum. One ancient saint might be worth thousands of dollars. The excitement of Monuments work lay in the fact that you could never tell when you might hit a jackpot. Among the treasures to be sought were the crown jewels of the Holy Roman Empire, the Ghent altarpiece, the stained glass from the Strasbourg Cathedral, and the treasures which had been taken from the Cathedral of Metz. You weren't apt to find any of these on the outskirts of Germany, but you never could tell. Somebody might have been careless or overconfident.

X

The car was brought, and some of the lighter stuff loaded into it and taken to the shelter of the lodge. The first painting from which they took the wrappings was a Cranach Madonna, and Lanny said, "Maybe this shipment was for Göring. He had set himself the goal of owning every Cranach in Europe." The next was one of the finest Watteaus that Lanny had ever seen, a lovers' tryst in that same garden of Versailles where the P. A. had been walking only two days ago. Next came a heavy roll of unframed paintings, which, when unrolled, revealed one after another of modern French examples. It wasn't necessary to investigate any further. The experts wrote a telegram to headquarters in Versailles, saying that this was the real thing and asking that a storage

place be named and two covered trucks or vans sent. A courier took
this to regimental headquarters, and meantime the expedition settled
down to enjoy a cultural holiday.

It was a most agreeable place for a winter sojourn. When snow stopped
falling the air was crisp and bracing. Firewood could be had for the
asking, and the GIs didn't wait to be asked. The elderly German couple,
once convinced that they were not going to be led out behind the icehouse and shot, labored diligently to oblige their new masters. The
country-born fellows among the troops needed no orders to go hunting and came back loaded down with hare and pheasants and presently
a huge wild boar, riding in a jeep and ready to be cut up into chops
and ham slices.

Meantime the main room of the hunting lodge blossomed forth, as if
under a spell of enchantment, with the culture and charm, the history
and religion, biography and topography, of every part of Europe for
half a dozen centuries. Blazing color, magnificence of costume, beauty
of person, elegance of surroundings—farm boys from Maine and the
Carolinas, ranch boys from California and Texas, stood awe-stricken
and whispered, "Jeepers, I never knew there were such things in the
world!"

XI

In three days of this idyllic life all but the heavy stuff was sorted out
and listed, repacked and marked. Word had come that transportation
was under way and that the treasure trove was to be taken to a storeroom in Reims. The Monuments officers were pleased with themselves;
it would be a story to tell their colleagues, and perhaps their grandchildren. Rain had started to fall, and a heavy fog came up out of the
river valleys. The art experts, who had talked of taking more time to
go hunting, discussed the chances of the weather's clearing up.

The top sergeant who commanded their small squad was worried.
There had been enemy planes overhead, and until these it had been a
long time since he had seen any. "Didn't think they had so many left,"
he said. Before dawn everybody was awakened by heavy firing, not from
the north, where it had been going on for weeks, but directly east, where
it had been only scattered. "That's not hunting," said the sergeant.
"That's a barrage, and it covers the whole front." It was an unceasing
thunder, familiar to Lanny because he had listened to the same thing,
exactly four months ago, from the hills above the French Riviera.

An elegant breakfast had been prepared of broiled hare and hot cakes with syrup, not to mention real coffee, the aroma of which made the old Germans almost weep with joy when they served it. But in the middle of the meal the sergeant came in and reported, "Sirs, there is an enemy offensive under way. I believe it is our duty to get back to our unit."

"But, Sergeant," said the senior officer, who was Lanny Budd, "we can't leave all this stuff."

"It won't do any good, sir, to stay with the stuff if the enemy comes."

"You really think he can penetrate our lines?"

"It depends on how badly he wants to. The line in front of us is thinly held. About half the 28th are green troops, fresh out of basic training, and you can't count on them too much in action."

The Monuments officers got up and went outside. It was a battle, no question about it; there was incessant firing all along the front. They couldn't judge if it was approaching, but the sergeant who had been listening for hours declared that it clearly was.

Lanny suggested, "Surely we ought to leave a guard to watch this treasure. It is worth millions of dollars, maybe tens of millions."

The reply was, "No guard can save it if the Jerries get here, and if they don't, I doubt if this old couple has any way to steal the stuff."

The sergeant was the man whose job it was to know about military matters. Being officers of assimilated rank, the Monuments people really had no right to give him orders; he was there to protect them. Lanny, the oldest and highest ranking of the art experts, could say nothing but, "OK, Sergeant."

XII

It took but two or three minutes to shove their belongings into bags and throw them into the trunk of the car. They told the old German couple that they would be back soon, and to take the best of care of the treasures. This couple, of course, knew what was happening, and the gleam in their eyes told what their real thoughts were. The invincible German Army was coming back, and once more there would be real *Hoheiten* in the hunting lodge.

The noncom assembled his little squad and gave them orders. "We're hightailing it out of here, as fast as the big car can stand it. Follow my jeep, and keep as close together as you can. Keep your eyes peeled and be ready to shoot first. Get it clear in your minds, Jerry isn't wasting metal like this for nothing; it means he's coming, and that means he has put down paras all over this district." The sergeant stopped, then explained, for the benefit of the civilians, "Parachute troops. And the worst of it is, some of them will be wearing our uniforms—that's one of the Huns favorite tricks. Remember, we weren't sent here to fight, but to take care of these gentlemen; we have to run away, no matter how little we like it. If we can't make our own post, we'll turn west, away from the enemy. If I raise my arm straight up, it means stop, and stop quick. That's all."

The sergeant rode beside the driver of the leading jeep. Then came a second jeep, then the car, and the third jeep brought up the rear. The cortege sped fast over the snow-covered track, which wound snakelike through the forest, avoiding rocks and large trees. They were heading north with a westward trend; that was about parallel to the enemy front, as well as Lanny could guess it. While everyone but the drivers peered anxiously into the thickets and through the forest vistas, Lanny was busy with the papers he had grabbed from his bag. Any one of those would have identified him to the Germans, and there were few persons near the front whom they would have been more pleased to capture. The P.A. worked at tearing them up into the smallest pieces and dropping half a dozen at a time from the speeding car. They were inconspicuous in the wet snow and would soon disintegrate. It hurt him to destroy the precious letter from his Boss, but he could get another—assuming that he got out of this trap alive.

They came to a small open space, and a track crossing their own. They came upon it suddenly, and the sergeant swung up his arm. The four vehicles ground to a halt, only a few feet apart. At the crossing of the tracks stood four infantrymen in American uniforms and carrying "burp" guns; they had been taken by surprise and stood staring. "Who are you?" shouted the sergeant, and the reply came promptly, "Second Battalion, 318th Infantry, 106th Division."

The voice sounded American; but then many Germans had lived in America, and they had plenty of prisoners from whom they could learn accents. "You, squad leader, what's your name?" demanded the sergeant.

"Pete Collins."

"What state do you come from?"

"Iowa."

"And what is the river that forms the eastern border of Iowa?" It was a trick that had been taught to many of the combat troops, and geography lessons had been held especially to prepare for it.

Perhaps the enemy had heard of the trick and perhaps he hadn't. The reply of this squad leader must have been a whispered order, for the four men swung up their weapons together and poured a blast of fire

into the column of vehicles. There was a crash of splintering glass and
dented steel. It happened so quickly that Lanny saw only part of it; he
saw the sergeant drop, and saw the man who sat beside the driver of
Lanny's car with blood spurting from a hole in his head. Other men in
the jeeps leaped out and flung themselves flat in the snow and began
shooting; the enemy guns were turned upon them, and in that second
or two of respite the driver of Lanny's car threw it into gear, swung
past the jeeps in front of him, turned off the track and went crashing
through a thicket in low gear. In another second or two the car was on
the cross track, headed west.

XIII

That was orders, and nobody could object. The three horrified art
experts sat speechless while the car hightailed it out of there, swinging
this way and that, leaping over the bumps and down into the ruts, toss-
ing the three passengers up to the roof and hitting their heads, then
dropping them half dazed into their seats. The dead man's blood was
spattered everywhere, and you would have thought he was alive by the
way his body behaved.

That went on for a mile or two until they came to a place where
there was a turn and soft mud covered a stretch of road; the car started
to slide, and the driver jammed on his brake, enough to slow the car
but not to stop it. It skidded and hit a tree, with force enough to jolt
their necks and bruise their arms but not enough to injure their legs—
thank goodness!

They got out and examined the damage. The front axle was bent, the
wheel jammed, and the car immobilized. The soldier said, "Sorry, sirs,"
and they could readily believe him. Being polite persons, they assured
him that it wasn't his fault.

What to do next? Should they walk back and rejoin their party in
the hope of getting a jeep? But maybe their party hadn't won the battle;
or maybe more Germans had come up. Walking back, they would be
going toward the enemy. Furthermore, the soldier pointed out, it would
be a grave risk to drive a jeep where paratroopers were about. Walking,
they could travel in the forest and have a chance to stop and listen and
hide. There were villages and farms scattered through this district, and
American troops were in all of them.

Lanny took the carbine from the dead man; it was a Budd, whose
development he had followed for forty years; he had been taught to
take Budd Gunmakers products apart and put them together again at

an age when other children were building houses out of blocks. One of the other officers took the automatic pistol, and the third took the sheath knife and a couple of grenades. Assimilated officers were noncombatants, forbidden to carry arms; but when the enemy was breaking the laws of war by wearing American uniforms it seemed useless to expect consideration from him and better to fight back.

The others wanted to lug their bags, but Lanny persuaded them against it. They might have a long and rough journey, and they were not outdoor men, hardened and tough. They would have to travel fast because they were leaving plain tracks, and enemies might be trailing them, using the captured jeeps.

What became of their escort they never knew. They had no chance to go back, and probably couldn't have found the spot if they had tried. This patch of forest, hills, ravines, and ice-covered streams became the scene of some of the wildest fighting in the history of a blood-soaked earth. A million men were coming from all the points of the compass, prepared to trample this ground, to stain fresh layers of snow with blood and track them with the treads of monstrous machines. Armies would advance and retreat and advance again; men would die by the hundreds on every hillock and ridge. Reinforcements would be rushed up, on foot, by truck and train, or through the air. For a full month the struggle would rage; it would be known to history as the Battle of the Bulge, and it would be the Gettysburg of the western front, as Stalingrad had been of the eastern.

As for three art experts and one soldier boy from Brooklyn, they would be like four grains of salt in a shaker. They would be hurled here and there, hardly knowing what was happening to them. They would be in the midst of uproar and racket, chaos and confusion. They would know only what they saw with their eyes and heard with their ears, and would have to wait until near the end before they began to form an idea as to which side was gaining. It was two or three weeks before even the commanding generals knew, and four grains of salt counted for nothing whatever in their calculations.

CRISIS CONFESSION

3

No Rest Day or Night

I

THREE highly trained art experts and one very young garage mechanic from Brooklyn stole through the rough Ardennes Forest, putting their feet down softly in the snow and turning their eyes this way and that incessantly. When they came to an open spot they would stop before emerging from the brush and stand with their ears cocked, listening attentively. A twig crackling beneath their feet would make them jump; a partridge taking flight would leave them with hearts pounding. It was Indian fighting, which all four of them had read about but had enacted only as children at play. Now it was reality, and far more deadly, for no Indian had ever dreamed of such weapons as the enemy here had made.

The fugitives avoided the roads, on which the enemy was most apt to travel; they avoided the thickets because they could not see through them or penetrate them without making a noise; they preferred stretches of forest with great trees because they could stand behind trees and see a long way. The land was cut up with ravines, and these were bad because, both in descending and climbing, you might set a loose stone to tumbling, and were a helpless target because you couldn't move fast. Frozen swamps were bad too, for they wouldn't hold your weight, and if you got your legs wet, how would you get them dry? These and other things you had to learn, and your first mistake might be your last.

They were not left long in doubt as to the presence of the enemy. They came in sight of one of the tracks—you couldn't really call them roads—which crisscrossed this wild region. They heard the sound of engines and backed away into a thicket and lay flat. Peering out, they watched a terrifying procession going past, perhaps fifty yards away: first a clanking steel monster, one of the new Tiger tanks, weighing as much as seventy tons, and with a long gun barrel sticking out in front. This land battleship carried eleven-inch armor and was capable of a speed of forty miles an hour; now it was moving with majestic slowness, and behind it, walking in the tracks left by the tank treads, came two columns of men. They carried automatic guns and about their waists a string of grenades, objects like gourds with long necks. They were the Panzer grenadiers, whose job was to protect the tanks against men who might try to sneak up on them with explosives or combustibles. Behind them came Panzerfaust teams and officers, then medical-aid men, all precisely spaced.

There came another tank and another marching column, then another tank, and so on and on—good God! it was the whole German Army, thought the cowering fugitives. But it wasn't; it was just one Panzer Grenadier Battalion, and the Germans were sending in four whole divisions of them, about sixty thousand men; also four Wehrmacht Panzer Divisions, that is, of the regular Army, and four SS Panzer Divisions, who were Hitler's own chosen troops, his private army, as you might say, trained from childhood to be cruel and deadly killers.

The four Americans couldn't know all that; but one thing they understood clearly, that the enemy had broken through the thinly held American lines. Somebody had blundered, somebody had underestimated the reserves the enemy could command. It was also clear that this tank column wasn't just wandering blindly through the forest; it was heading for some town where there were known to be American forces—and that was surely a town at which the fugitives did not desire to arrive.

The Germans had had every opportunity to make themselves familiar with this territory; they had driven through it in World War I to capture Sedan and rout the French Army; they had done the same thing thirty years later and had held the land until the American First Army had driven them out a couple of months ago. It was a commander whom Lanny had met at Berchtesgaden, Field Marshal Karl Rudolf Gerd von Rundstedt, who had performed the feat in 1944, and Hitler had picked him for this new offensive, meant to rout the American Army and win the war.

II

When the column of steel pachyderms had passed out of sight and sound the fugitives conversed in whispers. They realized now how serious their plight was; they were no longer fleeing from a sprinkling of parachutists but from the German Army. No Panzer column like that would go without infantry to follow; no such column would go without other columns proceeding close by. In short, one such column meant an army. To have arrived where it had so early must mean that it had by-passed towns and villages held by the Americans, leaving them to be cleaned up later on. This was to be a surprise attack, and to go far. "They'll be all over these woods," Lanny said, "and it'll be hard to dodge them."

They started again, choosing a route slightly more to the north. They had no detail map of this district, but the soldier had one priceless possession, a tiny compass dangling from a chain at his waist. "If anything happens to me, don't fail to get it," he said; "and don't forget that it's the blue end that points to the north. I forgot that once and I was sunk. I have made myself a word that I say to myself—bengas— blue north, gray south."

He was a Jewish boy named Abramson; he had been one of those who had shyly asked permission to stand and gaze at works of European art. He knew all about cars and internal combustion engines but was dubious about his abilities as an Indian fighter; he admitted that he had never fired a shot at a human being. He was taking the advice of an art expert who had more than twice his years. Like all GIs, he addressed such learned persons as "Doc."

They came to another woodroad—that seemed the best name for such crude forest tracks. Taught by experience, they hid in a thicket and listened, and this proved a wise precaution. There came a distant rumble, and it grew into a roar, and here was another column of tanks, bigger yet; they must be the Royal Tigers, of which Göring had boasted but which Lanny had not seen. They were going faster, and behind them came armored cars loaded with grenadiers and Panzer- fausts. These were in a hurry and not yet near enough to their foes so that they had to take precautions. They went by like a storm, while the watchers clung to the earth like so many baby rabbits or quail.

The four got up and started again, more anxious than ever. They had taken it for granted that if they got to some American military group they would be safe; but now they were not sure. They might find the group in the midst of a battle—and not winning it. But what else could the fugitives do? They had no food, it was turning colder and starting to snow again, and how could they spend a freezing night without blankets or shelter? To build a fire would be suicide. What they wanted was to find some Americans who were not yet under attack; vehicles would no doubt be bringing in reinforcements and would consent to take out a load of Monuments on the return trip.

Where were the Americans anyhow, and why were the roads left

entirely to Tigers and Royal Tigers? Where were the General Sher-
mans and the TDs—tank destroyers? The fugitives soon got their
answer, for straight ahead of them there burst a solid mass of sound,
big guns and little guns roaring together, and continuing so that it was
all one sound. It had been like that pretty much since dawn, but the
sound had been behind them, and distant, whereas this was near, and
ahead. Evidently one of the tank columns was making an attack and
being resisted. The four fugitives chose another point of the compass.

All this was hard on the two younger experts, for they had lived
soft lives and had had little basic training. Lanny, although he was
some fifteen years older, had been climbing mountains, escaping from
the Vichy militia, and before that from the Gestapo in Germany and
Italy. Soft snow and mud clung to his feet and made heavy going;
a carbine in one hand and an overcoat over the other arm did not
make things any easier; but he stuck it out, and it was one of the
younger men who first called for a breathing space.

III

They came to a stream and drank, which refreshed them slightly;
but the periods of rest grew longer and those of walking shorter. Snow
was falling again, and the light was growing dim; the short day was
ending. It was the 16th of December, and the longest night of the year
was only five days away. They had dreamed of a cave in which to hide,
but they had found none. They had dreamed of a hollow log into
which they might crawl, but they found that fir and pine trees rarely
grew that big and the oaks didn't seem to rot. There was firing all
around them now, and no longer any hope of escaping beyond the
battle; the Panzers had been too fast. The four were reduced to imitating the life of rabbits, hiding in one patch of undergrowth and peering
out for another patch to run to.

Traveling thus, they came to a clearing and saw a little farm. They
hid and studied the place carefully, to make sure whether it was in the
hands of friends or foes. So far as they could see it wasn't in anybody's
hands; there was no sign of life. Perhaps the peasants had fled to some
hiding place they knew about. They were accustomed to war, an
invasion every generation and perhaps oftener. The Germans had come
in 1914 and stayed nearly four years; they had come in 1940 and
stayed even longer; then the Americans had come, and now the Germans were coming again. No wonder a farm was deserted, not even
a duck or a chicken left!

They discussed in whispers what to do. There was a barn, extremely tempting. A barn has a place for the cow and the horse below, and a high place above where the hay is stored, and hay is marvelous to hide in. No one there had tried it in winter, and they weren't sure how warm it would be, but if you burrowed deep it would surely be better than remaining out in the open, to be covered with snow or soaked with rain if the weather turned warmer. They weren't sure now whether they were in Luxembourg or Belgium; in either case the peasants would probably be friendly; but you couldn't be sure, for there were Germans in both Belgium and Luxembourg, and Germans were always Germans—so declared the Jewish boy from Brooklyn, who surely didn't like them.

They decided to wait until dark and then sneak into the barn. If there was a cow they might get some milk; one of the art experts had been raised on a farm in Wisconsin and understood the technique, so mysterious to a city dweller. If there was no cow one of the four might approach the house and try to buy food, not mentioning that there were others or where he meant to spend the night. All that sounded good, and four votes were cast for the program.

There was a council of war, discussing both strategy and tactics and including all the eventualities they could think of. They weren't there to fight but to get away, and they would resist only if they could be sure of success. Somebody might have to decide in a split second, and they chose Lanny for their leader because he was the oldest and knew more about both the natives and the enemy. He did not tell them his special reasons for being unwilling to surrender; he warned them that in an offensive like this, where the enemy's chances would depend entirely upon speed, prisoners would be an inconvenience and the enemy might be taking none. "A nice cheerful thought!" said the farm boy from Wisconsin who had become the assistant director of an art museum in his native state.

Stepping softly, in Indian file, they stole across the clearing, climbed a stone wall, and came to the barn. There was no sign of life; the door was padlocked. They quickly pried it open, went in and stood listening, then groped around and found the nailed-on boards which served as a ladder to the loft. It was half full of hay, as they had hoped, and they dug themselves into it and piled the stuff over them, all but their faces. Lying side by side, they kept one another warm, and it was bliss compared to the snow and wind outside.

Obviously this place wasn't going to be left deserted all through a battle. The fugitives had discussed the chances and decided that it was fifty-fifty whether friends or enemies would come first. Anyhow, that would be better than lying out in the open on a freezing night without blankets. Such would be the problem of tens of thousands of other Americans who had been overwhelmed by this enemy onslaught and scattered in groups large or small. They would survive the night as best they could, and get together again and fight, or surrender when they had fired their last cartridges. Most of them were well trained and had been taught how to meet emergencies; but few of them would know much more than the art experts about where the enemy was, or in what force, or what was going on beyond the reach of their eyesight.

The Monuments party slept for a while, then were awakened by a crashing sound and the roar of heavy engines. They lay with hearts pounding, trying to make out what was happening. They realized that oncoming tanks had crashed their way through the stone wall. Spotlights playing over the barn shone through the chinks, and the refugees dug their way deeper into the hay, pulling it over their faces until they were barely able to breathe. They listened to voices, and their hearts sank. "*Halt! . . . Wie heisst der Ort? . . . Hier bleiben wir über nacht. . . . Heraus mit Euch—zum Donnerwetter! . . . Panzerfäusten mitnehmen!*" Even the boy from Brooklyn, who didn't know the meaning of these raucous sounds, knew what language they were in. It was the language of the Adolf Hitler Schutzstaffel Panzer Division and the Grossdeutschland Panzer Grenadier Division.

The door was flung open, and men tramped in, spitting out their many crowded consonants and flashing torches about. "*Niemand hier.*" The four Americans cowered and held their breath. Would the intruders climb up and investigate the hay, perhaps stab into it with their bayonets? Sound military practice would have called for that; but they had had a hard day and half a night, driving, marching, fighting; also, the makeshift ladder did not look too strong. They did not climb but settled down to gulp their hard rations and get ready for the night. Their talk was of the day's adventures, and their mood was of exultation—mind triumphing over the exhaustion of the body. They had driven *die amerikanischen Schweinehunde* in rout before them; this time they were really going through with it—they would cut off the enemy from his base and pin him against the sea as they had done with the French and the British four and a half years ago. *Sieg Heil!*

IV

The newly appointed commander of three other pig-dogs lay still and thought hard about his duty. It seemed certain that when sleeping time came—and that would be but a few minutes—some of these men would climb into the hay. Then it would be either fight or surrender. A single grenade tossed down might eliminate most of the group in the barn; but what about the greater number outside, and the tanks with their powerful spotlights and deadly machine guns? Lanny and his friends would surely die; and was that their duty? Only one of them had been trained to fight, and he had been told not to.

On the other hand, what were Lanny Budd's personal chances if he surrendered? He had destroyed all his papers and could give a false name and might get by with it. But he had traveled all over Germany, ever since boyhood, and had known literally thousands of Germans, especially of the officer class and among the Nazis of the ruling group. He had met them at Berchtesgaden and Karinhall and in the Berlin Chancellery; he had spent a week at the *Parteitag* in Nürnberg the year before the war and been introduced wholesale. Everywhere he had been conspicuous as the Führer's one and only American friend; and now, in all probability, they knew that he had been a spy and traitor to their cause. Was it conceivable that he could become a prisoner and pass under a false name? And if he were recognized, would they be content to hang or shoot him? Wasn't it certain that they would apply all the fancy kinds of scientific torture they had devised to make him reveal the names of his accomplices? So why not die quickly and take a few highly trained enemy troops along with him?

But what about his three companions? They had a chance for their lives and might wish to take it; but he couldn't ask them, he had to decide for them, and that was a delicate ethical problem. He had to think fast, for at any moment one of the weary Germans might decide to hit the hay. To live or not to live, that was the question. To save his companions and take a chance on being able to kill himself if and when the Nazis found him out? If only he had had one of those tiny cyanide capsules with which the OSS provided its agents when going into enemy territory!

As it happened, this decision didn't have to be made. The door of the barn was suddenly thrown open, and a commanding voice shouted, "*'Raus! Alles 'raus!*" Without so much as a mutter or a groan the well-disciplined troopers scrambled to their feet, gathered up their gear, and filed out into the sifting snow. Lanny's heart leaped; they were going away, leaving this comfortable shelter to the American pig-dogs!

But that hope lasted only a minute or so. There was another stern command, in another voice. *"Herein, Ihr Hurensöhne!"* Then more shuffling feet; other men coming into the barn, a great many, for the sounds went on and on, the angry voice still shouting, *"Hier herein fahren!"* This time the men were not silent and humble; they muttered and grumbled, and what they said was, "The goddam bastards, what do they think we are—sardines?" No difficulty in identifying those voices: the barn was being filled with prisoners of war.

After much shouting in German the Americans were packed in to the satisfaction of their captors, and then the door of the barn was slammed shut. Half a minute later came an ominous sound, unmistakably hammer and nails—the door was being nailed up. "Holy Christ!" exclaimed a voice. "They're putting us in here to suffocate!" Then another voice, "Maybe they're going to set fire to the place!" There was a babel of protests, cries, and curses.

The four refugees scrambled up out of their hay nests. Their impulse was to call to the men below, but Lanny cautioned, whispering, "The Germans may have spies among them." He went to the ladder, made by nailing boards onto one of the supporting posts of the barn. He went down a couple of steps, then reached and touched one of the men on the shoulder. The startled man reached up, and Lanny took his hand and shook it, then guided it to the boards, which had not been discovered in the darkness. That was enough; the man started to climb, and Lanny preceded him.

V

Up in the loft there was a whispered conference. "What unit are you?"

"Combat Command R of 9th Armored Division. Who are you?"

"One soldier and three Monuments officers; art experts, not fighting men. But we have weapons; one carbine, one automatic, two grenades, and two knives."

"Fighting knives?"

"Sharp as razors."

"That's what we need. If we have to fire a shot we're sunk. How can we get out of this barn without waking up the whole Kraut army?"

Peter Morrison, ex-farm boy from Wisconsin, spoke up. In this man's Army there was always somebody who could answer any question. "Every barn has to have a hay window, to pitch the stuff in; it's always at the front, and all I ever saw open inward."

"You look for it," was the reply, "and I'll get the lieutenant."

It took Morrison but a minute to find the window and come back and report: it was oblong in shape, made entirely of wood, and held in place by a strip of wood which turned at the center. When the strip was turned crossways the cover was fastened; when it was turned vertically the cover was loose and could be lifted down. It should be possible to perform this operation noiselessly.

The combat man came with three others, who gave their names as Lieutenant Hutchins and Sergeants Carvalho and Eckart. Lanny never saw their faces; he knew them only by voice. They talked fast, and it was evident that they knew their business down to the last detail; they had spent two years learning it and half a year acting what they had learned. With quiet competence they laid out the procedure. First, get as many men as possible into the loft and instruct the rest to climb up as fast as room was made; then open the hay window as softly as possible and listen for the sentry below. There would probably not be more than one because of the door having been nailed. The most powerful and active of the Americans, one trained in commando work, would drop upon that sentry's back, bear him down, and slit his throat with the knife. Another commando would be a second or two behind, prepared to help.

Everything of course depended upon that first action. If the sentry succeeded in giving a cry or firing a shot, it would be all up with the project—and probably with the projectors. But the job was a simple one, a hundred times rehearsed. Other men would be dropping fast and they would look for other sentries at the sides of the barn or behind it. If you could steal up behind a man, you would grab him by the face with the left hand, pull his head back, and pass the knife across his neck. If the sentry was facing you, you said "*Heil Hitler! Ein Freund!*" and when he saluted you clasped him to your bosom with your left hand and cut his throat with the right. All that presupposed darkness, of which there was an unlimited quantity outside.

"And when your men have all dropped, what then?" asked Lanny. The answer was, they would scatter and run for it. But the P.A. countered, "Why not march out in good order? If the alarm is not given, the Germans won't turn on their searchlights and won't see our uniforms. I have listened to a thousand German officers giving orders, and I'm sure I can talk your men all the way across a barnyard and out into a forest."

"God Almighty!" exclaimed the lieutenant, pleased but uncertain.

"Most of the officers will be in the farmhouse, eating supper and resting. No German common soldier dares to challenge an officer or anything he does. Their units have probably been scrambled up, just like our own, and an unfamiliar voice won't attract attention."

"All right, sir, we'll put our fate in your hands."

"One thing more: have each of your men start questioning every man around him and make sure he knows the identity of everyone he puts his hands on. The enemy may have put spies in with you to pick up information regarding units and their disposition."

"OK, sir," said the young officer; "and if we find a stranger we'll make sure he doesn't tell tales."

VI

This was the program, and it was carried out with all speed, for who could tell at what moment a squad might appear to set fire to this barn? A horrid idea, but Lanny wouldn't have put it past these black-clad SS men with the death's head insignia on their sleeves. The orders were passed in whispers, and the Yanks stood in dead silence. The cover was carefully removed from the hay window. Lanny and his friends stood near, holding their breath while the commando dropped. Fortunately there was a tank running its engine near by; also, there were firing in the woods and the rumble of distant artillery— enough to drown out whatever groan or cry the sentry or sentries may have made.

The men were dropping out of the window, a steady stream of them. The lieutenant told Lanny and his friends to go; he would follow, and they would keep together. The drop was nothing, for the barn was small, and when you were hanging by your hands from the window you were only three or four feet from the ground; a pair of strong arms caught you by the knees and set you down and shoved you to one side. Lanny didn't count the procession, but there must have been thirty or forty. When the last one was on the ground the young officer took Lanny and his friends to the front of the group. He whispered, "OK!"

So there was Hauptmann von Buddow, or maybe it was Buddenbrooks or Buddenburg, commanding: *"Habt Acht, Kompagnie! Vorwärts marsch!"* They started: tramp, tramp, all in step, and hitting the ground hard. And meantime the commanding officer was pronouncing an oration: *"Diesmal gehts ums Ganze, zum letzten Mal gehen wir ran an den Feind! Die amerikanischen Schweinhunde sind in voller Flucht. Wir werden sie ins Meer werfen. Wir kämpfen für Führer und Vaterland. Mag der Kampf auch heiss sein, diesmal wird ein schneller Sieg winken. Sieg Heil!"*

A bit flowery, perhaps, but this was a Hitlerjugend SS group, and its officers were in a mood of glory; the world was theirs, and why shouldn't they repeat the familiar slogans to troops called upon to march out and fight in darkness and cold? We fight for Führer and Fatherland! The battle may be hot, but a quick victory will greet us! Hail victory! Thus inspired, the detachment marched across the barnyard, and over what the tanks had left of the stone fence, and out into the forest by the same track which Lanny and his group had entered by. No alarm was given, no lights were flashed, and they were left to imagine what happened when the Germans discovered how their cageful of birds had flown.

Deep in the forest, the lieutenant ordered them to break up into groups of three, get off the road, travel as far as they could in the darkness, then grope their way into the thickets. The moment daylight came they would start traveling, and collect weapons from the many dead bodies which lay about. They would try to reach the American lines, though nobody had much of an idea where the lines were. The young officer invited Monuments to come with him, but they thought that four was as large a group as could easily hide, and there was a difference of methods between hiders and fighters. They exchanged addresses and promised to write and let each other know how they had made out; but Lanny never heard from this able young shavetail. They were a rank in which many replacements were needed; they led their men into the fight and many did not come back.

VII

The P.A. had exchanged a few sentences with members of the fleeing group but had not learned very much. They did not know where they were; they could only say that there had been an overwhelming offensive. The 9th Armored had been ordered to hold at all costs and they had done so; the noncombatants—the cooks, clerks, mechanics, and even members of the band—had caught up weapons and stood fast until their last cartridges had been fired. They had fallen back, got more ammunition, and fought again. They had surrendered only when they found themselves surrounded and helpless. The Germans had taken everything they had, so they could not offer the Monuments officers so much as a can of bully beef.

Men who are well fed and well clad can perhaps dig into snow and sleep without danger; but men whose bellies are empty, and who have been floundering through snowdrifts to the point of exhaustion, dare not lie down and lose consciousness. They established a system, whereby three lay down to rest and one stood guard and kicked their feet and made them answer. After a while there would be a fresh kicker; so they all managed to keep alive until a pale, ghostly light began to spread through the fogbound forest. It was one of the most beautiful forests in Europe, but they wholly failed to appreciate it. They did not admire the snow-laden fir trees which now and then dropped loads upon their heads; they did not like the high ridges, strewn with rocks behind which snipers might hide and take potshots; they did not like the deep ravines which filled up with snow, and sometimes with treacherous ice-covered water. If you slipped you might lose all your toes when you stopped walking and started freezing.

But the Lord must have loved the Ardennes because He had made such a lot of it and kept it going for so long. It stretched well into France, covered the southern part of Belgium and the northern part of Luxembourg, and into Germany as far as the Rhine. Many thousands of square miles of it—no one could say exactly because it petered out at the edges and there were stretches of cultivated land, with scattered towns and villages. There were a few paved roads connecting these, and many bridges over the streams and gullies; now the Americans were busily blowing the bridges up wherever they could get a chance, and the Germans were establishing defense posts to prevent it.

Early dawn was the time to get started, so the fugitives figured; and evidently the fighting men had the same idea, for the sounds of battle broke out all over the region. Every kind of explosive, big and little and in between; it was like a symphony in which the sound never ceases but the instruments change and the individual notes are hardly noticed. The ignominious men who didn't want to fight no longer knew which way to turn. They crouched and discussed the problem in whispers. They had been going west with the idea of outrunning the Panzers, but they had failed; the enemy was driving a deep wedge, and might it not be the part of wisdom to turn south, with the chance that the wedge might not be as broad as it was long, and that American resistance might be stronger at the sides?

They decided on this tactic, and for a while followed the gray needle of the Brooklyn boy's compass. When they heard shots ahead they crouched in snow-covered underbrush and tried to peer through the heavy mist which veiled the forest all that day. It seemed like a joke to remind themselves that this was Sunday morning and that soon, when the sun got up over the States, people would be eating eggs and hot toast and coffee, and putting on their best clothes for church. "They will be praying for us," said Georgie Bradford, the other art expert; he was real Beacon Street, and a devout Episcopalian. He believed it was the prayers of his wife and mother that had saved him last night, rather than the training of the commandos and the quick thinking of the son of Budd-Erling.

VIII

They came to a paved road and kept away from it in well-schooled dread. Anything might come dashing along that highway, and before they could make sure whether it was German or American it would have disappeared or else have wiped them out with a burst of machine-gun fire or grenades fired from a rifle. They were at a disadvantage because their overcoats were brown, and there was nothing else of that color in the forest, unless it was the hair of the deer. Lanny knew that the Russians wore white camouflage in winter, and had heard that the Germans had taken up the practice, covering their helmets with pillowcases and their bodies with bedsheets whenever they could get them. The P.A. had asked about this at the front and been told that the doughboys had called for it but the stuff had not arrived.

They held another conference in whispers. The road led west and obviously must come to a town; should they keep just out of sight of it and parallel to it? What would they find at the end, friends or enemies, a battle between them or a siege? Manifestly they had to find something; they couldn't stay out in the open indefinitely without food. They had had a chance to shoot a deer, but they were afraid to shoot or to build a fire, and hadn't yet reached the stage where they could drink raw blood or devour raw meat.

"Hush!" whispered the sharp-eared Morrison. They listened and caught a new sound—axes. What did that mean? It wasn't likely that anybody was cutting firewood—unless it was in a well-guarded strong-post. Several axes going at once, and fast—that would mean that men were cutting trees to block a road, and the chances were ten to one that it was Americans. The enemy wasn't blocking roads, he was using them, while the GIs were trying desperately to delay him.

The sounds came from the west, where the road led, and they followed its course, but at some distance away, crouching, darting from thicket to thicket—the life of the Belgian hare, a large and meaty animal destined to make *Hasenpfeffer*. There had been fighting here, a lot of it; there was blood on the snow, the ground had been trampled, and branches of trees shot away and scattered. Presently, under a young fir tree, a body, covered with snow; they brushed it away with their gloved hands and turned the body over. The face had been shot away, a terrible sight; the knees were bent and frozen stiff as rocks. They took the man's belongings and his dogtag, the little identification disk he wore about his neck. They would turn these things in when they had a chance; they would not turn in the can of K-rations they found in one of the victim's pockets. They opened that and cut it into four parts; it was frozen hard, and they ate it like popsicles.

IX

The ringing of axes is a pleasant sound, especially to a man from Wisconsin where there are lumber camps; it brings memories of hunting and fishing trips, and now it brought hopes of more ration cans, and even of hot food and coffee. When they got near Ike Abramson volunteered to do the scouting; he had been trained for it, he was younger and fresher, and called himself expendable. If he found it was the Army, he would shout "OK"; if he didn't shout within three minutes by the watch, they had better make a "sneak," as he called it. Let them go north away from the road, and if he could make his escape he would look for them there. The code word would be "*gefüllte Fisch*"—one of the Kraut phrases most familiar to a Brooklyn Jew.

He crept away, and they lay hugging the snow and keeping one eye on their watches. The hands moved, and their hearts began to fail them. The three minutes were up, and they were in the act of starting their sneak when they noticed that the sounds of chopping had ceased; a moment later came the gladsome shout, "OK, Monuments!" They turned and ran toward the road and came out into sight of it, holding their hands in the air.

It was the Army! They didn't shout, for it was no time for that. They came running, with all the strength they had left, and with joy in their faces. There were half a dozen woodsmen with double-bitted axes, and other GIs with various weapons mounting guard. What they had done to the road was a crime, at least from the point of view of Jerry, otherwise known as Heinie, the Hun, or the Kraut. The woodsmen had cut trees on both sides of the road so that they fell across the road and made a tangle of branches that would take a lot of chopping to remove. Smaller trees underneath and bigger trees on top, an ungodly mess covering perhaps a hundred yards of road. It would hold the Tigers for at least a couple of hours.

The gang had been just ready to call it a job and get out of there when Ike had put in his appearance, calling his name and his unit. Now came three noncombatants, holding their hands high lest they be taken for an enemy masquerade. There was no need of explanations, for such groups were coming in everywhere, in numbers from one to a thousand, and they all had the same story to tell. The three introduced themselves to the sergeant in command, who saluted and gave his unit: Task Force D, 10th Armored. "We are holding on at Longwilly," he said. Like all Americans below the commissioned ranks, he was contemptuous of French pronunciations. If they wanted you to say "Lonhveeyee," why didn't they spell it that way? These GIs, no doubt, thought of this village as belonging to somebody named William who happened to be tall and thin.

"Will you take us in with you?" asked the assimilated colonel.

"Sure thing, sir, if we can. Heinie's all over the place, and we never know where he'll show up in force. We sneaked out by a side road and hope to get back the same way. Pile in, boys."

Each of the Monuments had a seat, and then took a man on his knees. The man was armed with a "burp" gun, and he had to be prepared to use it in the tenth part of a lightning flash. There were six jeeps, and they started with a rush; they turned off the highway onto an unpaved track, and just then there was a tremendous explosion behind them. "Tank," said the man in Lanny's lap. "We put some of his own Tellers there for him, and I hope they got it." The Teller was a German land mine, round and flat like a plate; in a paved road you chipped out a chunk of the pavement of the right size, set the mine in the hole, and laid the block of pavement gently on top. When a tank came along and its tread hit that spot—"Zowie!" said the man with the "burp" gun. He was talkative, but all the time he sat with his head high, turning it swiftly this way and that, for all the world like a scared partridge on a tree branch.

The jeeps bounced and almost threw people out, but not quite. Their axles did not break, they went through snow and mud, and if ever they got stuck you could lift them; they were marvels for dependability, and the Army loved them. They sped through the forest, down into ravines and up again, and presently came to open fields with houses; presumably that was the town of the man named William who was tall and thin. Shots were fired at them and bullets whined overhead; they hit it up to sixty or seventy miles an hour, and it was most exhilarating. "We're surrounded," shouted the "burp" man, "but we don't know it!"

X

So here was Lanny Budd, back with the Army, where he had wanted to be, and right in the midst of action, which he hadn't wanted. Now and then a shell came in and crashed near by; the line was out on the ridges beyond the village, the GIs explained. They stopped in front of the town hall, which was the CP, busy as a beehive. The passengers got out and announced themselves.

The commander here was Lieutenant Colonel Cherry, who came from Georgia and was courteous, like all Southerners; he was a much worried officer and looked as if he hadn't slept or eaten since the day before yesterday. "I hope that I can send you out, gentlemen, but at present all communications are cut, including our telephone lines." He turned the visitors over to one of his staff officers, Captain May, who took them into an improvised dining-room, it being lunchtime. They tried to remember their manners in the presence of a plate of hot beef stew, coffee with milk and sugar, and bread with canned butter. Never had there been any food like that!

"Let us be of use while we stay here," Lanny said, and the staff officer asked what they could do. The P.A. told how he had served as an interrogation officer with the Seventh Army, all the way up from Cannes to Lyon; having lived most of his life in Europe, he knew French and German well, and the other two Monuments officers had scholars' knowledge and could soon pick up various German dialects. "If you have prisoners," Lanny added.

The other replied that they had not a few; some had come in of their own impulse, anxious to get out of the mess. "But they're right in it," he added. "If we're forced out of here we may not be able to hold them. Meantime, of course, the more we can get out of them the better. We've been pretty well blinded; we have only the radio-phone and have to be careful what we ask or tell over that, since the enemy will be recording everything."

Lanny said, "The weather is against us," and the answer was, "Oh, God, yes! If it were clear there'd be a swarm of planes helping us. As it is, we've heard some but we haven't seen a single one."

The three "Docs" bade good-by to the eager Brooklyn boy who had been so great a help to them. The boy would have a sleep, and then he would go into the line, which now had men from a score or two of units who had come straggling in. Lanny told him, "When the war's over, go and see my father in Newcastle, Connecticut, and he'll give you a good job." It was the first time the boy had known that this "Colonel" Budd was Budd-Erling, and he was quite awe-stricken.

The three officers also had a sleep, undisturbed by the thunder of guns all around them. Out there in the woods and thickets tanks and tank-killers were chasing one another about like prehistoric pachyderms; men crouching behind trees and rocks and in trenches were shooting streams of steel at one another and throwing deadly grenades when they got a chance. Guns small and medium were hurling shells into the village and out of it—that was referred to as "arty," meaning artillery. Here, as everywhere in the Ardennes, the American forces knew only what was within a couple of miles of them, and had no idea what might be coming in the next half hour. "Intelligence" had failed; or, rather, as Lanny learned later on, "Topside" had failed to pay attention to what "Intelligence" had sent it. This "Bulge" represented the greatest defeat the Army had sustained since Bataan, and its greatest peril since the beginning of the war.

XI

The three Monuments officers received only the briefest briefing. Lanny knew the job, and the other two listened, and after they had learned how to proceed they were put off in a corner by themselves. A stern-faced soldier brought in a prisoner and stood on guard while the officer asked questions. There should have been a stenographer, but in a jam like this each interrogator had a pad on his knee and made his own notes of what seemed to him important. What is your name? Where do you live? How long have you been in the service? What is your unit? Who is your commander? Where did you start from? What other units have you seen? Where were you captured? And so on.

Some of the men lied, of course; some were cocky and defiant, victory being in their hands at last. Others were humble and talked freely, hoping to win favors; for the promise of a cigarette they would betray the German Army. Many of them were sick of the war; many of them hated the Nazis—when they got behind the American lines. It was necessary to speak sternly because that was what they were used to. *"Ich bin ein einfacher, gewöhnlicher Mensch. Was konnte ich tun?"* Lanny had heard it a hundred times. I am a poor, common man. What could I do? Lanny didn't say that he had heard a hundred thousand such poor common men yelling their heads off for Hitler in the old days.

When you put all this together a pattern emerged, its outline blurred and dim, but still it was there. The offensive had been in preparation for weeks, with extraordinary precautions being taken to keep the troops hidden in forests. The assault had been made on a front of at least fifty miles, and there were more than a score of divisions named as taking part: Paratroopers, Panzers, Panzer grenadiers, Volksgrenadiers, everything the enemy had. Field Marshal von Rundstedt was commanding, and the Führer himself had come to the Rhineland and briefed the higher officers, telling them that this was the great crisis of the war, that they were going to take the huge American supply base at Liége, break through to the port of Antwerp, cut off the American First Army and the British to the north and annihilate them. Word of this had been spread among the troops, and now they were sure it was all coming true. Their great armored forces weren't bothering with small towns and villages like Longwilly, but were leaving them to be mopped up later; they were driving straight through for the great strategic bases, Sedan and Namur and Liége. *Sieg Heil!*

4

Deeds of Courage

I

THE Allied armies were facing the Germans over a front of some four hundred miles, extending from the North Sea, first eastward and then southward. There were, in order, the Canadians and the British, then the American Ninth Army, then the First, then General Patton's

Third, and then the American Sixth Army Group, including the
Seventh Army with which Lanny Budd had traveled in the late summer. Farthest to the south were the French, closing the Belmont Gap,
near the Swiss border. The Ardennes lay at about the center of this
four-hundred-mile line, and the divisions which had been caught there
and were fighting for their lives were a part of the American First
Army. About fifty thousand men had been holding fifty miles, a
thousand men to the mile, or one every five feet, and no reserves; that
was spreading them thin indeed. There was a group of highly trained
brass at SHAEF—Supreme Headquarters Allied Expeditionary Force—
who had been quite sure the Germans would not attack through such
uninviting country; they had overlooked the fact that to be so sure
was the way to invite an attack.

Now it had come, with every division the enemy could spare from
the rest of the front, plus all the reserves he could scrape together in
besieged Germany. He had rolled over the American 28th and 106th
Divisions and the 9th Armored, which had been directly in front of
him; he had scattered them, driven them back, captured perhaps half
of them; but the rest had reassembled and were making a stand wherever they found themselves. The tactics were to destroy bridges and
culverts and block and hold the roads. It was possible for tanks and
heavy vehicles to move through snowbound forests, but only at great
expense of time and fuel, and both these were vital to the Germans
if they were going to reach Namur and Liége, to say nothing of
Antwerp.

There was a paved road running east and west through the little
town of Longwilly, and that made it vital. Out there on the ridges,
behind rocks and in hastily dug trenches, men of many different units
and types of training were fighting where they stood and dying where
they fell. It was a wild kind of brawl because neither side was sure
what it held, and when the Americans were surrounded they fought
their way out and got more supplies and then fought their way
back in again. "Hold on at all costs," was the order, and they held,
day and night; every hour they denied the use of this road to the
Germans was that much time for the defense to rally and for new
divisions to gather on the sides of the Bulge. Apparently there was
nothing much at the tip; the enemy could go fifty or sixty miles, and
farther if he dared.

II

Sleep when you can is one of the first lessons a soldier learns. Lanny slept two or three hours that Sunday night, and before dawn he was awakened. "Come," said a voice. "We have to move." The three Monuments sprang awake, gathered up their pencils and records, for no army can exist for even one day without what it calls "paper work." Headquarters was moving, they were told; they were surrounded in force and would have to fight their way back westward and take another stand. Tanks and halftracks were going ahead to clear the way, and troops would spread out into the forest to protect them.

The three sat on a bench and waited. There was an incessant thunder and rattle of guns, all kinds and sizes. Apparently the three had been routed out too soon; the fighting men were having a harder time than had been expected. The three conversed for a while in whispers, then they dozed. When they were told "All out!" they bolted outdoors, and there was an armored car waiting. Office people of all sorts were packed into it, a halftrack preceded it a length in front, and away they went down the main street of Longwilly. It was good-by forever—at least so far as the son of Budd-Erling was concerned.

Out into that dark forest, with only a dim light to guide the driver. A ride not soon to be forgotten, with shells exploding here and there, and the rattle of machine guns on both sides, and the thought every moment: Are we going to hit a mine? Are we going to turn over in a ditch? Shall we meet a Tiger, or a Royal Tiger? Shall we find the road blocked and have to get out and tramp in the snow again?

Their destination lay some five miles to the west, a larger town called Bastogne. It too was being defended with desperation; it too might be surrounded now, or in the next hour. The headquarters staff would go there, but the fighting men would stay out on the ridges, in the trenches and foxholes which the defenders had dug. Bastogne was of supreme importance because no fewer than eight roads ran out of it, and five of them were paved; it lay pretty close to the middle of the Bulge, and so long as it was held the enemy would be greatly handicapped. It had some four thousand inhabitants; just one more Belgian town, dull and dingy, but it was destined to immortality, like that other one called Waterloo, and another called Ypres.

III

The procession of cars arrived without serious losses, and Monuments found themselves established in a new headquarters. The commanding officer was Colonel William Roberts, of the 10th Armored; Longwilly might have been named in anticipation of him, for he was tall and lean. He came from Louisiana, and was scholarly in appearance, quiet in manner—but he was called "the Stone," because he was so hard to move when he didn't want to go. "Gentlemen," he said to the new arrivals, "we are being pressed hard, but we are staying and we are going to stay. Confidentially, we have been promised help. At all hazards, we must deny these roads to the enemy."

It was the biggest battle that Lanny Budd had ever been near, and it was much too near for comfort. Five enemy divisions surrounded the town, and their artillery was pouring shells into it; also, they seemed to have a new-style rocket bomb, smaller than the V-2 but more precisely directed. Houses crumbled on top of the terrified inhabitants crouching in the cellars. The Americans were out on the high ground; they had tanks and tank-killers, but the biggest German tanks carried 88 mm. guns, so heavy that they could knock out even the tank destroyers. Expert marksmen fought them with rifles, aiming into the firing slits, and men hidden in foxholes threw bottles of gasoline. Forests were good places for the American style of fighting, every man ready to be on his own and to think for himself.

Heavy fog lay everywhere, and it began to rain again; how the officers and men cursed this weather! If only there had come one hour of sunshine the fighter-bombers would have been all over the place, knocking out enemy tanks and paralyzing his communications. As it was, this might have been an old-time battle, before air power existed. No doubt the Germans had planned it so; their weather stations in Greenland and Spitsbergen had been captured, but they got the same information by wireless from their submarines, so they knew what kind of weather was coming. Lanny could guess that the Führer's meteorologists had promised him what he wanted, and that the date of the blitz had been set by them.

Soon after Lanny's arrival in Bastogne a terrible item of news was reported to him. On the previous day, near the town of Malmédy to the north, a group of a hundred and twenty-five Americans had been surrounded by tanks and forced to surrender. The 12th SS Panzer had disarmed their captives and taken their valuables from them, then

herded them into a vacant space and turned machines guns on them;
men had fallen in heaps, and afterward officers had tramped among
them, shooting all who showed any signs of life. A score of men had
thrown themselves down when the shooting began and were buried
under the heaps; these escaped to tell the story. It spread quickly,
and American soldiers made note of the designation of those black-
uniformed murderers.

Soon afterward came an episode in Bastogne, showing again what
kind of battle this was going to be. There was a large hospital in the
suburbs, to the northwest, and it was full of wounded soldiers. There
came a group of tanks and some Nazis in civilian clothes and began
shooting up the place in the darkness and rain. A doctor went out
with a white flag and asked them to stop. The reply was that they
would give him and his staff a half-hour to pack up and get ready
to move. They carted off not merely the staff and the supplies, but all
the wounded men.

IV

Monuments resumed work on interrogation; it was the way they
could be most useful, setting free the military men for more urgent
duties. In this mixed-up fighting a number of prisoners were gathered,
and it called for some knowledge of German character and disposition
to get out of each one as much as possible. The work was interesting,
because it brought revelations as to how the battle was going; sometimes Monuments knew more than the commander and his staff.
Lanny's interest was the keener because his own life was at stake.

In his progress up the "Route Napoleon," from Cannes to Lyon,
he had met just one Nazi who recognized him, an SS man of the
Führer's own bodyguard. Now he wondered how long it would be
before this happened again. Many whom he didn't know would know
him, for he had been a conspicuous figure wherever he went in Naziland, the American whom the Führer trusted. Why the Führer trusted
him was a mystery to all Germans, except those few who understood
the Führer's peculiarity, that persons whom he had known in the days
before he became great constituted a chosen band, above suspicion of
self-seeking. In some seventeen years of acquaintance Lanny Budd had
never asked a favor, and when a favor was offered he had refused it
unless it was one of small importance.

During the first crowded day came the sort of thing he had anticipated. The GI whose assignment it was to bring in prisoners and stand

guard during the interrogation remarked, "We have just nabbed a staff car with three officers; the chauffeur was shot and the car upset in a ditch." Lanny asked the rank of the officers, and the answer was, "Two colonels and a major." Lanny's curiosity was aroused, and he went to the room where the prisoners were sitting and looked in; then he went back to the cubicle in which his work was carried on and said, "Soldier, go and bring that SS colonel to me."

The GI went away and came back with a black-clad SS *Oberst* in his middle forties, pasty-faced, stoutish, and carrying a paunch which a tight military belt could not conceal. Ordinarily he would have been dignified, but now he was mudstained, wet, and crestfallen—for one is not thrown out of a car into a ditch during a rainstorm without loss of social status. His round face had always been amiable in Lanny Budd's presence, but now he was obviously taken back by this confrontation.

"*Oberst*," said the P.A., speaking English, "I offer to put you on parole. Will you give me your word of honor not to attempt to escape while you are talking with me?"

"Certainly, *mein Herr*," replied the German at once. He was quick to guess that Lanny might not wish to be known as his friend.

"Soldier, you may wait outside," said Lanny. It wasn't the soldier's business to ask questions, and he went out, closing the door. Lanny held out his hand. He did it with some misgiving, for when he had done the same thing to another prisoner, his old friend Kurt Meissner, Kurt had spat in his face.

But Heinrich Jung was a different sort of Nazi; much milder, and always awed by a wealthy and elegant playboy from overseas. He accepted the handclasp, although his face wore a pained look. "You have turned against us, Lanny!"—this in German.

"No," replied the other, "you have been misinformed, Heinrich. I am not a military man and have never fired a shot against a German."

"But you are wearing a uniform!"

"The Army has given me what is called an assimilated rank, to enable me to travel with it and to have proper treatment. I am an officer of what is called the Monuments, Fine Arts, and Archives Section. My duty is to seek out the treasures of art and culture and protect them as far as possible from damage in this war."

"To be taken to America?"

"No, to be returned to their lawful owners when the war is over. Of that I am authorized to give positive assurance. You must know that as an art expert I could not refuse to render such a service. But what about you, *alter Freund?* You have become a military man?"

"As it happens I am in much the same position as yourself, Lanny. I am doing morale work only. I am attached to the Hitlerjugend SS Division. As you know, those are my own boys; I have been helping in their education since they were five years old, and I could not refuse an assignment to guide and inspire them at the front. Like you, I can say that I have never fired a shot."

"Well, Heinrich, that makes it about even; we can still be friends." Lanny wasn't really that naïve, but it was his job to appear so; it had been his job for the past seven or eight years, ever since he had become a presidential agent and had turned his acquaintance with Heinrich Jung to the service of the anti-Nazi cause. So now the P.A.'s face was wreathed in smiles; between the son of Budd-Erling and the *Oberförster's* son from Schloss Stubendorf it would be as if there had never been any war. They were still in the happy days when Lanny would come to Berlin on a visit, and invite Oberführer Jung and blond Frau Oberführer to an elegant dinner at the Adlon, and send them home loaded with presents for the eight little Hitlerjungen and Hitlermädels.

V

What did Lanny want from this rather dull Nazi patriot, and why was he willing to spend an afternoon chatting about old times and risk his personal safety still further? To be sure, Heinrich was a prisoner, and his two fellow officers were prisoners—but who could say for how long? Heinrich would be sure to tell the others about this wonderful rich American. And if the Americans in Bastogne were forced to surrender—something which would surely happen if help did not come soon—the Germans would know about him and would learn quickly that he was one of the most wanted of enemies.

It was what the military men call a "calculated risk." Lanny would collect information from Heinrich and then would find some way to get out of here, or to get Heinrich out of here; it would be a battle of wits between them, and Lanny was sure he had the better set of wits. Now he assured his old friend that it was all a cruel misunderstanding, the reports which had been spread in Germany that he had turned against his Nazi friends; he had been terribly distressed about these reports, and only recently had come upon what he believed was the true explanation. Reichsminister Himmler, head of the Gestapo and now of the SS, had interviewed Lanny on the latter's last visit to Berlin. Lanny had assumed that Himmler was suspicious of an

American friend of the Führer; but since then he had found reason to believe that Himmler himself was planning to turn against his Führer and replace him, and had been sounding Lanny out with the idea of inviting him to join in the conspiracy. Only when Himmler had found that Lanny was completely loyal to Hitler had he set out to poison the Führer's mind against him.

The worshipful Heinrich was, of course, horrified by this idea and assured Lanny solemnly that it couldn't possibly be true. Lanny insisted that he had come upon convincing evidence. The ruthless Reichsminister had become certain that the war was lost and was trying to save his own neck.

Heinrich's answer to this was, of course, that the war wasn't lost; quite the contrary, it was being won right now, and Lanny himself must be aware of it. Lanny admitted that his confidence had been shaken, and that started Heinrich off to boasting about his wonderful Führer and what that Führer had done to turn the tide and snatch victory out of defeat, exactly as his predecessor Frederick the Great had done under similar circumstances. Heinrich boasted about his own Hitlerjugend Panzer Division and how far it had penetrated, and as he named town after town and village after village, Lanny expressed surprise. The P.A. would ask whether the Americans hadn't broken up this unit and that, and Heinrich would laugh and tell him it wasn't so. Heinrich himself had nothing to fear, he insisted, for Bastogne was completely surrounded, and the Americans couldn't get out if they wanted to; Heinrich would soon be liberated, and when that happened he would at once take Lanny to the Führer and give him a chance to warn the Führer about Himmler's treachery.

VI

Yes, the *Oberst Oberführer* was a rather inept person. He was tremendously proud of his friendship with the greatest man in the world, and indeed the greatest man in all history—not that Heinrich knew much history. He told how he had had the honor of attending a meeting with this greatest man at his headquarters at Ziegenberg, a castle in the Taunus Mountains, just east of the Rhine. Heinrich had gone there to make a report on the morale of the Hitler youth in the Army; he didn't have to explain to Lanny why he had been singled out for this honor, for Lanny knew that Heinrich was one of the Nazi "old companions"; he had visited Adolf Hitler when Hitler had been imprisoned for his part in the Putsch in Munich just twenty years ago.

That had given him something to talk about for the rest of his days, and also a safe and sure career in the Nazi bureaucracy.

"How is the Führer?" asked the P.A. with the solicitude of a friend, and Heinrich said that his spirit was still that of the eagle, but physically he had never recovered from the shock of the dastardly attempt upon his life last July. His hands shook so that he would no longer eat in the presence of others, and he was obliged to wear spectacles when he read, something he had never done in public hitherto. During Heinrich's visit had occurred the conference with all the army, corps, and division commanders at which Adi had announced this present offensive, which he had planned all by himself and made known as fixed and final.

Heinrich himself had not been invited to this session, but there had been so much talk about it among the Führer's personal staff, both preceding it and afterward, that it was as if he had been present; he couldn't resist the impulse to tell Lanny all the gossip. Imagine, if you could, those high and mighty Wehrmacht generals and marshals being compelled to leave their pistols and briefcases in the cloakroom of a hotel, and then enter busses and be driven around in pouring rain for half an hour, so that they wouldn't know where they were! They entered a heavy bunker between a double row of SS men and sat at a table with a line of SS men behind them, watching every move; those old fellows didn't even dare to draw a handkerchief out of their pockets! For an hour the Führer told them the history of the National Socialist party and how much the German people owed to him.

After the first hour of history there was another of tactics and strategy. Everything was to be put into this Ardennes offensive, and it was going to win the war; nothing else must be thought of for a single moment. Each commander received his precise orders. General Dietrich, known as "Sepp," which is short for Joseph, was to go in a wide curve to Liége and take possession of its enormous stores of supplies, thus crippling the enemy and building his own power. General Manteuffel—which means "man-devil," exactly what Hitler thought of him—was to go on to Antwerp, the port upon which all Allied power depended. General Montgomery's entire army of British and Canadians would be cut off and destroyed, and the loss would so discourage America that it would quit. To the Führer's devoted servant this was a clear outline of what was in progress now, and his heart swelled with exultation as he recited it; the art expert served as a proper foil, now looking dismayed and discouraged, then expressing doubts which brought out more details. That was the way to interview an enemy prisoner.

VII

When the session was over Lanny asked, "How do you get along with those two Wehrmacht officers you are with?" The answer was, "They look down on all party people and show it as much as they dare. Besides, they blame me for what happened, because I insisted on taking the road that we did."

Lanny thought for a space. "Suppose I could arrange for you to be paroled, Heinrich?"

"Oh, could you do that? You could surely trust me, Lanny. I wouldn't break faith with you for anything."

"The point is, you're not really a fighting man, any more than I am. You might put on civilian clothes and help take care of some of the German wounded we have here."

"I'd be happy to do it, Lanny. I'd help any wounded men, regardless of which side."

Lanny called in the GI and told him to keep this prisoner until Lanny returned. He sought out the staff officer to whom he was reporting and told him the whole story, explaining why he didn't want the Germans to know who he was, and didn't want Heinrich to go back with the two Wehrmacht officers. There was no special reason why a "morale" *Oberst Oberführer* shouldn't be paroled; he was too fat and soft to be a fighting man, even if he wanted to be.

The result was that he was put in Lanny's custody and went to work in an improvised hospital, wearing a dead civilian's suit much too small for him. He solemnly promised not to mention the name of Lanny Budd to anyone; and this seemed all right to him, for the reason that Lanny wouldn't want anybody in the American Army to know that he was a friend of the Führer. It pleased the SS *Oberst Oberführer* to be keeping so deadly a secret from his foes. When the Germans took Bastogne, which was bound to happen in a day or two, Lanny would give a lot of priceless information to the German forces.

VIII

Things did look pretty black for the Americans that Monday night. Fog hung over the battle scene, so thick that you could put your hands in it. Sometimes it rained and sometimes it snowed, and there could be no help from the air. All over that black forest groups of men were fighting, and between times blocking roads and blowing bridges, doing everything they could to delay the enemy hordes. Small groups would join themselves to larger groups—there were some who had fought with as many as nine different units before the month-long battle was over; they were caught there, and had nothing to do but fight, and then fall back to some other crossroads and fight again.

Bastogne was completely surrounded; but the wireless telephone was in use, and headquarters told them to hold on at all hazards. Headquarters of the First Army had been at Spa, a luxurious springs resort to the north. It was uncomfortably near to the enemy's line of advance, and the staff had got out in a hurry, some not even stopping to pack their duds. Where they had gone to now was not being told over the radio, even in code, but they had code words to identify them, and they kept saying, "Hold at all costs." Bastogne kept saying, "We are holding."

Somewhere just outside the Bulge, to the north, was the 101st Airborne, known according to its insigne as the "Screaming Eagle" Division. "Airborne" means that its members are flown in transport planes or towed in gliders; they are tough guys and have been taught all there is about combat. This division had been put down in Normandy and had fought all the way to Holland. They were supposed to be resting now, and it was only a few days to Christmas; they had been planning a football game, the most wonderful ever, and they were greatly excited about it—but it was never played. On Sunday morning had come telephone orders, in double-talk, telling them to be ready to move on Tuesday; a little later it was changed to Monday at fourteen, which is two in the afternoon. Nothing could be "airborne" in this weather, so their SOS—Service of Supplies—scoured the neighborhood for trucks big and little and all sizes between.

The commanding officer of this division happened to be in Washington. The second in command was Brigadier General McAuliffe, a little man, quiet but determined, known to his men as the "Old Crock"—although he was young. He got his twelve thousand men under way at the time specified, using all the north-south roads there were. Plenty of Germans were in the way, but led by tanks the Americans broke through everything. It was like an episode in a movie, the grand climax where the cavalry comes galloping in with flags flying and is welcomed with frantic cheers; the only difference was that the Screaming Eagles came packed in trucks, and had no flags, and there was nobody to cheer, because the Belgians were hiding in their cellars and the fighting men were out in trenches and foxholes and didn't even know what was happening.

The way they found out was that fresh men kept sneaking up behind them and joining them in the trenches; very cocky fellows who called themselves "paradoughs" and thought that nobody else knew very much. Presently they began charging out and driving the enemy back, with the help of shells from their batteries posted behind the lines. Something new began to happen to the Germans then, and most of them never knew what it was. There had come to the rescue of Bastogne not merely some thousands of paradoughs and their artillery, but a large group of scientists and engineers working in laboratories three or four thousand miles away.

IX

It was one of the great secrets of the war, and one of the engineering marvels of all time; a thing known as a "proximity fuse." Lanny had been given a hint of it by his friend Professor Alston, the presidential "fixer"; but he hadn't asked any questions, for it wasn't his job. Now the talk went round among the officers at Bastogne, the amazing things that were happening out there at the front, and so Lanny heard a strange phrase, "pozit ammunition," as the new device had come to be called.

When a shell is fired at an airplane in the sky, the gunner has to calculate or guess the spot where the plane will be when the shell arrives; then he has to set the fuse of the shell so that it will explode in the number of seconds required for it to reach that spot. A tremendously difficult task, and experience showed that a gunner fired twenty-five hundred shots to bring down one plane. But suppose a fuse could be made with some sort of radar equipment that would send out signals as it sped, and when these signals were echoed back with sufficient strength from some object in the sky, the shell would explode near the target?

There would be no trouble in devising a fuse that would go off at a radio signal. The problem lay in the fact that it had to be fired from a cannon, and had to be tough enough to withstand the impact of an explosion that would hurl the shell a distance of many miles. Moreover, the shell on its way revolves 475 times a second, and it takes some toughness to stand that. Literally thousands of scientists and engineers had been working at this problem for years, even before the war; in the end they had come up with a marvel called the VT-fuse, an object no bigger than your hand. Inside it was a radio sending and receiving set, so resistant to shock that the shell in which it was set could be fired from a gun big or little. The fuse was set to detonate the shell a certain number of feet from an object which sent an echo back from its radio signals.

This was a secret so precious that those in command decreed that it should be used only over the sea. Some shells are duds, and when they hit the sea they sink out of an enemy's sight and he will never know what missed him. But when a shell hits the ground it buries itself not too deeply, and the enemy might dig it up and get the benefit of all those years of research and hundreds of millions of dollars of expenditure. Now, however, this situation in the Bulge was so critical, the danger of Adolf Hitler's dream coming true was so imminent, that orders had come to use the VT-fused shells. So here they were, and Germans crouching in trenches and foxholes in the good old way, thinking themselves safe from everything but a direct hit, suddenly discovered that howitzer shells were going off directly over their heads and pouring death and ruin among them. There was no longer any way to be safe; and dazed prisoners were brought in, who exclaimed to Lanny Budd, "We don't know how you do it, but it must be contrary to The Hague Convention!"

X

At this time there were five German divisions attacking Bastogne; at full strength that would have been seventy-five thousand men. Pozit shells couldn't kill them all, especially as Bastogne's supply of them was limited. The battle was fought fiercely, day and night. The Americans would sally forth and seize a ridge; the Germans would attack and cut it off, and the Americans would fight their way back. Then it would be the Germans who got cut off and they would fight *their* way back.

The bombarding was incessant, and the town was gradually being reduced to rubble. A shell would come screaming and hit the house next to yours and shatter all the glass in your windows; if you were an American officer you were not supposed to bat an eye. You would make some supposed-to-be humorous remark—"Good eye, Jerry," or "Wrong number!"—anything to show that you didn't in the least mind being blown to flinders if it happened to be in the cards. The truth was, you were afraid you might lose your self-control, and you mustn't show it; the other fellow might be on the verge of losing his, and you had to set an example.

Every rainy night the besieged men told one another, "Tomorrow we'll have better weather, and the planes will come." But day after day the weather stayed the same—they were marvelous meteorologists that Adi Schicklgruber had in his service. The men in the trenches lay in icy cold water, and at night it froze and maybe they froze with it.

They got used to the sight of huge tanks looming up in the mist, and when they got mixed up in the woods it was hard to tell which was theirs and which was ours. It was sure-enough Indian fighting, and many a time a man was on his own and had nobody to give him any orders or help. A man named Beaster went out in a newly arrived tank-killer, and he came up over a ridge and there were five enemy tanks which had turned to get away from him. He fired five quick shots and knocked them out like so many stupid partridges sitting on a limb; then two more came into sight and he hit them. Over his telephone he reported, "I have just killed seven tanks." A moment later a shell from a German 88 hit his tank and knocked him out; but he lived to get more tanks.

Stories like that were all over the place. Men kept sneaking in through the enemy lines at night with the wildest tales of what had happened to them; enough adventure stories to keep the movies going for a hundred years. A young headquarters clerk from New York and two medics had sought refuge in a hayloft, exactly like Lanny and his Monuments. When they opened their eyes in the morning they discovered Germans cooking breakfast below; the barn had become a command post. Four days they had to stay there, without food or water, and one of the medics had to keep the wretched clerk from sleeping because he snored. By the time that Americans came the man was half out of his mind.

XI

In the headquarters was a maproom, and a Monuments colonel who had rendered special service was entitled to go there. The German units were marked with little red flags and the American with blue. By this time a lot of information had been accumulated, and you could see clearly what had happened. The Bulge was about sixty miles wide at its base and just about as deep; it was a triangle with irregular, curved sides. The Germans had got within fifteen miles of Namur, and within twenty of Liége; there they seemed to have been stopped.

The two exposed sides of that triangle, a front of a hundred and fifty miles, were one incessant battle. American units had been rushed up from every direction, with orders to stand and hold at all hazards; the Germans, probing here and there for soft spots, trying desperately to reach the goals which their Führer had set, found themselves encountering newly arrived columns, deploying quickly and not waiting to be attacked but attacking. So in the north there were battles at Malmédy and La Gleize and Werbomont and Marche, and in the nose of the Bulge at Rochefort, and behind that at Ciney and Celles and Beauraing; it was the same along the south side of the salient, only fighting was not so heavy, because the Führer had set the goals to the northwest.

Thursday, the 21st of December, the shortest day of the year, was the sixth day of the offensive; that longest night, instead of fair weather there was a high wind and heavy snow, what in America is called a blizzard. In the midst of it the Germans attacked Bastogne with renewed fury; evidently they had realized that unless they could have the use of those eight major roads they could no longer supply their troops that had plunged on to the west. They even recalled some of their armored forces to complete the encirclement of the town. By the next afternoon they had made such progress that they sent a major, accompanied by a captain and a couple of common soldiers, out into a field waving a flag made of a bedsheet. An American sergeant south of the town, getting ready a mortar barrage with some of those wonderful new proximity-fused shells, observed the flag and held up his fire. The Germans requested to be taken to an officer, so they were escorted to the nearest command post, and from there driven to town and into the presence of General McAuliffe.

That small-sized man with one star on each shoulder was very busy and probably not very elegant in appearance just then; he hadn't been expecting company. The German major handed him a letter, and he took time off to read it. It was in English and employed the very formal style which Wehrmacht officers considered protocol. It informed the American commander that: "The fortunes of war are changing, and this time United States Army forces in and near Bastogne have been encircled by strong German Army units. . . . There is only one possibility to save American troops from total annihilation, and that is honorable surrender." The letter went on to say that the Americans would be granted a two-hour period "in order to think this over," and it took the opportunity to offer a moral sentiment, pointing out that civilians might be killed in the bombardment, that the American Army would be to blame for this, and that it was not in line with "that well-known American humanity."

Was this a touch of irony, or was it just hypocrisy? Did they really think the Americans hadn't learned anything about German humanity, from Warsaw and Rotterdam on? The "Old Crock" may have felt a little bit sick at his stomach; anyhow, what he said was "*Nuts!*" He didn't have any idea that he was making himself immortal by that word; millions of American boys had said it, and continued to say it when they had grown up and wished to express the ultimate of boredom and disgust. McAuliffe wrote on a scrap of paper: "To the German Commander: *Nuts!*"—and drew two lines under the word. The German major knew English, but not of that inelegant kind. On his way out he asked the staff officer who was escorting him, "What does 'nuts' mean?" The answer was, "It means about the same as 'Go to hell.'" The German flushed and said no more. In his heart he would know that he was dealing with backwoodsmen, low-born men without breeding or manners; but unfortunately they could fight.

XII

The strange silence of the truce was broken, and the battle became still more fierce. The Germans attacked again and again, and shells poured into the town, making its lack of charm still more evident. Scores of fires were burning, many civilians were killed, and it was the Americans' fault, but they bore up under the burden. And next morning came a miracle—a decent day. The storm had blown itself out, and, actually, there was a sun in the sky!

So there came the planes; all kinds and sizes, on their various errands; more than five thousand flew from the Continent and England that day. Thunderbolt fighter-bombers dropped their stuff on enemy tanks, truck concentrations, and supply dumps; Budd-Erlings sprayed road convoys with machine-gun bullets; and the pot-bellied cargo planes, the C-47s, came in swarms, flying low and dumping off stuff with parachutes. McAuliffe had called for all sorts of supplies and now he was getting them. Red parachutes meant one kind, blue another, yellow a third, and so on. The men below did not fail to make note of the spot and to collect.

That wonderful weather held for five days, and the Air Force made use of every hour. It was the end of German hopes, and the higher-ups could not have failed to realize it. Their supply lines far to the rear were being bombed out; ammunition depots and oil dumps, railroad yards, locomotives and trains, bridges and culverts—the Germans were back in the days when their trains and trucks dared to move only at night and had to be hidden off the roads by day. They sent out the best they had against the Air Force, and their planes were shot out of the sky by the mysterious new shells, whose accuracy appeared to be supernatural. They couldn't, alas, make any appeal to The Hague Convention, for they had taken The Hague and everything in it; and anyhow, since when had the laws of war forbidden gunners to shoot too accurately?

The attack on Bastogne continued unabated. On Christmas Eve there was a fearful bombing, and it cost the young Monuments man from Wisconsin one of his arms. Fortunately a few surgeons had got into the town with Piper Cubs and gliders, and plenty of blood plasma had been dropped from the skies. Lanny's conscience troubled him, and he wondered if he should not have tried to take his little company out to safety. But where was safety, going or coming, in the Bulge?

At three o'clock on Christmas morning the Germans made their fiercest attack, throwing four full divisions against the fourteen-mile perimeter of the town. They broke through on a front of about a quarter-mile. There was the wildest kind of melee in the snow, men using bayonets and knives, which were supposed to have got out of date in war. Ten Tiger tanks broke into the town, and kitchen and office men and the wounded fought them with anything they could pick up, including bottles of gasoline thrown from windows of houses. During those two days the Germans lost a couple of hundred tanks and before darkness fell on Christmas night had had to give up the ground gained. But they didn't yield a foot without fierce fighting, and many chose to die in the trampled snow. Their Führer had ordered it, having told them that the loss of this battle would mean the loss of the war.

XIII

General McAuliffe might well have been worried, for his supplies were getting desperately low and he had to ration ten cartridges to each man in the trenches. But he knew that help was coming. It was another motion-picture finale, this time on an even bigger scale, and the hero of the event was that doughty warrior with the two pearl-handled revolvers, "Old Blood and Guts," officially known as General George Patton. His Third Army was next in the line to the south, a couple of hundred miles away. It had been facing east, ready for a grand slam, when the Battle of the Bulge began, and it was ordered to make a left face and go to the rescue.

Only a military man could conceive what that meant; an army has things that belong at the front and others that belong at the rear, and if any of them get mixed up there is confusion beyond imagining. When you have several hundred thousand men performing such a maneuver there are several hundred thousand things that may go wrong, and a headquarters staff has to work all day and all night and its members are lucky if they don't go mad. After it was all over, some of them figured up that in six days 133,178 motor vehicles had traveled 1,654,042 miles; 61,935 tons of supplies had been moved; and enough telephone lines laid, what is called "field wire," to reach six times across the United States. Some had to prepare and others had to distribute hundreds of thousands of maps, terrain analyses of the new battle area, estimates of the enemy situation, and detailed orders of battle.

The 4th Armored Division, deep in the Sarreguemines salient, was ordered to move at once to the Ardennes. The order came at midnight, and in black darkness the division withdrew, and by nine o'clock next morning was at Nancy, fifty miles behind its former position; this in the midst of the blizzard just before Christmas. The division sped northward, and by the next morning it was fighting enemy tanks at a town called Arlon, some thirty miles below Bastogne. The Germans knew all about the 4th Armored, for it had chased them all the way through Normandy, across France, and across the Moselle River. Apparently they didn't like what they had learned, for they called the men "Roosevelt's Butchers," which didn't annoy the men a bit.

And then came the 80th Infantry Division, who called themselves the "Blue Ridge Mountain Boys." They too had fought all the way across France. They had been resting at St. Avold, and had traveled forty miles on their way back into the line when the Ardennes battle started. The division was loaded into open trucks at one o'clock in the morning and traveled in bitter cold for fourteen hours. Then it got out and fought, and destroyed two-thirds of a German division which blocked its path. That helped to explain why the Germans did not succeed in their efforts to widen the shoulders of the southern salient and take the city of Luxembourg.

XIV

The fighting here was as tough as that before Bastogne, and it lasted as long. "Old Blood and Guts" was a fighting man, and so were all his officers; he had told them that they must *like* to fight. "If you don't like to fight, go back to Washington; you don't belong with the Third." The battle was going on all through the period of rotten weather, the blizzard followed by fog and rain, and the General, a devout Episcopalian, wrote a prayer and had it printed and distributed to all the troops:

"Almighty and merciful Father, we humbly beseech Thee, of Thy great goodness, to restrain these immoderate rains with which we have had to contend. Grant us fair weather for battle. Graciously hearken to us as soldiers who call upon Thee, that armed with Thy power we may advance from victory to victory, and crush the oppression and wickedness of our enemies, and establish Thy justice among men and nations. Amen."

And when this prayer was answered and five thousand planes shot up into the sky, the man with the pearl-handled revolvers danced with delight and exclaimed, "*Hot dog!* I guess I'll have another hundred thousand of those prayers printed. The Lord is on our side, and we've got to keep Him informed of what we need!"

Villages changed hands three times in the course of the 4th Armored's advance toward Bastogne. The enemy mined the roads and posted their Panzerfausts behind rocks and trees. American planes swooped down upon German tanks, thus revealing their position; the American "arty" would get them with the new pozit ammunition. The fighting advance went on for five days, and on the day after Christmas the commander of one tank battalion announced, "We are going into Bastogne today."

The tank men stepped on the gas, and they came to a little village only a mile and a half south of Bastogne. American artillery was firing into the town and knocked out several of the American halftracks. But the road was cleared and the Sherman tanks sped on. The Germans literally threw their Teller mines into the road, and the Americans lifted them off by hand. Then they came to a pillbox that had been knocked out and was still smoking; they didn't know whether it was American or German. They halted, afraid to fire, and both sides stared at each other. It was almost evening and the light was bad. Finally an American officer came forward, and when he had made sure who it was he said, "I am glad to see you."

XV

And that's all the drama there was to the second deliverance of Bastogne. Oddly enough, when the "Old Crock" got word that the tanks had come and rode out to meet them, he said the very same words, "I am glad to see you." Americans are a practical-minded people and as a rule lack a sense of drama. It probably never occurred to "Tony" McAuliffe that he was making history; he was just giving the Germans a licking, because they had declared war on his country and it was a job that had to be done. Anything beyond that would have been play-acting, and rather silly to him.

Such was the ending of the Siege of Bastogne. But right away another struggle began, no less fierce, which was properly to be called the Battle of Bastogne. The enemy couldn't give up and retire because Bastogne and the new corridor constituted a bulge driven into *his* bulge, and it imperiled all the forces he had sent far to the west. He had hoped to fight at Namur and Liége, but instead he was forced to fight at this dingy little town which was now a mass of rubble. He had to bring in troops from both east and west to meet those Patton was driving in from the south. It took two days to widen the corridor so that American supplies could be safely brought into the town, and after that there were ten days of ceaseless fighting.

Another blizzard descended, in spite of all Georgie's printed prayers, and three Monuments officers decided that this battle was one out of many still to be fought, and it was no point of honor to stay and risk any more portions of themselves. Convoys were coming in loaded and going out empty, and it was easy for assimilated officers to bum a ride. Morrison, the wounded man, was carried in an ambulance, and his two friends rode with him to see that he was kept warm and cheerful.

One last duty Lanny had: to bid farewell to Heinrich Jung. There was nothing to be done with Heinrich now but to put him with the other officer prisoners; he would be shipped to America and have a chance to grow still stouter upon abundant American food in one of many summer-resort hotels. Lanny no longer worried about being mentioned, for he was getting out of the Bulge and wasn't going to be captured.

A strange meeting that, between two enemy friends of twenty years' standing. The poor Nazi *Beamter* had tears in his eyes—not so much over the parting with Lanny as the parting with his dream of victory. He had been close to all this fighting and had known that the Germans weren't winning; now he knew that the corridor was open and new troops pouring in. It was the Americans' confident hope to cut off the Bulge and trap all those bold Nazi heroes who had set out for Liége and Antwerp and the ending of the war. Heinrich knew how Hitler had told his generals that if this offensive failed the war was lost; and after twelve days of fighting it was no longer possible to doubt that the offensive had failed. It was a *Götterdämmerung*, the end of Adi Schicklgruber's Thousand-Year Reich!

"Oh, such a tragic thing!" exclaimed the *Oberst Oberführer*. "It would have meant peace in Europe—it was the only chance. Do you Americans imagine you will be able to keep the peace in Europe?"

"I don't know," Lanny had to say. "We're hoping to set up a new League of Nations."

"*Ach, was Unsinn!* The Reds will have Europe, and you will be calling on us to help fight them."

"That's in the lap of the gods," replied the other, and didn't stop to argue because he had other farewells to say. He could understand that Heinrich's grief wasn't entirely altruistic. The *Oberführer* had sat in a fine office with a big desk and many push buttons and gadgets, and he had issued orders which determined the lives of hundreds of thousands of young men. Now all that glory was gone, and what would become of him? He might become night watchman of the building in which he had ruled!

Lanny said, "When you have a chance, write me in care of my father in Newcastle, Connecticut, and when the war's over we'll know more than we do now."

XVI

It was cold riding in an ambulance, even with blankets, and when they came to Arlon in the morning they got out to get hot coffee and brought some to their wounded friend. It was a command post at which they stopped, and one of the first things Lanny heard was that Georgie was there. All the men, high and low, called him this, and loved him because he fought for them as hard as he fought against the enemy. When a battle was on he did not sit on his backside and direct it in comfort; he was all over the place, mixing with the men, laughing, joking, exhorting, scolding. He rode in a plane when weather permitted, and when it didn't he came in a car; any GI could tell him his troubles and say "What the hell!" The old man himself rarely uttered a sentence without cussing, and that was the soldier's idea of soldier talk. It wouldn't have sounded good at home, but hell, "Old Blood and Guts" hadn't been home since the war began, and when he went home it would be in a coffin.

An assimilated colonel from Bastogne had no trouble in getting into the CP, and when Patton saw him he gave a shout in his oddly high-pitched voice; also, a crushing handclasp. "Budd, of all people! Are you with us again?"

Lanny told what he had been doing, interrogating for the "Old Crock," and added, "I'm expecting to see the President before long, and I'll tell him that you have a real man's army."

"Jesus Christ!" burst out the militant Episcopalian. "Tell him about these goddam blizzards, and here we are without snow camouflage for either men or tanks, and both are sitting ducks for German tanks and machine gunners. I put in my requisition two months ago, and those SOBs at SOS sit on their fat fannies and do nothing. Tell the Old Man I got a hundred and twenty-five thousand pairs of shoe pacs from Com Z and the inner felt linings were missing. My QM didn't waste any time complaining to those goddam bastards in Paris, he just cut up blankets to make liners. Imagine, if you can, I have to buy white cloth and have a salvage repair company turn out makeshift suits. I have bombarded Com Z for white paint for helmets, raincoats, and shoes, and for lime to whitewash vehicles. But do I get it? Like hell I do! They can't read the goddam calendar in Paris and they don't know the goddam winter has come. The best they can do is to send me five thousand mattress covers to make suits out of. There are seven hundred goddam tons of winter-warfare clothing in Le Havre, and I can have it if I send the trucks—and me trying to save you and your goddam heroes in Bastogne!"

That was Georgie Patton talking!

BOOK TWO

Love, and Man's Unconquerable Mind

5

What Friends Thou Hast

I

FROM Nancy, Lanny was flown to Paris, and there he found two letters from Laurel, the second telling him that she was worried at not hearing from him. Incidentally she mentioned the pleasant warmth she was enjoying, and he decided on an impulse that the combination of Laurel and sunshine was not to be resisted. Only now, when the strain was over, did he realize how great it had been; he had had very little sleep for two weeks; and fear repressed does not cease to exist but does its evil work in the subconscious mind. Lanny found that he would jump and quiver at a sudden sound, even though it bore no resemblance to the whine of an approaching shell. When he thought of the suffering and the broken bodies he had seen, there would be tears in his eyes.

There was no reason why he should not take a rest. Certainly a month or two must elapse before the American armies were ready for another offensive; the fronts would have to be realigned, and things that belonged at the front would have to be sorted out from those that belonged at the rear; half a million men would have to rest, and half a million tons of fresh supplies be brought up. Until the armies got farther into Germany, there would be no more work for either Monuments or Alsos. Therefore the assimilated colonel excused himself, and wrote a report to his Big Boss in Washington, telling where he was going and why. He thumbed another plane ride to Cannes, and then in an elegant Cadillac, a staff car, to the gates of Bienvenu.

He had debated in his mind what to tell Laurel. She was a writer of stories and needed material to feed her imagination; but she was also a wife, and would not feel the same about the perils of her husband as about those of her fictional characters. He compromised about telling her that he had sought refuge from the Germans in Bastogne, but he left out about the bombing and other perils; he talked about the battle lines as being remote from the town, which most of the time they had been. He admitted that it had all been uncomfortable and promised to do his best to keep clear of any more bulges. He doubted if there would be any, for Hitler had shot his bolt and would be kept on the defensive from then on.

Morning, noon, and evening they listened to the radio, in French and English. The official communiqués were kept deliberately behind the battle events, but the news they gave was dependable, as of a day or two previous. Lanny had his pocket map, and they marked the places, and saw that the Bulge was being steadily squeezed from both north and south. There was the possibility of a large-scale pocketing of Germans; but no, they kept backing out, contesting every step. Lanny could guess from this that Rundstedt was now having his way. The Führer, as military strategist, had a fatal weakness: he could never bear to give up territory that he had conquered and would sacrifice whole armies rather than admit a failure.

Lanny could keep himself happy imagining the fury in which this half-genius, half-madman must be at the present hour. A hyena cornered by a pack of fighting dogs could not emit more snarls and frenzied raving. A score of times in the course of his seven or eight years as presidential agent Lanny had listened to these sounds, and that sufficed him. He was content now to have between them and himself not merely the high mountains of the Alps, but also two or three hundred divisions of the AEF, the Allied Expeditionary Force.

II

Pleasant indeed was it to be out of the sounds of gunfire and the sights and smells of death; to walk on a road that was free from the rumble of tanks and heavy guns, to lie on a sandy beach that was not under shellfire. Cicero in one of his letters expresses the opinion that the remembrance of past griefs is a pleasure; but Lanny, whose fate it had been to live through two World Wars and many tumults and revolutions in between, thought that he had seen far too many griefs. Here in Juan he much preferred to remember his boyhood days, before the crowds had come pouring in and real-estate values had jumped to the skies.

Lanny told his wife stories about those days, when there had been a social life that was quiet and harmless, or so it had appeared; you gave small parties, different from the costly, promiscuous affairs of recent years. The people who came were your friends, and they rarely drank too much; if they did you left them out next time. But after

World War I a whole new population had swarmed to this Coast of Pleasure. They came from strange parts of the world and seemed to have unlimited money; they didn't tell how they had got it, and you didn't ask. They gave parties, and "everybody" went; there was something called "gate-crashing," and nobody cared about anything so long as food and liquor were free.

"A man could have stayed here at the Cap d'Antibes," Lanny pointed out, "and written a history of modern Europe. In my childhood it was the Russian and the British aristocracies. Now these Russians have been scattered over the earth like leaves in a whirlwind; some are serving as café entertainers in Shanghai, and others as waiters here at the Hotel du Cap. The British dukes and earls gradually gave up, because of income taxes at home; and it was the same way with the Spanish grandees, and then the German and Italian nobility, and those of the old Austro-Hungarian Empire. Their places were taken by munitions kings and oil and steel and coal magnates, many of them from America. After the depression wiped these out, there were cattle kings from the Argentine and Maharajas from India."

"Who will come after this war?" asked Laurel.

"All sorts of black marketeers," he ventured; "and French and Italian landlords who keep two sets of books, one for the tax collector and the other for their private information. Many South American countries haven't yet discovered the income tax, and their rich can come; also Hollywood stars who have good lawyers and can charge world travel and other pleasures up as advertising expenses."

"Introduce me to one of those lawyers," said the wife, much amused. She was traveling on an expense account herself, and her editors had been agreeably surprised to discover how little she asked for. If she had claimed several hundred dollars for the entertainment of the persons from whom she got information they would have paid it; they might not have blinked at an item for payment of a husband who gave information and revised manuscripts. Lanny warned her, "If you work too cheaply they won't have proper respect for you."

III

A fortnight of rest and the P.A. was himself again. Laurel wanted to go back with him to consult with her editors; so he sought out the OSS man in Cannes whose name had been entrusted to him and had a cablegram sent to Baker, the President's man in Washington. That was the way to avoid delays and uncertainty caused by the censor. Two days later the privileged couple were informed that they would be flown from Cannes to Marseille and from there to Marrakech, where they would have two days according to their request. From there the route would be Dakar in West Africa, Belém in Brazil, Puerto Rico, and Washington. Lanny would travel at government expense, and his wife would pay her fare and put it on her expense account. All that was routine, and a journey which in the old days of sailing ships would have taken several months now took about one day of actual flying time. It was a great help to the winning of a war.

To Marseille took about half an hour. Here was a great harbor, now restored, and hundreds of ships coming to deposit war cargoes; the stuff went by railroads, also restored, to armies all over France. Then from Marseille to Marrakech across the blue Mediterranean, in obligingly good weather, and along the coast of Africa, some of it barren and some pale green with new wheat. The high Atlas Mountains, snow-covered to their bases, framed the sky to their left, and down below Lanny pointed out little white dots which he said were marabouts, or Mohammedan shrines.

So into French Morocco, taken by the Germans and now by the Americans—but all had preserved the fiction that it belonged to the Moorish sultan. There was the ancient city of Marrakech, an oasis in a desert land, with red stone aqueducts bringing water from the mountains, and a great spread of orange groves and date orchards, both loaded with fruit. The brown Moors had built mosques of red stone, and white millionaires from all over the world had built elaborate villas of the same material. The poor lived in wretched hovels, as they had done for fifty centuries.

Here was the famous Hotel Mamounia, one of those palaces of luxury which had become standard in every part of the earth where there was agreeable climate or amusement for the excessively rich. Here Beauty Budd had lived in safety for nearly a year; she had made herself so agreeable that when others were turned out to make way for the top brass she had been allowed to stay. Don't tell anybody, but Beauty was in her sixties, and it didn't do much good for her to dye her hair, because her husband's hair was snow-white, and she had a little grandson here, and couldn't refrain from talking about a granddaughter nearly fifteen years old living in Connecticut; her son came along every now and then, and while he didn't look his years he was obviously no spring chicken. There was nothing a onetime professional beauty could do but rely upon kindness and knowledge of the world and try not to be jealous of the young things who, if they were aware of her existence at all, would pity and patronize her. They had the charms, while she, alas, had only memories.

But she still had money; Robbie Budd had sent her a thousand dollars every month for forty-four years, and the paintings of her former husband, Marcel Detaze, were bringing higher prices all the time. Also, she had that fine property on the Cap, which she had never mortgaged, because Robbie had fixed it so that she couldn't. She had fled here to get away from the invasion, and now it was over. "Don't you think so, Lanny? Is there any chance of a bulge on the Riviera?"

I V

In the guessing game of marriage people make the queerest choices; this is well known, but all Beauty Budd's friends thought that her present one was the queerest ever. Nobody could find any real fault with Parsifal Dingle except his name; but he was so different from Beauty, so completely out of this world, while she was so completely in it. The old gentleman differed from other religious persons whom Lanny had known in that he was seriously trying to live his belief; he went on tirelessly manifesting the power of love to everybody he met, regardless of what they might do to him or what they thought or said about him. It didn't matter whether they were rich or poor, whether their skins were white or brown, Parsifal talked to them about Divine Love and exhibited it in his benevolent pink countenance. In less than a year's stay in this luxurious hotel he had managed to convince high and low that they had a saint among them. The place was full of rich refugees from a war-torn world, and many of them hated one another bitterly; but the onetime real-estate agent from the Middle West went right on practicing his notion that if you loved other people you would sooner or later bring them to love you.

The third member of the family had been brought up under this system; now six and a half years old, he had never known anything but love. He was all over this establishment and was everybody's friend and playmate; every effort was made to spoil him, but it didn't seem to take. He sat at the feet of his stepgrandfather and listened to discourses about the Eternal Principle which made all the universe one, and he responded to it in the way a plant responds to moisture and sunshine.

It seemed a demonstration of the influence of environment over heredity; for Baby Marcel's father was a most unlovely person, a Fascist *conte* and *capitano* who was now a prisoner of war in the States. Beauty's daughter, Marceline, had quarreled with him, divorced him, and taken back her maiden name of Detaze; so this little chap bore the name of his grandfather, the French painter of whom everybody knew. An example of his work hung on a wall of the hotel, an African landscape with a brown-skinned peasant in a white burnoose. Now when Uncle Lanny came visiting it was one of his duties to stand in front of that painting and tell the little fellow more stories about his grandfather.

Where was Marcel's mother? This was a subject Lanny didn't mention to the child; but Beauty would take Lanny off and ask him if he had any news and beg him to give her some hope. Marceline was in besieged Naziland, and Lanny hadn't told his mother what he knew: that his half-sister had been in dire peril and had risked her life to warn Lanny that he too was in peril. There was nothing to be gained by telling either Beauty or Laurel about that incident; there was nothing they could do, nothing anybody could do, until the war was over. If the half-French, half-American dancer was in a concentration camp, nobody could help her, least of all her half-brother, now known to the Nazis as an American agent and spy. If she was in hiding, she would want to be left alone and not have attention drawn to her. In this dreadful war many millions of people had been separated from their loved ones and had no way of finding out what had become of them.

V

Beauty hadn't wanted her son to marry Laurel Creston; she had wanted him to marry an heiress, as his good looks and elegant manners entitled him to do. But one heiress had been enough, and the mother had reluctantly decided that perhaps a bluestocking was the second-best thing for him after all. Now there was a baby, and that settled it; for two days and nights Beauty labored to establish herself as the perfect mother-in-law. She was all honey and cream, and watched for any little sign of difference between the pair, so that she could place herself on Laurel's side. She took the literary lady aside and questioned her as to how matters were going; she told everything a mother could know about her son's peculiarities, and how to manage him—for his own good, of course.

Also she did not fail to ask questions about Baby Lanny. Men are so dumb about such matters; they don't notice details, and if you try to drag things out of them they answer vaguely and absent-mindedly. The little one was two years old and was talking, and a mother would know how he talked and what he said; she would understand that a grandmother who had never seen him couldn't be content with a photograph but had to know the color of his eyes and his hair, and what he ate, whom he played with, which parent he loved best, and so on.

The stepfather-in-law also had a claim upon Laurel which was not to be overlooked. He knew that she had discovered in herself the strange gift of mediumship; she went into a trance, and alien voices spoke through her lips. She didn't know what they were, and neither did Lanny, but Parsifal was firm in the belief that they were the spirits of the dead; he gave to them the same love that he gave to the living, and they responded in kind. It was necessary that Laurel should give him a demonstration of her power, with Lanny and Beauty sitting by, curious to observe what this new environment might bring forth.

Laurel lay back on her couch and closed her eyes, sighed a few times, and then there was silence. At last Parsifal inquired, in a low persuasive voice, "Is anybody present?" There came a woman's voice which they expected and recognized, or imagined that they recognized; it was the old Polish medium who had been a member of their household for fifteen years before her recent death. With the aid of Madame Zyszynski's psychic gift Parsifal had explored the ancient civilizations of India and Ceylon, and she had promised that if she were the first to pass over she would do her best to return. How was she in the spirit world? And Madame said, as all the "spirits" do, that she was well and happy, and had tried to reach him, but the mediums he had found in Marrakech did not have the necessary power.

"Is there anybody else present?" inquired the man of God. Lanny was expecting to hear the voice of Otto Kahn, the international banker who had been haunting Laurel's mind, to her own bewilderment and her husband's. But no, this time it was a newcomer. "There is an old gentleman standing by me," reported the voice. "He is rather a small man and has a little white mustache. He is very thin and frail and has deep-sunk dark eyes. He wears a black skullcap, and I think he is Jewish."

"Tell him that we welcome his presence," said Parsifal. "Has he something to say to us?"

"He is speaking French," said the voice, "but he will speak English if I wish. He says he passed over three years ago. He was a writer, and Lanny was interested in his books."

"Will he give us his name?"

"He says Bergson; Henri Bergson. He says that he despised the Nazis; they offered to make him what they call an honorary Aryan, but he would not accept any favor from them; he wore the Star of David and lived like the other Jews in Paris. He wears the star now; it was supposed to be a badge of shame, but now it is a badge of honor."

"Tell him I have studied his ideas," said Parsifal, a tireless reader of all books that took the idealistic view of philosophy. "I am one of his disciples."

"He says that he knows you. He says to tell you that he has been confirmed in his belief that—he is using long words that I do not know, but I try to repeat them as they sound—that mechanistic explanations include only a very small part of the real."

"You are doing very well, Madame," said Parsifal considerately. "M. Bergson is a great philosopher, and I once heard him lecture at the Académie des Sciences Morales et Politiques. It is an honor that he does in coming to speak to us."

"It is too bad that I am a poor ignorant woman," put in Madame, and went on, pronouncing syllable after syllable. "This polite old gentleman wants you to know that he is still experiencing that continuous creation of unforeseen novelty which goes on in the universe. He says, 'I feel it more vividly than ever, the action I will and of which I am the sole master. The inert world is solely an abstraction; and concrete reality comprises living conscious beings enframed in inorganic matter.'"

This went on for several minutes, with both Parsifal and Lanny diligently taking notes, just as if it had been a lecture at the Sorbonne or Oxford University. When it was over, and Laurel had sighed and moaned her way out of the trance, they sat and discussed what had occurred. Laurel assured them that she had never met the author of *Creative Evolution;* he was a mere name to her, and she couldn't have named one of his books. Lanny told how, in Paris just before setting out for the Ardennes, he had been strolling on the Quai and had stopped at a bookstall and picked up a paper-bound copy of Bergson's *L'Energie Spirituelle*. He had found time to read only a few pages and had left the book with other belongings in a bag at his hotel.

So you were at liberty to assume that Laurel had just dipped into Lanny's mind and given a little demonstration of "the continuous creation of unforeseen novelty"—it had surely been that! You didn't have to believe that the spirit of a departed French metaphysician had had anything to do with this creation—other than by creating a book, which you might properly describe as a bit of consciousness "enframed in inert matter." You were at liberty to assume that some part of the subconscious mind of Laurel Creston had the power to dip into the subconscious mind of her husband and take out a whole set of ideas and impressions and construct them into a fictional scene. Surely that was a startling enough discovery; Lanny, who had seen it happening with different persons over a period of a decade and a half, was waiting impatiently for some scientist to come along and tell him how these things occurred.

VI

The trip from Marrakech was in a luxury liner, with chromium fixtures and snakeskin-covered seats which were unfolded at night to make comfortable beds; excellent meals were served, and the detachable tables enabled a woman writer to revise her manuscripts and a presidential agent to make notes of what he wanted to tell his Boss. The wrinkled sea beneath them crawled, and Lanny recited this line and the rest of Tennyson's picture of the eagle. "He watches from his mountain walls and like a thunderbolt he falls." Edward MacDowell had composed a piano sketch on the theme, and Lanny said the fall was impressive, only the eagle hit twice on his way down.

At Dakar, the "peanut port" of West Africa, they got out and strolled in hot sunshine while men refueled the plane and tested its engines. They had taken this same route, but in reverse, when they had visited Palestine a few months earlier; so there was nothing new about the scene. Dakar had been a great French naval base, and Hitler had tried desperately to build a railroad across the Sahara to it, using slave labor; if he had got there he would have had South America at the mercy of his Luftwaffe. But now all that was over; the Americans had both ends of the dream railroad, and in South America producers and traders were eagerly accumulating North American dollars.

Another flight, from the bulge of Africa to the bulge of Brazil. Lanny's friend Professor Alston, once a geographer, had pointed out to him how these coast lines corresponded, and said they had been parts of one continent which had split apart in a gigantic convulsion. Many such events had occurred in the preparation of this earth for human habitation; had it all been accident, or had it been planned? Would the future be planned, or would that too be accident?—thus a student of Bergson, trying to understand his world, and not at all satisfied with the progress he was making. If only men would stop killing one another all over the earth, they might really pay heed to the claims of idealistic philosophy.

From there northward, across the equator and to the large island of Puerto Rico, which had been taken over by the United States half a century ago. Order had been maintained and democratic institutions were being taught, but poverty continued unabated. The population had grown beyond the ability of the island's agriculture to support it. A century and a half ago an English clergyman named Malthus had pointed out this unfortunate tendency; since his time the population of the earth had more than doubled, and there was still poverty and misery in all the backward lands, and insecurity and fear everywhere. The two amateur philosophers discussed the problem of birth control, or planned parenthood, as it was now being called. Puerto Rico is a Catholic land; its Church forbids the use and even the spreading of this priceless knowledge, and so these unhappy people are condemned to misery and degradation for generation after generation.

VII

From Bolling Field Laurel took a plane to New York, and Lanny telephoned to Baker, to put himself at the President's disposal. He rode into Washington and put up at the Mayflower, where Baker had made arrangements for him. The place swarmed with busy bureaucrats, carrying leather briefcases, and portly executives come to negotiate contracts for tens and sometimes hundreds of millions of dollars. Lanny had a bath and a shave, and then he called the President's man again, and was told that his appointment was for the evening of the next day. Baker added, "Professor Alston is at your hotel." Lanny said, "Oh, good!"

He would have company, and give a lot of information, and get a few items in return. This college professor, Lanny's first and only employer just a quarter of a century ago, was responsible for his having taken on the volunteer job of P.A., and the two were like father and son in their trust of each other. Alston was one of the New Dealers from the old days back in Albany who still addressed F. D. R. as "Governor." For twelve years now he had had a job in the Department of Commerce at which he did not work; it was an excuse for him to have a salary and an expense account. What he did was to flit here and there over the United States and sometimes abroad in the role of "fixer," otherwise known as "trouble shooter." He arbitrated disputes among bureaucrats and brass, he scolded executives who were falling behind schedules and patted them on the back when they promised to do better. He was one of those wiry little men who do not appear to age; his hair was white but he was still sprightly and could get along with very little sleep. Many people were in awe of him because he stood near to the throne, and he told Lanny that his morning and evening prayers consisted of repeating to himself Lord Acton's formula that "power tends to corrupt, and absolute power corrupts absolutely."

The meetings of this pair depended upon chance, and they made the most of each one. They had dinner together and spent the evening. Lanny told what he had seen of the Battle of the Bulge; it was over now, having lasted just a month, and Alston knew the results. "We were taken badly by surprise," he said, "but in the long run I don't think it matters. We have taken fifty thousand German prisoners and inflicted twice as many casualties as we suffered. We had to fight all those Germans somewhere, and they won't be on hand when we start our advance to the Rhine."

Lanny couldn't keep from smiling. "It seemed so different when I was in it," he remarked. "It was such a mean place to fight."

"Of course; but it was just as mean for the Germans. I was talking yesterday with an American officer who was captured at Celles, a place at the tip of the salient only four miles from the Meuse. A Panzer battalion made the rush, and then they waited three days for their army to bring them more gasoline and it didn't. They realized that they would be cut off, and there was nothing for them to do but to burn all their tanks and other vehicles and walk back. They were lost and had to fight all the way, hiding from Americans as you hid from Germans —and they didn't find it a bit more comfortable. They shot anyone who tried to lag behind."

"What happened to your officer?" asked Lanny, to whom it was a human-interest story.

"He had nothing to eat and was very tired. He waited until the Germans were busy in a fight and then just walked off to one side. Presently he came to an American outpost and made himself known."

VIII

Lanny told about the pozit ammunition and the tremendous effect it had had. Alston knew about it and said that it had knocked sixteen hundred Luftwaffe planes out of the sky during the Ardennes fighting. "I don't think they have many more planes," he said. "When fair weather comes we'll have their armies on the run." When Lanny remarked that the new shells had been scarce at Bastogne his friend replied, "That won't be true much longer, for we have sent three-quarters of a million of them over there. We haven't forgotten the Pacific either. The Jap air forces probably haven't the least idea what is happening to them; they just know that our gunners have improved miraculously."

Lanny told about his visit to Strasbourg University. Alston didn't know who had sent in the report, but he had got the substance of it—

that the Germans were making no progress toward atomic fission. "That is the greatest load that was ever lifted off our minds," he said, and added, "You understand, Lanny, this is the tightest secret in the world. We are going to have the bomb. I don't know when—I don't think anybody knows—but it's coming, and when it comes it will end the war."

"In time for the Germans?" inquired the P.A.

"We expect to finish the Germans this summer. If the bomb is ready before then, it will save a lot of American lives. That's all I can tell you, because it's all I know. I was sent to a place out West where one of the atomic piles is in operation, and I'm sure they would have told me the probable time if they had known. What they say is that everything is new and unprecedented, and nobody can guess what new bugs they may encounter."

They talked about the subject which was nearest to the hearts of both of them, the great man whom they served. "How is he?" Lanny asked, and the answer was, "The doctors can't find anything organically wrong with him; but he's overworking, and no one can get him to stop."

"He tries to keep too much in his own hands," Lanny ventured. "As a planner and inspirer he is the greatest man we have ever had in the White House; but a good administrator has to know how to delegate power."

"I said almost those words to him," replied the fixer. "He turned his shrewd eyes upon me and asked, 'To whom?' Then, of course, I was stumped. I didn't know who could carry the load. When he said, 'To you, Charlie?' I had to admit that I had all I could do. And poor Harry Hopkins is staggering along from one job to the next, slowly dying." Alston went on to name one man after another who had been tried and found wanting. "Everything that comes up appears to be vital, everything depends on everything else, and the war is all one."

"And the peace," added Lanny. "I am guessing that history will say that F. D. R. is doing better in the war than he did before it."

"That's because he has built a huge machine which is ready to hand —the Army, the Navy, the Air Force. Those men have learned their jobs, and know how to delegate authority; they give obedience and loyalty as a matter of course. But in peace you are scouting around, picking new men for new jobs—and the first thing they all do is to start fighting one another instead of the enemy, which is poverty and confusion and greed. Every day I give to politics I'm more sorry I ever left the field of geography, where things are fixed and you can count on them!"

IX

Lanny was taken into the White House by the customary "social door," which was really the front door but served the purposes of a back door. The orders were that persons brought in by Baker were not stopped or questioned; they went past the naval guards with no more than an informal sort of salute, made with one finger, and up a red-carpeted side stairway to the second floor. At the door of the President's bedroom sat Prettyman, his negro valet, ready and vigorous—he had to be, for he lifted a heavy load from wheel chair to bed or vice versa. "Evenin', gentlemen," he said, for he knew them both, and stood up respectfully as they approached and tapped on the door.

The P.A. knew that room and everything in it as well as he knew his own. It had been in the summer of 1937 that he had first been brought here, so this was the eighth year. A generously proportioned room, with old-fashioned mahogany furniture, and pictures of ships, for ship lore was one of F. D. R.'s hobbies. There was a reading table by the bed with a lamp, and on the bed a stack of documents and letters which the harassed man was supposed to read and perhaps sign before he went to sleep. There was a blue and white coverlet and the occupant wore a knitted blue crew-neck sweater over his pajama coat—he was subject to what he called "the sniffles."

What concerned Lanny was the face that he saw. He had been told that the President's health was failing, but even so he was shocked. It was the face of an invalid, drawn and haggard; where for years had been the glow of health and energy there was now plain exhaustion. It would, of course, have been the worst of taste for a visitor to reveal this reaction; he must wear a quick smile and be ready to respond to the playful greeting which would never fail while the spirit of F. D. R. remained in his body. "Hello, how's the old Bulge-battler?"—thus showing that he had received and read his agent's report.

"I've been a beachcomber on the Cap d'Antibes for two weeks," said Lanny, grinning. "I wish you could have been there."

"Never mind," said the Boss. "Someday I'm going to dump this load and go back to Hyde Park and write history. You shall come and visit me and tell me about all the great people you have known. Tell me about the Bulge."

In Franklin Roosevelt there was a boy who had never grown up. He really loved a story and wanted to hear all the details of this one. His heart sorrowed because he couldn't have been there himself—his old sturdy self that would have tramped through snowbound forests and carried any soldier's load. They were the dear dead days beyond recall but they lived in his memory; he was enraptured by the adventure of three Monuments men hiding in the hay and roared with delight when Lanny imitated the German exhortations with which he had marched a column of prisoners out of a farmyard. "That's where we beat the enemy," he exclaimed. "Our wits are quicker; our people are accustomed to thinking for themselves, and wherever there is an emergency there is always an idea to meet it."

"There are ideas busting out all over that Army," responded the grown-up playboy. "I keep running into them, and I'm as much surprised as the enemy." He went on to talk about the proximity fuse and the way it was knocking German planes out of the skies and German vehicles off the roads. F. D. R. in turn told about the co-operative efforts of scientists and engineers, literally thousands, who had been working on that project over a period of years, even long before the start of this war; for the last five years they had been working day and night, and the problems they had solved were beyond the comprehension of anybody but specialists. "It was a race between our science and Germany's, and we have won in every field."

"Not quite all, Governor," said Lanny, and discussed the terrible V-2, the rocket bomb which was now taking its toll of life and property in England; also the smaller-sized versions which the Germans had used in the Ardennes and which they were calling the V-1½. The President promised that it wouldn't be long before the launching sites of these weapons were taken. "We already have the secrets," he said, "and we'll improve on them. Our fellows refuse to admit that the Germans can do anything better than we can."

X

The Boss lighted a cigarette in the long thin holder which had made him look debonair in the photographs—but not now! Then he said, "I'll tell you a state secret: I am going to meet Stalin again. Don't say a word about it."

"Of course not. Are you going to Russia?"

"To the Crimea."

"That's a long trip, Governor."

"I know; but we absolutely have to meet and settle our problems. I have the advantage over Stalin in that I'm not afraid to come to his country, but he is afraid to come to mine. I suppose there are too many people who would be looking for a chance to pot him."

"No doubt about that," assented Lanny. Then, on an impulse, "You have many advantages over him, but there's one advantage he has over you. He knows a lot more about you than you know about him. Also, he understands your ideas better than you understand his."

"I suppose my education has been neglected." Roosevelt's face took on one of his smiles, but Lanny found it a wan and troubled one.

"In a poker game," the P.A. went on, "it is a great advantage to know your opponent's mind and how he plays his cards. If you do, you can figure out when he's bluffing and when he really has the cards. Stalin has written several books, and I'm venturing the guess that you haven't read any of them."

"You win, Lanny."

"Have you ever read Marx's *Capital?*"

"I picked it up, but I could only manage a few pages. I just haven't had time."

"In the days when you had time you didn't realize the necessity. It was the same thing as regards Hitler; he published a book twenty years ago in which he told exactly what he was going to do to the world. Millions of Germans read it—thousands of them over here. But how many in authority here read it?"

"They tell me it is a horrid book, Lanny."

"Of course, and Hitler is a horrid man. The reason we lose out in Europe is that so few of our people can believe how bad Europe is—I mean those who have power or are on the way to power in Europe."

"I got the impression after your talk with Stalin that you liked him and trusted him to keep his word."

"I wanted to trust him; but maybe I'm just one more naïve American. Stalin can be charming when he wants to; and when I interviewed him, nearly three years ago, he wanted to be, because he wanted American aid to save him from Hitler. What he lives for is his Russian revolution, and his hope to spread it over the world. Whatever will help that is his policy, and whatever opposes it is anathema to him."

"Then you don't really think we can trust him?"

"Three years have passed since I talked to him, and I have learned some new things since then. In Göring's home I was permitted to read the text of the negotiations which Molotov and Ribbentrop carried on in Berlin in November of 1940. Bear in mind that Molotov is Stalin's right hand—also his tongue. Molotov was willing to make a deal with Hitler on the basis that Russia was to have the Near East and the Balkans. Hitler was willing to give him the Near and Middle East—Turkey, Persia and the Persian Gulf, India, everything he could take. But Hitler wanted the Balkans for himself, and that was where the negotiations broke down."

"You feel absolutely certain that transcript was genuine?"

"I have had confirmation from several sources. Göring, of course, would lie freely, but he's not very good at it, because he's such a show-off, a bundle of vanity. His opposition to Hitler in this and other matters is the reason he lost favor and now is pretty much on the shelf —he has lost control even of his Luftwaffe. You recall, Governor, I reported those Berlin negotiations to you."

"Yes. But it's hard to make such cynicism real to one's self."

"Remind yourself how Tsar Alexander the First dropped his friendship with Napoleon and shifted over to Napoleon's enemies in the middle of a war."

"That is what keeps our General Staff from getting any sleep at night—the fear that Stalin may make a separate peace and release Hitler's armies for the western front. Also, we need his help to beat down the Japanese in China. I am taking this journey to persuade him that his true interests lie with us, and to get the best deal out of him that I can."

XI

The world was in very bad shape, and a warmhearted and idealistic President wanted so hard to believe there was something good in it. Pessimistic statements from his friend and trusted agent hurt him like a series of blows. They hurt Lanny too, because he had tied his whole life to the workers' struggle for justice, and he hated to have to admit that any part of this struggle could go wrong. But what good would it do to tear down one form of dictatorship and set up another?—one that used the Cyrillic alphabet instead of the Gothic, or Germanic, or whatever you called it. This exhausted man was going to travel ten thousand miles and carry on negotiations with a tough, hardfisted outfit; his decisions might affect the future of the world for centuries, and somebody had to warn him what he was up against.

Perhaps he realized his own weakness, for suddenly he asked, "How would you like to come along, Lanny?"

The P.A., too much surprised to think about dignity, exclaimed,

"Gosh!" Then, quickly, he added, "What you need are experts on Russia and on Communist tactics."

"You are an expert on all Europe," was the reply. "Harry is very optimistic about Stalin, and perhaps I need a pessimist in the bunch. You know how the Roman emperors used to have a man at their banquets to whisper '*Memento mori.*' "

"What I would whisper is the story of how Stalin made a neutrality pact with Japan early in 1941, and when it was signed he said to Matsuoka, very genially, 'You and I are both Asiatics.' "

"*Touché!*" exclaimed F. D. R. with one of his infectious grins. "You will make your plans to come along?"

"Of course, Governor, if you really want me. When is it to be?"

"We plan to arrive February second. We shall rendezvous in Malta a day or two earlier. If you are in Europe you can meet the party there; or if you are here we'll arrange a place for you. I am taking about six hundred persons."

"Good Lord! If you have that many you won't have any time for amateurs."

"I'll manage to make some time, and so will Harry. We can never know what will come up. Maybe I'll let you try your charms on the Red Marshal."

"He invited me to come back," said Lanny, amused; "but he's probably forgotten me by now."

"That I doubt," said the President. "And anyhow, you can be sure he keeps a card file. Be ready for a call near the end of January, and we'll go and see what happens to us."

6

No Place Like Home

I

LAUREL had talked with her editors in New York and reported that they wanted her to follow the Army into Germany and write about what she found there. Everybody took it for granted that the

Army was going in, and all plans were made on that basis. Laurel had the advantage of having lived in Germany before the war; she had written a book of short stories and a novel about Naziland, and so had a basis for comparison.

Baby Lanny was in Newcastle with his grandparents; they had begged and argued, on the ground that their country house was so much better than a city apartment. In happy days before the war Robbie had built his house big so as to have plenty of room for his family, and now he wanted plenty of family to fill his big house. Robbie's two sons, who had built their homes on the estate, had supplied children of various ages who would be interested in a tiny toddler. Now in January there was a white blanket all over the place, and he was bundled up and taken outdoors, where his life was one continuous ecstasy; he would stumble over himself, and everywhere he fell it was soft and delightful. He learned to fashion crude snowballs and throw them wildly. Presently he learned that a big snowball with a smaller one on top was a man, and he began right away to develop those art impulses which he had come by honestly.

In the house he was a quiet, rather shy little fellow. He had fair hair, like his mother when she was young; his eyes were brown like those of both parents. Laurel hadn't seen him for several months, and at his age that makes a great difference. Both she and Lanny had to start all over to make his acquaintance, and do it carefully so as not to startle him; two immense creatures in uniforms, calling themselves "Papa" and "Mama" but only vaguely remembered, and manifesting excitement for reasons not entirely clear. Laurel's maternal impulses reawakened, and she found herself wondering whether fame and success, even with the higher motives of the artistic and the social conscience, were worth the price they cost a woman.

But the little one was all right; he had exactly the right diet, he slept the right number of hours, and neither parent could find any fault with his regime—except that he had received too many Christmas toys, something that could not have been helped even in a New York apartment, for he had so many relatives. Laurel had never gotten along very well with her own family and had never taken her husband to meet them, but she couldn't keep them from sending Christmas presents, because that was the thing to do.

II

Esther Remsen Budd had had in the past some reason to find fault with her left-handed stepson, but now that he had settled down this was no longer the case. When husband and wife came to Newcastle they behaved in an exemplary manner and made themselves agreeable to the many people they had to meet. The Budds were a large clan, and everybody in this overgrown manufacturing town looked up to them and wanted to know them. There had been a lot of gossip and mystery about Lanny, but now he had a respectable job that he could talk about; it was natural for an art expert to be a Monuments man, and everybody knew that Esther's niece, Peggy Remsen, was in it, thus vouching for its social status. The fact that Lanny's new wife wrote stories had been kept secret, but now there was no longer any reason for that, and the report had created excitement in Newcastle.

Esther was an extremely conscientious great lady, aware of her position and the power it gave her. In her girlhood she had read a book by Andrew Carnegie called *The Gospel of Wealth;* she looked upon her own wealth in that light, and used her influence with the women's clubs and the churches to run the politics of the town and try to keep it clean. This was a heavy duty, and in wartime almost impossible, for swarms of new people had piled into the town; the airplane plant and the munitions plant had grown in a way suggestive of the *Arabian Nights,* and people from Texas and Oklahoma and Quebec and Newfoundland had more money than they had ever dreamed of in their stunted lives. They did not always spend it wisely, and worrying about this had put lines in Esther's kindly but rather stern face and had turned her hair gray. She held herself erect and never admitted any sort of weakness.

Her stepson had acquired in his youth ideas which she had considered "radical," even incendiary. But years had passed, times had changed, and the ideas had worked in Esther's mind and made more impression than she admitted to herself. When the greatly dreaded CIO, a so-called "industrial" union, had succeeded in organizing the Budd plant, it had seemed to Esther's stubborn husband like the end of his world; but there was nothing he could do about it, because "That Man in the White House" had forced laws through Congress legalizing the unions and ordering Robbie to deal with them. He worried and lost his sleep, and although he put on weight he did not look well; his hair was gray and thinning, and he was showing his age. This war was killing men thousands of miles from the battlefields.

Seeing all this, Robbie's wife had taken a bold resolve and invited half a dozen of the union leaders to have tea at her home. To her surprise she had found them to be both polite and intelligent; and when she told them that she was determined not to have any strikes in her home town, especially in wartime, they assured her they were in agreement. She invited them to tell her what could be done to make the workers' lives easier and to convince them that the company really appreciated their help. The union men proceeded to pour out a list of suggestions, most of which seemed to Esther quite reasonable: rest rooms and first-aid treatment; day nurseries where mothers could leave babies while they did riveting jobs; a cafeteria which the workers could run for themselves, to have what they wanted; busses to bring them to the plant, since the parking places had grown so big that they had a long walk in snow or rain.

The result had been a debate between Robbie and his wife, lasting far into the night. All this was "paternalism," a word that the son of Budd Gunmakers had been taught to hate at Yale University nearly half a century ago. He had forgotten almost everything he had learned there, but he remembered the perils of "coddling"; also a sort of Frankenstein creation known as "the economic man," and a deity known as "laissez faire," which meant in cruder language "each for himself and the devil take the hindmost." The devil had been taking them by the million, but Robbie's mind had remained untouched in the suit of chain-mail which had been forged and fitted onto it by Professor William Graham Sumner.

"Where are we going to get all these rationed materials?" demanded the overburdened executive. To this his wife answered, "Let the unions try to get them, and if they can't, they'll know you're not to blame." "Good God!" exclaimed the captain of industry. "We're going to invite these interlopers not merely to run our plant but to construct it?" Said the wife, "When they are chosen by your workers they are not interlopers but representatives; and if they offer to take a burden off your hands, why shouldn't you thank them?"

In the end Robbie had to give in, because he admired his wife, and he wouldn't have admired her so much if she hadn't had a mind of her own. If a rich man's wife insists on going in for crèches and cafeterias, at least it is better than if she took to cocktail parties, or gambling, or displaying her bosom in the "Diamond Horseshoe" and putting her legs up on the table in the refreshment room of the Metropolitan Opera

House. Robbie would have to stand some kidding from his friends in the locker room of the country club—but then he seldom had time to play golf any more. The thing to do was to take it with a grin; and presently it occurred to him that it might be turned into very good publicity. If he had to drink tea at his home with those union fellows —well, after all, they could talk shop, and if it really prevented strikes it would be a form of insurance. Budd-Erling was making so much money, and what it had to pay as excess profit taxes broke Robbie's heart; now he could charge off social services as expenses and thus pay less to a government that he hated almost as much as he hated the unions.

III

Lanny had written his father about Emily Chattersworth's will, and Robbie's law firm had been attending to the matter in New York. Now in Robbie's study they discussed the subject; the father chose to take it with humor and remarked, "You are in for it! You are a businessman now. You will have to hire help and learn to meet a payroll, and you will have all the crackpots of the whole world after you."

Lanny admitted ruefully that it might be so. Said he, "Tell me what you think I should do."

"You mean to end war in the world?" Robbie still had a twinkle in his eye. "I would suggest that you spend the million dollars to keep Budd-Erling going for a while after this war is over."

Robbie's son wasn't usually slow-witted, but he didn't get that one right away. He knew that he was supposed to bite, so he asked, "How would that help?"

"Well," said the father, "you know what the situation is going to be when this war ends; Russia is going to hold all the countries along her border, including part of Germany, no doubt. All the Nazis will turn Communist and proceed to shoot the Socialists like you and the capitalists like me. America will have to make up its mind whether to let the Russians have the whole of Europe or to stop them."

"In other words," said Lanny, "the way to get peace will be to fight a third world war?"

"Precisely; you will be for it when the time comes. And you know what happens to us makers of war goods: in wartime we are public benefactors and get huge sums of money and perform prodigies of service; but the moment the fighting stops all our contracts are canceled, our workers who have acquired skills are turned into the street, and congressional committees call us merchants of death. We have to learn to live on our fat, keep our temper, and bide our time till the next call comes."

"And how long would Emily's million keep you going?" inquired Lanny, entering into the spirit of the occasion.

"Maybe a week, maybe a month, depending how much of our skeleton we were trying to save. Every little helps."

"Well, Robbie, I'll see if Laurel can get in touch with Emily in a trance, and ask if that will be a satisfactory solution of the problem."

"Emily was a Budd-Erling stockholder, and Laurel is one, so between them they ought to be able to fix it up."

"Joking aside, Robbie, you wouldn't have much hope for my undertaking?"

The father shifted from gay to grave. "I'm sorry to have to tell you, but I think the project a piece of pernicious nonsense, and I'll be greatly embarrassed to see you undertaking it."

"You don't think there is any kind of educational work that might prepare people's minds for an international organization to keep the peace?"

"I remember a sentence once spoken by Grover Cleveland: 'It is a condition and not a theory that confronts us.' When this war ends the only active pacifists will be the Commies and their dupes. They will have the biggest army in the world and they will keep it; but they will preach disarmament for Italy and Germany, for France and Britain, for Turkey and China, all the countries they want to throw to the dogs. They will want our Army to disband right away, and then to rot us with strikes and discontent. They will be enthusiastic for your work; they will swarm around you, with or without false faces on, and you will be following their party line whether you know it or not."

IV

Lanny always dealt gently with his father on the subject of the Reds, for he knew the wound that was festering in the old man's heart. To have a dearly loved son who was a parlor Pink was bad enough; but to have a daughter who was an out-and-out Communist party member was beyond endurance. Bessie Budd Robin came at long intervals to see her parents out of politeness, and they talked about her husband, her children, and her music, but never one word about her ideas. Now that the Soviet Union was an ally in the war, many people thought it was proper to be tolerant of Reds in America, but the president of Budd-Erling was not one of these. He knew that the Communist program was revolution throughout the world, and he made no compromises with those who advocated it. He would call them bad names and then suddenly stop and fall silent. Lanny would know what was in his mind, that one of these evildoers was his own flesh and blood!

Bessie was his only daughter, and in the early days her parents had laid the blame upon her marriage, which they had opposed. Hansi Robin might be ever so fine a violinist, but he was a Socialist and a Jew, and the Jews, a homeless people, were prone to internationalism and radicalism—so said Robbie. But now poor Hansi had been left far behind in the march to the future; Hansi was an idealist, a gentle soul, a lover of all mankind, and he was as unhappy over his wife's course as were Robbie and Esther. Where had Bess got such ideas, and how could she possibly believe in them?

The father couldn't bear to talk about it, but the proud mother asked this question, and Lanny answered, "She got them from you, Esther, and from your forefathers and their creed."

"What nonsense, Lanny! My forefathers never heard of Communism, and it was nothing but a vague bad word to me."

"You are an ethical person, Esther. You have convictions from which nobody can budge you—not if you had to go to the stake for them. I once called you a daughter of the Puritans, and you smiled over it, and perhaps never stopped to realize how true it is. Your forefathers had a faith they would die for and many of them did; and the Communists are like that. Your forefathers wanted to save souls for heaven, and the Communists want to save them on earth, but at base all fanaticism is the same thing."

"Such cruelty, Lanny! Such dreadful, wholesale wickedness!"

"You have read New England history, dear, but you've let the ugly parts slip into the back of your mind. Your forefathers hanged helpless old women as witches."

"Yes, Lanny, but they believed the devil was in them."

"The Communists believe the devil is in the capitalists, the great landlords and others who monopolize the means of life and use them to exploit the laboring masses. It is a different set of ideas, but the fundamental attitude, the type of mind, is the same. Your forefathers put men in stocks, they ducked women in ducking stools, they drove Roger Williams, a gentle mystic, out into the wilderness."

"Surely they never murdered people wholesale as the Communists have done!"

"Are you sure? Just go to your public library and get a history of Ireland, and see what Oliver Cromwell did to the Irish people, the names he called them, and the wholesale ferocious slaughter. Ireland is a smaller country than Russia, but proportionately I doubt if the Communists have killed as many people in Russia as the Roundheads killed in the Emerald Isle. You and I are used to seeing social progress made by means of the ballot, but we have to bear in mind that some peoples haven't reached that stage of development and cannot get any sort of change without violence, and a lot of it."

"Lanny," said the stepmother with sudden anxiety, "you're not going to let Bess win *you* over, are you?"

He smiled gently, being sorry for her. "Mother dear, I am one of those unlucky people who have to stand in the middle and get the brickbats from both sides. I see the good in both and I see the evil. But if you point that out the fanatics on both sides want to kill you."

V

Hansi and Bess had a home halfway between Newcastle and New York, and Lanny and Laurel drove to see them and spent the day. All these four people loved one another, and the conflict of minds and wills that went on between the two musicians corresponded to that which went on inside the mind of Lanny Budd, and to a lesser extent in that of Laurel Creston. Could there really be in America such a thing as an orderly and peaceable change from a system of exploitation to one of co-operation, or were the Socialists just deluding themselves with a vain hope? Were the Commies—so determined, so unresting—helping to prepare America for the great social change, or were they hindering the change and putting weapons into the hands of the reactionaries?

Hansi and Bessie Budd Robin had labored unceasingly and made themselves true artists. They had given recitals for violin and piano all over America and Europe and had been hailed by uncounted numbers of people. They had made money and bought a beautiful home overlooking Long Island Sound; they had two lovely children, and everything that was needed to make them happy; but they were tormenting themselves because they couldn't agree on their political and social beliefs. They had argued, each trying to convince the other, until each could no longer endure the sound of the other's voice. The only way they could live together was by a strict agreement never to mention these subjects in each other's presence. They would listen to news over the radio and never utter a word about what they heard. If a Communist came to call, Hansi would excuse himself, and if a Socialist came, Bess would do the same. They cut their minds in half, and each put one half aside and kept it in a locked compartment. But of course the other knew where it was and what was in it!

They could talk about the war, since both of them wanted the same outcome. Lanny told about his Monuments adventure and about the art treasures he had discovered and then had to leave to the Germans. He told about Emily's bequest, and this interested them greatly, because it had been in her Paris town house that Hansi and Bess had met. Hansi had performed the Beethoven concerto, with Lanny playing the piano arrangement, and that had settled Bess's fate. But they couldn't discuss how Lanny would spend the money, for they knew in advance what Bess would say, that the only way to world peace was by the route of the Communist International. Stalin had abolished this organization, reportedly to oblige Roosevelt, but both the Hansibesses and the Lannybudds knew this was merely a temporary move and that the organization would be revived in some form as soon as the war was won.

Not even the topic of music was absolutely safe, for the Soviet rulers objected to musical compositions that were oversubtle and precious, and Hansi had remarked that Stalin wanted tunes the commissars could whistle. Better to leave out modern music and stick to the classics, by which the taste of all four had been molded. What was Hansi playing now? He had composed a little "Concert Piece" which he used as an encore, and the audiences gave evidence of liking it. He played that for his relatives; it was gentle, lovely, and a little bit sad, like himself. Could any Jew be really happy, knowing what had been going on in Germany for twelve years?

The composer was pleased by what Lanny and Laurel said about the piece, and he kissed Bess and exclaimed, "Let's celebrate our honeymoon again!" So they played the sweeping and grand first movement of the Beethoven concerto. Hansi could play it as only perhaps half a dozen virtuosos in the world, and that was a real treat, worth coming all the way from Juan-les-Pins to hear. It cheered them, and started the lives of two musicians over again.

VI

In the afternoon the two men put on their overcoats and went for a walk in the softly falling snow. Bess and Laurel stayed and talked, and then music was forgotten. Bess poured out her troubles. She had

the idea that Laurel was more radical than Lanny, or at any rate took
her social creed more seriously; perhaps she thought that Laurel might
be able to influence Hansi. He persisted in reading newspapers like the
New Leader, which filled his mind with all the evils that could be
found in the Soviet Union and never by any chance reported what was
good: the hundred and fifty million people who had been lifted out of
ignorance and superstition, who had been taught to read and write and
had had the world's classics put before them; the hundred or more
tribes and races which had been given cultural freedom, many of them
given an alphabet for the first time, and books printed in it. Bess would
tell things like this for hours, and had done so with Hansi—but how
much effect had it had? Nothing that next week's *New Leader*
couldn't wipe out!

Meantime there was Hansi walking and telling about Bess and the
evil company she kept. Nothing sexual—it wasn't like that, but something worse; conspiratorial persons who went about under aliases and
carried dark secrets which they mentioned in whispers; efforts to steal
the secrets of American weapons and plans to promote strikes after
the war. Lanny himself had been doing that sort of thing in Germany,
but he hadn't told Hansi and didn't tell him now. He listened sym-
pathetically to statements that his half-sister read poisonous papers like
the *Daily Worker* and the *New Masses*, which told her only the evil
things about America and never by any chance mentioned the good:
the New Deal and all the benefits it had brought to the public; the
Tennessee Valley Authority, a model of what a public service enterprise ought to be; the laws establishing social security and protecting
the rights of labor.

Wasn't it true, asked the violinist, that a revolution sometimes de-
generated and fell into the hands of men who used its slogans as covers
for their love of personal power? And when you had a one-party system and suppressed all criticism, how could any evil be corrected? Even
Stalin himself couldn't get truth, because the men around him, seeking
to please him, would tell him what they knew he wanted to hear.
Hansi insisted that the Communist world revolution had become a
tool of Russian power politics; every day it grew more narrow, more
limited, less open to modern ideas. Birth control, for example; wasn't
that a test of reaction versus progress? To suppress knowledge of birth
control could only mean that you were breeding soldiers for war. Just
as with the Catholics, the top classes had the knowledge and used it
but denied it to the poor underlings.

The Hansibesses had been in Russia for nearly two years, returning only a short time ago, so Hansi knew what he was talking about. On the concert platform he had been welcomed tumultuously, but in private life few Russians dared to be his friend. To associate with a foreigner meant to fall under the suspicion of the dread secret police; and even foreign Communists, who came to work for the cause in Moscow, found that they were watched, and only in a very few cases were they trusted.

Hansi told about Lanny's Uncle Jesse Blackless, who was Beauty's elder brother. Jesse had lived most of his life in France, and had been the fountainhead from which had flowed all this "radicalism" which had brought so much distress into the life of the president of Budd-Erling Aircraft. Just thirty years ago Jesse had taken his young nephew to meet a woman Syndicalist in the working-class quarter of Cannes, and the two of them had planted in a sensitive young mind the seeds of doubt which had sprouted fast and spread widely. Lanny had influenced both Hansi and Freddie Robin, and Hansi had converted Bess; so it had gone.

A lean, nearly bald painter of fair-to-average portraits, Jesse had espoused the cause of the Soviet revolution from the day it had occurred, and had risked his liberty in France to aid it during the Peace Conference in Paris. He had joined the party, and had taken as his companion a woman worker in the party office in Paris. He had gone to Moscow to help with the French Section of the International, and Hansi and Bess had seen a good deal of him. Like other foreign Communists whom the pair had met, he was too free-spoken, too independent; he was open to suspicion of having been infected with the heresy known as "Trotskyist deviationism." This meant simply that you were international instead of being Russian; it meant that you couldn't be trusted to react instantly and automatically to the party line, but might ask tactless questions and express dangerous doubts. So Lanny Budd's Red uncle had become a tired, discouraged old man who was given routine jobs of translation, but could never hold any power and knew that his few Russian friends were there to watch him.

VII

Laurel and Lanny drove back to New York in the car which Robbie always loaned them. That crowded island had become the center of the world's finance, and America's center of publication and publicity. Ideas went out from it in billions of printed pages and by short wave to the whole world. There was an incessant struggle for power between the lower part of this island and the center of government on the Potomac River. The Man in the White House had taken so much of the power from Wall Street to Washington that he had become the most hated President in American history.

New York remained the center of all the luxury trades, and among them was Lanny's trade, that of advising about art. Here he met his friend and associate, Zoltan Kertezsi, who had taught him how to judge paintings and how to persuade the rich that his judgment was correct. For more than two decades Lanny had been following this occupation, an easy one for him because he loved beautiful things, and studying them, and talking about them; also because, as the son of Budd-Erling, he naturally met the rich and might as well get something substantial out of the acquaintance. They wished to decorate their homes, and might better have good things than bad; they were going to take somebody's advice, and it would be wiser for them to pay Lanny a ten per cent commission than to be unconscionably cheated by some dealer.

Now these two amiable gentlemen wandered along East 57th Street and strolled in to see the exhibitions and chatted with the dealers, who knew them and gladly spread out the best of their wares. Quality and price were inseparably mixed in their conversation, and that had become the case also in Lanny's mind. Quality was something fixed, you might have thought, but what counted was the estimation of quality, and that varied like the ebb and flow of tides. Some schools were on their way in and others on their way out, and prices went up and down with them; the man who could tell what was of permanent value might build himself a marble palace.

Zoltan Kertezsi was a Hungarian, a very elegant person with iron-gray hair and wide mustaches. He was of a conservative turn of mind and looked with scorn upon those modern painters who slapped colors on canvas any old way and were too busy to finish anything properly. In these days a colossal fraud was being perpetrated upon the public by men who painted jumbles of objects as in a kaleidoscope; a face with the eye stuck on sidewise, or something that looked like telephone wire after a cyclone had passed, and was called "Man Asleep," or maybe "Daydream," or just "Etude." Such jumbles were given mysterious titles, and the public was left to guess at a meaning where there was nothing but idiocy. Worse yet were things called "collages"; you might see a board on which a piece of torn burlap was nailed, its beauty enhanced by pieces of string, newspaper, and broken glass glued on, the whole in a fine antique Italian frame.

The works of Marcel Detaze were stored in a fireproof vault, and now and then Zoltan would put some of them into a van and take them to a distant city for a "one-man show." He knew how to get them advertised, and he put prices on them which the dealers said were beyond reason—but how could you be sure? All over America were people who were swamped under floods of money and who were proud to say, "I paid twenty thousand for that Detaze"—and would be happy all their lives, knowing it must be good because of what it had cost. Ten per cent of the price would go to Zoltan, and thirty each to Lanny, to Beauty, and to Marceline—if she was alive to receive it.

VIII

In the previous October the Russian armies had come to a halt along the Vistula River, in front of Warsaw, and had begun preparations for a winter offensive. Tanks can move in snow, unless it is very deep; the only thing that really troubles them is sticky mud; and on the level plains of Poland everything freezes. The Russians brought up enormous masses of supplies, and artillery in such quantities as the world had never seen before. They had many thousands of American trucks and uncountable swarms of peasant carts—their advance was more like a migration than an army. They had all lived more than half their lives in cold and knew how to exist in spite of it.

Just as the Battle of the Bulge was ending, the second week of January, these vast hordes struck. Artillery barrages knocked down the German defenses, and the Russians poured through great gaps in the line, all the way from the Baltic Sea to the Carpathian Mountains, a distance of some four hundred miles. They had command of the air, and the supply bases of the Germans behind the lines were being pounded by British and American bombers flying from France. The Germans brought reserves from the western front and threw them into the battle, but in vain. Hitler had sent too many of his troops to the south, trying to keep the Russians away from Budapest and Vienna. That was Adi's way; he couldn't bear to give up anything, and so he was losing everything.

This Russian advance was going on all the time that Lanny was in Newcastle and New York. Wherever there was a radio he and Laurel would sit and listen. Morning and evening the newspapers printed maps showing how the great bulges were spreading all the way across the broad plains of Poland and up to the German border. The Germans had constructed immense defense areas and turned whole cities into fortresses, but the Russians by-passed most of these; they were so sure of their own strength and their enemy's weakness that they no longer feared counteroffensives. They were going straight through this time, their destination Berlin. The only thing that troubled the American listeners was fear that the Allied armies might be too slow in getting started and might take too long to get across the Rhine. The Russians might take all Germany; and what if they refused to get out? Uneasiness was spreading, and Lanny heard more than one of his rich friends express the idea that maybe there might have been something in Hitler's ideas after all. Wouldn't it have been better to make a deal with him? Perhaps he couldn't be trusted, but at least the armies would have been moving east instead of west!

7

Let Us Have Peace

I

FOR the assimilated Colonel Budd there came a War Department telegram, instructing him to board a plane at Mitchel Field, the Army airbase, two days later. He took the precaution to drive out there and check. He didn't need any passports or other documents; all he had to do was to identify himself, which was not difficult. He packed his bags and took his little portable; they put no weight limit on one of his status, for who could know what important documents or other impedimenta he might be needing? He reported at the field on time and found an assemblage of passengers, Army and State Department people, both men and women—secretaries, translators, specialists in various subjects. Apparently not one of them knew where he was going or for how long, and there was a lot of speculating and talking in low tones.

They were to be transported in a passenger plane and would be made comfortable; no bucket-seat job, for they must be fit to go to work the moment they arrived. Lanny found himself seated next to a young lawyer from Cleveland, now with the State Department; he was Russian-born, and read Russian books all the way—which would have helped Lanny to a guess if he had needed a guess. He asked no questions, and neither did the other man; they talked for a while about the news which appeared on the bulletin board of the plane. It was the end of January, and the Russians had reached a place called Kleinitz on the Oder, a river that flows within fifty miles of Berlin. Amazing!

Air travel had been routine to Lanny for a long time now. He had a bundle of newspapers and magazines and passed the time agreeably. Bermuda wasn't new to him, except for the extensions of the airport; the same was true of the Azores, of Casablanca, and of Naples, with Mount Vesuvius for a background. It was interesting to see how quickly the Americans had restored the facilities of that port; a job of the Army engineers, who boasted of having hairy ears and of breaking schedules in all the places where they were turned loose. From Naples the party was flown to Malta, an island reported to be the most-bombed spot on the face of the globe. It is some twenty miles long and half as wide, and if there was one of its stone houses undamaged Lanny Budd failed to see it.

Those unhappy days were over now, and the RAF airbase at Luqa was in perfect shape. It needed to be, for big planes were coming in every few minutes, bringing what one of the pilots described as "heavy loads of brass." These were the six hundred people that F. D. R. had spoken of, and no doubt as many more British. A total of ninety four-motor aircraft—C-54s and British Yorks—were required for this job. The first person Lanny met was Baker, the President's man, and after that he felt at home. He forbore to ask questions, but was told that his plane was to be flown to a town called Saki, on the southern coast of the Crimea. Nobody could go by ship, because the enemy had mined all the harbors of the Black Sea.

Franklin Roosevelt's fourth inauguration had taken place in Washington, a brief and simple ceremony, and two days later he had been taken in his special train to Norfolk, the Army's secret port of embarkation, and had boarded the heavy cruiser *Quincy*; a week later he was in the Strait of Gibraltar. Those on board had held their breath, wondering how many German subs would be waiting for them. The last time the President had come there, on his way to the Teheran Conference, Franco had turned all his searchlights on the battleship *Iowa*, to give what help he could to the subs. But this time he hadn't done so, and the P.A. remarked, "He has found out how the war is going."

II

The trip from Malta was rough, and some of the passengers were airsick. They passed over the Isles of Greece, which brought back memories to Lanny, who had sailed among them just thirty years ago as a guest aboard a yacht. A fellow guest had been Marcel Detaze, who was to become Lanny's first stepfather. (If you went about in the fashionable world you might meet some lad who had had half a dozen stepfathers.) Lanny had had no cares, and the world had been wonderful; he had not dreamed that he was destined to live through the two most dreadful wars in history, or that when he passed over these islands again he would be two miles up in the air, on his way to do what he could to help prevent a third war that would dwarf the others if it came.

The Germans, after holding the Crimea for a couple of years, had wrecked everything before they left. The big planes had to be set down on what was called an airstrip, having but a single runway made by laying mats of steel. The first sight Lanny saw was snow-covered mountains, and then, on the field below, hundreds of women diligently shoveling freshly fallen snow from the runway. The plane circled until this job was completed, and then it came in to a bumpy landing. There were few houses left standing in Saki, and apparently most of the people lived in cellars and shacks built out of wreckage. You saw no young or middle-aged men, only the old, the children, and the women. Girls served as soldiers guarding the road to Yalta, releasing the men for the front now far away; the girls carried old-fashioned Springfield rifles, obtained by American lend-lease.

From there it was a two-hundred-mile drive along the coast to Yalta. The Russians had provided cars, but not enough for this great company; more were brought in by the Americans in cargo planes. Lanny and half a dozen of his party were driven by an American chauffeur through rolling country, lined with wrecked houses, wrecked cars, trucks and tanks, all the debris of battle as Lanny had seen it in the Rhône valley and in the Ardennes. Near Yalta it was mountain country, which might have been the French Riviera with its towns and villas; the road was like the Grande Corniche, the "great shelf" which runs high up above the Côte d'Azur, winding around the sides of one mountain after another, and looking down upon a boundless sea. This one was called the Black because it was so deep and dark.

Yalta had been a town, the summer playground of the tsars and their court. The Germans, before retiring, had reduced every building of the town to rubble, sparing only three palaces along the coast. The Livadia, assigned to the Americans, had been the residence of Tsar Nicholas II; it was an enormous place, which had been the headquarters of Marshal von Rundstedt, who had come so near to capturing Lanny in the Ardennes. The report was that Hitler had promised these palaces to three of his best generals, and so the historic buildings hadn't been blown up or burned. All that Rundstedt's men had done was to take the furniture and even the plumbing fixtures. The Russians had brought down trainloads of stuff and done their best to make fastidious Americans feel at home. Lanny was told that the medical corps had fumigated the palace; this because Churchill had radioed Roosevelt on the *Quincy*, reporting that it was swarming with typhus-bearing lice.

III

The building, immensely long, was of white stone and had two tall stories; at each end was a wide tower, twice as tall as the rest of the building. The front was indented to make wide porticoes, and above these were verandas and a sort of covered pavilion on the roof; the Tsar and his large family had come here for fresh air.

Lanny had been told how, just after the revolution, all these Crimean palaces had been turned into rest homes for the workers, and thousands of them had swarmed here, eating on long trestle tables set out in the court, in the porticoes, and in the very splendid formal gardens. The war had ended all that, and now there was a new picnic party coming to the summer palace in midwinter. Tsar Nicholas II had ardently desired peace but hadn't known how to get it or to keep it. Here came an American President, a British Prime Minister, and a Bolshevik Party Secretary become Marshal, to see if they could be any wiser and abler.

The United States Secret Service was on hand, Argus-eyed and all-foreseeing; they had politely told all the Russian servants that they were not needed, and the President's Filipino mess-boys had moved in and were busy surveying the premises, unpacking their gear, and getting ready for the great show. Everything had been planned in advance, like a battle; everybody knew his post and his duties, and it was like an army deploying.

Baker had given Lanny the needed credentials, and anyhow, the Secret Service had known him for a long time and gave him the run of the place. The Irish-American head of this super-body, Mike Reilly, told him about some of the precautions taken for this trip. All along the Black Sea coast, where the planes had to fly, were Russian anti-aircraft batteries, and the young soldiers manning these were apt to be "trigger-happy"; they wouldn't know American planes and might take one for an enemy. Before he let the President fly that route, Mike had decreed that there must be an American Air Force man stationed with every battery. To that the Russian military commander had said "Impossible," and Mike had replied, "Then no President." The issue had been referred to Stalin, who, to the obvious bewilderment of the Russian officer, had assented at once. So now there was a noncom in every battery, armed with a pair of binoculars, and he called the turn on all the approaching planes. He had been taught one Russian word, "*Stoy*," which means stop. All the Americans learned that word, for when a Russian sentry said "*Stoy!*" he meant it, and *stoy* you did.

IV

Having no duties the first afternoon, and being stiff from plane and car riding, Lanny went for a walk to inspect the ruins of Yalta. At once he made an interesting discovery—he was to have a shadow: a very tiny Russian man, presumably not big enough to carry a gun, and clad in very tight striped trousers which did not come down to the tops of his shoes. He walked when Lanny walked and stopped when Lanny stopped, and as soon as Lanny realized what this meant he turned back and joined him, greeted him politely and shook hands, to the man's evident embarrassment. That wasn't the orthodox way to treat a shadow.

But why not? "We are allies," said Lanny, and when the man didn't understand that, he said "*Tovarish*"—which did the business. Lanny had visited Leningrad, and on another yachting trip Odessa, and more recently Kuibyshev and Moscow, so he knew some words. When someone said "*Tchai?*" he could say "*Da*," meaning that he would have some tea. When they said "*Vodka*," he could say "*Nyet, nyet*"—and he knew he would have to say it many times during his sojourn in the Livadia Palace.

Knowing the war-torn lands, he had put chewing gum and chocolate into his bags, and now he offered a stick of gum to the odd little man, who accepted it gladly and put it into his mouth, paper, tinfoil, and all. So it was Lanny's turn to cry "*Stoy!*" and he showed the man what to do. After that they were friends, and grinned every time they saw each other; but the shadow would never walk beside Lanny, always a few feet behind—that, no doubt, being the regulation.

Lanny didn't want to do any harm to anybody; he just wanted to look at the old folks and the children, see them smile at the rich *Amerikansi*, and find out how they were getting along in a land which their enemies had so cruelly wrecked. There had been time for planting since the enemies had been driven out, so the people had food, and the climate here was mild enough so that they could work all the year round. They would survive, and presumably some of the men would come back from the war. This was no new story to the Crimea. They had lived through it all a generation ago, and again less than a century ago, when the British had been the enemy. Not far away was that "mouth of hell" into which "the six hundred" had ridden.

Lanny looked into several peasant huts, and invariably was greeted with broad smiles. Strange and rather alarming smiles they were, for many of the old people had lost their teeth and had dental plates of which they were proud. They were made of steel and shone like polished silver plate in the sunlight. He made another discovery, of great interest to him: on the wall of every hut hung a small radio set, and at first he didn't know what it was, for it had no dials. Then he realized that this was a totalitarian set; it could get only the wave lengths assigned to the official Russian stations. Lanny could guess that these people wouldn't know there was any other kind of set or any other wave length in the world. Lanny recalled the story of Caliph Omar in the Alexandrian library: "Burn all the books but the Koran, for their value is in that."

V

Roosevelt had a new plane, built especially for his travels, and this was his first trip in it. The Air Force men dubbed it "The Sacred Cow," and before long the symbol was painted on the nose. Also he had an armored car with bullet-proof glass, which was brought by plane and in which he made the drive from Saki to Yalta. This wasn't new; it had belonged to Chicago gangster Al Capone. The Treasury Department had got the car when it succeeded in sending Capone to jail for understating his income taxes due.

The President was put up in one of the Tsar's numerous bedrooms; War Mobilization Director Jimmy Byrnes slept in the Tsarina's room, and that was certainly an odd adventure for a country boy from South Carolina. The royal lady's boudoir was occupied by the very stiff and proper Admiral King, Commander of the Fleet. There was only one bathroom in this entire palace, and queues formed up; only the VGDIPs got showers.

Churchill and his outfit were installed in the Alupka Palace, about twelve miles away from the Livadia. He showed up at the conference wearing a round fur hat, Russian style, which he had had made in Canada; he had learned a few phrases of Russian to say to Stalin, but Stalin, alas, wasn't able to understand them. The Red Marshal came by train and was established in the palace which had belonged to Prince Yussupoff, the slayer of Rasputin. He brought a large staff, headed by Molotov, his Foreign Commissar. For the Americans, among themselves, the pair were "Uncle Joe" and "Auntie Mol."

The first day of the conference was Sunday, the 4th of February. Stalin and Molotov came to call on Roosevelt, bringing their interpreter. Half an hour later the first formal meeting began in the Grand Ballroom of the Livadia Palace. There was an immense round table in the center, and around it sat about thirty men: the heads of the three governments, their secretaries of state, and their chief military officers, army, navy and air force. They spent nearly three hours in discussion and then adjourned for dinner, with Roosevelt as host; there was consommé, sturgeon with tomatoes, beef and macaroni, plus the fixings. It was not an elegant menu, but the diners presumably made it palatable with vodka and five kinds of wine.

VI

The son of Budd-Erling wasn't invited to this banquet, and he rather wondered why he had been brought to this secret state affair. Had F. D. R. acted on an impulse of friendliness, and would he now forget about it in the rush of affairs? Lanny stayed in his room, which he shared with three of the lesser officials; he was resolved not to force himself upon anybody, and studied diligently a little Russian phrase book he had bought in New York. In the middle of the morning he was summoned to Harry Hopkins, who said that the Boss wanted Lanny to give Harry what help he could, pending the time the Boss would have some leisure. Nothing could have given Lanny more pleasure, for he knew no better company than this harness-maker's son from Iowa, keen-witted and at the same time warmhearted, grimly determined for the cause of the world's downtrodden, and loyal to the great man who was trying to lift them up.

Helping Harry consisted of sitting by the bed while the tired man lay and chain-smoked cigarettes and talked about the events of the day. He was an extremely sociable person, and perhaps talking aided his mind to work; he respected Lanny's opinion and wanted to hear his reaction to this and that. Lanny was careful never to force his ideas upon these overworked official persons; he listened until they had propounded a problem, and then, if he had any answer, he gave it once. He too was impatient of bores and took pains not to be one. As a result people invited him to stay longer and to come again.

Harry the Hop told how in Malta our military men had had a tough argument with the British, who had a different plan for the advance upon Germany; it had become so hot that Marshall, Chief of Staff, had advised Eisenhower to say that he would resign if the British plan were followed. Our Navy people were demanding more forces against Japan; but F.D.R. settled that one, sticking right to the program he had laid down at the beginning—Germany must be beaten first. Our main problem was to get the Russians' promise to help us drive the Japanese out of China. When would they undertake that job, and what price would they charge for it? This, alas, was not an altruistic world. They would want the Kurile Islands, and probably Dairen and Port Arthur, and they might want Manchuria, which would hurt. Chinese cities and provinces weren't ours to give away; but they weren't China's either; was it our business to pour out American blood to save China's possessions and lay them in China's lap? All we could do was to try to persuade Stalin not to keep too much.

The most important of all tasks, in the view of F.D.R., was the forming of an international organization to settle future disputes and keep the peace of the world. There must never be another war like this, if civilization was to endure. The President had called an international conference at a mansion in Washington called Dumbarton Oaks, and it had worked out the details of such an undertaking; now he wanted to persuade Stalin to agree to a time and place for a formal assemblage of delegates to organize and launch the project. That was the most important news that Lanny Budd had heard for a long time; it would mean a real chance of winning the peace as well as the war. He told Hopkins in confidence about the Chattersworth bequest, and they agreed to meet and discuss that later on.

VII

A tragic thing it was to Lanny to see this desperately sick man, holding on to life in a sort of frenzy, putting his last ounce of strength into the effort to render one final service to mankind. Every moment of his life was an effort; and when he could do no more he would sink back upon the pillow, gasping, and Lanny would turn himself into a manservant, put a blanket over him, bring him a glass of water, take notes of what he needed or what he wanted said to this person or that. Harry had secretaries with him, but they were busy every moment, and there were always unexpected errands turning up. He would start to apologize, and Lanny would say, "This is the most important thing I have ever done."

So it went for day after day. Lanny wrote down the day's agenda, he ran errands, he looked up passages in books and reports, read the morning paper and marked items Harry would need to see. *The Times* was flown from London every day of the conference, arriving the day after its issue date—this despite the fact that a two-hundred-mile motor drive was part of the route. Mail was brought daily by a special courier of the Joint Chiefs of Staff. Harry would read, dictate, and consult all morning, have lunch with Roosevelt, and then attend a conference with the American staff. At four o'clock would come the formal meeting of the three delegations, lasting about three hours. At eight would come one of those exhausting dinners, with numerous toasts, and discussion which had to be translated. A sick man had to be excused from these affairs.

That was the time Lanny sat by his bedside and got his orders, made his reports, and gave opinions when they were asked for. This was the culmination of the war for the art expert, and the best part. The war itself was a brutal thing, but here was conscience as well as brains being applied to human affairs. The powers which were going to rule the world, perhaps for the next century, were meeting here and learning to understand one another, to come to definite agreement about all possible differences, so that reason and fair play might at last take charge of the world.

Stalin was being very accommodating, Lanny was told. He was in agreement with all the military plans for the finishing of the war, and he promised to enter the war against Japan within two or three months after the German surrender. He agreed to all the plans for the demilitarization of both enemy lands. He was not so keen for the proposed international organization; he preferred to have the three nations which were winning the war keep the right to settle the peace; he couldn't see much sense in a proposal which would place the Soviet Union and Honduras, for example, on the same plane of power. He was persuaded to agree on the basis that the Big Three should retain the power to veto actions they didn't like—they being the ones who would have to supply the military force if it was required.

Harry had long talks with his underground adviser on this subject. They agreed that the principal reason the old League of Nations failed was because America had refused to come in; so now there could be no use in proposing at Yalta anything that the United States Senate would refuse to endorse. "Those old political pachyderms," as Harry called them, would demand the same thing that the Red dictator was demanding, the right to say NO to any proposal that would compel the United States to send its military forces out of the country. "That Man" and his New Deal crackpots might work up any fancy schemes they chose, but the decision would rest with elderly senators from the poll-tax belt who held all the committee chairmanships by virtue of the seniority rule.

VIII

Harry said that he had told the Boss of the help Lanny Budd was giving, and the Boss had expressed his gratitude. Lanny got his reward on the fourth day of the conference, when he was invited to lunch with F. D. R. and his daughter, Mrs. Boettiger, who was acting as his secretary. Present also was Pa Watson, the President's military aide, an elderly brigadier general whom he dearly loved and who was destined to die before this trip was over. Lanny listened to talk about the various personalities at the great affair and the decisions which were being taken. He had the honor of being asked for his opinion more than once, and ventured to suggest that it was an error to divide Germany into zones under Russian, British, French, and American control. It meant there would be four different Germanys, and many disputes among their administrators. It would be far wiser to have one joint administration, and then the disputes could be settled at the council table before the various measures were put into effect. Roosevelt replied, sadly, that this was his own view, but Stalin and Churchill had ganged up against him.

Lanny said, "Of course, each will want to have his own way in his own zone."

"No doubt, but they have agreed that the principles of the Atlantic Charter shall be applied in all the lands they control."

"I hate to be a pessimist," was the reply, "but it is hard to bind men to agreements when they do not give the same meaning to the words they are using."

The tired man could not face this thought and Lanny did not press it. He knew that Roosevelt was acting as moderator between two political extremists, who had been denouncing each other ever since each had heard of the other—a longer time in Churchill's case than in Stalin's. The descendant of the first Duke of Marlborough had leaped into prominence during the Boer War, almost half a century ago, at which time Joseph Djugashvili, the cobbler's son, had been a wretchedly poor theological student in Tiflis, unknown to anybody in the great world. Now they were in agreement on only two things: the desire to wipe Nazi-Fascism from the earth and the desire to do the same to the Japanese Greater East Asia Co-Prosperity Sphere. What they were going to put in the place of these two systems was something it was better not to mention in each other's presence.

IX

After the formal dinners broke up there was some standing around and chatting, and some of the lesser lights were welcome to enter and enjoy glimpses of the great. Lanny kept in the background, because the Navy had brought along photographers who took pictures of everyone they thought might be of interest to posterity, and Lanny didn't think of himself as belonging in that class. He watched both Stalin and Churchill, and thought how much older they looked; the war was wearing all these old men down. Churchill was still round and rosy, but he had shadows under his eyes and was almost entirely bald. Stalin's hair was gray, and his face was sallow and lined; he looked ill at ease in a military outfit cut too big for him—perhaps with the idea of concealing the fact that he was a small man.

His eye caught Lanny's, and presently an aide came over and asked, "Are you Mr. Budd?" Then, "The Marshal would like to speak to you." So Lanny had not been forgotten, as he had imagined.

He went up and was greeted. "Why did you not come to see me again?" When this had been translated by the young man who never left the Marshal's side, Lanny smiled and said that he had had the idea that the Marshal must be busy these days. He added, "This is the occasion to which I have been looking forward for many years."

"I too," replied Stalin. "I am always happy to meet your President, who is a very great man." Nothing could have been more gracious; and Lanny, seeing Air Marshal Khudiakov waiting to speak to his chief, moved tactfully on.

With the Prime Minister there was less formality, for they had sat more than twenty years ago by the swimming pool of Maxine Elliott's villa at Cannes—Churchill wearing a red dressing gown and a big, ragged straw hat. Then the onetime Liberal turned Tory had been sure that his political career was over and that he was destined to spend his days writing what he called "hist'ry." When Lanny reminded him of this he remarked, "In those days I had never heard of Adolf Hitler, damn his soul." He added, "You don't come to see us any more, Budd."

Lanny explained, "I used to come to visit my little daughter, but now I have her in Connecticut, away from the buzzbombs."

"We shall soon make England safe again," declared the Prime Minister. "And Jimmie can sleep in his own little room." He was quoting from a popular song expressing the English yearning for peace.

When Lanny told Harry about these greetings the latter remarked with a smile, "These things come naturally to you, Lanny; but for me, I have to rub my eyes when I wake up in one of the Tsar's bedrooms. You know, I was a poor boy in Sioux City, Iowa."

Said the son of Budd-Erling, "I never went in for genealogy, but I've been told that the first Budd who came to New England was a tinker. I dare say that if you went back far enough in Winston's past you'd find chimneysweeps and charwomen."

"More likely thieves and harlots," said Harry.

X

The Yalta Conference lasted eight days, from Sunday to Sunday. Everybody was happy, because the Russians were continuing their drive to the Oder and the Baltic, and on the western front the Americans, British, and Canadians were beginning their drive for the Rhine. Even Lanny's shadow was happy, because every day when the American stranger went for a walk in the clear cold sunshine he gave the little man a package of chewing gum or a five-cent bar of chocolate. Shower baths were scarce, but internal libations were abundant—even at breakfast the Russians had ten different sizes and colors of glasses for the drinking of different wines and liquors, and if there were blunders in the conference proceedings Lanny attributed them to this state of affairs. He remembered that Lenin had been an abstemious man, and that one of the first acts of his revolution had been to prohibit the manufacture of alcoholic liquor. What a change in twenty-eight years!

When the conference adjourned, a simultaneous issuance of a statement was arranged; the Americans expended a lot of energy making sure that the other two groups agreed on the meaning of that word "simultaneous." In previous instances there had somehow happened to be a leak from London, and all American newspapermen were sore about it. This time it didn't happen; the declaration to the world was given out from the three capitals at the same hour.

Said the conference: "It is our inflexible purpose to destroy German militarism and Nazism, and to ensure that Germany will never again be able to destroy the peace of the world. We are determined to disarm and disband all German Armed Forces; break up for all time the German General Staff that has continually contrived the resurgence of German militarism; remove or destroy all German military equipment; eliminate or control all German industry that could be used for military production; bring all war criminals to just and swift punishment and exact reparations in kind for the destruction wrought by the Germans; wipe out the Nazi party, Nazi laws, organizations, and institutions, remove all Nazi and militarist influences from public office and from the cultural and economic life of the German people; and take in harmony such measures in Germany as may be necessary to the future peace and safety of the world."

All that gave great pleasure to Lanny Budd, the more so because he had a chance to see it three days before the rest of the world. Harry Hopkins wrote the preliminary draft, and Lanny read it; it was Lanny who suggested the words "and from the cultural and economic life of the German people." The whirligig of time had brought this quiet form of revenge to a man who had known Hitler, Göring, Hess, and Goebbels for a matter of a decade and a half, and who had watched them forcing Nazi laws, organizations, and institutions upon the deluded German people.

XI

Completely absorbed in these important matters, Lanny was surprised by the arrival of a noncom belonging to the military guard. The man said, "There is a Russky that wants to see you, sir. Says he has a letter for you."

"Why didn't he give it to you?" asked the officer.

"Says he has to put it in your hands, sir. He's waiting outside one of the back doors."

Lanny had no idea what that could mean. He followed the man to a door which led to the elaborate court behind the palace. The door was well guarded, and when Lanny stepped out to confront the waiting Russky, one of the soldiers turned a flashlight upon the man's face. The man shrank and put his hands over his face, exclaiming, "*Nyet! Nyet!*" Lanny, who had no reason to fear any danger, told the soldier to shut off the light, and said, "My name is Budd. You have a letter for me?"

Without a word the man put a small envelope into his hand, and Lanny stepped back into the building to read it. He found five words: "I must see you. Pugliese." He knew the writing well; it was that of his Uncle Jesse, and the name was code which nobody in the world but he could have understood. Pugliese is a rather unusual Italian name, and Barbara Pugliese was the name of that Syndicalist woman to whom Jesse Blackless had taken Lanny at the age of fourteen, and who had made such an impression upon the mind of a sensitive lad. The Fascists had murdered her in San Remo twenty years ago.

Uncle Jesse in Yalta, and secretly! It meant something serious, and Lanny couldn't in decency hesitate. He went out to the messenger; he couldn't recall the Russian word for "wait," but he could say "*Stoy!*" and he said it twice for good measure. The man said, "*Da,*" and Lanny went to his room, which was upstairs, and got his overcoat, cap, and gloves.

It was a cold night, cloudy and dark. The man walked very quietly, and Lanny did the same. He wondered how the man had got past the Russians who guarded the park so carefully; but he had no way to inquire. No word was spoken, and they walked for several minutes on a snow-covered path. Then the man stopped. Lanny saw nobody, but a voice spoke the code name, Italian fashion, Pool-yay-say. Lanny said, "How are you?" And an almost invisible form stepped out from behind a tree and clasped his hand.

"I am in danger," whispered the old man with no preliminaries. "Don't speak my name. I want you to take me out with you."

"Good God!" exclaimed the nephew, astounded. "I couldn't do that!"

"Why not?"

"I am not my own master here. I haven't the right to ask such a thing."

"No one knows that I am here. I traveled with a forged permit, and I paid money to get here."

"Yes, Uncle—" Lanny checked himself. "You would surely be recognized, and it would cause a frightful diplomatic scandal. We are here to guarantee the peace."

"You are here to be swindled out of your eyeteeth."

"You have lost faith in your cause then?"

"I have lost faith in the men who are supposed to be serving it. I am one of the old Bolsheviks, and an unpleasant reminder to them. Most of us have been put out of the way. I am an old man, and sick, and I cannot do any good here, or any harm outside."

"Have you applied for a permit to leave?"

"There would be no sense in applying. I know too much, and they would never trust me. Others have applied, and they have disappeared."

"What sort of citizenship have you now?"

"Many years ago I took French citizenship in order to stand for the Assembly. You know that."

"Yes. Unfortunately there are no French here."

"You might ask your President to take me out."

It was the toughest decision Lanny had ever had to make, but he could not even hesitate. "I would be asking our President to risk all that he is trying to accomplish. It would be improper for me to ask him, and if *he* asked *me* I should have to advise against it."

"That is your last word?"

"I will ask him to intercede for you if you wish; but I can't ask him to take you out without Stalin's permission. You must understand our position—"

But Lanny was talking to empty air. The old and sick man had turned and disappeared into the darkness. The nephew went back into the well-lighted palace, feeling somewhat old and sick himself.

Later in the evening he told Harry what had happened. Harry knew about Jesse Blackless, for there had once been a controversy over his right to re-enter his native land. Harry said, "It's too bad, but of course we couldn't attempt to smuggle him. The old man has made his bed and he must lie in it."

XII

When the conference ended, on the second Sunday, F. D. R. said to his agent, "Tell me what plans you have."

Lanny replied, "Unless you have something special in mind, I had better go back to Paris. Our Army is on the move again, and I promised the Monuments and the Alsos people that I'd be there to give them what help I could."

The Boss said, "OK"; and then, perhaps feeling guilty because he hadn't had more time for a friend, he added, "Would you like to ride out with me?" The friend grinned and said, "You must know the answer to that."

A long cortege set out from Livadia along the coast to Sevastopol. The Stalin party led the way; he had a whole division of MVD men guarding the route, all the way to the railhead. Roosevelt followed, in Al Capone's armored car; his daughter and Mike Reilly rode with him, and Lanny rode in one of the later cars. In Sevastopol they saw a sight never to be forgotten—what the Germans could do to a city when they had advance notice and plenty of explosives at hand. The motor cavalcade entered the city just at twilight, when it all looked mysterious and awful; miles and miles of rubble, and here and there steel girders sticking up, or a wall standing alone, like a billboard. Lanny was told that only six buildings had been left intact.

The harbor had been cleared of mines, and the naval auxiliary *Catoctin* was waiting for them. The party spent the night on board, and in the morning Lanny had the pleasure of making a flight in that wonderful new plane, "The Sacred Cow." A thousand miles to the Deservoir Field, which lies by the Great Bitter Lake, a part of the Suez Canal. Fighter planes accompanied them—the Armed Forces were taking first-rate care of their "Cominch." The *Quincy* was waiting there, and that was like getting home. Lanny was interested to see what the war had done to a cruiser; it was hard to walk on the decks for the ack-ack guns that had been stuck here and there.

F. D. R. was a tired man, and looked thinner than ever; but there were visitors he felt he had to see. First came the King of Egypt, a young snip whose principal joys in life were eating and racing about in American motorcars. He stayed for three hours, including a hearty lunch. Roosevelt told him to raise more long-staple cotton, much needed in America, and presented him with a two-motored transport plane. Egyptian neutrality had been valuable in the days when Rommel's hard-bitten troops had been standing at El Alamein, less than eighty miles from Alexandria. It wasn't so important now that Rommel was dead—killed in an automobile accident, so the papers had it, but later it was learned that he had been ordered to take poison, having been involved in the attempt on the Führer's life.

Later in the afternoon came another dark-skinned potentate, who stayed for tea. The thin and frail old Emperor of Ethiopia presented a contrast to fat young King Farouk. Haile Selassie, Conquering Lion of Judah, claimed to be a direct descendant of King Solomon and the Queen of Sheba, and maybe was. Mussolini had killed his people with poison-gas bombs and driven the Emperor into exile; now he was back, and eager for close relations with the powerful President of the great republic overseas. He had gold in his country and presented the President with a gold cigarette case and a gold globe. In return he received something much more useful—four American automobiles.

XIII

Next day came the really big show, one of the oddest that Lanny had ever witnessed in his much-traveled life. An American destroyer, the *Murphy*, had made a journey of some eight hundred miles to the port of Jidda, where it had picked up a third Oriental potentate, whose difficult name in Arabic was 'Abd-al-'Azīz ibn-'Abd-al-Rahmān al-Faisal ibn-Su'ūd, King of Saudi Arabia. He was a very important potentate indeed, for he owned what was perhaps the greatest oil pool in the world, and was being paid some fifteen million dollars a year in royalties—no pun intended. His oil was the lifeblood of the American defense forces in the Mediterranean area, ships, planes and tanks, and so Ibn Saud could have anything he wanted to make him happy.

What he had wanted was to bring along his two sons, his brother, his Minister of Finance, his Deputy Minister of Foreign Affairs, his Minister Plenipotentiary to Great Britain, his Privy Counselor, his Physician, his Astrologer, his Imam, or Chaplain, his Commander of the Guards, his Adjutant of the Guards, his Assistant Minister of Finance, and so on, for a list of forty-seven persons, not forgetting the Official Food Taster and Caterer, the Royal Purse Bearer, and the Chief Server of Ceremonial Coffee. He wanted this company to live in the style to which they were accustomed, and this meant turning the deck of the *Murphy* into a desert-Arab encampment. Nobody would go below, for they were an open-air people.

The first thing was to cover the fo'c'sle of the destroyer with brightly colored awnings and to spread many thousands of dollars' worth of fine rugs on the deck. The nights being chilly, there were many charcoal braziers, very picturesque. Then there must be food for the party, so they brought a flock of sheep which were pastured on the fantail of the vessel, and Negro slaves wearing large silver earrings cut the throat of one of them every now and then. Most people had the impression that slavery had been abolished throughout the world some time ago, but when a king is also an oil magnate he can carry on a semi-secret slave trade across the Gulf of Aden, and his slaves are not automatically set free when they board an American war vessel. Or maybe they were free but nobody mentioned it to them!

Now came the *Murphy*, to take its place alongside the *Quincy*. F.D.R. was sitting on deck, and Lanny came to him and whispered that he really must not miss the sight. This great man was eager for fun; he wheeled his chair to a position behind a stanchion, so that he could hide and watch the show. He shook all over with laughter, and had to put his hand over his mouth to keep from being heard during the transfer to the cruiser. Having been fed on fat sheep, His Majesty was an enormous man. He was in his seventies, badly crippled, and walked with difficulty; also, he was half blind, because of cataracts. He looked like something on the Metropolitan Opera House stage, in flowing black robes and a red turban with gold head ropes and a sort of tailpiece hanging behind.

His guards accompanied him, and they wouldn't move unless and until the Secret Service men also moved; they all went away together, leaving the two rulers with only an interpreter. Afterward F.D.R. told Lanny that this old Arabian was the toughest proposition he had ever tackled; he hated the Jews and was not the slightest bit moved by the President's appeal for those hundreds of thousands who had fled from the Nazis and wanted to get into Palestine. But host and guest preserved the amenities; Ibn Saud presented the President with four Arabian costumes, and one each for his wife and daughter. Roosevelt presented the King with a two-motored transport plane and, more important yet, with the wheel chair for which His Majesty had expressed admiration. Fortunately there was an extra on board the cruiser.

XIV

Dispatch planes brought mail and newspapers, and the tired man worked on these while the vessel sailed through the Suez Canal and the Mediterranean to Alexandria. He had a long sea voyage before him, but this he loved, and he was hoping to catch up with his manifold duties. The stack of documents which had been piled up in his cabin made Lanny's heart ache; a President of the United States just couldn't go away from home for a month without being swamped under the accumulated load. Nobody else could sign documents for him, and if he made a single mistake there were thousands of Republican eyes watching, eager to exploit the opportunity.

This was the longest period that Lanny had ever spent with his Boss, and he did what he could to make himself agreeable. He couldn't help with the documents and correspondence, but at mealtimes and rest periods he tried to divert Roosevelt's mind with cheerful topics. Every evening they had a movie, the latest products, gladly loaned by the studios. "When Irish Eyes Are Smiling" was a long way from the war, both geographically and spiritually; it put no strain on anybody's mentality and gave great pleasure to Michael F. Reilly.

But nothing could keep the President's mind off Europe for very long, and he picked Lanny's mind for details and for guesses as to what might lie before the world. Would Hitler give up when the Rhine had been crossed, or would the Allies have to fight all the way to Berlin? And what would the Führer do personally: would he be taken alive, or would somebody kill him, or would he kill himself? Would there be any way to reach Göring and persuade him to turn against the gang? And what was the answer to the difficult question of immunity to be promised to any of these gangsters?

Lanny said he had never dared to put the idea of defeat before any of them. Hitler had become persuaded that if he were captured the Allies would lock him in a cage and put him on public exhibition. His plan was to retire to the Alpine Redoubt in the Bavarian Alps and make a last stand; undoubtedly the Nazis were building fortifications there and piling up supplies, but there were no factories in the region, and it wouldn't take an army very long to use up what they had been able to store. When Roosevelt asked about the so-called "werewolves," the threat of underground terrorism after the war, the P.A. said that the bulk of the Germans were law-abiding people, and if they got any sort of decent treatment they would surely not support criminals.

Said the President, "We will give them enough fighting to satisfy them; we'll take no chances on their being able to say that it was a stab in the back that defeated them. All the stabs will come from the front."

"From the two fronts," said Lanny with a smile. By this time the Russians had overrun the whole of Silesia, a district second only to the Ruhr as a source of war materials—a hundred million tons of coal and eight million tons of steel every year, and many tank and munitions factories which the Allies had not been able to reach with their bombers. From such losses there could be no hope of recovery.

XV

The *Quincy* was due to stop at Algiers, and it had been arranged that Lanny was to take his departure there. General de Gaulle, now head of the French government, had been invited to consult with the President; but instead the American Ambassador came on board and reported that *le grand Charlie* had made lame excuses. The truth was his *dignité* did not permit him to travel to see anybody. He hated Roosevelt almost as much as any Wall Street tycoon hated him—Robbie Budd, for example.

This incident caused Mike Reilly to entrust Robbie's son with an account of what had happened when these two strong-willed men had had their first meeting, during the Casablanca Conference. They had talked in French, and Mike didn't know French, but he knew an enraged man when he saw one, and as he watched the Frenchman's long nose coming nearer and nearer to the American's projecting chin, he had considered it his duty to draw his pistol and hold it in his hand for the half-hour the interview lasted. The Secret Service chief was half hidden behind some drapes, and neither of the two men knew what he was doing. It was the first and only time that Mike had had occasion to do this in the four years that he had been guarding the President.

Lanny thought it was just as well that F.D.R. didn't have to undergo the ordeal of another interview with that hysterical Frenchman, who called himself a successor to Joan of Arc and whose mind had come straight out of that period of history. When the time came for the P.A. to leave the deck of the cruiser he exchanged a strong handclasp with his friend and said, "You have done a grand job, Governor. Take a rest now and delegate the hard work."

F.D.R. did not say "To whom?" He was too tired for joking. He just smiled wanly and said, "I'll try."

BOOK THREE

Come the Three Corners of the World in Arms

8

O Peuple Deux Fois Né!

I

IN PARIS the presidential agent found a letter from Laurel, saying that she was still waiting for the Army to get far enough into Germany to make it worth while for her to come. When he went to talk with the Monuments and the Alsos people he found the same thing: they were making elaborate preparations, but they hadn't yet moved.

Monuments told him about those art treasures that had been left behind in the Bulge. As soon as the Third Army had driven the enemy out a couple of the experts had returned to the hunting lodge and found it burned to the ground—not a stick left standing. There was no way to know whether the Germans had done this on purpose or whether it was the result of shellfire. The wooden and stone saints were still in the hidden shed, but of paintings and other treasures there was no trace. Some of the parcels had been bound with wire and some of the boxes had had metal fastenings; a careful search for these was made in the snow-covered ashes, but without result. The presumption was that the Germans had carted the treasures away as soon as they had begun to have any doubt of being able to hold the district.

Lanny went to talk with the scientists. They were busy, for new information was continually coming in and new teams were being organized for research. A strange sort of job these learned professors had, part scientific, part military, and part detectical, if one may coin an adjective for which the language has no equivalent. They were making material for a whole sequence of movie melodramas, mystery stories, whodunits; the sort of thing that Woodrow Wilson had used, and that F. D. R. still used, to put himself to sleep at night. But it surely didn't put any of the Alsos physicists, biochemists, biologists, astronomers, engineers, and what-nots of the Alsos mission to sleep at any time, day or night. They got along fairly well so long as they were out in the field where nobody could get hold of them; they were less happy in Paris, where they might receive alarming pink radiograms from Washington, marked TOP SECRET, and worse yet, stamped ACTION COPY, which meant that there was a time limit on it, perhaps as little as twenty-four hours. And what if the action was wrong?

General Groves in Washington—known as "GG"—was a military man, and his staff was composed of military men, corporation executives, lawyers, and such, and they found it hard to understand nuclear physicists and their ways of working. How could physicists know so much which they couldn't explain to military men, corporation executives, and lawyers? How could they say, in advance, that this German physicist was important, while that German physicist couldn't possibly be of any use whatever? How could they say that if the Germans actually had an atom-bomb project, Werner Heisenberg and none other must be the head of it? Soldiers, corporation executives, and lawyers were shifted around and told to do what they were told; might not the Nazis have done the same thing with their A-bomb people? "Yes," replied Professor Goudsmit, "but in that case their A-bomb plant won't be worth bothering about. It is Heisenberg or nobody."

II

The Germans, overlooking nothing, had had their own Scientific Intelligence group in Paris, using as camouflage a firm and business called "Cellastic." Oddly enough, they were in the Rue Quentin Beauchart, right next door to the supposedly secret American OSS. They had cleaned their place out but hadn't been able to conceal the fact that they had had soundproof rooms and interphones of a special type which could not be tapped. Also, they had left a lot of litter around, including a floor plan with the names and technical interests of the various occupants. A doorman's list gave the names and addresses of callers, and a switchboard record gave a list of call numbers. All that was straight out of the latest detective-story magazine, and so was the use of this information in the tracing down of traitor scientists in Holland.

Or take the story of Professor Joliot-Curie, son-in-law of the Curies who discovered radium. He was a leading nuclear physicist, and the Germans confiscated his Paris laboratory. The rumor spread that he was collaborating with the Nazis, and he let it stand that way, for he was secretly helping the Resistance. The Germans sent a competent physicist, Dr. Gentner, to take charge of the laboratory, and Gentner was an anti-Nazi at heart, a man who had worked in California with the inventor of the cyclotron. Gentner knew about Joliot's political activities and protected him from the Gestapo. Later the Alsos people uncovered a Gestapo report on the German physicist, who had fallen under suspicion because his wife was a Swiss. Gentner was recalled to Germany, and managed to get word to Joliot in Paris, warning him that the man who took Gentner's place in Paris was a genuine Nazi and to be on guard against him.

Movie plots all ready but the shooting script! In a French internment camp for German civilians the Alsos came upon a German chemist who had saved all his notebooks, which were full of valuable information. A Jew who had fled to Switzerland, the Nazis had lured him back by promises of special treatment, which promises they did not keep. He had ducked out of Berlin and got to Paris after a series of adventures which warmed Lanny's heart—they were so much like Lanny's own.

Also there was the great mystery of the Auer-Gesellschaft, a great German chemical concern; it appeared to be an A-bomb matter. There was a French company called Terres-Rares, which dealt in rare chemicals and owned a monopoly on the world's supply of thorium; Auer had taken this company over and hurriedly removed all its thorium to Germany. This element could be used in a late stage of A-bomb manufacture, so Washington went crazy with fear and kept hounding Alsos to trace the matter down among the French employees of Auer and find out what the Germans had meant to do with the thorium.

So began an elaborate research, a study of catalogues and scraps of letters, also a telephone list obtained from the French government; it was learned that two former employees were now in the Belgian town of Eupen, just north of the Bulge. Alsos went there, brought the two culprits to Paris, and put them through a grilling. Alsos couldn't give any hint of what they were looking for, and the employees couldn't imagine what all the excitement was about. It turned out that the Auer people had been collecting thorium in order to prepare for the end of the war, when they would no longer be making gas masks and other military products; they had a patent on a toothpaste containing thorium oxide, supposed to make the teeth shine, and they were planning to go in for American-type advertising. Like Bob Hope, promoting Irium toothpaste!

III

One important group of Alsos was on the trail of the V-1s and V-2s, the robot and rocket bombs which were still wreaking damage in London, and the dread V-3s which might be starting up any day. The launching sites of rockets were mostly in Holland, the British and Canadian zone of fighting, but the factories and laboratories might be anywhere, and these were the most eagerly sought targets of the whole Army. The son of Budd-Erling looked back upon the days when he had been helping in this field and laid stress upon the idea that German labor, especially the Social Democrats, would have knowledge of locations and processes and techniques. Nothing could be hidden from the men who had to do the work, and thousands must by now be cured of any Nazi infection they might have acquired during the past dozen years. One such worker might be able to pass the investigator on to a score of others.

The scientists who specialized in jet propulsion plied Lanny with questions. Among other things, he told them about his old friend Bernhardt Monck, who had begun life as a sailor and Social-Democratic leader, had risen to be a *capitán* in the Spanish Republican Army, and now was an OSS man operating under an alias in one of the neutral lands. Lanny wasn't at liberty to say what alias or what land, but he suggested that Alsos should apply to OSS for Monck to be brought to Paris, and Lanny would add his recommendation in the matter.

General Donovan's organization in the old brick building in Washington was one branch of the bureaucracy that had very little red tape. "Oh So Secret" and "Oh So Social," the wits called it, and said that it was made up entirely of "sportsmen, sporting men, and sports"; but at least they were men who were used to having their way and getting things done. So it came about that three days later an unresting secret enemy of Nazi-Fascism telephoned Lanny at his hotel, using the name of "Trudi's friend," which nobody in the world but Lanny would understand. He had been flown from Stockholm to London by a secret route and from there to Paris. Over the telephone he said, "The Geneva place, twenty hours."

That too was code, because in the past they had been wont to meet in the public library in the Swiss city. At eight that evening Lanny strolled into the reading-room of the great Bibliothèque Nationale, and there was the sturdy German, with bullet head and gray hair close-cut, busily making notes from a book of French history. Their eyes met, Lanny strolled out again, and the other followed; they went into an ill-lighted street, and since it was too cold for sitting down they walked. Such precautions had become second nature to them both, and they did not relax because the enemy had been driven out of Paris. The enemy was expecting to come back and seldom failed to plant his espionage system in any important place he abandoned.

This pair would have stories to tell each other when the war was over; but meantime they talked only about necessary things. Lanny told how he had had to get out of Germany, because he had reason to believe that Himmler was onto his game. He had been helped by the old Social-Democratic watch repairer, Johann Seidl, whose name and address had been furnished by Monck. It was important for Monck to know that this man was still alive and true to the cause, although he had been posing as a Nazi. Lanny had been hidden in the cellar of a woman named Anna who ran some sort of leather-working shop. Monck said, "Anna Pfister; another old-timer."

Monck was ready and glad to meet the Alsos people. He thought it would be all right for him to come to Lanny's hotel room, provided that he didn't have to go to the desk; Lanny gave him the room number, and next morning he met an Alsos man there, also an OSS man and an officer from Army Intelligence, G-2. Monck's memory ranged over all the years of anti-Nazi struggle; he had never written anything down, but had learned it by heart, and now he gave the names and last known addresses of some twoscore men and women who could be depended upon to get and to give information—if they were still alive. One of them was found in the Rhineland within a few days and gave information concerning a huge rocket-assembly plant, eight hundred feet deep in the heart of the Kohnstein Mountains, near Nordhausen, where the Germans were making a V-2 that could fly three thousand miles and hit with pinpoint accuracy.

Lanny was proud of his friend Monck, proud to see him "delivering the goods." For more than ten years the pair had been working hand in glove against the Nazi-Fascists, and whenever Lanny had had an impulse to get tired and take it easy, he had thought of Bernhardt Monck, alias Capitán Herzog, alias Braun, alias Anton Vetterl. Lanny would be ashamed, because he hadn't had so many aliases or so many perilous escapes in the imminent deadly breach.

Monck's wife had fled to the Argentine with their children and now wished to come back. Monck had entrusted a considerable sum of money to Lanny for safekeeping, and Lanny had left it with Robbie. Now he undertook to have two thousand dollars forwarded to the wife; the man didn't want any for himself, the OSS was taking care of him, he said. They exchanged a warm handclasp at parting, and Monck said, "See you in Berlin, at the home of Johann Seidl."

"Or at Göring's Residenz," replied Lanny with a chuckle.

IV

The armies on the western front had begun their offensive while Lanny was on the way to Yalta. Hitler had elected to fight west of the Rhine, which meant that his troops no longer had much ground to give; they had to stand where they were and win or die. There were snow and ice, and then would come a period of rain and mud, then overnight another freeze; both sides had to learn to live without shelter and to take weather as it came.

It was a land of large rivers and small streams, now full flooded in early spring; each was a barrier, defended to the last. Artillery pounded the enemy lines, and heavy trucks brought up boats of all sizes and materials, rubber, canvas, wood, sheet metal. A crossing would be forced, by night or day; a bridgehead would be established and a bridge built of pontoons. The tanks would come clanking across, and troops marching in double lines behind them. They would go up into the high ground, the vineyards, the orchards, the forests, shooting as they went, the men taking shelter behind trees and rocks, throwing grenades with the skill they had acquired in happier days with base-balls. If the enemy had a pillbox, the "walkie-talkie" men would call the tanks. If weather permitted, planes would be overhead, spying out the enemy and sending word by radio to batteries of mortars; they were all using the pozit ammunition now, and the shells would burst over the entrenched Heinies, and those who were left alive jumped up and scattered quickly.

Behind the lines was that marvelous SOS, the Services of Supply. There was a system called the Red Ball Express, coming by one set of highways and returning by another; an unbroken line of trucks, properly spaced, speeding at forty miles an hour. All the drivers had to do was follow the Red Ball markers; two men on each truck, and they never stopped driving, day or night. They rested while the truck was being unloaded and serviced, and then back they came to Antwerp, Cherbourg, Marseille, or other ports which had been taken and re-stored. The great ships came with their loads, and there were cranes and other great machines, and longshoremen by the thousands to put the stuff onto the trucks.

Also there were the C-47s, known as "flying boxcars," big freight-carrying planes that swarmed everywhere, landing on what seemed no more than a cow pasture, and bringing gasoline, ammunition, and food to the men right up at the front. This was American industry, put into uniform and transported across three or four thousand miles of water. The Germans had been sure it couldn't be done, at least not in time; but here it was being done, and the result was a striking force—something superhuman, unimaginable, that blinded the enemy, dazed him, and either destroyed him or routed him.

Hurry, hurry, hurry!—that was the motto everywhere. Time was of the essence. Once pried loose, the enemy must have no time to rally, to reorganize; wherever he went, the pursuit must be at his heels, keeping him on the move. It cost an enormous amount of matériel and many American lives, but in the long run it would pay off. The more Germans you killed or captured on one side of the river, the fewer you would find when you got across. So it was, all along the Meuse and the Roer and the Neuss, the Prüm, the Sauer, the Saar, and the Moselle; all through February and early March, unceasing attack and dogged defense. Retreat was forbidden to the Germans, and there were SS men behind the lines with machine guns to turn on stragglers.

V

Lanny waited in Paris, a pleasant place even in the midst of war if you knew where to go and what to look for. Physically the city had not sustained much damage; it was no longer *la ville lumière*, being blacked out by scarcity of fuel as well as by war regulations; but by daylight it had its beautiful vistas, its splendid buildings, its river, and its parks. Comforts were scarce, but the Americans were bringing in food, and nobody was starving. Most important of all, the people had hope; the war would be over, and the great President Roosevelt was promising that never again would the Germans have the chance to start another.

Lanny had been neglecting his private business for long periods, and he had been told by his Boss that he was free to carry it on when he could. There were many people of property who now were short of cash and who had thought of old masters as a form of investment, as safe as diamonds and jewelry. They were pleased to meet a former acquaintance who was known to have access to money. He would inspect their treasures and politely ask if they would care to put a price on this or that; he would write by airmail to some of his clients at home, telling what he had found, and if a deal was made he would pay a deposit out of funds he had had in Cannes and Paris banks before the war; the rest would be paid as soon as freedom of trade had been restored. The franc was steadily going down, and as the franc went down the dollar went up.

French painters, who for the most part had small chance of ever becoming rich, had gone on painting through the war; it was an occupation that didn't cost much, and it kept a man off the streets, where the enemy might pick him up and ship him off to work in the coal mines. According to French custom, the products of art labor could be seen in humble tobacco shops, cafés, and other places in Montmartre and Montparnasse, as well as at the elegant dealers in the neighborhood of the Place Vendôme. A fastidious American Army officer would stop and inspect them—provided that the painter had chosen to represent something that the Army officer could recognize. If he found something that he thought was good he might buy it, and get the address of the painter and seek him out in his attic atelier. Quite apart from questions of money, Lanny would be welcomed as a colleague, because he was the stepson of Marcel Detaze and son of a onetime painter's model who had lived in this very Quartier Latin almost half a century ago. *Eheu fugaces anni!*—or, as we say nowadays, How time does fly!

VI

Lanny had written to his friend Rick in England, telling him the news about Yalta, no longer a secret. Rick's father had died, and he was now Sir Eric Vivian Pomeroy-Nielson, but he wasn't using the title; he was going to stand for Parliament as a labor candidate in the elections which were to be held after the war had come to its now certain end. Rick told the news about his family, and among other things mentioned that his elder son, Alfy, was an RAF captain stationed at Amiens. Having long since made his allotted number of flights, he was grounded, and if he had a leave coming he would visit Paris.

That was good news, and when Alfy showed up it was an occasion to be celebrated. Lanny had known this dutiful and generous-minded Englishman for all twenty-eight of his years and loved him like a son. When only nineteen Alfy had flown in combat for the Spanish Republican government, and Lanny had helped him get out of a Franco dungeon. From then on the young officer watched for a chance to do anything to express his gratitude, without violating that reticence which was a part of his nature and training.

They went about Paris together, and looked at paintings and listened to beautiful music—something that had been kept safe from all the devastations of war. Many English men and women were here, and Alfy had friends among them, and they all had interesting news to relate, and personal adventures if you could manage tactfully to extract them. Normally, a war wound or a parachute descent into the Channel would be worth only a sentence or two. There was a girl friend who was feeding American food to French children, out in one of the factory districts that ring the show parts of Paris; the two men went by the *métro*, and it was a sight not soon to be forgotten: a hundred or two of eager French youngsters, their faces smeared with good food and beaming with delight.

There was an English officers' club, a place to tell your own children about. It had belonged to Baron Maurice Rothschild, and after he had fled Göring had taken it and shipped all the paintings to Germany. Later he had given it to his Luftwaffe as an officers' club, and now the British had taken over where the Luftwaffe had left off—in a hurry. The place had forty-three rooms, all on a magnificent scale, the kind of rooms that made one think of public buildings. It had a two-acre back yard and an air-raid shelter built by Göring, camouflaged as a garden walk. The Baroness's bathroom was as big as an ordinary house, all of green marble—even a door of marble. The tub with its gold faucets could have served as a swimming pool, and as you swam you could look up at a ceiling of engraved crystal. On the other side of the house was the Baron's bath, and that was the same except that its marble was white. There was a theater, and a cardroom papered with the skins of oriental tropical snakes.

The two friends had lunch in the dining-room of white and gold crystal. At one end of the room, on a pedestal of black marble, stood a life-size figure of a man, exactly the way nature makes man, and clad in the costume which nature provides. This, Alfy reported, sometimes caused embarrassment to English young ladies, so their escorts took the trouble to seat them with their backs to this elegant *objet d'art*. The lunch which Lanny ate was well cooked but small in size, so it didn't take long. They adjourned to a terrace in the rear, where they could enjoy early spring sunshine and look upon the British Embassy on their right and the French Presidential Palace on their left. They were in the very midst of the *grand monde de Paris*.

VII

Le Capitaine Denis de Bruyne had been wounded again, this time in the fighting at the Belfort Gap, close to the Swiss border, where the French Army was maintaining pressure upon its ancient enemy. France, disgraced by the treachery of her leaders, betrayed into cowardly surrender, was now redeeming her honor; so Denis felt, and the scar of a bullet which had barely missed his lung was to him like a medal, a testimonial to the world that Frenchmen were still worthy of their heritage. He was recuperating at his home, with a devoted wife attending him, and it was Lanny's obvious duty to go out there.

The head of this wealthy and aristocratic family, now in his eighties, had sustained a stroke, losing the use of his right leg. He was taken about in a wheel chair, but his mind was still alert, and he looked out for his business interests by telephone, and by a secretary who came every day from Paris. France was coming back, and with one leg in the grave this aged capitalist was behaving as if he had arranged to take all his stocks and bonds into the next world. He had invested heavily in Budd-Erling Aircraft and had a large amount of dollars in the First National Bank of Newcastle, Connecticut. He wanted Robbie's help in cutting red tape and getting some of this money to France; he wanted Lanny's help in urging Robbie to manage this.

Lanny had never had any admiration for this aged man who was lecherous as well as greedy, but he had pretended friendship because a representative of the "two hundred families" was a source of information valuable to a presidential agent. Lanny played the role of a loyal son of his father, a member of his father's class, and both the elder and the younger Denis talked to him freely about the political and business affairs of their country. They were deeply indebted to him, because he had persuaded the father to come over to the American side in the very nick of time to save him from the fate of a *collaborateur*. This shift had cost the life of the younger son, Charlot, who had been shot as a traitor by the Vichy gangsters. Lanny listened to the *père de famille* chuckling over his success in outwitting his enemies; it would seem that the old man felt more joy over having saved his property than grief at the loss of his son. Possibly, however, that wasn't a fair judgment, for he no longer had the son but did have the property.

There were two daughters-in-law, one of them a widow, and five children, living in this lovely old red-brick house called a "château," though it was hardly big enough to deserve the title. There was a considerable estate, and they could live comfortably, not too much troubled by war shortages. What the war meant to them was that the Germans had been driven out of France, and so people of property could resume their pleasant lives where they had left off five and a half years ago.

Two things were of paramount importance to them: first that the Americans should guarantee them against another German invasion, which would be the fourth in less than a century; second that there should be a dependable authority in France, Catholic and conservative, to hold down the labor unions. To all members of the *deux cents familles* that spelled the name de Gaulle; but their idol had been collaborating with the Reds, and that worried them. Of course it must be a wartime maneuver, compelled by the pressing need of resisting the German occupation; surely now the great General would be quick to break with his dangerous allies. Neither the stricken father nor the wounded son had been able to visit *le grand Charlie* and make sure, so they were reduced to asking their American friend what he thought. Lanny was able to comfort them with the assurance that the head of their Provisional government would never forget the fundamentals of his St. Cyr training.

Returning to Paris, Lanny found a long letter from his friend Raoul Palma, who had stood as a Socialist in the municipal elections in Toulon and had been victorious. Raoul took it as one of his duties to report to Lanny, in order that Lanny might report to his friends abroad, and especially to the great President Roosevelt. The news, alas, was bad; already, before the war was over, the Communists were beginning to break the people's truce; they were demanding all power for themselves and pushing the Socialists out of the way. Nobody could trust them, they admitted no loyalty save to their party. They had tried to seize power in Marseille when the Germans fled, and they were organizing now for a coup in Toulon the moment Germany surrendered. "We Socialists are caught between two millstones, Lanny"; and then the inevitable question, "What will President Roosevelt do about it?" President Roosevelt was going to solve all the problems for all the people of the world.

The son of Budd-Erling gazed at the future of France as if in a crystal ball, and what he saw saddened him greatly. *La patrie* was going back into the past, into that social strife which had paralyzed her and put her at the mercy, or rather the lack of mercy, of her hereditary foreign foe. There would be the extremists of the Right and those of the Left, at deadly social and political war; and there would be a middle party, pleading in vain for compromise, for understanding, for orderly social progress. The de Bruynes of France wouldn't pay income taxes; the farmers of France insisted upon hoarding their produce for higher prices; the politicians of France, elected under fraudulent labels, would choose the easy way of inflationary spending. And woe to the man who took his political stand in the middle, out in no man's land between the fighting fronts of Right and Left!

9

Joyful News at Hand

I

ORDERS for Mr. Lanning Prescott Budd, and not from Monuments or Alsos, but from G-2 of SHAEF, most imposing; he was to report "for special interrogation purposes" to Colonel Koch of G-2 of Third Army, in the city of Luxembourg. Mr. Budd needed no powers of divination to guess what that meant; Patton's forces had captured some German of importance, whom they hoped by tactful persuasion to convert into a source of information. It was to Colonel Koch that Lanny had been sent a few months previously to meet his old friend General Emil Meissner, and Lanny's magic had worked dependably. He wondered who it would be this time and tried to think of some German who was likely to be at the western front and to have mentioned the Führer's onetime American friend.

A flight to headquarters of Third was a matter of no more than an hour. The weather in early March was bad, and the passenger was tossed about and instructed to put on his parachute. He was shaky in the knees when the plane landed; but one didn't say anything about that in the Army. He was set down in a valley close to a very old city, on cliffs along a river lined with breweries and distilleries. He was driven through a viaduct to the headquarters from which Patton's war was directed, a former home for the aged; quite an elegant place, but now damaged by shells. There he met the scholarly Intelligence officer who had so well justified his right to the title.

The weather being what it was, there was no need to ask the visitor if he had had a pleasant trip. The colonel seated him in a comfortable chair, offered Lanny a drink to steady his nerves, and then asked, "Mr. Budd, do you know a German officer, General-Major Furt-wängler?"

"Very well indeed." Lanny had guessed that name among the first. "I have known him since thirty-three, when the Nazis took power. He had just been made an *Oberleutnant* on Göring's personal staff."

"He was shifted recently to the line and commanded the 117th Division, 53rd Corps. He got separated from his main body escaping from Trier, and he and a couple of his officers were looking for their headquarters. They came upon a group of our tanks and mistook them for Panzers; by the time they realized the mistake we had them covered."

Lanny said, "Furtwängler is an amiable fellow, but not especially bright. He was humbly devoted to Göring, and I think was a loyal Nazi. Of course I don't know what the recent defeats may have done to his mind."

"He seems very melancholy. He tells us he has a family in Germany. He is greatly worried about their safety—asked us to give it out that he had been taken in combat, as otherwise the Nazis might punish them. We obliged him, since we had hope that he might be able to give us information."

"On Göring's staff he had opportunity to get a great deal. In the line, of course, he would be apt to know only local conditions."

"He seems to like talking," said the G-2 officer; "but so far he hasn't told anything of importance. He mentioned that he knew you very well."

Lanny explained, "My father had business dealings with Göring from almost the beginning of the regime. He took me along, and Furtwängler was the staff officer who had us in charge. We did our best to make ourselves agreeable, and he the same. Then a young Jewish friend of mine in Berlin got into trouble with the Nazis, and I went to Göring to try to intercede. The General, as he was then, seemed to find me amusing; of course I never could tell how much of that was policy, but he invited me to come back and I did. In 1937 President Roosevelt learned that I knew Göring and he commissioned me to go and try to get information. I was authorized to give Göring some in return, provided it wasn't too important. *Der Dicke* has his attractive qualities, and I made much of appreciating them. I always met Furtwängler on these trips, and I am sure he genuinely liked me. For a time I had a rich wife, and I persuaded her to invite Furt-wängler and his wife to dine with us at the Adlon. That ravished their souls; they thought they were moving in *die grosse Welt*."

"All that sounds promising," said the colonel, smiling. "We'd be glad to have you talk to him as long as it seems worth while. Bear in mind the Army's policy: we do not promise immunity, but you can promise him special treatment—we are keeping a group of ranking officers separate. It wouldn't do to expose those who give us information to the anger and possible abuse of the others."

II

The son of Budd-Erling was esconced in what had been the very small bedroom of a superannuated Luxembourger. It was provided with two armchairs and a table with a bottle of "liberated" schnapps and a package of American cigarettes, better than money in any part of wartorn Europe. The captured General-Major was brought in, spruce and elegant—his uniform had been cleaned and pressed for him, as part of the process of winning him over. He had lost a little of that *embonpoint* which he had been accumulating in years of good living at the Berlin Residenz and at Karinhall, but still he was rotund and hearty. He had been told Lanny was coming and had got over his melancholy, at least for the moment.

Lanny rose. It was forbidden to shake hands with captured enemy officers—that was "fraternizing"; but the rule didn't apply to interro-gation men, who were free to use whatever technique they thought might work. Lanny behaved as if nothing had happened, as if the war was all a bad dream. "*Ja, Günther, bist Du's wirklich? Wie freue ich mich Dich wiederzusehen!*" They spoke German, as always, and were *alter Freund* and *lieber Lanny*.

Furtwängler had been told that Lanny was not a regular military officer but only an art expert in uniform; so Lanny didn't have to explain that he hadn't harmed any dear Germans but was doing what he had always done, trying to save beautiful works of art and put them in places where people might have a chance to enjoy them. He asked after Furtwängler's family and told about his father's health, and that of Irma Barnes and their little daughter. He asked after the Reichs-marschall and other friends on the staff and at Karinhall.

Said the art expert, "I don't know what you have been told about the terrible thing that happened to me in Germany. Tell me what you heard."

"I was informed that you were supposed to be an American spy."

"And did you believe that?"

"I didn't know what to believe, Lanny. How could I?"

So Lanny began the spiel that he had studied carefully and tried out successfully on Heinrich Jung. The most dreaded chief of the Gestapo and of the SS, Reichsminister Heinrich Himmler, had come to Lanny in the New Chancellery Building and begun an elaborate siege of his mind, trying to find out what would be Lanny's attitude, and the attitude of the American government, to Himmler's assumption of power in the event of the Führer's death. Himmler had said that the Führer's health was failing fast; but Lanny had doubted this and felt certain that Himmler knew of some plot against the Führer's life, or perhaps was instigating one himself.

"Anyhow, I knew that my life wasn't worth a pfennig in Germany after that. I had no way to get word to the Führer without Himmler's knowing it; and how could I expect the Führer to take the word of an enemy alien against that of his most trusted friend, the man who had charge of his protection. I had no means of guessing whether Himmler was trying to test my loyalty to the Führer, or whether he was the man behind the plot which came to a head last July in the bomb attempt on the Führer's life. I didn't know then and I don't know now. I asked the help of friends in getting out of Germany, and I got out, and of course I can never go back."

What means had a general officer of humble origin, neither a prominent party member nor a favorite of the Junker elite, of judging the truth of such a tale? He could have no means, and that was why Lanny told it. The General-Major was like a man who, walking, suddenly sees an abyss opening before his feet. He said, "I know these dreadful intrigues—*diese fürchterlichen Verschwörungen.* After all that the Führer has done for these men, the heights to which he has lifted them! He was all right so long as he was sweeping them to victory; but now that he encounters troubles—" The speaker stopped, because he didn't want to say too much.

"It has been a bitter experience to me," declared the American. "I took risks for the Führer. I jeopardized my own position. I want you to know that in my heart I have not changed; but my father was greatly distressed and insisted that I had no right to risk the ruin of my whole family. So I gave up; I am not going to fight National Socialism, but have gone back to what I was long ago, an art expert and lover of beautiful things. Some of these, I hope, can be saved out of the wreckage of our time."

"I can't say I blame you," replied the German. Had he accepted Lanny's tale, or had he decided to pretend that he did? In this game of cross and double-cross you could never be sure. Anyhow, they would start from there.

III

It was Lanny's tactic to throw this captive officer into a still deeper state of melancholy. He told how, since joining the American Army half a year ago, he had been able to see from the inside the plans for the annihilation of Germany and had become convinced that the Fatherland had no choice but surrender. Lanny, who had loved the German people since childhood, thought only of saving German lives, and the old German towns and splendid modern cities. Furtwängler must know that these last were being reduced to rubble by thousand-plane bombing raids, something the Germans had declared to be impossible, even after the first one had visited Cologne.

Now Lanny was in a position to know that the bombing was no haphazard affair, but was planned scientifically, on the basis of exact knowledge. He quoted from a list which Colonel Koch had shown him: Duisburg on the Rhine, the largest inland harbor in Europe, was in ruins; the marshaling yards at Hamm, which had handled ten thousand cars a day, were smashed beyond repair; the same with the three-miles-long Badische Analin works at Ludwigshafen, the optical works at Jena, the artificial rubber works at Huls, and all the airplane factories which Göring had boasted could never be destroyed because they were so scattered. They had all been located and were being steadily bombed—Siemens, Dornier, Heinkel, Argus, and Daimler-Benz in Berlin, Junkers at Leipzig, Messerschmitt at Nürnberg and Stuttgart, Heinkel at Warnemünde, Dornier at Friedrichshafen, Focke-Wulf at Hamburg.

Lanny argued, "All these plants could be turned to the production of peace goods; their destruction means that the German people are being condemned to destitution for a generation, perhaps for a century. And what is the sense of it? If the war is hopeless, in the name of common sense why not recognize the fact?"

"Germany is fighting for her existence, Lanny!" exclaimed the other. "We have been attacked—"

"*Stellen Sie sich nicht dumm, lieber Günther!* You know that Germany attacked Russia and thus made a two-front war for herself. And has somebody succeeded in keeping from you the fact that Germany declared war upon the United States?"

The General-Major passed this over, for it would have been embarrassing to admit that he had forgotten the fact. Instead he complained of "unconditional surrender" as a barbarous demand. Lanny assured him that it was an empty phrase; there were conditions imposed by American standards. "We do not kill the troops that surrender; we feed them, and if they are wounded they get medical care. It will be the same with the whole German people; there will not be a shot fired or a bomb dropped from the minute the surrender is signed. Do you realize that we have taken two million German prisoners since we landed in Normandy, and all those will some day be returned to the Fatherland?"

"I see that you have turned against the Führer!" lamented the SS-trained officer; to which Lanny repeated, "I have been forced to recognize the fact that the Führer's cause is lost, and the only question is, how many more German cities are going to be destroyed and how many more German people are going to be killed to no purpose."

IV

This argument went on the rest of the day. A Nazi-warped mind had to have a hundred delusions taken out of it; and once wasn't enough—they popped back in and had to be removed again. Like Heinrich Jung, Furtwängler had been certain that the Battle of the Bulge would mean the capture of Antwerp and the annihilation of the American First Army and the British and Canadian armies. Now Lanny had to pound into him the fact that this dream was dead. Trier, in front of which Furtwängler had been captured, lay east of the southern shoulder of that Bulge; so now there was an American Bulge instead of a German. Lanny had seen recco photographs of Trier and offered to bring them to his friend; there was nothing but a few smoke-blackened walls of this, the oldest city of Northern Europe, a city founded by the ancient Romans. It had had ninety thousand inhabitants, and now they were scattered all over the German countryside, sleeping in cellars, in chicken houses, in caves or holes in the snow-covered ground.

Now Patton's armies had turned to the east, headed for the Rhine. Coblenz was in front of them, and the airmen were reducing that to rubble. Coblenz, being on the west bank, would fall easy prey—

"But you will never be able to get across, Lanny!" exclaimed the Nazi and quoted "The Watch on the Rhine": *"Lieb' Vaterland, magst ruhig sein!"*

Lanny answered, "You were taught that as a child, *alter Freund*, but you must realize it is hopelessly out of date. The Third Army has crossed thirty-two rivers this year, and the Rhine is not so much bigger than the Moselle. We have a score of different devices, all of which have been well tested. We will have half a dozen bridgeheads on the right bank before this month of March is past."

"What do you want me to do, Lanny?" demanded the despairing General-Major. "Turn traitor to my country?"

"I don't want anything, Günther—I am just putting the facts before you and leaving it to your common sense. The quicker this fighting is over, the more Germans will be left and the more homes for them to sleep in and factories to work in. I should think that you would come to the same decision as General Meissner, for example—"

"Du lieber Gott!" exclaimed the Nazi, reverting to his childhood. "You mean that Emil Meissner has turned against the Führer?"

"I mean that he stood in front of the entire staff of the Third Army and gave them a detailed lecture on the fortifications of Metz, thus enabling the Americans to take it quickly and to make thousands of Germans into prisoners of war instead of corpses. There are several score high-ranking officers who have come to the same decision—I am not at liberty to name them all."

"We have known, of course, that many of the Wehrmacht officers are traitors at heart—"

"There are some SS officers among them, Günther."

"What have you done with them?"

"They are living very comfortably in a villa behind the front, and when we need information we go to them and get it."

"What information have I that I could give you?"

"Surely you must know. I am here to save the art works of Europe from destruction. We take the position that these are the heritage of all humanity, and we shall do everything we can to save and preserve them."

"And take them to America!"

"I give you my word of honor, I know the policy and can speak with authority. Everything is to be returned to its former owners."

"Including German owners?"

"Certainly, unless they are persons convicted of war crimes. Works that were in German museums will go back to those museums. Those taken from France or other countries will be restored to those owners. That is the fixed policy, and the terms on which I came. You, Günther, must know where Göring has hidden all his acquisitions"—Lanny was careful not to say "loot"—"and the quicker we can find these things, the more chance we'll have to save them from bombs, and from dampness and mold, and from fanatics who might think it a noble action to destroy them. Unless I know Hermann Göring less well than I think I do, he would approve this program; he must know by now that his last card is played and must be worrying about what will happen to his priceless treasures. You know he meant to turn Karinhall into a museum and make the art works accessible to all the people of the world."

V

General-Major Furtwängler had to have time to think this over, to let it soak into his mind. So the art expert went out and met some of the officers of CP of Third, whose code name was "Lucky Forward."

G-2 had a spacious and elegant workroom with a lot of the plaster missing, and the commander had a solarium with broken glass patched with boards. The officers were quartered and messed in rehabilitated hotels near by. First you smashed things in a hurry, and then you repaired them in a hurry! They talked shop, and this was the way to know how the war was going, and to realize that it was being fought by human beings, not by machines. How the fellows on this staff didn't like that bugaboo known as "Monty," the British commander up north who was getting "gas" and "ammo" that Third so desperately needed! Monty wanted to win the war and reap the glory for himself, and so he sat on his backside and prepared and prepared, and when he advanced and got stuck in the mud of Holland he stopped and prepared some more. Meantime Georgie Patton fought and scratched, and called on Jesus Christ and God Almighty to help him get more supplies and kill more of the minions of Satan out there near the Rhine.

Georgie was like a wild horse that wants to gallop and goes crazy kicking against its hobbles. Georgie was fighting not merely the Germans but also an organization known as "CCS," Combined Chiefs of Staff, consisting of elderly brass in Washington who sat on their backsides—Georgie's favorite expression, only he used a shorter and uglier word. They sat four or five thousand miles away from the battlefront, evolved elaborate, beautiful-sounding plans, and communi-

cated them to the Army as if they were a voice from Sinai, the ten
tablets of the law. But that wasn't the way you fought a war, the
two-gun General insisted over and over to his staff. The way you
fought it was to be right on the spot and to make split-second decisions
based on your enemy's reactions; you found a weak spot and you
plunged through and poured in everything you had and kept him
running like hell. "Old Blood and Guts" had a vocabulary, most of it
unprintable, to describe his contempt for those officers who sat in
padded armchairs in paneled offices and told the fighting men what
not to do.

Early in last November, Lucky Forward had had the Germans on
the run, and Georgie had wanted to drive to the Rhine and cross it
and keep the enemy from reorganizing. But SHAEF had ordered a
sitdown, and Georgie had sat and made the air blue with his rage.
Again, just recently, while Georgie had been on the point of taking
Trier, the goddam down-sitters had tried to take his 10th Armored away
from him—the very spearhead of his striking force—because CCS had
decreed that SHAEF must keep a reserve against the possibility of
another Bulge. Patton was sure the Germans didn't have the forces
for another Bulge, and the way to prevent it was to keep them on
the run, goddam 'em.

It was really funny, if you could keep your sense of humor while
so much blood was being poured out. The two-gun General's little
private war with SHAEF was being waged with such infinite subtlety;
he would wangle another division the way a small boy wangles another
cookie. He would lure SHAEF into giving him permission to "probe"
the enemy, and he would turn a probe into the taking of Trier; he
would get his superior, General Bradley, to admit that of course if
a "break-through" should occur, it would be his duty to take advantage thereof; and now he was making the "break-through," and would
use it to drive all the way through the Eifel Mountains to the Rhine.
He would keep out of reach by telephone in order that nobody might
stop him.

VI

Right at this juncture, as if to help Lanny with his arguments, came
one of the most picturesque developments of the war. He had told
Furtwängler that the Americans would get across the Rhine, and he
had imagined a mighty battle to achieve it; never had it occurred to
him that they might get across by accident. A detachment of the

2nd Armored, heading for the river at the town of Remagen, on the far side of the Rhine, came over the ridge and were astounded to discover a great bridge intact. Hitler's orders had been that every bridge was to be blown under penalty of death; but no bridge should be blown until all the troops were across—that also under penalty of death; it was a trifle confusing. This time someone had blundered; charges had been set, and two had gone off but weren't big enough, and the Ludendorff Bridge, as it was called, was still usable.

The order was given, and the Americans charged across; the engineers, trained in demolition work, knew wires when they saw them, and had cutters in their belts; there were no more explosions. There was no German armor in sight and the German engineers had no means of resisting tanks; the tanks proceeded to clear the town and the shore both north and south—the beginning of a bridgehead. Field telephones carried the magical tidings, and more troops came racing to the scene.

When General Eisenhower got word of the lucky strike he ordered five divisions to the spot, two of them armored. An American armored division is quite a show. It consists of fourteen thousand men, with some three thousand vehicles and four hundred and fifty heavy armored vehicles, tanks and tank-killers, halftracks and self-propelled guns. That makes a procession the like of which you do not often see. Traveling on highways, the rule was fifty yards between the heavy vehicles, to avoid piling up, and that would make a column a hundred miles long. This, however, was an emergency, and the only rule was to get across fast and make room for the next fellow. Day and night for ten days that bridge roared and rumbled with vehicles and fast-running infantrymen. Then the Germans succeeded in knocking it out with artillery, but it was too late; the engineers had built pontoon bridges, which served even better.

The Germans had no Panzers in that neighborhood and very few reserves, for they had had to send everything up north to stop the British and Canadians. By the time they got troops there the American First Army had built a strong bridgehead, ten miles along the river and five miles back into the hills. Plenty of room to maneuver, and to set up depots of supplies, and to get ready to charge out and capture Frankfurt, and to form the right side of a pair of pincers to surround the Ruhr, with Germany's greatest coal mines and steel mills.

Lanny took this news to his friend the General-Major and remarked, "There is one point at least that we no longer have to argue."

VII

Lanny had asked for information about works of art because that would be the easiest way to get Furtwängler to talking. After his tongue was loosened, after he had told all the hiding places of Göring's treasures, then it might be possible to lead him gently into another line of revelation. Asking permission to make notes, Lanny listened while the General-Major told how the fat Reichsmarschall's cherished paintings of naked ladies and velvet-clad great gentlemen, Spanish and Italian, French, English, and Dutch, had been removed to an immense bunker especially built near the old hunting lodge on the Karinhall estate. At least ten thousand paintings, including all those from the Museum of Vienna, had been stored in one of the great salt mines, that at Alt Aussee, in Austria. Lanny remarked, "I went through one of those mines some time ago." He didn't say that it had been less than six months ago, in the course of his escape from the clutches of the Gestapo.

The art expert plied his friend with questions about the various persons who had had to do with the accumulating of these art treasures. Baron von Behr, corrupt aristocrat who had put himself in the service of the Nazis and become head of the Einsatzstab, the "task force" which was charged with the seeking out and appropriating of art treasures in all the conquered lands—what had he done with the share he had kept for his own? And Herr Hofer, Göring's shifty-eyed "curator"? And Dr. Bunjes, art authority who had justified the seizure of the art works in Paris museums on the ground that they "might be exchanged for planes or tanks"? And Bruno Lohse, handsome young Nazi zealot, one of the few really sincere ones Lanny had met—what was he doing now and where would he be hiding? Lanny pretended to have a human interest in the various persons he had met at Karinhall, and that was easy enough, for they were interesting from various points of view. Esthetics dissociated from ethics has produced some of the most extraordinary human types, of concern to psychiatrists and criminologists as well as to secret agents.

Der Dicke himself was such a type. He was one of the greatest criminals in history, and at the same time one of the most passionate lovers of great art. His crimes did not trouble him in the slightest; on the contrary, he was one of the most self-satisfied of men, vain to the point almost of lunacy; a showman displaying himself and everything he had, and certain that it was the greatest spectacle ever offered to the world. At the same time he had a keen sense of humor, and would even be capable of laughing at himself, provided the comment was offered by one of the few persons he considered his equals. One of these was the rich and well-informed son of Budd-Erling, and at some of Lanny's "kidding" Göring would throw back his head and burst into a bellow of laughter. He would stuff himself with food, and then belch, and then guffaw over that—and yet never doubt that he was one of the most elegant of persons.

"How do you suppose he will take defeat?" Lanny asked; and the former staff member—really a higher servant—replied, "He is a sensible man and will manage to enjoy whatever comes. As you know, most of his power has been taken from him already; he has had very little to do with running the Luftwaffe for some time. He has retired to Karinhall, which your airmen have left alone."

"We do not bomb art galleries," Lanny said. "The last time I saw Hermann he was terribly depressed. I was able to cheer him up by telling him that the Führer had spoken kindly of him." Then, after a pause, "Tell me, how did they come to give you a command?"

"My wife is related to General Keitel," explained the General-Major; "and I suppose they have a hard time finding officers who are party members and can be trusted. I had never had a command before and was frightened by the responsibility. I did the best I could, but, as you see, it wasn't good enough."

"Nobody in the world could have done better," replied the American soothingly. "It was a fundamental mistake to try to hold west of the Rhine. You were bound to lose a large part of your troops; and you must admit it is better to be captured than killed."

VIII

This amiable conversation went on for a couple of days, and, just as Lanny had thought, the more Furtwängler talked, the easier he found it. He had told so much, he might as well tell the rest and reap the benefit of his frankness. He told of an enormous collection of art works in Neuschwanstein Castle near Munich. The treasures of the great Kaiser Friedrich Museum in Berlin had been hidden in the Merkers copper mine in Thuringia; and so on for a long list. Lanny collected everything that could be of use to Monuments, and then he went to work for Alsos and plied his old friend with questions about the newest jet-propulsion engines and planes. Göring was no longer running the Luftwaffe, but he knew about these matters, and members of his staff had picked up bits of conversation and had talked freely among themselves. Yes, there was a tremendously fast new jet, expected to knock the Americans and British out of the skies, if only it could be produced fast enough. Also, there was a multiple rocket gun that would discharge one hundred of the V-1½s in ten minutes. Lanny said, "We captured one of those in the Bulge, I am told."

Such things as "Schnorkel" submarines and "booster" guns a hundred yards long were outside the General-Major's province; but he might have heard some talk, or taken a look at some "*GeKdos*" (top secret) report. Atomic fission must never be mentioned by the P.A.; but it was possible to skirt the subject carefully, and perhaps the captive officer would say, "We have something even more deadly, which will give us the victory if we can get it in time." But he didn't say that.

He did tell about the V-3, the immense rocket that would leap into the stratosphere, travel several thousand miles, and deliver a load of explosives that would destroy most of London or even New York. There was Peenemünde, where these deadly experiments were being carried out. It wasn't far from Karinhall, and officers in charge had come now and then as guests, and had been disposed to make friends with a staff officer of the man whom Hitler had designated his successor. Even though he had put Göring on the shelf, he had never withdrawn that designation; with the well-known breakdown of the Führer's health, the *Nummer Zwei* went to sleep every night with the knowledge that he might wake up in full command of Germany's war effort.

Then there was the subject of the German forces confronting the Americans: the Second SS Mountain Division and the 11th Panzer, known to the GIs as the "Fireman Division" because it showed up in place after place where there was trouble for the Hun. Furtwängler revealed that Army Group B, fronting this part of the Rhine, had just been placed under the command of Field Marshal Walther Model. Lanny didn't know this, and didn't know if the CP here in Luxembourg did. He knew that Model was on the list of war criminals for the killing of prisoners of war and civilians; he was the most fanatical of Nazi generals, known as "*der kleine Hitler.*" Lanny remarked, "I suppose that means war to the finish," and Furtwängler replied, "It does."

10

Die Wacht am Rhein

I

MONUMENTS in Versailles telegraphed Lanny; they would like to see him as soon as he could be spared. His work for Third Army was done, and Third thanked him cordially and invited him to come again whenever the spirit moved him; he replied that it might be soon, whenever they got deep enough into Germany to uncover either art or scientific treasures. He turned his Nazi friend over to their tender mercies, and they promised to handle him as if he were made of damp tissue paper. With new developments might come the need of new information, and Furtwängler agreed to give it. Theoretically, that didn't mean "immunity" for anything, but in practice it probably would.

Lanny was put into a plane for Paris, and then by staff car to Versailles, and there in the Royal Stables he found his friends wanting to know if he would be willing to travel to Rome for them. Art treasures had been stolen by the Nazis in Italy, and some had been left behind and hidden. There was a Monuments group looking for them, and it was a problem, because some Italians had been bribed to keep them concealed, and might be planning to keep them permanently in the event of a German collapse. Somebody had come on the trail of an American art expert who had been in Rome less than two years ago and had met numbers of artists and collectors of art. Everybody was sure he was an agent of some sort, but nobody was quite sure whether he was Nazi or American. His name was Lanny Budd, and could Paris Monuments find out anything about him?

Paris Monuments had a good laugh over this letter and over the fact that they had got a bit of a scare themselves and had taken the precaution to refer the question to OSS Washington, which had put the stamp "OK" on this man of mystery. So now they wanted to know if Lanny would be willing to fly to Rome and give the people there advice about their problems. It promised to be exciting, and several of the

153

young Fogg Museum lads were eager to go along; but a call might come from the Rhineland or the Saar at any moment, and nobody could be spared.

It was one of those roundabout air trips, like flying to Africa and Brazil when you wanted to get from Washington to London. The direct route would have taken him over enemy territory; so it was Marseille, Algiers, Tunis, Naples, Rome. Army and Air Force planes were shuttling between these places day and night, so there was never any trouble in getting a lift if you had proper credentials. Lanny read his mail and answered it—including a note to Laurel, who wrote that she would soon leave for Paris. He got himself a load of London and New York newspapers and magazines—very expensive—and when he had read them he could get all sorts of favors by giving them to mentally starved American officers along the route.

He had flown most of these hops before and hadn't much to see. Dingy and crowded Marseille was being restored as by magic. White Algiers on the hillslopes had been turned into an American naval, military, and airbase. Tunis had been rebuilt, and white-robed Moors were working hard for American dollars. Naples and its beautiful bay with a smoking volcano for background was full of ships from many ports being unloaded at newly restored docks. As for the Eternal City on its Seven Hills—Lanny was set down at the Ciampino Airport which he had seen bombed into hills and craters by several hundred Marauders and Mitchells in July of 1943. Now it was in perfect order, lined by rows of big Liberators and Flying Fortresses, taking off every day for raids on Vienna and Budapest and Munich.

II

Victory is a pleasant thing, for which men strive mightily. When Lanny had been here before he had been playing a dangerous double role and had cringed in his heart; he had walked warily, fearing the worst at every moment. Now he wore the uniform of an American Army officer, and all Romans were his friends, some of them real and more pretending. He could meet his old acquaintances, worldly, cynical, corrupt, but cultivated and agreeable. He wouldn't go into explanations, but just smile, and everyone would understand that what he had been doing was war. "*Cosi fan tutti*" was a common saying, as well as the title of an opera; it means "Everybody does it," and excuses everything, provided that you have good manners and spend money freely.

He reported first to the Monuments, who welcomed him gladly. Scholarly and naïve young Americans, they could hardly conceive of the sophistications and intrigues of Roman society; it was like a shell of translucent pearl, iridescent and lovely, through which they could not chip their way. They had come here for the altruistic purpose of restoring property to its owners, without price and without bribes; they had a hard time persuading anyone that this was so, and persons to whom they told it began at once to figure how to get some advantage from this unprecedented situation. How could well-bred boys and girls from Boston know how to set about persuading a red-ribboned *commendatore* to betray the criminal secrets of an aged ex-minister of state?

The Monuments were installed in the mansion of a nazified Italian wine merchant who had fled with his friends to the north. The place was elegant, with spacious rooms and high ceilings, but fuel was hard to get. There was no bathroom in the building, and Lanny had goose pimples all over him while he bathed and shaved with cold water in an elegant crystal hand basin. Meantime his uniform was pressed by an Italian woman servant; then, spruced and elegant, he went to have coffee with his friend Julie, Marchesa di Caporini—not failing to bring the coffee.

The Marchesa, French-born cousin of the deceased Marie de Bruyne, was married to a Roman proprietor of landed estates and slum tenements, and was a dissatisfied lady of fashion at the "dangerous age." She had been pleased to introduce an American art expert posing as a Frenchman into her social set, and now she was delighted to have him come down out of the sky to relieve the boredom of her days. Italy was crushed and poverty-stricken, "society" was dead, and the only compensation for Roman ladies was the presence of elegant, conquering gentlemen in American, French, British, and Canadian uniforms.

While coffee was brewing they chatted, and while sipping it they went on chatting: all the latest gossip concerning the many ladies and gentlemen Lanny had met at the oddly named Acquasanta—Holy Water—Golf Club. Who was loving whom and who was hating whom; who was in power and who was struggling to oust him—such are the subjects of conversation among ladies of fashion all the way from Rome to Tokyo, and back by way of Hollywood and Washington. "And you, Lanny? What are you doing in a uniform—in which you look so very handsome?"

Lanny explained that it was still art. Possibly Julie had heard of the

Monuments, Fine Arts, and Archives Section; they had a depot here, and he was trying to help them. "But why bother with art works when you haven't won the war?" was the Marchesa's reaction. "Why don't you finish driving these wretched Germans out of Italy?"

Lanny had to tell her that the Allied strategists considered Italy as a secondary front; men and supplies had been taken from it for the invasion of Southern France, and now everything was being put into the crossing of the Rhine. Since the coming of winter the Allies had sat confronting the Germans on their so-called "Gothic Line," which crossed the Italian boot at its top, where it widens out into a knee, or whatever it is that composes Northern Italy. "But your troops are so miserable, up in our mountains in the snow, or down in the coastal plains in the mud!" So protested Julie Caporini; and Lanny assured her they would be moving in the spring. He added, in the proper style of light banter, "Some of them are having a very pleasant time here in Rome, I am told."

Tactfully he approached the subject of restoring stolen art works to their proper owners. There were reports that certain persons had made deals to hide such works for the benefit of the German plunderers; in some cases there had been fake sales. Of course such works wouldn't be found hanging on people's walls; they would be hidden in cellars or attics. But servants would know about them, and for a small fee would tell; the Army would not hesitate to make a search wherever there were good grounds for suspicion.

"Oh, Lanny!" laughed the Roman lady. "Your people are so altruistic you embarrass us! We have no such moral fervor!"

He answered that it was a police duty; the Nazi plunderers, and all who aided and abetted them, must be taught that war did not pay. Surely all decent Romans would want to punish thieves. Could not Julie think of some person interested in art who had access to society and would take the trouble to ask questions, not too pointedly? Lanny didn't suggest that Julie herself might do it; he waited to see if she would offer, as that would reduce the price.

She was just as shrewd as he was and forced him to make the overture. But the price wasn't exorbitant. Ten thousand lire a month sounded impressive but it was less than a hundred dollars and going lower. There would be five thousand additional for tips to servants, and Julie would keep most of this, and it would provide her with the cosmetics so necessary to ladies when their charms begin to fade. Lanny knew that her husband was a niggard and that they quarreled over the subject of money. He guessed that the husband would help her, and that this small nucleus might expand into an efficient intelligence outfit. He wouldn't have to ask Monuments for the money, for he had received some out of the President's secret funds and was authorized to spend it in any way that would promote the American cause. He would tell Roosevelt what he had done and get a prompt "OK."

III

Lanny spent a pleasant fortnight in Rome. That was time enough to sit down with his colleagues and tell them all he knew about this ancient "Holy City" which for a thousand years had had as worthless idle rich and as miserable starving poor as any place that Lanny had seen in the world. It was time enough for him to call at the magnificent palace of the Princess Colonna, the Levantine lady who was the social leader of the city, and be taken to the Holy Water Golf Club, where all the lovely ladies repaired on pleasant afternoons to gossip and flirt with the conquering Allied officers as previously they had flirted with the conquering Germans. Here nothing succeeded like success, and *amore* and *arme* were close together in the Italian dictionary.

When Lanny had been here some twenty months ago the king rooster of this well-feathered flock had been the loud-crowing Galeazzo Ciano, son-in-law of Mussolini and just-deposed foreign minister. Those whom he had cast off were known as "Galeazzo widows." He had taken up residence in Vatican City, but that had not saved him; his treason had been discovered and he had been court-martialed and shot. Now all that was a bad dream; *Il Fascismo* was forgotten, and the password was *Democrazia*, but it was a new style, adapted to a country having ancient traditions of Royal and Papal infallibility and threatened by blood-red Communism. The property-owning classes were afraid, and the ladies of smart society were devoting their best efforts to winning American diplomatic and military authorities over to their point of view. The English were already won; it was Winston Churchill's program to maintain the Italian monarchy by setting aside a widely hated old lecher and put in his place a handsome tall prince who couldn't be blamed for anything and was too stupid ever to interfere with what the politicians might want to do.

It didn't take Julie very long to come upon support of the rumor that an ex-minister of the Badoglio government had concealed a roll of stolen paintings in a secret compartment in his wine cellar. The GIs made a raid and found them, and of course that made a tremendous scandal in fashionable Rome. Some other persons lost their nerve and brought in stuff they had thought was safely hidden. The Marchesa got an extra fee, and the promise of more.

Also, this highly placed Roman lady told him the life story of Italy's crown princess, fit theme for some tragic dramatist. Fair blond daughter of the King of the Belgians, she had been married in a week of nation-wide festivities to the handsome son of the pint-sized Italian king. Dissolute like his father, he had humiliated her, and she had had to live in silent loathing of the whole House of Savoy, as well as the Fascists whose puppets they had become. Secretly she had carried on intrigues against them—how interested Lanny would have been to know it, in those days not so far in the past when he had been doing the same thing in Rome! When the Americans had surged into Italy the Nazis had taken over Rome, and the Princess Marie José had gone into exile in Switzerland, where she still was. "Go and see her," said the Marchesa; but the Monuments man had no time for royal visits now.

The American communiqué reported that the Seventh Army had forced a crossing of the Rhine not far north of Heidelberg, which lies twelve miles east of that river. There was a great university there, and it had a physics laboratory. *Wuwas* were more important than paintings these days; so Lanny said a reluctant farewell to all the Holy Water ladies, who had now decided that he was a far more fascinating person than any Duce's son-in-law. He picked out the most competent of the Monuments men and entrusted him with the secret of Julie Caporini; he arranged to get some funds to this man—making plain that they were government funds and not the gift of a modern Maecenas. He got some coffee and cigarettes at the PX and gave them to Julie, shook hands cordially but did not kiss her, and flew away by the same route that he had come, a god out of one machine and into another.

IV

Back in Paris, Lanny found his wife, champing like General Patton, because she had been promised access to Germany and the Army kept stalling. Lanny couldn't blame them too much; he had found out what it was like to be caught in a bulge, and he wasn't going to get his wife into one—she being a notorious anti-Nazi novelist, wanted by the Gestapo since the year 1939, and guilty of the even greater crime of having entered Hitler's Berghof under a false name.

Lanny found that both Alsos and Monuments would be glad to have his company in Heidelberg. There were bound to be art treasures hidden in the neighborhood, and there was a physics laboratory, with a famous nuclear experimenter, Professor Bothe, and also a famous chemist, Professor Kuhn. As to the question of Laurel, Lanny soon made up his mind that the danger was slight; the Germans just wouldn't be able to make any counterattacks. All their good reserves had been rushed to the north; and then had come the Remagen coup, and half a dozen divisions had been hurried to that spot, where they had made no headway whatever. Farther to the south Patton's armor had made hash of all the enemy forces west of the river. These were mostly the Volksgrenadier and Volkssturm troops, last-ditch organizations made up of the old and the very young, the sick and the crippled; many of them had no uniforms, only armbands, and obsolete weapons with very little ammunition. The Third's north and south prongs had formed pincers and gathered them in by the tens of thousands—so many that the depots behind the lines refused to take any more.

Now, at the beginning of April, all the various Allied armies had got across the Rhine, and the real collapse of Germany was underway. Lanny went to see the Seventh people in Paris and agreed to assume responsibility for his wife; also, Monuments put in a request on her behalf, because she had offered to write her first article on the search for art treasures. Everything that Alsos did was top secret, but Monuments, Fine Arts, and Archives had no military value, and their devotees were free to splurge in newspapers and magazines. It was good publicity for the Army, because it showed these tough guys appreciating culture, and knowing that beauty was truth, truth beauty. "What the hell does that mean?" asked the commander of a tank battalion to whom Lanny quoted it; and Lanny had to admit that he didn't know just what it meant, but it had a fine sound.

V

The P.A. knew the Seventh well; it was they who had "assimilated" him when he had come down out of the hills above the Riviera, a few hours after that magnificent Army had stepped out of its LCIs and LSTs on the 15th of August last. He had volunteered to serve as interpreter and interrogator, and they had needed many extras, having accumulated such an unexpected load of prisoners. He could hardly expect the luck to hit upon the same armored outfit that he had ridden with all the way from the Côte d'Azur to Dijon by way of Grenoble—known as the Route Napoleon, because it was the one the Emperor had taken on his return from Elba. He inquired and learned that his old outfit had taken Mannheim and was on its way eastward. He took the liberty of putting in an application for his friend Lieutenant Jerry Pendleton to be loaned on behalf of both Alsos and Monuments; he and Jerry had worked together against the Nazis, and Jerry was not merely an interpreter but also a top-class secret agent and sleuth.

So it came about that when the husband and wife were motored to the famous old university town on the River Neckar, Lanny's ex-tutor and fishing and tennis companion was waiting for them, and had seen the billeting officer and secured a comfortable cottage for the three of them, with a non-Nazi maidservant—at least she said she was that. He had even managed to get a goose, and proudly displayed it hanging up in the kitchen. Military life seemed to have agreed with Jerry; he was fifty, and his hair was gray, his skin weather-beaten, but he was in good health and full of the glory of the great adventure on which he was engaged. He had been given the rank of captain—and no longer just assimilated. This was a load off his mind, for after World War I he had got sick of sitting round and was one of thousands of soldiers in France who just went off and forgot the Army. He had married a French girl and settled down to help run a pension in Cannes.

Captain Jerry had been interrogating men from a Stalag on the west bank of the Rhine, where some fifty thousand Russian and Polish prisoners of war had been kept by the Germans under wretched conditions. Many were staying on after the Americans had come because they had no other place to find shelter and be fed. Among them were a number of Germans, accused or suspected of anti-Nazi ideas, and Jerry had taken a leaf out of Lanny's notebook and sought out the Reds and Pinks among these. Before leaving for Heidelberg he had consulted his card file and got the names and addresses of several who lived in the town. When you found one Socialist you could soon find others, for under the Nazis they had been a secret society, knowing one another, and knowing who had really gone over to the Nazi enemy and who were only pretending to.

Now they were coming out of hiding, denouncing their former persecutors to the Americans, and ready to help get information. Did the *Herren* want to know whether the Kaiser Wilhelm Institute for Medical Research had any secret laboratory outside the town? Did they want to know where the art works of the Museum had been taken and who had done the taking? *Ja, ja, meine Herren, so schnell wie möglich!* Thus it quickly came about that Monuments went scouting in a jeep, looking for a cave in the high hills of the Elsenzgau, and that one of the house servants of Professor Phillip Lenard, head physicist of the University, was interviewed and set to finding out where that eighty-year-old nazified scientist had fled to. All that for about one carton of American cigarettes, judiciously distributed.

VI

The seven-hundred-year-old town of Heidelberg is on the Neckar River, where it comes out of a gorge and enters the flat plains of the Rhine. There are hills on both sides, very lovely with vineyards and forests. There is a medieval castle on the heights, now a ruin, and there was a town hall until the British bombers destroyed it. They spared the University, the town's main source of livelihood. Someone had written a sentimental play about it, and that brought more students, looking for pretty girls, and tourists, looking for both students and girls. "Alt Heidelberg" was a name of magic, and both scientists and art lovers trod gently when they walked down its Hauptstrasse—which nobody was so irreverent as to translate into "Main Street."

Alsos was concerned about two institutions, a branch of the Kaiser Wilhelm Institute and the Physics Department of the University of Heidelberg. The former had a cyclotron, the only one in Germany, and it was important to know what had been done with it. The Institute had been constructed by Professor Bothe, a nuclear physicist of renown, and a former friend of Goudsmit, encountered at various international conferences. Now he was an enemy alien and might be made a prisoner of war at Goudsmit's direction. They talked, and Bothe told about the work in theoretical physics he had been carrying on; but when asked about war work he refused to talk and declared that he had burned all his papers under orders. The same statement was made by Professor Kuhn, director of the Institute, who, so he said, had been working exclusively on the chemistry of modern drugs. Were you to believe this professor, who had started all his classes with "*Sieg Heil*" and the Hitler salute? A problem for the supersleuths!

Lenard had fled to an unknown destination; and the search for him got Lanny Budd into an amusing adventure. This old man was the most rabid Nazi scientist in Germany, having been one before Hitler was born; of course he hadn't had the name then, but only the spirit; he had been a pan-German fanatic, and at the end of World War I had been jailed for making violent monarchist speeches. On this record, Adi Schicklgruber had declared him the leader of German physical science and had assigned to him the noble task of eliminating the poison of Judaeo-Einsteinian relativity from the intellectual life of young Germany. *Hitler hat immer recht!*

Word came that this prize scientific bird was roosting in an obscure village some ten miles back in the hills, and that he might soon be off on another flight. It so happened that Professor Goudsmit was out on another expedition and could not be reached by telephone. Jerry said, "Let's go and bring the bird in." It was a pleasant day, with promise of early spring, and Lanny gave his OK. They got a fine new Cadillac, suitable for an imitation colonel, a real captain, and a captive super-scientist. A GI with a tommy gun rode beside the chauffeur, and four others in a jeep rode ahead to be sure the way was clear.

They drove through charming scenery and meantime discussed their problem. "What if he won't come?" inquired the ex-tutor. "Shall we put irons on him?"

"Lord, no, Jerry. You can't get scientific secrets by force."

"But can you get anything out of that old fussbudget anyhow?"

"You go out and shoot hares in the woods," said Lanny with a grin. "Let me try some of my tricks on him."

VII

They found the white-haired old Nobel Prize winner—he had really been a capable scientist back in the year 1905—living in a forester's cottage, and greatly agitated at the arrival of an armed contingent. Perhaps he really thought the barbarians from overseas might stand him up and shoot him on sight. Lanny's good German and good manners calmed him down, and when they were left alone in the room he listened with amazed incredulity to an American in an officer's uniform assuring him that he, the American, was no fighting man, but was a National Socialist at heart and had been that for nearly twenty years. Obviously this must be a trap to persuade the Fatherland's greatest scientist to part with his learning; but the plausible speaker went on to tell about visits to Berchtesgaden and the New Chancellery, to Karinhall and the Berlin Residenz, and even to the Bürgerbräukeller in Munich, a shrine of the early days. *Erstaunlich!*

The old bird was wary. He knew that he was one of the greatest prizes of the war, and he knew that the enemy was sly and unscrupulous. The head of the Physics Department of Heidelberg University was not going to be taken in by a cheap swindle, and he spent a good hour cross-questioning this alleged art expert and trying to trap him. The professor had been to the Berghof himself and was surprised to discover that the American had undoubtedly been there too. He could describe the furniture, the paneling, the art works in the great square central room; he could describe the Führer's private study, with its immense window looking out over the Austrian Alps; he could describe the long dining-room and the refectory table with twenty chairs along each side. He mentioned the rules on the door of each guest room, as in a summer hotel; no smoking inside the building, and you had to be on time for a meal if you wanted that meal. The names of the Führer's personal staff, his secretaries, his physicians, and the treatments they gave him! *Höchst sonderbar!*

In the end the old man had to give up and admit that Oberst Budd had been the Führer's friend, and had bought Defreggers for him in Vienna and sold him the Detazes which were in the Bechsteinhaus at Berchtesgaden. He had actually been taken to the top of the Kehlstein and to the bottom of the Führerbunker in the New Chancellery garden, two places which the Professor had heard about but assuredly never seen. He knew the party history, the party doctrines, the party language, the party leaders and their personal habits. He had shot stags with Göring and swapped astrologers and spiritualist mediums with Hess. *"Nun, Herr Budd, was führt Sie zu mir?"*

Lanny answered that he had been sure the American scientists would wish to talk with Germany's most eminent physicist, and it had been his idea to spare an elderly *Gelehrte* any possible shock and discomfort. He wanted Professor Lenard to know that he had a friend at court, and one who would be glad to mediate for him. The Professor was to know that he would be treated with the respect due to a Nobel Prize winner and true discoverer of the Röntgen rays. (Lenard so considered himself, and blamed a political plot for the fact that he was not given credit for this achievement.)

"They will want your papers and records, of course," ventured the interrogator, and received the expected answer, that the scientist had burned all his papers, in compliance with strict orders from the Führer himself.

So Lanny had to lay another siege. He had to tell the story that he had told Heinrich Jung and Günther Furtwängler—that the war was lost, and that the best thing for the German people and *Kultur* was to get it over as quickly and cheaply as possible. That said, Lanny turned himself into Robbie Budd, president of Budd-Erling, who hated the Bolsheviks and considered them the great menace to civilization. Sooner or later the Western world would have to put them down; and the question for a great German physicist to consider at this moment was whether he wished the treasures of German science to come into the possession of the Western world or the Eastern. There would be only two countries, America and Russia, in a position to make use of them.

VIII

Lanny knew exactly the words with which to present this argument to a Nazi zealot. He spent a whole afternoon hammering it into this white-headed one, and he won what he thought was a glorious victory. The great physicist would unload all the treasures of his knowledge to the American scientists—and he did not change his mind even when it was revealed to him that the head of the American mission was a Jew! He would even tell the priceless secrets having to do with uranium, heavy water, and atomic fission!

The old gentleman packed his belongings, and a GI stowed them in the car trunk, and they set out for Heidelberg. When they came out of the hills it occurred to Lanny that it might be a good idea to prepare his friends for what was coming, so he stopped at a near-by Army Post and telephoned. Professor Goudsmit had returned, and Lanny told of his achievement. He was greatly disconcerted when the Professor said, "Thanks, but really we have no use for that old man."

"But," protested the art expert, "he has agreed to tell everything he knows."

"Yes, but he doesn't know anything worth listening to."

"How can you be sure of that?"

"I have read his publications, and I know his mind. He hasn't had a new idea in thirty years. He spends all his time scolding at Einstein's formulas, which are the basis of all modern physics. How can such a man know anything?"

"That applies to uranium, heavy water, and atomic fission?"

"It applies to everything. The man is crazy. One reason the Germans have lost this war is because Hitler was ignorant enough to be persuaded that Lenard was a great physicist."

"Then what do you want me to do with him?"

"Do anything you please. Just ignore him."

Lanny hung up the phone and sat thinking it over. He loathed the Nazi ideas as much as anybody, but when it came to a showdown he lacked the impulse to hurt the feelings of an old man. He went back and told the Nazi avatar that the Americans had decided, in view of his age and past services to knowledge, not to trouble him with questioning. He drove his passenger back to the forester's cottage and left him with the pious non-Nazi formula: *"Gott behüte Euch!"*

IX

After that fiasco the art expert decided that he had better confine himself to his own specialty. He became for several days an ardent Monuments man. They had found the cave, and truckloads of paintings and other treasures were being brought down to the depot—a public building of which one-half was wrecked and the other half sound. No pleasanter form of amusement in the world than unwrapping these treasures, inspecting them, checking the signatures, and in many cases the names of owners. A surprising thing how many people would possess a valuable painting all their lives and never bother to put a name and address on the back. A pretty set of problems they had prepared for an organization of American altruism!

Most of the works were Dutch and had come from Holland. The British and Canadians had liberated a part of that country and were working fast on the rest; a group of Dutch art experts had been assigned to co-operate with Monuments, and Lanny renewed his very special liking for this people. He found them honest, kind, and generous, and he asked no more of human beings. How many, many times he had got less!

Word had come in of a "pile" laboratory in a village in the Thuringian forest, to the northeast; also in that region was the Merkers mine, stuffed full of art treasures. Near Stuttgart, toward the southeast, was the laboratory of the great Werner Heisenberg; and here also were castles full of paintings. The Seventh Army was heading for both these places, and it was a question which would be reached first. Both the scientists and art lovers were on tiptoe, ready to start their small caravans at an hour's notice.

Lanny's wounded feelings had been soothed, and he was ready to help either group. Laurel was ready to go too; she had written about Heidelberg, old and new, and about the strange phenomenon of bandits and pirates who were passionate lovers of beauty. She didn't know anything about science, and couldn't tell a cyclotron from a wind tunnel, but she did know great paintings when she saw them, and she was tempted to stick by Peggy Remsen the rest of the way across Germany. Peggy was now in Heidelberg, in charge of records and the setting up of record systems at all the new depots.

X

Lanny was going where his wife went, or so he thought; but at this juncture came a message which knocked out all his plans. Only ten words, but they were packed with import: "You are wanted immediately OSS Paris will arrange transportation. Baker." That meant Roosevelt, of course. All the P.A. could say to his wife was, "I am called to Washington." He saw her cheeks blanch and tried to comfort her; the time of danger was past now, except for the fighting men. Laurel had to pretend to believe it, for no woman of character would sap her husband's courage by fears.

The trip to Paris took half a day, most of it spent in getting to one airport and from another. He reported to General Donovan's organization; they were expecting him—all he had to do was to indicate the route he preferred. He would have voted for England if he could have taken the time to see Rick and Nina, but he assumed that the word "immediately" meant just that, and he said, "The quickest way." They did some telephoning and studying of charts, and gave him a schedule via Lisbon, the Cape Verde Islands, Bermuda, and Savannah, Georgia. This last city was where he was to be delivered, they didn't know why. Lanny could guess that the President was resting somewhere in the South, a fact that would not be mentioned in the press.

All the way on this trip, very pleasant in early April, the P.A.'s imagination was busy with the problem of what was coming. F. D. R. would never have jerked him away like this unless it was something of top importance. Surely not art works, and hardly any scientific matter—for the Alsos people could do anything that Lanny could, and more. This was a war of infinite variety, and Lanny's imagination lighted upon a truly exciting idea. At their last meeting the Boss had done a lot of fishing around the subject of Adi Schicklgruber and his hideout in the mountains of the wild witch Berchta. Wasn't it reasonable to assume that the Führer would retreat to that Alpine Redoubt his troops were preparing for their last stand? What forces would he have in the neighborhood of his Berghof? What was the character of the land? How near were the guardhouses and how strong were the gates?

It must be that! They were going to kidnap Hitler and pay him back for the stunt he had pulled off in snatching Mussolini from the prison of the anti-Nazi Italians! It would be a job for General Donovan's commandos, the most carefully trained fighting individuals in the world. They would be dropped by parachutes in the night, protected by bombing planes overhead; they would raid the Berghof and grab its master, while at the same time another bunch would be seizing the airfield at Berchtesgaden. The Führer would be put into a car and rushed to that field, and the Germans would have a hard time deciding whether to shoot at the car. The commandos might be "expendable," or they might hole up and defend themselves, with planes dropping supplies, and perhaps an armored task force rushing to join them. The Führer's summer home might be turned into a bridgehead in the Alps, a redoubt within a redoubt!

A marvelous *coup de guerre*, a legend for the rest of time. They would take Lanny along because of his knowledge of the whole layout. But no; perhaps they just wanted to pump his brains and then leave him behind. He would put up a battle for the right to go. But then he remembered that he was no longer a playboy; he was a married man with a son. Moreover, he had just been willed a million dollars to end war in the world—and here he was planning to go and get himself killed, and all his peace projects along with him!

With such thoughts he beguiled himself while a transport plane carrying convalescent officers set him down near the Portuguese capital by the Tagus River, and then again on a Portuguese island, and again on a British island which had become an immense American air and naval base—a ninety-nine-year lease in exchange for fifty out-of-date four-stack destroyers, desperately needed to hunt submarines. There were beautiful amphibious views at each of these places, and also at warm Savannah, with its great live-oak trees decorated with gray Spanish moss. But Lanny didn't have much of an eye for natural beauty, being busy imagining himself at Berchtesgaden on some dark night, pouring slugs out of a machine gun into the snappy, green-clad zealots of the Leibstandarte, who had always been so exactly *korrekt* with him, even though they must have hated him as an interloper.

Tears from the Depth of Some Divine Despair

BOOK FOUR

Tears from the Depth of Some Divine Despair

11

A Living Sacrifice

I

A CUB PLANE came for Lanny, and he asked the pilot where they were going. The reply was "Warm Springs," and the passenger needed to ask no more. It was the President's favorite vacation resort; there was a pool of delightfully warm water, heavily mineralized, so that it was as easy to swim and float in as the Great Salt Lake in Utah. This was the best form of exercise for crippled legs, and Roosevelt had built himself a cottage, called "the Little White House." He had made the resort known, and the public had organized what was called the "March of Dimes" and contributed great sums of money. So now there was an elaborate free treatment place, to which sufferers from polio came from all over the country.

Being known to the Secret Service men, Lanny might have gone to the President's house, but that wasn't his way of working. He went to the hotel, called Baker, and was told to be in front of the hotel at eight that evening; the Boss went to bed early, or was supposed to. That gave the visitor time to take a long walk in the pine woods of Western Georgia, and then to come back and bathe and shave, listen to the war news over the radio in the hotel lobby, and eat half a Georgia fried chicken with cornbread and turnip greens. Promptly on the second he strolled in front of the hotel and stepped silently into the car that stopped for him.

Pine Mountain was the name of the site, and a graveled road led up to it. Two Secret Service men stood at the door, and no doubt there were others in the shrubbery. Lanny was taken into a cluttered study—all sorts of people sent the President gifts, and he was amused and tried to make room for them. From there into a small anteroom, and then into the bedroom, with its maplewood bed, large mahogany desk, and a ship's chronometer. The crippled man spent his evenings in bed, where he had room for papers and books, and his fountain pen and cigarette holder and what not. Nearly always Lanny had seen him thus, wearing a striped pajama coat, and sweater or blue cape if it was chilly. But this was a warm spring night, and the thin pajama coat was open at the throat. The little Scottie, Fala, lay at the foot of the bed and wagged his tail as if to tell the visitor he was welcome.

Lanny had become used to the fact that his Boss was haggard and gray, his face thin and lined with care. Always he had picked up when he came to this resort; but perhaps he hadn't been here very long, for he looked terrible. The sight of him filled the P.A. with mingled grief and fear, but he put a grin of welcome on his face, and the tired President did the same. "Hello, old Geiger counter!" he exclaimed. Lanny chuckled at this reference to a forbidden subject.

"The Germans are clean out of that race, Governor," he replied. "They stumbled at the start."

There was only one chair in the room, a large one by the bed. Lanny took it, and told the story of Hitler's greatest physicist and how he had been spurned by the Jewish head of Alsos. Roosevelt, who had a Jew in his cabinet and another helping to write his speeches, did not miss the racial angle of this episode. Also, it was a joke on Lanny, and we can always enjoy a joke on our friends more easily than one on ourselves. The story was in the nature of a gold medal awarded to Franklin D. Roosevelt—the man who had gambled two billion dollars of his country's money on atomic fission, while Hitler had put his money on rockets. Rockets were good all right, but now the British and Canadians were plunging northward into Holland, seeking out the launching sites, and a *Wuwa* hadn't fallen on London in a fortnight.

Lanny had the idea that talk about Hitler might lead to the subject of how to kidnap him. But no, it wasn't that at all. Suddenly the Boss looked grave and said, "The reason I sent for you: I am worried about Stalin."

"Oh!" exclaimed the P.A. and couldn't keep the disappointment out of his face. He explained the reason, and the other replied, "We made elaborate preparations for that; but the trouble is, Hitler stays in Berlin and apparently intends to direct the war from there."

"He has an elaborate bunker there, and I can tell the OSS all about it. I was in it, you know."

"Yes, but it's this way—the Russians are so close to Berlin, and if we went in there with parachutes or any other way, they would get the idea we were trying to snatch the prize away from them. It really doesn't make any difference to us who gets Hitler; and above all things we have to avoid giving offense to Stalin."

II

So they were back at the Red Marshal again, and stayed there. "We are all very much puzzled about it," explained F. D. R. "We made what we thought were clear and explicit agreements at Yalta; but apparently it is as you said, words don't mean the same thing to the Russians as they mean to us. There has been a series of actions over a period of two months which seems to us to indicate that they are paying no attention to what was supposed to be settled at Yalta. I thought I had won Stalin's trust, but now it appears that I'm mistaken."

"It is hard for Stalin to trust anybody in the world, Governor. You must realize that he has been a conspirator from his youth. He grew up in a movement that was outlawed, and he always knew that the Tsarist police were sending spies and provocateurs to burrow into his party and betray it. He had a few friends that he trusted, but even some of these turned traitor—or changed their minds, which was the same thing from Stalin's point of view. The moment they came in sight of power the internal struggle began, and the only way he has been able to hold power has been by liquidating everybody who set up ideas contrary to his own. It is hard for an American to comprehend the suspiciousness which has been molded into the Russian character by ages and ages of despotism—so far back that I guess there never was anything else."

"And yet we have to live in the world with them, and have to come to some sort of understanding."

"Of course, Governor. I have the belief that you can do more with Stalin than anybody else in what he calls the capitalist world."

"Our agents in Italy have been carrying on discussions with some of the German military men who are sick of their Führer and want to surrender. Of course those discussions have to be secret, or these Germans would be taken out and filled with lead. What possible harm can it do to Stalin if we save some thousands of American lives and release our troops to come north and go at the Germans? But he got wind of the procedure and sent me a red-hot telegram impugning the good faith of my advisers. I sent him an equally hot reply; but I realize that what is needed in this situation is not heat but light; a cool head and a clear vision."

"Yes, Governor; you need somebody in Moscow who understands Stalin and his language—I don't mean his Russian language but his revolutionary language. Also, somebody who understands the New Deal and can explain to Stalin what that means to the future of the world. You may have to do it yourself."

"I can't possibly go to meet him again at present. I came here to rest and accumulate a little strength for the San Francisco Conference that I hope will establish the United Nations. That is to be the keystone of the arch I am building, and without it all the rest will be rubble. That meeting is just two weeks off, and it is important that the Russians should come there in a mood of co-operation and not of suspicion and fear. We are not setting any trap for them; we are trying to build a world in which all the nations, great and small, can be left in freedom, each to work out its destiny in its own way."

"Yes indeed; but suppose that isn't what Stalin wants. Maybe he wants to compel the other nations, at least those near him, to abolish capitalism and capitalists and come into a Communist system."

"If he wants that, Lanny, it can mean only another world war. What I hope to do is to persuade him that if he will let the free nations alone, their people will find their own solution to their problems. If they want a Socialist state, surely I have no desire to stop them; only let them get it by the democratic process and not by repression and dictatorship."

"What you are asking, Governor, is that Stalin shall cease to be a Leninist and become a Kautskyist, or a Blumite, or shall we say a Norman-Thomasite? But Stalin hates the very names of these men; he calls them Social Fascists and teaches his people to liquidate them."

"You think the problem is hopeless then?"

"I don't say that. Lenin was always ready to shift his party line—he set up the NEP, you remember. And Stalin is his disciple; Stalin was ready to make deals with Hitler, and even with Hirohito. He will make a deal with you, for the time being—until his industry has recovered. It might even be that he would make one with you and mean it, provided you could convince him that you were actually going to unhorse your economic royalists. Wall Street is his real enemy, and he knows it well." Lanny paused for a moment and then asked, "Why don't you send Harry Hopkins?"

"In the first place I need Harry in San Francisco; he is at the Mayo Clinic resting up for the ordeal, as I am. If I ordered him to Russia, I should feel that it was a death sentence. The poor fellow hangs onto life with his teeth and toenails."

An alarming idea had come into the P.A.'s mind. "You're not planning to send *me!*" he exclaimed.

"Why not, Lanny?"

"I'm not equal to a job of that size."

"I have thousands of men doing jobs they aren't equal to. They just have to brace themselves and become equal. You have the health and the time. You know Stalin, and he remembers you—he went out of his way to indicate that. He asked you why you hadn't come again—and now why not come?"

"I would go as your representative?"

"Not to take any action, but to inquire, and explain, and report to me."

"And what am I to say?"

"Say whatever you think may persuade Stalin to trust me and make a trial of real friendship. You understand his ideology and you understand ours. Try to show him that if he will make a real peace and let the democratic countries alone, they will be traveling the road toward social control of industry, and may surprise him by the speed with which they move. I can surely answer for the next four years. Believe you me, the economic royalists are not going to be running the U.S.A. while I am alive."

III

Of course Lanny had to say yes; he had never said no to Roosevelt in the eight years they had been working together. He would diligently bone up on the problems of the peace settlement, the control of Germany and Japan, and of capitalism and Communism in a constantly shrinking world. He would retrace the long flying route to Sevastopol, and from there to Moscow. He would sit in the Kremlin room, oval-shaped, with white oak paneling and a vaulted ceiling; he would summon all the tact and knowledge of human nature he had acquired in his forty-five years; he would gaze into the heavy-lidded eyes of the Georgian dictator, solemnly puffing on his pipe; he would pause while the bespectacled young translator Pavlov put the words into Russian. It would be a slow process and would give Lanny time to shape each sentence in his mind. He would do it conscientiously, hoping that some well-chosen word might be the means of averting the greatest calamity that had yet befallen the unhappy human race.

The Boss said, "My first thought was to send you to Washington and arrange for the striped-pants boys to give you a briefing; but I decided against that for several reasons. They are not at all pleased with my idea of sending personal representatives; they take it as a sign that I am not entirely satisfied with their routine, and in that I am sorry to say they are correct. Also, I am afraid the newspaper fellows might get on your trail. I want this to be strictly between us two."

"Of course, Governor."

"You understand, you are not to make any decisions, not even any proposals. What I want you to do, or try to do, is to explain our country to Stalin. Make him realize our intense desire for good faith and good feeling between the two countries. Make him understand the seriousness with which we take our agreements, and that we intend to follow them, not merely to the letter but in the spirit. We have been his allies in this war, and we want to be his friends in the peace. Tell him I have sent you for that purpose and that alone: not to complain about particular breaches of faith so much as to re-establish the spirit of friendship in which we met at Teheran and Yalta."

"I understand that perfectly, Governor. I am not well enough informed to go into the details with Stalin."

"You must know about the breaches of our agreements, to deal with them if he brings them up. I will give you confidential documents which you may study on the trip and then destroy before your plane reaches Russian territory. In addition, I will set aside an hour or two tomorrow afternoon, the fore part. I shall be busy with the mail in the morning, and later in the afternoon I have promised to go to a barbecue; one of my friends, a peach grower, is going to make me some of his good Brunswick stew. Do you know what that is?—chicken and corn, with some fixings. In the evening the patients here are putting on a minstrel show for me. A President is not allowed to live entirely as a recluse, you know."

"I can't see you very well as a recluse," replied Lanny, returning the smile.

"There is a Russian lady who comes to paint a portrait of me; she sits and works while I attend to the mail. I'll manage to get rid of her while we have our confidential talk. Shall we say half-past one? I won't invite you to lunch, as there will be other people here, and I don't want any talk about you."

"Of course, Governor."

Roosevelt handed him a sheet of paper and took one himself. "I'll make notes of what I want to tell you, and you make some so that you can be thinking the points over. I have mentioned Italy. Then there is Poland: we had a perfectly clear understanding at Yalta that the Polish people were to choose their own government in free, democratic elections; but the Russians have gone right ahead setting up a Communist regime there. I know their antagonism to the Polish government-in-exile; but it is for the Polish people as a whole to decide what sort of government they want."

"Right," said Lanny.

"We also had the same agreement regarding the Greek people. Now the Russians are sending arms to partisans in the Greek mountains; and if they are to fight Germans, that is fine, but all our information indicates that they are getting ready to fight other Greeks, the existing government."

Lanny hesitated, then decided to speak. "I don't need to travel to Moscow to know what Stalin will say to that; and you might as well give me the answer now. He will say the existing government is a stooge for Winston Churchill, who is trying to set up a puppet king to maintain Greek landlords and capitalists."

"Remind Stalin that I am not Churchill. He knows perfectly well how I have stood between Churchill and himself. I would not let Churchill send our armies into the Balkans, to occupy them and keep Stalin out; but neither do I want to see Stalin keep Churchill out. I want the Greek people to decide what sort of government Greece shall have."

"But suppose the Greek people want to have a civil war?"

"We don't want to let any people have wars. We want to establish an international authority, which will order a free and fair election, and compel people to submit to that decision. That goes for Italy, for Poland, for Greece. It goes also for Iran, where the Russian agents are working now to undermine the British position. We buy oil from Iran, and so do the British. We are perfectly willing to let the Russians buy their fair share. What we don't want is to see an oil war built up between Russia and Britain."

"And don't forget Turkey and the Dardanelles."

"So far they haven't brought that up; but we are informed that Russian agents are stirring up the Kurds—which is a way of making a civil war in Turkey. In short, Lanny, the present Russian government is coming to look more and more like the old Russian government, with exactly the same aims the tsars had—warm-water ports and all the rest. We thought they had dropped their old national anthem."

"Yes, but their new one says: 'The international party shall be the human race.'"

"Our answer is, if they mean to be human, let them come into the United Nations Organization and make provisions for the settlement of international disputes by negotiation and arbitration. What we fear is that inhuman part of the race which aims to take what it wants by force and fraud."

IV

Lanny had always been careful never to overstay his time with this overburdened man. Now he saw exhaustion in the gray face, and several times he had noticed that the jaw quivered, and had turned his eyes away to avoid embarrassing his host. He said, "All right, Governor. You have given me enough to think over till tomorrow. Shall I go now and let you get your sleep? You have my promise, I will take the mission and do my best."

"Be assured," replied the President, "I shall give great weight to what you tell me. I have many friends, but only a few who can say that they have never asked me for anything." He paused, and then added, "I lost one of my closest friends on the trip back from Yalta. I suppose you heard that Pa Watson died on the *Quincy* soon after you left us."

"I read it, and I knew what a loss it would be to you."

"A great sorrow. He had a cerebral hemorrhage, a terrible thing. It strikes like lightning, and the doctors can neither foresee it nor do anything when it comes."

"Take care of yourself," Lanny said, and put all his heart into the words. "Get your full sleep now."

"You talk like Doctor Mac," said F. D. R., smiling again. "He'd give me a terrible scolding if he knew about this conference. I promised him I'd have none here."

The two exchanged a warm handclasp, and Lanny went out.

V

A storm had come up, and he was driven back to the hotel through rain. Baker said, "The Chief looks bad," and Lanny replied, "He carries a heavy load."

That was all; he went up to his room, undressed, and lay on the bed, thinking hard about the load that had been transferred to his shoulders. He felt no pride in the honor that had been done him; only fear that he would not be equal to the duty. Perhaps no man could be equal to it; perhaps it was a task beyond anyone's power. Perhaps those who ruled the world were not ready for order and justice and peace. Perhaps too many of them wanted to have their own way, cost what it might. Perhaps there were too many Hitlers, big and little, loose in the world.

Lanny slept over the problem, and in the morning, the rain having stopped, he went for a long walk among the peach orchards of Georgia, now in fresh pale green, and the pine forests, always a dark green. He thought as hard as he ever had in his life, and his decision was that he dared not spare this man of many cares but must put the painful truth before him. To go on this mission and come back and report defeat, or doubt of success, would be humiliating, but Lanny was not moved by fear of that. The point was not to go blindly or to let Roosevelt send him blindly. On that long walk Lanny prepared a speech which it was his painful duty to make:

"Governor, if Stalin were to send you a confidential emissary and tell you that in his opinion the principal factor creating the danger of another world war was American big business with its search for raw materials all over the world and for markets for its finished products—what would you answer? You would say that you doubt it, and that even if it were so, there is nothing you could do about it. Private enterprise, as we call it, is our way of life and of doing business with the rest of the world; our whole economic system its committed to it; our people, all but a small minority, believe in it and intend to maintain it. You are President of the United States and head of the Democratic party, but you are not omnipotent, and you could not change America from a capitalist to a co-operative economy even if you wanted to. That is what you would say, is it not, Governor?"

So Lanny asked in his imagination, and his great friend nodded assent. The discourse continued:

"If Stalin really talks straight to me, if we ever get down to brass tacks, he will tell me that the situation is the same in his case. His is a revolutionary country, and his party is committed to abolishing the capitalist economy and all its ways. Stalin is not alone, he is one drop of water in a gigantic rolling wave. He has helped to train millions of young Russians, a whole generation of them, to believe in Communism and to hate and fear capitalism. If I, the plausible and friendly Lanny Budd, were to succeed in persuading him to accept Kautskyism, or Blumism, or Norman-Thomasism, how much success would he have in persuading the thirteen devotees in the Politburo? How much success would *they* have with the army of fanatics they have trained and sent out to every country of the world, and who now see their hour at hand, the people awake and eager for change, asking only for leadership. 'Arise, ye pris'ners of starvation; arise, ye wretched of the earth!' Stalin would say to me the same thing that you, Governor, have said: 'I don't want to do it, and if I did want to, I haven't the power. I am Marshal of the Soviet Union and head of the Communist party of the Soviet Union, but I am not all-powerful.'"

"But," countered Roosevelt in Lanny's imaginary conversation, "does that mean that he has to give pledges and then break them?"

"For the answer to that," said the P.A., "you have to consult the works of Lenin, who told his disciples that everything was right that furthered the cause of the proletarian revolution, and that Communists must be prepared to lie and cheat for the cause."

VI

Lanny lunched at the hotel and then went for a stroll. He had arranged to meet Baker on the road, to avoid attracting the attention of any of the "newspaper fellows." Lanny had diligently studied his notes, and now went over in his mind the sentences he meant to speak; it was almost as important to get them right with Roosevelt as it would be with Stalin. Halfway to Pine Mountain he met Baker and got into his car; they drove slowly, so as not to arrive too soon. Baker spoke of the war news; the Germans were really on the run now, and would they give up? Lanny gave his opinion that Hitler would never give up—they would have to fight their way into his house. All Americans were asking one another questions like that. Americans wanted the war over; they fought hard, but they didn't like to fight. General Patton was unique in his enjoyment of that activity.

They parked in the wide driveway in front of the Little White House. Lanny, in uniform, rated a salute from the guards. Baker led the way and Lanny followed. In the entrance hall Baker hung up his hat and Lanny his cap; they went into the ample study, and one swift glance told them there was something wrong. Three ladies sat on the far side of the room on a couch, the Russian painter and two cousins of the President; they were silent, staring before them, seeming not to see the new entrants. The latter went into the anteroom of the President's bedroom. Near the study door were three other persons, Reilly, Grace Tully, the President's confidential secretary, and Hassett, who had charge of documents; they too were behaving in the same strange way. Nobody greeted them—only stared.

The two halted of course. "What is it?" Baker asked in a low voice, and Reilly answered, "The Boss is ill."

Then Baker, "Serious?"

"He was unconscious."

"Who is with him?"

"Doctor Bruenn has just come."

Baker signed Lanny to a seat and took one beside him. There was nothing they could do or say; they just had to wait. From the open door of the President's bedroom came sounds of heavy breathing. They followed the sounds, and never took their eyes off the doorway.

The two most agonizing hours of Lanny Budd's life followed. It was like falling into a black abyss, endlessly falling, as if to the center of the earth, or into hell itself. Fear grew upon him; sometimes despair, but very seldom hope. Those words the President had spoken echoed in his brain: "...a cerebral hemorrhage...a terrible thing...it strikes like lightning, and the doctors can neither foresee it nor do anything when it comes." Were they words of prescience, words of doom? The President had known his own condition, and Lanny had known it too. He didn't see how anybody could have looked at that exhausted man and failed to know.

He had given his life for the cause he was trying to serve—just as surely as any man who went into battle. He was trying to save his country and the world. Rightly or wrongly, he had believed that no other man could do it. There might be others who had the knowledge, the understanding; but who else had the prestige, the political skill? Who else knew how to manage bullheaded and recalcitrant men? Who else was known to the people of the whole world and trusted as their friend? F. D. R. had told Lanny that he was going to San Francisco to make the speech of his life; he was going to establish the United Nations Organization—he had chosen the name for it himself. He had said that if he did not succeed in this, everything else he had done would be rubble. And now, if he were to die, what a tragedy for mankind, the blackest in the history of the world!

Lanny's grief and horror had nothing to do with his personal self and fortunes. The lightning stroke would reduce him to a nobody, but he didn't mind that; he had no craving for prominence or glory. He didn't mind if his trip to see Stalin was knocked on the head; he didn't really want to go, he didn't have any real hope of success. He was prepared to take a plane ride of some fifteen thousand miles just to oblige his great friend. He would have a talk with the Red Marshal, and the Marshal would be polite, even affable, as he had been at Yalta; but when it was over, would it mean a thing? Stalin is a *nom de guerre*, and means steel; you could talk to steel ever so politely, but you couldn't change the shape of it—except if you melted it in the white-hot furnace of war.

VII

There is a belief, widely held, that a drowning man reviews in his mind all the events of his life; time is abolished, and a year happens in a second, as in dreams. With Lanny there was no need of such speed; he had nothing to do. He didn't wish to go out, and he didn't consider it decorous to get up and look through the open doorway. He recalled his meetings with this great man of history, over a period of almost eight years; he saw in his mind the different places: the White House, the Hyde Park mansion, "Shangri La" in the Catoctin Mountains of Maryland; more recently Casablanca and Marrakech, Yalta and the cruiser *Quincy*. He reviewed all the errands upon which he had been sent, a score or more, many of them dangerous; he recalled the reports he had sent in, and what the Boss had said about them, always kind things—he was one of the kindest men Lanny had ever known. He could not bear to hurt the feelings of his friends; that was the basis of his weakness as an executive.

Tears started into the P.A.'s eyes again and again. There was no use trying to stop them, he just had to let them flow. He could not summon any hope, search as he would in the corners of his mind. For a young man, for a strong man, yes; but for this gray ghost, this man who had been driving himself and had been driven by his enemies beyond the limits of endurance, no. He had lost consciousness, and he must be staying unconscious, or surely the doctor would have come out and spoken some word of cheer. No, this was one of those lightning strokes, and it had wiped out the best hope of the world.

Baker whispered, "He may pull through." Lanny did not try to answer, for it was not fair to destroy another man's spark of hope. He thought for a moment about this faithful servant, who had carried out so punctiliously every secret order of his employer. He was always on hand, ready for any duty. Many times Lanny had wondered, What life did he have apart from this service? He had never spoken of it; rarely had he spoken of anything but his job. Now he too must see the ruin of everything that had been important in his life.

The Russian painter took her departure, and the two cousins went, presumably, to their rooms. But the three White House employees did not move unless they were called. Lanny stole glances at them; they sat rigid, their eyes closed most of the time. All three were Catholics, and he knew they were praying, perhaps the same prayers. He had done his praying for Roosevelt over a long period; now he confronted the fear that his prayers were vain. This must be death.

A cruel, a terrible thing, a fact of the universe which man confronts with dismay, and for which he makes up whatever explanations and excuses he can find. For a great and good man like this it seemed something monstrous, intolerable. Millions of people, hundreds of millions, were depending upon this man for their happiness, their hope of life. He had labored half a century and more, building a mind, storing it with knowledge, with skills, to fit himself for the task of abolishing strife and establishing justice in the world; then suddenly, in a lightning flash, all that was wiped out of existence. Some little pipe broke in his body, some tiny vein no thicker than a cotton thread; and in that instant his mind ceased to exist, his career was over, his voice was silent, his task abandoned—as he himself had said, "All rubble!"

But was death the end? F. D. R. himself didn't believe it; at any rate he acted as if he didn't. He belonged to St. James' Episcopal Church in Hyde Park and went dutifully on Sundays and said prayers and sang hymns and listened to rituals based upon the certainty that his soul was immortal and that he would meet his friends and loved ones in a hereafter. But did he really believe it? Lanny in his life had met very few persons who acted as if they really believed it. If they did, why the grief, and why the fear of death, the agonized efforts to escape its reaching fingers?

Lanny had tried hard to make up his mind about it. He tried now, sitting here listening to the hoarse breathing of his unconscious friend. Had that consciousness ceased to exist, or had it gone somewhere else, and was Franklin Delano Roosevelt watching from some near or distant place and wishing he could tell his friends not to worry, not to suffer so much about him?

Lanny and his wife were interested in psychic research and had conversed amiably and with curiosity with voices which called themselves spirits of the dead and played the role with verve and conviction. But were they really spirits of the dead? Many people devoutly believed so, and had built a church upon their faith. But in spite of all his good will Lanny could never bring himself to believe that these entities really were what they called themselves. He couldn't explain them, but thought they were products of subconscious work of his own and other living minds. Somehow we were not solitary beings, as we thought ourselves; somehow we were bubbles floating on an ocean of mind stuff; beautiful bubbles, but they burst, and their substance dropped back into the sea of which they were made.

Would the mind stuff of Franklin D. Roosevelt go to make other minds, as the stuff of his body would go to make other bodies? Were thoughts, impulses, aspirations, prayers, the basic stuff of the universe, more real than calcium, magnesium, iron, and the other ninety-odd elements which modern physics had discovered to be nothing but waves? The physicists called them that, without having the least idea what it was that was waving, and the possibility had dawned upon many of them that the waves might be thoughts. Could it be that Franklin D. Roosevelt was only thoughts, and that God had been thinking him?

VIII

A break in the thoughts of Lanny was provided by the arrival of a heart specialist. Dr. Paullin, summoned by phone from Washington, had driven the eighty miles from Atlanta over back-country roads in a little more than an hour. He strode in with his black medical bag, straight into the bedroom, with no more than a nod to the watchers. Hope picked up for a few minutes; surely this esteemed person must be able to do something—or why had he been called? The breathing sounds continued, and while there was life there would be hope. Let the Catholics say their formal prayers, let Lanny pray with his heart and without words. It meant so much to America, so much to the world. Spare this happy thought of yours, dear God, and let him stay with us just a short while longer! Let him be able to send at least a message to the San Francisco Conference, upon which so much depends, which he has called the keystone of his work! Even if somebody else has to write it for him, and all he has to do is to hear it and whisper "OK"!

But it was all in vain. God had other plans. Thy will, not mine, be done! Commander Bruenn, the naval physician who had had charge of the President on this vacation, was making a report over the phone to the White House, and Lanny heard the dread words, "massive inter-cerebral hemorrhage." The phone talk was interrupted by a call from the bedroom, and the Commander ran in. The sounds of breathing had stopped, and when he came out he couldn't speak, but just let his head fall on his chest and shook it slowly from side to side.

Then an extraordinary thing happened. That little black Scottie who was the President's adoring friend, who lay by his chair or his bed, followed his wheel chair, leaped into the car ahead of him, and had even been a part of his political campaign half a year back—Fala had been lying out of the way under the bed all the time, still as a mouse, and now suddenly he leaped up and let out the most awful howl that Lanny

had ever heard in this world. He didn't stop; it was one howl after another, and he rushed like a mad thing out of the room, across the study,
and into the screen door; he crashed it open, and went, still screaming,
out into the woods.

That was the end for one silent watcher; he couldn't stand any more.
Sobs convulsed him, and he got up and went out, following the dog. He
didn't see Fala; he walked along a forest path, and when he could walk
no more he sat down on the pine needles and wept unashamedly.

IX

Lanny did not go back to that house of mourning. No one needed
him there; they all had their duties and would do them, in death as in
life. Mrs. Roosevelt was in Washington. With the courage and calm
which made her a great woman, she excused herself from the charity
function she was attending, put on a black dress, and was flown to the
bedside of the man she had married forty years before and to whom
she had borne four sons and a daughter. There would be public ceremonies, necessary in the death as well as the life of a public man. In all
this Lanny would have no part; he was no longer a presidential agent,
but a mere complimentary colonel, of whom there were hundreds in the
State of Georgia, and thousands in Washington and New York. The
Boss had trained him to keep out of the public eye, and if the inquisi-
tive newspapermen should ask, "Who was that officer?" the reply would
be, "Just a friend of the family."

Lanny walked down to the village. He was so distracted, so full of
despair, that he didn't know what he would do or where he would go.
For eight years he had been a satellite of F. D. R., revolving about him;
now suddenly there was no F. D. R., and Lanny was an asteroid or something, wandering alone through space. He took the night train north,
and, lying in a Pullman berth, he contemplated his destiny and tried to
imagine what the world would be like without that genial yet commanding presence in the White House. It was truly impossible for him
to picture politics, government, or the war without Roosevelt.

In Washington he learned from the papers that most of the world felt
just as he did; the world was dazed and lost. The news had gone everywhere in a few seconds, by telephone, telegraph, and radio, and the grief
was like nothing that had been in the world before. Reports kept coming
in from all over; it was a universal chorus. People walked the streets,
sobbing; taxicab drivers pulled up at the curb and sat with tears in their
eyes; barbers left their customers half shaven because they could not

control the shaking of their hands. Night clubs were closed, restaurants were darkened. People put on mourning as if for a relative; they went about downcast, unsmiling. The radio was one incessant dirge. It was a spontaneous, unrehearsed religious ceremony, in which all took part and by which all were awed. People who hated Roosevelt—had there been people who hated him?—fell silent even among their own groups.

Abraham Lincoln had been mourned like that all over the North; but this was the first time in history that a man had been mourned like that all over the world. For days the stories kept coming in by radio and cable. For the first time in history the British House of Commons adjourned out of respect for an American; Lloyd's rang the famous Lutine Bell. Over the Kremlin was raised the black-fringed red banner of mourning, hitherto sacred to the Soviet Union's own greatest. Italy declared three days of national mourning. All the way from Belgrade to Buenos Aires people stopped Americans on the street and poured out their grief in tears. Strangest thing of all, the Japanese radio expressed the people's grief! Roosevelt had vowed the extermination of the Japanese government, and his planes were showering bombs on their cities; yet, somehow, behind their steel-barred barricades, the people of Japan had managed to find out that they had good things to expect from this great-hearted man, and they managed to get their feelings spoken!

X

Eighty-five hours elapsed between the President's death and his interment in Hyde Park, and all that time the national mourning continued. The body was placed in a hearse in Warm Springs and driven slowly past the Foundation Building, with the crippled children in their wheel chairs watching the marching troops and listening to the muffled drums; the minstrel show they had been rehearsing would never be given. At the station the coffin was placed in the last car of the funeral train, the car brilliantly lighted so that the people could see it; the train went slowly, and the country people came from many miles, lining the tracks; they did not wave, but wept, and many fell on their knees; at all the stations great crowds assembled to pay the last futile tribute to the leader they loved.

In Washington, Lanny was one of that vast throng which lined the streets, the men bareheaded and both men and women in tears. They watched the caisson with its black-draped coffin, drawn by six white horses, proceeding slowly up Pennsylvania Avenue, where six months ago Lanny had stood in the rain to see the newly re-elected President riding in an open car and waving gaily to the shouting throngs. In the White House a private service was held, attended by the family and by Washington's great. The Episcopal bishop, at Mrs. Roosevelt's request, quoted the dead man's words: "The only thing we have to fear is fear itself." That was what he would have wished the people to remember and put into action.

Then the funeral train moved on to Hyde Park on the Hudson, the home where Franklin Roosevelt had been born and had lived his happiest years. It was Sunday morning, and the sun shone bright; violets and apple trees were in bloom. There was a place which Franklin himself had set aside for his grave, a hemlock-bordered space between the mansion and the new library he had built to house the papers and souvenirs of his life. An honor guard of six hundred West Point cadets attended, and a battery of guns behind the garden fired a salute of twenty-one guns. With the band playing Chopin's funeral march, the caisson rolled slowly into the garden. By the grave stood Mrs. Roosevelt, her daughter, and one of her sons—the others being far away at the wars.

The casket was lowered, and the Episcopal service was read a second time. Again at Mrs. Roosevelt's request, the rector of the local church read one of the President's favorite biblical passages, from the First Epistle of Paul to the Corinthians: "For now we see through a glass, darkly; but then face to face: now I know in part; but then shall I know even as also I am known. And now abideth faith, hope, and charity, these three; but the greatest of these is charity." Out of such words the Christian religion had been made, and by them the character and career of Franklin D. Roosevelt had been shaped.

12

Gifts of an Enemy

I

THE United States of America had a new President. He succeeded automatically, the moment the old President died, and two or three hours later he took the oath of office, administered by the Chief Justice of the

Supreme Court. Everybody in the country, indeed everybody in the conscious world, wondered what kind of man he was and what sort of President he would make.

His name was Harry S Truman and he came from a small town in Missouri. He had been brought up on a small farm and, like many other Presidents, he had had to make his own way in the world. In World War I he had risen to be a captain of artillery. Then he had gone into the haberdashery business and failed. He had been made a district judge, and the boss of a very corrupt political machine had picked him as Democratic candidate for United States senator. Elected, he had been made chairman of a committee to investigate frauds in war production, and the success he had made at this job had caused him to be singled out for the vice-presidential nomination. By American tradition such candidates are chosen because they come from a different part of the country from the presidential candidate, and because they haven't made too many enemies in the political pulling and hauling.

Everybody agreed that Harry Truman was personally honest. He was a kindly and likable man, folksy and unpretentious. He liked to play poker with the boys, and he could play the "Missouri Waltz" on the piano, an unusual cultural attainment. He had had no executive training and possessed little knowledge of international affairs. Everybody agreed that he was now having a dreadful burden dumped onto his shoulders; he was obviously frightened, and people were sorry for him and wanted to help him. In the country's public life a new "Era of Good Feeling" was promised.

Like most Americans, Lanny Budd had never seen this new man and had to learn about him from newspapers and radio. His voice had a flat, hard tone and his Middlewestern accent suggested crudity; a contrast with the golden voice to which the country had become accustomed. The newspapermen and politicians who knew Harry Truman seemed to be at one in the idea that while he had been elected as a New Dealer, he wasn't one at heart; he was a mild man, anxious to please everybody and disposed to let things stay as they were. Of course that might be wishful thinking on the part of some; but the impression seemed so widespread that Lanny's heart sank deeper and deeper with each day's reading. The war had forced the government into an enormous program of production for use; and now would Lanny have to witness the same spectacle that had tormented his young soul after World War I, seeing these magnificent plants turned over to the service of private greed at a price of ten cents on the dollar or less?

Apparently all Big Business was counting upon that. In California a

Republican congressman made a speech before the Chamber of Commerce of his home town. With the body of Franklin Roosevelt not yet underground, this congressman declared that he knew Harry Truman, and that Truman would "go definitely to the right." This statement was considered to be of interest, not merely to Americans, but also to people abroad; it was cabled to London, and a couple of days later Lanny received a cablegram from his friend Rick. When properly paragraphed and punctuated it turned out to be some verses:

> The shepherd is dead, and the sheep
>   Wander alone in the hills;
> The night comes on, the black night,
>   And the heart with terror fills.
>
> The wolves slink in the shadows,
>   They who must be fed;
> Their breath is hot and panting,
>   They know that the shepherd is dead.
>
> Oh, sorrow beyond telling!
> Oh, sheep that none can save!
> Oh, heartbreak of the future!
> O shepherd, speak from the grave!

Lanny thought that these verses said something to the American people. There would be no use submitting them to any of the big-circulation magazines, for, one and all, their proprietors hated to pay income taxes and would surely not consent to refer to their two, three, or four million subscribers as sheep. In New York were several small-circulation magazines which called themselves liberal or progressive, and Lanny submitted the verses to them. The effort brought polite rejection slips, and increased the depression in the soul of a former presidential agent. These magazines supported the New Deal on political and economic issues, but when it came to cultural matters, to drama and art, to literature and especially poetry, their editors were victims of intellectual snobbery, some of it age-old and some ultramodern. If the product contained anything in which the ordinary man could find meaning, that automatically stamped it as beneath editorial notice. Praise was reserved for works which were so subtle, obscure, or eccentric that only a chosen few could form any idea what they were about. If you asked the editors, you would find that no two of them could agree what the work in question meant, and it was a toss-up whether the creator of the work thought that he knew, or was just slinging paint or words in a mood of hilarity.

II

All Lanny Budd's magic was dead, or dying. No longer was he a privileged character, no longer was the path made smooth before his feet. They knew him at the Mayflower Hotel and consented to give him a bed to sleep in, but there would be two other men in the room and he would be limited to five days. Perhaps they thought he had something to do with the funeral; he could guess from their manner that after it he would have to present new credentials, fresh evidence of being a VGDIP. Sooner or later it would be that way with all the New Dealers.

He stayed on in Washington because he had no other place to go. He wanted time to think and to decide what to do with the rest of his life. He walked the streets of this grief-stricken city, and saw how, after the funeral, people dried their tears and resumed their daily tasks. The King was dead, long live the King—the word "long" meaning three years and nine months, the time which Harry Truman would have to serve. Lanny walked by the White House, where people stood gazing through the iron fence, remembering the old and perhaps hoping to get a glimpse of the new.

Lanny could have got an introduction and gone in and told the new King what he had done for the old. But he knew that Truman would be swamped with problems and harassed by fears, and would be forced to use the help of persons he already knew. The trip to Stalin was off, and the job of being a friend to the great was done forever. Charlie Alston happened to be somewhere out West and when he came back would find that he too was a "has been." Harry the Hop would get the rest he so desperately needed, and the "social door" of the White House would open for a new set of favorites, mostly from Missouri.

Lanny was soon to have that million dollars, and perhaps it was his duty to settle down to the problem of how he meant to spend it. He went over the idea in his mind but found that he could not get up the courage. His mind was haunted by grief; this bereavement was the most tragic thing that had ever happened to him, and he couldn't bring himself to face the fact that he would never see that great friend, never hear his voice again. Tears would well into his eyes unexpectedly, from despair deeply buried in his soul. He was restless and distracted; he couldn't settle down to any desk job, he couldn't get up any interest in the idea of changing the world—at least not until he knew definitely what part Harry Truman was going to play in it.

An active job was what he wanted, and he found his thoughts turning to Europe. If he couldn't go to Moscow, at least he could go to Paris, and later to Berlin. If he couldn't be a presidential agent, at least he could stay an assimilated colonel and carry out some of the earlier tasks his Boss had assigned to him. He could keep on the move and distract his mind. Laurel was somewhere in Germany, and he could join her; he could still have a roving commission, and use it to try to run away from his sorrow.

III

He telephoned Robbie. No use talking to him about grief, for Robbie, while outwardly polite and considerate, would in his heart be vastly relieved at having got rid of his worst enemy. A wonderful thought, that there might be in the White House a man who could be persuaded to reduce taxes and let Robbie refuse to raise wages! The less the son probed into the father's mind on the subject of F. D. R., the better for both of them.

Lanny, equally polite and considerate, said that he was studying paintings in the National Gallery and would Robbie please forward his mail. There was a cablegram, and Lanny said, "Open it and read it to me." It was from Laurel: "Courage. Remember we still have each other. Come soon." Lanny had a hard time keeping his voice from choking. He asked about the health of the baby and Frances, and then said, "My love to everybody," and hung up.

Yes, the place for him was Germany. He could still be somebody there, still watch events and perhaps influence them ever so slightly. He could see this war to its end, at least as far as Europe was concerned, and by that time he might have clearer ideas about how to prevent the next war. He went to see the Monuments people in Washington and told them his story; he was inclined to operate under their auspices, because theirs was the subject he knew best. They were glad to have his report and his promise of help.

He went to Alsos and introduced himself; they had heard good reports of him and wanted him in their department. Art works would keep, they argued, but scientific secrets might shorten the war with Japan by a year. He went also to General Donovan, the head of OSS, who knew most about what Lanny had done for F. D. R., and was

pleased to give him credentials. The genial Irish-American lawyer
wanted Lanny to pose as a Nazi again and find out about the plans for
the Alpine Redoubt, and for activities of the "werewolves"! Lanny
had to say no; he no longer had any faith in his ability to pose as a
Nazi. He would interview important Germans behind the American
lines.

He had his choice of routes and preferred the northern this time;
he wanted a day in New York and one in London. Hansi and Bess were
giving a concert that night, and Lanny got there in time for it. Afterward they sat in a hotel room, talking for hours; for the first time
Lanny was free to tell what he had been doing for Roosevelt and what
he thought of him. To Hansi the dead President was a hero-statesman,
for Bess he was a bourgeois politician, admittedly a cut above the
others. She politely refrained from arguing, however; all three of them
wanted the Nazis licked, and all approved the salvage of art works, so
they thought on these things. ("Finally, brethren, whatsoever things
are true, whatsoever things are honest, whatsoever things are just,
whatsoever things are lovely, whatsoever things are of good report
. . . think on these things.")

Hansi mentioned that his nephew, Freddi junior, had had his heart's
desire and been shipped overseas. Being tall, he had misrepresented his
age, volunteered, and taken the stiff training of a private soldier. Now
he was what had been called a "replacement," but the Army had decided that the word sounded suggestive of death and destruction, so
he was a "reinforcement." His grandfather, Johannes Robin, had
pulled wires and got him into the Seventh Army. Young Freddi had it
as a dream of his life to be in at the capture of Dachau and perhaps
meet some survivors who had known his father. Lanny said with a
smile, "Maybe I can take him there." He made note of the lad's unit
and promised to look him up if possible.

I V

Next morning Lanny dictated business letters, had a talk with Zoltan,
then took a taxi to Mitchel Field, from which he took off in a passenger plane for Gander Lake in Newfoundland: a place of many memories for the onetime P.A., including a strange psychic experience to
which he had paid no heed. Amazing how the place had grown in three
or four years; it was now one of the great airports of the world,
through which the giant bombers from American factories were
streaming to the battlefronts.

Lanny's plane stopped only for refueling, then set out over those cold waters where he had come so near to losing his life. This time the weather was foggy but quiet, and they did not stop at Greenland but went on to Iceland, that strange country of glaciers and hot springs. Here was another immense field, where unwanted Americans were being carefully polite to the natives. Since the Icelanders didn't want to be taken permanently by Nazis they had to be taken temporarily by Americans, and both sides had to make the best of the trying situation. Geography was to blame.

Again the plane was refueled and flew to another great base, near the little village of Prestwick, Scotland, celebrated as the birthplace of Britain's greatest golfer. From there you could take a train to London, or, if you were in a hurry, you could be flown to a nearer airfield. Lanny had cabled to Sir Eric Vivian Pomeroy-Nielson, Baronet—you had to give full names when you cabled in wartime and pay for every word. Now he telephoned and learned that the cablegram had not yet arrived. Rick and Nina, delighted, would take the first train for London and meet him at the Savoy; he was no longer a secret agent, meeting his friends clandestinely, but a perfectly respectable assimiliated colonel, wearing a uniform but without insignia.

"What friends thou hast and their adoption tried, grapple them to thy heart with hooks of steel." Some of the commentators make it "hoops," but in either case it is sound advice, and Lanny had followed it. Thirty-two years had passed since the baronet's son and the grandson of Budd Gunmakers had met at the Dalcroze dancing school at Hellerau, near Dresden, and there had been few of these years when they had not met at least once. In the beginning Rick had been a tall dark-haired lad, intense but reserved, and very positive in his views; being a year or two older than Lanny, he had taken charge of Lanny's thinking. Now he was still tall and slender, his hair turning gray, his face thin and lined. He wore a steel brace and walked with a limp because he had a bad knee, sustained in an airplane crash while fighting over France in World War I.

Ever since the Paris Peace Conference of 1919 Lanny had been quietly passing inside information to this English friend, who had been causing it to be published in the Socialist and Labor press of his country, from which sooner or later it found its way to the thinking world. If there were any political or social questions on which these two differed, Lanny had never found out about them. The threads of their beliefs had been so woven together that neither could have said who had contributed the greater quantity or the better quality.

Nina, whom Rick had married during World War I, was now a grandmother, but didn't look it. A gentle quiet little body, she would sit and listen while the masterful males expounded their ideas; then, unexpectedly, she would make some remark that would surprise them by its pungency. How much *she* had contributed to her husband's clear-sightedness would have been another problem for a psychologist.

V

They wanted to talk, first about Roosevelt and then about Truman. Rick had meant every word of his verses, and more; it was a tragedy without parallel in history; like seeing the driver of a team of wild horses drop dead while they were at full gallop. Lanny said, "*Trio* of wild horses," and told his friend what F. D. R. had said at their first meeting, comparing himself to the driver of a Russian troika. His three horses were the Southern Democrats, a whole generation behind the rest of the country in their thinking; the hierarchy of the Catholic Church in the great cities, such as New York, Boston, Chicago, and Los Angeles; and finally, the labor unions and their "intellectual" sympathizers. Three of the wildest steeds imaginable, each desiring to travel to a different goal; yet the Democratic party could never win a victory without all three, and it had been Roosevelt's task to keep them in harness and on the highway.

"And now they will fly apart!" exclaimed the Englishman.

Lanny could only say, "I fear so; but I don't think the reactionaries, if they come back, will dare repeal more than a small part of the New Deal. That's the way America travels, two steps forward and one step back."

"It's not only a question of your domestic affairs, Lanny; it's a question of saving Europe and Asia from Bolshevism. The only way it can be done is by American support to the democratic Socialists everywhere; and what is your Harry Truman going to make of that problem?"

"God knows," Lanny was forced to reply. "I am afraid you Englishmen will have to teach him, and teach the rest of America. I mention the subject now and then to one of our brass hats, and he looks at me hard, trying to make up his mind whether I am a secret Communist agent or just a harmless nut."

That brought them to the subject of the Chattersworth bequest and what Lanny was going to do. He had written his friend long letters about it and now he said, "Whatever plan we choose, whether it's a newspaper or a magazine, or pamphlets and books, you are to come and be the editor, the boss."

Rick answered gravely, "I couldn't do that. You know I have agreed to stand for Parliament for the Labour party."

"Yes, Rick, and I know how much that would mean to you and how much you could accomplish. But there are many who could serve competently in Parliament, while there's only one man who can help me with this big job."

"It would be absurd for me to come to America and give advice to your people. I have never even been in the country."

"If we have any idea of preventing the next war we shall have to reach the entire world, and not just America. It isn't in any sense a local job. And what legwork has to be done I can do for you; I am good at meeting people and picking up information, but I'm no good at writing and I don't know the first thing about editing. I know you and your outlook on world affairs. We'd never have to argue about policy; we did all that thirty years ago."

Rick said, "I'd feel like a deserter if I quit my job here. We have a real chance to carry the country at the elections which must come as soon as this show is over."

"It's all one job," argued Lanny, "whether you are doing it in London or New York. As a matter of fact, I have the idea that we should have our office in some small place, where rents would be cheaper and labor easier to get. Ours is a long-term job and not spot-news journalism."

"I see you've been thinking about it," said the Englishman, still with the serious look upon his thin nervous face. "Have you invented any way to get me out of my agreement with the Labour chaps?"

"Indeed yes. Let Alfy take the job."

"Alfy!"

"He's young and he doesn't have your handicap of lameness. What I'm offering you is a desk job, suitable for a man of middle years. Cultivating a constituency would wear you to skin and bones. Alfy knows the movement, and he has a fine record, flying first for Spain and then for Britain. The fact that Franco threw him into a dungeon ought to be good for several thousand votes. Take him around and introduce him, hear him talk a few times and coach him. Tell your committee that you aren't physically equal to the job and get them used to Alfy."

Rick smiled for the first time. "You make it very plausible. But it would be a serious matter for us to pull up stakes and emigrate."

"It won't be a lifetime job. I plan to spend all the money in five years, and I hardly think we'll find an angel to keep us going. Your boys are grown, and you can leave the place to them for a while, or maybe bring one of them with you. We'll pick out some village in New Jersey or Long Island, and find you a one-story bungalow where you and Nina can be Darby and Joan."

"What do you say, Joan?" inquired "Darby."

"I say we'll think it over," she replied. "We'll let you know." And so they left it.

VI

It was Lanny's duty to telephone to Irma Barnes Masterson, Countess of Wickthorpe, his onetime wife, and tell how their fifteen-year-old daughter was faring at Newcastle. It was an entirely good report; she was doing well at school, and was happy with all her associates. Irma told her former husband that there had not been a V-bomb on Britain for nearly a month, and Lanny said, "I think that is probably all over; if your troops haven't got the last of the launching sites they must be close to them."

"Then, Lanny, you are going to bring the child home to me! You promised!"

"Surely not until the end of the school year," he protested. "She is doing well and it would be a shame to interrupt her." He added on the spur of the moment, "Why don't you and Ceddy go over and pay her a visit? The last of the U-boats will be out of the seas before long; and you would get a royal reception. You are still a Budd-Erling stock-holder, I suppose, and it should interest you to see where the money is coming from."

"I'll propose it to Ceddy," she answered. "He thinks about nothing but his crops these days." His lordship had come pretty close to trea-son, as Lanny knew, because of his sympathy with Nazi ideas. Did his conscience trouble him, or was he just trying to square himself with his neighbors by turning his great estate into a model agricultural project?

Lanny didn't offer to come out to the Castle and make a fuller re-port. He had a good excuse, that he was flying to Paris that afternoon. He dutifully inquired about the health of his former mother-in-law and about Irma's two little boys, the Viscount and the Honorable; they had pink cheeks and golden hair like the earl, their father—only his hair, alas, was touched with gray.

"He says that England is going to be a poor country when this war is over," remarked the daughter of a Chicago traction king.

Lanny couldn't restrain a chuckle. "Save your money, old dear," he said. "Robbie is expecting the government to begin canceling orders any day now."

"Oh, surely not!" exclaimed Irma in distress. "Won't they be needed to fight the Japs?"

"Yes, but those in Europe can be flown to the Far East or taken by carriers."

"Oh, putrid!" exclaimed the hostess of the "Wickthorpe set."

VII

When Lanny arrived in Paris, ten days after the death of Roosevelt, Georgie Patton had plunged all the way across Germany and reached the western tip of Czechoslovakia. The Seventh had reached Stuttgart and Nürnberg, the First had reached Leipzig, and the Ninth was spread along the Elbe River. The British were nearing Bremen and Hamburg, the Canadians were all the way up through Holland and close to the German naval base of Emden. A million prisoners had been taken in three weeks. If Germany had not been in the hands of a madman, she would have given up long ago.

It was Lanny's duty to report to the three organizations with which he was to co-operate. He found a letter from Laurel, telling him that she was at Frankfurt; a wonderful thing, they had brought all the art works of the Kaiser Friedrich Museum which had been found in the Merkers mine in Thuringia; they had been two thousand feet underground, in galleries half a mile long. The place was dripping wet, so there was a lot of repairs to be done. Laurel was studying the art works and writing an article about them. "Your cousin Peggy is supervising the inventory," she wrote, and added, "I hope you got my cablegram. I knew you would be heartbroken. I cried a whole night. I doubt if there is a person on our staff who didn't shed tears."

Laurel explained that she was going back to Heidelberg and make that her headquarters because she had a comfortable place in which to write. Lanny joined her, and it was a sad meeting. Stopping only to ask about Baby Lanny, Laurel wanted to hear about Roosevelt's death, and what this change of leadership was going to do to America and the world. Later, of course, she asked about the families and friends he had met; Hansi and Bess, Rick and Nina, Robbie and Frances. And then back to that extraordinary project of a trip to Stalin, and what he would have said and perhaps accomplished if he had taken it!

Laurel told of the sights she had been enjoying in the Reichsbank building in Frankfurt. Imagine, if you could, several hundred of the world's greatest paintings lined up against the wall of one immense room; a polite GI had set them up, one after another, for her examination. Others were boxed and had to be opened for inventory. Leatherbound cases contained the most marvelous etchings she had ever seen. In other rooms were all the Egyptian treasures. Upstairs, in a vault, were priceless gold and silver church vessels looted from Poland.

The old masters from Berlin had brought back poignant memories to Laurel, for she had visited the Kaiser Friedrich Museum in Berlin in the company of a competent art expert who had given her the benefit of his learning. That had been some eight years ago, and she had found the gentleman fully as interesting as the paintings; but she had never thought of the idea of marrying him—or had she? Pinned down, she admitted with a touch of mischief that it was barely possible the idea might have crossed her mind once or twice; but she had thought that he was much too well satisfied with himself. Under her tuition he had greatly improved.

She had foreseen the mood of heartsickness against which he would be struggling. She tried to awaken his interest in an art cache which had just been discovered in the neighborhood of Heidelberg; it included Holbeins, a treasure indeed. An expert had been flown from the Rijksmuseum in Amsterdam to inspect them, and the next day Lanny would meet this gentleman. Later on husband and wife would arrange for a trip farther into Germany—the Army brass had decided that it was safe for ladies now.

VIII

Such were the plans; but plans of mice or men didn't always work out in wartime. Next morning came a call from an Alsos team; they had been informed that Mr. Budd was on the way, and could he make it convenient to come over to their depot and hear about a project of importance? They would send a car if he wished. But Lanny didn't mind walking in the upper town of Heidelberg, with its lovely views of the Neckar valley and hills covered with early spring foliage. He had met this Alsos bunch and liked them; he couldn't deny the argument that their projects came first. *Objets d'art* could be locked up in a Reichsbank and studied later, but German weapons and techniques could be flown to Washington and put to immediate use. Always one had to bear in mind that whatever the Germans had the Japanese might have also, and the Allies had better get ready to counter them.

This time it was a metallurgist from the laboratories of Westinghouse in Pittsburgh. Dr. Allan Bates was his name, and he had just got word that a research man from the Kaiser Wilhelm Institute for Metallurgical Research in Stuttgart had sought refuge in a small village in the Swabian Alps and was believed to have with him priceless records. Dr. Bates wanted some competent man to go with him. Just now the teams were spread all over Western Germany—more than half the land had suddenly been opened up, and everybody was called to several places at once.

Lanny said, "What I don't know about metallurgy would fill all the records in the Stuttgart Institute." But they answered that Dr. Bates had the special knowledge; what Mr. Budd would supply was a knowledge of Germans and how to deal with them. "Please come. It is really a top matter."

Lanny couldn't say no to such a request. So they put him into a jeep and ran him up the winding river valley to Stuttgart, one of the worst-smashed cities he had yet visited. The bombers had been working on it for a couple of years, for it had key industries; their procedure was to smash them, give the Germans time to get them in repair, and then smash again, until the time came when the Germans no longer had either labor or materials for another job. French colonial troops, Algerians and Moroccans, had taken the city.

The scientist proved to be an agreeable companion. He was very short and broad, with a close-cropped black mustache; he had been an acrobat and tumbler, and although he was Lanny's age, he was still ready to take on any youngster who fancied himself as a wrestler. He was waiting with a little Opel car, all packed and ready; a GI was to drive them. Other escort was not thought necessary; the Heinies here in the southwest area knew they were licked, and besides, they had been the least nazified of all the tribe. The unarmed scientists in uniform went where they pleased and were treated as the lords of creation.

A delightful trip up the valley of the Neckar River. Lanny had traveled it once before, in the company of Laurel Creston before their marriage; he had been helping her to escape from the Gestapo, which had seized her trunk in her Berlin pension and surely couldn't have been pleased with her opinions of them and their regime. The art expert had been under great strain then, but now he was having a holiday, or so he thought. He had pleasant company. The scientists of

America were no longer locked up in their narrow specialties but had been rudely forced out into the world; they were thinking hard about politics and economics. Dr. Bates expressed ideas about the future of Germany and how mankind might prevent another cataclysm like this.

IX

The road signs were down, but they had a good map. For some reason the population of this part of Württemberg had chosen to have their towns end in "ingen"; Reutlingen, Ergenzingen, Eutingen, Bieringen, Kietingen, Derendingen, Tübingen, Wurmlingen, Metzingen, Neckartenlingen, Neckartailfingen—the woods were full of them. They came to a small tributary river, the Erms, now running at full flood; they turned southward, into densely wooded mountains. The stream wound and the road wound, up and up. *Auf die Berge will ich steigen!* They came to the summer-resort town called Urach, with its very old Gothic church, and its two hotels on the market place, just as you would have found them in the southern part of the United States. There was the inevitable *Schloss,* and this you wouldn't have found anywhere on the North American continent, which had escaped the age of feudalism.

Even before they got to the center of the town they saw that something was wrong. Groups of men were entering the houses, and there were screams from inside; men came out carrying food and other articles, and at the market place there were crowds and some fighting with sticks and stones. An old, old story of war—pillage and rape. And here suddenly arrived two godlike personages, symbolically clad in power; one tall, one short, but both in spick-and-span uniforms, gazing in stern disapproval at the tumult. This could only be the American Army, come to the rescue. *Gott sei Dank!*

Germans came running, Germans terrified, breathless, with staring eyes. They didn't wait to be asked, but poured out their story. *"Die Arbeiter vom Lager! Sie sind frei!"* The foreign laborers, Russian, Polish, and Czech, who had been brought here as semi-slaves, had broken loose and were pillaging. *"Beschützen Sie uns, General!"* The humble townspeople were sure the strangers must be generals at least, and might be field marshals—who could say?

Lanny said to his companion, "You won't be able to do much work with this going on. They might burn the town."

"It must be stopped," declared the other, and ordered the petitioners, "Bring us one of the officials of your town."

They ran off and presently came back with a stoutish, middle-aged, and evidently educated man. With Germans you didn't argue or persuade; you gave orders. Dr. Bates said, "Go pick out twenty men you know and can trust and bring them to us."

The official hurried away, and Lanny set out to find an educated Frenchman—for apparently the French workers had also been misbehaving. One was brought, and Lanny spoke in his language. With him, too, Americans had authority. Were they not allies and liberators of *la patrie*—two-time liberators? And had not the great General Eisenhower and *le grand Charlie* both demanded order and good behavior? "Go find me twenty Frenchmen who have self-respect and decency."

Presently came the two squads. "*Haben Sie Waffen?*" demanded Bates of the Germans. *Ja, ja,* they had weapons hidden in the Town Hall. "*Vorwärts, marsch!*" commanded the general, field marshal, or maybe admiral. The ex-gymnast commanded the Germans and the art expert commanded the French, and just marching and keeping step made them all a military body, disciplined and obedient to commands. Into the Town Hall and past the *Goldne Saal* which was the town's pride, then upstairs and up a ladder to the attic. Guns and ammunition were passed down, just enough. "Germans will not fight Frenchmen and Frenchmen will not fight Germans," commanded the metallurgist, as sternly as any *Feldwebel*. "*Wir wollen Ordnung in diesem Dorf.*" The son of Budd-Erling echoed, "*Nous voulons de l'ordre dans cette ville.*"

Order in this town! The word was magic. It went everywhere. Lanny marched one way at the head of the French, and Dr. Bates marched another way at the head of the Germans. As a rule commands were sufficient; one or two who replied with insolence felt the physical force of a trained gymnast, and others who had stolen liquor and got drunk were ordered to the *Gefängniss*. In half an hour the rioting was over—and two assimilated officers were in command of a German town, and, oddly enough, a French town also.

X

The two commanders called a town meeting of the Germans and addressed them with paternal authority. This town must have a responsible government, adapted to the new conditions, and excluding all Nazis and Nazi sympathizers. The result was a clamor, and Dr. Bates was unanimously elected *Bürgermeister* of Urach. With stern mien he commanded that all former Nazis should be *hinausgeworfen,* and he appointed new officials who were declared to have been non-political in the evil days that were past.

Lanny acquired the title of *Bürgermeisterstellvertreter* (deputy), and went off to a town meeting in the compound of the easterners. Poor devils, they had been kidnaped outright or lured here by promises of fine treatment—promises which had been shamelessly broken. They had been in effect slaves, and their emaciated condition showed that they had been on short rations for a long time. With the help of translators the American explained that they could not be returned to their homes because no transportation was available until the war was won. In order that this might happen quickly, they must govern themselves and not make it necessary for Lanny to summon American soldiers to keep order. He appointed educated and trustworthy deputies of the various nationalities to run the camp.

Next came the job of bringing all the leaders together and helping them to understand one another. Let all the laborers go back to work in the town's small factories, and let food be collected and fairly divided among them. Let there be a committee to consult and decide such matters; and let both sides pledge their good faith, so that it would not be necessary to call American troops away from their duties in order to preserve order in the Emsthal.

Yes indeed, Lanny Budd was a busy man during those days that he spent in the Swabian Alps! He had no time to visit the Urach *Wasserfall,* or to take more than a glance at the *Goldne Saal* or at the Gothic fountain in the market place. Dr. Bates soon found his scientist, and was busy interviewing him and getting the precious records locked up in the trunk of the car. Lanny discovered an anti-Nazi worker who informed him of a large cache of arms hidden in near-by farm buildings, and these were confiscated and put under guard. After that, the ex-P.A. was occupied in arbitrating and adjudicating, fixing the price of potatoes and bacon, getting multilingual proclamations printed, deciding whether German girls should be allowed to marry foreign laborers—in short, engaging in all the activities which AMG, American Military Government, would be performing in Württemberg for years to come. He hoped he was getting them off to a good start and not establishing too many bad precedents. Certainly he managed to please the population, for when the time for departure came they presented their deliverers with two swords which had been captured from Napoleon's armies and had been among the town's cherished relics for almost a century and a half.

XI

Dr. Bates reported that he had got material of great importance, and he didn't want to take it through Stuttgart, because the French held that city, and the Americans were keeping scientific secrets for themselves. Lanny thought that French colonials would be more interested in pigs and chickens than in metallurgy; but he assented to what the scientist thought safest. They headed west, toward the Rhine, and when they came into Strasbourg they turned the papers over to the Alsos people there, with instructions to ship them at once by air to the OSRD—Office of Scientific Research and Development —in Washington.

In this town they encountered a so-called T-force of Alsos, under the command of Colonel Boris Pash, the capable officer who had charge of guiding and guarding scientists. The force consisted of two armored cars, a dozen or so jeeps, and several covered trucks with supplies. It would not plunge in haphazardly as the Bates-Budd force had done, but would proceed with military caution, telephoning ahead to each town and village to demand its surrender. The scientists would come along half a day or so later; Sam Goudsmit, who enjoyed a sense of humor, said this wasn't to protect them from bombs and shells, but to make sure the Nazis didn't get a chance to wring atomic secrets out of them.

The ultimate destination of this T-force was Munich, and Lanny Budd could think of half a dozen reasons for wishing to travel there. Next to Berlin, Munich was Germany's greatest art center; also it was close to Berchtesgaden, and to Dachau, and to that Alpine Redoubt about which G-2 had been getting so many secret reports. Lanny wanted to see that show if it came off, so he bade good-by to Dr. Bates and waited for the Goudsmit party to come along.

He had taken a shine to this Jewish professor and was welcomed cordially. They could make room for an extra man and one suitcase, and they promised him an interesting time. They were heading back into that "ingen" country from which he had just come, their destination being a town called Hechingen, in which they were told that the great Werner Heisenberg had his secret atomic laboratory. Goudsmit was sure he hadn't got very far with his project, but whatever it was the orders were to go in and get it.

On the way they told him what had been happening in Europe while he had been Deputy *Bürgermeister* of Urach. Russian troops had reached the center of Berlin and were fighting to capture Gestapo headquarters. British planes had dropped six-ton bombs on the Berghof, Hitler's Berchtesgaden chalet—no doubt on the chance that he might have fled there. British troops had reached the River Po in Italy. Most interesting of all, Heinrich Himmler had made an offer to surrender Germany to the Western Allies alone—which offer the Allies were ignoring. VE Day couldn't be very far off!

They turned off at another of the swift streams which flow down into the Neckar. This one was the Starzel; tall, steep mountains on both sides, and a winding road suffering from lack of upkeep—like everything else in Germany now. Hechingen had been the eyrie of the Hohenzollerns—the high toll-takers—that dynasty which had got control, first of Prussia and then of the Fatherland, and had led both to their doom.

No trouble this time! When you had a real T-force with armored cars the population of the town came out waving bedsheets on poles. There was no delay in finding the Heisenberg laboratory; part of it was in one wing of a textile plant and another part in an old brewery. Several miles away was a small underground cave containing the uranium pile. The Army had got to the cave and removed all the apparatus and blown it up. No more scientific hocus-pocus there!

XII

The great Heisenberg had skipped the town, or, rather, had rolled out of it on a bicycle. He had left half a dozen of his colleagues, including Otto Hahn, the discoverer of uranium fission; also that Professor von Weizsäcker, the Prussian aristocrat who had lent his services to the Nazis and had skipped out of Strasbourg before Alsos had got there. Another of the group was Professor Plötzen, whom Lanny had met at the Kaiser Wilhelm Institute in Berlin. Posing as a friend and secret agent of Hitler, Lanny had gone to spend an evening at Plötzen's home, and there to his consternation had discovered Bernhardt Monck, who had managed to get a job as the wealthy gentleman's butler and was having his papers secretly photographed at night.

So Alsos did not fail in its promise to provide the art expert with an interesting time. He spent hours with this worldly and genial physicist, who was a member of the Herrenklub as well as of the Kaiser Wilhelm Society. Did he accept Lanny's story that he had remained a friend of Germany until Himmler had tried to draw him into a conspiracy to get rid of Hitler? The story was no longer so fantastic, since all the world had been told over the radio that the Reichsminister and head of SS and Gestapo had deserted his Führer in an effort to save his own skin.

What Plötzen said was, all that was water over the dam; what he was interested in was trying to save scientific knowledge. He thought it was silly of Heisenberg to run off to hide in the Alpine Redoubt, because that stronghold wouldn't be able to hold out more than a week or two. Plötzen didn't mind saying that this famed colleague—of whom he was perhaps somewhat jealous—had gone to join his family at their summer home in the town of Urfeld, on the Walchensee, south of Munich. Confidentially he was willing to tell his friend Budd where Heisenberg had had the materials of the laboratory buried. The cache was dug up: a ton and a half of uranium, a ton and a half of heavy water, and ten tons of carbon. The first item was of tremendous value and would be transported to a secret place in New Mexico as quickly as it could be loaded into a flying boxcar. The heavy water had been produced at great expense in Rjukan, Norway, a place whose name Lanny had obtained a couple of years ago at the expense of a great deal of his nervous energy.

At first Goudsmit had thought he had all the documents of this small laboratory. But then doubt seized him—there wasn't enough about Heisenberg's own atomic experiments. Plötzen vowed that he didn't know anything about secret papers, and it was quite possible that Heisenberg hadn't trusted him. One of the other physicists was persuaded over to the American side and revealed the curious fact that the documents had been sealed in a large can and buried in the latrine of the outhouse used by the scientists. The GI Joes didn't relish the job of rescuing that treasure and showed their sentiments by depositing the can under the open window of the room where Professor Goudsmit spent the night.

In the morning it was cleaned and opened up, and there were the real secrets. They were sealed again and taken to Heidelberg to be shipped to Washington. Thousands of such treasures were pouring into that center, and thousands of scientists of all specialties were waiting to study them and decide if any immediate use could be made of them. The half-dozen German scientists were put into cars and taken to Heidelberg for a very special and polite sort of internment, which consisted of living in a steam-heated villa and having long technical conversations with their former colleagues—American, British, and French.

XIII

Colonel Pash proposed to head a small task force to dash into the Alpine Redoubt and grab the much-wanted Werner Heisenberg. They would avoid Munich, which had not yet fallen but might be falling at this very hour. Lanny saw in this the quickest way to get where he wanted to be, so he offered to go along, and the military officer, who had been diverted by the story of Lanny at Urach, replied, "Sure thing!" They were taking only two cars and half a dozen well-armed men, including a young lieutenant named Hayes. They would be crowded if they captured their man, but Lanny said he wouldn't object to having Germany's greatest physicist sitting on his knees. Photographs in Heisenberg's office showed an amiable and not too large person with somewhat unruly hair.

Lanny had captured the Swabian town of Urach, and now he was going to capture the Bavarian town of Urfeld. The syllable *"Ur"* means aged, having to do with one's remote ancestors; it is a difference between America and Europe that on the old continent the most delightful summer resorts may have buildings and history going back five or six or more centuries. In many valleys along the northern Alpine slopes are lovely little blue lakes, and Munich is fortunate in having a score of them within easy reach. There couldn't have been a pleasanter motor trip; only two or three shots were fired at them, and they might have taken great numbers of prisoners if they hadn't had more important work in hand.

They traveled fast, not stopping for anything. They cut up into the foothills to avoid Munich. They had passed not far from Dachau, but had no way of knowing what had happened or might be happening there. Americans had found it difficult to believe the atrocity stories, but now that they were liberating one after another of these packed concentration camps they were horrified by the conditions they found.

XIV

They raced into the small town of Urfeld, on the Walchensee, a lake three or four miles long, at the head of that River Isar which flows through Munich, and down whose clear green waters Lanny had once been floated on a great raft, in company with a score of Nazi *Bonzen*, a picnic party with baskets of *Leberwurst* sandwiches and a cask of beer. That had been in the days of "Munich"—in the special sense of the name which history will always remember. Lanny had motored through this pleasureland, enjoying the good life which fate had assigned to him.

Now he and his party came with no little trepidation, not sure what kind of welcome they would get. The war was coming to its anticipated end, but many men were still dying every day, and nobody could guess in what remote valleys the fanatics of the Redoubt might be hiding, or through what forests the "werewolves" might be sneaking. The ancient German legend of men who sometimes turned into wolves at night was deeply rooted and was now being used to inspire terror in the population, in much the same way as the hooded Ku-Kluxers had done in the American South after the Civil War.

The little T-force had no trouble in locating their quarry. He was a dignified gentleman, very conscious of his scientific standing. He had, of course, no idea what progress the Americans had been making in the esoteric field of atomic fission; he took it for granted that what he knew must be far ahead of what anybody else in the world knew —it had been that way in so many branches of science. The news that they had been to Hechingen and had found his uranium and his heavy water and his can full of atomic secrets must have seemed to him like the invasion of ancient Rome by the barbarians from the northern forests. When he was told that he would have to accompany the task force to Heidelberg where his colleagues were interned, he yielded politely, since there was nothing else he could do.

While preparations for departure were under way an amusing incident took place. Two high SS officers presented themselves. They had learned that American officers had arrived in town, and it did not occur to them that the Americans might have come without an adequate force. The SS men stated that they had six hundred troops up in the mountains; the snow was deep and they had little food, and, recognizing that the war was over, they desired to surrender. Very gravely Colonel Pash agreed to accept the surrender and specified the spot at which the Germans were to present themselves.

At this moment the young lieutenant happened in. Perhaps he failed to grasp the situation, or perhaps he was one of those persons whose wits do not work quickly. He blurted out, "But we are only seven men!"

Colonel Pash answered quietly, "Our troops will be here in an hour or two, and that is before these gentlemen can get back." He sent the enemy officers away, and the tiny T-force hightailed it out of Urfeld to find a larger American force and send it up there.

As he promised, Lanny took Germany's greatest physicist on his knees. They chatted on the way, and Lanny didn't say who he was or that he had been coached on the subject of atomic fission by Professor Einstein. He just remarked that he had had the privilege of knowing Professor Plötzen for some time, and had called several times upon Professor Salzmann at the Physics Laboratory of the Kaiser Wilhelm Institute in Berlin. That caused Heisenberg to open up and say that he took little stock in the talk about the possibility of an atomic bomb, but that there existed a real possibility of the development of atomic power for use in industry; he had been working on this problem, and now that peace seemed near he would be glad to give the world the benefit of the knowledge he had acquired. Lanny said that was the attitude he had been sure a true scientist would take. Colonel Pash listened and must have smiled quietly to himself, for he knew more about what was going on at Oak Ridge, Tennessee, and at Hanford, Washington, than had ever been confided to a presidential agent.

13

Walls of Jericho

I

LEARNING that Munich had been captured that day, Lanny did not ride back to Heidelberg but left the T-force and made his way into the city. This shrine of Nazism was full of memories for him—but he had to travel some distance into it before he could be sure where he was. The heart of the city, a circle about a mile and a half in diameter, was a mass of rubble, hurled out into the streets and blocking them. All the factory districts had been bombed out of existence, also the railroad yards. There had been an attempt at revolution, and the SS troops had been attacked front and rear; so the city had held out only one day, but the Nazis had succeeded in blowing up most of the bridges in their retreat. Nearly half the population had fled, and the rest were in such confusion as Lanny had never seen before.

It was the Seventh Army which had taken the city, having come down from Nürnberg on a broad front in about ten days. Meantime the Third had reached the tip of Czechoslovakia. Presumably having orders to leave that country to the Russians, they had swung south to the Danube and deep into Austria. At all hazards the Americans meant to possess that Alpine Redoubt, and block the enemy's plans to fortify it. To hold any city requires only a few troops, and the rest would go on, looking for the enemy's armed forces. That would include six hundred SS men holed up in a snow-filled valley above the Walchensee. This time the six hundred wouldn't ride into the valley of death, but into a valley of K-rations and warm stoves.

There was so much news in Munich that an assimilated colonel, coming into headquarters of Seventh, could hardly assimilate it. The Hamburg radio blared with solemn fanfare the tidings that on the previous day Adolf Hitler had died in battle for the Fatherland. The crooked little *Doktor*, Josef Goebbels, had poisoned himself, but his spirit lived on in the solemn official lie. It was several days before the world learned the truth, that the Führer of the Germans had shot himself in the head in the underground bunker of the New Chancellery in Berlin.

Admiral Doenitz had been appointed his successor—but nobody that Lanny met seemed to care about that, since there was going to be nothing left for any German to succeed to. The Allies weren't dealing with governments, but only with troops that wished either to fight or to surrender. The Russians had broken through the defenses of Berlin and their artillery had been tearing the New Chancellery to pieces when the Führer had at last made up his tortured mind that his cause was lost.

Soldiers had no time to stop and think about him, but an art expert did. Lanny had been taken down into that Führerbunker during an American air raid, and had sat on an overstuffed sofa feeling the earth shake around him but knowing that he was safe under a twenty-foot covering of concrete and steel. An entire house built underground, an office and a hospital, all with every convenience, a heating plant, a lighting plant, an air-conditioning plant, a telephone switchboard, a radio sending and receiving set—Hitler had been prepared to govern all Germany and conduct its many-front war from that safe retreat. He would make his foes take Germany foot by foot—and they had done just that, and in another day would have been standing over his head and smoking him out like a rat in its hole.

II

Wonderful, wonderful, and after that out of all hoping!—Benito Mussolini likewise had been removed from the scene of history. Il Duce of the Italians had been conducting a sort of mock government in the northern part of his country, under the protection of the German Army. When the British and the Americans closed in on him he fled toward Germany, with his latest mistress, Petacci, and a group of his henchmen. The Partisans had caught them, given them a drumhead court-martial, then lined them up against a wall and shot them. That wasn't enough to express their sentiments concerning this odious usurper; they took the bodies of Duce and girl down to Milan, and from a scaffold in the old Piazza Loreto hung them by chains, feet up and heads down, to be stared at by all the city and photographed for the rest of the world.

Lanny Budd had taken that pair of dictators for his special and personal foes; he had called them two foxes whose brushes he wanted to hang over his mantel. How they died and what worms ate them was no matter; the point was they could no longer torment mankind with their ignorance, their insolence, and their blind lust for power. It was Lanny's fond dream that the whole people were wiser than any self-appointed leaders; that if they could once get power and manage to keep it, they and the products of their toil would no longer be at the mercy of evil creatures spewed up from the cesspools of society. So long as such existed, so long as they could seize the wealth of great nations and turn them to fanaticism and aggression, they had to be fought—which meant that the adult life of a lover of art and music and poetry had to be turned to spying and betrayal.

Exactly a quarter of a century had passed since Lanny Budd had had the agitator Mussolini pointed out to him in a café in San Remo, being cursed by one of his Socialist followers whom he had betrayed. Later Lanny had been present when Rick had interviewed him for a British newspaper. Still later the American had heard Il Duce bellowing from his balcony and had tried to tell the world about his cold-blooded murder of Matteotti, the noblest personality that Italy had produced in Lanny's time. Now the murderer was hanging by his feet in the market place, like a butchered pig!

Lanny hadn't heard of Adolf Hitler quite so early, but had spent half his life in learning about that genius-madman, realizing what a menace he meant to the future, and practicing to deceive him and pick secrets out of his mind. It hadn't been such a difficult task, for Adi had been an extraordinarily frank liar and cheat. He had put it all into a book, but few outside his own land had bothered to read it. He had adhered steadily to his theory that the bigger the lie, the easier to get it believed. Again and again he had said that he had no further territorial demands upon Europe; each time he had been believed, and each time he had presented another demand within half a year or less. His opponents had been so stupid that you were tempted to say they deserved what they got—if only it hadn't meant such hideous suffering for tens of millions of innocent and helpless people.

Now the evil pair were dead; but not until they had caused the loss of some thirty or forty million human lives, and an amount of treasure difficult to estimate but that couldn't have been less than half a million million dollars, a sum so astronomical that the figures brought no realization to the human mind. How many lives and how many dollars would it take to remove the next set of dictators from the world? And where was the statesman who was going to supervise that job? Was it Winston Churchill, immovable arch-Tory, thinking about nothing but the protection of his "Empah" over all the other empahs of the world? Was it General Charles-André-Joseph-Marie de Gaulle, trained militarist keen for his calling and Catholic zealot proud of his superstition? Or was it the kind and modest little man in the White House, who knew Independence, Missouri, and liked to play poker and the piano, but who knew little more than the average high-school student about the manners and immorals, the greeds and insanities, of the old continent of Europe?

III

Lanny stayed in Munich because he knew that Alsos was on the way and that Monuments wouldn't be far behind; meantime he could scout around and get information for them both. Most of his acquaintances were Nazi leaders who had fled or were in hiding; the Americans were throwing them into jail as fast as they could be caught. This was a convenient place to interview them, because they were badly scared, expecting the mistreatment which they themselves had meted out to captives during twelve glorious years. Most of them were men of no principles, thinking only to save their skins; they knew that the jig was up and fell over themselves in the effort to oblige their captors. It made one a little sick to hear them protest that they had never been "real" Nazis but only employees obliged to obey orders.

Knowing headquarters of both Third and Seventh Armies, Lanny had no trouble in getting a billet and a meal ticket, and permission to go where he pleased. He asked some help from the Seventh on an emergency job; there was a University of Munich, and it had a Physics Department. He got a T-force, consisting of himself and three GIs with a car. Having learned the technique, he took it upon himself to drive up to what was left of the group of damaged buildings on the Ludwigstrasse. Everybody bowed low before American authority. There had been no academic freedom in Germany for a dozen years; from janitors to president they had all trod the goosestep and heiled Hitler. Now they would all heil Eisenhower. The president, a Doktor Walther Wüst, was also professor of Sanskrit and Persian, and director of Scholarship in the Ahnenerbe, a semi-lunatic organization founded by Heinrich Himmler for the purpose of collecting and cherishing knowledge about the ancient Germanic tribes, the forefathers of the "Aryan" world.

It was with the administrative head of the University that Colonel Budd had his dealings. This gentleman was SS Colonel Wolfram Sievers, an especially ardent Nazi enthusiast and propagandist. He counted it a rare good fortune that his name began and ended with S, since this provided him with a unique opportunity to demonstrate his loyalty to his Aryan heritage. The insigne of the SS, worn as their shoulder patch, looked like a pair of parallel lightning strokes, and the outside world in its ignorance had taken it for granted that these strokes symbolized a military threat; but no, they were the ancient Runic form of the letter S, and so Colonel Sievers of the Schutzstaffel signed his name this way: ⚡iever⚡.

This learned university administrator was obsequious to a conquering officer of co-equal rank and offered to introduce him to the heads of his various departments, which included Genealogy, the Origin of Proper Names, Family Symbols (*Sippenzeichen*) and House Markings, Speleology, Folklore, and *Welteislehre*—which meant the important Nazi discovery that the inner core of all the planets and all the stars consisted of ice. Among the correspondence which Professor Goudsmit turned up in this institution of learning was a letter from Colonel ⚡iever⚡ to an official lady named Piffl, instructing her to send a representative to Jutland immediately—this in the very midst of a two-front war— because Reichsführer Himmler had heard a report that there was an old woman living in the village of Ribe who had knowledge of "the knitting methods of the Vikings."

Lanny didn't want knowledge of the Vikings or yet of the inner core of the planets and the stars. He wanted to be taken at once to the

Physics Department, and there he wanted to collect and impound all papers and records of whatever character. This was a task of some magnitude, and both janitors and professors were pressed into service. The documents were all stacked in one room, and the door locked, and a day-and-night guard set up by the obliging Seventh Army, pending the arrival of the Jewish-Dutch-American discoverer of the "spin of the electron"—something in which real Nazi physicists of course did not believe.

IV

Having done this important job, Lanny ventured to ask another favor of Seventh headquarters; he wanted them to let him have one of their PFCs named Freddi Robin for a week to act as his bodyguard and general handyman. One Joe being the same as any other to this busy Army, they were willing to cut the red tape and give Doc Budd an order, a jeep, and driver for a quick run to Rosenheim, where the Jewish boy's unit was now—but of course nobody could be sure how many moments it would stay there. The Seventh was on its way down through the Brenner Pass—they being the fifty-eighth conquering force to travel that route during recorded history. They could cut off the retreat of the Germans in Italy and bring them to a quick surrender.

So Doc had another holiday drive, with a chauffeur who told him about the delights of dashing across Germany from the Rhine to the Danube, with some of the enemy fighting like devils and others standing by the roadside holding up their hands and waving any sort of white rag they could get. The war was fun at that stage; but Jesus Christ, what a lot of misery it had meant in the winter time, driving the Huns back against the Rhine! Private Jack Forrester had had enough of it to last him for a lifetime, and all he wanted was to get back to Abilene, Texas, where there was a girl waiting for him. From first to last Lanny didn't meet a single "dough" who had any thought about solving the problems of Europe; what was worrying them was that there mightn't be enough jobs back home to go round, and the guys who got there first would get the pick. "How soon do you think they'll start shipping us back, Doc?"

Lanny's appearance in the town of Rosenheim was truly like a miracle to young Freddi. He had joined up at Saarbrücken, and had helped count prisoners all the way across the Rhineland and South Germany. He had by-passed Dachau and Munich—nobody had had time to listen to his plea that he might as well count prisoners in a concentration camp. Now he was going to be with his friend Lanny Budd, whom he adored as the greatest man in the Army, not even excepting General Ike.

Lanny had a magic piece of paper which did the business in a minute or two, and it took the boy not much longer to stuff his belongings into his kitbag and throw it into the back seat of the jeep. Away they went, not stopping for even a glimpse of the swift-flowing Inn River, along which Lanny had driven with Laurel Creston, getting out of Germany with Hitler's permission on the day the war broke out. Then the road had been crowded with German troops going to the front, and now it was crowded with Americans doing the same—but a different front!

Lanny wasn't going to Dachau just on young Freddi's account. Freddi's father was dead and gone and there was no way to help him. Lanny was interested in helping the living, by ending one war and making another impossible. He knew that Dachau had been the first of the concentration camps, Hitler's own. Here he had sent his special enemies, those who threatened his regime—beginning on the 30th of January 1933, the day that he took power, and continuing for exactly a hundred and forty-seven months, up to the 30th of April 1945, the day that he put a bullet into his disordered brain. In Dachau he had assembled his most skilled torturers, to wring secrets out of the prisoners and to render them incapable of acting, or even of thinking, against his regime. Here he had assigned his most fanatical zealots, to inflict in the name of experimental science the most hideous sufferings upon these unfortunate wretches; freezing them, baking them, injecting drugs and poisons into them, depriving them of food, of water, of sleep, and keeping exact records of how much they could endure and how they could be brought back and got ready for the next set of experiments.

In this enormous prison pen, several miles in circumference, had been confined the flower of Germany's political and social idealism: those leaders who had been guiding the toiling masses and those younger men who had been trained at the labor school which Lanny and the elder Freddi had helped to keep going in Berlin. It was possible that he might find Ludi Schultz, husband of Trudi, the woman whom Lanny had married after he had been told that Ludi was dead. It was conceivable that the Nazis might have immured one of their most hated foes for twelve years and never permitted the outside world to hear a word from him. It was even conceivable that Trudi might be here! Rudolf Hess had had the records looked up and reported that she had died in Dachau. But then, there were probably as many Trudi Schultzes in

Germany as there are Mary Smiths in America, and suppose Hess had got the wrong one?

There were not only German Social Democrats in Dachau, there were Communists and democrats and liberals and pacifists and in general all friends of mankind. Their crimes had been such as listening to foreign broadcasts or speaking disrespectfully of the *Regierung*. There were more than a thousand Catholic priests, and perhaps as many Protestant pastors, accused of practicing their religion. And not merely Germans, but Frenchmen and Dutchmen and Norwegians and Czechs and Danes, and perhaps some British and Americans; all the finest spirits of the world who had got caught in Adi Schicklgruber's death trap.

Lanny was moved not merely by friendship and friendly curiosity; he hoped to get a mass of information from these different kinds of people, and from the records of this enormous *Lager*. The inmates could put their fingers on the guilty and defend the innocent, inside and outside the camp. They could tell where treasures were hidden, and paper secrets more precious than treasure. Those who had enough life in them were the persons who would redeem the soul of Germany and guide its future. G-2 of Army would be there, busily asking questions about war criminals; but Lanny Budd knew special questions to ask, and tactful ways to ask them. He might help not merely Alsos and Monuments, but also AMG and the government of Germans by Germans which AMG was already setting up in conquered territory.

V

Dachau lies some ten miles to the northwest of Munich, and there is a railroad but it wasn't working. Lanny got a Daimler car which one of the Nazi *Bonzen* had left behind, presumably because he couldn't get gas; it was odd to hear how these masters of the Thousand-Year Reich had hitched horses, oxen, cows, and even Poles and Russians to their rubber-tired chariots in order to get their corpulent selves hauled away toward the east. They fled from General Patch's Seventh Army, only to run into Georgie Patton's Third, headed hell-for-leather into Austria. And believe it, those were real man-sized armies! Patton alone had more than three hundred and fifty thousand men.

Before setting out on this journey the two investigators had had to have typhus shots, and have their hair and clothing well dusted with DDT. There were reported to be two thousand cases of typhus in the camp, and a visitor could not touch anyone or sit in a chair or lean

against a wall without getting lice on him. The inmates could not have
been turned loose without spreading the plague all over Germany; they
would be kept under quarantine until they were safe to move. Doc
Budd was urged against going, but he was a special sort of Intelligence
man, and if he felt it was his duty no one would forbid it.

Dachauerstrasse from Munich had shell holes, and was crowded with
displaced persons and military traffic; bridges were down, and you de-
toured into small streams. It was Army etiquette for the private soldier
to drive the car; but Lanny wouldn't trust his young friend, who was
so excited that he couldn't keep his hands from shaking. "Chillon! Thy
prison is a holy place," the poet Byron had written, and so this sensitive Jewish lad felt about the place to which he was bound. If he
could manage to find the building where his father had been confined
he would search every inch of it for traces of writing. "May none those
marks efface! For they appeal from tyranny to God."

Lanny remembered the gates, and the wide street inside, lined with
tall administration buildings. To keep his Thousand-Year Reich safe,
Hitler would need thousand-year prisons and cages for his opponents;
he had known that and planned with German thoroughness. The officers in charge must be comfortable; they must have well-built homes
with all modern conveniences, crystal and silver and linen, books and
radios and music, all elegance and all culture for the *Herrenvolk*, those
whom the Creator had chosen to rule the inferior races of the earth.
These homes must be situated in beautiful gardens remote from all
scenes of horror.

In the course of his visit Lanny was escorted into one of these by the
American officer who had that day moved in and had barely had time
to look around. A bit crude by American taste but pleasant; on the center table lay a volume, and Lanny picked it up; Goethe's *Lieder und
Gedichte!* The visitor's mind was swept back to his early youth when
he had discovered the young Goethe of the lyric days, a godlike being,
singing of all things lovely and noble in human life; *im Ganzen, Guten,
Wahren resolut zu leben!* Then Lanny noticed the reading lamp, with
a shade of a peculiar sort, a tissue like parchment, yellowish in color
and ornamented with crude designs in red and blue—German eagles,
flags, heraldic coats of arms, mermaids, quite a collection. "What is
that?" he asked, and the answer was, "Somebody had a bright idea; that
is tattooed human skin."

"Good God!" exclaimed the visitor. "Do you suppose they killed
people to get it?"

"We haven't made sure about that," was the answer. "Maybe they just made note of men who had good tattooings and waited for them to die. In this place they were dying at the rate of two every hour."

VI

"You should go and see the train first," remarked the officer at the gates. "If you want to know what death is, go see it and smell it." So the visitors went outside and around to the north, where the train stood on a siding. What had happened was that at Buchenwald, a camp near Weimar, to the north, the Americans had been drawing near and the Nazis apparently had the idea that things were going to be safer in the south. They had loaded some four thousand of their Russian and Polish slave laborers into a long freight train—thirty-nine cars, said the officer, more than a hundred men to the car. But the railroad had been bombed, and of course military traffic had the right of way; the journey to Dachau took twenty-one days, and it was early April, with cold and rain, and most of the cars were open flatcars, "gondolas" as they are called in America. Half the prisoners perished on the way, and most of the rest in the few days after reaching Dachau.

The track was curved, making it possible to view the whole train. Lanny and Freddi looked into the uncovered cars and through the open doors of the boxcars, and saw the ghastliest sights of their lives: rows and piles of human bodies, many naked, others covered with rags and bits of filthy blanket, lying as they had fallen, because they could no longer stand or sit; a few out in the fields where they had been shot trying to escape. Many of the naked bodies bore the marks of whips.

There is a familiar phrase, "mere skin and bones." It is an accurate phrase, for in starvation the body does not give up easily, but protects itself by drawing all the substance out of the muscles and putting it into heart and lungs and blood vessels. These creatures who had once been men were now skeletons covered with skin; their bowels had shrunk to nothing, and the skin of the belly lay against the backbone; their eyes had sunk into the sockets, and their skulls were like those of mummies. They gave out a sickly sweet odor that threatened to set you to vomiting.

There was no getting away from this odor in Dachau. The whole vast *Lager* was pervaded by it, and it drifted out into the countryside, paying no heed to barbed and electrified wire. It was like the smell of the Chicago stockyards, except that these bodies hadn't all been cooked. The visitors went into some of the barracks, where the narrow bunks were in tiers, and discovered that many of the inmates had reached that stage of exhaustion where they could not move anything but their eyes; they had lost the power to assimilate food and lay waiting for merciful death. They lay in their own excrement, and so there was a new kind of stench.

When they died they were placed in stacks exactly like cordwood, until they could be carted to the crematory; there they were stacked again, for crematories were overcrowded and fuel was getting scarce. The American Army had too many things to do in conquered Germany and still needed its men for the unconquered portions. They were going to order the townspeople of Dachau to bury the bodies that were in the freight cars, so they informed Lanny.

It was interesting to note that the town's five thousand people appeared well fed and sturdy. There was no lack of food in rural Germany; the starvation policy had been deliberate and followed from the beginning. The non-working prisoners had received one slice of bread and one dipper of thin soup twice a day; this amounted to about five hundred calories, about one-fourth of what it takes to maintain the weight of an average person at rest. From first to last there had been a hundred and twenty-five thousand captives in this hellhole, and about half of them had died of starvation and disease.

VII

It was a sunshiny day, and all the inmates who could move were out enjoying the warmth. The liberation had occurred two days ago, but the pitiful creatures had not yet got over their excitement; the sight of American visitors filled them with emotions beyond control. They came running or tottering, weeping, babbling incoherently; they wanted to touch the visitors, to be sure they were real; they wanted to clutch them with clawlike hands; they wanted to kiss them with unshaven faces, and to press stinking and verminous clothing against them; they wanted to thank them in Serbian and Russian, Italian and French, Norwegian, Polish, and even Hindustani.

There was an immense open compound, big enough for a parade ground, with a high wooden wall. It was crowded with men, and was really dangerous to go into. A cheer started and ran all over the place; a mob came crowding, pouring out their thanks, questions, requests. They wanted cigarettes, liquor, food—they had been fed, but of course not as much as they wanted, or they would have killed themselves. Thirty-two thousand men in this place, and nothing could be done for them individually; they had to be treated en masse. But they were individuals, with their individual hopes and fears, worries and needs; they wanted news of the outside world, of their families and friends; they wanted to write letters, to send messages; they wanted to tell their stories; they wanted just to have a contact with the wonderful free world, to know that it existed, to touch some fragment of it. They had all been lousy and stinking for so long that they had forgotten how this would affect normal men.

The visitors got out of the compound; no use trying to carry on conversation there. They walked through the narrow lanes between the low barracks, and here living skeletons, too weak to get to the compound, sat or lay against the walls and made feeble efforts to greet the visitors, a sickly grin and a lifting of the hand perhaps six inches, perhaps a foot. Their faces all looked alike and aged. Here and there lay a different sort of body, normal in size and vigorous, but dead; they were clad in black uniforms with the SS insignia. These were the guards of the camp, and until three days ago they had lorded it over their victims; wherever they strode with their snarling dogs the victims were required to stand at attention, hats in hand, if they had hats, and never closer than six feet. If anyone failed in this ceremonial he was seized, his hands bound behind his back, and hung to a wall hook by the cord; there he stayed for one hour. On the Sunday when the Americans came the mob rose and killed every one of their tormentors they could lay hands on. In the frenzy of the first minutes men had torn themselves on barbed wire, breaking through it, and some had been killed by electrified wire, or just by the violence of their excitement.

The GIs had never seen anything like this; they had heard stories but hadn't believed them. Now they wanted to tell the world, and they started on one buddy and one "Doc"; ask them one question, and they would pour out a flood of horror and rage. Look in this barrack where the Poles had been herded, the poor devils who had been hated worst of all. Triple-tiered bunks just deep enough to slide into, and five feet wide; five men had slept in each bunk, and a lot of them were still in there, dead. Or this place where a group of Jewish women had been herded three weeks ago; things here that could not be put into print.

A noncom on duty at the crematory undertook to escort the visitors through that large brick building. There was a big "office," where the victims had been stripped, there was a gas room where they died, and there were two large furnaces where they were turned into ashes, excellent for spreading on German fields. There was a punishment room where they were hung on hooks and whipped, and this had thoughtfully been arranged so that while they were hanging they could see bodies being thrown into the furnaces. In the early days of this concentration camp Lanny had been shown through it, or so he had been told; but he hadn't seen any of these sights, only the barracks in which the important prisoners lived.

All such persons had been taken away two nights before the Americans arrived; eight thousand had been taken in a huge caravan, and no one had any idea where they had gone. All the records of the *Lager* had been burned in the crematory. Later on Lanny found that some records had been secretly kept by some of the prisoner doctors, but these related only to medical matters, the number of prisoners who had died and what they had died of. The doctors were from all the nations of Europe, and were among the most intelligent of the men Lanny met; they had done the best they could with few instruments and almost no drugs. They had been given enough food so that they could work— they and the male nurses, who also had to practice medicine to the best of their ability.

They talked about the alleged medical experiments which Nazi doctors had been carrying on in the camp, under government orders. The son of Budd-Erling had been told about these at Karinhall, by one of the "scientists" who had planned the work. Eleven thousand men had died from being infected with malaria, in order to test various cures which didn't succeed. With the idea of helping Nazi airmen who parachuted into the North Sea or the Baltic, the Luftwaffe had sought to discover how long a man could survive in freezing water and how he could best be revived. To make sure, they had a tank here at Dachau, whose temperature could be lowered at will, and prisoners were immersed for exact times and careful records kept; these records were burned, but copies were found later at Luftwaffe headquarters. They were grotesquely thorough; among the methods of revival was putting the victim in bed with a young woman; the records of "Section H" showed "rewarming by one woman," "rewarming by two women," and "rewarming by women after coitus." Six hundred victims had died in spite of such rewarming. Dr. Rascher, who conducted these unique experiments, had requested that he be transferred to Auschwitz, because it was colder there and "patients" could be frozen in the open; also because they made trouble in Dachau, they "roared while being frozen."

VIII

Lanny and his young friend spent two days and three nights in this inferno, sleeping in one of the officers' homes. They questioned everybody they met regarding prisoners named Freddi Robin and Ludi and Trudi Schultz, but without results. Twelve years was a long time ago, and when sixty thousand human beings have died and been burned to ashes, who can remember names? Who even tries? Here human beings had been deliberately deprived of personality and had become bundles of bones, to be stacked like cordwood. All the intellectual persons had been killed or taken away. Freddi went tirelessly into the compound and was passed from one Social Democrat to another, but he did not find anyone who claimed to have been in this camp from the beginning; men did not last that long, they said.

Lanny asked concerning an officer of the Wehrmacht, Oberst Oskar von Herzenberg, but nobody had heard of him. That was a long shot, of course; Lanny had had no tidings of Marceline's lover, and it was just a wild guess that he might be here. He had known about the bomb plot to kill Hitler last July. Several thousand men had been shot or hanged for that; but it might be that others, against whom there was nothing but suspicion, had been incarcerated. It might even be that Marceline was among the few women prisoners at Dachau. Lanny met a man who had seen her dancing in a night club, but that was the nearest he got to her.

He questioned the doctors, and then the religious groups. It was hard to imagine anyone with less religion than Marceline Detaze; but who could guess what might happen to a man or woman facing the tortures of a hell like this? They were deliberately designed to break the human spirit; and to what extent had they succeeded? He discovered that the political groups had not stood the test very well; they had some heroes and saints among them, but many others had broken and had accepted jobs to lord it over the less fortunate inmates, the Jews, the Poles, the Slavs. They had squabbled over a bit of bread or a cigarette butt—even though possession of the latter involved the penalty of being shut up in the "box," a place the size of a telephone booth in which four men were locked and left for three days and nights without food or water.

The religious people, it appeared, had done better. There were all sorts of clergy in this *Lager*: orthodox Jews, and every sect of Christians—Catholic, Greek Orthodox, Old Catholic, Mariavite, and a score of different Protestant creeds. They were objects of especial hatred to the Nazis and were exploited in every way. Three hundred and fifty were crowded into a single dormitory, managed by "capos," convicted criminals who were sent here because of their dependable brutality. In winter the priests and ministers shoveled snow and removed it from the camp; inverted dining tables were put upon long wheelbarrows to carry the snow and it was dumped into the river which flows past the camp. They had stood it all and kept their faith.

This involved a psychological problem of interest to Lanny. How had they managed it? Obviously, if you call yourself a materialist, you have your body and your body is all; if it is weakened, you are weakened, and if it is destroyed, that is the end of you. You resist that happening in physical ways, but when you are caught and penned up and your foes have all the weapons, what more can you do? You can hate them, but you realize that your hatred is impotent, and sooner or later that saps the power of your will.

But how different if you believe that your body is a purely temporary and relatively unimportant thing! All flesh is grass, and whether it withers early or late matters not at all. When it is dead, an immortal soul escapes from its bondage and flies to heaven to have a martyr's crown put upon its immaterial head. Meantime God is with you, the Holy Family and all the heavenly host, the cherubim and the seraphim, the blessed saints and the goodly company of martyrs; you pray to them, they give you spiritual strength, they enable you to defy your oppressors, to laugh at the worst that Satan can do. As your physical strength wanes, your moral strength grows.

IX

The Catholic clergy especially had the advantage in an ordeal such as this. Their religious life had been a training for it; their traditions were full of martyrdom, and also self-punishment. Their St. Simeon Stylites of Antioch had lived his life on top of a stone pillar, a sort of old-style flagpole sitter—and surely a dormitory in Dachau was no less comfortable. Catholic zealots had practiced flagellation, tearing their own backs with barbed steel whips—it was still done in Mexico. Catholics mortified their flesh in various ways and denied its claims; their orders practiced celibacy, they wore unlovely and uncomfortable clothing, they went without food on occasions, and learned not to be bored by the repetition of prayers and ceremonies. When they were put in any sort of prison they were like well-trained troops going into battle; they knew exactly what to do, and their new life was like their old, only more so.

Lanny talked with a Father de Coninck, a Catholic priest from Belgium. His offense had been lecturing to other priests concerning the incompatibility of Nazism with the Gospel. When he arrived at Dachau there were some twenty-five hundred Catholic priests, and now after three years there were only eleven hundred, the rest having died or been killed. He had reason to believe that he was one of those destined for the gas chamber, and for two months he shared the life of the condemned. He was saved through a chain of circumstances in which, as he said to Lanny, "the protection of the Virgin was obvious." To the non-believer, that seemed polytheism, but Lanny kept the opinion to himself.

This long-enduring priest went on to explain that he had succeeded in obtaining some consecrated Hosts, meaning wafers which by the process called transubstantiation had been turned into the mystical body of Christ. He had broken these into tiny particles, twenty to each Host, and wrapped them in cigarette papers. A dying man who confessed his sins, repented, and ate one of these crumbs in reverent ceremony had his sins forgiven and his soul transported to heaven. This gift was called the Viaticum—"provision for a journey"—and Father de Coninck was able to give it to many on the way to execution. They died, as he said, "with true saintliness."

To Lanny this host seemed true fetishism, but again he held his peace. What did he, man of the world and art lover, have to say to the two thousand victims of typhus locked up here in quarantine, and would he be willing to have himself locked up with them, as many of the priests had done? He had had himself well dusted with DDT, and knew that the hard-working Army was doing the same for the whole camp as quickly as possible. If you ended war, poverty, and ignorance all over the earth, you could end typhus and all other plagues, and Lanny had taken that for his job. But meantime here were two thousand men, most of whom had to die, and if anybody could make them happier while dying, even by telling them a myth, by all means let it be done. So Lanny said to young Freddi, and discovered that the new generation was shocked by this idea. Let men be told the truth, even though it made them unhappy!

"But what is the truth?" asked this modern Pilate, driving the Daimler back to Munich. "Can you be absolutely certain that no portion of your father's psychic being has survived? You can say that the probabilities appear to be against it; but can you say that it positively is not so? And what was your father's psychic being, anyhow?"

BOOK FIVE

Appeal from Tyranny to God

14

The Mighty Fallen

I

WHEN Lanny and Freddi got back to Munich the war with Germany was close to its end. First the German armies in Italy surrendered; two days later those in Holland and Northwest Germany, and next day those in Berlin. And what were the Allies going to do with this colossal victory? Young Freddi wanted to know, but Lanny couldn't help him much; he didn't know that new man in the White House and had no way to find out about him. Subconsciously, perhaps, he resented having him there, as a child resents a new baby in his mother's arms. What Lanny wanted was to get a bath and a change of underwear and to have his uniform cleaned and pressed; it seemed to him that he stank of carrion, and he imagined that people looked at him queerly. He wanted to see something different from Dachau, and it didn't do him much good to wander about the streets of Munich and watch ill-clad and undernourished citizens shoveling rubble into Army trucks. Burnedout buildings reminded him of human skulls with blackened eyesockets, and girders sticking up into the air were the bones of dead buildings.

He sent the younger man back to his outfit, telling him not to be too sad over the outcome of their expedition. He had done his best, and no one could have done better. Whatever else might happen, Nazi-Fascism was dead in Italy and Germany. That was what the elder Freddi had given his life for, and he would surely have given it gladly. The new generation must carry on from there.

Professor Goudsmit and his party arrived in Munich, and with them Jerry Pendleton. Jerry had been out with a T-force to a small town named Celle, north of Hannover, where it had been reported that the Germans had a centrifuge laboratory. They had found it in some rooms of a parachute-silk factory, and like everything else the Germans had done along the line of atomic fission, it was on a small experimental scale. They had found some important reports by Professor Walther Gerlach, a physicist whom Hitler had named as the man whom Lanny should see at the Kaiser Wilhelm Institute in Berlin. Now Gerlach had fled to Munich, and Jerry was to help in the hunt for him.

II

Lanny wasn't needed and decided that he would turn Monument for a while and look at something beautiful. He would cultivate his old-time Munich acquaintances—assuming that any of them were alive and had not fled the bombs. His first thought was of Freiherr von Breine, Bavarian landowner and art collector from whom he had purchased a painting as a cover for his presence in Munich while working up a scheme to get the elder Freddi out of Dachau.

He went walking and saw the great Deutsches Museum, a burned-out shell. He saw the Nazi Braune Haus, where he had met Hitler; he remembered the red-leather chairs studded with bronze nails and the big bronze initials on the office door. In the entrance hall had been a marble statue of Dietrich Eckhard, sot, drug addict, and Nazi philosopher, a large benevolent-looking Aryan god with an immense head, bulging forehead, and surprisingly small eyes. Now the building, a shrine of Nazism, was one heap of wreckage. Farther on was the enormous white-colonnaded Haus der Deutschen Kunst, which the wits of the town had called "the Greek railroad station"; here Hitler had housed the commonplace art works of which he approved. He had had it covered with a huge fish net, dark green in color; now the net flapped in the wind, but it had done its work, making the bombardiers think it was a park.

Lanny went on to the residential district in which the Freiherr had his fine home. Such districts had been spared, except where they were too close to military targets. The Freiherr's house was intact, but he wasn't living there; the Nazis had turned him out, and he was living in the gardener's cottage in back. The Americans had taken over the mansion, which pleased the owner greatly, because they would pay him rent and make it possible for him to patronize the black market.

He was a round-headed, dark-eyed Bavarian, with dark hair turned gray. He was no longer plump and rosy, but still kept his worldly grace, his bonhomie, and tried his best to take a humorous view of the experiences he had been through. Never tell your troubles, for if you do your friends will stop coming to see you! He said: "*Grüss Gott!*" and added, "Thank Him we no longer have to talk about blood and soil, blood and race, blood and iron, blood and guts!" Bavarians of his generation had watched a kaleidoscope of history during the past fifty years: a monarchy with mad rulers, a world war, a Socialist republic and a Communist revolution, a democratic republic, and a Nationalist revolution. "And now," said he, "we have an American Military Government—and what are you going to do to us?"

"We are going to treat you politely," replied the assimilated colonel; "that is, unless you have been a Nazi. I'll be pleased to give you a clean bill of health, and you can have a position in a new civil government when it is formed."

"*Gott behüte!*" exclaimed the pious gentleman. "No politics for me! But if I dared to ask a favor I'd suggest very humbly that your government might return my paintings that the Nazis got from me."

"*Lieber Baron*, that happens to be exactly what I am in Munich for. Any *objets d'art* that you can prove were yours will assuredly be returned."

"Technically speaking, they are not mine, for I had to sign a document parting with them. Herr Walter Andreas Hofer came to see me—you know that gentleman, perhaps?"

"I have had the pleasure of meeting him several times." Lanny didn't say "at Karinhall," for that would have taken too much explanation.

"Such a visit was never a pleasure to any German who owned paintings. Herr Hofer would say, 'Reichsmarschall Göring's birthday comes next month, and we think it would be a gracious act to make him a present for his planned National Museum.' If you owned a good painting, he would suggest that you give it. If you didn't own one good enough for the great Museum, he would tell you about one, and the price; all you had to do was to pay for it. Nobody ever had to be told how dangerous it would be to refuse."

"You were fortunate in owning good ones," Lanny said, smiling. "You will get them back if we can find them. If you had paid money, you might not have stood so good a chance. That question has not come up."

The elderly aristocrat gazed earnestly at this handsome American officer, no doubt trying his best not to look incredulous. "You really mean, *lieber Herr Budd*, that our property will be returned to us, and not seized for reparations?"

"I am telling you the policy of the organization in which I am serving; the Monuments, Fine Arts, and Archives Commission."

"You Americans are indeed an extraordinary people!"

"We are hoping to set a standard for international conduct. We shall hang many war criminals, I hope, but we do not plan to rob innocent civilians."

III

The Freiherr let it rest there. Did he remember how he had said to Lanny, in days before the war, that Germany had to expand? Most Germans had said that, but not one would say that civilians had any sort of responsibility for the hideous things that had been done in the Fatherland. One and all they would assert that they hadn't known what was going on, and that, anyhow, there was nothing they could have done. *Ein einzelner, machtloser Mensch!* No one of them ever stated whether he had been among those crowds, sometimes a million in one spot, which whooped and roared for National Socialism and its Führer.

"What can I do in return?" inquired the Freiherr, and Lanny said, "You can help us to find where art treasures have been hidden, so that we can return them where they belong. Do you have any idea whether Göring kept any of his accumulations in the South?"

"I am informed that all his Karinhall collection was put into freight cars and brought south, and that the train is somewhere near Berchtesgaden. The French got to it first, and so you had better hurry if you plan to do anything altruistic."

"That is indeed most interesting," said Lanny.

"Also, Emmy Göring visits in a *Schloss* belonging to a rich South American at Zell am See. It is very unlikely that Hermann has failed to trust her with a few old masters, as a safeguard against mischance. I have heard that they are there."

"*Besten Dank, Baron.* May I ask how you learn things like this?"

"Oh, we Bavarians are great gossips, and when we meet in one another's homes we talk fast, always in whispers. What other pleasure have we? A few of us who trusted one another maintained a sort of underground against the Nazis."

"Will you maintain it against us Americans?"

"If you behave in the decent manner you have told me, there will be an underground to help you. I assure you, the news you have just imparted will create a sensation in the proper social circles, and information will be poured in upon you. There is more I can tell you now."

"May I make notes?" asked the Monuments man. He had brought a pencil and some paper, on the chance that there might be none in a wealthy Münchner's home. He made a note of the Göring train and of the castle at Zell am See. He noted that there might be treasures hidden in Ribbentrop's castle at Fuschl, and also in one of those built by the mad King Ludwig II of Bavaria. There was a colossal hoard in the salt mine at Alt Aussee, high up in the mountains southeast of Berchtesgaden; it was said to contain ten thousand paintings, including most of, and perhaps all, the treasures from the Vienna Museum. And so on and on, until Lanny had a sheet of paper full of notes and the promise of more in a few days.

"But don't mention me," added Freiherr von Breine. "I can do much more for you that way."

IV

The first outfit of the art seekers arrived, and there was a great scurrying round to get billets, an eating place, and a headquarters big enough to hold all the treasures which would be brought in. They were allotted the Verwaltungsbau, the Nazi administration building, one of those immense massive structures which the world's greatest architect had erected for his Thousand-Year Reich. Everything was built of stone, solid, square, plain, useful, and ugly. It was three stories high and occupied nearly a whole block facing the Königsplatz. Inside were two large central courts, from each of which a marble stairway led to the floor above. The building had not been hit by bombs but had been badly shaken; the skylights had been smashed, and rain had poured in; but very quickly they were boarded up. The doors wouldn't lock, but they too would be repaired, and the smashed windows covered with translucent plastic.

There was a second building, a duplicate of the Verwaltungsbau, the Führerbau, where Hitler's own Munich offices had been; it was only a block away, and the two buildings were connected by underground passages. It was in the Führerbau that Chamberlain had signed the Munich Pact, which was supposed to guarantee peace for our time; the table on which the signing had been done was now to be used as a conference table by these art experts from the Fogg Museum in Cambridge and other museums of America. Less than seven years had passed, and the Lord had put down the mighty from their seats and exalted them of low degree!

The plan was to engage a staff of German museum technicians and clerks to carry on the enormous work which lay ahead, and here as everywhere was the difficult task of excluding Nazis, in a land where everybody had been compelled to be a Nazi in order to survive. The Monuments were working under pressure; they had already learned about the train full of Göring's paintings and realized that this was probably the most valuable collection ever assembled in the world. Something had to be done about it without delay, and they were re-

lieved to learn that Lanny had already discussed the matter with headquarters of Seventh and had procured the necessary permits and arranged for a T-force to lead the way. There wasn't supposed to be any
more fighting, but there were bands of Nazi fanatics holding out in the
forests and mountains, and nobody could tell where they might make
a raid. That treasure would call for a night-and-day guard, and a train
of trucks to bring it in.

V

Lanny had a claim to go with the first outfit, and it was granted.
They were exceptionally nice fellows, informed about all the subjects
which he loved best. Two jeeps and a command car sped rapidly over
the *Autobahn* toward Salzburg; already the shellholes had been filled
up, smashed Panzers thrown into ditches, and temporary bridges built;
the engineers with hairy ears did such things overnight. It was almost
mid-May, and the sun was warm, the fruit trees in blossom, and the
snow-clad mountains a glorious background to every scene. From this
far-off perpetual snow flowed torrents of water, running clear green in
the many streams, except for the creamy foam. When you got off the
Munich plain there were rolling hills, and then the rise into the Austrian
Alps.

At this southeastern corner of Germany a lumpy peninsula-shaped
piece of land juts into Austria, so that at once place you can go west
into a land that lies east of you, and at another you can go north into
a land that lies south of you. Adi Schicklgruber, onetime wastrel of the
Vienna slums, had chosen this region for his mountain retreat and had
purchased a property looking out over the land of his birth. He had expanded a modest villa into an establishment suitable for the occupancy
of a future ruler of the world.

They passed the wide blue Chiemsee, and soon after passing Traun-
stein they left the *Autobahn* and turned southward. The road sign
said "Berchtesgaden, 30 Kilometers." The road followed a winding
stream and was beautifully balanced, so that you could drive fast even
on the curves, and the forests sped by as if in a motion-picture film.
Lanny did not tell anyone how familiar this road was to him; how
many times he had come here, by day and by night, in sunshine, rain,
and snow. In the first place they would not have believed him, and
if anyone did, that one would never have ceased to wonder what sort
of man was this, and which side had he really been on.

They came into the pleasant little summer-resort town, with many hotels and some baths. Up to three days ago it had been swarming with Nazis, and now it was swarming with "Amis," as the Nazis called their principal foes. These particular Amis wore a shoulder patch consisting of a blue triangle with a yellow triangle inside and a red triangle inside that, and this meant they were of the Seventh; their unit was the 101st Airborne Division, very cocky and proud of themselves. They would tell you that the reason the SS were coming down out of those snow-clad Alps so fast was that they wanted the honor of surrendering to so renowned an outfit.

The Monuments hunted up the CP and asked about the Göring train. It developed that somebody had waked up to the importance of a possible billion dollars' worth of paintings, and the stuff was now being unloaded and taken by a back road to a little place called Unterstein, where there was a rest house until recently used by German officers. This had some fifty rooms, all that could be needed to sort and catalogue nine freighter-car loads of art treasures.

So there was no longer an emergency, and the Monuments man in charge of the T-force decided that the thing to do was to go on to Alt Aussee, some seventy miles farther east, inspect the salt mine, and make sure the thousands of paintings there hidden were not in danger from either pillagers or dampness and mold. The CP wasn't sure whether their men had got there or not, but they or others from the Third would surely do so in course of the day; anyhow, it didn't matter so much, for word had just come that in Berlin the three German commanders—of Army (Keitel), Navy (Friedeburg), and Air Force (Stumpff)—had that morning signed a formal surrender of all German Armed Forces, to be effective at one minute past eleven o'clock that night. Lanny asked the officer who gave them the news, "Why that extra minute?" The officer, who came from the Bronx in New York, answered, "Dunt esk!"

So this was VE Day, so long desired, so long postponed! There was wild rejoicing at home, but not much in the Army; people were too tired. War was no fun, and don't let anybody tell you different— so said the doughs, the Joes, the sad sacks. Here and there the officers shook hands, and a few of them took too many drinks. The enlisted men repeated their old question, "When do we get to go home?" Don't talk to any of them about picturesque and historic buildings, without plumbing or central heating or other comforts! Let the Frenchies and the Heinies have their art and culture, and give us the corner drugstore with the soda fountain, and the movie palace with a new program twice a week—in the American language!

VI

The Monuments studied their maps, and meantime Lanny thought it over; then he said, "I don't suppose it will make any difference to you if I stay here. There are some people I can talk to, and maybe get information of importance." They knew what he had already got and wished him luck.

For eight years Lanny Budd's thoughts had been swinging, pendulumlike, between the White House in Washington and Hitler's Berghof, up on the heights to the east of this little town. He had seen the Führer in many other places, but this was the place of his own choice, the place that revealed his soul. Berchtesgaden had been named for a wild witch, and Adi loved all the imaginings of the *Urgermane* who had worn bearskins and lived in the dark forests of this land. Deep in his soul he believed in all these creatures, the witches, elves, giants, ogres, gnomes, dragons, Lorelei, Valkyrie, and even gods; he took the *Niebelungenlied* for history and the *Ring* for the whole of music and poetry. The old bloody legends had worked in his subconsciousness, and made him willing to exterminate some ten or twenty million people for the crime of not being German. Almost in sight of his retreat was the village of Braunau, in the Austrian Innviertel, where he had been born, and beyond it was the town of Linz where his mother had been born, and where he had meant to erect in her memory a temple of art that would cast Karinhall into the shade.

Now he was dead, it appeared, and his Thousand-Year Reich and all his other dreams. His Berghof was a burned-out ruin, and Lanny had seen enough of these. But up on the Obersalzberg was a living woman —or so he hoped. A year and a half had passed since he had called upon her and she had given him food and a guide to help him escape into Italy. He hadn't been able to write her a bread-and-butter letter, but now he could pay a visit and see how she was. As a source of underground whispers she was even better than Freiherr von Breine. She had had her summer chalet here ever since she had married, unhappily, the Fürst Donnerstein much older than herself; that meant some thirty years, and she knew all the *grosse Welt* which had sought refuge in these mountains, and her servants knew their servants.

It was a pleasant afternoon's walk from the town, and Lanny proposed to enjoy it on a delightful bright day. But Major Jennings of G-2, to whom he broached the project, said that it was out of the question. The war wasn't even over yet, and any German soldier had the legal right to shoot any American in uniform. In these woods were hiding not merely Nazi fanatics but displaced persons and escaped prisoners from a dozen nations and plain bandits on the rampage. Mr. Budd's OSS credentials were of the best, and if he had business that called him to the Obersalzberg the Army would provide him with an escort; it wouldn't let him go strolling off as if this were the Adirondacks.

VII

So the ex-P.A. rode in state in a Mercedes car, with an armed chauffeur and a tommy gunner in front, and nobody took a shot at them. There was the familiar chalet, intact, and there was Hilde, Fürstin Donnerstein, out in her garden, picking caterpillars off her cabbages like any peasant woman. In the old days she would have had a wide basket and been cutting roses for her dinner table; she had loved roses, and now she loved cabbages. She had been beautiful and gay, and now her hair was gray and her face lined and the skin of her hands freckled and toughened by outdoor work. She was sad, for her mother had died in the bombing of their Berlin palace and her sister was ill in the house. There was no doctor to be had—they were all tending wounded and dying men.

She was delighted to see this vision from the free world. "I knew that you would come, Lanny. But you are in uniform!"

He explained that he was a noncombatant, and she said it was all right with her either way—all the decent people of Germany were sick of the Nazis and their works. She took him out to the summerhouse built on a point of rock where they had sat in happier times. From there you could see where the Berghof had been, and she offered to get her opera glasses and let him inspect the ruins. He said no, it saddened him to think of the house being bombed, for it had been a beautiful place; but it would have been a Nazi shrine, of course, and the Americans didn't want to leave any monuments to that evil creed. They would be careful not to make any martyrs either; nobody would be punished until he had had a public trial and been proved a criminal.

"That will include your neighbor, *Der Dicke*," he said with a smile, and she told him the amazing story of what had been happening to Göring in the last week or two. He had gone to Berlin and tried to convince Hitler that the war was lost, but Hitler would not be convinced and had flown into one of his rages; Göring had come away and told his friends that the Führer was insane. Later he had telephoned Hitler, proposing to take over Germany and carry out the surrender; Hitler in return had called him a traitor and scoundrel and had ordered the SS to seize him and shoot him at once. The SS had obeyed the first half of the order, but they had hesitated about the second half, for the Reichsmarschall with his jeweled baton was a majestic person in their eyes. In the confusion of defeat there had been a conflict of authority, and a group of Göring's paratroopers had dashed in and rescued him and carried him off somewhere into the mountains.

"What a story!" he exclaimed. "What a world we are living in!"

"I have a hard time making up my mind that I want to go on living in it," said Hilde. "But I see you looking well and happy. Tell me how you got away."

He told the story of his walking and hitchhiking southward, and how by the combined magic of Italian Partisans and American secret agents he had been carried out into the Adriatic on a fishing boat and picked up by a seaplane. Now he was looking for art works hidden by the Nazi plunderers, and she was the one who was going to collect information for him in this neighborhood; he had some secret funds which he was authorized to pay out for such services, and there was no reason in the world why she shouldn't have some. "Moreover," he said with one of his cheerful grins, "I'll get you some insecticide from the PX, and you'll be able to spray your cabbages instead of picking off the bugs with your aristocratic fingers."

"There won't be anything aristocratic in Germany any more," she mourned; and he said he wished he could believe that, but feared it wasn't so.

"Hold onto your stocks and bonds," he told her; "especially industrials. Roosevelt is dead, and my guess is that America is going to uphold what it calls the private enterprise system all over the world. When the factories start up again you will once more be able to live in luxury on the toil of the German workers."

"Lanny, how horrid!" she exclaimed in English, for her speech was cosmopolitan, like her taste and acquaintanceship. "I thought you got over all that Socialism long ago!"

"I was only posing, old dear," he told her. "I am still as Pink as the roses that you used to grow."

"Some roses are Red," she warned. "And, *lieber Gott*, those awful Russians! Are you going to let them get hold of us?" He promised to use his best influence in Washington, provided that she would tell him all that she could about the hiding places of art treasures in the Bavarian Alps.

VIII

That suited her, and she went to work without delay. She told him about several places on the Obersalzberg where Göring would be apt to have such works hidden. "You know his hunting lodge here?" she asked; and he reminded her how he had sat before an enormous log fire in that sumptuous place and heard *Der Dicke* discourse upon the joys of sticking a spear into a wild pig. "You should have a search made in those forests," she said; "undoubtedly he has hiding places there. Emmy went to Berchtesgaden when he was arrested and has fled to the mountains with him. She will be pretty sure to come back to Zell, and there is where she would have her paintings—unless they are in the trunk of her car. I don't need to tell you that a single Rembrandt might be enough to keep a woman in comfort the rest of her life."

Also, there was Ribbentrop; he fancied himself as an esthete, in art as in every other way, and would undoubtedly have hidden old masters. Goebbels had a place here, and Rosenberg, for whom the Einsatzstab had been named; there had been the bitterest rivalry between him and Göring as to who should get the first choice of prizes, and if those two men were caught they would no doubt tell on each other. Adolf Wagner, lame Nazi boss of Munich, was a great plunderer too, but Hilde didn't know what had become of him. Hofer, Göring's so-called curator, was in Berchtesgaden, a red-headed rascal who cheated everybody, including his master.

Lanny said, "I met him at Karinhall; he is a great talker."

"They say he has a remarkable memory and knows the owner and price of every *objet d'art* that ever passed through his hands. All he will want is a promise of immunity for himself."

That went on for an hour or so; Lanny didn't trust to his memory, but made quick notes. He didn't linger in her house, for he knew that she was a woman with an empty heart, and she had once propositioned him, to use the New York phrase. He gave her a box of delicacies from the Army PX, and he promised to come again and not forget the insecticide. This was a product unobtainable in Germany, because the materials had gone into the making of poison gases for war. The Nazis had prepared enormous quantities but had never used them, because they knew that the Amis had them too.

IX

The investigator went back to Berchtesgaden and talked with Major Jennings, the top Intelligence officer of the outfit stationed here. He told this man what information he had got; and now that the fighting was to end in a few hours, G-2 had more time to think about Monuments and their problems. "Mightn't it be a good thing to raid that hunting lodge?" Lanny asked, and Major Jennings replied, "I'll suggest it, and I'm sure it will be done. Any of these people you want brought in for questioning, just say the word."

Lanny answered, "Thanks, but it will be better to approach them first as an art expert. They realize that their game is played out, and they want to make friends with their new masters."

"They make me sick to my stomach," was the other's comment. "Here in this vulture's nest you can't find a single one that ever wore so much as a vulture's feather."

The officer went off and talked to his commander, and when he came back he had an important item of news. "A report has just come in—Göring has surrendered. Sent out a white flag, and we went into the mountains and got him. He was more afraid of the Russians than he was of us."

"Where is he?" and when Lanny heard "Kitzbühel," he added, "I believe I could get more out of him than anybody else in the Army. He has counted me as a friend for more than a dozen years and has told me many secrets."

"Won't he hate your guts?"

"I have a perfect cover story—that Himmler tried to get me to turn against the Führer. I was afraid it would sound fishy, but Himmler has made it true by actually doing just that."

"We have been alerted to look out for that bird; he may have come this way, looking for his Redoubt."

"Nothing he says can do me any harm, for no one is believing any Nazis now. I think I ought to go to Kitzbühel right away, Major. I may be able to get Göring to talk, not merely about paintings but about all the gangsters he hates, and where his confidential papers are, and a lot of other things. Can you spare me a car again?"

"Sure thing. I'll give you a note to Major General Dahlquist, who commands our 36th Division. It's a great feather in his cap to have captured the Number Two."

"Poor old hulk!" said Lanny. "He ceased to be Number Anything

some time ago and was terribly humiliated about it. Will you mark the
note 'personal' and instruct one of your men to deliver it? There is
bound to be a swarm of newspapermen at the place, and my specialty
has been operating on the q.t."

"Sure thing," said Major Jennings again.

X

Lanny delayed only long enough to get his overcoat and a few other
belongings, including a box of rations which he would eat while being
driven in the car. Major Jennings had obtained permission to go along,
which would facilitate matters greatly. It was late afternoon, but the
days were long, and the sun had not yet disappeared behind the
mountains.

Kitzbühel is a winter resort to the southwest of Berchtesgaden, well
inside the Austrian border. They traveled by secondary roads, winding up valleys and through mountain passes for three hours. Meantime
Lanny talked about this extraordinary man he was going to meet, the
man who had interested him most of any of the Nazis, not even excepting Hitler—for he had a better mind than Hitler and a far better education. Hermann Wilhelm Göring was a combination of vile qualities
and great capacities; a first-class brain and a perverted soul. He was
a slave to greed and lust for power; he was an exhibitionist, a bundle
of vanities; but at the same time he had a sense of humor and could
laugh at jokes about what he was doing to the German people.

He had been brought up in a school of military cynicism and as a
young flight officer had known the bitterness of defeat; he had become
a drug addict and had suffered the loss of the woman he adored. Then
had come Hitler, a master hypnotist, a mass hypnotist; Göring had
seen success and glory there, and had climbed into Hitler's war chariot,
and lent this man of demonic fury the use of his organizing brain. He
had climbed to the height of what was called greatness in Germany;
he had devised for himself a whole wardrobe of fancy uniforms and
had covered his expansive chest with medals and decorations; he had
taken unto himself so many offices and titles no man could remember
them all. Lanny amused his traveling companion by seeing how many
he could call to mind:

Marshal of Greater Germany, Field Marshal General, Supreme War
Economic Authority, President of the Reichstag, Chairman of the
Council for Defense of the Reich, Commissioner in Control of Trans-
portation, Chairman of the Wartime Ministerial Council, Chief Hunter,

Governor of Prussia, Chief of Prussian Secret Police, Infantry General of the Reichswehr, Minister of the Forests, Minister of Aviation, Premier of Prussia, Nazi Minister without Portfolio, Member of the Secret Cabinet Council, Director of State Theaters and Operas . . .

From all that he had become a prisoner at Hitler's order, barely escaping execution by the SS; and now he was a prisoner of his enemies, those who, he had said, would never be able to set foot on German soil or even drop a bomb thereon. Now he knew that he had brought destruction to the Reich's great cities and death to the flower of its young manhood. He knew that his armies were shattered, his titles emptied of content, his medals turned to junk. He had reached the depths of humiliation; and how would he take it? Lanny said, "I am guessing he will have a new role and have found a way to bluff it through."

XI

The command car arrived long after dark, and Lanny sat back in his seat, waiting while Major Jennings went into headquarters and talked with the officers. He came back saying "OK," and the car was driven around to a rear entrance of the commandeered Grand Hotel. There was Göring's own car, a sixteen-cylinder Maibach, with steel plates two inches thick and glass twice as thick as that. There would, no doubt, be newspaper correspondents in the hotel lobby, but Lanny didn't see them and they didn't see him.

He was escorted to a room and introduced to Major General Dahlquist, commander of this division, whom he had met before when the Army had come ashore on the Riviera; also to Brigadier General Stack, the officer who had gone up into the mountains to accept the surrender of this VGDIP. They inspected an ex-P.A.'s credentials and put questions to make sure that he really did know the *Nummer Zwei* Nazi. He gave them his pledge to report everything of importance that Göring might say; they assented to his idea that he should talk with the prisoner alone and that he should fraternize. So far, nobody had shaken hands with "*Unser Hermann*," but Lanny would do so, and perhaps even pat him on the back. "He will probably cry," said the art expert.

And, sure enough, he did! He had been all alone in the hands of his enemies for nearly twenty-four hours; he had been stripped of his medals, his weapons, and his jeweled baton of authority. His field-gray coat was unpressed and dingy looking, and his features flabby and ashen gray. To be sure, he had had a good dinner of chicken with peas and potatoes, and that meant a lot to him; but what food for his mind and soul? Not a particle!

"Lanny Budd!" he exclaimed as the visitor walked into his suite. His face showed surprise and a flash of pleasure.

Lanny said, "*Lieber Hermann!*" Then, seeing a shadow darken the other's face, he spoke quickly, "Don't tell me, *alter Freund*, that you have been believing false reports about me!"

"You are wearing an American uniform!" replied the other; and Lanny began his routine explanation, that he was only an assimilated officer, bearing no arms and concerned solely with the protection of art works. That was a humane occupation, and surely not one that his German friends could take ill.

"*Hören Sie, Hermann,*" he went on, speaking German as they always did. "I came to you the moment I heard you were here, for you are the friend whose good opinion I most value. Hear my story with an open mind. I am sure you will not take the word of Heinrich Himmler against mine."

The ex-P.A. had perfected his alibi by careful study and had tried it out on Heinrich Jung and Günther Furtwängler. It was a story cut to fit the Reichsmarschall, who hated Himmler beyond any other Nazi, as the man who had supplanted him in the Führer's favor and had kept him out in the cold for a couple of years. Only a few days ago this odious usurper had publicly tried to sell out his Führer to the Allies, and it was easy to believe that he had been cherishing this idea for some time. Lanny told how he had been waiting in the New Chancellery Building for the Führer to return from the front when the former poultry grower had come in and put him through a shrewd cross-questioning, designed to find out his attitude to the Führer and to the war, and leading up to the question of the Allies' attitude to the peace, and what that attitude would be if they no longer had Hitler to deal with.

"It froze my very bones, Hermann," declared the art expert. "I had heard rumors of plots to kill the Führer and had warned him about them; and here was this most dangerous man in Germany trying to draw me into them. I couldn't be sure whether he was in such a plot himself or whether he would just permit them to succeed and take advantage of the event. What he was trying to find out from me was what the attitude of the Allies would be toward a German regime headed by a dependable non-political person such as Heinrich Himmler."

"What did you tell him?" inquired *Der Dicke*. He fixed his small, hard blue eyes upon his visitor—and this was unusual for him, for his eyes had a way of darting here and there while listening.

"I told him that I was a non-political person, like himself, and I didn't know the answer to his question. I realized that from that moment my life was in danger. I had come into Germany because the Führer had asked me to, and I was anxious to help him; but what could I do now? Could I imagine the Führer taking the word of an alien enemy against that of the man whom he most trusted, the man upon whom he depended for the protection of his life?"

"Why didn't you come to me?"

"What right did I have to put such a burden upon any friend? I knew that if you took my side it might be your life against Himmler's; and you yourself had told me that you had lost favor at court. I took it that the kindest thing I could do was to keep out of your way."

"How did you get out of Germany?"

"I had a friend from the old days, an entirely non-political person. I went to him, and he let me stay with him for a week or two and then sent me to Italy as his business representative. What troubled me most was that I knew false rumors would be spread about me and that my friends would believe them. You know how many people were jealous of my position as the Führer's friend and were eager to see me ousted."

XII

Would Göring swallow this tale? Lanny knew that he was nobody's fool; but he couldn't be certain that the tale was false, and anyhow it might please him to pretend to believe it. After all, what did it matter now? He was lonely, and Lanny had always been good company; especially so at present, because he came from the outside world. If he had been a rascal he had been a shrewd one, and that didn't make him any the less interesting to talk to.

The prisoner wanted very much to know what was going to happen to him. He had the idea that he was to be taken to General Eisenhower; he thought his military rank entitled him to that, and Lanny promised to support his petition. Then he wanted to know, should he carry his baton, and should he wear a pistol? Lanny said that these were questions for a military man, not for a mere Monument. This was protocol, and he took it gravely; in his own mind he doubted very much whether Hermann Wilhelm Göring would ever see General Ike and whether he would ever again wear a pistol in this life.

Kindness and joviality had been the fat man's role ever since Lanny had known him, and he played it exactly as in old days. He had had a rare adventure, being rescued in Berchtesgaden and fleeing up into the snow-covered heights, surrounded by a company of his own trusted officers and men. He told about it with zest, admitting that he had a bad scare—for that belonged in his role of frankness. He was furious against Hitler. Ungrateful wretch! After all that Hermann had done for him! The last time Göring had seen him, April 22, with the Russians pounding at the gates of Berlin, his behavior had indicated a cracked mind. Later on, over the telephone, he had screamed like a maniac.

"You know, he often raved at people, but he always knew what he was doing and stopped when he was through. But now he couldn't control himself; his disappointment was too terrible. He issued orders to divisions and corps that no longer existed; he jumped them about as if they were chessmen, ignoring the fact that they could not travel the roads by day on account of your airmen. When I told him that the few planes we had left were grounded for lack of fuel, he shouted at me, 'I order them to fly!' Of course, one does not get planes off the ground just by words."

"Do you think he is dead, Hermann?"

"I do not doubt it. He had told me many times that he would never be taken alive."

"But might he not have escaped?"

"He couldn't bring himself to face the thought of defeat, and when at last the idea was forced upon him, it was too late. The Russians broke through suddenly, and it was the same here in the south; we had planned to set up a Redoubt and make a last-ditch stand, but your General Patton cut the country in half."

Lanny thought it good tactics to remark, "I think I ought to tell you, Hermann; in order to get permission to come here and see you, I had to promise that I would tell our officers everything you said."

Der Dicke shrugged his heavy shoulders. "What difference does it make now? *Alles ist kaput.* You will have all our records; we Germans are great keepers of records, you know, and here, too, the speed of your armies governs the situation. There has been no time to burn very much."

XIII

This was the occasion for a Monuments man to explain the special purpose for which he was here. To talk about art was the best way to cheer up an old-style robber baron, threatened with melancholia; to appeal to him as a fellow esthete was the way to gain his heart. To be sure, it took a lot of persuading to get him to believe that the American government had gone to the trouble and expense of picking out a large staff of experts and sending them over to Germany in order to return art works to their former owners whether these owners happened to be French or Dutch or Polish or even Jews. Hermann had had a vision of his vast collection being shipped to New York and Washington and other American cities; he had been sure that would happen to the treasures of the Kaiser Friedrich Museum of Berlin, the Gemäldegallerie in Dresden, and the other priceless public collections. Lanny had to swear upon his honor as an art lover and a friend that this was not so, that all such collections were considered to be the property of the German people, upon whom the Americans had never been waging war.

You couldn't expect Hermann Wilhelm Göring to have any honor as a politician or a man; but, oddly enough, he still dreamed of perpetuating his name as a connoisseur of art. Once Lanny had convinced him on that level, he agreed that the wisest thing he could do was to entrust his priceless possessions to the care of this well-informed member of the conquering nation. He pointed out how conscientiously he himself had guarded the treasures, even in the confusion of defeat. The railway cars in which he had shipped the Karinhall collection had all been air-conditioned, and never once had they been kept in any building that was not fireproof. "It was my intention to present Karinhall as a museum to the German people on my sixtieth birthday, in 1953," said *Der Dicke*; and no fat face could have looked more mournful when he said, "Now I wonder where I will be on that date!"

Lanny exclaimed, "*Nur Mut, Hermann!* Eight years is a long time these days, and I cannot prophesy; but I can tell you that several springs hotels in Virginia and North Carolina have been set aside as dwelling places for the higher German officers, and since most of the rooms have private baths, they are far more comfortable to live in than any German castle."

The ex-P.A. asked permission to make notes. He jotted down the fact that the Karinhall collection had first been transported to Göring's castle of Beldenstein on the Pegnitz River in Northern Bavaria. When Patton had got too near to that, it had been removed to Berchtesgaden. Lanny could give the assurance that it would be taken to the Führerbau in Munich, and that the same thing would be done with the Vienna and other collections now in the Alt Aussee salt mines. Lanny told how the treasures of the Kaiser Friedrich were safe in the vaults of the Reichsbank in Frankfurt; his wife had been there and inspected them. Thus encouraged, Göring imparted the fact that the crown jewels of the Holy Roman Empire had been taken to Nürnberg and walled up under the Paniers-Platz; these included the crown of Charlemagne, which the Pope had placed upon that emperor's head in the year 800. The Prussian crown jewels had been placed in a sort of shrine, along with the bones of Frederick the Great and of Frederick William the Great Elector, and buried deep in a salt mine in Central Germany.

And that wasn't all. There were those Nazi rascals who had dared to try to have collections rivaling the Reichsmarschall's. That scoundrel Ribbentrop, and that upstart and nobody Martin Bormann, who had managed to worm himself into the Führer's graces—imagine such men setting up as art authorities! And Himmler, if you please; and that deranged mentality Rosenberg—"He got his name on the organization, but I got the best of the stuff—ha, ha, ha!" said Hermann. He was alluding to the ERR, the Einsatzstab Reichsleiter Rosenberg, which had been set up to handle the art plundering in foreign lands. Göring told where each of these collectors had kept his treasures; he told where they would probably be hidden; and when he didn't know he told the names of subordinates and advisers who would tell if they were well frightened.

Evidently the Third Reich was breaking up not merely militarily but morally. *Der Dicke* didn't have a good word to say for a single one of the men with whom he had been co-operating for almost a quarter of a century. Not even for his Führer! Göring was free now to say what he really thought, and he pointed out that Hitler had never traveled and was both narrow and ignorant; that was why he had let himself be lured into the frightful blunder of a two-front war— that turned into a multiple-front war before it finished. Imagine attacking Russia, and then six months later declaring war on the United States—and just to oblige Japan! "As if Japan would be able to give us any help!"

"Did you know the attack on Pearl Harbor was coming?" asked Lanny; and the answer was, "We were as much surprised as you. I was still in the Führer's confidence in those days, and I am sure he would have told me if he had known. I suppose the Japs were afraid to trust us."

The prisoner of war went on to recall how bitterly he had opposed the attack upon Russia. "You can bear witness to that, Lanny," and Lanny could and did. "I think that my fall from grace began at that time. The more I turned out to be right, the more it annoyed the Führer, until he could no longer bear to confront me. You see, in the early days he acted against the advice of his generals and was proved right so many times that he came to think of himself as infallible, and he had to prove it, even if it meant the ruin of all Germany. The evidence of his rightness was the territory he had taken, and he couldn't bear to give up a single foot of it—at Stalingrad, or in France, or the Rhineland, or the Ruhr."

"A terrible set of calamities," Lanny agreed—to keep him going.

"What beat us was your country's industrial power. I warned the Führer about it, but even I had only a slight idea of what you could do. Your father must have a colossal plant by now."

"He has indeed; but I haven't seen it for some time."

"From the beginning I pleaded with the Führer to recognize that this war would be won by air power and to concentrate on that. But I suppose he thought I was just trying to get glory for my own branch of the services. He spent our energies on rockets, when it should have been engines for planes. And meantime you built bombers, bigger and bigger. I knew you would do it, but I must admit I never thought you'd be able to get a fighter-bomber that could fly to Berlin and back."

XIV

This post mortem went on for a long while. There was no further need for secrecy, and Lanny mentioned the proximity fuse, and the radar and Loran devices that had enabled night-fighters to find and hit their enemy in complete darkness. He said, "I don't suppose you waste any love upon the Japs; and if you have new things, they might be useful to us in that part of the world." So Göring talked freely about new German war devices, and where they were being made, and who would know about them. That was the thing Lanny had come for, and he did not fail to make careful notes.

Thus there was a V-2 rocket that could be fired from a submarine— and the submarine didn't have to come to the surface but could fire from three hundred feet under water. "That would have been pretty good off New York harbor, *nicht wahr?*" said Göring with one of his old-time smiles. Lanny answered, "It may be pretty good off Tokyo harbor."

Also there was an improved V-2—the "flying telegraph pole"—almost ready for service, and having a range of eighteen hundred miles; and there was the dreaded V-3, which was to fly through the stratosphere from Berlin to New York and even farther. "It's really too bad we couldn't have had a try at that!" said the genial Reichsmarschall; but now *alles* was *kaput*, and the Americans were free to dig out all these secrets at Peenemünde and at the huge rocket-assembly plant built eight hundred feet deep in the Kohnstein Mountains near Nordhausen.

Then Göring asked a question that startled Lanny, though a practiced intriguer didn't show it. "Did you ever visit a place called Oak Ridge, Tennessee?"

The other replied, quite truthfully, "No," and then added a dutiful lie, "I don't think I ever heard of it."

"Our Intelligence Service in America hasn't been anything to brag about, but we were told that at that place you have built a tremendous plant with the idea of making an atomic bomb. Of course it may be just camouflage for some other line of activity."

Said Lanny, "That is something outside my father's province, and I wouldn't know about it. If it comes off, we can be glad it won't be over Germany."

"Our physicists tell us it's a delusion," said Göring. "They were happy to know that you were wasting your resources on it."

"It may have been one of Roosevelt's hunches," said the ex-P.A. "He had them, you know, and followed them, just like Hitler."

XV

It was late, and the fat man's eyelids showed signs of drooping. The visitor remarked tactfully, "I am keeping you too long. You have been generous as always, Hermann. You may rest assured that I shall do everything in my power to see that your precious paintings are kept safe for the benefit of posterity."

"Thank you," said the old-time robber baron. Lanny had thought of him thus the first time they had met; later, when Lanny knew him better and became aware of his love of art, he had called him a "Renaissance man," and this had pleased him greatly—he had even taken up the phrase. Now he remarked, "I had the best of those paintings in my home, Lanny, and never a day passed that I didn't look at them; they became a part of my being. Now you will send me to Virginia, where there are no paintings except bad ones. It will be like being marooned on a desert island."

Then it was that tears came into the eyes of this Renaissance man; not for the great German cities that had been blasted to rubble, not for the millions of German youths who had been turned into carrion, but for the Cranachs and the Rembrandts, the Rubenses and the Holbeins and the Van Dycks, that he was never going to see again; for the greatest art collection that had ever been assembled in the whole of history and that had been planned to earn the gratitude of posterity and carry the name of Hermann Wilhelm Göring down through all the ages of mankind! "Lorenzo di Medici would have been a mere footnote to the history of that bright name!"—so he said.

15

Art Is Long

I

DRIVING back to Berchtesgaden, Lanny thought about the mail he might get there, and one letter in particular that he had been expecting for a year and a half. Now, if ever, was the time when he should get word from his half-sister Marceline. Now she would have come out of her hiding place and be trying to get in touch with her family. She would have no way to find out where Lanny was, but she would write to her mother at Bienvenu; Beauty had come back from Marrakech and was waiting in painful suspense and perhaps joining her husband in prayer. Marceline couldn't be sure that her mother was still alive, or that the villa at Bienvenu was still in existence; but she could be sure that Budd-Erling Aircraft Corporation was functioning and that a cablegram to Robbie would reach him or, if he had died, some member of his family.

Marceline was a capable person and knew her way about in the world. Lanny had informed her as to her status; she was an American citizen, if she chose to enter that claim, by virtue of her mother's being of American birth. That she had voluntarily gone to Germany after America was at war with that country, and had taken a position as a dancer in a Berlin night club, would give her a black eye with the American public, but it could hardly interfere with her citizenship status. And in the confusion of the present moment who would remember dates or bother to ask questions on such a point? Marceline would go to the nearest American Army post and report herself as an American citizen who had hidden out during the war. She would request and obtain permission to write through Army channels to her mother on the French Riviera and to cable her half-brother in Newcastle, Connecticut. Somehow or other word would surely come.

But there was no word; Lanny with sorrow made up his mind that there was never going to be such word. Someday, perhaps, in the records of the SS or the Gestapo, the mystery might be solved; some day Heinrich Himmler might be captured—he was reported as having fled to Norway—and Lanny might go to him and get the answer. Meantime there were the living; a letter from Beauty, saying that all three of them were back home, safe and well; a letter from Laurel, reporting that she had been working on the overworked officers of the Seventh in Heidelberg and had extracted from them the promise that in a week—"*about* a week," they said—they would consider it safe to let a lady writer travel to Berchtesgaden and report what she found in the haunts of the wild witch and the wild wizard.

II

Lanny wrote a report for Professor Goudsmit and one for Monuments, of which he sent carbon copies to the chiefs in the various collecting points, Munich, Frankfurt, Marburg, and one to the headquarters in Versailles.

That duty done, he was free to ride in a Monuments car to Alt Aussee, some seventy miles southeast of Berchtesgaden—the distance being made greater by winding through mountain passes and down into valleys. Beautiful scenery, with snow still in the high places, but melting fast and turning small rivulets into rushing torrents. Endless vistas of evergreen forests, and in the valleys lovely little villages with irregular streets and brightly painted houses with many gables—"gingerbread houses," the Americans called them. This was not a strategic area, and war hadn't come here, except in the last hours.

The GI who drove him had been going back and forth and knew

the landmarks. Soon after leaving Salzburg, there was Lake Fuschl,
with the castle that Ribbentrop had stolen. Then came the Wolf-
gangsee, with the Weisse Rössel, the inn famed in musical comedies.
Would Doc like to get out and see the old church, with the Pacher
altar? And then Bad Ischl, where the old Emperor Franz Joseph had
had his summer home. There he had bought a villa for an actress.
Then a steep pass, and Bad Aussee, and after it Alt Aussee, on a deep
dark lake, where the world seemed to come to an end, lost in mountains. The Third Army, Lucky Forward, had got here first, and its
11th Armored Division was guarding the mine. Lanny had no business being here without a permit; he had to go at once and explain
himself and get one, and be warned not to travel anywhere in Third
territory without getting a permit first. Georgie Patton was rigid on
the subject of regulations: wearing your cap, keeping your coat
collar buttoned, saluting snappily—all those Army things which the
doughs contemptuously called "chicken." You couldn't have more
than five gallons of gas at a time, and the rule against officers driving
cars was rigidly enforced.

The mine was high up, in the Salzberg—the salt mountain. It was
the steepest road Lanny had ever traveled. Near it was "House 71,"
as it was called, a villa with a heavy iron fence and padlocked gates.
Here two OSS men had taken up their abode, and they welcomed
Lanny as a colleague. They had brought with them for questioning
no less a personage than Herr Walther Andreas Hofer, the Berlin art
dealer whom Göring had chosen as his number-one expert and super-
visor of plundering. The OSS had discovered him in Berchtesgaden
and had brought him to this remote region to keep him away from
evil influences. Lanny, who had known him at Karinhall, was greeted
as an intimate friend. A stocky little redhead, dressed in gray tweeds,
Hofer was to all appearances perfectly happy; he was loquacious, a
show-off, and here were important persons who were willing to devote all their time to listening to him.

This was the man who was credited with having invented the ingenious scheme of inviting wealthy Germans to give art presents to
the Reichsmarschall on his birthday. Hofer had a most extraordinary
memory; he knew the name of every such donor, what he had given,
and the price he had paid for it. He could remember every art trans-
action he had carried on since the coming of the Nazis; the name of
the painting, the price asked and the price paid, the size of the work,
and sometimes even the kind of frame it was in. There were some
things that he professed to have forgotten; but when Lanny told him

how he had visited Göring only the night before last and obtained the great man's approval of the American program, Herr Hofer suddenly remembered a lot more.

Lanny spent the night at House 71, and the agents told him the exciting story of the last few days. The balked and frenzied SS, seeing the Americans drawing near, had brought large cases containing dynamite, preparing to blow up and flood the mine and destroy all the art works in one grand bust. But the miners had risen and had blown up the mine entrances, making it impossible for the Nazis to get in. The American Army had arrived in the nick of time—"ten, twenty, thirty," said one of the OSS men; there was so much melodrama in this war that the movies would be telling about it for a thousand years. In this case it was not a virtuous maiden who was saved but a hundred thousand *objets d'art*, many of which were quite literally priceless.

III

A space had been chopped into the mountainside to make level ground, and a group of clean white two-story buildings had been erected, buildings with steep roofs to run the snow off, and with many gables and chimneys. These were the administration buildings of the salt mine, called "Steinbergwerke." Lanny wondered just where the mine was, and the guide opened a back door in the lower floor of the building, and it was the main entrance to the mine.

Lanny had been through a salt mine of the same kind, escaping from Germany, so it was no novelty to him. The salt is not mined in the usual sense of that word; enormous basins are dug inside the mine and water is pumped into them; the water absorbs the salt out of the heavy clay and then the water is pumped out and evaporated outside. That process has been going on for three thousand years, so legend declares; it is definitely known to have been going for six hundred. For that long, at least, imperial Austria had been breeding a race of men who specialized in working a mile inside a mountain and with another mile of mountain over their heads. The men were small but sturdy and had queer wizened faces; it was impossible for the Americans not to call them gnomes, and that didn't hurt their feelings, for they spoke and understood only a medieval German, difficult even for other Germans. They wore at their work an odd costume of white duck, the jacket having a collar like a cape, and large black buttons up the front. Germany and Old Austria were disciplined countries,

and everybody worked cheerfully if he could have a uniform to sym-
bolize his special abilities and obligations.

Salt mines had been chosen as art shelters because the salt absorbs
moisture and makes them comparatively dry; also the temperature is
uniform, about forty degrees Fahrenheit, and, oddly enough, slightly
warmer in winter. The systematic Germans had come, curators,
restorers, and a great staff of clerks; for there had to be exact records
of everything. There were 6755 paintings, 5350 of them being old
masters. More than half bore tags reading "A.H., Linz," meaning that
they were the property of Adolf Hitler, intended for that thousand-
year museum that was to end all museums.

IV

A little train run by a gasoline engine took you into the mine.
There were tiny flatcars, called *Hunde*—dogs—with just room enough
for two men facing each other. The jagged rock ceiling of the long
tunnel was menacingly close, but it would never hit you unless you
were taller than the gnomes. The tunnels ran immense distances, and
every now and then there was a locked iron door at the side. You un-
locked the door and there was a grotto. It might be full of Louis XV
chairs and tables, arranged as in a drawing-room; or you might find
yourself confronted by Michelangelo's statue of the Madonna, carved
in 1501, and stolen by the Nazis from the Bruges Cathedral; or by the
marvelous Van Eyck altarpiece, called "The Adoration of the Mystic
Lamb," dating from the fifteenth century, taken from the Ghent
Cathedral. There might be mysterious sealed cases; or boxes full of
gold and silver Renaissance armor; or stacked-up bales of tapestries;
or vegetable baskets piled with all sorts of miscellaneous art objects.

Many of the paintings were carefully wrapped and lay on numbered racks; others had evidently been brought in a hurry and were
just stacked against the walls. In the part of the mine called the
"Springerwerke" there were no doors to lock, and here stood GIs on
duty, wearing the long fleece-lined coats which the Germans had
made for use on the Russian front. Inside these places Lanny inspected
paintings which he had come to know at the Berghof; they now bore
that sacred label: "A.H., Linz." In other rooms the marking was
"ERR," Einsatzstab Reichsleiter Rosenberg. There were rooms divided into small compartments, and here the art treasures bore the
names of various Jewish families in Vienna; their return would be
easy—if there were any members of those families left alive.

There appeared to be no limit to the kind of stuff in this strange repository: Egyptian tombs, Greek and Roman portrait busts, Gothic relics, gold and silver church vessels, manuscripts, books and prints, furniture, rugs, jewels, coins, porcelain. Lanny had seen the like only once before in his life, in the Bronx, New York: the property of an American multimillionaire who had built an enormous warehouse to contain the treasures he never had time to look at. William Randolph Hearst had paid for the stuff with the pennies he had collected from newspaper readers over a period of more than half a century; under the laws of the business game that made it proper, and you could not indict him for the mass of crime, scandal, and political reaction he had fed to the American people through those years.

The Monuments men were at work here, measuring, estimating weights, and figuring how to handle this precious material; how many trucks it would require, and what size. The miners would give willing help, for they wanted to clear the stuff out and get back to their proper business. Whatever had been got in somehow could be got out somehow; it would be carted to those two immense buildings in Munich and there classified and ultimately returned to the land from which it had come. The plan was to put off the job of finding the original owners upon each country; American responsibility would end when the stuff had been turned over to that country and a receipt signed by the proper official.

V

Back in the town of Berchtesgaden, he found a letter from Laurel, saying that she had got permission and was coming. So he waited, indulging himself meanwhile in the pleasure of walking in these foot-hills and talking with the German people, not in the guise of a Nazi but as he really was. One and all they were polite, even obsequious, and one and all denied ever having had any sympathy with the Nazis. What they really thought was impossible to know. At home were people who talked blithely about the project of making the German people over according to the pattern of democracy; but the ex-*Bürgermeisterstellvertreter* of Urach had to admit to himself that he would hardly know how to set about it.

The magazine writer in search of copy put in her appearance. Her first question was, "Any news about Marceline?" He told her that he had about given up hope, and that cast a shadow over their meeting. But nothing could take away Laurel's relief that this most dreadful of wars was over. The whole world took on a different aspect, and she could draw a free breath for the first time in nearly six years. Lanny's reply was peculiar; he said that he felt let down; the war had kept him in a state of tension, and now he missed it. The wife said, "How like you men! I believe you are all as bad as General Patton!"

For the first time she could ask him questions and he was free to answer. He did not tell her everything at once; there were some painful experiences that he would never tell. But he satisfied her curiosity about his friendship with Hitler, something which had been a mystery to her since she had first come to know him. How had it been possible, and what had Hitler seen in him?

An ancient Roman emperor had made the remark, *"Pecunia non olet"*—money has no smell; but Adi Schicklgruber had proved that this was an error. He had developed a sharp sense of smell for money, and especially for that which might be obtained for his cause. In the early days he had diligently cultivated Frau Bechstein, widow of the piano manufacturer; and so on up to Stinnes and Thyssen and the other steel kings who had given him both money and arms and set him up in his business of conquering first Germany and then the rest of Europe.

To a Führer on the make the grandson of Budd Gunmakers had seemed a likely prospect; he was eager and alert, as well as polite and friendly. And then he had married Irma Barnes, heiress of twenty-three million dollars, so reported in the press. He brought her to visit Berchtesgaden, and Irma had listened to the Führer and declared outright, "I agree with every word you have said." Lanny didn't go that far, but had played the *Moonlight Sonata* for the Führer, and admired his taste in paintings, and been entirely agreeable company.

When Lanny's old friend and employer, Professor Alston, had heard about this contact, what more natural than that he should tell Roosevelt about it, and that Roosevelt should propose that Lanny become a presidential agent, and bring the information to him? Laurel asked if he would be willing to do the same thing for Truman, and he told her no. He wanted to be a normal man for a while and say what he really thought. "I have a sort of psychosis on the subject of secrecy," he declared. "I can't bear to talk about what I have done, and I have a shrinking from any sort of publicity."

Said the wife with a smile, "Wait till you start spending Emily's million dollars!"

VI

They were driven to Unterstein. The Karinhall art works, so many of which Lanny had learned to know and to love, had been spread out in the forty rooms of the rest house. The colonel in charge of the outfit on duty had the bright idea of diverting the minds of his troops by getting up an exhibition. "You know," he explained, "our boys were all keyed to the war, and now they have a let-down feeling; they don't know what to do with themselves." Laurel exchanged an amused glance with her husband; it was just what he had said about himself.

An art expert who was the stepson of a famous painter and had helped to get up art shows was the right person to be called upon. So husband and wife inspected the treasures and tagged those which they thought most likely to raise the cultural level of farm boys from the southern tip of Florida to the northern tip of Washington and points in between. It involved much shifting and carrying of paintings in heavy frames, and some conversation with the GIs who performed this labor—no gnomes from the salt mines here!

In the course of this experience an assimilated colonel and an assimilated lady captain came upon a curious discovery concerning the standards of propriety that prevailed in their native land. Castles and palaces, elegant furniture and gorgeous costumes, armor and weapons, lace and furs and jewels—all these things America had grown used to by way of the movies, and especially since the technicolor days. As for naked men, one saw plenty of those in the Army; but if ever you had seen naked women, it was at some place you did not mention in the presence of ladies. If you saw pictures of such, they were the "feelthy postcards" which were an industry in Europe, or in magazines which you called "cheesecake" and kept hidden from your mothers and sisters.

But here in this Göring collection of paintings was a sort of explosion of nakedness; the taste of the fat man had run to the buxom fleshiness of Rubens and the Flemish school and the delicate and graceful sensuality of Raphael and the other Florentines. There were even some that Lanny himself would have considered prurient, such as two panels by Boucher showing the rustic maidens of Marie Antoinette's France submitting to the amorous advances of elegant courtiers. And boys from the very proper South and the Puritan Middle West had to carry these paintings about and wait while a lady and a gentleman, their military superiors, stood and discussed them from a strictly esthetic point of view. The GIs would stand silent and embarrassed, and if they were asked a question they would blush to the roots of their hair. When they were among themselves they called the Monuments crew "the Venus fixers."

One amusing episode: there was a lifesize statue of the Magdalene, beautifully carved in fine wood and polychromed some four hundred years ago. Her bosom was covered by a flood of blond hair, but there was nothing to cover the rest of her. It happened that her features were identical with those of Emmy Sonnemann, German stage star who had become Göring's wife, and whose picture had been widely published in newspapers and magazines both German and American. Just recently she had been arrested with her husband, and again more pictures; so now all the GIs at Unterstein took to calling the statue "Emmy." They put her in the entrance hall, and that night when a cold wind was blowing from the snow-clad mountains Lanny observed that one of the sentries had put his overcoat over the figure. Lanny warned him, "You may get into trouble, soldier. You know you are forbidden to touch any of the art works."

"Sorry, Doc," said the man—he was young and really looked innocent. "I didn't mean to break the regulations, but I thought that Emmy looked chilly."

VII

From the rest house you could gaze across the valley to the Obersalzberg, site of the Berghof, and far above it, the top of the Kehlstein, where Hitler had built his solitary eyrie. It was a sight not to be missed, and Lanny borrowed a car and an Army driver who knew the road. Lanny himself had been taken there by the Führer, one of the two or three foreigners who had had that honor. It was perched right on the top of a mountain, built of stone hewed out in leveling the site. The road to it was terrific; in the village Lanny had recently been told that three thousand men had worked on it for several years. There were three tunnels on the way. Laurel held her breath and wished she hadn't started, but there was no way to turn until you got to the end of the road, where there was a turnaround for cars and a parking space.

You left the car and entered the mountain by a tunnel with bronze doors. The American Army was on guard, and had put up a sign to the effect that the elevator was for field-grade officers only; that meant majors and those of higher rank, but nobody objected when a colonel took a captain, his wife. You went up seven hundred feet through solid rock, and when you came out there was a dwelling with all the comforts of home, though it looked like a fort. On the second floor was an immense eight-sided room, with windows so that you could look out over Germany, Austria, and Italy. Here this mountain-loving man had come to commune with his dreams of a Thousand-Year Reich and everlasting fame. On the stone-paved loggia outside he had sat with his American friend and revealed his belief that there was recorded in the entire world's history only one man as great as Adi Schicklgruber, the onetime wastrel from a home for the shelterless in Vienna. That other great one was the camel driver Mohammed, who had known how to found a religion and make it stick for thirteen centuries. Adi was out to break that record, so he declared.

VIII

Hermann der Dicke had been taken to Augsburg, and Emmy— not the wooden but the real one—came to stay with her South American friend in the castle at Zell am See. Lanny went there with a T-force—one car and a "pickup"—to look for paintings. The Monuments asked him to take charge of the operation, since he knew her, and they didn't want any scenes with a woman. The chatelaine of Karinhall had always been cordial to the elegant son of Budd-Erling, and once Robbie had warned his son not to be too cordial to her. Now she did her actress-best to be pathetic and touching, and to play sad melodies upon his heartstrings. Those paintings were her personal property and were all that stood between her and outright starvation, herself and her little girl, so sweet and innocent. She produced the little one, now seven years old, and the little one wept with her mother, having been frightened by the strange events of the last two weeks.

Lanny played a mean trick upon this former First Lady of Naziland. (She had been that because Hitler was supposed to have been a bachelor and a virgin.) Lanny said to her what all the Nazis had been saying to him, up and down and across Germany, "I am sorry, and very much embarrassed, but you must know I cannot help it; I am merely carrying out orders; I am an employee of the Army and have no say in the matter." So she produced fifteen paintings, enormously valuable, of the Flemish school of five hundred years ago; they had been taken from the famous Renders collection in Brussels. Lanny appreciated them, and saw them carried out; then he said, "And now the rest, *gnädige Frau*."

She protested that that was all, and they had a quite ugly scene. He didn't really know, but he felt sure that she would not give up everything at the first try. She broke down and wept hysterically, and Lanny ordered the GIs to search the castle. Thereupon the child's nurse went without a word to a closet in the room and from behind a lot of clothing drew forth a lightly framed canvas about two and a half feet square and handed it to Lanny. He took one glance, and his heart gave a jump; it was Göring's famed "Vermeer," which he had shown to Lanny at Karinhall and for which he had traded a hundred and thirty-seven other paintings, valued at more than a million and a half guilders.

Lanny said nothing but took it out and saw it packed carefully. Back at Unterstein he placed it before the Monuments men, and right away there started that controversy which had shaken all Holland. One of those present was Tom Howe, handsome and genial director of San Francisco's municipal art museum; he was vehement in calling the work a fraud. "Look at the flat greens and blues and the lack of subtlety in the modeling of the flesh tones! It lacks that total visual effect which Vermeer so completely mastered." Lanny, who didn't feel so sure, pointed out that half the authorities in Holland, Vermeer's native land, had pronounced the work genuine. At Karinhall Lanny had of course said the same thing; he might have ruined his career as a P.A. if he had done otherwise.

The painting, called "Christ and the Adulteress," showed a half figure of a beardless Jesus, with hair falling over both shoulders. The woman taken in adultery, a subject eternally popular with painters, stood before him in profile, with head bowed and eyes cast down; two angry Jews stood behind the Christ, they being the ones who were ready to stone her. The painting would be taken back to Amsterdam, and before long would be proven to be the work of an obscure Dutch painter named van Meegeren, who had made a fortune out of painting and then "discovering" a number of "Vermeers" —a seventeenth-century old master whose known works were very scarce. Even when van Meegeren confessed, many of the authorities would refuse to accept his story, and he would have to do yet one more "Vermeer" in prison before they would give up.

IX

Next came a trip to Salzburg, and beyond it to Lake Fuschl, where the most odious of champagne salesmen in all Europe had a castle full of art works. What fun it had been to send armies into a foreign land and take possession of everything; to set yourself up in some-body else's castle on the shore of a blue Alpine lake, in the shadow of mountains covered with fir trees, and then proceed to fill the establishment with the lovely and beautiful things that you and your agents could find in Austria, Poland, and Czechoslovakia, France, Holland, and Belgium! It had been a popular form of diver-sion in Europe since the days of Greece and Rome, and some people had naïvely assumed that it was over for good—but Joachim von Ribbentrop had shown them, and now the armies had shown *him!*

His castle had become a recreation ground for American troops, and a string of Army trucks came and carted the treasures off to the Munich collecting point. After watching this operation, Lanny and his wife were driven back to Salzburg on a mild spring evening, a full moon lighting their way. They stopped in this small mountain city with the foaming river through the middle of it. This "Salt Castle's" name was famous all over the world because of the music festival that had been held here every summer. Adi Schicklgruber had changed it into one of his *Kraft durch Freude* festivals; he was not keen for internationalism, and especially not the kind that gave jobs to Jewish musicians and conductors.

Sitting in the familiar Mirabell Gardens, having supper, Lanny told his wife what this place had meant to him. In the little town of Hal-lein, a few miles to the south, his first marriage had come to an end. Irma had quarreled with him because of his ideas and associates, and when he had put her in the position of having to help Trudi Schultz escape from Germany, that had been the last straw; at the railway station of Hallein she had said good-by to him and gone back to her mother on Long Island.

So then, feeling very desolate, he had driven up to Salzburg. (Those wonderful days when you could have a car of your own, and pur-chase fuel for it in any town or village!) Lanny had tried to drown his sorrows in music; and, sitting in these pleasant gardens, he had found himself in the company of another sorrow-smitten gentleman, who had poured out his domestic troubles to an entire stranger. Lanny hadn't reciprocated; but now he remarked to Laurel that he often wondered whether the ruling-class reticence which had been impressed upon him since childhood wasn't really a great strain upon the emotional life.

The music had been delightful, also the dramas and the music dramas; and after each performance the crowds had emerged, everybody excited and pouring out volumes of art gossip, more about the artists than about the works they performed. He had boarded for a couple of weeks with the family of a civic official—everybody took "paying guests" for the festival and lived the rest of the year on the proceeds. Here again were people who vented their emotions freely, and the sixteen-year-old daughter of the family had fallen head over heels in love with a cultivated and wealthy American gentleman, who was greatly embarrassed. He had escaped with his conscience intact—otherwise he surely wouldn't have been telling the story to his wife. He could tell her everything except the physical dangers, which would have frightened her.

16

Sorrow's Crown of Sorrow

I

THIS art-loving couple were having a pleasant holiday, living in Europe's central playground and having a couple of million young American males to keep them safe and comfortable. The war had ended—"just like that," instantly, really unbelievably. The Germans had gone on fighting for a few days against the Russians in Czechoslovakia, but that was all. There wasn't any Alpine Redoubt, there weren't any "werewolves," and if there was a Nazi underground it dug in so deep that nobody knew about it. All the Germans suddenly became willing and obliging; a large part of them became anti-Nazi, and the rest non-Nazi, all at a few strokes of a pen in the hands of an admiral, a general, and an Air Force commander.

The old Germany had come back to life, and it was safe to go walking, to go driving, to go into any German's home, or what was

left of it, and ask him or her how things were and how they had
been during the past six years. Back in America were millions of
people curious about such details, and a practiced woman writer
could sell all the copy she could turn out. As for an art expert, he
couldn't do business yet, but he could inspect and discuss and come
to a gentlemen's agreement as to what would be done as soon as the
barriers against trade were lifted.

Lanny recalled the half-dozen Detaze landscapes in the villa called
"Bechstein Haus" on the Berghof estate. He had sold them to the
Führer at a proper price, so he had no claim upon them; but who
did? Hitler was dead, or said to be, and surely his property should
be in the hands of the American Army until such a time as the question was decided. Lanny led another task force, consisting of a car
and a jeep, and took Laurel along because the Berghof would be
"copy"—and also because she had a special and personal interest in
this ogre's den.

The once lovely chalet was a pitiful sight. It had been hit several
times by six-ton bombs, and a few days later the SS had set fire to
it on the approach of the American Seventh Army. Both its elaborate
wings had been reduced to ashes, and the central part, which had
contained the immense square living-room and Hitler's study above,
with the "largest window in the world" looking out over Austria—
all that was burned-out shell. The GIs who stood guard reported that
everyone who came to the site carried off a souvenir, and Laurel
chose a bronze doorknob which she found in the ashes. She remarked
that perhaps it was the one under which she had propped a chair to
keep the door shut tight—there were no locks on any room in that
strange establishment. It had been a true ogre's castle to an American
woman guest; it was the first and only time that a man had ever laid
forcible hands upon her, and the experience was one never to be forgotten.

The barracks where the SS guards had lived had been spared, and
were useful to the Americans. (In the last days of the war General
Eisenhower had issued an order against the bombing of any barracks,
because they would be needed, and they were.) The Bechstein Haus
still stood, and the lovely Detaze paintings were where Hitler had
ordered them hung. They were landscapes and seascapes of the Riviera, and one of ruins in Greece. Each was a separate story for Lanny,
who had watched them being painted and knew the places they represented. He had told his wife many stories of this gentle-minded
Frenchman who had been Beauty's lover for ten years or more, and

whom she had married when he had got his dreadful wounds in World War I.

Marcel Detaze had been a French representational painter whom the Führer could tolerate. He had ordered these examples because he wanted to honor the French and make friends with them, so that they would trust him and let him take Poland; also, perhaps, because he wanted to bribe the reluctant Herr Budd and bind him to the Nazi cause. Marcel would have loathed Hitler beyond all the French bad language that he knew. He had painted awful caricatures of the Germans—but apparently the Führer's agents in Paris had failed to inform him of that fact. Now the American government would turn these landscapes over to the French government, and they would be hung in the Luxembourg, along with Marcel's indictments of the *furor teutonicus.*

II

Lanny had subscribed to a newspaper in Paris, and there was a radio set in the Unterstein rest house, where he and his wife were privileged to listen to broadcasts from Paris and London, and from a station which the Americans were using in Luxembourg. So the pair followed the fates of those evil persons whom they had hated and feared through so many years. Quisling was in jail in Norway, weeping and raging by turns. Edward Waiter, director of the horrors of Dachau, had fled to the château which was part of the prison system, and there put a bullet through his heart; when that didn't kill him quickly enough he put another through his eye. Max Amann, head of the publishing house which printed Hitler's works and paid him his fortune, poisoned himself, and so did Frau Gertrude Scholtz-Klink, head of the Nazi women's movement. From that ardent soul at the outbreak of the war had come a proclamation: "Dear Führer, we German women give you the fruits of our fertility—our children—to do with as you wish." Adi had taken them!

And now came the news about Heinrich Himmler, most sought of all the party survivors. An odd turn of the wheel of fate; this most mild-mannered of fanatics, head of the SS and the Gestapo, had driven Lanny Budd into secret flight with false papers and a disguise, and now the tables were turned and it was Heinrich who was fleeing under the same circumstances. Only two differences between the cases: Lanny had fled southward while Himmler fled westward, and Lanny had succeeded while Himmler failed. Two British soldiers guarding a bridge at Bremerwörde, west of Hamburg, stopped three men in civilian clothing who were trying to pass. The leader was a shortish, smooth-faced man wearing thick horn-rimmed glasses and a patch over one eye; he had perfectly good papers and a pass identifying him as Herr Hitzinger, member of the German Field Security Police.

His papers were too good, for in these days of turmoil few refugees had any papers whatever. The trio were turned over to the British Field Security Police, and after a grilling the gentle Heinrich admitted who he was. He was searched, and protested against the indignity—he who had had so many millions of people searched, all over Europe! The British doctor ordered him to open his mouth, and he did so, and rolled his tongue around his teeth to show that his mouth was empty. But the doctor wasn't satisfied and put his finger into the mouth, whereupon the man clamped his teeth down and broke a tiny capsule of cyanide which he had hidden there.

He fell, and for a few minutes slobbered into a tin basin, and then was dead. The British put him into what they call a "lorry" and carried him out into the woods. They had no coffin, and didn't waste even that much wood on him; they dug a deep hole and dropped the body in. "A worm to the worms," said the British sergeant, and they shoveled in the earth and carefully leveled the ground and scattered leaves over it, so that there would be no martyr's bones for the SS to cherish.

III

These tidings were important to Lanny for a special reason: they took from his mind one more faint hope that he might find out something regarding his half-sister. The ex-Reichsminister might have been willing to tell him if he remembered the case. The only other chance would be the Gestapo records in Berlin. Millions of displaced persons and other millions of German refugees were all over this tormented land, and who was going to remember anything about a Franco-American night-club dancer who had been the mistress of a Junker officer and had disappeared from public view when places of entertainment had been closed some three years ago?

No, he might as well give it up, write his mother to give it up, and say that Marceline was dead. He had just about decided on this, and composed in his mind a letter to Beauty, when there came to Unterstein a letter for him, forwarded by Monuments in Paris. It was from Bernhardt Monck and had been mailed in Leipzig. It read:

"Dear Lanny: The censor permits me to tell you where I am, and that I have resumed my own name. You can reach me in care of G-2 of First Army Headquarters here. You told me about your sister, and I promised to make inquiries wherever I saw a chance. I have come upon the following case, which I think may be worth reporting to you:

"A woman was found in the women's hospital of the Leipzig Concentration Camp. She was one of a thousand or so who had been working twelve-hour shifts in a near-by munitions factory. She was wearing a canvas skirt and jacket, nothing else, and no identification marks of any sort. I am guessing that she is young, but it is hard to be sure. She had been through the torture mill; all her teeth have been knocked out, her back and legs are a mass of welts which the doctors say have been there for some time, and her finger ends show scars of fire, probably caused by shoving matches under the nails.

"Apparently she suffers from complete amnesia; she does not know who she is or where she came from. She answers everything about her past with 'I do not know.' When let alone, she sits perfectly still, and cowers when she is approached. Her eyes and hair are brown, the hair with some gray. She has a strawberry mark on her left leg; no other peculiarity that I can see. She is about five feet seven, and is fearfully emaciated, but not beyond the point where she can be restored. If these details correspond to your sister, you might come and have a look at her. If you are too far away, or if it is not convenient, I will arrange to get a photo for you. She goes by the name Martha and the number F1147.

"The sights in this place exceed anything that even I imagined, and I had thought I knew the Nazis after almost twenty-five years of keeping out of their clutches. For your sake I am hoping that this is not Marceline; perhaps you have already found her, and if so this letter will not trouble you. If I have to leave here I will give a forwarding address. As ever, Bernhardt Monck."

IV

Lanny read that letter with a sinking heart. One sentence struck him like a blow: the strawberry mark! He had seen Marceline's a thousand times, for they had worn bathing suits a good part of the time at Bienvenu. As a toddler she had learned dancing steps from him, wearing nothing but a tiny pair of trunks; the strawberry mark had been there and had grown with her, and he had teased her about it.

He had had every opportunity to watch that lovely body growing; she had added to the bathing trunks only a brassière—no more was called for on the Coast of Pleasure. They had practiced dancing steps by the hour; she was tireless, and her vigor and grace had been a marvel to him. After she divorced her Italian *capitano* and had made up her mind to a professional career, she had worn Lanny out making him rehearse with her. And now the fiends had knocked all the teeth out of her jaws; they had poked burning matches under her finger nails and lashed her back bloody with steel whips.

He took the letter to Laurel, saying, "This is Marceline." She read it and then sat gazing at him, speechless for a while. "Oh, Lanny, how awful! How awful!" she whispered at last.

"They must have been trying to make her tell about me," he said. "And she wouldn't!"

"She couldn't even if she had wanted to. She had warned me to get out of Germany, but she had no idea how I would do it. I didn't know myself until I had time to think it over."

"You mustn't torture yourself over this, Lanny. You couldn't have helped it. And it may not be Marceline."

"It is hardly possible that there could be such a set of coincidences. Leipzig is not far from Berlin, and she may have sought refuge there. It is even possible that she may have been there when she telephoned me the warning."

"You must go and make sure about her of course."

"She may not recognize me. Her amnesia is a retreat from pain and terror."

"What will you do if it is Marceline?"

"It depends upon her condition. If she is able to be moved I must get her back to Bienvenu. This will be no new story to Beauty." He didn't need to explain what he meant, for Laurel knew all the details of the story of Marcel Detaze, how he had had his face burned off in the exploding of an observation balloon, and how Beauty had stuck to him through it all. She had married him, in spite of his having to wear a silk mask over his face. Marceline had been the fruit of that marriage.

"Can you spare me that long, dear?" he asked, keeping the delicate balance between wives and in-laws.

"Of course," she answered. "I would come with you if I could be of any use. But I am not much more than a name to Marceline, and it is possible that in her subconscious mind she resents my having taken her beloved brother away from her."

"I don't think that," he said. "She had her own affairs and was quite cold-blooded about going after what she wanted. She never asked my advice except in matters of art and how to meet rich people who would take an interest in her dancing."

"But she stood by you in Germany, Lanny!"

"Of course, and I have to stand by her. It will be painful, and there's nothing you can do to make it less so. I am guessing that what she needs is psychological care, and the person to give it is Parsifal. He knows her and loves her, and can give her suggestions all day and half the night without ever being bored. You go on getting your material; then come to Juan to do your writing, where you can be warm."

V

Lanny packed his bag and got himself transported to Munich. At the dusty airport it didn't take him long to find a pilot who was flying to Berlin and could get permission to drop an assimilated colonel off at Leipzig. The trip was a couple of hundred miles and took only an hour. He looked down on another bombed-out city, and when he got a jeep to run him into town he saw the familiar sight of tall, crowded buildings, which had stood for a couple of hundred years, turned to rubble and, where it blocked the streets, being shoveled into trucks. The British had done what was called "area bombing," coming by night and hitting anything; the Americans had come by day, and had boasted that they could drop a bomb into a barrel—but many times, aiming at a factory, they had leveled five- and six-story tenements or rows of barrack-like workers' homes.

Lanny knew nobody in the First Army, but he had his credentials and his pitiful story. Intelligence here knew Bernhardt Monck and valued him; they gave Lanny the requisite permit and a car to take him to the *Lager*, which was far in the suburbs, so that residents of this ancient and honorable city might not be bothered by the stink. Leipzig had been the center of the German publishing industry, and from it had come the seven million copies of *Mein Kampf* which so many Germans had taken for their national and racial Bible. Now you would have had a hard time finding any man or woman who would admit having read it through; you would be tempted to believe them, since no book less readable had been published in the modern world.

All the *Lagern* were alike; they had been brought into being on a mass-production basis, and when you had seen Dachau, the prototype, you had seen them all. At Leipzig the American Army had had about six weeks to clean up; there were no longer cordwood stacks of human skeletons covered with skin, and so the stinks were reduced in intensity. The hospital was clean, and the German doctors no longer tried "scientific" experiments on the patients but worked under American direction to restore blood and tissue to nearly starved bodies. The patients were getting orange juice made from canned powder, and canned milk diluted, and broth and gruel, and when they were able to walk and to digest solid food they were turned loose if they wanted to go. But many had no place to go to and were terrified by the thought of confronting a world in which they no longer had relatives or friends or homes. Millions of the homes had been destroyed, and millions of families had been scattered over the face of Europe, so that parents had no way to find children and children no way to find parents.

VI

Here, in a place that was the same as a barracks except that the bunks were not in tiers, Lanny found his half-sister. It was Marceline beyond question, in spite of the dreadful changes. Only once before had his heart been wrung in the same way—when he stood on the Rhine bridge between Kehl and Strasbourg and took from the hands of Nazi stormtroopers the broken body of Freddi Robin. That had been twelve years ago, but he had never forgotten the pangs, and never would he forget these. Marceline was a woman, twenty-eight years old by the calendar, and something of an artist; Freddi had been two years younger at the time; a scholar, musician, and idealist, almost a saint. For which of them would you feel the greater grief?

This woman was one of the near-skeletons; her jaws were sunken, her hair unkempt and streaked with gray, her eyes full of fear. She didn't know Lanny, and for a long time she manifested no interest in him. She was well enough to move about, but apparently all she wanted was to sit in a corner and be let alone. She had been working twelve hours every day filling cases of small-caliber artillery shells, and the doctors had thought it unwise to leave her idle, so they had had a woman teach her to knit. That was all right with the patient; they had given her a sock for a model, and now she turned out socks with machine-like regularity. She was afraid of new persons who came near her, and it was some time before she could be convinced that her half-brother was not another torturer.

He told the doctors who she was, and told them her story as far as he knew it. They said it was a familiar case; they had others here. They used long technical words, as doctors do; the substance of it was that her personality had retreated from unendurable suffering and had sought refuge deep in her subconsciousness. Perhaps it was the last dreadful climax that had caused it. When the American Army had drawn near, the infuriated SS had locked all the doors of the men's hospital and set fire to it. The building was just across the street from the women's, and they had heard the screams of the men and smelled the odor of burning flesh. Half a dozen of the half-burned men had managed to crawl out of the building and into the women's hospital. Marceline had fled into the typhoid ward, where nearly three hundred women were huddled, expecting the same fate as the men; she had been found hidden under a bunk—and perhaps that was where her sense of identity had taken flight.

Lanny sent telegrams to Laurel, to Beauty, and to Robbie, telling what he had found. Then he settled down, patiently and tenderly, to try to bring back his half-sister's memory. He told her who she was, but the name meant nothing to her. He told her about her mother, her stepfather, her little boy, and the home where she had been raised; she had no trace of recollection and seemed not to want to have any; she resisted the disclosures, as if they were an attack. He thought it the part of wisdom not to mention Oskar von Herzenberg, or her dancing, or anything that had happened in Germany, because that would be bringing back her fears. Better to go back to her childhood, to memories that meant peace and joy. But nothing made any difference that he could observe. Marceline wanted to remain Martha F1147.

They were feeding her every two hours on limited quantities of liquid foods; he arranged that he should perform this service, and while she ate he sat and talked to her gently. She had to be re-educated, as if she were a child. He explained to her that the cruel war was over, that the evil Nazis were gone and had no possibility of returning; she was in the hands of people who loved her and would never do her harm. He tried his best to interest her in the strange idea that she had a mother, and a lovely little dark-eyed half-Italian son, and a beautiful home on the Cap d'Antibes, in a country called France. That country meant nothing to her.

She would sit and knit with her half-crippled fingers—better not to look at them, or you would want to go out and hunt for a few SS men and shoot them. He managed to make friends with her, so that she accepted his statement that he was her half-brother; but he failed to awaken a single memory. She was hungry and ate her food, and that was a sign of life; for the rest, she did what he told her, or what anybody told her. If they said "You should sleep now," she would lie down and sleep. If they said "Come with me," she would come. It was the well-known German *Ordnung und Zucht!*

VII

In the evenings he went out and looked up Bernhardt Monck, who had been away on a mission and now had returned. For the first time since war had come, these two men were able to talk frankly to each other. One of the strictest rules which OSS and other secret agents had to keep was against telling anybody anything that didn't have to be told. What any agent knew might be wrung out of him by torture, but what he didn't know was beyond any power of the enemy to get.

This pair had made contacts a dozen times during the war, and each time had strictly obeyed the rule. Monck, stationed in Stockholm, had given Lanny the name of a faithful German Social Democrat, an old watchmaker, and it was he who had put Lanny in touch with the underground which had passed him part of the way to Italy. Now Lanny could tell Monck about Johann Seidl and ask what had become of him. Monck didn't know, for he hadn't been to Berlin; it was the "Russkys" who had taken the city, and Americans went there only on official missions. He wanted to know if Lanny thought that Hitler was really dead, and Lanny told about his interview with Göring and what the old-style robber baron had said on the subject. Of course you couldn't know what Göring really thought.

Two veterans back from the wars, fighting their battles over again! Monck owed his position in the OSS to Lanny's endorsement, and now he felt that he was making a report to a superior. He had reason to be proud of the work he had done. In collaboration with Eric Erickson, Swedish oil man secretly in sympathy with America, Monck had been in charge of collecting information concerning the synthetic oil plants of Germany, their location and condition before and after bombing. The destruction of these plants had had as much to do with bringing the war to an end as any one thing a man could put his finger on. A year ago General Spaatz, Air Force commander, had cabled the order: "Primary strategic aim of U. S. Strategic Air Forces is now to deny oil to enemy air forces." From then on oil plants were top priority targets and were dealt with under the familiar system: put them out of use, wait until they were repaired, and then smash them again.

Monck, in Stockholm, had had some thirty agents, men and women, working under his command in Germany, and only four of them had been lost. They had reported on eighty-seven vital targets connected with oil, and in the last ten months of the war General Spaatz's airmen had dropped nearly two hundred thousand tons of bombs on or near those targets. When he had started the war Hitler had had on hand only two or three months' supply of oil, but he had made tremendous efforts to increase his supply and had succeeded for five years, as all the world knew. Synthetic oil was the answer, and by what was known as the Karinhall Plan he had raised Germany's oil production to eight million tons per year.

Listening to Monck's story, Lanny realized that this had been an oil war. Lack of oil was the reason the mad Führer had had to drop his program of bombing Britain out of the war and to fall back upon a defensive program. He had made the mistake of building too many of his plants in the west and had to build new ones in Silesia and Poland. The plants were the most secret places in Germany, the most carefully camouflaged and most heavily defended. Vital machinery was put under heavy concrete, blast walls were built around the rest, and every plant was surrounded with smoke screens, searchlights, and solid rings of anti-aircraft batteries. This had been a life-or-death war for the Nazis, and they had all known it.

"We got the information," Monck said quietly, and went on to tell the story of the tremendous Leuna works near this city of Leipzig. The plant had produced more than one-third of all Germany's aviation and motor gasoline, and during the last year there had been twenty-two knockout air raids upon it. The first, on May 12, 1944, had dropped five hundred tons of bombs and stopped production entirely. But the Germans had their plans to restore full production in a month—"We got a copy of those plans," said Monck; "I had them in my own hands a week after the raid."

So the bombers had come again in sixteen days, and this war between destroyers and repairers went on for the full year. At the end of July, after the landing in Normandy and when the rout of Rommel and Rundstedt was beginning, the Leunawerke was hit by nearly three thousand tons of bombs in two days. There had been an attack every fortnight, and nine total knockouts of production. "I have just been looking over the records," reported the secret agent. "Our bombs caused more than five thousand breaks in pipe-lines at Leuna, and every one of those had to be repaired and fully tested before they could carry the highly inflammable gases and liquids. In the end we had the Nazis reduced to building little plants in the forests, like what you call moonlight stills in America."

"Moonshine," corrected Lanny with a smile. "I was told about one in the Black Forest that was run by the power of a steam locomotive. I saw tanks and armored vehicles that had been hauled into the Ardennes by horses and oxen; and they didn't get out again. Also, there were Tiger tanks that had been fitted with gas generators, to burn charcoal."

Said Monck, "That was why the Luftwaffe didn't appear to defend the Rhine; and why the Führer shot himself, and Goebbels and Himmler took poison."

VIII

Lanny went back in his memory to the books he had read on the subject of psychology. That had been a decade and a half ago, when his stepfather had discovered a spiritualist medium in a tenement on Sixth Avenue in New York, and had become excited about the subject of psychic research. For years after that he had experimented and read the best books he could find. This included several on hypnotism, a powerful weapon which the doctors of an earlier generation had taken seriously but which had dropped out of use, apparently because it took too much time and trouble.

Lanny had the time now and was willing to take the trouble. He arranged to take Marceline into a quiet room and seated her in a chair and tried every way he knew to hypnotize her. He told her to gaze into his eyes, but he found it impossible to fix her attention; she was uneasy and afraid, and her eyes would wander. He tried having her gaze into a pinpoint of light, but encountered the same difficulty. No one can be hypnotized without his or her consent, and he could get no real consent from this shell-shocked mind. The very fears which he was seeking to heal prevented any approach to the healing.

He decided that a new environment might solve the problem, and when she was physically strong enough to be moved he wangled per-

mission for a flight to Paris; that took only about three hours and was
not too great a strain. He knew that the hospitals would be crowded,
but he got a hotel suite and a nurse to watch over her while he went
about the business of begging another plane ride, this time to Cannes.
No private motorcar could get gasoline for such a trip, and the trains
were slow and irregular and packed to the very platform steps.

Lanny judged that neither Monuments nor Alsos would be able to
help him in a case like this. He went to OSS, a privileged institution,
of which few questions were asked. He told his story, and they said
it would be necessary to appeal to one of the high brass, and whom
did Lanny know here in Paris? When he said that he had served in
both the Third and the Seventh, they mentioned that General Patton
was in town. Lanny said, "He's the man!"

IX

No trouble for an assimilated colonel to see Georgie, especially
when it had been Lucky Forward which had done the assimilating.
They were on terms of banter, for when they had first met the son
of Budd-Erling had presumed to tell Georgie it was his duty to take
Paris at once, and Georgie had been as mad as hops, and then had had
a second thought about it. Now the old boy was sitting on top of
this world, but perhaps a trifle bored, there being no longer any new
worlds to be conquered. His troubles were far from over, because
his Army had been picked to serve as occupation troops, and he and
all of his officers were begging to get to Japan. He was always having
arguments with SHAEF, and perhaps that was why he had come to
Paris now.

He looked old and tired, and Lanny could guess that the strain
of the past three or four years had done something to his kidneys.
But he stood tall and straight, in a tight-fitting battle jacket with
shiny brass buttons and four silver stars on each of his shoulders,
and four on each side of his shirt collar; he wore trousers creased to
a knife edge and tucked into polished battle boots. He still wore the
two pearl-handled revolvers and the swashbuckler's air, which his
high squeaky voice somewhat oddly belied. "Well, Budd," he said,
"what's biting you now?"

"General," said Lanny, "you know the services I rendered at Bastogne. And Colonel Koch has twice thanked me for help I gave him,
once at Nancy and once at Luxembourg. Now I am asking a favor in
return."

Georgie signed him to a chair, then said, "Shoot!"

"I have a half-sister, Marceline Detaze, daughter of the famous French painter Marcel Detaze. She is twenty-eight, and was a professional dancer. She was caught in Germany. Not quite two years ago I was in Berlin, on a special Intelligence mission for President Roosevelt. Marceline found out that the Nazis had got onto me and risked her life to telephone me to get out, which I did. The scoundrels must have caught her and tried to make her reveal my whereabouts; they knocked out all her teeth, they stuck matches under her fingernails, and they whipped her till her back looks like a washboard. I found her in the Leipzig *Lager*; they had been working her twelve hours a day in an underground munitions plant. She is a victim of amnesia and doesn't know who she is or anything about herself."

"The goddam SOBs!" exclaimed Georgie. He used cavalryman's language so freely that when he was really mad he had no way to show it but in his face and with the clenching of his hands. "What is it you want?"

"I have got her as far as Paris. I want to take her to our mother, at our home on the Cap d'Antibes. Marceline was born and brought up there, and I have hopes that the familiar scenes may bring her memory back. She has been starved to less than a hundred pounds and she couldn't stand a train trip. I want to fly her to Cannes. I'm not asking for a special plane; I just want a couple of seats on any plane that's flying there, and I'm perfectly willing to pay transportation."

"Nonsense, man; the Army isn't that hard up. I'm glad you came to me. I'll have one of my staff men see that it is arranged." He added, "Never mind the thanks, it's the Army." He leaned back in his chair and beamed. "Well, we licked the goddam bastards!"

"*You* did, General," said Lanny, who knew the right way to say thanks. "A wonderful thing to see them come pouring in to give up. I was in the heart of what was going to be their Redoubt, and I had a hard time keeping them from surrendering to me."

"We wouldn't have minded your having a few. We took more than a million and a quarter."

"You'll be interested to know that I had a talk with Göring the night after he came in."

"That bundle of hogsfat! Tell me about him." Lanny told that story; then he told how he had become *Bürgermeisterstellvertreter* of Urach, and Georgie chuckled.

The ex-P.A. knew better than to continue with his own exploits;

he asked the two-gun General what had been happening to him, and the squeaky voice turned loose on the "old women at SHAEF," who had been so timid they wouldn't let him win the war last winter; at the very end they wouldn't let him go into Czechoslovakia for fear of displeasing the Russians, and they almost wouldn't let him go into Austria. The only reason they did was that it was part of the Redoubt and they were afraid the blankety-blanks might hole up there. And now they had turned down his request to be sent to the Pacific. All because of jealousy at headquarters!

When they were parting the tired man said, "My work is done, Budd. The Lord can take me any time." Lanny remembered the words, and thought of them a few months later when he heard over the radio that the commander of the Third Army had been killed in a motorcar crash.

X

Lanny succeeded in telephoning his mother to tell her that he was coming. The flight from Paris was without incident, and at the landing field there was Beauty herself with a horse and buggy. The former was experienced and sedate, and the latter had stood in a shed on the estate since the days before motorcars had been invented; they hadn't even been able to get paint for it until Robbie had mailed them a can from Newcastle. The fine car that Beauty had been driving had been taken by the Légion Tricolore, and what had happened to it they would never know.

Lanny had said over the telephone, "Don't kiss her, for that may frighten her. Don't show any emotion, just be gentle and quiet." So Beauty blinked the tears out of her eyes—she had been prepared, but the reality was beyond imagining. She drove, and Marceline was helped into the seat beside her, and then Lanny climbed in beside Marceline. There wasn't enough of her to crowd them.

The nag ambled along, and it took them nearly an hour to get to Bienvenu, a drive which they had been accustomed to make by car in six or seven minutes. They talked about the beautiful day, the wide spacious Boulevard de la Croisette with its rows of palm trees, the blue waters of the Golfe Juan, the swarms of GIs filling all the fashionable hotels, the buildings which had been damaged and were now nearly all repaired. Topics like that, harmless, and likely to bring back memory; but all the time Marceline said not a word. She had been told that this was her mother, but the statement meant nothing to her, and if she had ever swum in these blue waters or sailed over them she did not know or care.

It was the same with the white-haired old gentleman of seventy and the dark-haired little boy of seven. The strange situation had been made known to the child; his mother, of whom he had no recollection, had lost her recollection of him; he must be gentle and quiet with her and help her get well. Since he was gentle and quiet by nature, this was not difficult. He took seriously his duties as assistant nurse. He had been impressed by the information that she had been almost starved to death and that food would help to restore her to a more agreeable aspect. He would sit and watch every spoonful that she put into her mouth.

For Parsifal Dingle this was a situation made to order. He was like the Catholic priests in Dachau: he had been in training for the job. His benevolent aspect impressed the sick woman at once; he was a man of God, and he wasted no time in preliminaries but took a seat before her and began to explain his faith. She, Marceline Detaze, was God's perfect child, and all she had to do was to put her faith in Him, and He would restore her to peace and happiness. Parsifal did not undertake to explain why God had let her get into her present state, or why He had created, or permitted to come into existence, those fiends in human form who had brought her there. The problem of evil and how it comes to be is one which has baffled the world's greatest philosophers, and what Parsifal Dingle did was to ignore it. God knew the answer, and perhaps in His good time would reveal it. What Parsifal had to do was to turn evil into good, a power which God gave him and for which he was duly grateful.

So, day and night, he recited the prayers which he had composed for the help of other suffering persons and which now had become routine. Monotony did not trouble him, and the idea of boredom did not occur to him, for this was the presence of God. He did not tell God what to do, or even ask; he told Marceline what God could and would do, because God was good and could do nothing else. He told her that God was the living Principle that had made her and sustained her, and if she had faith in this certainty the process of restoration would go on and she would have peace and health and happiness. He told her that God would cast out her fears if she would believe that He would do it. She, being docile, believed it, and it happened. A little boy sat by, listening and watching with his wide dark eyes, deeply stirred, because this was the first miracle he had seen. He was told that his presence was important, for Jesus had said,

"Where two or three are gathered together in my name, there am I in the midst of them."

XI

Laurel came, having got all the material she needed, and being glad of a place where she could sit in the sun with a writing pad on her knee. Laurel had never been religious, but this was a new kind of religion, something which could be taken as psychology. If faith healed as Parsifal had insisted he had been proving for thirty years, was it not advisable for men and women to acquire some? It was, the old gentleman insisted, something different from reason; it was something that you proved by experiment. You had faith in peace and you had peace; you had faith in health and you had health.

Up to a certain point it worked admirably with Marceline. She was getting confidence and was restoring her starved tissues. In this household where only love was spoken she came to feel at home and accepted their statement that this was her family and the house in which she had been born and raised. She never went away from the house; she stayed in her room when strangers came, which happened seldom because transportation was so difficult to get. She would knit or she would do any household task that was set before her. Only now and then was there a relapse, as when a thunderstorm caused her to crawl under the bed and refuse to come out. Apparently God was not in the thunder.

But no effort had any effect upon her memory; no suggestion and no prayers could carry her back behind that curtain which had fallen in the Leipzig *Lager*. Lanny tried again and again to hypnotize her; he was sure that if he could plant the suggestion that her memory would return it would happen. But his best efforts failed; the fears still blocked the way.

Then he bethought himself of an idea which had occurred to him many years ago, that it might be possible to implant suggestions during normal sleep; he had tried several experiments, but the monotony had bored him—he lacked his stepfather's firm conviction that God was speaking through his voice. But now, apparently, this idea had occurred to others; Lanny had read an item to the effect that the Army was dealing with shell-shock cases by means of suggestion implanted by a phonograph record played while the patient slept. They had a device to make radio records audible under the pillows of airplane pilots in training, and when they woke up in the morning they knew their lessons. If the Army was doing such things, that made them respectable.

Lanny searched in the attic of this villa for a phonograph he had used in giving dance lessons to Marceline and young Freddi and other children. It had a device which shifted the needle and played the same record over and over as long as you wanted; it was run by electricity, so that it could keep going all night. Lanny dusted it off and made sure it was in order; then, with Parsifal's help, he composed a spiel. He rode in a crowded bus to the city of Nice where there was a recording studio; he had a twelve-inch recording made and tried out, and took it home and tried it there, and let Marceline hear it, so that it would not make her uneasy.

After that she went to sleep every night to the sound of Lanny's voice murmuring gently, and all night long it continued to murmur reassuring suggestions. "I am your brother, Lanny Budd, and I love you and want to help you. You will remember me, and how I taught you to swim and dance and play tennis. Beauty is your mother, and she loves you, and you will remember all the kind things she did for you. Your father was Marcel Detaze, and you will remember his beautiful paintings. Little Marcel is your son; you will remember how he was born and how happy you were with him. Parsifal is your other father; he loves you, and you will remember how he taught you. Laurel is your sister, and she loves you too. Bienvenu is your home, and you will recall your childhood here and all your friends and the happy times you had. Everybody here loves you and wants to help you, and you will trust them and remember all your happiness . . ."

And so on and on. To have had a human voice repeating that for eight hours would have been a great strain upon the voice, but it didn't worry the phonograph a bit, and it didn't use up much of the scarce electrical power of the Midi. Nor did it trouble Marceline's sleep; she had been brought to the point where she wanted to remember these agreeable things that were told to her. Her past life had become a sort of fairy tale, to which she listened gladly and asked questions. After the treatment had continued for two or three weeks she began to exclaim, "I believe I remember that!"

How could they be sure? They had told her much. But the day came when she cried: "Oh, I remember Vittorio! He was such a horrid man!" Then they knew that the suggestions were really taking effect, for they had agreed never to mention her divorced husband—he being one of the painful memories which might cause her to shrink away from her past.

Memories did not come in a rush, but little by little; and perhaps that was just as well. She was getting back her interest in life, she was learning to live in this new-old world and be useful in it, much more so than she had been in the past, for she had been a self-centered person, ravenous for pleasure and praise. The day before Lanny and Laurel went away he tried a fascinating experiment. The radio was playing *Tales of the Vienna Woods,* and he took her hands and began to lead her gently into a waltz. The result was amazing; she began to follow his steps, and a light of happiness came into her eyes. "Oh, I know how to dance!" she exclaimed.

And dance she did, with mounting delight, until her breath gave out and she had to sit down, panting. And how happy she was then! What a marvelous discovery! "I know a lot about dancing! I remember it! I love to dance! I can be happy dancing!" And so Lanny knew that she was cured.

BOOK SIX

'Tis Excellent to Have a Giant's Strength

17

Earthquake and Eclipse

I

THE terrible World War had been shifted now to the Pacific; the time had come for the Japanese to feel the weight of America's power. The Philippines had been retaken after half a year of the toughest kind of fighting. The small island of Okinawa, close to Japan, had required nearly three months to capture; a hundred and twenty thousand Japanese had been killed or driven to suicide, and only eight thousand captured—which showed the kind of war it was. This island was crucial because it immediately became a base for the big bombers; they could make what the airmen called a "milk run" to the Japanese cities and do to them what had been done in Germany, destroying their oil and munitions-making centers.

But Lanny knew no military man who believed that this fanatical enemy would give up until the homeland itself had been taken. He knew that armies were being transported from the Mediterranean to the Far East and that the invasion was set for November. Patton had told him that they were reckoning upon a million casualties, more than the British, French, and Americans had sustained in all the European fighting. A terrible prospect indeed, and one that weighed upon the consciences of two idealists dreaming peace on earth and good will toward men.

Lanny found himself thinking continuously about his million dollars and what he was going to do with it. He talked about it with Laurel whenever her mind was not on her own work. He decided that he had done all he could for the United States Army in Europe; he had got all the information he could get for both Alsos and Monuments, and the rest was up to others. The scientists would study and appraise the documents; the museum people would collect the works of art and transport them and classify them and deliver them to the owner countries, with banquets and ceremonies for which Lanny didn't especially care.

281

The day came when Laurel said, "I have written all about this war that I care to write. From now on I want to give whatever power I possess to your project." That was important indeed to Lanny; it meant that for the first time his marriage and his job would be one and the same.

One decision they had come to: this was not going to be a long-term job. If anybody was going to prevent World War III, about which many of the big brass were speculating, it would have to be done soon. Lanny had decided that they would divide the money into five equal portions and spend one portion every year. Whatever seed they had to sow would be sown in that time; when the harvest would be reaped was beyond guessing. Anyhow, they wouldn't establish a foundation and set up a group of chairwarmers for life.

II

The next move was to England, to have things out with Rick and Nina. Transportation for a concentration-camp victim had been hard to get, but for Lanny and his wife it was a simple matter; they were officers in uniform, with permission to go where they pleased. They were flown to Paris and from there to London; they went by train to The Reaches, Rick's home in Buckinghamshire on the River Thames. Lanny hadn't seen it for more than eight years. While he posed as a Nazi sympathizer, his meetings with a well-known Labour journalist had taken place in an obscure hotel room which one or the other would rent for the purpose.

Nothing changes much in the English countryside. This old brick house had been added to at several periods in different styles; it had many gables and dormer windows, and a chimney with a pot on top for every tier of rooms. In the old days that had meant a slavey carrying coals and ashes all day in cold weather; but now the slaveys were working at munitions, and most of the rooms had been left unused of late. There were few modern comforts, because the old baronet had spent all his money on "little theaters," and since he had died Rick had spent his paying the old gentleman's debts.

From the house a graveled path between a double row of oak trees led down to the river; there was a boathouse, and a punt in which two boys had explored a historic waterway, meantime expressing firm convictions about all the problems of mankind. On the grassy banks of this river Lanny had sat in the evening, listening to Rick playing the piano in the house; Rosemary Codwilliger—pronounced Culliver, please

—had sat by his side, and a fourteen-year-old lad had felt the first touches of a magic wand. Rosemary had come to the Riviera one winter and had seduced him but refused to marry him, because she preferred to become a countess. Now she was a grandmother several times over, and Lanny went to see her—but only when she was hard up and had persuaded her husband to sell another of his ancestral portraits.

Memories, memories! Beauty Budd had come to the Henley Regatta, the boat race between Oxford and Cambridge; all in pink, a lovely rose in full bloom, attended by a young millionaire from Pittsburgh, who was begging her to marry him—but the young Lanny had begged her to stick to Marcel and stay what she called poor, with no more than the thousand dollars a month that Robbie sent her. Beauty and her fast, free-spending friends—Sophie, Baroness de la Tourette, and Margy, Lady Eversham-Watson, rich Americans married to titles, and both of them old ladies now. Decked out in their fashionable finery, and with a world war hanging over their heads, they had been a swarm of gaily colored butterflies in a garden that was about to be struck by a lightning bolt. Most of the boys Lanny had played with here, slightly older than himself, had died in Flanders. The sons they had left behind had died in the recent war; but the breed went on—generation after generation born, raised, educated at great expense and trouble, only to be slaughtered on some foreign field. To the pair of English parents at The Reaches it did not seem rational, and the American pair agreed.

III

It was summer, and Britain was in the midst of the hottest of political campaigns. Their unwritten constitution required a general election every five years at the maximum, and this time the war had forced a breach of the rule. Now that the land was safe, they did not wait until the Japs had given up. The Conservatives thought they would stand a better chance before the glamour of victory had faded from Winston Churchill's brow; Labour thought that he was a grand old man for warmaking but they didn't want any of his peacemaking. They were "going to the country," as they phrase it, and the polling was to be in late July.

Following Lanny's suggestion, Rick had invited the Labour party leaders to consider Alfy, already well known to them. It was obvious enough that campaigning would be hard on a man who could not walk or stand without a steel brace on one leg; service in Parliament wouldn't be any picnic either. Alfy had got a leave and come home, and his personality had charmed everyone. He had entirely recovered from his wounds, his legs were long and sound, and he had drawn in the Labour program with his mother's milk. He was only twenty-eight, and the movement kept talking about "new blood." He knew how to talk to servicemen, and to the young women who had toiled in the munitions plants to keep the war going. At the end of World War I they had been promised homes fit for heroes to live in, and they had assuredly not got them. This time they meant for things to be different.

So this twice-wounded Royal Air Force hero had been put up as the candidate and now was in the midst of a whirlwind, speaking at several meetings every night and at noon-hour meetings in factories. His mother and father came to the more important meetings and spoke for him. Nina went to gatherings of the women and explained to them what it would mean to have a government of their own kind of people, familiar with their needs. The Labour party was campaigning on a carefully studied program, telling the people exactly what they would do during five years of office: the nationalization of basic industries, coal, transport, communications, steel, and so on. The campaign was one of education, to show the people what such a program would do for them and what a difference it would make in their lives. Security from the cradle to the grave was the slogan.

IV

In the midst of these excitements the family hadn't much time to give to problems of the future; but Rick said that he had canvassed the situation thoroughly and was ready to go in for the five-year deal if Lanny still wanted him. What attracted him, he said, was Lanny's assurance that, whatever the program decided upon, it would be some sort of job that he could do in part at home. At the age of forty-six, he was beginning to be troubled by his game leg, and he had been attracted by Lanny's picture of Roosevelt lying in bed without his braces and with a stack of documents beside him. If Rick could read, edit, and dictate that way, he would get a lot more out of his mind. Lanny said, "Come and do it."

They took a morning off to thrash out their problems. Their first job would be in New York, where they would rent an apartment, if one could be found, and set to work to get the best advice from persons who knew the movement for peace and social justice. When they had chosen their course, they would pick out some small town not too far away and there would establish a small office and two homes. Rick said, "I understand there's a terrible housing shortage and you can't rent anything." Lanny answered, "You can't rent but you can buy, and we'll have to pay the price. I'll find you a bungalow-type house so that you won't have stairs to climb, and it won't be far from the office."

They assented to the ex-P.A.'s proposal that he was to stay in the background. He didn't want to involve Budd-Erling, and besides that, his own record was dubious; he was supposed to have been a pro-Nazi and he didn't want to bother with public explanations. Laurel would use her pen name; she would be Miss Mary Morrow and would be the one who was supposed to have the money; a woman's money was like her age, she didn't have to talk about it unless she pleased. When the publicity started there would be a lot of it, and Laurel would stand it as best she could. There would be a mysterious gentleman in the background, carefully keeping out of the way of reporters. A lady had a right to end war in the world if she could, and she also had a right to have a gentleman friend.

V

Far away to the west, across the American continent, there had been an assemblage of major importance to anybody interested in the keeping of the peace. Delegates had come to San Francisco from most of the governments of the earth, to form a new version of the League of Nations. Roosevelt hadn't lived to see it, but he had given it a name, the United Nations Organization. Having completed its work and adopted a charter, it dropped the last word, but for some reason the British preferred to retain it and kept writing and talking about UNO. Lanny hadn't been able to get adequate accounts at Bienvenu, but now in the British newspapers and magazines he studied the details.

There had been a long-drawn-out struggle over the proposed charter. The Soviet representatives had been leery of any proposal which would give power to the small nations; their position was that Russia, America, and Britain had won the war and would have to keep the peace. How farcical to pretend that Honduras, for example, should have a say about it! The strategy of this was clear enough; Russia had swallowed all the small nations about her and didn't want them to have any say about anything. The other small nations were capitalist small nations and looked for financial favors to the capitalist big nations; obviously they would vote the way the big nations said. In this argument the discerning reader could see the pattern of all the disputes of future years; these four trained Socialists did not fail in discernment.

The dispute had grown so warm and the blockade so serious that President Truman had sent the ailing Harry Hopkins flying to Moscow to talk to Stalin about voting procedure and other questions that had arisen between the two countries. That poor man was the only one who could do this job, because he had been present at the previous conferences, and knew what had been in Roosevelt's mind, and what had been in Stalin's mind as far as Stalin was willing to reveal it to Americans. So in the end a compromise had been worked out. The Soviet Union got three votes, and it was agreed that the Soviet Union, Britain, and the United States should each have the right to veto any action of the Security Council that involved their affairs. The Soviet Union reluctantly agreed to permit the General Assembly to discuss whatever problems were brought before it, but would not let it have any power to take action. Such was the new instrument to preserve world peace—like a horse with hobbles on, and no way to get them off. It took no powers of divination to say that UN, or UNO, would not travel very far on the road to Utopia.

The four peace conspirators agreed that they would have to study that charter, and probably spend more than five years pointing out to the world what was wrong with it. Rick said, "It all depends on the thirteen men of the Politburo. If they are willing to take what they've got and settle down and develop it with loans from America, then we're all right until the next slump comes. On the other hand, if they insist upon taking the rest of Central Europe and making a try for Western Europe, then all the charters in the world won't bind them, and it won't matter how Honduras votes."

"Funny thing," added Lanny. "In the early twenties Stalin was all for Socialism in one country, and it was Trotsky who was for world revolution. Now that Trotsky is dead, it will be odd to see Stalin adopting the program of his hated rival."

Rick said, "Don't let Sister Bess hear you say that!"

VI

Lanny and Laurel were flown by the familiar Iceland route and set down gently on the tip of Long Island. Robbie had a car waiting, and they went by ferry to the Connecticut shore. There was that large Budd family, scattered over a township, each subgroup with its own comfortable home and its own sense of importance. They ranged in age from ninety-seven to two-and-a-half; Baby Lanny was the latest addition, the new generation being not so prolific as the old had been in its time. The old grumbled about this, and the young smiled.

Nearly three months had passed since mother and father had seen their little one; he could run faster and more safely, and he knew many new words. He had been kept reminded of his parents, and was ready to tell them his adventures and show them his rabbit. Far-off lands and wars didn't mean much to him, but a rabbit was alive, and would eat lettuce leaves, and wrinkle his nose, and learn to follow you about. Life is a source of wonder, to a child as well as to a philosopher. A part of it is rhythm; and when Lanny sat at the piano and played little tunes with strong accent his son behaved just as Baby Marcel had done, and Frances in her time, and Marceline in hers. Frances would take Baby Lanny's two hands and teach him the same dance steps that Lanny had taught her; so it is that the torch of culture is passed down the corridor of time.

Frances was fifteen, a very lovely age, where the brook and river meet, womanhood and childhood fleet. She too had a world of her own and delighted in telling about it: the school she had attended, the friends she had made, the boat they sailed on the river. Her crushes had been girls, and now they were boys, and her cheeks took on color when she was teased about them. That was according to nature's scheme and was understood by parents. It was early July, and she was going with her cousins to a mountain camp, and later her mother and stepfather had promised to come and take her back to England. She had been so happy in both countries that it was hard to choose; she thought she would like to divide her time between them.

One half of the war was over, the worst half, as people believed; but nearly everybody, high or low, had some relative in the Far East. Everybody read the papers and listened to the radio, trying to guess how long the Japs would hold out and would the Russians come in. Lanny wasn't free to tell what he knew about the matter. He said, "It will be bad if they don't," and his skeptical father answered, "It will also be bad if they do." Robbie was in a state of dissatisfaction with that New Man in the White House. New Man and True Man, you could make puns about him, but they weren't funny to the president of Budd-Erling; he said it was like turning a high-powered automobile over to a child. Robbie wanted the war to be won, but you couldn't expect him to be too eager about it, considering what the end was going to mean to his business.

Esther of course wanted to hear about her niece, Peggy Remsen, and what she was doing. The returning couple made it sound quite fascinating, but really it was hard work, and messy, like cleaning up after a fire or an earthquake. However, Peggy was enjoying it and was meeting very nice young fellows, of the sort that her aunt would approve. Barely four years ago Esther had been thinking of her stepson as a possible nephew-in-law, and maybe Peggy had had thoughts along the same line, but that was all over now. There was Baby Lanny, and Esther hoped they would let him stay on, for the summer at least. Esther disapproved of big cities on many grounds, hygienic, moral, esthetic, political. It saddened her to see her own little river port growing at so insane a rate, and the money her husband was making out of it weighed little in her balance.

VII

The couple drove to New York, in the car which Robbie always loaned them, and with gasoline coupons of which he had a plentiful supply. They opened up their apartment, and Laurel went to see her editors and find out what else they wanted her to write. Lanny took off his uniform, not wishing to advertise his past. He wanted to report to some of his clients about conditions in Europe, and what he had found there, and the prices. Zoltan was at the seashore, but came to town to meet his colleague; the Hungarian-born art expert had wanted to join the Monuments, but they wouldn't take him because he was too old. He was familiar with all the places Lanny had visited and with the art works he told about. His heart ached for the old continent and its tragedies.

Also Lanny had to visit his father's lawyers and find out about the money he was going to get. All the legal formalities had been complied with, and one of the great Wall Street banks had an order to turn over to him the securities specified in Emily Chattersworth's will. Lanny identified himself and arranged to leave them where they were and let them accumulate interest and dividends according to their nature. The Sept Chênes property in Cannes was in charge of caretakers, and he would wait for conditions to improve before putting it on the market.

Major Jim Stotzlmann came to town. He had been out in San Francisco attending the birth pangs of the United Nations. It was his practice to be in all places where important things were happening; he could always pull some wires and have some brass hat or bureaucrat or newspaper publisher send him, and he would write accounts of the event which showed that he knew everybody connected with it and enjoyed the confidence of the most exalted. That made him good company, and he brought his newest young wife to the Budd apartment, and they sat and swapped gossip until the small hours of the morning. Life was so exciting that it always seemed a shame to go to sleep; you raided the icebox and ate a snack and then went on talking, and just as you were thinking about leaving you flushed some new and delightful item of gossip.

It was the first time Jim and Lanny had met since Roosevelt's death, and they mourned together. Naturally Lanny wanted to know all about the New Man, the Tru-man, and naturally Jim possessed the information. Harry was a kind and decent sort but tragically unequipped to run the affairs of the world. When word of the death had come he had been like a man caught under an avalanche; he had exclaimed to one of his friends, "Look what's fallen on me!" He wanted to follow in F. D. R.'s footsteps, but the steps were too far apart for him. Of necessity he wanted people he knew to help him, and he had brought from Missouri a bunch of friends who didn't know any more about world affairs than he did; they were a pretty crude sort, according to the scion of the Stotzlmanns. The new President had been a captain of artillery, so he had a great respect for the high brass; he seemed also to trust the Wall Street fellows. F. D. R. had been able to manage them, but now they were managing Truman, and the prospects for the New Deal looked dark indeed.

"What are you going to do now?" inquired Jim, and Lanny said he was going back to buying old masters; he wouldn't mention Emily's money to one of the town's most celebrated gossips. Lanny said that he had lost his status, and when the other offered to introduce him to Tru-man he declined politely; he wouldn't promise to serve any man until he knew what sort of service the man would ask. If things in Washington were going to be as bad as Jim feared, Lanny would stay away. They went back to mourning their dead Boss, the greatest man they had ever known, the greatest President the country had ever had—so they agreed. Lanny recited the verses which Rick had written, and they sorrowed for the sheep wandering alone in the hills.

VIII

Another mourner was Charles T. Alston, who also had lost his status by that apoplectic stroke in Georgia. The old gentleman had been in San Francisco, not as a leading adviser, but as a humble assistant to one of these; his advice had been asked occasionally but rarely taken. Now he was going back to his old occupation; he had accepted a position in one of the smaller New England colleges, this time to teach, not geography, but industrial relations, in which he had become something of an expert. A summer session was just starting, and Lanny drove out and sat in on one of his old friend's lectures, then spent the night in his home. Alston was a widower and lived with a widowed sister.

He was well content to have a rest, he said; after the hectic life he had been living a college campus was an Elysian field and a lecture room a sanctuary. But he was dreadfully unhappy about the world. He judged that the charter adopted at San Francisco was wholly inadequate, and in some ways worse than a disagreement, because it lulled the world with a false sense of security. There was looming a conflict between the capitalist and the Communist worlds, and the UN would be powerless to prevent it. What was the sense of a police force if any would-be lawbreaker had the right to veto what the police proposed to do? And where was the leadership that was going to work out a compromise among greedy and self-willed great powers?

Inevitably this led to the new President—all roads led to him, for he controlled the greatest single lump of power in the world. Alston said, "The man's an enigma to me. He says he believes in the principles of the New Deal and means to carry them out, but apparently he has no use for any of our crowd. One after another, our policies are disapproved, and we find ourselves shunted aside; when we ask politely if our resignations would be welcomed we are answered coldly. I think perhaps the Governor spoiled us; he let us have our own way too much, and we set too high a value upon our attainments. Anyhow, we see our duties being turned over to men who don't understand the New Deal and would hate it if they did."

Again Lanny recited the poem "The Shepherd Is Dead," and this time it brought tears to the eyes of a man whose hair had turned white in the service of Franklin Roosevelt. Alston had given sixteen years to helping the "Governor" plan his programs and carry them out. He said now, "We have to keep our faith in democracy and believe that the people will raise up a new leader."

IX

This pair had lost their influence over affairs, but they had not lost their interest. They were like parents who have seen their children go out into the world; the parents' advice is no longer sought, but their love and their fears follow the children in whatever they do. Both Lanny and Alston worried about what was left of the war. Would the Japanese yield to the air attack, or would their home islands have to be invaded? And if the Russians got into China would they ever get out? Alston had thought it a great mistake to invite Stalin to declare war upon Japan; he felt certain that when the Emperor gave up, the troops in China and on the conquered islands would follow his lead. Alston was troubled by the idea that the revolutionary fervor of the Soviets was evolving into plain Russian patriotism of the old imperial type.

The ex-P.A. told of the discoveries he had made in Germany, and said that he felt frustrated because he could no longer take them to the man at the top. "I'm back in my old days," he said. "I take them to my English friend, and he puts them into the Socialist press. Apart from that, I'm out of everything."

Alston sat in thought for a space. "Lanny," he remarked suddenly, "I consider that you have earned a reward."

"I'm not worried about that," was the reply. "I can always earn what I need, and I don't care anything for publicity."

"That isn't what I mean. There is a story about to break, the biggest in the world, and you have the right to be in on it."

There was a special look of seriousness in the ex-geographer's eyes, and Lanny read it. "You mean—?" he said, and stopped as if he couldn't quite bring himself to say the words.

"Yes, I *mean*!" replied the other, smiling. "You ought to be there and see it, and when the news comes out your wife will have a story like nothing else ever."

"Where should I go?"

"To a place called Los Alamos, in New Mexico."

"Would they let me in?"

"I think I can fix it so that they will. You should go quickly because the event may happen any day. They don't give me anything but a wink, but that's enough."

"I'll start tomorrow," Lanny said. A wink was enough for him too.

"I suggest that you make sure by calling on Einstein. Ask him to give you a note. He's the king of the whole shebang."

"The word being a pun?" inquired Lanny, and they both grinned.

Alston took one of his visiting cards and wrote on the back of it: "Dear Oppy: Trust Lanny Budd as you would trust me. He was Roosevelt's confidential agent for eight years. Let him tell you his story, and you will understand why I have sent him. C.T.A." He handed the card to Lanny and asked, "Does the name J. Robert Oppenheimer mean anything to you?"

"I don't think I have heard it."

"He is a young Jewish physicist, the top theoretical brain in the project. He headed the group that took Einstein's formula and turned it into physical reality. At the beginning F. D. R. called me in to help in the picking and choosing. Oppy won my confidence, and I hope I won his. You will find out for me."

"You mean a young physicist has been running that enormous project?"

"Not in the business sense. That was General Groves. You have been talking about him for a year or more; but you don't know Greek. The Greek word for grove is Alsos."

So then Lanny saw. All he said was, "*Oh!*"

"General Groves is an Army officer and an executive; he runs the business. But he is not a physicist, and has to do what the physicists tell him. They tried the experiments and laid down the processes, the engineers worked out the techniques, and G. G., as they call him, let the contracts, paid the money, and protected the job. I am sure that never before has two billion dollars' worth of labor and materials been risked on the basis of formulas worked out in a few mathematical brains. There had been laboratory experiments, but there wasn't a bit of assurance that things that happened on an infinitesimal scale in the lab could be made to happen on a colossal scale in hundred-million-dollar factories."

"People call F. D. R. a gambler," remarked Lanny. "If the gamble succeeds they will call it genius."

X

Lanny went back to his apartment and told his wife, "I have a chance to get in on the biggest thing going. Unfortunately it's top secret; but some day soon it'll be a story I can tell you and you can write it. Want to go along?"

"Where to?"

"A place in New Mexico that I never heard of before."

"When do we start?"

"Early tomorrow morning. I have to get a trailer from Robbie. You can spend the time at his New Mexico plant and watch his new jets shoot up into the sky, and maybe make a story about them."

"Righto," said Laurel, who had recently visited Rick's home on the Thames.

The ex-P.A. went to the phone. Robbie was purchasing new aluminum trailers every week, for he was still hiring new people and had to have a place to put them. Lanny said, "Laurel and I want a trailer, to start tomorrow for New Mexico. I can't explain."

"No harm in my guessing?"

"Not a bit, but don't do it out loud. Laurel will stop at Budd"—the name of the plant where Robbie was trying out his jet engines.

"How early do you want it?"

"As early as you can get it here. Laurel doesn't like to ride in city traffic with a trailer attached, so suppose you have your man meet us in front of the post office in Newark at nine tomorrow morning."

"He'll be there, unless the traffic is too much for him."

"Newark, New Jersey, not New York," said Lanny.

His father chuckled. "I have heard of it."

XI

They left their apartment at eight. At that hour the traffic was mostly into the city, so they had their half of the tube and the Skyway pretty much to themselves. They got to Newark ahead of time. Robbie's man had had the same idea and was waiting for them. They drove south on Highway 1 until they found a place where there was plenty of room on the side, and there the expert unhitched the trailer and attached it to Lanny's car, which had been prepared with a "ball" when they had taken this same trip the previous year. Lanny handed the man a ten-dollar bill and all was well.

They turned off the highway and took the road to Princeton, and in that lovely old college town Lanny found a shady spot for car and trailer, so that Laurel could read comfortably. Then he walked to the imitation Gothic building where Professor Einstein had his sumptuous study. The Institute for Advanced Study has nothing to do with Princeton University; it is a separate affair, supplied with an endowment of five million dollars by two Jewish department-store owners. Here great thinkers in all branches of learning use their minds, free from other duties and cares. From here Albert Einstein, refugee from the Nazi lunatics, had written to President Roosevelt, calling his attention to the fact that recent discoveries in physical science had created the possibility of atomic fission on a significant scale. A curious sort of revenge which the whirligig of time had brought: it was upon Einstein's formula governing the relationship between matter and energy that all these discoveries were based; and it was this formula which Lenard and the other Nazi lunatics had been banning by force from Germany.

Four years ago Lanny had come here to be briefed by one of the

Professor's assistants, preparatory to his going into Naziland in an effort to find out what progress they were making in atomic fission. The elderly cherub, as Lanny thought of him, had taken a liking to his pupil—something that he did frequently, being among the kindest of men. They had played Mozart's sonatas for violin and piano, and Lanny had come back long afterward and been surprised to discover that this man who was trying to evolve a theory that would include the whole physical universe had room in his mind to remember which sonatas they had played. A sweet and gentle person as well as a great one, and these qualities are not always found together.

He received his visitor in an oak-paneled room containing a large center table, used no doubt for seminars. He was cordial, and deeply interested to hear what Lanny had seen of physical science in Germany. Having been director of the Physics Department at the Kaiser Wilhelm Institute in Berlin, and having attended congresses of physicists for thirty years or more, he knew all the men whom Lanny had helped to run down and question—Hahn and Weizsäcker, Bothe, Heisenberg, Plötzen, Salzmann. He listened with glee to the story of how Lanny had captured old Phillip Lenard and then been ordered to turn him loose because he was no good. A special and peculiar sort of vengeance over an ideological enemy, a sort which even the kindest-hearted scientist might enjoy.

After listening, he said, "Why don't you stay, Mr. Budd, and we will play some music."

Lanny explained, "I can't stay. My wife is sitting outside in the car."

"But why didn't you bring her in?"

"What I want to speak to you about, Professor, is not for wives." Lanny showed him the card which Alston had written and said, "He thought that I had done so much for the project that I was entitled to see what is expected to happen in New Mexico. He suggested that I should stop by, on the chance that you too might be willing to give me a note."

"Indeed yes, Mr. Budd. Certainly you have earned that right." He took a sheet of paper and wrote: "Lanny Budd is my close friend and has earned your confidence. A. Einstein." So he always signed himself, and Lanny thought, A. Einstein and A. Lincoln.

The great man waved aside the ex-P.A.'s thanks. His face was deeply lined and his soft brown eyes were sad as he said, "I gave my sanction to this Manhattan District project, as they call it, because I felt it was my duty. Now that the war is so near to being won I find myself half wishing that the effort may not succeed."

Said Lanny, "Our military people estimate that it may cost us a million casualties to take the Japanese home islands."

"So I am told; and this project might be the means of saving them. But it is a moral question which I shall never be able to resolve to my satisfaction—whether we scientists have the right to permit our knowledge to be used for destruction on such a frightful scale."

XII

The two travelers returned to Highway 1 and drove on to North Philadelphia, skirting the great city and heading westward on the famous turnpike that leads to Harrisburg. On their previous trailer trip it had been winter and they had got as far south as they could; now it was summer and they stayed north. The shiny new trailer followed obediently behind, and they drove through lovely farming country lush with ripening crops. Past the Gettysburg battlefield, where guides waited to show them the monuments, but they did not stop. Then the steel and coal country—Allegheny County, the heart of America's industrial power; it was ugly and depressing, but you couldn't afford to look down upon it in wartime. Rather you must marvel and rejoice, while your car and trailer ran for miles past one single plant that turned out steel for guns and tanks.

The travelers crossed the Alleghenies by a broad pass, and then it was the level farmlands of Ohio, and now and then a great city throbbing with industry. They stopped for dinner and drove on until late, then found a trailer camp and had a sound sleep in their little one-room home. It was furnished completely, and they wondered how Robbie had managed to arrange that at such short notice. Perhaps he had them all fixed up in advance, so that mechanics and lady riveters wouldn't have to go shopping when they might put in the time on a fighter plane.

Through Indiana and Southern Illinois and then across the Mississippi by a long bridge. They were in Missouri, from which President Truman and his cronies had come. When you said "I'm from Missouri," it meant that you were of a skeptical disposition and wanted to be shown. All the world was waiting for Harry to show them, and ardent New Dealers like the son of Budd-Erling were cherishing no great expectations. He turned on the radio in the car and listened to news of the latest bombing raids over Japan, comforting himself with the thought that at least an artilleryman-haberdasher couldn't lose the war.

There was a hot spell, and perspiration gathered on their foreheads;

then came a thunderstorm, and it was pleasanter. They bought food in a grocery and did not stop for meals. Lanny was in a hurry but didn't say why; Laurel might guess but didn't ask. She dozed while he drove, and then it was turn about. Presently they were in Kansas, a wide state, with seemingly endless fields of wheat and corn. Trending southward, they came into the Panhandle, and then to a corner of Texas. The roads ran straight most of the time, and the men also ran straight, they would tell you. Lanny had seen them all over Europe, proud of themselves and certain that Texas was winning the war, with just a little help from Oklahoma and Kansas.

In West Texas the hills begin, and presently there are mountains, always bare and rocky, so different from the forest-clad ranges of the East. Nothing useful grew here, except in irrigated valleys. It was hot in the month of July—Mark Twain had joked about hell and Texas. They stopped in a town and bought a dishpan and a chunk of ice to go in it, and set that on the seat between them and persuaded themselves that it made them cooler. A thermometer would have made them feel hotter, so they did not buy one.

Then it was New Mexico, and the mountains were gray, brown, red, black; sometimes green, but it wasn't verdure, and sometimes white, but it wasn't snow. The highway wound here and there, finding its way up through passes and down again. The breeze of the car's motion dried you out but didn't cool you; if you put your hand on one of the rocks by the roadside you would take it away in a hurry. The ice melted fast, and they drank large draughts of the cold water.

XIII

So to the new-paved road that led off to the wartown of Budd. Lanny had phoned, and they were expecting him; he and Laurel had been there before. They drove to what is called a mesa, a plateau, and what they saw astonished them; only a year and a half had passed, and what had magically become a town appeared now to be a city. A flying field as big as La Guardia, and along one side a mile or more of one-story office buildings and hangars and sheds, and back of them block after block of dwellings, all in the Spanish style of this region, of adobe brick or tile. The government had built all this and the government owned it; they would offer to sell it to Robbie for ten per cent of its cost, but what would Robbie or anybody else do with it when the war was over? Especially with the UN proposing to prevent any more business opportunities of the sort!

Everybody was working here like all-possessed, knowing that the Germans had been ahead. New types of planes were being assembled, the component parts coming in caravans of trucks. New types of engines were installed in them, and then they were wheeled or towed out to the field. "Jet buggies" they were called, and weirdly accoutered pilots would be fitted into them—the jokers said they had to be fitted in sections on account of the small space in the newest models. The jets were getting well over five hundred miles an hour now; they flew five or six miles high, and the plexiglass covers the pilots fastened over themselves had to withstand heavy outward pressures. When everything was ready there would come a roar and a flash of white flame. Stand a good way off and always at the side; if you stood in the rear you would be burned completely black. The little plane would leap and go roaring down the runway, and then shoot into the air and become a streak in the sky. Faster and faster! There was a saying: "If you can see them, they're obsolete."

18

Blood on the Moon

I

LANNY saw his wife comfortably settled in an air-conditioned guest house, and then he set out by himself. He drove faster now because there was nobody but himself to watch the speedometer. The school site called Los Alamos lies about forty miles northwest of Santa Fe, and when he got into that neighborhood he looked for road signs, and there weren't any. He stopped at a filling station and asked, "How do I get to Los Alamos?" The answer surprised him. "You don't get there, buddy; there's no such place." For a moment he thought the man was joking and answered in kind, "There must be some mistake on my map then."

"Listen, brother," said the man. "The Army says there ain't, and what the Army says goes around here."

"Oh, I see," replied the traveler. "It happens that I have important business at Los Alamos."

"If you think you have business, buddy, just go ahead and try. If you find it, you'll be the first one."

Lanny, a mere civilian now, said no more but drove on. There was no law against scouting round in this mountain and desert land, so he drove and kept looking. There were road signs directing him to Santa Fe, and others to the little town of Española, so from the map he was able to figure out pretty well where he was. He came to the deep White Rock Canyon of the Rio Grande. Behind it were tall mountains, and a road went winding up to what might be a plateau. At the entrance were heavy gates and a guardhouse, but no sign of any sort.

There stood a sentry with a tommy gun, and Lanny could guess what that meant. He stopped his car. "Soldier, I'm looking for Los Alamos." The answer was, "Have you a pass?" When Lanny said, "I have credentials," the answer to that was, "There's no such place." The man was polite, but there was a weary tone to his voice, as if he had said the same thing a hundred times before and might have to say it another hundred. "Very sorry, but you know what orders are. There's no such place as Los Alamos. You have to write to Box 1663, Santa Fe."

It was a drive of forty miles, and slow, because it was a shelf road winding up a cliff, and there was a surprising lot of traffic. The cliff was of volcanic material, porous and easy to dig into, and the Indians had known it for centuries. There were whole colonies of cliff dwellings, and anyone might collect arrowheads and bits of pottery by the bushel. So to Santa Fe, the capital city of the state, built in Spanish adobe style; it was a favorite haunt of artists and tourists—but seldom in the month of July. Lanny got a room in an air-conditioned hotel and on its stationery wrote a note to Dr. J. Robert Oppenheimer:

"I have come here with cards of introduction from Charles T. Alston and Albert Einstein. I do not want to entrust these to the chances of the mail, but hope that you will give me a chance to present them to you in person. The cards read as follows"—and Lanny quoted the messages, adding, "I have just returned from Europe where I have been doing secret work in connection with the project in which you are especially interested. I have credentials from the OSS." He signed himself "Respectfully, Lanning Prescott Budd," addressed the letter to Box 1663, and took it to the post office.

Then he came back and had a bath and a shave and a meal. He didn't know how long it would take the letter to reach its destination, but he guessed that mail would be carried frequently to the top-secret place, possibly by air. But Oppy might not be there, and his secretary might not have authority to deal with a stranger. In the lobby of the hotel the stranger bought newspapers and magazines and then stretched himself on the bed for a comfortable wait.

II

It was midevening before the call came. A voice, high-pitched and young-sounding, inquired, "Is this Mr. Budd? This is Dr. Fairchild. Could you arrange to come to the confidential place in the morning?"

Lanny said, "I was there this afternoon, but they wouldn't let me in."

"If you will go to U.S. Engineering Office Number Three, in Santa Fe, and identify yourself, they will give you a permit. When you get here you will be brought to me."

Lanny had a well-earned sleep, and in the morning the hotel porter told him where to go; everybody knew that something important was going on at that address but had no idea what. At the office he was escorted into a cubicle, where he presented his Connecticut driver's license, his calling card, his two cards of introduction, and a bunch of letters which he happened to have with him. He had to fill out a questionnaire, giving his name, his age, his place of birth, the names of his parents, and a lot of other details. They took his fingerprints and then made out a pass which, they told him, would be valid only until six o'clock that day. Hard luck if his car broke down!

He retraced the hot, sandy drive on the cliffside road; downhill most of the way, descending into dry riverbeds and climbing again, with heavy traffic all the way. He came to the gate, and it was a different soldier. Others came and inspected the pass, the passee, and the car; a minute inspection—they lifted the seats, rummaged in the trunk, looked under the hood of the car; Lanny wondered if they were going to open the cylinders. Nobody was going to carry any bombs or weapons, and perhaps not any opium or heroin or marijuana, into the world's greatest nuclear research laboratory.

They asked him to slide over in the seat and let a soldier drive. They went through the gate and climbed a winding road up to the top of the Pajarito Plateau, backed by the high green Jemez Mountains. The soldier said, "Sir, the regulations require that visitors shall look straight ahead." Lanny promised to comply.

They went through another pair of gates, and he couldn't help seeing a high industrial fence topped with barbed wire on each side of the street. He did not look at the low buildings. When he got past the fence there were the stores and dwellings of a very ugly, higgledy-piggledy town. Lanny had never seen so many queer types of dwellings, and could guess that it had grown haphazardly and in a hurry. Later he was told that Oppy, who ran this place, had estimated that they would need accommodations for three hundred persons; now, at its maximum, the town had twelve thousand.

The place had been an expensive ranch school three years ago when the government had taken it over. There had been no time to level the ground; the graveled roads went winding up and down and into canyons, and were lined on both sides with more queer kinds of emergency houses than Lanny had ever seen in one place: hutments, a dozen kinds of pre-fabricated buildings, two-story, four-apartment, board houses painted dark green, and more kinds and sizes and colors of trailers than anyone could imagine. Trucks whirling around corners kicked up dust.

The visitor was taken into one of the dark green apartments. It was cool and pleasant, with an electric fan going. It was a study with a flat-topped desk, comfortable chairs, reading lamps, and many books. Rising to greet him was an almost comically young and bouncing lad with curly golden hair, bright pink cheeks, and horn-rimmed spectacles. Lanny would have taken him for eighteen, and learned that he was twenty-three. "I am Dr. Fairchild," he said, and Lanny would have liked to answer, "How well you are named!" Instead he inquired with a grin, "Do I have to have shots?" The other replied with a smile, "I am not that sort of doctor. I am one of those the soldiers here call 'long-hairs,' meaning a physicist."

III

Seated, the youngster began ceremoniously, "Mr. Budd, I am one of Dr. Oppenheimer's assistants. I told him over the phone about your letter, and he told me to see you. Unfortunately the regulations require that you be cleared by the Army Security Forces. Will you come with me to Captain Smith's office?"

Said the visitor, "By all means. I have been a secret agent for eight years and I know about security." He noted that the GI who had driven him was staying right there by the door; and when he went out with the young scientist the soldier followed a few steps behind. No doubt everything had been planned in advance.

They walked several blocks through this strange town and came to a substantial building, which had been a part of the boys' school. Ushered into an office, Lanny was introduced to a severe-faced gentleman who looked like a prize-fighter with his nose broken. The ex-P.A. turned over all his papers: the two cards and the OSS credentials, a driver's license and such letters as he happened to have with him. The officer studied them and then said, "So far, so good. But you understand that such things can easily be forged; also, I have to consider the possibility that the real Mr. Budd might have been slugged and buried somewhere out in the desert."

"True," said the other, smiling. "What you want are psychological tests, which cannot be forged."

"Would you mind telling me how you came to know Dr. Einstein?"

"It is all one story, and I had better begin at the beginning. My father is Robert Budd, president of Budd-Erling Aircraft. They have a new town called Budd in this state, and I have just come from there; one of the things you can do is to telephone to the superintendent and get a physical description of me. I was born in Europe—"

"In what country, sir?" The stern officer was making notes.

"Switzerland. I was raised in France and traveled all over Europe. After World War I my father brought me back to France, and on the steamer was Professor Alston, on his way to advise President Wilson at the Peace Conference. Alston had been in my father's class at Yale, and he invited me to become his secretary because I knew the languages so well. I didn't see Alston again until 1937; meantime he had become a member of Governor Roosevelt's staff in Albany and had been taken to Washington with him. Alston sent me to Roosevelt, who invited me to become what is called "presidential agent." I was Number 103, but I doubt if he had that many. Have you heard of them?"

"They are not within the Army's province, sir. Proceed."

"It happened that I had a boyhood friend in Germany who knew Hitler. I pretended to become a convert, and brought out information which F. D. R. said was of value. In the summer of 1941 I was trained to go into Germany to find out what they were doing about atomic fission, and that is how I came to know Einstein. I spent the summer in Princeton, and my instructor was Dr. Braunschweig." Lanny turned to Dr. Fairchild. "Do you know him?"

"I am sorry, Mr. Budd. I'm a country boy and got my education at Cal Tech. I have never been East."

"I have never been to Cal Tech, but I visited the Huntington Library. I am by profession an art expert, and that was my camouflage in Germany. I never finished my mission because my plane was wrecked on the way to Iceland and I had both legs broken. You know how it is, Dr. Fairchild, when you bone up for an exam you forget a lot of it quickly; but some of it is still in my mind. It began, I remember, with E equals mc squared, and you write the E with a capital, and the m and c in small letters, otherwise they mean other things than mass and the speed of light. The E is energy expressed in ergs, the mass is in grams, and the speed of light in centimeters per second. I could recite a number of formulas, I believe. I have things like this floating through my mind: 'The separation factor, sometimes known as the enrichment or fractionating factor of a process, is the ratio of the relative concentration of the desired isotope after processing to its relative concentration before processing.' Does that mean anything to you, Dr. Fairchild?"

"Of course, Mr. Budd."

"Still more important is the fact that I played some of Mozart's sonatas with Einstein. If you are musical—"

"Unfortunately I am not."

"I called on Einstein only five days ago, to get that card. I told him what I had been doing in Germany in recent months, helping the Alsos Mission dig up atomic secrets. I worked with Professor Goudsmit and Colonel Pash, the military head of the mission. Pash and I drove up to a village called Urfeld, in the Bavarian Alps, to get hold of Werner Heisenberg."

"He was at Cal Tech, and I saw him."

"So then we have a point of contact! Heisenberg is a medium-sized man, smooth shaven, pleasant mannered but oversure of his own importance. The principal thing I remember is how warm his buttocks were, for I had to hold him on my knees all the way on a drive out of the mountains, and his weight seemed to double. That is perhaps not very convincing—"

"The way you tell it is, sir." The young scientist was grinning.

"The main point is what we found. The German efforts at atomic fission were judged amateurish. Their apparatus was good, but it was the wrong kind. They appeared to have the idea that a chain-reaction pile might be a bomb, and they were sure we couldn't have anything better than they had, because they were Germans. However, we got some materials that were useful; at a place called Hechingen, in the Swabian Alps, we got a ton and a half of uranium, a ton and a half of heavy water, and ten tons of carbon. I suppose all of it was shipped to this country."

"We did not see the Goudsmit reports," said Fairchild. "I suppose General Groves thought there was nothing in them that we needed."

"Goudsmit was absolutely sure the Germans had nothing of importance. I captured Phillip Lenard for him, but he didn't think it was worth while even to talk to the old man. Perhaps you have seen pictures of him, so I will describe him—"

The Security officer had been listening, never taking his eyes off the visitor. Now he broke in, "I think I have heard enough to be sure of your identity, Mr. Budd. I should tell you that last night, when your letter came, I checked at once with Dr. Einstein and Mr. Alston by telephone, and also with OSS Washington, and they gave me various details by which I might identify you. This morning I phoned General Groves, and he authorized me to clear you provided that I was satisfied you were the right person. Nobody ever gets in here without the General's OK."

"I am very obliged to you both," said the visitor politely.

"I might also tell you that you will be the only person present at the Base Camp who is not actually working on the project. It will be better if you don't say what you are there for or how you got in; that will avoid hurt feelings. There are a number who would have liked to be present but have been sent to a place twenty-seven miles away."

"Thank you again, Captain. I'm used to keeping my own counsel."

The captain made out the pass and handed it over. They shook hands, and Lanny went out with Fairchild. The latter remarked, "We are at the very top of our crisis, the thing we have been hoping and praying for and at the same time dreading. I am so nervous myself I can hardly sleep or eat. You are to drive to a place called Alamagordo, in the southern part of the state. I am expecting to go there myself. I have to make certain records."

"Why don't you ride with me?" suggested the ex-P.A. "That way I can be sure they'll let me in."

"You are very kind, sir. I'll phone Oppy and tell him we are coming."

IV

The road followed the valley of the Rio Grande, which in its early stages flows south. For the most part it flows through canyons, and the road runs along the edge. Presently it was Highway 85, and then they made better time. A wild and lonely country; Fairchild said that the United States was fortunate in having great spaces in which dangerous modern experiments could be carried out. At Alamagordo there was an air-bombing range, with thirty or forty miles of unbroken desolate country. It was in the remote northern part of this that the all-important test was to be made.

The barriers were down now, and the eager young scientist talked freely. He told about himself; he still considered himself a student, but now he was learning by doing. The need for persons who understood modern physics was so extreme that you could have a job the moment you were fit for it, and you could have promotion as fast as you could equip yourself for new duties. Fairchild had been a pupil of Oppy at the California Institute of Technology, and he adored his teacher, calling him the greatest man in the world—then correcting it to say perhaps the second greatest, Lanny's friend Einstein being number one. Time would decide between them, for the elder sage was nearing seventy, while the younger was only forty-one.

The pupil described Los Alamos, an extraordinary shrine of science, the most secret place in the world, the place where the most deadly force in the world was being created and controlled. It was the force that made the heat and light which the sun had been scattering for millions of years and would continue to scatter for millions more; the force that created all the uncountable suns in uncountable nebulae through a billion light years of space. For the first time on this earth this force had been harnessed and would be put to use—and all in a space of five or six years. It was as if that amount of time had been allowed between the discovery of fire and the building of a great steam locomotive.

The "stuff" came from two enormous plants, a different kind from each. The Clinton Engineer Works near Knoxville, Tennessee, covered nearly a hundred square miles and had more than four hundred and twenty-five industrial buildings, some of them more than two miles long. Mostly they were low, flat structures of brick or tile or corrugated asbestos, without windows. Near by was the city of Oak Ridge—code name "Dogpatch"—with about seventy-five thousand population, and both this and Clinton had been built in less than three years. The plant made a uranium isotope, U-235, by a minute and delicate process known as "electromagnetic separation." Electrically charged particles of uranium were fired through a powerful electromagnet in a curving course; the lighter particles were bent more than the heavier and were caught separately. This had been done on a minute scale in laboratories, but never on a scale above milligrams until the Clinton plant had gone to work.

The other plant extended for twenty miles along the Columbia River in the State of Washington. It was known as the Hanford Engineer Works, and covered more than six hundred square miles of gray sand and sagebrush. Scattered over it were long, windowless concrete structures, many of them in the form of rectangles the size of several city blocks. Near by was a new town for seventeen thousand workers. Here was located a huge "uranium pile," in which atomic processes transformed part of the uranium into the newly discovered element known as plutonium, this too being fissionable. No one knew which would make the more powerful bomb, if any.

It was to Los Alamos that all the stuff came, and they worked over the problem of how to control it, how to shape it into a bomb, how to keep the bomb from going off too soon, and how to make it go off when they so desired. They had determined that there was a critical size for a nuclear chain reaction; too much of the stuff and it would go off spontaneously; too little of the stuff and it wouldn't go off at all. Ordinary methods of detonation had no relation to this nuclear material; what you had to do was to release some neutrons into the stuff—these neutrons, having no electrical charge, would penetrate the uranium nuclei and knock out other neutrons which in turn would do the same. How fast the chain reaction would be, a minute fraction of a second, was something that had been determined by mathematical formulas only.

They were dealing with the deadliest material known, and had to do their work behind thick lead shields, and handle the stuff with long tools specially contrived. Everybody wore electroscopes that would tell instantly if they were getting too heavy a dose of radiation. Oppy was the boss of all this—Oppy, the man with the chain-reaction brain, the boy who had given his teachers the answers before they had had time to formulate their questions! Oppy trusted his mathematics, those "beautiful, wonderful regularities" which had ravished his youthful mind. Calm and serene, Oppy drove this furious atomic blast; it couldn't exactly be said that he was performing the Almighty's orders, but he certainly was riding in the whirlwind and directing the storm. From the beginning he had been given everything he asked for, and everything had top priority; he had been free to take up the telephone and call for a cyclotron that cost a million dollars. He and his fellow scientists had caused the expenditure of two billions, upon the basis of their nebulous theories and hopes. Now, in this lonely and baking desert of Southern New Mexico, they were going to put it to the touch and win or lose it all.

V

It was a long drive, more than three hundred miles altogether. Lanny related stories about the German scientists he had helped to intern and question; Fairchild talked about life in this secret utopia in which he had spent the past year. It was a comfortable life, for the Army saw to everything, heat, light, water, even food and recreation. There were huge cafeterias where you could get a wide choice, and there were movies and dances, and any sort of concerts, shows, and games you chose to get up; also there were hunting and fishing.

But your mail was censored and your telephone conversations listened in on, and you were restricted to an area with Taos, Santa Fe, and Albuquerque at the corners. If you went elsewhere it had to be on business for the project, and you couldn't let anybody know you were in town, not even the members of your family. Your children could go to school inside the project, but if they went to boarding school outside they couldn't come back. This was hard on families, and on friends who couldn't know anything about your affairs but a post-office box. In Berkeley, where Oppy had taught, the report was that he had been arrested as a German spy.

The scientists were a secret society, a consecrated order, which included no fewer than ten Nobel Prize winners. Among themselves they spoke a code, so that workingmen or others who overheard them wouldn't pick up hints. Codes were made up on the spur of the moment, and it took alertness to follow a conversation. Special codes would be made up for trips and for communications by telegraph or phone. Men with famous names changed them; Lawrence was Larson, Fermi was Farmer, Compton was Comas, the Danish Niels Bohr was Nicholas Baker, called "Nick" by everybody. General Groves had been "GG," but that seemed too obvious; a clerk had misread it as 99, and now that was his name. All these men would be at the scene of the test, and Lanny made mental notes about them.

He also listened attentively to statements about the nuclear processes, and his old knowledge began to come back. He was able to form some idea of the developments that had taken place in four years; that much of the war had been a century of ordinary time. He could compare what he learned now with what he had heard from Salzmann and Plötzen, from Bothe and Hahn and Heisenberg and Weizsäcker. The Germans had been back in the Dark Ages so far as nuclear physics was concerned. All the rest of the world except Canada and Britain would stay there until America chose to lift the curtain.

VI

They came to the Alamagordo reservation, an area so big that the rocks and sand and cactus and sagebrush seemed to go on forever. As you approached the test site there were the same security proceedings to be gone through. Lanny's pass was OK, but that didn't keep his car from being searched, including the engine, and he was fingerprinted again; this test site was even more top secret than Los Alamos.

They drove in for some miles, and there were a couple of small buildings and many Army tents, having to do not with the air base but with the test; it was known as the Base Camp. The physicists had come here, traveling separately, and if they had met one another on a train they had carefully refrained from giving any sign of recognition. A few of them were middle-aged, but most were young, for in the department of nuclear physics it was possible to become world-famous in your twenties. The field was open, and all you had to do was to take one step farther into the dark chamber where nature's mysteries had been mysteriously hidden.

There were Army and Navy officers also, and specially chosen enlisted men who did the hard work. The Army's Security officer took the son of Budd-Erling aside, not to put him through another grilling, for they respected the clearance from Los Alamos, but to inform him as to the regulations and administer a solemn oath that he would speak no word about what he had seen here until the story was officially released; then, if he wrote anything about it, he must submit a copy to the Army in advance. Lanny had made all sorts of promises and kept them, but this was the first time he had had to swear.

Lanny's host was Oppy, a very much preoccupied man. He said, "We are taking you in on Einstein's say-so, Mr. Budd; make yourself at home." The scientist had kind blue eyes and wavy dark hair, which he seldom let grow long. He was about Lanny's height but weighed only a hundred and fifteen pounds at the moment—no doubt he had forgotten many a meal. His shoulders were stooped and his manner intense and nervous, for he was approaching the crisis of all his labors. He had a chain-lightning mind that could run all around other men's; he could evolve long equations and remember them forever, and all that had come easily. But for the past three or four years he had been doing a job far more difficult from his point of view, the managing of an enormous undertaking, and the guiding and reconciling of a great number of men, some of whom were prima donnas and all of whom had their own fountainheads of ideas.

Robert Oppenheimer was the son of German-Jewish parents who had come to New York and made a modest fortune. All his life he had had all the money he wanted, and what he had wanted was a marvelous education, which he received at the Ethical Culture School, then at Harvard, Cambridge, and Göttingen. He was still a student, he liked to say, and was getting education from everybody who could teach him. He lectured at a breakneck pace, and there were only a few people in the world who could understand him; his pupils tried, and at least they could imitate his peculiar mannerisms: wearing blue shirts, smoking cigarettes endlessly, running their fingers nervously through their hair while they talked. Oppy spoke with quick excited gestures, and when he could get to a blackboard he soon had it covered with a maze of mystical symbols.

Just now he was like a man balanced on a tightrope over an abyss. A terrible moment: some miles out there in the desert was an old ranch-house, where a crew of highly trained men were engaged in putting the parts of the bomb together. They were under the direction of a Cornell physics professor, Dr. Bacher, who was Goudsmit's "first Ph.D." These parts had been made in different places and brought here in well-guarded caravans. Never before had the parts been joined; never before had there been an atomic bomb in this world. The parts had been machined to the ten-thousandth of an inch, and now the damn thing was stuck; it wouldn't go together and it wouldn't come apart; if it blew up, that would be the end of the Cornell professor and all his trained crew, and of all the labors and hopes of the ten Nobel Prize winners and their hundreds of assistants. Indeed, it would have been the end of the entire bomb project.

Oppy would go to the phone every few minutes and call the ranch-house while the others held their breath. Then he would grunt and light another cigarette and start his stoop-shouldered pacing of the floor. That went on for a while, and then at the phone a smile broke over his face, and he said, "That's fine!" and reported to the company, "They've got it." So it was possible to breathe again.

VII

The most dangerous job was done, but there were many other prepa-rations to be made, and the finale was set for three days later, before dawn. Ten or twelve miles out in the desert a steel tower had been erected, and Lanny drove Fairchild and a couple of other late arrivals out to see it. A drive over the desert road, and there was the tall tower on which the bomb was to be hung. The best—or should one say the worst?—results were to be expected from an explosion in the air, and in military use the weapon was to be used with a special timing device so that it would explode in the air. Men were busily hanging instru-ments on the tower, by which it was hoped to record the various effects of the explosion. The scientists disagreed widely as to the force the ex-plosion would develop; they guessed all the way from two hundred and fifty tons to twenty thousand tons of TNT. On the latter basis, a hundred and twenty-five such bombs would have equaled the damage done by the two-and-a-half-million tons dropped by all the Allied air forces over Europe. On the chance that the instruments on the tower would be destroyed, others were being placed at intervals on the floor of the desert.

From the conversation Lanny could guess that there was a trigger device which shot one section of the U-235 in between two other sections, thus bringing the whole to a size beyond the critical. The explosion would go off with the speed of light, and it was a question whether the whole amount of the stuff would react or whether it would be blown apart and scattered in fragments. Many uncertainties for these learned gentlemen. One and all, they felt that their reputations were at stake; one and all, they were going to be shown to the world either as miracle men or as the world's most costly bunglers.

When they learned that the new arrival had been with Goudsmit, they stopped work for a few minutes to question him. Not one of them had been abroad during the war, and apparently none of them had seen the reports. They were surprised to know how completely the Germans had failed in their efforts at atomic fission on a large scale. The story of poor old Lenard was good for a round of chuckles. These men of the free world all shared a loathing of fantastic creatures such as Osenberg and Sievers whom the Nazis had set up as directors of the great physical laboratories of the Fatherland.

Oppy no longer had to pace the floor; he joined these groups and revealed himself as a genial person. He seemed sure that the test was going to succeed; but many of the others had grave doubts; they were sure their formulas were right, but what the formulas indicated was too colossal, too awful, for the mind to face. They discussed the consequences of the release of atomic energy, the greatest step in the whole history of science. Many were troubled in conscience because the first use of this colossal power had to be for the destruction of life. All agreed that, properly used, it would make man the master of the physical world. Once this power was harnessed to industry, production would become for practical purposes unlimited, and poverty could be banished from the earth.

Lanny brought up the subject whenever he found a chance and collected the opinions of many of these wise gentlemen. He didn't say what use he expected to make of the ideas, but he got the men to talking about the subject of war and what steps mankind would have to take to end it. One and all, they said that this discovery, if it proved to be real, would make war impossible; an atomic war would end only with the destruction of civilization as we knew it. More than one man said, "I am hoping the thing may fail, and that an explosive chain reaction may be proved impossible. Mankind is not far enough advanced, politically or morally, to be entrusted with such a weapon."

What Oppy said was, "We shall have to educate the people. We scientists have hidden ourselves in our laboratories and forgotten the rest of the world. Now we have to come out and take part in politics, and make both the politicians and the public realize what this discovery means, in happiness if it is used wisely, and in misery if it is used evilly."

VIII

On Saturday, the 14th of July, the bomb was raised to the top of the steel tower and hung there. That dangerous job was witnessed only by the men who performed it. The test was set for four o'clock on Monday morning, and on Sunday night few slept soundly. Lanny lay on his Army cot in a tent he shared with young Fairchild; he wasn't sure if his tentmate was asleep, so he lay still, his mind roaming over a score of different aspects of the world-shaking event he hoped to witness. Even if the bomb did not explode, even if a sudden and violent chain reaction proved impossible, still there could be no doubt that the world was on the threshold of a new age of power. First fire, then steam, then electricity, then the internal-combustion engine, and now the nuclear chain reaction.

Only two and a half years had passed since Roosevelt had confided to his P.A. the fact that the first atomic pile had been put into successful operation. Roosevelt hadn't said where or how; but here Lanny had heard the story of how Professor Compton of the University of Chicago had set up a laboratory in the squash court, under the stands of the football stadium, and there had managed to solve this most difficult problem. It was undoubtedly the most deadly contraption ever born of the brain of man. Bars of uranium oxide and of pure uranium were placed with spaces between them, so that bars of graphite could be slid in. Six tons of specially purified graphite were provided; and you didn't just poke those bars in by hand, you had hooks operated by machines, with the operators staying behind heavy lead shields. Rods of cadmium, a metal which strongly absorbs the neutrons, could be moved in and out of the pile to control the chain reaction.

The design of the pile was computed from the results of small-scale experiments, and no one knew how accurate these were. Therefore, blocks of cadmium were suspended from the ceiling and could be dropped into the pile at once, in case the reaction threatened to get out of control. At this time they did not know enough to be sure that they would not blow up a few blocks of the city of Chicago. So said Fermi, the Italian who was here under the name of Farmer; he was the man who had first proposed the chain-reaction idea, three years earlier, and had tried it out with a microscopic quantity of U-235. In those happy days it had been the custom of scientists to publish their discoveries at once, and Fermi had set the whole world of physics to speculating and experimenting with this force that was the parent of all the heat, light, and motion in the world.

Lanny had his private thoughts for this crucial occasion. He couldn't say to these scientists, "I have a million dollars with which to prevent an atomic war"; but he could feel them out and judge which men would be most useful for his purposes; he could make friends with them, so that later, if he wrote to them or went to see them, they would know who he was. Whether nuclear fission was to be used in war or only for the purposes of industry, these were the experts whose say-so the world would have to heed. He found them in a grave mood, ready to speak.

IX

On Sunday evening General Groves arrived; a heavy-set West Pointer just turning fifty, with a small mustache and thick black hair beginning to show gray. His face wore a rather grim expression, and Lanny could guess that he didn't welcome meeting strangers at this busy moment. He brought with him President Conant of Harvard and Dr. Bush of the OSRD.

Lanny talked with his well-informed young tent companion. What would happen if lightning struck that steel tower? Fairchild couldn't be sure, but he said it was just as well that nobody should be near. Rain, he was positive, wouldn't hurt it, for this was not the kind of fire that water would have any effect upon; when a chain reaction got going, water would disappear as steam or perhaps be changed into atoms of hydrogen and oxygen.

One of the uncomfortable ideas these long-hairs had discussed was that a large-scale chain reaction might not stop with the isotopes of uranium. Suppose it were to start off some other heavy metal, iron, for example, and there should be a vein of it under this desert floor! Or suppose—just supposing!—that it should set off a chain reaction of the lighter elements? In that case a medium-sized planet of the solar system would disappear in one bright flash—though not bright enough to be observed by inhabitants of other planetary systems, if such inhabitants might be in the vasty deeps. In that case Lanny would never get to carry out Emily Chattersworth's mission; in that case, where would Lanny be, and where would Emily be? He tried his best to persuade himself that somewhere, or out of all wheres, might be still existing the millions of millions of souls that had lived upon the earth during its last million or so of years, and that he had been hearing the voices of a few of these through the lips of Laurel and of Madame Zyzynski. The best he could do was to say that he would believe it when he woke up in that new state of being.

From the tent opening he saw the lean figure of Oppy and the burly figure of GG, alias 99, wandering about in the diminishing rain. He knew they couldn't sleep, and he could imagine their discussion. They wanted aerial observation, photographs, and instrument recordings of the great event; but pilots couldn't see anything in this weather. More important yet, if the explosion came off, and the enormous radioactive cloud were brought down to the earth by rain, what would be the effect upon towns and ranches and growing crops? These were new questions, and new fears for the authors of unprecedented destruction. Oppy lighted more cigarettes, and wandered about, peering up at the clouds and looking in vain for a star. The test was postponed from four o'clock to five-thirty. Later than that would spoil the chance for photographs in darkness.

One star appeared, then two, and they were enough; the storm was passing. Oppenheimer and Groves consulted their meteorologist and decided that five-thirty would be H-hour. The lieutenant of the Military Police Detachment guarding the tower reported by telephone that all was well. The control station from which the bomb was to be detonated was ten thousand yards, about six miles, from the tower, and here a shelter of heavy logs and earth had been built, with a sloping side toward the explosion. The place assigned to the observers was a slight rise of ground, seventeen thousand yards from the tower, and their orders were to lie flat on the ground, face downward, and heads away from the blast. All were provided with dark glasses, but did not trust to these; they buried their eyes in the sleeves of their forearms crooked in front of them.

X

A tension such as Lanny had never seen before in any group of men. The control room and various observation points were all tied in by radio, and twenty minutes before H-hour one of the scientists took control and began calling—minus twenty minutes, minus fifteen minutes, and so on until the last five minutes, which were called minute by minute from a loudspeaker. Not a sound from any of those prostrate forms; some, no doubt, were praying, others shuddering, all finding them the longest minutes in their lives. At minus forty-five seconds an automatic mechanism took over, and from then on all the complicated procedure was out of the hands of human beings. There was a reserve switch with a soldier-scientist sitting before it; he could have stopped everything if he had been told to—but he wasn't.

At the precise second there came a flash of light, the like of which had never been seen on this earth, many times the brightness of the sun at its brightest. A blind girl a hundred miles away perceived it somehow, and before the sound reached her she asked, "What was that?" The scientists leaped to their feet and looked through their dark glasses at an enormous half-bubble of light that had been shot up into the sky. They braced themselves for the blast, the mass of air pushed from the explosion, with the greatest force ever created by human beings. At ten miles distance it was not serious, but it knocked flat two men who had stood outside the control room. A few seconds more and there came the sound, a thunderous all-pervading roar like nothing anyone could imagine.

A huge cloud of many bright colors had surged up into the sky. Explosions seemed to be going on inside it, and the shock waves and sounds continued. It billowed and boiled and became an immense mushroom, emitting light like the sun and growling and roaring like the monsters of primeval time. The watchers were stunned at first; then exultation possessed them, and they shook one another's hands, they hugged the nearest man, and cried out with wonder and delight. They had done it! Their formulas were right!

A sight never to be forgotten by anyone who was there. The light turned the whole landscape to day; the mountain range near by stood out as if in a dawn of many suns. The light shifted and changed, from golden to red to blue to violet, then to gray; nobody dared look at it without the dark glasses. The cloud continued to rise and boil until it became a tower some eight miles tall; then slowly the light faded out of it, the grumbling ceased, and the wind began to shift it, fortunately away from the Base Camp and with no rain to bring it quickly to earth.

The learned scientists stood chattering like a group of schoolchildren. Their satisfaction was beyond bounds. One and all, they had staked their time, their thought, their health, their reputations, upon this, the most costly of all scientific experiments. Up to the last second they had had no surety of success, and now, all of a sudden, they had it in overwhelming quantity and quality. Nobody could have asked more, nobody could have imagined more. There was a story about a pilot who had been sent up to make observations from a long distance and report by radio. When he saw the flash and felt the blast he shouted, "The damn long-hairs have let the thing get away from them!" But it wasn't so; it was "Operation according to plan." One of the scientists confided to Lanny the astounding fact that the bomb which had wrought this colossal effect was slightly larger than a baseball and weighed no more than twenty or thirty pounds.

Specially equipped tanks, with thick lead covering, were wheeled to the scene in course of the day. One of them carried the quiet Professor Fermi; he came back and reported that the steel tower, with all its instruments, had completely disappeared; the steel had been vaporized and must have gone up in the cloud. At the base of the tower was an immense crater with sloping sides. The sand of the desert floor had been fused and was now a sheet of green glass, upon which nobody would dare to set foot for many a day, perhaps a year.

"If we drop this over Japan it will end the war," said 99; and Oppy added, "I hope it won't end civilization."

BOOK SEVEN

Thy Friends Are Exaltations

19

Powers That Will Work for Thee

I

LANNY drove back to the town of Budd and reported to his wife that he had seen something important which he was not permitted to disclose; he thought it wouldn't be long before the story was released, and then she would have an eyewitness account to write up. In return, she told him that she had taken up the idea of writing a story about Robbie's number-one test pilot, a daring fellow who flew everything that was made and was still alive in spite of having been doing it for twenty years. When he had flown a plane for an hour he knew more about it than its makers. His job was to get what he called "the numbers": how fast the plane flew at level flight and how fast when rising; how fast at sea level and at twenty thousand feet; its engine temperatures, its gallons of fuel consumed per hour, and many other details. After he had got them, the Army came and made the tests all over again before accepting the plane. No wonder Budd was a busy field!

It amused Lanny to hear his wife telling him things which he had been hearing from Robbie for a couple of decades. Did Lanny know what it meant for a plane to "snake"? Yes, he had heard the expression. This pilot had a new model that snaked so that it almost yawed, and he had decided it was the fuel sloshing in the tank; they were putting in baffles, which they hoped would stop the trouble. Laurel went on to describe the man's pathetic little wife, who had never become reconciled to his dangerous job, not even at fifty dollars a day. Laurel said, "I wanted to tell her how sorry I was for her, but I thought I'd better not." Lanny answered with a smile, "Robbie wouldn't have liked it."

He teased her for inconsistency; she, a hater of war, and preparing to start out on a crusade against it, was a Budd-Erling stockholder; she was making blood money out of these engines of destruction. She had inherited the stock from her uncle, so it wasn't of her own choice; and if she sold the stock, somebody else would get the profits, but it wouldn't stop the making of the engines. "Thou shalt not kill," said

317

the Commandment; the Episcopalians had softened it to read "Thou shalt do no murder." This illustrates the fact that moral problems are complicated, and not even God has been able to make them plain and simple.

II

President Truman had gone to Germany, to sit down with Churchill and Stalin and try to solve those problems which had been troubling Franklin Roosevelt on the night before his death. Lanny had been free to tell his wife about this interview, and now, driving their little aluminum house back to New York, they listened to broadcasts speculating as to what might be going on at the Potsdam Conference. The fate of the world for many years to come might be decided over there in the large quadrangular palace full of relics of Frederick the Great. Certainly it would have a great deal to do with what the Budd couple would be thinking and doing in course of the next five years.

The conference lasted two weeks and two days, and that gave the newspapers and radio commentators plenty of time to speculate, and gave the couple time to get their affairs in order. They took the trailer back to Newcastle, duly thanked its owner, and reported what they had seen at his town. They talked about the trip and about jets, but not a word about bombs. A dutiful son did feel free to say this much to his father, "Don't quote me, but I think you can make your plans on the basis of the Japs giving up very soon." The wise father looked at this man of mystery whom he knew so very well and saw a steady look in his eyes and a grave expression on his face. "You really mean that, Lanny?"

"I mean it positively. I can't say more."

They found Frances in a state of excitement because her mother and stepfather were coming to pay a visit and take her on a trip across the continent. Ceddy had bought a big ranch in Western Canada—with Irma's money, of course. It was raising wheat for England, a worthy purpose, and now harvest time was at hand, a great sight. They were going to make a grand tour, through the Canadian Rockies, and returning by way of California and Budd, in which Irma too was a stockholder.

In the course of that trip the girl would make up her mind whether she preferred going back to England to school or staying in Newcastle. Lanny didn't want to influence her decision. He was aware that the elder Budds were extremely sensitive on the subject of divorces and would consider it a theme for gossip if Irma and Laurel were to be in the same town or if Lanny were to meet his former wife there; he needed no hint, but remarked that he and Laurel had to go back to New York in the next day or two. He knew without being told that the arrival of a genuine English earl and countess would constitute a colossal social event, adding to the prestige of the Budd tribe. He looked with distaste upon such snobbery and had no desire for a close-up view of it.

He took his eager young daughter for a sail on the river and listened to the outpouring of her small adventures and her hopes. He told her that she was to make up her own mind about her future. There was an agreement between her mother and himself that neither would ever do anything to influence her against the other, and this meant that Lanny couldn't tell Frances his opinion about titles of nobility or about the false glories of inherited fortune. She would have to live in Irma's world. She would see all the excitement over the almost-royal pilgrimage, be kowtowed to and admired and photographed, and must make what she could of it. He did feel free to tell her that he hated war and was going to do what he could to end it. She, of course, could have no idea that hereditary privilege such as her own was among the causes of social and national strife.

They left the baby in the care of Agnes, the skilled trained nurse who had been a second mother to him from his birth. It was summer, and cool breezes blew off the Sound; also Laurel wanted to write an article about test pilots of jet planes—of which she disapproved. Lanny said she would have to leave her disapproval out of the story, for jet planes might have given the victory to Germany if Britain hadn't been able to build them faster and better. Jet planes were now knocking the Japs out of the skies, and so the American reading public thought them very excellent indeed.

III

Back in the great city, Lanny went on a hunt for an apartment for Nina and Rick, and thereby extended his distrust of the profit system into a new field. Owing to the housing shortage, Congress had passed a law fixing rents of houses, apartments, and even hotel rooms at the prices which prevailed before the war. The effect of this had been to direct the mental energies of landlords and agents to originating devices to get money from would-be tenants for something that couldn't be classified as rent. The landlord had just installed a fine piano in the apartment, and would Lanny's friends be willing to pay fifty dollars a month extra for the use of this piano? In another case, would they be willing to pay the agent a hundred dollars a month extra for his services in finding them a competent cleaning woman—this above what they would pay to the woman?

Lanny didn't mind paying a high price so much as he minded being forced to connive at breaking the law. After answering several ads and running into various forms of trickery, he decided that he would make use of that snobbery which he had discovered to be so powerful in Newcastle. He inserted in the most highly regarded newspapers an advertisement with a box number, reading: "English baronet (genuine), a well-known playwright visiting city with his wife, desires to rent comfortably furnished, centrally located apartment two months. Middle-aged couple, no children, no pets."

Two days later there was a reply, offering him just what he wanted, not far from his own apartment. A telephone number was given, and he called it; a pleasant woman's voice answered and asked for the name of the prospective English tenants. Lanny replied that he didn't care to give the name of the tenants until he had seen the apartment and been told the price. They sparred for a while over this, and he was asked for his own name and gave a part of it, Mr. Lanning.

The lady consented to meet him and take him to the apartment, and he met her in the lobby of a near-by hotel. She was young, well dressed, and smart, and devoted her smartness to trying to get him to name the baronet; he in turn devoted his to an effort to persuade her to show the apartment, which could be had for only three hundred dollars a month, a price he was willing to pay. The effort was of no avail, and in the end she laughed and told him she didn't think he had any baronet, and she didn't have any apartment. She was a newspaperwoman who had smelled a good story in the coming of a titled Englishman who was a well-known playwright!

The problem was solved by accident when Lanny mentioned his trouble to Zoltan Kertezsi. The art expert said, "They can have my apartment. I am going to be away." Zoltan had been invited to study and prepare a descriptive catalogue of the art collection of a wealthy retired banker in Princeton—none other than that Mr. Curtice who had given Lanny a hiding place while he was boning up on atomic fission. Mr. Curtice was going to the Adirondacks, and Zoltan would have his lovely old mansion with the smooth green lawns and white peacocks on them—all to himself except for some of the servants. "Come and see me," Zoltan said. "Mr. Curtice will agree that our two heads are better than my one."

IV

In the midst of these small affairs came an event of electrifying import to the two rich friends of the poor: polling day in Britain, and the Potsdam Conference adjourned for three days to enable Winston Churchill and his large staff to fly back home to vote. Winston went— and he didn't come back. The most amazing thing, a parliamentary upset the like of which had never been known in British history. The common people of that land of hope and glory adored their war leader, but they didn't want him as a peace leader—a distinction that was clear to them but must have been confusing to Winnie. The Labour party obtained a majority of almost two to one; they got it upon the basis of a definite program calling for the nationalization of the five most important of the nation's industries: coal, steel, transportation, communications, and finance.

It was the program to which Nina and Rick had devoted the labors of their youth and maturity. The same thing was true of Lanny; and while Laurel was a later convert, she was none the less ardent. Their jubilation was unbounded, and they held a brief celebration over the transatlantic telephone. Alfy was "in," and by a large enough vote so that he could speak with authority. And Winnie was "out"—and immediately, by the marvelous system which they have on that tight little island, where statesmen can get to London quickly. There was a new man flying to Potsdam to help decide the fate of Europe, a man by the name of Attlee, of whom few outside of Britain had heard; a quiet, rather frail-looking man, with no booming voice and no polished periods; but he knew what he wanted and had most of the British working class and a good part of the middle class behind him.

So now it was possible to go ahead with the ending of war, and not merely in Potsdam but in London and New York. Nina and Rick had procured their passports and made application for visas; they were coming as visitors, which gave them six months, and then, if they wanted more time, they would make a new application. The land of the free and the home of the brave had become rather choosy in these later years. Lanny had to fly down to Washington to stir up the cookie-pushers in the State Department, assuring them that a British baronet was really a Socialist and not a Communist, and that he wasn't going to advocate the overthrow of the United States government by force and violence.

V

A tense and exciting time in the world's history, and nobody in his right mind could complain of being bored. The B-29s were keeping up their milk runs over Japanese cities, and the Navy's task forces kept coming closer to Tokyo, shooting down the enemy's suicide pilots and sending swarms of divebombers against ships and other targets. That was supposed to go on for a long time yet, perhaps a year or two; but Lanny kept waiting for the big news that was due any day. His imagination pictured those terrific new bombs being transported to a base on some island near Japan. Would they go by plane or by ship, and how long would it take? Only a few persons knew, and none of these had given Lanny a hint.

He developed the habit of turning on the radio every hour on the hour and looking at newspaper headlines whenever he passed a stand. He couldn't give up the habit because, obviously, with each day that passed, A-day must be one day nearer. Everybody who knew anything about the A-bomb agreed that there wasn't going to be any hesitation; the enemy was going to learn about the bomb in action. Of course after that there would be no keeping the secret—the enemy would tell even if we didn't.

The Potsdam Conference came to an end on the 2nd of August and a summary of its results was released. Japan was called on to surrender, and warned of dreadful things to come. Germany was to be divided into four zones, each to be governed by one of the four nations, America, Britain, France, and the Soviet Union. To anyone who really wanted peace this arrangement was ominous, for it could mean only that the Big Four distrusted their ability to agree and had agreed upon a series of arguments and squabbles for an indefinite time. Each of the four would have its own idea of what Germany and the Germans ought to be and would proceed to make them over in its image: a Communist East Germany, a Socialist North-central Germany, a Big-Business, Private-Enterprise South-central Germany, and a Bourgeois Southwest Germany, hated, feared, and kept as poor as possible.

President Truman came back to Washington and put the best face possible on what he had done. Most people thought he had been hoodwinked, and this wouldn't have been surprising, since he had had no previous experience with international affairs. America had the strange practice of putting its possible substitute President away on a shelf, as it were; he had no special way to learn what was going on, and when his Chief suffered a massive brain hemorrhage, all he could do was to wring his hands and say, "Look what's fallen on me!"

VI

On the 6th of August, a day never to be forgotten, Lanny turned on his radio. It meant having to listen to odious commercials, and he loathed them, but in times like these he had no choice. His heart gave a leap as he heard the announcer say, "Ladies and gentlemen, we interrupt the program to give you a statement which has just been issued from the White House, signed by the President of the United States. Give it your close attention. The statement follows."

He called to Laurel, who was pounding the typewriter in her room. She came running, and they listened to these portentous words: "Sixteen hours ago an American airplane dropped one bomb on Hiroshima, an important Japanese Army base. That bomb had more power than twenty thousand tons of TNT. It had more than two thousand times the blast power of the British 'Grand Slam,' which is the largest bomb ever yet used in the history of warfare. The Japanese began the war from the air at Pearl Harbor. They have been repaid manyfold. And the end is not yet. With this bomb we have now added a new and revolutionary increase in destruction to supplement the growing power of our Armed Forces. In their present form these bombs are now in production, and even more powerful forms are in development. It is an atomic bomb. It is a harnessing of the basic power of the universe. The force from which the sun draws its powers has been loosed against those who brought war to the Far East."

So at last the secret was out, the secret that Lanny had been keeping from his family and friends for four years, the secret that had come near to burning a hole through his brain. Now at last he could tell Laurel where he had been in New Mexico and what he had seen there; why he had set out on a plane four years ago and come near to losing his life; what he had been doing in Germany, both before the war's end and more recently. "Oh, what an awful thing!" she exclaimed. "What an awful thing we have done!" As usual, she thought about human beings and failed to take the military attitude. "It makes our task more urgent," she said, and Lanny answered, "It also makes it more possible, perhaps."

He telephoned his father. "Have you heard the news?"

"Someone in the office just told me," was the reply. "So that's what you've been doing all this time!"

"Don't mention it to anyone else," he said. "There are reasons."

"This finishes Budd-Erling," said the father. "They won't need us any more." He never failed to take the business point of view; but he would tell you it was the human point of view as well, for what was going to happen to those thousands of men and women he employed?

Laurel was so shocked it was hard for her to think. A paralyzing thing to know that such a horror was loose in the world, and that she had been living with it for the whole of her married life! Of course Lanny hadn't been allowed to tell her; but what about those psychic gifts she thought she had discovered? They had failed her so utterly just when they had the most important material to work on.

Lanny brought her back to earth. "Don't forget that you have an eyewitness story," he remarked, and her writer's instinct began to stir. She went in and sat by her typewriter, and Lanny stretched out on the bed and started to talk, sentence by sentence, while her fingers flew over the keys. They agreed that the way to handle this thing was as a straight reporting job, with no attempt to elaborate or philosophize. Said Mary Morrow, "This is an account of what happened at the first atomic-bomb test at Alamogordo, New Mexico, as told to me by a friend who was present." Then came the story, and instead of what Mary Morrow thought about it, or what her friend thought, there was what the different scientists and military men had said.

When the job was done she wasn't willing to entrust it to anybody else; she stayed up part of the night to make a set of clean copies, and in the morning she took one to a newspaper syndicate. At the same time Lanny took a plane to Washington to carry out his promise to the Army. He had put on his uniform again, and that helped; he had no trouble in seeing the right man. Since he was already familiar with what was called "Security," there wasn't much to object to; a couple of phrases which the censor thought might be questioned, and Lanny agreed to change them. The OK was given, and the husband went out and phoned his wife. She reported that the syndicate had grabbed the story and was ready to put it on the wires the moment it was released.

VII

Two days later a second bomb was dropped over Japan, this time on the great seaport of Nagasaki. No one could say how many lives were destroyed, but the airmen took photographs, and these appeared in the newspapers and showed nothing left standing except a few heavy concrete buildings and part of some steel frames. It was said that the second bomb was even more powerful than the first; Lanny could guess that the material of one was U-235 and came from the Oak Ridge plant, while the other was plutonium and came from the Hanford plant.

Everybody agreed that no civilized state could stand such punishment, and least of all Japan, whose cities were so largely of wood and paper. From Potsdam the United States, Britain, and China had issued a call to the last enemy to surrender, threatening "inevitably the utter devastation of the Japanese homeland." Now the Japanese knew what that meant better than anybody else in the world. The toad beneath the harrow knows exactly where each tooth point goes! The statesmen and their Emperor were also able to guess exactly where the next bomb would be dropped.

It was believed among the Allies that the Emperor desired to surrender, but there was a question whether the fanatical military clique would let him; they wanted to do what Hitler had done and go to their ancestors with glory. There was a plot to assassinate members of the cabinet and seize the person of the Emperor, but this was thwarted and the moderate party won out.

On the day after the bomb was dropped over Nagasaki a message came to the government of Switzerland, saying that "in obedience to the gracious command of His Majesty the Emperor" the Japanese government was ready to accept the Potsdam terms, "with the understanding that the said declaration does not comprise any demand which prejudices the prerogatives of His Majesty as a sovereign ruler."

To this the United States replied next day that the authority of the Emperor would be subject to the Supreme Commander of the Allied Powers. Four days later the Japanese government bowed to these terms, and on the second of September millions of Americans listened over the radio to the elaborate ceremony of signing the surrender document, which General MacArthur had arranged on board the battleship *Missouri* in Tokyo Bay. Such was the formal and dignified ending of World War II.

VIII

There was a new world, so everybody felt. Decent people could breathe freely again and turn their thoughts to whatever interested them. Everybody in the Army wanted to get out and come home by the first ship, no matter how crowded. The Army worked out a system of points, based on the period of service, and the great war forces began to melt away; the *Queens* brought double loads of men, one lot sleeping by night and the other by day, and nobody complained of the discomfort. Production would be shifted to civilian goods, rationing and price-fixing would be ended, taxes would be reduced, and everything would be the way it had been before the war, only much better. So the papers said.

Nina and Rick were on the way; and meantime Lanny went to work in the library of the Rand School of Social Science, learning about the history of American Socialism. He read old books and bound volumes of magazines and refreshed his memory as to facts which he had almost forgotten. In his youth his great-uncle Eli Budd, a Congregational clergyman and scholar, had told him a lot of things about the land of his forefathers. American labor didn't have to go to Marx and Engels, to Fourier and Proudhon, for its ideas of social reconstruction; America had had its own thinkers from the earliest days, who had ideas in accord with American character and institutions.

That didn't mean that students should be ignorant of European ideas; they were necessary to the understanding of European problems and events. But to understand American problems and events one had to know American ideas, and this meant a knowledge of the writings of Robert Owen and Albert Brisbane—not Arthur, but his great and noble-minded father; of Wendell Phillips and Horace Greeley, of Edward Bellamy and Henry George, of George D. Herron and Charlotte Perkins Gilman and Gaylord Wilshire and J. A. Wayland and Eugene V. Debs. These writers and many others had put American ideas into circulation, had shaped the minds of several generations of Americans, and had become the wellspring of innumerable movements and programs. Practically everything in Roosevelt's New Deal had been included in the "immediate demands" of the Socialist party of America for thirty years, and the Tennessee Valley Authority had been the dream of every home-grown utopian since the invention of hydroelectric power.

One of the formulas that Lanny had fixed in his mind was to "talk American." This devastating war had left America the one country in the world that had money in quantity enough to speak and be heard. Whatever was going to be done to prevent the next war would have to be done with American support and under American guidance; the task was to help the American people to know what to do. Second in importance would be the British people, and Rick would know how to speak to them. As to the Russians, they had chosen to be an enigma, or rather their rulers had chosen that role for them; what part they would take in the organization of the new world was something which could not be foreseen but could be known only when the thirteen men of the Politburo revealed it in action.

IX

Lanny Budd had been watching wars since the age of fourteen, asking questions and reading what the world's accepted authorities had to say on the subject. He had made note of the many factors involved: the natural belligerence of the human male, a quality which had come down from his animal past; the vast weight of ignorance and superstition brought from that same past; the hatreds and prejudices which had been acquired through the centuries and the memories of wrongs which the peoples had committed and had suffered—it being human nature to remember the latter and forget the former. All these had played their part in the past and must be dealt with in the future.

There were two other factors which in Lanny's mind had come to assume predominance. The first was pressure of population, and for that there was but one permanent remedy, the universal knowledge and practice of birth control. Manifestly, if any species of living thing, animal or vegetable, were permitted to reproduce itself unchecked, it would in time cover the earth and leave no room to move about in. What had checked the human family was three things: pestilence, famine, and war. Modern techniques had suppressed the first two, and thus made the third the more inevitable and more deadly. Populations increased the faster, and the resort to the third remedy became more certain, quick, and extensive.

The other major factor was the private ownership of the means of production and their use for private profit. This meant the exaltation of greed into the most powerful motive in human society. The survival of the masses of any nation was dependent upon the ability of the private owners in that nation to find markets for their products; so each nation was organized as an instrument of private greed, seeking raw materials and markets where the products could be sold at a profit. Failure to find either of these meant unemployment and starvation at home, with the threat of revolution. Driven by these fears, international rivalry grew more intense and led inevitably to war, which relieved the pressure of population, the unemployment, and the threat of hard times. There was plenty of work until the damage had been

repaired, and then the old troubles would loom over the land once
more. Under the system of production for profit a world war every
generation was automatic.

X

Rick and his wife arrived. Having been a successful playwright
many years ago, and being now a baronet, he found the newspaper
reporters on hand with their scratch paper and their questions. Had
Sir Eric ever been to America before? What had he come for now?
What did he think about the country? What would he say about the
British elections? What hopes did he have for the United Nations?

The tall, slender Englishman, who had been dealing with newspapers
all his mature life, revealed himself as a gracious and obliging person.
He had decided that the future of the world lay in the keeping of the
United States of America, and he had come as a student to learn what
he could about this great country. Everybody in Britain had been
filled with awe at the demonstration of power America had given in
the past four or five years. Britain was grateful for lend-lease—and so
on. Yes, Sir Eric and his wife were members of the Labour party, and
had campaigned in the recent elections; their eldest son, Colonel
Alfred Pomeroy-Nielson of the Royal Air Force, had just been elected
to Parliament on the Labour ticket. No, Sir Eric had no plans to lecture in America, but might be happy to do so if invited. He would
deal, of course, only with British and European subjects; he would
never feel himself competent to give advice to the people of any country but his own.

So it went, and next morning all the newspapers were respectful,
and the four conspirators felt that their enterprise had got off to a
good start. One of the papers stated that the visitors would be staying
at the Chiswick Arms, and before the morning was over there came
a telephone call from the Rand School inquiring if he would consent
to give a talk in the school's auditorium on the significance of the
recent elections. Rick said he would be happy to do it, and he was,
for this was the way to meet the intellectuals of Pinkish inclination and
get started in the field of his endeavor.

What neither Rick nor Lanny understood was the number of queer
people there were in America, each with a cause of his or her own and
the firm conviction that it was the most important cause in the world.
Before that morning was over Rick had several callers, and each time
he went down in the elevator to the reception room of this large

apartment hotel. First, an elderly sweet-faced lady who was interested in a movement to forbid the use of animals in medical experiments; she had a handbag full of pamphlets with horrifying pictures of things being done to dogs that might have been her own beloved pets. She besought Rick to read these, and she also pressed upon him a copy of the previous day's Hearst newspaper, from which Rick learned that an immensely wealthy press lord, who in his early days had promoted many causes on behalf of human beings, now was crusading to let human beings perish in order to spare the feelings of dogs.

The next was a threadbare old gentleman with trembling voice, who had had some difficulty in getting by the august, resplendent doorman of an apartment house just off Park Avenue; he had said that he was a friend of Sir Eric, and it was true because he was a friend of all mankind. He had a plan to end poverty by what he called the "Bacon and Eggs Plan," in order to distinguish it from the "Ham and Eggs Plan" which had been put on the ballot in California a few years before. It involved the distribution of paper money to the aged and needy, for both of which classes this gentleman appeared eligible. He was ready to start publication of a paper, he said, and all he wanted was for Sir Eric to put up the money.

Also, before the day was over, there came a severe-looking, pale-faced man about seven feet tall—at any rate he towered over Rick. He had a trace of Swedish accent and announced in solemn basso profundo, "I have a revelation direct from God."

"Indeed?" said the Englishman politely. "What is it?"

"It is a manuscript," replied the man—he had a large parcel under his arm.

"And may I see it?" asked Rick, still more politely.

The answer was given in a voice as near like God's as possible. "No human eye has ever beheld it. No human eye ever will behold it."

Rick took care in extracting himself from that situation, for he knew from ancient Hebrew days that God had sometimes given alarming instructions to his prophets. Rick gave instructions to the girl at the switchboard that in the future Sir Eric would receive visitors only by appointment and that strangers were to write and tell him what they wanted.

XI

It took the couple no more than a day or two to get settled in Zoltan's comfortable apartment, full of books and *objets d'art*. The four collaborators would go out for one square meal each day and feed one another in picnic style for the rest. A cleaning woman would come once a week, and the rest of the time they could have the two places to themselves. People who set out to change the world need all the time there is; and perhaps if they knew in advance what a small amount of success they would have, they wouldn't make a start. However, it is clear that the world would never change at all if nobody tried to change it; and you would have a hard time finding any adult person in the present world who would say that he or she was entirely pleased with things as they stood.

What these four persons wanted was to put a set of important ideas before as large a number of people as possible; and what was the best way to do it? By the spoken voice? They might all four have become lecturers and taken to the platform and the road. It was a slow and trying way, and for Rick it would have been especially hard. They might write and publish books, or offer prizes for the best books by others; but that too was a slow way, and the A-bomb had filled them all with a sense of urgency.

Pamphlets were easier and quicker; but how would you get them circulated? In the old days people had read pamphlets; Tom Paine had helped to make the history of America with his *Common Sense* and his *The Crisis*. But pamphleteering had been by-passed as the American way. What the masses in America read was newspapers and low-priced magazines; also, they listened to the radio and went to the movies. If you wanted mass circulation, those were the ways to get it. They were all enormously expensive and conducted for the profit of private owners; a genuine liberal among the owners was as rare as a white blackbird, and that was why opinion in America lagged so far behind mechanical development—including the aforesaid A-bomb.

Lanny said, "Whatever we publish ought to look like what the people are used to reading."

To which the experienced Rick replied, "The trouble with that is, everything the people are used to is produced on a mass scale, and to reproduce it on a smaller scale would be very costly. You could use up your million dollars in a few months."

"The people want to be entertained, and only a few want to be instructed"—thus pronounced Laurel. Such was the barrier, and to break through it was possible only to top genius, to which none of the four laid claim. Rick suggested gallantly that maybe Laurel had it; anyhow, she was the only one of them who had managed to get mass circulation for her work. "My plays were written for the carriage trade," he declared. "You can laugh at such people, and make them enjoy it—if you are a Bernard Shaw; but when you become too explicit they drop you—or the producer does it for them."

XII

They needed figures and expert advice, but they distrusted the publicity people and the promoters, who charged fancy fees and whose advice might be shaped by their own interests. Laurel went to her magazine editors, who thought highly of her and passed her on to others in the trade who had experience of different kinds. She also interviewed printers who could tell her about prices—and about the difficulties of getting paper in these times.

Rick went to the Socialists, whose job was carrying on various kinds of small-scale propaganda; they were glad to tell a British comrade about it, especially when he consented to write something about the miracle that had just been produced in his homeland. Rick found the American Socialists in a somewhat discouraged state because they had not been able to achieve either mass circulation or a mass vote. They were inclined to lay the blame upon F. D. R., who had misled the masses with doles and delusive promises. They thought now that things would be going better for the party, because Harry Truman was turning rapidly to the Right, and the returning soldiers would surely be ready to consider the need for fundamental change.

As for Lanny, he got into his car and went scouting, first on Long Island and then among the Oranges—so called not because they grew there, but because the Dutch had been there. He wanted a place where they would have access to a moderate-sized library and where they could find a printing establishment, an office with half a dozen rooms, and a residence large enough—they had decided to keep house together since they got along so well and it was a nuisance visiting back and forth. These things were easier to find since the war had come to an end, and a lot of people had the idea fixed in their heads that there was going to be a slump and widespread unemployment. It had happened a couple of years after the last war, and few of the rich put any faith in those taxing-and-spending techniques which they hated and which obliged them to earn their money over and over again instead of salting it away the first time they got it.

That left Nina, and she didn't sit at home. She put on her best clothes and, looking very much the lady, went visiting the business offices of radio stations. She had the idea that the radio was a more important social force than her friends realized, and she didn't let herself be bluffed by the statement that the cost of a single coast-to-coast broadcast would be something like five thousand dollars for a single quarter-hour. Why did you have to reach two coasts? Why not start on one and see what happened? Maybe there were radio managers who were worried about business prospects too.

The English lady discovered that there were a number of small independent stations in and around New York, and they were glad to talk with anybody who looked like money. They were not too choosy about programs; if you paid for the time in advance you could oppose the vivisection of cats and dogs, you could advocate government printing and distribution of paper money, or you could tell about a revelation direct from God. You could even advocate birth control, provided you didn't go into detail as to how it was done—and of course you mustn't offend the Catholic Church.

No less important, some of these stations had friendly relations with others scattered over the northeastern part of the country, and they sometimes hooked up when they had a program of wider interest. You could build up a temporary chain that way, and if you had something the public really wanted you would accumulate a clientele; have a regular period once or twice a week, and people would get into the habit of listening to you. For a thing like ending war there were thousands of people who would be interested, and if you had something convincing to propose you could ask them for money, and it might pour in. That was the way Father Coughlin had built up his influence, back in the twenties; station by station, he had put together his radio chain, and it could still be done. "It don't matter if it's an idea or a soap powder," was the slogan that Nina brought away with her.

XIII

This research went on for several weeks, and by that time they had a dossier which might have cost fifty thousand dollars if they had bought it from one of the concerns specializing in business research. But they were learning by doing; their questions awakened interest, and it was pleasant to discover how many business people showed an interest in the idea of ending war in the world and wanted to be told how it could be done. Americans, it appeared, weren't nearly as bad as their business system tried to make them. They were friendly and genial and glad to take time off to give information when they were approached in the right way. They even wanted to have their names put down and to be informed when the enterprise got started. If the four had been soliciting subscriptions they might have taken in enough to keep them going.

The lecture at the Rand School came off. This institution, founded by the wife of George D. Herron some forty years earlier, was dedicated to the cause of democratic Socialism. The Communists, dedicated to the cause of Socialism by dictatorship, hated the Rand School more than they hated any capitalist institution. Their headquarters were only three blocks distant, and the organs of the rival parties gave a good part of their space to pointing out each other's errors.

The auditorium, which could accommodate close to a thousand, sitting and standing, was crowded that evening. The victory of the British Labour party was perhaps the most sensational event in the history of the movement. How had it been won, what did it signify, and what use would be made of it? A good part of the audience was made up of Jews; their fathers had been educated at this school. The families had moved to the Bronx or Brooklyn, and now the sons and daughters went to City College or Brooklyn College by day and to the Rand School in the evening. They came with alert and eager faces, taking the intellectual life seriously; the awful things which had been happening in Central Europe had made them into a thoughtful generation.

The chairman explained that Sir Eric Pomeroy-Nielson had lost a part of one knee when he had been shot down as a pilot fighting over France in World War I; therefore he was accustomed to speak sitting. He sat behind a small desk as if he were a college professor giving a lecture. He had known personally the men and women of two generations who had built the British Labour movement: Keir Hardie, Ramsay MacDonald, Tom Mann, H. M. Hyndman, and the Webbs of the past, and Herbert Morrison, Ernest Bevin, Clement Attlee, Stafford Cripps of the present. Sir Eric himself had written for Labour papers and spoken at Labour meetings for the past quarter of a century; he told how the movement had been built, how the workers had been educated, the extremists restrained, and a large part of the middle classes won over. He said that in his opinion this taking over of the British Commonwealth of Nations by its organized workers was the most important single event of modern times.

What was Labour going to do with its victory? It was going to do what it had promised in an official campaign pamphlet which had been studied by the voters. It was going to make a basic portion of the nation's industries into national properties, paying for them at the market price with government bonds. It would reorganize them, abolishing the wastes of competition, and turn them to public service. It would do this in peaceable and orderly fashion under the constitution, without killing or robbing anybody. The task wouldn't be easy, for Britain had spent the greater part of her resources on the war and now was a poor country; everybody would have to work hard and make sacrifices, and anybody who thought that Socialism was going to mean ease and luxury at once was doomed to bitter disappointment.

The Labour movement would explain this to its people, as it had explained other problems and dangers in the past. What the Webbs had called "the inevitability of gradualness" was something that emanated from the national temperament; the British people were not extremists or revolutionists, and they didn't trust people who bragged and made large promises. Said Sir Eric, "If you watch our movement for the next five years you will see that we do what we were elected to do, no less and not much more."

XIV

The question period is the most interesting part of any lecture, and there were many who wanted to have their doubts cleared up, and others, the Commies or fellow travelers, who wanted to put the speaker in a hole. Many of the questions had to do with the application of British tactics to America, and the speaker said he had no competence to discuss that. The general principle of achieving socialization by popular consent would apply to all the peoples of the world who possessed democratic institutions and were accustomed to using them. That meant the Anglo-Saxon lands and the Scandinavian, also Belgium, Holland, and Switzerland. It would include France, Italy, and Czechoslovakia, provided that the Communists would allow it to happen, which he thought was doubtful.

The Communists, who put an end to free speech wherever they can, found it suited their purposes in the Rand School auditorium. A bespectacled young woman arose and wanted to know if the speaker really thought that the capitalist class of Britain would permit the abolition of their privileges without forcible resistance. The speaker answered that they had already done it. The Coalition government was out and the Labour government was in, and Winston Churchill had already taken his place as leader of His Majesty's Loyal Opposition. He would criticize and he would scold, as the free institutions of Britain permitted him to do; but he wouldn't dream of sedition, and if in 1950 the Labour party carried the elections with a program for further socialization, he would submit as he had done before, regretfully but politely.

Again and again someone wanted to know how these lessons applied to America. Rick said that the problem was different because America's political ways were different. America had the primary system, which enabled the people to select their party candidates by direct vote. That made it possible for the people to take possession of an old party and use it for a new purpose. By that means it had been possible for Roosevelt to take and use the Democratic party, and had thus made it difficult to interest the workers in a new, or third party.

Then, of course, the fat was in the fire. What relationship did the New Deal bear to British Socialism? Lanny, who had placed himself at one side where he could watch the audience, saw that everybody was sitting forward on his or her seat; this was the topic of debate of which you never heard an end in the Rand School. Sir Eric quoted the saying of an old-time British political leader, that the Tories had caught the Whigs in swimming and stolen their clothes. Rick said, "We Labour people have always felt that our business was to have our ideas stolen by our opponents. For half a century they have been taking our programs of social security and putting them into effect. You in America didn't feel the need of such measures until fifteen years ago; then the Democratic party began putting them into effect, and I should think you would let the Republicans do the worrying about it."

Did the speaker think that the Socialists should use the Democratic party? An earnest young girl student asked the question, and Rick smiled and said he wouldn't tell even if he knew, which he didn't. Americans knew their own institutions best, and they wouldn't need an Englishman to tell them how to go to work.

An old-time Socialist whom Lanny remembered from the days when he had visited the Rand School before the great depression inquired whether the speaker thought there was any prospect of the socialization of basic industry in America. Rick said that basic changes would come only when there was basic need for them. American industry was now at its peak of prosperity, and only when the next slump came would drastic action be forced. And did he expect a slump soon? He answered that this depended upon whether international understanding could be achieved. If there should be another war, of course there would be no slump; even preparation for war would postpone it, perhaps for years.

"So," said the Englishman, "if our Communist friends who antici-
pate a slump are wise, they will keep hands off and let this country
follow its normal boom-and-bust cycle, as it has been doing for more
than a century. What I fear is that the Kremlin will yield to the temp-
tation to grab while the grabbing looks good. In that case they will
compel the capitalist world to rearm, and thus will keep the capitalists
in the saddle for nobody knows how much longer."

Oh, how mad that made the Communists! They got up and started
an argument, and the audience started to hiss and boo them. But Sir
Eric said, "Let them ask their questions. We Englishmen are used to
being heckled. It is a difference of opinion that makes horse races, and
if nobody disagrees with me I'd be sure I hadn't said anything worth
listening to." So they laughed and listened, and the meeting was a
success.

20

Multitude of Counselors

I

PROFESSOR GOUDSMIT went to Washington to make a report, and then he came to New York and phoned Lanny. They had a
lot to talk about, and he came to dinner and spent the evening. The
atomic bomb, which had been the most closely guarded of secrets, was
now something you could sit and chat about in drawing-rooms—and
this the old-timers found hard to get used to. Nina and Rick came,
and Lanny answered the Professor's questions about what he had seen
in New Mexico, and what Einstein had said, and Oppy, and the others;
all the things that had been top secret until the 6th of August.

Goudsmit had been to Berlin, of which the American Army had
taken over a sector in July. He drew a depressing picture of the center
of that great capital, almost entirely destroyed; the Russian artillery
had done even more damage than the British and American bombs.
That huge New Chancellery, which Hitler had built for a thousand
years, was partly smashed and completely looted; the garden, in which

the Führer's body was said to have been burned, was trampled and littered with junk, and the underground Führerbunker was now a place for souvenir hunters. Only the main thoroughfares had been partly cleared of debris, and the wind bore clouds of plaster dust and the smell of burned wood and rotting bodies.

The Alsos men, of course, were interested mainly in the Kaiser Wilhelm Institute, especially the building known as the Max Planck Laboratory. Several years ago Lanny had gone there as a pretended friend of the Nazis, in peril at every moment. He had talked with a grim old Prussian physicist, Salzmann, and had revealed to him secrets deliberately designed to mislead him as to what the Americans were doing. It was a large building, two-and-a-half stories high, with a rounded corner and a tower, and having a basement with steel-barred windows opening to the street. Goudsmit reported that the place had been completely plundered by the Russians; they had taken even the electric wiring and the plumbing. They had dumped a lot of trash into the back yard, and there Alsos had found blocks of pressed uranium oxide, probably the most valuable property that had ever been in the place.

In charge was the "Director of Intelligence of the U.S. Control Council," and he told them that there was in the sub-basement what appeared to be a swimming pool. Goudsmit recognized it as the "bunker laboratory" of which the German physicists had been so proud. The "swimming pool" was the sunken pit in which they had built their atomic pile, thinking it might become a bomb; the metal frames which were to contain the uranium cubes were standing near by. Goudsmit called it "the physicists' symbol of the defeat of Nazism."

II

Hardly less interesting was the story the Alsos head had to tell about the fate of the German scientists whom Lanny had helped to find and intern. They had been delivered to the American military, and apparently these non-scientific brass hats hadn't known quite what to do with them. The British had kindly offered to take them off our hands, and so were getting the benefit of the best German brains. These brains were housed in a fine estate not too far from London, with a radio, a piano, a tennis court, newspapers and books, and the best of food.

Goudsmit hadn't seen the place, or even been told where it was, but he had talked with an English scientist who happened to be visiting them at the time the news of Hiroshima came over the radio. The reaction of the Germans was of utter incredulity: the American claim was absurd. The Germans were the people who knew better than anybody else in the world, for they had been trying and had made sure how difficult it was, impossible in that short space of time. The Americans had no doubt invented some new and more powerful chemical explosive, and they were calling it "atomic" in order to frighten the Japanese. Dr. Goebbels' fellow countrymen were familiar with that method of carrying on warfare.

No, the so-called "atomic bomb" could have nothing to do with nuclear fission or with uranium—"oo-rahn," as it is in German. The ten were so certain of it they could eat their dinner with enjoyment. But later in the evening came a more detailed report, and the effect upon the Germans was devastating; their own little world came to an end. For six years they had been working, and they had failed, while the despised Americans, the Jew-ridden upstarts, had succeeded. How dare the radio claim that Lise Meitner, a Jewess, had discovered uranium fission when everybody knew it was Otto Hahn, a pure Aryan German?

Most depressed of all was Walther Gerlach; he had been in charge and was the one who would carry the blame for all time. He sat with his head in his hands and talked as if he were contemplating suicide; his colleagues had to gather round and argue him out of it. They tried to interest him in the problems that were tormenting them, the statements over the radio that made no sense at all. What was this talk about heavy water, and the pride the Allies took in having destroyed the Rjukan plant in Norway? Heavy water could be used in making an atomic engine, but surely not a weapon!

To the Germans the word "bomb" meant the thing they had been trying to build in the Max Planck Laboratory's sub-basement, an atomic pile. What was it the Americans used in place of heavy water, and how on earth had anyone managed to get an atomic pile into the air? The stuff was heavy, heavier than lead, and had to be protected with heavy lead shields. No plane ever built could have carried such a load. Could they have used fast neutrons in pure uranium? But that would have made it even heavier. Or had they been able to separate uranium-235? But how was this possible in just a few years? And what was this nonsense about plutonium? There was no such element as plutonium. Did the ignorant newspaper and radio people perhaps mean protoactinium? This would make a bomb, but there wasn't enough of the substance in the whole world.

Hour by hour the ten listened to the world-shaking news, and little by little their leading theoretical man, Heisenberg, was able to solve the mystery. The atomic pile wasn't the bomb; it was merely the means of splitting uranium atoms and making new and more highly radio-active substances. That must be what the talk about plutonium meant. A new element! And new isotopes! How had the Germans ever failed to discover the clue, and how could their science stand such a blow to its prestige? It began to dawn on these renowned gentlemen that they were safe and comfortable where they were. If they went back to Germany it might occur to some of the frenzied werewolves to punish them for the humiliation they had brought upon their native land!

III

There came a letter from Beauty with interesting news. The Army's wonderful sleep-talking machine had brought back Marceline's memory almost completely. They had got her a set of dental plates, and she was able to eat normally and had regained her strength. They had refrained from asking her questions about painful events, but the day had come when she chose to talk to her mother about them.

There had been several different plots against Hitler's life, and hundreds of Reichswehr officers and officials of the old regime had known about them. Every now and then Himmler's agents would stumble on a new clue, and there would be new arrests and shootings of the guilty, and often of those whose ill luck it was to be related to the guilty or acquainted with them. All Marceline knew was that she had been sitting quietly one afternoon in front of the cottage she had rented on the grounds of what had been a girls' school and was now a hospital for wounded officers. She was enjoying the sunshine when she heard a low whistle and saw an elderly war cripple who worked as gardener on the place beckoning to her from the doorway of her home. She got up and went inside, and the man whispered the dreadful news that the Gestapo was coming for her; they had stopped in a near-by village café to have lunch, and a waitress had overheard their talk. Being the daughter of this old gardener, and having heard of Marceline's kindness to him, the girl risked her life to telephone her father.

Marceline stopped only long enough to put on her hat, snatch up her purse, and pay a sum to the old man. Being fond of walking, she knew the paths about this neighborhood and was able to get away unobserved. She got to a town and phoned Lanny at the Berlin hotel where he was staying; then she sought refuge in the home of friends, and they kept her in their attic for a couple of weeks. A servant must have betrayed her; the Gestapo men came and took her and the whole family to the old red-brick jail on the Alexanderplatz in Berlin.

At first they pretended to be friendly. They told her they had arrested her lover and had him in this same jail; he had confessed everything, including the fact that she and Lanny had known about the plot. Of course the statements about Oskar might be true or not, Marceline had no means of knowing. They told her they realized she had taken no active part in the conspiracy, and all they wanted of her was to know the whereabouts of her half-brother. She said she had no idea and had not heard from him for weeks. They traced her telephone call and confronted her with that, and all she could say was the truth, that she had no idea where Lanny would go.

Of course they didn't believe her and tortured her near to death in the effort to wring the secret from her. They told her that her lover was being tortured too and that there would be no respite for either of them until she gave up. "Perhaps I might have," Marceline said, "but I couldn't tell what I didn't know." So in the end they quit and put her in with the herd of women who were driven every day to the underground munitions plant in Leipzig, to slave until they died.

Such was the answer to the riddle that had been troubling Lanny's mind for two years. He did not get the last detail of it until another year, when he had access to the Gestapo's voluminous records and learned that Oberst Oskar von Herzenberg had been taken to Lichterfelde. There in the courtyard of the old military cadet school, scene of the Blood Purge of 1934, the handsome, arrogant Junker had been hanged.

IV

Rick's talk in the Rand School and his article in the *New Leader* served the purpose of launching him in that movement for social change which it is difficult to name because it has many different groups and labels. The two Budds and the two Nielsons sought the advice of older and more experienced campaigners for peace and social justice, and found that the town was full of them. All appeared pleased to be asked for their opinions and would start to pour out ideas, always with positiveness. The only trouble was the ideas differed so much and often were contradictory.

However, certain types emerged, the most common being the "tired radical." Always he was the idealist who had grown gray in the service of his cause, and the high hopes with which he had started had failed of realization. Perhaps he had hoped for too much and in his disappointment was unable to realize to what extent his program had actually been accepted. The social climate of America had changed, but so slowly that the day-by-day observer had no way to notice it; there was no social thermometer by which you could get the exact measure of progress.

It was amusing to notice how each of these war-worn veterans advised you to eschew the activity in which he himself had made his career. The writer of pamphlets said, "Don't write pamphlets, there is no way to get them circulated." The writer of books said, "People don't read serious books any more; the radio and the week end at the farm have put an end to reading." The orator said, "People don't come to meetings any more; they stay at home and drink gin and listen to imbecile shows." The editor said, "For God's sake, don't try a paper. The slicks and the pulps have all the stock and the advertising and circulation; you're licked before you start."

Yes, there was need of a thermometer, a clock, a Geiger counter, a device of some sort to register the effects of propaganda and to help social-reform writers and publishers and editors keep up their spirits. Somebody was needed to point out to them that even though they had had to quit, they had not failed entirely. If they had published sound ideas and had found readers, their ideas would live in other minds and spawn and reproduce themselves after the manner of ideas.

Alfred Bingham, sensitive and high-minded son of a former governor of Connecticut, had published a little monthly called *Common Sense*. Now he said, "A dozen years as editor and publisher left me with a feeling of futility. No magazine in my line has had a noticeable effect on events, except perhaps for Henry Luce's."

To which Laurel answered, "But I read your magazine and learned a lot from it. Why do you assume that I have forgotten it?" This cheered the good soul not a little.

It wasn't so different with the *New Leader*, a twelve-page weekly paper that was still speaking for the Left Wing New Dealers and Right Wing Socialists in and around New York. The four newcomers invited the staff to a dinner in a private room and told them about the problem they were facing. The editors were generous in their attitude; they had no fear of competition—the harvest was plenteous and the laborers were few. But on the whole they were discouraging as to what could be accomplished. William Bohn, most amiable of veterans, expressed himself: "Anything really good in the way of a movement or publication will require much more than a million dollars." When

Laurel referred to the so-called "Garland Fund," a million dollars which a young man had donated to the cause of social justice, the editor gave his verdict: "The world would be just as well off if young Garland had spent his money on chorus girls."

V

In all these researches the "Peace" group, as they had taken to calling themselves, were careful to preserve the roles they had agreed upon. Sir Eric could be himself, and so could his wife: he the writer and old-time Socialist and she his loyal partner. Mary Morrow was the lady of mystery and money; a popular writer, eccentric in that she refused to wear high-heeled shoes or to smear red grease on her lips—but then writers are allowed a certain amount of oddity, and so are rich persons. Mr. Budd was her gentleman friend who sat quietly listening, now and then asking a question but never arguing, and leaving you to assume that he wasn't much of a personality. Rick was the brains and did the talking; it was natural that, having never been in America before, he should be trying to understand the country and its ways.

Talk about him spread, and before long it reached the press. When reporters came Sir Eric was tactful, as ever. He had recognized the fact that New York had become the intellectual as well as the financial center of the world, and he was feeling out the possibility of getting together a few friends of international order, to speak and write on behalf of progressive and humanitarian ideas. It would be a program of co-operation and agreement, along the lines of the United Nations—which had made up its mind to settle somewhere in the United States, if the country would have them.

Such interviews brought more letters and more visitors, and already a card file was accumulating; a secretary and a temporary office had to be engaged. Rick and Nina did the interviewing, while Lanny went to the library and continued his research. He wanted to know all there was to know about the collectivist ideas and movements in the past of his country. There was little about it in the regular histories, but there was a vast special literature, now mostly forgotten. At the turn of the century there had been a Socialist monthly, *Wilshire's Magazine*, which had achieved a circulation of three or four hundred thousand. It was run by a "billboard" man from Los Angeles who had made a fortune and then been converted to the new-old religion of human brotherhood. The experts in the publishing field had told him that if he got a circulation of that size he would meet expenses; he found it wasn't so. Big advertisers would have nothing to do with a publication whose slogan was "Let the nation own the trusts." *Wilshire's* died when its owner's money was gone.

There had also been a weekly paper, *Appeal to Reason*, with a circulation of more than a million. This paper had been started by a real-estate dealer named J. A. Wayland, who had fifty thousand dollars to spare and bought a press. He built up the paper by the policy of supporting the cause of labor, right or wrong, and of never asking for donations but only new subscriptions. World War I wiped it all out, and the "little old *Appeal*" was remembered only by a few old-timers.

It took the researcher no little trouble to find out that the former editor of the *Appeal*, Fred D. Warren, was living in Kansas, a retired owner of oil leases. Rick wrote to him, expecting to get advice as to the launching of a paper in these new times. The reply he got was, "As an old newspaperman I can see no possible chance to build up a circulation of a weekly or monthly that would reach the folks we need to reach. Only by the media that are now established can we do the job quickly. I would buy space in such widely circulated magazines and newspapers as would accept the things I wrote. I would use material from the columns of the old *Appeal*, because I am convinced that Wayland had the right ideas as to what was wrong and what should be done."

When Nina read that she remarked, "In other words, we turn our million dollars over to the capitalist press and increase its power!"

Lanny added, "Whatever we have, it must surely be our own."

VI

For many years a presidential agent had been dealing with men of action, those who held power and determined immediate events. Now he was meeting with men of ideas, who were trying to determine the future. Very certainly Franklin Roosevelt would never have been able to launch his New Deal if men such as these had not been sowing the seeds of collectivist thought for a couple of generations. When you met the sowers, and discovered what a variety of seeds they carried, you were better able to understand the confusion and groping of the early New Deal. It might be true that in the multitude of counselors there was safety, but there was also an appalling amount of waste.

The four called in a quiet and conscientious thinker who had been troubled by this confusion. After publishing a number of Socialist books, Stuart Chase had taken up an English notion called "semantics," and spent an evening explaining to the quartet the importance of knowing the meaning of the words you used in talking about social problems. Early in the century the Russian revolutionists had invited the soldiers to shout for a constitution, and they had done so gladly, having the impression that *Constitutza* was the Tsar's mistress. And now the sons of these same men were shouting for a thing they called "*Democratzia*," understanding by it that they voted a ballot which had only one set of names on it.

What Chase wanted in social reform was "more light and less power." He said, "Too many reforms amount to attempts at predicting with insufficient data, and if such predictions ever work in the social field it is by accident." He admitted that a more even distribution of goods throughout the world would be a big help for peace, but added, "Nobody yet knows how it can be achieved, in a realistic political way." When Rick suggested that perhaps they hadn't time to make the elaborate investigation proposed, the answer was, "We haven't time not to."

After their guest had departed the two couples sat discussing his point of view. Rick, who had lived through the rough and tumble of British politics for most of his life, exclaimed, "Insufficient data, my eye! You have the data of a score of depressions in a century and a half. You have the data that with each depression thousands of little businessmen were forced into bankruptcy, and millions of workers had to part with their savings and their homes. You have the data that a hundred men, or maybe two hundred, have incomes of a million dollars a year. What more data do you need in order to know that your society is in a state of perpetual civil war, with strikes and revolts and crime waves and all the other products of a blind competitive system?"

That was the way the impatient ones talked.

VII

Another impatient one was Emanuel Haldeman-Julius, editor and publisher from the Middle West. They heard that he was in town and sought him out; they found in him the first and only man who still believed in the pamphlet as a weapon. He went into a sort of ecstasy over the very word. "A pamphlet is cheap, effective, and popular with the masses. It is not big enough to frighten them off. A pamphlet gets its job done because, if it is properly written, it covers a theme thoroughly and brings the reader to a definite conclusion. A pamphlet has the power to move mountains."

When he heard about the million dollars he pleaded, "Don't make the mistake of wasting your money on fat, expensive books. Learn from the work of Voltaire, Paine, Ingersoll, Kropotkin, Goldman, Debs, and hundreds of others. You must go to your job with the passion and sincerity of Diderot, d'Holbach, and the other French encyclopedists. You must take all culture as your field—politics, economics, finance, social evolution, free thought, anti-clericalism, democracy, science, history, philosophy. You must conduct the greatest battle of the pamphlets in all history. The people have been misled and confused, and you must rebuild their minds; they will come to you with the innocence of children, and you must give them understanding. The encyclopedists brought enlightenment to the top layers of society; a set of their books cost about two hundred dollars. They found their readers even in the palace of the King, and among skeptical members of the Church hierarchy. Theirs was a revolution from the top, an aristocratic movement; but yours will be a cultural revolution from the bottom up. You have the brains and the money, and you can buy the right machinery and the know-how. You have a staggering opportunity!"

This lover of cheap books spoke as one having authority, having made himself the greatest creator of pamphlets in history. He had sold more than three hundred million "Little Blue Books" at the price of five cents each, which meant that he had handled fifteen million dollars. He had more than twenty-five hundred titles, including every subject of importance you could think of. He advertised this list in all the important magazines and newspapers that would accept his copy—many wouldn't because his list included attacks on superstition and clerical power. In course of time his list had come to include eight hundred "Big Books" also; his was a going concern, and he was the one man who had been able to make money out of selling the masses what were supposed to be unpopular ideas.

This dreamer of unlimited education ended his excited discourse with a smile. "I suppose that what has stirred me so is the idea of a million dollars. Even though I don't expect to touch any of it, still it works on both my mind and my senses. I have a nose for news, and another for money."

This large and prosperous lover of books went on to relate amusing stories of what he had learned about his business. He had published a short story by Maupassant entitled "The Ball of Tallow" and had sold fifteen thousand copies a year; then it occurred to him to give it a different title, and as "A French Prostitute's Sacrifice" it sold nearly four times as many. Théophile Gautier's *Fleece of Gold* sold only five thousand a year, but when it became *In Quest of a Blonde Mistress* its sales were multiplied by ten. That wasn't supposed to be ethical, or at any rate dignified, but the publisher's conscience did not trouble him. "The people get a recognized masterpiece, and they learn something about the world they live in. Believe me, I know what the discovery of great literature means to people who are poor. I began earning my living as a boy, driving an elevator in a school, and I devoured good literature in between passengers. I read books and wrote books a long time before I began selling them, and when I sell a thousand I am reading every copy in my imagination."

VIII

Then came another Jew and another book lover: Sam de Witt, old-time New Yorker, old-time tennis champion, a poet who published his own poems and plays, and a prosperous dealer in tools and machinery. Sam was one of the five elected Socialists who had been expelled from the New York legislature during World War I. He was in his mid-fifties now, but as full of liveliness as ever. He knew all about the different "causes" in New York and the quarreling party lines. He became eloquent as he described the situation.

"There is the curse of the 'angle.' Having edited a Socialist weekly for years, and in that time read Communist, Trotskyist, anarchist, liberal, and every other tint and twist of sociological publication, I learned to distinguish a clipping without reference to its source. Wording and tone fell into their pattern at once, whether dealing with the future of the Swedish thermos bottle or the holy tetractys of Pythagoras. Each publication developed a planetary system, around whose hub some twenty to forty thousand votaries swirled or trailed in self-righteous assurance."

Rick ventured mildly, "It has been our hope that we can hold ourselves above party and faction." To which the answer was, "To do that you will have to hold yourselves so high that nobody will know you are there."

The speaker went on to tell the sad story of Marshall Field, benevolent multimillionaire, who had subsidized an afternoon newspaper called *PM*. He had succeeded in fusing some of these rival groups into a circulation of a hundred and fifty thousand; as Sam classified them, "Forty thousand Stalinists, twenty thousand Socialists with various shades of hatred of Joe and all his works, five thousand Trotskyists, and the rest confused goodhearted lads and lassies who just can't stomach Hearst and Luce and the rest of our press masters. The paper has lost several times as much money as you lads and lassies have to put into the pot. Here you are with one million dollars, proposing to save two billion human beings who are standing on the verge of extirpation."

"What would you advise us to do?" asked the American "lassie," not without a touch of acid in her tone.

The discouraged Socialist thought for a bit and then said, "I can tell you—but you won't do it."

"Give us a chance," urged Rick.

"All right. You rent yourselves a large tract of land somewhere out beyond the Jersey marshes and put a heavy steel fence around it and turn loose a lot of savage dogs to guard it. You erect some low, flat, sinister-looking buildings and take extraordinary precautions to swear all the workingmen to secrecy. You install a lot of queer machinery which I can buy for you—that's my business and I won't charge you a profit. Gradually rumors will spread, and reporters will come; you tell them that you have employed the world's greatest physicist, and he has discovered a process for producing atomic fission in ordinary rock, and so you are going to make the world's most awful bomb. This is a free country, and you don't have to let anybody into your plant that you don't want to. Gradually awe and terror spread—nobody doubts that you have something, because who would spend a million dollars on nothing? That is reasonable, isn't it?"

"And then?"

"This goes on for three or four years, until the whole world knows about your project and the suspense has become extreme. By that time the United Nations will be on the verge of its final break-up. You come before them and say, 'Gentlemen, there is not to be another war. I have decided to save you the trouble. I have created a rock bomb that will destroy everything within a hundred miles of it, and probably start a chain reaction in all the rock in the earth. I have a dozen of these bombs, and my agents have them hidden in a dozen of your great cities—New York, Washington, London, Paris, and, believe it or not, Moscow and Leningrad. I give you one week in which to submit your dispute to the arbitration of the World Court, to abolish all armed forces and all national boundaries and tariffs, passports, visas, vetoes, and other obstructions to peaceful intercourse. You will immediately establish an international government run by the majority vote of the nations here present. If you don't take this action the bombs will go off at the same instant in all the different places. They will be time bombs, and the agents will have time to escape. Nor will it do you any good to arrest me, for in that case my agents have orders to get the bombs started, and may God have mercy on your dumb souls!"

They all had a chuckle; and Laurel, somewhat mollified, remarked, "You ought to make that into a play, Mr. de Witt."

"If I do," countered the tool merchant, "will you use part of your million dollars to produce it?"

IX

All this was America, and they were learning about it at first hand. For Rick, all the reading of his lifetime was not equal to this face-to-face contact. He found the American accent fascinating; he was amused to note that whereas the Americans all knew he had an English accent, they were surprised to learn that they had an American accent. It is, apparently, the habit of all peoples to assume that the earth revolves around their particular spot on it. "Everybody but thee and me is queer, and sometimes I have doubts about thee."

For Lanny, too, these encounters were stimulating. For nearly a decade he had had no personal contact with the movement he had been trying to serve. He had been living in the enemy's country, not merely physically but ideologically; he had been living capitalism and luxury, while cherishing democracy as a secret dream. Now he could sit among his real friends and listen to their talk and observe what life had been doing to them, and especially what war had been doing to them. There had been more than ten years of war, for it had begun in Spain, and even before that, when Hitler had advanced into the Rhineland.

For anyone with a critical sense it is easier to love the people in imagination than in reality. These "radicals," these "Leftists," or whatever name you chose to give them, were opinionated persons and didn't mind repeating themselves over and over—they couldn't have carried on their work otherwise. They had strongly developed egos, and strong resistance to other egos. Along with their sense of justice it was possible for them to have more or less envy; they would have had to be superhuman in order not to enjoy having a little success, even a little luxury in their lives. Those who had forced their way upward in the world had found it rough going, and they hadn't always had time to practice the amenities, or even to think about them. Some didn't have good table manners, and some didn't always remember to brush the dandruff off their coat collars. In short, a leisure-class person could find numerous reasons for disapproving of them.

These facts stood out when the leisure-class person took a day off and went among his own sort. Lanny and Laurel took Rick and Nina up to Newcastle; a delightful drive in bracing autumn weather, and there was a large household, living in accord with completely accepted conventions which removed all friction and made every human contact agreeable. Nobody tried to force his opinions upon you; nobody forced anything upon you, you were assumed to know what to say, what to do, what to wear, what to eat and drink. If it was golf, you knew how to play; if it was cards, you wouldn't dream of cheating; if it was at the table, you knew how to hold your knife and fork, and you were offered a second helping once and only once. Friction of every sort was avoided like a plague. Of course it existed; Lanny told his friends about bitter family quarrels, but no visitor would ever see a trace of them. There was the story of a haughty Budd dame who had said to her husband, "Take me into the closet and spit on me if you must, but show respect for me when we are in public."

The way Lanny got along with the highly developed egos of the wealthy was to let them say their say and never oppose them. What was the use? You could never change them, only make them angry. Rick and Nina had grown up on this course, and so the four dwelt in the enemy's country, ate the enemy's food, listened to the enemy's conversation, and conformed to the enemy's proprieties. The enemy became a friend, and all the Budd tribe came in to meet a British baronet (genuine) and his wife (also genuine). There was a tea for them at the country club, where they met "everybody," and they might have stayed on as guests indefinitely. But after three days of it they were bored and wanted to get back to that uncomfortable world where crude, imperfect people argued and squabbled over party lines and programs. (Incidentally, Baby Lanny had the measles and was shut up in a darkened room, and Frances had gone back to England with her mother; so two reasons for staying were canceled.)

X

The work of delving into the American mind went on. Lanny looked into the story of the Garland Fund, an experiment which came closest to the one he was planning. Some twenty years ago a young radical had inherited from his father a share of a fortune and had announced that he did not believe in the right of inheritance and would not touch it. Thereupon his fellow radicals and mentors had gathered about and persuaded him that this was a mistake; if he refused the money others would get it and make no good use of it. How much more sensible to take the money and turn it over to the movement!

So Charles Garland announced that he had changed his mind. He would keep a quarter of a million for himself and give the rest, slightly over a million, to a trusteeship called the Garland Fund, directed by tried and true friends of social justice. There had followed a process of consulting and planning, like that which the Lannys and the Ricks were carrying on. Gifts were made to civil liberties and labor groups, and a large sum went into the reprinting of cheap editions of the classics of the social protest movement.

Lanny collected all the details that were available. A total of fifty volumes had been agreed on: Tolstoy and Kropotkin and Lenin, Marx and Proudhon, Blatchford and Ruskin, Shaw and Wells, Paine and Veblen and Jack London, Henry George and Lester Ward—a widely varied list. They had been made available in large editions at fifty cents a copy, and the question was, how many people had they reached and what had they accomplished? Seeking this information, Rick went to see the man who had launched the publishing venture and guided it for the Garland Fund—only to learn that the man was now engaged in private business and was of the opinion that the only enterprise worth considering was the overcoming of "the great totalitarian sweep" that was under way.

"Assuming that that is true," said the baronet, "how are we going to set about it? If we try to do it with capitalism, we will presently find ourselves the ally of Franco and the Catholic hierarchy, of Greek royalty and the Chinese landlords and moneylenders; in short, of reaction everywhere in the world. It will be one kind of totalitarianism against another, and we democrats will lose out either way. The only way to fight Communist totalitarianism is to show the people how they can get a just co-operative order by peaceable means. That way we can get all the peoples of the world on our side, including those whom Stalin is taking over by force; in the end we may win even the Russian people."

But it was of no use; this worried radical thought that there was no longer time for anything of the sort; the Communist menace was too immediate.

Next they got the name of a man who had assisted with the Garland Fund books. What would he have to report? Again Rick paid a call, and he heard the opinion, "World War III seems to me so certain, so absolutely inevitable, that it seems to me far more constructive to devote ourselves to preparation for winning it than to attempts to prevent it. For if this country loses World War III, I foresee a dark age that will last for at least five centuries."

This time Rick avoided arguing. He was dealing with a publisher in active business and could ask definite questions. The man pointed out that anyone who tried to sell low-priced serious books faced tremendous competition from magazines, both slicks and pulps, from comic books, from twenty-five-cent mysteries, and so on. He had found it easier to sell quantities of old books that had stood the test of time than to sell anything new. He estimated that from seventy-five to ninety per cent of radical publications were sold to radicals, which meant that the works had little effect on the general public.

Finally he spoke these depressing words: "No consideration of this kind would be honest if it failed to take into account the damned low intelligence quotient of a considerable segment of the American public. How large this segment is, and how low its intelligence quotient is, I leave for others to say, but any study of the extremely popular radio programs will prove that the programs with the highest rating, with extremely few exceptions, are directed at the ten- to twelve-year-old mind."

XI

Variety is said to be the spice of life, and certainly it was making life spicy for these four. They made notes on each set of opinions and tried to classify them, but it couldn't be done—there were so many more differences than agreements. They saw themselves in the position of the farmer and his son in the fable of Aesop, trying to get their donkey across a bridge. So many persons told them how to do it, and they tried to please everybody, with the result that they pleased nobody and lost their donkey into the bargain.

Lanny and Rick, according to their temperaments, were disposed to concentrate upon economics; but Laurel ranged farther afield and invited a young poet who had been present at the *New Leader* dinner. Richard Armour contributed brief satiric verses to the paper, and now he said, in substance, "I hope that your economics will be politico-social and not merely the economics of price and distribution. I understand the feeling that if physical wants could be supplied, everywhere in the world, everything might be well. But I am increasingly distrustful of a world dominated by economists and scientists, who make us comfortable—and narrow and dull and thankless. Your publications should have a column of relief from material things."

Here was a new angle, and Laurel decided to look into the spiritual side of their task. The American people were religious by tradition, and there had been a Christian Socialist movement of great influence. Because some Church machines had become corrupted and had sold out to landlords and moneylenders was not sufficient reason for going over to the atheists. As Bernard Shaw had said of his own early career, he had thrown out the baby with the bath, and now he had lived to be ashamed of his folly.

There was a minister in New York to whom all thoughts turned when it was a question of applying the religious impulse to political and social affairs. John Haynes Holmes had been for years the pastor of a Unitarian church in a fashionable part of the city; after World War I he had made it a "Community Church." He had been a pacifist through the two most dreadful wars in history; he had defended the rights of oppressed minorities and been a tower of strength for civil liberties. His voice was familiar on all forum platforms; he would say, "I am no orator"—and would say it oratorically.

Now to his study came two ladies, one American, the other English, and introduced themselves. They told him of their unusual project and asked his advice. All the ardor of an old crusader blazed up in his soul; yes, he knew exactly what to tell them to do. "You and your husbands must make a pilgrimage to Gandhi. *He* is the one who has the gospel; *his* way is the way to put an end to war."

They were surprised, and Dr. Holmes expatiated. He was planning himself to make a pilgrimage to this shrine; the Mahatma was frail and it was hardly likely that he would last much longer. He was the true "Great Soul" of modern times; in his shrunken hands he held the secret of the future. His technique of non-violent resistance was the truly spiritual, and at the same time a political, doctrine. It had been prepared in solitude, with fasting and prayer, and had been tried out in the rough and tumble of mass struggle. All the power of the British Empire had been unable to prevail against it; in the end the proud rulers had bowed before it, and the freedom of India had been won. The way to world peace lay in a study of this technique and its application to the affairs of Western imperialism.

All this was interesting, but the wife of an English baronet could hardly be expected to swallow it without some gagging. Said she, "Don't you think, Dr. Holmes, that at least a part of the credit for Gandhi's victory might be given to his opponents? You must know that the British treated him with the utmost tenderness; when they arrested him he had every comfort, and care such as he could have had only in a modern hospital."

"That may be true, Lady Nielson—"

"Suppose for a moment that it had been with the Nazis he was dealing. Do you think he could have driven them out of India? They wouldn't have waited for him to open his mouth! They would have put him in a poison-gas chamber and burned his body in a furnace and scattered his ashes to the winds. His followers wouldn't have had so much as a fingernail to cherish."

"Yes, but his message—"

"They would have slaughtered every one of his followers, they would have burned his writings—"

"You cannot burn a message, Lady Nielson. That was proven in the case of Jesus. The blood of the martyrs was the seed of the Church. All through the ages—"

"But we are not talking about the ages, Dr. Holmes, we are trying to prevent the destruction of our present world in an atomic war. We have to use the symbols and the mechanisms that our people understand, here and now."

"Mechanisms are one cause of our trouble; we have built so many that they have become more important than men. The machine is the master of our world."

Nina would have liked to ask this friend of mankind whether he used a car in the course of his pastoral duties, and whether he took the subway when he had to speak at "Town Meeting" on Manhattan Island. But she was afraid that wouldn't be polite. There was no need to travel to India to find a "Great Soul"; this was one—but, like his Hindu exemplar and many others throughout this ugly world, he found difficulty in keeping his actions in accord with his holy faith.

XII

There were great numbers of sacred creeds taught and solemn rites practiced in this megalopolis; they were contradictory, and couldn't all be true. The skeptical Rick was sure that no one of them would have any better solution to offer. Some might try to send the researchers to Rome, some to Mecca, and some even to Tibet. These faiths had had centuries in which to show what they could do to bring peace on earth; they had brought innumerable wars—never more bloody than when they were carried on in the name of the Prince of Peace.

There were a number of modern religions which originated in America, and had their churches and groups of devotees in New York. One of them was based upon faith in immortality, as something real and not just a formula to be recited on Sundays. The souls of the dead existed, and it was possible to communicate with them; it wasn't just fraud but something that could be proven and practiced. Laurel had talked with Nina about the strange gift of mediumship, and Nina knew about an old-time English medium who had settled in New York. Eileen Garrett was publishing a monthly magazine, *Tomorrow,* so there were two reasons for consulting her; she could tell them about costs and other business matters, and maybe the spirits would also make their appearance and have advice to give. This was just after their evening with Haldeman-Julius, and Laurel said with a smile, "We won't tell *him* about it!"

They wrote, introducing themselves, a playwright's wife and a woman novelist who was a medium. Naturally the editor was interested, and they called at her office, and later she came for an evening. Mrs. Garrett, retired head of the British College of Psychic Science, began by telling them the surprising news that Emily Chattersworth's bequest was not unique; there was a World Federation group to which a rich woman had just bequeathed a million dollars to be used in the effort to prevent the next war. "Indeed and indeed!" said Laurel. "We shall have to get in touch with those people and find out what they are going to do."

Then, unannounced and still more surprising, came a remark to Nina. "You have been having trouble with delayed menstruation, and you have been afraid of the possibility of cancer."

"How wonderful!" exclaimed the younger woman. "It is true."

"You don't need to worry about cancer, for you don't have it."

"How can you know that, Mrs. Garrett?"

"I don't know how; it has been happening to me all my life. The moment a person comes into my presence and I touch his hand, something comes to me. I give it instantly, spontaneously, and that puts me in touch with people, so that I can help them if they need it. I have found it a wonderful thing in my life, for it makes human relationships light and easy. I don't need a couch and a dark room to persuade people to tell me what's in their hearts."

So this was a clinic as well as a magazine office, something of a novelty in a commercial world. It was something of a church too. Said the editor, "Everyone, from the President of the United States to the street cleaner outside the White House, is in need of a new religion.

The dollar sign is not enough. Men earn their first thousand, and then they strive for five thousand, and it's a rat race until they get a million. Cars, refrigerators, and a hundred luxuries do not make peace of mind; neither Russia nor America has it today. People sense that Gandhi has it and speak of him as a saint. He is a shrewd politician who has the clarity of goodness; but I have no doubt that future generations will be portraying him with a halo about his head."

Nina and Laurel looked at each other and smiled. They told this unusual editor about their talk with Dr. Holmes, and she said, "You don't need to travel to India. God is here also. All you need is to believe in spiritual power without dogma or superstition, and you have it. Tell people that, and they will pay more heed to what you say about peace and social justice."

21

The Sheep Wander Alone

I

THE wars were over, and into all the harbors were coming transports loaded with men. For a weary year or two, or perhaps three or four, these men had been looking forward to the hour when they would set their feet on the soil of God's country, and now they slapped one another on the back and shouted or laughed for joy. They, the lucky ones who had returned, had money in their pockets and girls waiting for them. Many of the girls had money too; they had been earning as much as two dollars an hour in factories, something out of this world, as their lively phrase had it.

Only a thoughtful student of economics could understand the hidden forces that were conspiring to cause this happiness to fade and these bright hopes to turn gray. It wasn't anybody's devilment, but just the normal operation of a competitive business system, so highly lauded in newspaper and magazine editorials. The country was flooded with money, and goods were scarce; prices were bound to be forced up, and those who had the most money would, as always, be the first to be served. Government statistics, based on wholesale prices for basic commodities, would show a gradual rise; but that wouldn't mean anything to the housewife, who knew that she was paying two prices for meat and butter and three or four for fresh fruits and vegetables.

Just as the soldiers were clamoring to be "demobbed," so the businessmen were clamoring to be freed from price controls. The big fellows sent their lobbyists to lay siege to the Seventy-ninth Congress—supposed to be Democratic, having been swept in with Roosevelt's last victory; but a good part of it was made up of Southern reactionaries, and others were carried away by the tide. "Back to normalcy," was the cry, and the confused new President accepted the solemn assurance of the businessmen around him that if he would let them have their way reconversion would be swift and a flood of civilian goods would soon be pouring out of the factories.

One by one the controls were being lifted; and so it came about that lumber and cement went into the building of night clubs and race tracks instead of homes for the veterans. You could get a twenty-five-thousand-dollar home built, provided that you were willing to pay fifty thousand for it, but you couldn't get a five-thousand-dollar home built at any price; such homes just ceased to exist, and when they came into sight again they were eight- and ten-thousand-dollar homes. So the young married couples crowded in with their parents, or they fixed up a shed, if they could find some scrap lumber, or they lived in a trailer, or in one room in a lodging house, cooking on a gas burner. That wasn't very happy, and moralists were shocked by the increase in the divorce rate.

To the returned veteran the whole of America presented itself as a gigantic conspiracy to get his money away from him as quickly as possible; and again there was no malice about it, just the normal operation of free enterprise. He could not turn on the radio without hearing a clamor of profit-seekers beseeching him to purchase gadgets on easy credit terms, or patent medicines and processed foods in "economy-size packages"—meaning big ones. The originators of fashions were in a conspiracy to make him uncomfortable in his perfectly good clothing; he must throw it away and get a new outfit, because a vague "they" were wearing two-button coats instead of three-button coats, or vice versa. Despite the fact that cloth was scarce and millions in Europe freezing, women's short skirts would suddenly become long. That would be called the "new look," and women with the old look would feel passé and humiliated.

Few businessmen in the country were harder hit by the bad news of peace than Robbie Budd; all his contracts were canceled and his country needed him no longer. There was going to be peace all over the world, protected by a United Nations, and nobody would ever again want those marvelous swift engines of destruction which Robbie had been pouring off his assembly line. As it happened, the president of Budd-Erling was an old man and had been through it once before; so he hadn't paid out all his profits as dividends but had salted them away as reserves, invested in the hated Roosevelt's bonds. Now he could sell them, a few at a time, and pay his taxes and keep his head above water.

But that magnificent machine of production that he had built up just faded away, not exactly overnight but in a few weeks. The workers were turned off wholesale, with a very sincere "Thank you," and a "Sorry." If they had paid for their trailers they rolled away with them; or they went in their ten- or fifteen-year-old jalopies, or by train, back to Quebec or Maine or Arkansas or Texas. They had their savings, hidden under the car seat or made secure with a safety pin inside the women's stockings. They would hunt jobs in peace industries, and whether they would find them was a subject about which the economic experts argued without ever coming to agreement.

To what could you reconvert a huge plant for making fighter planes? Next door was Budd Gunmakers, and they could turn to tack hammers and frying pans—they still had the old jigs and dies, carefully preserved. But what could Budd-Erling make? A few cub planes for the civilian trade, a few luxury jobs for the rich—and what else? Robbie had canvassed the field with his experts. Gas heaters? Refrigerators? Radios? Every field was covered by patents, and you would have to buy them or pay royalties; you would have to learn a new business and install complete new equipment at enormous expense; and just when you got started the market would be glutted and the slump would come. Robbie Budd suddenly decided that he wanted to sit back and rest.

There were his two boys, now nearing their forties, vice-presidents of the company. They would want to go on, and Robbie would let them run the old portion of the plant, the part that predated the war. As for the rest, they would seal up the machinery in cellophane or coat it with grease and let it wait. If Robbie was right in his guess that World War III was only a few years away, all right, the boys could start things up again. Meantime Budd-Erling would live on its fat, like

a bear in wintertime; the stockholders would have to reconvert themselves or else learn to be bears. If they hadn't saved part of the huge
dividends Robbie had paid them they were fools and deserved what
they would get.

A tough decision, for the town as well as for Robbie and his inves-
tors. All the little merchants, the grocers who had sold food to the
workers, the café and lunch-wagon proprietors who had fed them,
these would have to fail or move away or both. The slum part of Newcastle would become a ghost town, or at least an invalid town, half
alive. A topsy-turvy world, in which war meant prosperity and peace
meant stagnation; in which slaughter and waste were good, and mercy,
kindness, and love were intolerable. That was the way it was, and if
you talked about changing it you were a dreamer, a crackpot.

III

In this world of confusion and uncertainty people fought to get to
the top, where money was plentiful and there were pleasure and luxury
for all. If you were known to have money, or any form of distinction,
you were besieged by persons on the make; your mail was full of begging letters, salesmen and agents knocked on your door, "climbers"
tried to make your acquaintance, and poor relations came to stay with
you. The quartet of reformers had put themselves in especially exposed
positions: Lanny as a rich man's son, Rick and Nina as titled persons,
Mary Morrow as a writer, and all four of them as idealists and easy
marks.

Laurel came to her husband, looking worried, and said, "My sister
Flo writes that she is coming to town, so I have the unpleasant task of
telling you about her."

Lanny had heard very little about Laurel's family. He had known
well her Uncle Reverdy, a Baltimore capitalist, and his daughter Liz-
beth, who had traveled to Hong Kong on a yacht which had been sunk
trying to escape from the Japanese. Lanny knew that Laurel's mother
had died when Laurel was young, and that her father had died as an
old man, not long before Lanny had met her. Laurel had said, "I never
got along with my family, and there is no reason for you to be bothered with them."

But now Sister Flo was coming and would force herself on Laurel,
and Lanny too, if she got a chance—but he mustn't let it happen. He
listened to one of those ugly stories of parasitism and what it did to
families. Laurel's father had been a considerable landowner on the

Eastern Shore of Maryland; he had lived to what is called a ripe old age and had had three grown daughters. The youngest, Laurel herself, had come to New York and lived in a boarding-house, making herself into a writer. The middle one had visited her wealthy uncle in Baltimore, and there had made a "catch," marrying a man of wealth and fashion who made her wretched by drinking and persistent infidelity. Flo was the eldest, and the least good looking, and she had stayed in the old family mansion with her father.

At the age of seventy-plus this respectable church elder had horrified her by getting hurt in a motorcar accident, going to a hospital, being nursed by a designing young woman, and then bringing her home as his wife. Flo had flown into a fury and made it her task in life to punish that vile interloper. Even the fact that the new wife bore two children didn't help; it made matters worse by diminishing the share of the inheritance that Flo could expect to get. She left her father's home, and when he died soon afterward she took up the notion of proving that he had been mentally incompetent and that his will was invalid.

"Of course she had no case," said Laurel. "Reputable lawyers told her so; but there are always shysters ready to prey upon a woman, and Flo has paid most of her inheritance over to them. If she isn't mentally deranged she is close to it, and spends all her time hating our stepmother and trying to figure out ways of punishing her. Nothing can keep her from talking about her grievance, and she is always in debt and trying to borrow money. Now she has the idea that I have married a rich man, and she will want to try you, and to meet your family, and tell her troubles to them. I want you to be out when she calls, or stay in your room and read."

That was the sort of story you ran into anywhere you went among the rich in America. Children were brought up to believe that the world owed them a luxurious living, without their making any sort of return. Servants waited upon them, all the world was at their beck and call; they were taught to believe themselves superior to other people, all but a very select few. By the time they were grown they were hopelessly spoiled and doomed to unhappiness for the rest of their lives. Money was everything to them; if they had plenty they used it to dominate the lives of others, and if they didn't have it they became parasites, little brothers or sisters of the rich.

Lanny didn't meet Flo; he went to the public library and did research, had lunch in an Automat—amusing product of a mechanical age—and then took a long walk in the park. He took the precaution to phone before he went home. There had been a scene of some sort; Laurel was upset, but she didn't want to talk about it, and he respected her right to keep her family skeletons locked up in her own closet.

IV

Lanny Budd, halfway through his forties, had become a serious-minded gentleman, brooding over the sorrows and perils of the world. But there had to be some form of recreation, and Hansi and Bess would come to town and they would attend symphony concerts. There was a piano in the apartment, and the two artists would play— they were just as happy playing for two or three persons whom they loved as for a large audience. In the old days they had helped their cause by playing for political groups, but now Hansi wouldn't play for Communists and Bess wouldn't play for Socialists. They played for charity, especially for the refugees and displaced persons. Hansi chose sorrow-laden music by Ernest Bloch and other Jewish com-posers, and the listeners would sit with tears running down their cheeks.

This married pair had reached a state of tension that was pitiful. There was hardly any subject they could talk about without trouble. Just as all roads had once led to Rome, so now all conversations led to the class struggle. It was history, it was geography, it was current events, it was literature, it was even getting to be music. "We can't agree now about the shape of a phrase of Mozart," said Hansi sadly; and Lanny couldn't joke about there being a party line for Mozart, for he knew that the Soviet authoritarians kept close watch over their composers and gave even the world-famous ones a dressing down now and then.

The violinist said this only when his wife had gone off, presumably to meet some of her party comrades. She was getting more severe all the time, he reported, more doctrinaire and less devoted to the art of music. "The comrades think the world is theirs," reported Hansi, "and they grow more and more avid. They don't talk much in front of me, but I pick up a phrase now and then, and it bodes ill for us dreamers of peace."

The gentle idealist was in a state of profound depression. He hated the militarists, yet he was coming to believe that they were necessary; the world was going to belong to them, perhaps for a long, long time. Hansi was more in fear of violent revolution than even the former publisher of the Garland Fund books. He was beginning to fear that the so-called democratic world had no weapons with which to meet the offensive of the grimly determined Reds.

Said Lanny, "You mean you really think that Russia could beat the United States if it came to a showdown?"

"It won't come to a showdown, Lanny; the Reds won't let it. They will use the much more deadly weapons of propaganda and intrigue. You know that they have got the Balkans; and does anybody imagine they won't know how to root out the opposition and put those peoples under the dictatorship of the Politburo? We invited them into China; and that means they will have four hundred million hard-working people thoroughly indoctrinated. Britain is going to have to get out of India, and how long will it be before the Communist propaganda will begin to show its effects there?"

"We democrats have some propagandists too," suggested Lanny mildly.

"Yes, but we go into the fight with one hand tied behind our backs. We believe with all our might in democracy in politics; but what about democracy in industry? Can you seriously believe that our Big Business masters are going to give up their privileges and their power for the sake of being able to counter the Reds, or for any other reason on earth?"

"Their power has been very much trimmed down of late. Haven't you heard their squeals?"

"I know, Lanny, but that's all over now. Big Business is riding high. And what have we halfway democrats to offer the depressed peoples of the earth—the Chinese, the Hindus, the Indonesians? We offer them free speech, but what they want is to get the landlords and the money-lenders off their backs."

"You have been listening to Bess too long!" was Lanny's serious answer.

V

The one who listened most patiently to Bess was Laurel. Somehow Lanny's half-sister had got the idea that she might make a convert of Lanny's wife; perhaps it was because Laurel had a Southerner's deeply ingrained politeness, and perhaps it was because she liked to hear all sorts of people and try to understand them. Someday she might want to put a Communist into a story.

She even let Bess take her to meetings, at which she was introduced as "Miss Creston." She sat and listened to the speakers and watched the audience, many of them foreigners or of foreign descent. What suffering had driven them to these extremes of bitterness, of fixed and implacable rage against the system which true-blue Americans glorified under the title of "free enterprise"? Under that system a few had risen to the top and settled themselves and found the view pleasant. If you questioned the arrangement, individuals who had recently managed to shove their way up were pointed out. Wasn't that fair? Laurel would tell them the fable of Pestalozzi, about the carp in the pond who had complained of the voracity of the pike. The pike held a meeting to consider the grievance and admitted that the complaint was well based. A program was adopted agreeing that every year thereafter two carp should be permitted to become pike.

It was remarks like that which caused Bess to decide that Laurel was "coming on"; but the truth was Laurel would come on for a step or two and then retreat as many. She admitted the justice of the Communists' indictment; it was their methods which repelled her. Why couldn't Stalin stick to the program he had talked about, of "Socialism in one country"? Why not take American loans and machinery and develop that vast land, show the greater economy of the cooperative method, and convert the rest of the world by example? Certainly American capitalism could do nothing to interfere with such a program, and the needed social changes could come about by peaceful means—

"Peaceful, hell!" said Bess—from whose language you would never have guessed that she was the daughter of Esther Remsen Budd. "American capitalism can talk about peace because it has the money, the natural resources, the know-how—everything in its greedy fists. All that Big Business wants is to have the game go on under its rules, and in a few years it will have the whole world in its debt as it now has America. That's what 'peace' means to capitalism—ownership and debt; the masses become well-trained slaves, and the masters build an industrial empire with the fraudulent label of democracy."

"I don't mean that the masses are to submit tamely to any such program, Bess. I mean that they can use the political power they have to win industrial power."

"It's a pipe dream, Laurel. Capitalist power builds a civilization and then capitalist war destroys it. The people are sick and tired of being robbed by exploiters and cheated by slick politicians."

Lanny had on his dressing table a picture of his "little sister" as she had been as a girl—some eight years younger than he. She had been a lovely pale blonde, with gentle features and a sweet smile, adoring when she fixed it upon Lanny. At the age of seventeen she had met the shepherd boy out of ancient Judea, as Lanny had called Hansi, in Emily Chattersworth's drawing-room; Hansi had played, and she had listened to the most entrancing sounds she had ever heard on earth. That had been twenty years ago, and Bess had made herself a competent pianist for her husband's sake.

Now she would tell you that she had become a Communist for humanity's sake; her face had become lean and her expression severe—don't think she didn't suffer over the chasm that had opened in her marriage, don't think she didn't know what tragedy she was preparing. She was, as Lanny had told Esther, a true granddaughter of the Puritans. Her forefathers had sailed in a tiny vessel across a turbulent sea and landed on a cold, inhospitable coast; they had risked their lives for the sake of freedom of conscience. Now Bess was ready to give her happiness for the sake of this new religion which despised religion but which manifested all the symptoms and practiced all the zealotry of those who had received a revelation direct from God.

Nothing made Bess madder than for anybody to tell her this; Lanny kept teasing her with it, in the hope of taming her down just a little. "What are you going to do when your friends have taken control of America and are ready to shoot Hansi and me in the back of the neck? Will you try to save us?"

"I am trying to save you right now," replied Bess. "Make note of it and remember that I gave you warning."

VI

Harry Hopkins, retired to civilian life, had got himself a house on Fifth Avenue, New York, and Mayor La Guardia had appointed him "impartial authority" for the garment trade, an arbitration job. Perhaps the friendly labor leaders understood what a sick man he was, for they settled all their disputes without bothering him. Lanny went to see him, intending to invite him to take part in a broadcast, but when he saw that wasted frame he turned it into a purely social call. Harry the Hop was losing the ability to assimilate food and was just fading away.

But he couldn't let go. There were two or three books he wanted to write; he had a man sorting out his forty cases of records, and he would make efforts to study them and revive the past. Lanny's presence rekindled the old fires. A dealer friend had loaned him some modern paintings for his room, and they talked about these: Utrillo, Picasso, Yves Tanguy, Serge Ferat, Marsden Hartley. Lanny entertained him with stories of the Monuments work, of Göring's monstrous collection and of how the false Vermeer had taken him in—a forger getting the better of a bandit!

Old memories came to life, and Harry talked about his last visit to Stalin, a trip he had taken at the other Harry's request, and which had prepared the way for the Potsdam Conference. Both Harrys had done their best, but apparently the job had been too much for any number of men. Hopkins said, "I have my doubts whether Stalin himself could check the revolutionary drive of world Communism. He has raised up a genie."

When the visitor asked, "Do you think it is destined to conquer the world?" the answer was, "I think it's touch and go. It depends upon whether the blind greeds of capitalism can be chained. I believe that another depression would mean the end of our system."

There had just been a general election in France, and the middle group, including the Socialists, had won power. Harry thought that encouraging; it showed the soundness of the democratic process. Lanny remarked, "The French will have to learn to pay taxes," and the other replied, "If the Russians make us start rearming, the whole world will learn something new about taxes."

They talked about Churchill, incorrigible old Tory who had been relegated to the position of Leader of His Majesty's Loyal Opposition —a title that appealed to the sense of humor of an American but apparently not of a Britisher. Harry told of their combats over the issue of Normandy versus the Balkans, "Overlord" versus "the soft under-belly of Europe." Throughout the war the issue was never quite settled, and Harry again and again would have to be flown to London. He described one of the scenes with a flash of his old humor. "Winston would throw the British Constitution at me; but as it isn't written, no damage was done."

VII

In between conferences the four Peace conspirators would thresh out what they had got and try to draw conclusions. They had accumulated a dossier on every suggested plan, and it seemed to be the opinon of the experts that all plans were impossible; apparently this group of novices would have to choose some one impossible plan and blunder along with it.

After many hours of discussion they found that each had settled upon a different method of getting rid of Emily's money. Laurel wanted a monthly magazine, small but distinguished in appearance. Being herself a fastidious person, she argued that few people would pay attention to reading matter that looked cheap and shoddy, no matter how excellent its content. She wanted to take time and get material of the very first quality, which people would treasure as literature; so, even if the magazine ran for only a year or two, it would have a permanent effect on men's minds.

Rick, long-time Labour propagandist, had no more use for the carriage trade in the field of literature than in that of the stage. He said that leisure-class standards were wholly corrupted by snobbery, and it was no use paying any attention to them, either in the appearance of a magazine or in its content. The highly esteemed writers of the time were sophisticated persons, motivated by delicate, well-camouflaged self-love. They wanted to show how much more they knew, how much more subtle and elegant they could be, than anybody else in their field. They wrote for small select groups and had very little to say; that little was pessimism and futility. What Rick wanted was pamphlets for the masses, telling them exactly what they needed; not many titles, but many copies of one title—like that by which the British Labour party had fought the election.

Nina was clinging to her idea that all printed matter was out of date; what counted was the radio. She was still collecting data about small stations and the possibility of building up a chain. "Work out an interesting program once a week, advertise it widely, and ask the people to help. If they like it they will tell their friends and it will spread. Even one of the big chains might take it in the end."

Lanny, thinking about a small cheap paper, had been down at the post office, making inquiries about postal rates, and had learned of a quirk in the regulations which he thought put books and pamphlets out of the running. On a single copy of a book, no matter how small, you had to pay four cents. On a leaflet, or anything classified as printed matter, you had to pay a minimum of a cent and a half on each separate piece. But on newspapers or magazines having "second-class entry" the postage was figured in bulk instead of on the individual parcel, and the rate in the first zone was only one and one-half cents a pound; a small four-page newspaper might weigh less than an ounce, and the postage would be only a small fraction of a cent. What this regulation amounted to was a government subsidy to newspapers and magazines, on the theory that they were educational; the subsidy amounted to hundreds of millions of dollars every year, and surely a foundation ought not to fail to take advantage of it.

What Lanny had in mind was a weekly newspaper, smaller than tabloid size. Its material would be packed, every sentence made to count, and, coming to the people once a week, its effect would be cumulative. Addressed by a stencil machine, such papers could go out at very low cost. Lanny had learned from the files of the "little old *Appeal*" a way to get circulation—by bundle orders. Persuade your readers to order the paper in hundred- or thousand-copy lots for distribution from door to door or at meetings. Make your paper so interesting that people would read it, talk about it, and pass it around.

VIII

Rick admitted that this provision in the postal laws put his pamphlet idea on the shelf. A weekly paper could be of use, no doubt about it; there had been the London *Clarion* in Blatchford's day, and now there were the *Tribune* and the *Socialist Leader;* from time to time there had been many smaller papers, put out by the "ginger" groups. But how were you to get the subscribers to start with?

Lanny answered, "My idea would be to put the price of the paper below cost, because we're not trying to make money but to spend it. Fifty cents a year for a weekly sheet is a price that no commercial concern could meet; at that price people will take up collections for us at meetings; workingmen will go about in shops and union halls; people will make lists of their friends and send us five or ten dollars. All the post-office people require you to have for a second-class entry is a list of paid subscriptions. We could get up a meeting at the Rand School and let Rick explain the plan to the audience; we could hand out blanks and get such a list in one evening."

Nina said, "You're forgetting my radio. For the same money you can hire time on a small station, have an interesting program, and tell the audience you are going to print such programs every week in a small paper and mail it to them for less than one cent a copy. Ask them to send you a dollar bill with two names, or a five dollar bill with ten names, and you may find yourself swamped."

So they came back to the radio: that marvelous discovery, not more than a quarter of a century old, whereby a person could save carfare, or wear and tear on the family "bus," and sit quietly at home and listen to voices from the other side of the world. People hunted for worth-while programs, and sometimes they got one—sandwiched in between the praises of soap powders and cigarettes that their own manufacturers couldn't have told from any other brand. If people

heard an interesting discussion of some important topic and at the end
a quiet persuasive voice invited them to subscribe to a paper along that
line—well, it surely wouldn't cost much to try.

Laurel said to Rick, "You can be the quiet persuasive voice." He answered, "It mustn't be a voice with a foreign accent. You be it,
Lanny." And when Lanny reminded them of the plan that he was to
keep in the background, Rick said, "Be Mr. Bienvenu." It was the
name Lanny had been using for camouflage with some of his friends
in Europe, and he had told these three about it.

Nina said, "It mustn't be a foreign name. It has to be one that people
know how to spell and that they can remember. Be Billy Budd." They
all laughed, and the name stuck; thereafter when they talked about the
radio idea the announcer bore that name. "Good evening, ladies and
gentlemen, this is Billy Budd!" It was the name of a book by Herman
Melville, but the radio public wouldn't know that.

IX

It was their practice to invite somebody to dine with them and
spend the evening: somebody who had been recommended as likely to
have ideas. There came a dignified grandfatherly gentleman, tall, and
holding himself erect in spite of his years. Ben Huebsch was the son
of a rabbi, and for thirty years had been a pillar of the American Civil
Liberties Union. He was editorial head of a publishing house and knew
hundreds of persons who had to do with the writing game in the great
metropolis.

He gave it as his opinion that American periodicals were floundering
about; as he said, "partly because of uncertain policy, partly because
of weak financial support, but mostly because there is no great editor.
You can't make a great editor, you can't go into the market and buy
one. But there are good men writing, and if the market for their work
were enlarged the supply might increase."

Rick put in, "Don't you think, Mr. Huebsch, that the reason there
are no great editors is because there are no editors? Policy is determined by publishers and owners, and the editors take orders."

"It may be," admitted this man of authority, and went on to explain
that the magazine of opinion was fighting a losing game. Under present
business techniques only those periodicals which circulated by millions
and had the support of the big advertisers could survive. "Writing for
other magazines, you write for a small number of scholars and experts,
and if you devote your capital to that, you can become effective only

after the work of the scholars has seeped through a generation of students who have sat at the scholars' feet."

"And by that time we may not have any civilization to write for," said Laurel.

The publisher nodded assent. "In my youth," he continued, "the *North American Review*, the *Forum*, the *Arena*, the *Outlook*, the *Independent*, *McClure's*, the early *American Magazine*, *Everybody's* and *Collier's* under Norman Hapgood—all influenced the public. *Everybody's*, also, as a muckraker, helped people to recognize corruption that called for remedy. But now all that is gone. Unless a magazine represents Big Business, and is conducted on the scale of the Curtis-Crowell-Luce publications or the *Reader's Digest*, it is out of the running."

Mr. Huebsch went on to the book field, which he knew even better. An occasional good book met with success, but it was always a gamble, a matter of luck; an equally worthy book, with identical promotion methods, might fail. The book-club world had the same ideas and ideals as the big magazines, and therefore was out of consideration. "The twenty-five-cent books which you see on every stand and stall do not pay dividends unless they are reprints of best-sellers. There are a few exceptions, and you might find one of the amiable gentlemen who run these concerns and would be willing to co-operate with you on some particular title; but you will have to look elsewhere to spend your million."

"We have canvassed that field," Lanny ventured; "we seem to find red lights on every highway."

"I know of one road that may still be open to traffic," said the publisher.

They wondered, was he going to suggest prize essays or debates, scholarships, lecture courses—any of the things they had considered and rejected as too small in scale? But it wasn't those; Mr. Huebsch wanted to tell them about newspaper syndicates, which were highly competitive and were free because it didn't take such a great amount of capital to start one. These syndicates sold material to newspapers, all kinds and sizes of papers, daily and weekly, and they sold all kinds of material: articles, stories, interviews, popularizations of anything historical, biographical, medical, scientific. It could be in any form, even comic strips and cartoons; the only requirements were, it had to be brief, well written or drawn, and not highbrow; in a word, good newspaper stuff.

Said this observant publisher, "If Paine had written *Common Sense* in the twentieth century it wouldn't have been a pamphlet but a newspaper article or series of them. If you want to get something over quick and big, you put it in a daily and get it read by millions before the ink is dry. All you need is the Tom Paines; and if there aren't any you do the best you can with fellows who can write and who believe as you do. Set them to work on all the different kinds of stuff I have named, and then have it submitted to one or two thousand newspaper editors."

"But will the syndicates handle material of our sort?" asked Rick, who wasn't familiar with this aspect of journalism.

"The syndicates will handle anything the newspapers will buy; and don't forget that thirty per cent of our newspapers supported Roosevelt all the way through. Thirty per cent of American newspapers is an awful lot of both papers and money. They want variety, they want things that will hold the interest of their readers; there is always a market for live stuff. I don't mean that you can feed them straight propaganda for your cause or any other, but you can feed them stuff that is shaded that way. What you have to get is a staff of working journalists with a soul above shoe leather. You can find them in the offices of the most conservative papers in the country, men of scholarship and ideals who would welcome the emancipation which a job with you would constitute."

"Those are the most hopeful words we have heard yet," exclaimed Laurel.

"They are true. You can find writers among those who have names, and you can discover and develop others by letting your plans become known through your staff and through certain college professors. If you take my advice, don't mention your million dollars; that might have a demoralizing effect. Just set out as a business concern with ideas. You can't expect to succeed with a rush; material which a syndicate can sell to hard-boiled editors doesn't spring ready-made from the brow of Jove. You and your board of editors will have to plot out the big scheme, work it out in sections, interest your first squad of writers, and learn by trial and error. If you find the right syndicate you can get a lot of guidance from it; they know what will go and what won't, and they will tell you because they want their share of the money."

"Tell us about the business side," said Rick.

"The syndicate will put a price on the articles, as high as they think they can get. They will keep a percentage, about forty, and you will get the rest; you probably won't make a profit, because you will need a large staff; but if you meet expenses you can keep going indefinitely.

If after you have learned the business you think you can do better, you are free to start a syndicate of your own. All sorts of material would come to you, and you could sell it, even though it had nothing to do with your propaganda. You might find yourselves making money. If my scheme is good you will be feeding articles, stories, poems, essays, and cartoons to millions daily. It will be neatly camouflaged, but not dishonestly. There is nothing dishonest about *Anna Karenina*, or 'Ozymandias of Egypt,' yet they are camouflaged moral tales from which publishers have made money. The same is true of Aesop's fables and the parables of Jesus."

"This sounds quite wonderful," said Nina. "We visitors find it hard to realize how big America is."

"The field is enormous," replied the publisher, "and the old maxim applies, the room is at the top."

"That is what frightens me," said the fastidious Laurel. "Can we get good enough material?"

"Your standards mustn't be too high, Miss Morrow. Good means good from the popular point of view: things that will touch the public's heart or its conscience, or that will answer questions that are in the public's mind. It has been my business to know writers for some forty years, and I can start you off with a dozen good men whose names mean something to newspaper readers and who sympathize with what you're after. They would find it quite marvelous to write what they believe in—and get money for it. It means a risk, of course; that would be the proper use for your capital, to carry the risk while you are experimenting and getting an education in the business."

X

All four of them agreed that this was the solution to their problem. They would set up a staff of editors and writers and feed material to the insatiable American press. Mr. Huebsch agreed that they could have their homes and offices in a near-by suburb. In its earlier idealistic days the *Cosmopolitan* had been conducted from Irvington-on-Hudson, and Doubleday had built up an immense business at Garden City, Long Island. "The writers will come to you if you have a better mousetrap."

Nina hated to see her radio idea go glimmering, and Lanny the same for his little paper. Each told his idea briefly, and the publisher responded, "There is no reason why three such plans might not be dovetailed. Your writers may bring you material that is entirely too propagandistic for the syndicate to handle, and you could put that into a paper or make it into a radio program. Certainly it's a good idea to have a radio program to promote a paper, and a paper to promote a program. If you begin on a small scale, both these experiments could help you, and either might grow of its own impulse. Why not have three departments and let each of you run the one he likes best?"

"Me for radio!" exclaimed Lady Nielson. She had begun her career as an Army nurse in World War I. For almost thirty years she had run a household, raised a family, and been the severest critic of a playwright and Labour journalist. She possessed an observant mind and had got her education on the run, as it were. Lanny, who had seen her during almost every year since her marriage, had acquired respect for her judgment and was pleased by this autumnal flowering. A woman's reach must exceed her grasp!

Lanny didn't say much about his own plan in the presence of any visitor; but he had his quiet intention. He called himself an old-fashioned person, used to getting ideas from the printed word, and he knew from experience what papers could do to young and new minds. He was determined to have one, and Laurel had tactfully dropped her idea of a dignified and highbrow magazine; after all, it was to Lanny that Emily had entrusted the funds and not to any of the others. If all Rick's time was to be taken up with the syndicate idea, let Mr. Huebsch suggest an editor to carry out Lanny's plan under Lanny's direction.

So there they had their set-up; they would be an organism with one body and three heads. Rick would run a writers' bureau, feeding material to a syndicate; his wife would run a radio program; Lanny and Laurel would run a small weekly paper, hoping to break through the barriers and achieve mass circulation. Three in one and one in three, holy, blessed Trinity! Laurel, who had been brought up as a devout Episcopalian, said, "Don't be sacrilegious."

To which the reverent Lanny replied, "By no means! We may be calling for Divine assistance before we get through."

22

The Laborers Are Few

I

THE sun of peace had risen and was shining upon a new America. Everybody had been rationed and restricted, everybody had been making sacrifices, or at any rate telling others to make them—and now all that was over. Everybody was free and could do what he pleased. Anybody could drive into a filling station and say "Fill 'er up"—provided only that he had the price, and practically all had it. There had never been so much money in circulation since the beginning of the world—real money, dollars! Everybody wanted to buy everything he had been doing without; everybody wanted to make more money to buy more things; everybody wanted to go to Florida for the winter, or perhaps load up the old jalopy and move to Southern California for good.

And of course everybody who was abroad wanted to get back to God's country; nobody wanted to stay and teach democracy to Germans or Japanese. The humiliating truth was that many Americans had but an imperfect idea of democracy; many were Republicans and thought of democracy as the opposition party; it meant Roosevelt, whom they had been fighting and would go on fighting long after he was no more. Army officers, and Navy officers even more so, believe in giving orders and having them obeyed. How to reconcile American Military Government with notions about the rights of man was not so simple as it sounded to political orators at home.

Captain Jerry Pendleton wrote his friend Lanny about this. Jerry himself was well content, he reported; they had sent him to Mondorf-les-Bains, near Luxembourg, to help watch over the higher-ups among the war criminals—this on account of his knowledge of French and German and of European ways in general. The Army had taken over Jerry's boarding-house in Cannes, and his wife had come to join him. They had a comfortable apartment, and Jerry had a car—what more could an American want?

In course of the years Jerry had become slightly infected with his ex-pupil's notions—more than he would have admitted, and perhaps more than he realized. He wasn't so well pleased with the way things were going in the captured lands; the denazification program just wasn't working out. The big bugs were going to get it in the neck all right, but their underlings were getting by with excuses and evasions, and many of them were back in their old positions of authority. Here indeed was a problem, for it was hard to find anybody who would admit that he had really been a Nazi, and it was hard to find anybody with any experience in administration or management who hadn't really been a Nazi. The Army couldn't manage Germany without the help of Germans, and the tendency was to say "Oh, to hell with it!" and turn the job over to anybody who could and would do it properly.

Said Jerry: "The people we ought to be working with are your kind—the Social Democrats. But the average Army officer is accustomed to thinking of any kind of Socialist as a nut. He looks down upon such fellows at home and can't understand why he should bother with them abroad. The people he looks up to at home are the Big Business crowd, the executives, those who have good manners and the right sort of homes to invite him to. The same sort of people are here, and he can't understand that they are the people who put the Nazis in power and would bring them back tomorrow if they could."

Interesting to Lanny was his ex-tutor's account of the way the Nazi big shots were living. Their home was the former Palace Hotel, seven stories high and once a resort of fashion, but no more. Its windows were all barred and the glass had been replaced with unbreakable material. The elegant furniture had been taken away. "This is a jail," said Jerry. "We have rules, and they are obeyed. Our fellows call it the 'Big House,' and the Germans have learned that much of the American language. They do not have newspapers and not one of them has sent or received a letter since he came. 'Ashcan' is our code name."

Here fifty-two of the top Nazi officials and military officers were being held until their fate should be decided by the War Crimes Commission. Here were Reichsmarschall Göring, Foreign Minister von Ribbentrop, Grand Admiral Doenitz, Field Marshal von Kesselring, Field Marshal von Keitel, Finance Minister Count von Krosigk, and so on down the line. Few of them whom the son of Budd-Erling had not met at one time or another through two decades, and now he read with interest the account of their behavior.

Göring, that huge bulk of vanity, half emperor and half clown, had imagined that he was going to be taken in state to call upon General

Eisenhower; now he was living in a room furnished with a cot, a straw mattress, a chair, a toothbrush, and an aluminum drinking cup. He was having hospital care to break him of his drug habit; he had been taking twenty times the normal dose of paracodeine, and now he complained bitterly that the Americans were cheating him. When he had sat down in his chair it had broken down, and they had got him a bigger one. Today he was in the dumps and tomorrow he would be haughty, appealing to posterity in his thoughts.

Ribbentrop, that egregious wine salesman who had displayed his insolent manners in so many of the council chambers of Europe, was now wearing a loose-fitting lumberman's shirt without a tie and his gray hair was shaggy. He was careless about making his own bed and had to be reprimanded frequently. He was greatly concerned about his fate and had fired volleys of questions at Jerry: when would the trials start, where would they be held, what would the charges be and who was preparing them? Jerry had answered nothing, because that was orders.

The prisoners were permitted to see movies, but only of one kind, those taken of scenes in the concentration camps. Doenitz had viewed some of them and had written a letter, blaming Allied air raids for the emaciated condition of the inmates. The American commander had replied that no doubt the Allied air raids were also responsible for the fat and sleek condition of the SS guards who had watched over the concentration-camp inmates.

Another curious detail was the class feeling which manifested itself among the prisoners. The ranking officers played cards with one another, but never with the low-caste civilians. Everybody disliked Ribbentrop and ignored him. When Julius Streicher, vile anti-Jewish propagandist, was brought to the place, Admiral von Doenitz had refused to eat at the table with him. He had been given the choice of eating there or not eating at all.

Streicher was cut by everyone, as was Dr. Robert Ley, Nazi Minister of Labor. That drunken beast was the one who had grabbed Johannes Robin, just after the Nazis took power, intending to plunder him of his fortune; but Göring had heard about it and taken the wealthy Jew for himself. Jerry knew about this and understood that Lanny would be interested in hearing how the beast was living now. Ley and Streicher were inseparable; the GIs called them the "Gold Dust twins." Ley had got a pair of GI trousers, Class X, meaning that they had been discarded by the Army; they were freshly pressed, whereas Streicher's were knee-sprung. Streicher had made a fuss, but Jerry had told him to be glad he had any trousers at all.

II

This punishment was part of the job of making the peace of the world secure, and it was to Lanny's satisfaction. No one knew better than he how evil these men had been, and how little right they had to put the cloak of legality over their deeds. Let the precedent be established that the beginning of aggressive war was a crime against mankind and that it would be punished by world authority. Law had to have a beginning, and there was no better time than the present.

The United Nations delegates were about to assemble in New York and set up a world legislature and a court to adjudicate disputes and make fighting forever unnecessary. The United States was assuming the leadership and paying a good part of the bills. What kind of example was America going to set, and what were the world delegates going to find when they came here? These were questions the four Peace conspirators kept asking themselves.

In the days when Lanny had been playing the role of Mister Irma Barnes, he had gone about with the smart set on Long Island and in the New York night clubs; he had come to know scores of these people well and perhaps a hundred of them casually. Now they were middle-aged like himself; many had been in the Armed Services and were coming back; others had had civilian jobs—it wasn't good form for anybody to be idle in a crisis such as the country had been passing through. He ran into them in hotel lobbies and on the street; they recognized and greeted him. Where had he been keeping himself all this time? They invited him to their cocktail parties, and sometimes he went, for he had to know America, high and low, and what people were saying and thinking and planning to do with the new world of peace.

One thing that Americans were doing, and that nobody could miss, was drinking liquor. It was alarming to see them pouring it down, and a mystery how they got away with it. No wonder you read of automobile accidents and that some of your acquaintances were taken to the hospital or the morgue. Women sat in bars with the men, or they sat alone, drinking themselves into a dull stupor. Drinking places called "night spots" were springing up on the outskirts of every town. In New York there was one opening up on New Year's Eve whose cover charge was seventy-five dollars per person. Food and drink were in addition.

Millions of women had been left alone for one year, two years, three. They suspected that their men, in Britain, France, North Africa, or on lonely Pacific islands, hadn't been living lives of plaster saints; the women had been experimenting also, and now the divorce rate was mounting fast—one marriage in three went on the rocks. In New York State, where the Catholic Church had succeeded in limiting the grounds of divorce to adultery only, there had been worked out a friendly arrangement of professional co-respondents; for the sum of ten dollars a nice respectable lady would consent to be discovered in a hotel room with you and be named as your partner in adultery. You would conduct yourself as a gentleman and not assume that any impropriety was expected.

In this period while Daddy had been overseas, the children also had been running wild. In California were "zoot-suiters," who wore strange-looking clothing and fought in gangs with rocks and knives— not seldom they fought the police. They smoked what they called "reefers," meaning marihuana. There were "bobby-soxers," who gathered in radio studios to hear their favorite crooners and screamed like maniacs. They mobbed the movie stars for autographs and tore the buttons off the men's clothes for souvenirs. Those who were not quite old enough for such exploits sat at home studying their lessons, but couldn't do them unless the radio was running; they read with their eyes and listened with their ears. If you mentioned John Milton they looked blank, but they knew the names of scores of hot trumpeters.

This new generation had invented a fantastic language all their own and kept improving on it. At the moment all phrases had to rhyme, and so a youth would remark that his dream beam was a chill bill, meaning that she didn't yield quickly to the seductions of the hot trumpet. Or he would call her a dull skull and say that she wasn't alive to the jive. If she got tired of him she would tell him to drop dead, or perhaps just to get lost. You had to know all the subtleties of this new jargon, for if she said "Leave us get lost," it meant that she wanted to take him out into the woods or upstairs to a bedroom.

Yes, there were things that needed to be changed in America; and the people who didn't know it wouldn't thank you for calling their attention to it; they would call you a drip or a droop or a jerk, or, worse yet, an unhep. They would put the rope up on you, a phrase which might puzzle you unless you knew the snooty night spots where they had a velvet rope across the entrance to the tables and you

THE LABORERS ARE FEW

couldn't get by unless the headwaiter knew you and was sure that you were prepared to spend several hundred dollars during the evening. People young and old wanted to go to hell in a hurry, and wouldn't stop to think about the consequences to themselves, to say nothing of the rest of the world. "Nobody bothers about me," Sister Flo had said. "Why the hell should I bother about them?"

III

The four crusaders set their course grimly and reconciled themselves to being unpopular. Perhaps in course of time they would discover some new friends and allies—there must surely be some old-fashioned people in this hard-pressed world. So far in human history there had been at least a score of great civilizations which had been built with hard toil and had gone down in ruins because of luxury and corruption at the top and misery and revolt at the bottom. Always there had been prophets crying doom and being stoned. What was new in this case was that the prophets had a million dollars, and that might make a difference in the outcome. There was no way to find out but to try.

Preparing to become a radio expert, Nina spent her spare time in front of the instrument in their drawing-room. It was, she said, exactly like the little girl who had a little curl; when it was good it was very very good, and when it was bad it was horrid. Mostly it was bad; but from it you could chart the American mind, and you had to know what anything was before you set out to change it. Radio was supported by the advertisers, and the advertisers spent millions studying the public, seeking ways to shift it from one brand of cigarettes to another brand, as like each other as two peas. The words that the public loved, the ideas the public accepted, were in those commercials. A generation of American children was being brought up on them. There was a story of a little girl of five who was taken to church for the first time by her father. When it was over he asked what she thought of it, and the answer was, "The music was very good, but I thought the commercial was too long."

Early in the morning people apparently wanted to open their windows and do calisthenics with imaginary company. Then they wanted to hear the news, and plenty of hot jazz while they ate their bacon and eggs and swallowed their coffee. After that the men went off, and the women of America owned the radio. They had loud music while they swept and dusted, and they had menus for the day's dinner, and fashion notes to guide their shopping or sewing or trimming of hats.

They listened to gossip about their favorite movie stars and praise of the pictures they might choose to see in the evening.

And always commercials, a double dose every fifteen minutes. Music had its charms, and so they sang them; and before you shut one off, stop and recall the days when you were bounced on your grandmother's knee and listened to Mother Goose rhymes. They had delighted both grandmother and child, and now it was the same thing for the same stages of mentality—first childhood and second. In those days it had been the cat and the fiddle and the cow that jumped over the moon; now it was Duz soap powder and somebody's face lotion. Lanny had once asked a great lady of society why she persisted in taking a dangerous kind of "alkalizing" drink, and the answer came without a trace of a smile, "The man who tells about it has such a pleasant voice."

IV

After her pick-up lunch it appeared that the American housewife liked to settle down for a good cry. For a matter of three hours she was fed soap operas, serial stories of the unending perils and romantic entanglements of heroines exactly like herself. As fast as the heroine got out of one trouble she was in another; she was unjustly suspected, her marriage was breaking up, her children were about to be taken away from her. Did Charlie love her or did he love the other girl? It went on and on; the listeners knew these different families and the characters involved and could hardly wait for the next day to learn what was going to happen to their favorites. Zoltan Kertezsi, who had been brought to New York as a child and had lived in a tenement, said that in those days there were papers issued weekly with much the same sort of stories; they were pushed under the grilled doors of areaways, intended for servant girls, and were free because the revenue came from advertisements of patent medicines and abortion mixtures and other things that servant girls were supposed to need.

Toward evening the men came home, and there was news, and horror dramas to frighten the children before they went to bed. Then came the comedies, with laugh meters to test the reaction of the audience in the studios to each and every joke, old or new. Also there were programs in which members of the audience competed for prizes. "Take it or leave it," the master of ceremonies would say, and the audience would shout the warning, "You'll be sorry!" This program gave the American language a new phrase, "the sixty-four-dollar question." Nobody could foresee the horrid developments which were about to come out of the many "give-away programs." How often was it that anybody could foresee the consequence of any action to which the big-money motive was driving this greedy world?

With Mr. Huebsch's advice, Nina found a radio announcer who would come in his off time and teach her the ins and outs of this business. She wanted to know it all, even though she herself would never be an announcer, on account of her English accent. It was a fact that puzzled and hurt her but that she had to face, that the English weren't as popular in New York as they deserved to be. English lecturers weren't wanted, nor English advice. Perhaps it was the influence of the Irish, and of the Germans in past years; or perhaps it was what the children had read in their schoolbooks. The redcoats had burned Washington, and lecturers had come over and collected dollars and then gone back and written impolite books about the domestic manners of the Americans. England was a land of kings and queens and dukes, pronounced "dooks"; the new England of the Labour party hadn't managed to register yet, and when it did the former Anglomaniacs wouldn't like it.

V

Sir Eric Pomeroy-Nielson spent his time inviting editors and authors to lunch or dine with him—those men and women whose names had been supplied by the heaven-sent publisher. The Englishman would tell them about the plan, and if they were interested they would sit and chat for an hour or two after the meal. Rick wanted first of all a tiptop man as assistant, one who knew not merely New York but America. It had to be one who had been trained in the newspaper game and yet who was capable of independent judgment; a man who believed in world order and co-operation and would have his heart in the job of promoting them.

Rick also wanted writers, many of them, and they had to believe what they were putting on paper. If they were successful writers they would have to take less money in return for freedom of expression. They would have to have conscience enough to give their best work to the cause and not try to palm off the stuff they had put away in a bureau drawer. Rick had done many kinds of writing, and had been around in a big city, and wasn't an easy man to fool.

Word got about town that a titled Britisher had a wallet stuffed with money and a new scheme up his sleeve. Reporters and executives out of jobs came to see him, and he listened to what they had to say and made notes; poets and storywriters sent him manuscripts, and he promised to read them and did. Already the mill was beginning to grind. A secretary was busy, files were accumulating, and pretty soon there would have to be an office somewhere.

That was Lanny's job. He went scouting in the car, to one town after another, interviewing real-estate agents. Nothing acceptable could be rented; he would have to buy, and that was a serious matter: an office with room enough for four busy managers and their staffs, secretaries, files, and what not; also a home for the four, plus a youngster and his governess. Each of the four would have to have a workroom, and there would have to be at least a couple of servants to keep the place in order. Quite an outlay, and a million dollars didn't look so big as it had sounded.

Also there had to be a printer in the neighborhood; someone who could make letterheads and circulars and such things for an office, and could start with a small paper and be willing to expand. For Lanny that meant learning the printing business and getting bids; it meant putting Sam de Witt at work locating a fast press that could be purchased if need developed. If you meant to succeed you had to be ready to hoist anchor and set sail while the breeze was fair. If you were stuck in the mud you might stay forever, mourning your lost opportunity.

VI

While Lanny and Freddi Robin had bummed around in Munich, Lanny had told about the bequest, and Freddi had gone off like a chain reaction. He would give his services for the cost of food and lodging; he would be office boy, janitor, chauffeur, anything that would enable him to be within earshot of this wonderful enterprise, to learn about it and show what he could do. Since then he had written not merely to Lanny but to his Uncle Hansi to plead his cause. He was wild to get out of the Army now that the job was done; he begged his grandfather to pull wires, and to ask the president of Budd-Erling to do the same. This youngster had a keen mind and could get his education by reading copy and listening to his elders just as well as by sitting in a crowded college classroom.

And now at this crisis came a wonderful event: Freddi came home! He came with his uniform newly pressed and himself well and fairly bursting with eagerness. How his discharge had been managed he had no idea; his grandfather, the ex-*Schieber*, the onetime multimillionaire, wouldn't tell. Johannes just smiled and said there were wires that could be pulled if you knew where to look for them; the boy was here, and now put him to work and keep him out of mischief.

Freddi didn't know a thing in the world about the printing business or the real-estate business; but it was with him as it had been with Jerry Pendleton when he had come to be Lanny Budd's tutor a full generation ago. Beauty had asked what he could teach and he had answered, "Anything, if you give me two weeks' start." He was keen and amazingly well informed for his age. He would run errands and bring back the right answers; he would get people on the telephone and make notes of what they said; he would hop in and out of the car, he would type letters with two fingers, and all the while he would keep you cheerful with his faith and hope—he was the new generation. Lanny would have trained him for a business manager, only it was obvious that he was the intellectual type.

Also there was Laurel. She was going to be writing for all of the three departments, and every day she would go for a walk in the park —that was where and how her mind worked. Stories, poems, essays, news material—Mr. Huebsch had specified all these, and Laurel's imagination would race from one form to another and weigh and test the ideas that came to her. She would come home and make careful notes before anything else had driven them out of her mind. For years she had been writing novels and stories exposing and ridiculing the Nazis, and she could feel that she had had something to do with putting them in the hotel-jail at Mondorf-les-Bains. Now she would use her talents against the profiteers, those who turned not merely industry but also government to the service of wholesale greed. She would write against these with all the energy she possessed, knowing in advance that the critics would say she was wasting her talents upon propaganda. There was a war between ethics and esthetics, and it had been going on for a long time. One side would say that you couldn't have civilized life if you didn't have moral standards; the other would say, what was the good of having any sort of life if you didn't have beauty?

VII

Lanny found what he thought would serve them in the small town of Edgemere, in Jersey. You took the train at the Pennsylvania Station and it carried you under the Hudson River. In a little more than half an hour you got off, and a car would meet you and take you about three miles; or you could motor the whole way, via the

Holland Tunnel and the Pulaski Skyway. Lanny showed his colleagues the layout. On the edge of the town had been a fine old mansion; the family had decayed and so had the mansion, becoming a rooming-house for workers in a war plant not far away. The plant had shut down suddenly and most of the occupants had gone. The place could be bought for twenty-four thousand dollars, which was high, but then everything was high.

It was depressing at first glance, as he had warned them; it was dirty and run down. But the Army had discovered a wonderful device, a DDT-bomb; you set one of them in the middle of the floor and turned a little knob, and it began to shoot a fine spray; you left it there, and a fog spread through the house. With three or four such bombs in different parts you would never have to think about vermin again. Then you would have everything scrubbed and cleaned, and the rooms redecorated if you could find workers to do it. There was a furnace in the cellar, and a man would come night and morning to tend it. There were rooms enough; a suite with bath on the ground floor for Rick and Nina, a second story with two bathrooms in it, and a wing with a room where the youngster could play without disturbing anyone else. They could make it do.

The big factory in the town had been making incendiary bombs—the small boy who pointed out the place to Lanny called them "incinerator bombs." Now it was shut down, and so was a small place near by which had been making fuses for the bombs. This latter was a one-story stucco building about a hundred and fifty feet long and thirty wide. There was a front office, and all the rest was one long room. Work had stopped one day, and they hadn't even bothered to sweep out the scraps of metal; you could imagine that news had come of the ending of the war and everybody had rushed outside and never come back. Through the center of the main room ran a long table with a moving top, a "belt," it was called, and women workers had sat on stools; the table could be taken apart and the lumber used to build partitions; they could make as many small rooms as they needed, and put in small gas heaters with vents in the roof or the outside walls. The company was asking twenty thousand for the place, and Lanny proposed to offer ten and expected to pay from twelve to fifteen.

There was a printing plant in the town, and the owner was a much-worried small businessman, who thought this was going to become a ghost town. He would do their work cheaply, just to keep going; or he would sell them the plant and run it for them. He was sure that a panic and a big bust were coming, and he was indiscreet enough to reveal his fears. It was astonishing how many people, big and little, had that conviction; they lived with a sword of Damocles hanging over their heads. The respectable newspapers and magazines rebuked this state of mind severely, but the pessimists took it for granted that this was propaganda.

The two places would do, the friends decided—ethics winning out over esthetics, at least for a time. The essentials were here in both places: water, electricity, gas, telephones. There was a post office and mail delivery; telegrams would be delivered by phone, and there were a couple of cafés in the town, not elegant but clean. Their guests could come on the train and be met at the station, or they could motor if they wished. The four could do their work here and have their chance at success. There was labor in the town, and so long as they had money to spend they would be welcomed with open arms.

Lanny made his offers and his deals; they were put into escrow at the local bank, and that was as good as ownership. Freddi Robin was all over the town, digging up people to do the various jobs; some who had been on the point of moving back to New York were happy to learn that the town wasn't going to die after all. The girls who had made bomb fuses would now learn to make stencils and mail papers.

The legman for the town's newspaper came running; what was it all about? They told him they were going to set up a literary bureau and publish a small paper, but not a newspaper, so he didn't have to worry. He wanted the story, of course, and an agreeable gentleman named Billy Budd gave it to him; there was a big-name novelist, Mary Morrow, and a real English baronet and his lady—oh, my goodness! You could see the reporter's eyes pop and you could be sure that the town would take fire. They had been mourning the demise of an incinerator-bomb plant and a fuse factory, and here they were going to be made famous. Actually, there was to be a radio studio right in the fuse building, and Edgemere, N. J., would be put on the map!

VIII

It was flat country, bleak and desolate in winter, with snow everywhere, and nothing green but a few straggly pines. But that wouldn't worry them, they knew that spring would come, and a gardener would plant flowers at both places. "The Willows" was the name of the mansion, and the big trees would make shade when it was needed. Freddi moved in and saw that the furnace was kept going—otherwise the water pipes might have burst. Some of the lodgers hadn't moved out yet, but a few ten-dollar bills brought action, and then the scrub-women came—they had already cleaned up the office building. The decorators started work, and in the office the carpenters began hammering; lumber was almost unobtainable, but by good fortune they found some plasterboard for partitions. The tinsmiths came, but they didn't have any pipe, and you couldn't get any gas heaters, unless it was in junkshops, so Freddi drove to Newark and looked up such places. So many things to think of and to oversee, and so many shortages—you might have to drive miles to get a few pounds of nails.

Freddi's mother heard about what was going on. Lanny had met her for the first time when he had been a guest on Johannes Robin's yacht, cruising in the Mediterranean. Rahel had then been a gentle and conscientious girl, with a sweet contralto voice; her husband had played the clarinet, and as Hansi and Bess had been along it had been a musical voyage. The future had been mercifully hidden from them, and they had had no idea of the horrors it contained. When the Nazis seized Rahel's husband and shut him up in Dachau, Lanny had been the one who possessed the magic to get him out, and for that he would be forever a hero in Rahel's eyes. Now she had a new husband and a new family, but she could leave them for a few days in care of Mama —that was the grandmother, Johannes's wife.

They wanted furniture for both the home and the office, and the prices the stores were asking were simply scandalous. Rahel, now a plump, middle-aged woman, had her own car, and she took over the job. She put up in a near-by hotel, and she hunted up all the second-hand shops in Newark and near-by towns; she argued and scolded, and went from one to the next, and by the time the painters had got out of The Willows and the carpenters had got out of the fuse plant she had accumulated two vanloads of new and used furniture at about half what Lanny or Laurel would have had to pay.

And not only that, she took care of having the well-chosen stuff unloaded and put in place. She interviewed cooks and housemaids and got one of each, and saw to the arrangements for electricity and tele-phone and water and gas and coal and garbage and trash disposal— so many things does it take to keep alive in a civilized world! Those literary folk in New York could go on working on their plans to save the world, and meantime Rahel and her son would see that they had a home to move into, one that was warm and clean, and had groceries in the pantry, and sheets and blankets on the beds, and coffee or orange juice ready for them when they woke up in the morning.

What was more, Rahel would come once a week, she promised, and see that the servants were not neglecting them and the tradespeople not cheating them, and that all their bills were properly checked before they were paid. The world was full of people who were ready to take advantage of any weakness they found; they would assume that people who were trying to save the world were easy marks. Let Rahel be the one to deal with them, and they would find out the difference!

Both Laurel and Nina thought this a gift from heaven. Laurel liked housekeeping as little as anything in this world, and Nina, who had had to do it for many years, now wanted to put her mind on a radio studio. By all means let Rahel feed them and warm them, and be forever blessed; when it was necessary to have a party or a reception, let her be caterer and hostess. No cocktail parties, they were at one about that; they would have coffee and fruit punch, and those who didn't like it could wear their hip-pocket flasks and retire to the lavatory for a nip.

IX

Nina had made the discovery that they didn't have to go in to the radio station in the crowded city. They could install a microphone at very small expense in one of the rooms in their office; at the appointed hour the telephone company would give them a connection, and they would speak by remote control. That way they could avoid travel and have everything in one place. A stenographer could take down an ad lib program and type it off for the paper. They would give Edgemere as their address for fan mail and orders, and the post office in the town gave them an imaginary number—Box 1000, Edgemere, New Jersey. The slowest mind could remember that.

Mr. Huebsch had recommended Station WYZ as one that was likely to be interested in their project. This station went in for what is called "class," or "side," or "swank," or "tone"—there were many fancy words for it; the rich catering to the rich, trying to make themselves feel important. The publisher said, "The rich are bored and are looking for something new. Be very elegant and impressive."

Nina and Laurel had an argument as to which of them could make a better deal for the radio time. Laurel insisted that a genuine baroness was a far more imposing personality than an author, of whom there were thousands in the city. Nina, on the other hand, argued that this was a professional and not a social matter, and that a foreign accent might awaken distrust. Rick agreed with her, so Laurel took up the duty.

She wrote, being careful to use fashionable stationery; she introduced herself as the author of novels and magazine stories, desiring to talk to them about a program series. She gave her telephone number, and her phone rang at eleven the next morning—that being the hour when fashionable business begins. A cultivated voice explained that this was Mr. Archibald, the program manager; he would be delighted if she would call that afternoon and let him show her the studio.

The place was on the top floor of a hotel facing Central Park. It had a private elevator, and you were whisked up swiftly. There were all the appurtenances of luxury: velvet rugs, overstuffed sofas, a lady receptionist with the voice of a Hollywood duchess. Everybody was dressed to kill—and you may be sure the visitor also had on her glad rags. The manager came, morning coat and pin-stripe trousers and a boutonniere—you might have thought you were in the queer old State Department building opposite the White House. He led her along a marble corridor with a crimson carpet and canaries singing in sunlit windows, and showed her the studios and the control rooms and the machinery, of which she understood nothing. They operated by remote control, their sending station being in Jersey.

In Mr. Archibald's private office Laurel made a tactful approach to the subject she had in mind. She had lived in Germany before the war and had been back there immediately in the wake of the Army; she had seen horrible sights and had resolved to help prevent such things in the future. She had ample backing, and her idea was to take a quarter-hour, once a week at the outset, and invite competent authorities in all branches of thought to come and be questioned as to the causes of war and what could be done to remove them.

"A most interesting idea," agreed Mr. Archibald cordially. The skeptical lady couldn't help wondering what his expression would have been if she had been asking him to donate the time.

"What I am in doubt about," she said, "is whether your special audience would be interested in a program of that sort."

"We have a highly intellectual clientele, Miss Morrow. We have accustomed them to hearing ideas discussed from every point of view."

"We should want a period when we could expect to find both men and women in their homes; somewhere between six and nine in the evening."

"Those are the very choice hours, you understand; they are rather expensive."

"What would they cost us?"

"Somewhere in the neighborhood of two hundred dollars for the fifteen minutes. Of course if you had a sponsor—"

"No, we don't want a sponsor. It is our idea to reprint the program in a little weekly paper, along with other material bearing on the subject, and we would tell our listeners about this paper and invite them to subscribe to it."

"That is something we look upon with great hesitation, Miss Morrow. We try to maintain a high-class atmosphere, as you know if you have listened to our programs."

"I understand, and I assure you we would handle the matter in a dignified manner. We would never try to high-pressure people. We would simply say, 'If you are interested in what you have just been hearing and would like to have it in print, you may subscribe to our weekly paper which contains it.' Our idea would not be to cover the cost of the programs but merely of the paper. Surely it is as dignified to sell ideas in print as it is to sell perfumes or cigarettes."

"I suppose that would be all right," admitted Mr. Archibald. This was a keen-witted lady, and he knew that a smart magazine was among the sponsors of his programs and that it solicited subscriptions quite shamelessly. Said he, "If you have doubt about our clientele taking an interest in your idea, why not make a try and find out. Let me give you a microphone now, and you tell them about it."

"*Now?*" exclaimed Laurel in sudden panic.

"We have music periods which we can always displace in favor of anything of special interest. We have one beginning in the next few minutes."

"But I have never spoken over the radio, Mr. Archibald!"

"There always has to be a first time. You won't find it such a trial as you imagine. Just think of some friend whom you would like to inform about it and imagine you are talking to that person. Use your ordinary tone of voice and pretend that you are in your own drawing-room."

X

Laurel picked out henna-haired Sophie Timmons, who had come from Cincinnati and married the Baron de la Tourette and been wretchedly unhappy with him. She had had a lovely villa on the Cap d'Antibes and been Beauty Budd's playmate and partner in mischief for some forty years. The Germans had almost caught her during World War I, and she had fled from them again in World War II, and was now back in the land of her fathers. The Germans had built a gun emplacement on the grounds of her villa, and American battleships, trying to hit the emplacement, had knocked the villa to flinders. Yes, good old Sophie would surely want no more war, so Laurel would tell her about the plan.

Seated at a table with the mike in front of her, a foot or so away, Laurel had her voice tested and was told that it was all right. The announcer stood at another mike near by; to him it was all in a day's work, but to her it was something that made her heart thump and the rest of her inwards sink. A little red light flashed, and they were on the air. The announcer said, "Ladies and gentlemen, we are setting aside our Cocktail Hour music in order to hear a very distinguished visitor who has honored us with her presence." He went on to name Laurel's books and articles and to tell of her visits abroad. "Miss Morrow tells us of a very interesting radio program which she has in mind, and we suggested that she might tell you about it and find out whether the audience of WYZ would like to have it become a permanent feature of this station. Miss Morrow tells us that she has never before spoken over the air; we mention that she is speaking quite impromptu and without any time to prepare. If you note signs of nervousness, you will make allowance, we are sure. Miss Morrow."

The listeners noted no such signs. Laurel, in her mid-thirties, was a sedate and self-possessed person. The pretense of Sophie was needed only for a minute or two; after that she was launching the plan which she had been pondering and discussing for close to a year. The world had been devastated by wars, the like of which had never been known before. There must be some fundamental reason for such terrifying outbursts of destruction, and if there was anything in the idea of the democratic process, the people had the duty of finding out what caused world wars and what measures were needed to stop them. A group of friends had set themselves the task of conducting such an inquiry; it was their idea to have a regular period over the air and invite the wisest and best-informed men and women they could find to come and submit to questioning on the subject.

"As the announcer has just told you, ladies and gentlemen, I didn't come here to make a speech. I just dropped in to inquire if time would be available and what it would cost. I asked whether it was likely that the audience of WYZ would be interested in such a program, and I was advised to ask you and I am doing so. We have financial backing, so we are not asking for money. It is our idea to print a little paper containing the week's program and other material bearing on the subject, and some-day we may invite you to subscribe to this paper at a price so low that you may want to put all your friends down for a subscription.

"What I am hoping at the moment is that you will tell us if you would listen once a week to a program discussing the causes of war and its prevention. These wars seem to come about a generation apart, just in time to get our sons and then our grandsons. We take up the notion that the last one was too terrible ever to be repeated, and so we lull our-selves to sleep, and wake up only when it is too late. This time it is my hope that some of us will stay awake and will use the time to dig into the roots of this subject and find out exactly why the nations of the world cannot stay within their own borders and solve their own prob-lems and let their neighbors alone. Will the United Nations be any more effective than the League of Nations was? Or is it true, as the late Gen-eral Patton declared, that wars are inevitable and natural to us humans? 'Mankind is war,' he said; and is this so, or are there factors, psychological or pathological, political or economic, which can be discovered and remedied, so that it will be possible for nations to disarm without fear?

"I have some ideas on this subject, and no doubt you have some also; the question is, would you like to check your ideas by the opinions of the wisest and best persons we can manage to bring before you? I should like to know your answers to this question, and so would those who conduct this station. If you have something to tell us, please write at once to Mary Morrow, in care of this station. I will read your letters and so will the others who have to help make the decision."

XI

So that was that; Mr. Archibald beamed and said she had a very good radio voice, and would she be interested to hear how it sounded. She was surprised, and he told her that in course of nature no one ever hears his or her own voice; a speaker hears from inside the mouth more than by the ears. He took her into another room, where there was a phono-graph, and he put a platter on and set it going. A strange experience—there was her speech, word for word and clear as a bell; but it was a different voice, and she would hardly have known it. It was like look-ing into a mirror and seeing another face there. "So that is the way I sound to the world!"

They gave her the record so that she could take it home and play it for her friends. "We always make two recordings," said the elegant Mr. Archibald; "one for the speaker and one for our files." Laurel thought of some lines of the English poet Clough which Lanny was fond of quoting—supposed to be spoken by the devil or some evil spirit: "How pleasant it is to have money, heigh-ho, How pleasant it is to have money!"

It was pleasant, too, to have a live idea, as Laurel discovered when she went back to the studio next day to see if there was any mail. The most astounding thing! there was a table piled with letters addressed to Mary Morrow, and all from persons who had written and mailed their letters on the previous afternoon or evening! She had to pick some of them up and examine them before she could believe her eyes. There were so many they filled a big carton box, and a boy had to carry it down and put it into a taxi for her. At home she would sit and open them, trembling with delight. When Lanny came in they would do a little dance together.

No, the American people very certainly didn't want World War III! They wanted it so little that they would pay handsomely to escape it; they would put checks and dollar bills and ten dollar bills into envelopes and mail them to an unknown voice out of the air! Apparently the way to get money in America was to say that you didn't want it. The flood lasted a week, and it brought enough money to pay for the opening quarter-hour. It also brought no fewer than three proposals of marriage from gentlemen who declared themselves to be eligible. But Laurel was not.

BOOK EIGHT

Tell Truth and Shame the Devil

23

New World Coming

I

THE four Peace conspirators had the task of choosing names for their various enterprises. "What's in a name?" Shakespeare had asked, and America's answer was, "Everything." Give a thing a good name and people would remember it and talk about it. A good name must be short and must tell you what it was all about. "Monuments, Fine Arts, and Archives Section"—how could anybody remember that? The result was that few people had heard of it, and those who had would describe its purpose rather than try to remember its name. But people remembered the "Blue Eagle," the "New Deal," the "GOP."

Lanny said, "What our program boils down to is Public Ownership and Peace. Let's call it POP." But Laurel, all for dignity, said they would confuse it with a concert of light music. They tried other combinations but without finding one that pleased them all, until Nina remarked, "Peace is what we want, and that seems to me a good word, short and sweet. Why not call the paper *Peace?* Move into the class with *Life* and *Time*."

From the point of view of circulation that prospect appealed to them and they agreed upon it. They would use General Grant's immortal words, "Let us have peace," as their slogan, putting it at the masthead of the paper and opening and closing their radio programs with it. The "Peace Program," it would be called. As for their syndicate proposition, that must look as little like propaganda as possible; it wouldn't really be propaganda, for they would take any good writing they came upon provided it wasn't antisocial. They would help to circulate it, and make it pay if they could. They wanted a neutral title and decided upon the "Edgemere Bureau."

Rick had taken to that job like a swan to the little pond at The Reaches. He liked nothing better than to lie propped up in bed with a stack of mss. by his side. And oh, how easy it was to get such a stack in the great metropolis of Mammon! So many people thought of writing as a "settin'

393

down job," easy, dignified, and sumptuously rewarded. Send out one call, and it spread all over the land; envelopes large and small poured in, frequently without return postage and sometimes without the author's address.

But a skilled editor learns to save his time. The wine taster does not have to take a single swallow, and an egg taster surely does not have to eat the whole egg. Rick knew what he wanted, and his quick eye roamed over page after page. It didn't necessarily have to be the work of a skilled writer; it didn't even have to be someone who knew how to spell; it just had to be somebody who had something worth while to say. Somebody who had had an experience and had felt it deeply; somebody who knew the world and had thought about life, whether his thoughts were sad or gay, hopeful or desperate. Copy could be edited and fixed up; but intensity, novelty, significance—these were qualities that were not kept on tap in editorial offices, and editors were like placer miners, hoping for nuggets and mostly getting sand and silt.

II

Rick and Laurel had paid a visit to the offices of the Acme Syndicate. Laurel had gone along because this was the concern which had handled her New Mexico bomb story and done very well with it. They were pleased to meet her English editor friend and to hear about the project for a writers' bureau. Needless to say, the two adventurers didn't say anything about their idea of changing the world; they hinted mildly that they were interested in material of a forward-looking nature, and these business people replied that they would handle anything their papers would take, and they would be glad to consider anything a successful playwright and a popular novelist thought it worth while to submit. New talent? Yes indeed, they were eager for it, and if this competent pair were willing to serve as talent scouts, on a percentage basis, what could be gladder news?

They were going to have a radio program and a little weekly paper to reprint its text, together with other material. They would use both these media to promote the writers' bureau. Mr. Adams and Mr. Mackenzie said "Fine!" and called in Mr. Smythe and Mr. Goldfarb to hear about the setup; they too said "Fine!" They were businessmen; and when anyone looked at this couple he could see that they had money, and when anyone listened to them he could see that they had brains. When the word "Peace" was brought in it didn't frighten anybody; of course, everybody wanted peace, and if you could manage to make readable copy out of it, the newspapers would want it too. When Rick asked if it would be permissible for them to use some of the syndicate copy in their paper, subsequent to the newspaper date, the answer was that no one would object to that. With newspapers, copy was alive one day and the next day was in the morgue.

So the happy pair went off and reported to their respective spouses. With the advice of their publisher friend and a lawyer recommended by him, they worked out a contract to be submitted to authors. They would deal in first serial rights only, and not try to rob the author of book or motion picture or other rights. With small stuff, they would buy the first serial rights for cash. With other material, such as a series, or something that they felt was speculative, they would pay the author ten per cent of the purchase price for a thirty-day option, which would give them time to try the manuscript out with the syndicate. They adopted a statement of program to go on their letterheads:

The Edgemere Bureau is a non-profit organization, established to promote the output of material of a liberal tendency. It does not seek to make a profit out of its authors, but to recover the costs of its operation. Its books will be audited and an annual report will be sent to its authors. If the enterprise is so fortunate as to make a profit, the sum will be turned over to the American Peace Foundation, for use in its Peace Program and the weekly newspaper *Peace*.

The very agreeable elderly lawyer who prepared their contract and checked all their business arrangements did not send any bill, and when they reminded him about it he told them that he was a poet and would be pleased if they would help to circulate his verses. He didn't want to be paid for his legal services because he too was interested in peace. They would have that sort of experience more than once.

III

When Rick wasn't reading mss., he was interviewing writers and editors. He chose for his top assistant a rewrite man on one of the big dailies. Philip Edgerton had been classified 4-F by the Army because he had flat feet, but that wouldn't interfere with the reading of manuscripts. He was in his early thirties, a chap after Rick's own heart, nervous, high strung, and keen as a rabbit hound on the scent of good writing. He was chained to a desk, reading stuff in which he had no sort of interest, and the idea of being able to read copy along his own line of thinking

sent him zooming, as he phrased it. He knew the newspaper game, having
been in it since leaving college. He was from the Middle West and had
earned his education as a book agent, selling good literature to farm
wives and eating with the harvest hands. Now he had a wife and two
children and was living in New York on eighty dollars a week; if the
Foundation would pay him that he would work double hours, and
maybe write something himself.

Each of the four conspirators had to have a secretary—four well-
trained ladies, two of them young and two middle-aged, and all willing
to be separated from the bright lights and eager to try living in the country for a while. It would be a safe guess that at least half the people in
Megalopolis were yearning to get out of it—or at any rate they said they
were. Edgemere was near enough so that you could go in now and
then, and your friends could come out week ends. It wouldn't be bad
at all, and they would hunt up a boarding-house, or two of them set
up housekeeping in a small apartment if they could find one.

Edgemere was willing to welcome them all. The day came when they
moved, bag and baggage, and that was a day of uproar. Before they had
time to get their things unpacked, Edgemere arrived, in the form of a
dairyman who wanted to sell them milk, a vegetable man who made the
rounds twice a week, a baker the same, and so on. Most important of
all was Comrade Tipton, who came to ask for their laundry, and at the
same time to welcome them in the name of the working class of this
community. Comrade Tipton drove the laundry wagon, white painted,
but a long time ago, paint having been scarce in wartime. He had white
handlebar mustaches and abundant hair and some one of his forefathers
must have kissed the Blarney stone.

What a life story he had to tell—and he told it! Nina happened to be
outdoors and received him, and later passed the tale on to the others.
He had emigrated to Australia. Then he had become a vendor of patent
medicine; that was how he had learned psychology and absorbed his
radical ideas.

"I'm really a philosophical Anarchist," he said, "but my wife is a Socialist, so I have to belong to the local and help them with a few libertarian ideas. My wife is a Methodist too, so I belong to the church, and
we have converted a few of the people. Also, I deliver an idea or two
along with the laundry, so you'll find that you have a lot of friends and
well-wishers in this town—but not among the well-to-do, God forbid.
They're not at all sure they want you, but the money you've been spending has carried the day, and they won't ride you out on a rail. You're
from England, I'm told, Comrade Nielson, and we're proud of what the

English are doing. When you get settled you must all come and get acquainted with the local. My wife cooks the bean suppers, and that's the way we get the young folks; they're not so keen for idealism as we oldsters, but they have good appetites. My wife works in the laundry, and I call for and deliver it—they were glad to have an old man do it in wartime, and I'm hanging on, expecting the next war. I'm not so optimistic as you folks but I'm ready to do my share of trying to wake the people up. I come to this part of town every Friday, but I'll make it another day if it's more convenient for you. We Reds have to stick together."

"Comrade" Nielson told her friends, "That could hardly have happened in England."

IV

The bureau was already working; it didn't need much paraphernalia, just a secretary and a file of large cards to keep track of manuscripts. Laurel had written an article about Göring in defeat, based on Lanny's interview and Jerry's letters. She had written another about the German scientists, their failure with the atomic bomb and how they had taken the American success. These two were musts, as you might say; they were interesting and important, and the syndicate took them and so did the papers. Rick wrote a short article, strictly objective and factual, about the plight of the British Isles, which had fifty million people crowded onto a very small space, and living by coal, iron, and shipping. Their savings were nearly all gone, and they must export or die. It didn't matter very much whether they had a Labour or Conservative government, it would have to make them work hard and live on short-commons. Rick didn't mention how President Truman had abruptly and unceremoniously cut off lend-lease, for that would have been propaganda and might have killed the story.

The starting of the radio and the magazine was another matter. Both would have to be ready at the same time, and it wouldn't be like an automobile, which can start slowly, but like a jet plane, which has to leap into the air. They knew by experience that the day after they sent out a radio call there would be a flood of mail, and there must be the machinery waiting and ready to handle it. Haldeman-Julius obligingly wrote, telling them how these things were done in Girard, Kansas. There was a long table in the center of the room, and girls sat opposite each other and put the money in piles in front of them—thus making it a little more difficult to steal. Each letter or order must be marked with a colored pencil, stating the amount of money enclosed and whether it was cash, check, or money order, and also the initials of the girl who handled it. There must be a severe, stern-eyed forewoman to watch these proceedings, and every now and then another girl must take up the orders and the money, add up the total, and see to it that the money was there. If it wasn't, the erring girl's attention was called to it, and if it happened again she was fired. This didn't sound so pleasant, but you were in the business world now. The forewoman was a matron supplied by Mrs. Tipton from among her Methodist Church members; the matron had run an office before her marriage, and now her children were grown and she was going to run another.

The orders were turned over to another girl who put the names and addresses on stencils, which were filed alphabetically. When mailing time came these stencils were fed into a machine which picked up a paper, stamped it through the stencil, and then shoved it out ready for mailing. It was Sam de Witt who got that machine for them; you had to have pull to get anything of the sort in these days. It was quite a wonderful machine, which increased your respect for the age in which you lived. If only the age wouldn't plunge into war every now and then and destroy the millions of wonderful things it had created!

V

There was everything ready, except the papers that were to be printed and mailed; that was another job, an editorial job about which they were greatly excited. So much depended upon the first issue! It must justify the hopes of all the enthusiastic persons who had already written, and of others who would write after the first broadcast. The paper would be pitifully small and cheap, but the people who took it up and glanced at it must realize at once that here was something alive and significant, something they would want to read and keep on reading.

At the top was the title PEACE, and under it: "Let Us Have Peace.—General Grant." In one corner was the serial number, Vol. 1, No. 1, and in the other corner, "A Weekly Paper. Subscription Price, 50 cents per year. Bundle orders, 100 for one dollar." Beginning at the right was a "Statement of Policy," which Rick wrote and which they discussed and revised with care. In its final form it read:

PEACE believes that World Wars have causes, and that modern science should be able to discover these causes, and at least to suggest remedies.

PEACE is endowed, and is published by a non-profit trusteeship. It is published in the cheapest possible form in the hope that no one may be too poor to possess it.

PEACE will call upon the best minds it can find to contribute their wisdom on the subject of world peace and how to maintain it. The paper's policy will be that of an open forum. Within the limits of its small space an earnest effort will be made to cover all aspects of the question.

PEACE is conducted in co-operation with the Peace Program on Radio Station WYZ, New York, on Thursday at 7 P.M., and will include a reprint of the previous week's broadcast.

PEACE will take no advertising, except of publications and enterprises of a character allied to its program.

PEACE solicits your support, not in the form of cash donations, but of subscriptions. Under post-office regulations you may subscribe for other persons. You may send us a list of your friends, your club members, your schoolmates, any list whatever, remitting fifty cents for each name. You may even send a telephone book and have all the subscribers in your town receive the paper.

The publishers and editors of PEACE are undertaking a public service, and their interests and your own are the same. We shall all suffer alike in an atomic war if it is permitted to come.

That statement, in not too large or obtrusive type, was to appear in every issue of the paper. The radio program would go on the back page; they discovered by experiment that a typewritten double-spaced page took about two minutes to read, and so twelve minutes of program would be somewhat less than two thousand words, just about a page of their small paper. They would use one or two of their short syndicate articles published during the previous week. The editorial would deal as a rule with the broadcast, embodying such comments as the editors might think were called for. No doubt there would be letters coming in; and they would remember Richard Armour's injunction to have something from the poets. Most editors of reform papers kept handy an anthology called *The Cry for Justice*, in which the wisdom and passion of the ages were to be found. In Vol 1, No. 1 they would include some verses which had appeared in the *New York World* more than a generation ago, sent in on a crumpled scrap of paper by an author who gave his address as Fourth Bench, City Hall Park. The verses were addressed "To a Nine-Inch Gun," and read:

> Whether your shell hits the target or not,
> Your cost is Five Hundred Dollars a Shot.

You thing of noise and flame and power,
We feed you a hundred barrels of flour
Each time you roar. Your flame is red
With twenty thousand loaves of bread.
Silence! A million hungry men
Seek bread to fill their mouths again.

VI

The four decided to have a housewarming, to get acquainted with
their authors and let them know that there really was a plant and a business. The plant being out of town, the authors and their wives would
have a journey; those who lived on Long Island or in Westchester would
have a long journey, and it would be late at night and cold when they
got home. The decision was for Sunday afternoon at five o'clock, the
cocktail hour in Megalopolis. The invitation would read "to a denatured
cocktail party," which would give everyone fair warning; those who
couldn't live without alcohol could take a nip before they came in and
another after they had left. The hosts would serve a buffet supper, which
it was fashionable to name, Swedish fashion, a *smörgåsbord*.

That meant almost as much work as getting out a paper, but it was
taken off the editors' hands by Rahel and Freddi. They went to visit the
Tiptons, and the head of that household agreed to bake a ham and roast
a turkey and provide all the necessary fixings. The head was a large stout
lady, extraordinarily agile, and as full of conversation and fun as her
husband. "I'll take charge of everything," she said, "but don't let *him*
know it." By "him" she meant the man with the white mustaches. "He
thinks he runs things but he doesn't," she explained with a wink that
women would understand.

At the appointed hour a table was spread in the dining-room of the
mansion, and there were heaps of sliced turkey and ham, several kinds
of bread sliced and buttered, potato salad, celery, cranberry jelly out
of cans, pickles, jellied fruits, salted almonds and cashew nuts, olives,
chocolates, and other delicacies that belong on such a table. There was
a great bowl of grape and pineapple juice with a cake of ice floating in
it; also a steaming urn of coffee. The deceased Emily Chattersworth
was paying for all this, and she would have enjoyed it.

The authors came, bringing their wives or their lady friends. The
well-to-do came in their own cars and the poor were met at the station.
Some were short and stout and some were lean and spectacled, some

were smooth shaven and some had fancy little beards. Always they tried to look important, and their conversation was highly intellectual, even when it was shop. Most of them knew one another, but they didn't know this outfit and were curious about it; they looked closely at everything.

The place wasn't elegant, but it looked as if it was meant to be permanent, and that was the important thing. So many fly-by-night propositions tried to take up the time and energy of authors, especially those who had "names." All of these men had promised to write for the bureau, and several were already at work.

Sir Eric, who had interviewed them all, acted as host and introduced them to the others. They had seen a picture of Lady Nielson in the papers, and most of them had read something by Mary Morrow, though they hadn't seen her before and didn't know where she came from. The vague Mr. Budd was presumably the business manager or something like that. They didn't know that the tall, thin Jewish lad was a nephew of Hansi Robin; if they had they would have paid more attention to him, at least to ask if he also was a musician.

Hansi was coming but not Bess; she had a committee meeting that Sunday evening, and she said that what Lanny was doing was bourgeois futility. Another million dollars that might as well be spent on chorus girls! Johannes's chauffeur drove Hansi, and they had a flat tire and arrived late, after all the turkey was gone; fortunately Hansi was a reformed-style Jew and could eat ham. He had brought his fiddle, which he did only on occasions where he wanted to do his host special honor.

After the meal they sat around and chatted for a while, and then Sir Eric got up to make a few remarks. He thought they would be interested to hear from members of the new group about the ideas which were moving them. He apologized for coming, as a foreigner, to set up an educational enterprise in America; but the world had become one so fast that Britain and America were next-door neighbors. It was a fact that London was now as near to New York as Edgemere, New Jersey, had been when the American nation was founded; Peiping or Moscow was as near to New York as Philadelphia had been in those days. Also, the fates had tied London and New York together; they were allies whether they liked it or not.

The speaker went on to declare that the group was hoping to do a scientific job; not merely to talk about world peace and to yearn for it, but to work for it and get it. It was surely scientific to believe that world wars had causes. Given any set of phenomena, science set out to find the cause for them; that was just as true of wars as of cancer, and surely world wars killed many more people than cancer. They wanted to bring the best brains of the world to work on the problem of the causes of modern wars, and how to remove these causes or reduce their impact.

"It is our belief," said Rick, "that the main driving force to war in these modern days is economic; it is the result of a competitive economy and the race for raw materials and foreign markets. A profit economy cannot market all its products at home, for it does not pay its workers enough. A profit economy is a drive to expansion, and so it becomes a drive to war. After the war is won, there will be unlimited production until the wreckage is repaired; then again there will be overproduction and crisis.

"If this idea is correct, the public should surely have a chance to consider it. But the fact is that if you write along this line, no matter how well you write, you cannot get publication in any but a small-circulation paper. You cannot get it into any big daily; you cannot get it into the *Saturday Evening Post*, or *Collier's*, or the *Reader's Digest*—and so on down the line. All the big-circulation media are Big Business enterprises and they are committed to the Big Business side of every question.

"What we are trying to do is set up one or more media whereby the unpopular aspects of the war-versus-peace problem can get an airing, and to make it possible for independent men and women to live while doing such writing. Whether we shall be able to get mass circulation is a question; we propose to make a try for it, and we believe that our success would make a tremendous difference in the future of both America and Britain, which from now on have to sink or swim together. It will do us Britons very little good to put an end to profiteering in our country if you in America permit it to go on growing like a giant upas tree."

VII

That was Sir Eric's story; and then he introduced Mary Morrow. That small, birdlike lady wore a simple blue dress, and she had not smeared any goo on her lips or paint on her cheeks. She was so much wrapped up in what she was thinking that she had a tendency to speak too fast; having had this pointed out to her, she would stop, pause for a moment, and then make another slow start. What she said was:

"There is an aspect of the peace problem that especially concerns us women. If you read the books of our opponents, the defenders of war, or those who tell us that we have to reconcile ourselves to the fact that wars are inevitable, you will learn that nations have to expand because their populations have expanded, and they have to have more room—*Lebensraum*, the Germans call it. If you lived in Germany, as I did, you would hear these same gentlemen advocating large families—in order that the nation might be able to expand.

"I agree with everything that Sir Eric has said about the economic causes of modern wars, but I think that overpopulation is another cause and I know that we have the remedy right at hand. It is birth control, or what they are now calling planned parenthood. All you have to do is to let the women know about it, and the women will do the rest. No woman with even the beginning of a mind wants to kill herself with continuous child-bearing, as our Puritan and pioneer foremothers did. But when we try to talk about that subject you know well what opposition we encounter from the Roman Catholic Church, and from legislators who have been elected by its influence. This, it seems to me, is a challenge to the integrity of every writer in the world.

"If you investigate you find that the Catholic legislators themselves use the technique of contraception in their private lives—the size of their families reveals that, and polls have shown that more than fifty per cent of Catholic women defy the dogmas of their Church in this respect. But the dogmas serve to keep the information from the poor, who need it most; they cause the laboring population to reproduce unduly, and then when there is starvation in Italy or Spain or Poland or Bavaria or other Catholic lands, you hear rumbles of discontent and threats of revolution, and so the politicians and the military gentlemen decide that the country must expand, it must take some of the land of its neighbors, who are in the very same fix. They don't say that they must get some of their superfluous men killed off and keep some of their women childless, but that is what they do when they go to war, and they have to do it every generation or so in order to keep their evil system going. The surplus populations of Europe used to come to America, but now we have our own surplus, and our own threat of hard times and social discontent always hanging over our heads."

There was a scattering of applause when Mary Morrow ceased, and it was apparent that there were no victims of superstition in this gathering. Lady Nielson said a few words, just by way of welcome, and then she suggested that questions were in order. A woman writer asked if it was their program to give a hearing to all sides or only to their own; Rick answered, "We have discussed that problem. It sounds good to say that we are conducting an open forum, and if we had the circulation and the resources, say, of the *Reader's Digest* it would be fun to do it.

The *Reader's Digest* is a cleverly baited trap for its eight or ten million subscribers. It publishes interesting articles on every harmless subject; but when it comes to the profit system and its evil practices and consequences, there is silence. I think our proper answer is that when the *Reader's Digest* and *Collier's* and the *Saturday Evening Post* become open forums, we will too. But meantime our space is small, and costs a lot of time and money and labor, and we use it to provide an antidote to the widely circulated poison of the profit-takers."

The woman writer suggested that sometimes opposition had the effect of stimulating interest. Rick said, "Yes, of course. Both *Time* and *Life* occasionally print some saucy letter from our side. They do it by way of a joke, and to show how secure they feel in their citadel of power. We might do that also. I personally feel quite secure in my ability to answer the partisans of privilege."

VIII

Lanny and Laurel had brought their furniture from the New York apartment they were giving up, including Lanny's piano, and now he played the accompaniments for Hansi. This great virtuoso could play the most difficult music, but when he wished to entertain a mixed company he would choose a bit of *Salonmusik*, which they would enjoy. Now he chose Raff's *Cavatina*, which gave him a chance to reveal his passionate tones; and when they applauded, he gave them one of Fritz Kreisler's charming imitations of Corelli. After that Rick asked him to say what he thought about the peace enterprise, and Hansi replied modestly that he was no orator, but he had known these friends for a long time and believed what they believed; he would come any time they asked him and play over the radio for them, and would try to persuade other musicians to do the same. That was handsome, and calculated to reassure a group of writers who were embarking on a voyage with a captain and crew they didn't know very well.

After that everybody loosened up, and ideas were exchanged freely. When they took their departure they all appeared to be satisfied, and some of the prosperous ones took the unprosperous into their cars, which was according to the code of comradeship. When the last had departed the five conspirators—they were counting Freddi now—sat, according to custom, discussing their guests, what they looked like as well as what they had said.

The way for men to learn things is to listen to the women, and it was truly amazing what Laurel with her quick-darting brown eyes and Nina with her blue ones had observed. That Mrs. Edgerton, for example! She and her husband had been traveling about Edgemere with a real-estate agent, looking for some place to live. When they had arrived at The Willows, the husband had been carrying two suitcases, and the wife had gone upstairs to change her clothes. She had descended in state, wearing pink crepe de chine, far too showy for an informal occasion and too expensive for her husband's income—though of course she might have money of her own. As to looks, it must be admitted that she had them; a stately figure, real blond hair, and placid perfect features that might have served a sculptor as a model for a Juno. Unfortunately she was conscious of what she had and spent most of her time posing; she would give the men a chance to observe her placid full face and then her perfect profile. "I'm afraid she's not thinking about much else," said Nina.

"I'm afraid also that she takes her social position seriously," added Laurel. "She accepted Rahel as a lady caterer, but she took Comrade Tipton for the butler and didn't relish being introduced to him."

"Don't be mean," said Lanny, and his lady answered quickly, "A woman like that can ruin a man, or take him out of the movement. If you don't believe it I'll go out and buy a costume like that and let you see what it costs!"

IX

Yes, when it comes to women, it is better to take the word of women, who make it their business to know. The morning after this enjoyable party Lanny went into his wife's room, where she was supposed to be getting her things unpacked and in order, and he found her sitting on the bed, her eyes inflamed, and tears in them which she couldn't keep away. "For heaven's sake!" he exclaimed. "What is the matter?"

She tried to tell him it was nothing; she didn't want to talk about it, but he insisted, and finally she said, "It's Flo."

"Listen, darling," he said. "It's silly to hide things from me. You know I'm no worshiper of the family ideal, and I'll never hold you responsible for your sister's doings. Why don't you tell me, and maybe I can help."

"There's nothing anybody can do, Lanny. It's just utterly, utterly horrible!"

"What has she done—robbed a bank? Is she in jail?"

"She ought to be!" She handed him a letter which had just come from the other sister, the rich one in Baltimore. Lanny sat on the bed beside his wife and read it, and before he had got very far he gave a whistle and exclaimed, "Holy smoke!" The letter read:

"Dear Laurel: Perhaps you have heard from Flo telling you that she has made what she calls a catch. She is married to an old man who was one of our leading physicians. He is close to eighty and quite well-to-do. He has been living for years with two sisters, almost as old as himself, and Flo took the job of housekeeper, and I suppose she managed to seduce the old man. Naturally, the sisters opposed the idea of a marriage, so then the fight was on. Flo took him to a justice of the peace, and then drove him back to the town house and left him. With the marriage certificate in her handbag, she drove to their place in the country, where she knew there were many sorts of valuables; she loaded the car with everything it would hold—jewels, paintings, antique furniture, and other heirlooms—and took it out and sold it. She is proud of the exploit. She said, 'I got that much away from them anyhow!'

"Incredible as it may seem, the infatuated old man stands by her, and the sisters, being gentlewomen, will not make a public scandal. They have moved out of their home, and now Flo has everything. The story is all over town, and you can imagine how I feel, living in the midst of it, knowing that my friends are talking about nothing else. You are lucky to be a couple of hundred miles away. Myself, I would be glad to be a couple of hundred thousand."

Lanny couldn't help laughing as he read; perhaps that was the best way to take it. He repeated the pungent motto: "God gave us our relatives, thank God we can choose our friends." But that didn't keep the tears out of Laurel's eyes. "Those poor women, Lanny—to be turned out of their home by an adventuress!"

"She did to them exactly what her stepmother had done to her. She acted on the principles of the American Indian." Laurel, it developed, didn't know about the principles of the American Indian, so he explained that whenever a white man had wronged an Indian, the Indian avenged himself on the next white man he met.

"Darling," he said, "there's no sense in your tearing your heart out. You have absolutely nothing to do with it, and nobody with any sense is going to blame you. You have to tell yourself that it's the very thing you are fighting—wholesale greed. The higher the stakes in the gamble, the greater the pressure on frail human nature, and the crazier people go. It's the automatic effect of inequality of wealth, and the longer it continues the worse it gets. In the end it will destroy our whole society if it's permitted to continue."

That was the way to make it tolerable, to present it as a thesis in economics, a part of their crusade. Laurel would turn her shame into social rage; she would identify the two outraged old ladies with all the robbed and oppressed of the earth. It didn't fit quite accurately, because even in a co-operative society there would be no way to prevent the use of sex for purposes of parasitism—so long as men were fools and women were predatory! But at least you could keep from bringing women up as Flo had been brought up, to regard useful service as a disgrace and vanity and display as glamour.

X

A marriage in Lanny's family also! There came a letter from Beauty, telling him the news that Marceline had met an American lieutenant recuperating in Cannes and had fallen in love with him, something she had vowed would never happen to her again. But she was a new woman now, not so centered upon herself. He was a nice fellow, what there was of him; he walked with a limp and had lost his right arm. But Marceline had plenty of money, and they would get along. This time there was to be a proper wedding, and how Beauty wished that her only son could be present!

A letter from Parsifal was enclosed. He didn't write often, only when he had something he thought worth saying. Now he had a curious story, about a British Indian official who had been returning home on account of the breakdown of his health and had stopped in Cannes for the winter. Parsifal had told him about God—not Jehovah of the thunders, Lord God of battles, but the loving Father who was in his heart—and this latter God had greatly assisted the gentleman's health. With him he had brought two talking myna birds, alert and lively creatures like crows, about ten inches long, shiny black, with white patches on their wings and yellow bills and legs. They lived on fruit, and had been kept alive on the steamer voyage with grapes and other fruits frozen in the ship's refrigerator. Here on the Riviera, the nights being sometimes chilly, they had to be tied up in paper sacks every night, with little holes for ventilation; they seemed to enjoy this greatly and made a terrible fuss when taken out of the sacks, presumably because they didn't know it was daylight.

These were young birds, and they do not acquire the power of talking until they are a year old. The official, Mr. Jerrold, was beginning to teach them words, but found it monotonous. Parsifal had had a bright idea—the records that had been prepared for treating sick people in their sleep! Could birds learn lessons as a victim of amnesia had done and as thousands of American airmen had done? If so, it would be something to tell the world about!

They had loaded the phonograph in the buggy and the old horse had carried it to Mr. Jerrold's hotel. Every night thereafter, when the birds were put into their paper sacks, they heard the phonograph repeat, slowly and distinctly, "God is all and God is love." After it had said that about a dozen times it said, "God is alive and God is real." Next came, "God helps and God heals." And then, "God sustains and God restores."

Wonder of wonders, it worked! Now, when the birds were taken out of their sacks, and after they had stopped fussing and had gulped down their quota of Malaga grapes, they would sit on their perches and cry the formulas of the New Thought philosophy, New England Transcendentalism superimposed on Kantian Idealism. The only trouble was that the male bird would be speaking one formula while his mate would be speaking another. Their voices were not gentle and soothing, like their teacher's, but harsh and cackly; even so, all who heard them agreed that the unpious French Riviera possessed the two most pious talking birds that had ever come out of the land of Buddha!

XI

There came another letter, this time with an American stamp and the postmark New York. It was from Bernhardt Monck, and the postmark meant that he had entrusted it to someone coming home to America. Monck was in the American sector of Berlin and wrote that his wife and children were with him after many years. He was well and serving as adviser to AMG. His letter revealed that he was a greatly worried German Social Democrat.

"The American Army is going to pieces," he wrote; "the officers here are in despair, but there seems to be nothing they can do about it. Washington makes the decisions, and if you know people there who have influence, do try to make them understand what is going on. I know you have shared the hope that the Russians would settle down and content themselves with restoring their own country. God knows they have got enough out of this war, and if they were willing to stick by their agreements they could get American loans on easy terms and show the world what a planned economy might do. But you know, Lanny, they aren't that sort of people. I have information that after a struggle inside the Politburo the decision has been taken for a hard policy. They think they have a chance for world revolution, and they are going to plunge for it.

"Do pull some wires and try to get the top people to understand Communist psychology. You must know that they respect only force, and that as you weaken yourselves you increase their aggressiveness. It is a serious thing for us Germans who have been pinning our faith on the Allies. It means concentration camp for us Socialists; the Russians have reopened the former Nazi camps in their zone of Germany and in Poland and are filling them with people of our sort. It is a hard decision to have to come to, but we have to make up our minds that the revolutionary idealism is dead, and that what we are facing is the old Russian imperialism wearing a proletarian camouflage. That may fool some Americans, but it cannot fool Germans, for we have lived next to the Russians for a long time and have seen them in action in Berlin. For a quarter of a century we watched National Socialism stealing our name and using it to cover naked aggression. Few of us are likely to be deceived a second time.

"I do not think the Reds want war; they are in no position to fight, and will not be for a long time. But they mean to take everything that can be taken without war; they will test you to the limit, and only pull back at the moment when they see it means an open break. Agreements mean nothing to them; their diplomats look you straight in the eye and say the opposite of the facts, even when they know that you know the facts. It is dreadful to think of the world having to stay armed, or to start rearming, but if you don't it will be the Hitler story all over again. Every division you demobilize means new territory and new populations surrendered to the totalitarian world. Already I am sorry that I brought my family back, and I am thinking of sending them to some new place in South America—but we cannot be sure of any place. I myself mean to stay. As you know, I have dedicated my life to democratic Socialism, and I am going to stick by that cause, come what may."

XII

When Lanny read that letter he phoned Professor Alston, took his wife in the car and went over and spent an evening with the old gentleman. It was the first time that Laurel and Alston had met, and it was an occasion for them both; but not an entirely happy occasion, they being conscientious persons; they were two admirers of Franklin D. Roosevelt, and had made sacrifices for his principles. Just now things looked dark indeed for those principles, and New Dealers when they got together could do nothing but mourn.

"There isn't a thing in the world I can do," the onetime "fixer" declared. "There is a new crowd in Washington, and we are out; they hate us and fear us, and our influence works in reverse—if we are known to favor something, that damns it. All controls are off and everybody is making money; the business lobbies are swarming into Washington and have unlimited funds to distribute—hospitality, gifts, salaries, everything. I went down there for a look around and it made me sick. I have never seen such drinking or such a riot of greed. Everybody takes it for granted that the Republicans are going to carry Congress this year and that taxes will be reduced—the excess profits tax dropped entirely. Senator Taft will be the new boss, and that means isolationism—let Europe go to hell if it wants to."

"They are willing to let the Communists have it?" asked Lanny.

"Oh, they'll hate the Communists all right, and call them lots of names, but it'll be politics, meant for home consumption. Everybody is still fighting Roosevelt, trying to prove that he was wrong—Republicans and Southern Democrats alike. They damn the Yalta Agreement—because the Russians aren't keeping it. As if that was anything against an agreement, that the other side breaks it! How could Roosevelt know they would break it, and what could he have done if he had known? Turned against Stalin and joined Hitler? Do they think Hitler would have kept agreements better?"

These were rhetorical questions—rhetoric being all the three peace lovers had at their command. They could sit and lament, and reactionary senators and congressmen could rave and scold—but the Russian armies stayed on in Northern Iran and threatened to take Tehran unless their oil demands were granted. They were demanding the northeastern provinces of Turkey and forcing America to send arms to that country. They were making no pretense of allowing a genuinely democratic government in Poland, according to the Yalta Agreement. They were gradually ejecting everybody but Communists from the governments of Rumania and Bulgaria and Hungary. Everywhere they were pushing to establish their dictatorships, according to the technique which Lenin had taught and which Stalin was modifying by the addition of more roughness.

"Here we are, planning to talk about peace!" exclaimed Laurel. "Are we going to have to face about and call for armaments?"

All that the old Professor could answer was, "There is nothing so hard as to steer a middle course when extremists are buffeting you from both sides."

24

A New Song's Measure

I

MARY MORROW, popular novelist and storywriter, made an appointment and took her friends, Sir Eric Vivian Pomeroy-Nielson and his lady, to call on the management of Station WYZ. The names of the visitors were impressive, and so were their personalities. Manifestly they were cultivated persons, acquainted with the world and the canons of good breeding; every word they spoke was carefully chosen, and soothing to the feelings of radio officials, who are always nervous concerning an "ad lib" program—fearing that someone may speak a word that cannot be recalled, the consequences of which might be grave.

Almost equally important, the novelist laid on the desk of the program manager a check for nineteen hundred dollars, signed by the American Peace Foundation, Laurel Creston, treasurer. Mr. Archibald didn't know who Laurel Creston was, but he would deposit the check and find that it didn't bounce. It paid for ten periods, and a good slice would represent net profit to a prosperous radio establishment. Under such circumstances it is easy to have warm feelings, and the staff bubbled over and promised to telephone to various stations outside New York with which they had friendly relations, recommending that they make a recording of the broadcast and use it later. One such station was in Massachusetts, another in Pennsylvania, and Miss Morrow was inspired to say that her Foundation would be willing to pay for these additional broadcasts.

The well-satisfied trio went back to Edgemere and reported to their radio announcer, an amiable gentleman by the new name of Billy Burns. You might not at first have recognized him, and he would have preferred that you didn't. For weeks he had been getting used to himself as Billy Budd, but at the last minute he had been seized by a qualm. He knew that his father would hate what he was doing, and that his two half-brothers and their snobbish wives would hate it even

411

more. Also, Lanny had a kind of snobbery of his own; for a quarter of a century he had been making a name for himself as an art expert, and he wanted to be taken for that; he was bored and annoyed when people discovered that he was the son of Budd-Erling Airplanes and deferred to him on that account. Robbie had made the money, and let Robbie have it and use it, and not have anyone else trading on his eminence.

Laurel had taken a nom de plume, and innumerable people had taken stage names; if Lanny was going to become a radio announcer, let him start afresh and make what reputation he could. There was a Billie Burke on the stage, but there was no Billy Burns that he had heard of; so he would make his debut next Thursday evening, and if any of the Budd tribe recognized his voice, they would appreciate the delicacy of his feelings. So long as the sacred name of Budd wasn't spoken over the radio or printed in the papers!

II

Time marched on, and the fateful hour arrived. Two microphones had been installed at the onetime fuse factory and duly tested. The telephone arrangements had been made, and at 6:55 the connection would be established, allowing time for voice testing and the giving or receiving of last-minute instructions. The studio was small—it was to be used as a file room in the daytime, and the cabinets along the walls left just room enough for the two microphones in the center of the room and half a dozen chairs for guests. The honored ones were Nina and Rick, Hansi, Rahel, and Freddi—and Zoltan, in return for his having donated the use of his lovely apartment for three months.

Inexperienced people are always in trepidation at the approach of the fateful moment when the signal is given and they go on the air. It is as if they were to find themselves in heaven, invited to exercise the powers of the seraphim. Will their voices work, or will they find themselves suddenly tongue-tied? What if they have to cough or sneeze? Even if they have written down what they are going to say, what if their hand shakes so that they cannot read it? Here was Lanny Budd, forty-five years old, yet he found himself quivery in the knees. It was his first time, and so much depended upon it.

Watches had been synchronized, and they counted the seconds. Rick sat at a telephone, connected with the studio in New York. He heard the announcer say, "This is Station WYZ. The following is a

paid program, and this studio has no responsibility for what is said."
Rick had his hand raised, and now he dropped it.

Lanny, who had already cleared his throat several times, began in
his most polished tone:

"Ladies and gentlemen, this is Billy Burns, announcer for the Peace
Program. 'Let us have peace' is our slogan. We are a group of persons
who have lived through two world wars and do not want to live
through a third. We have set ourselves the task of trying to find out
what causes these terrible wars, and what mankind can do to prevent
them. All history as we know it is a record of wars, but those of the
present century have been unique in their extent and their cost in
both lives and property. Now the scientists, by the discovery of
atomic fission, have made certain that the next war will be something
so much worse that our imaginations are not equal to conceiving it.
An atomic war may wipe out our great cities and kill millions of innocent people in a single night. Such a war may bring an end to
civilization as we know it. And this is no fantasy, no nightmare; it is
something which I personally have heard from the lips of one after
another of the great physicists who brought this power into existence,
knowing that it can be used either to destroy us or lift us to new
heights of happiness and freedom.

"It is our purpose to call upon these scientists, and other leaders of
thought, to help us in answering two questions: first, what causes
world wars? and second, what can be done to prevent them? We have
planned a series of broadcasts, and as our first speaker we have invited
the well-known novelist, Mary Morrow, to tell us her views. Miss
Morrow is in a special position to discuss this subject because of the
firsthand study she has made of the recent war. She lived in Germany
and saw it coming, and did what one woman writer could do to avert
it. The war came and dragged America into its frightful whirlpool.
More recently Miss Morrow has been following the American armies
into Germany, and no doubt many of you have read her articles about
the suffering and destruction which she saw.

"Knowing one war so intimately, and disliking it so heartily, she is
making an early start in the hope of preventing another, many times
worse. Ladies and gentlemen, I present Mary Morrow."

III

That took nearly three of the precious minutes. Lanny would need
another three at the end, for the "collection talk"; so that gave Laurel

nine minutes in which to exercise whatever charms she might possess. She had refrained from preparing a script; she believed that the success of her trial had been due to human friendliness, and she was afraid that a written text would make her sound literary. To speak with feeling was natural; to read with feeling was acting, and she had no training in that art.

She had elected to have her microphone placed at a little table, on the chance that her knees might give out. Now she sat with the instrument in front of her and spoke quietly and simply, thinking of good old Sophie, thinking of thousands of Sophies, and of mothers and young wives. She had taught herself to speak slowly. She began:

"I have seen horrible things. I have seen things so cruel and wicked that I cannot rest for thinking about them; they haunt my mind. I have decided that what we need is not more emotion, but more thought. It is very hard to think; this is a new power that our race has acquired only a short time ago. We find it easy to weep or to rage, to shout for joy or scold in anger; but to think—just how do we begin? I have tried, and will tell you some of my thoughts.

"I believe that world wars do not come by accident; they have causes. They are made by men and women, by people like you and me. They take a long time in the making, and you can watch them being made. I watched the last war being made for years. I wrote about it, trying to warn people in Britain and America. These were years during which it could have been prevented; but then came the time when it was too late. The war began, and one country after another was dragged in, until there were seventy-two countries involved.

"The causes of that war were at work from 1918 to 1939. Twenty-one years, just time for a young woman to find a husband, marry him, bear him a son, and raise that son to fighting age. Then World War II took him. And now at the beginning of 1946 the process begins again. Don't let anybody lull you with false hopes. The causes are at work; and how long will it be before they produce the same results? Shall we have time to raise a new generation? Some give us five years, some give us ten, some twenty or thirty. The atomic bomb is a more terrible weapon; our rivals are more afraid of it, and we are more afraid that our rivals may get it before we use it. That may bring things to a head more quickly.

"I am not going to tell you that the causes of war are simple, or that I know them all. I am groping for knowledge, as you are, or should be. All I tell you is that the world wars have causes, and that the possibility exists for the human mind to find out what these are. Having used my mind earnestly on the subject, and read the ideas of many others, I have listed about a dozen factors which may be contributing causes of wars; but it seems to me that they all boil down to one cause, that our society is not organized, and is not ruled by reason but by blind chance.

"In the old days that did not matter so much. Here in this New Jersey plain where I am standing, if two Indian tribes fought for possession of the ground, the rest of the world knew nothing about it and was not affected; but within the past hundred years or so we have created railroads and airplanes, telephones and radios, and now atomic bombs; so the world has become one, and when a Hitler invades Poland, seventy-two nations are dragged into war. That being a fact, it seems clear that we have to have a world organization, a world government, complete as we have learned to know governments: that is, a legislature to pass laws, an executive to enforce them, and a court to judge and settle disputes.

"If you and your neighbor disagree about a boundary line, you do not get out your shotguns and go to war; you go to law. That is because the law is there, and you have learned to respect and obey it. Now we have the United Nations meeting in London, and we are all hoping for the best; but we know that this organization has a fatal defect, that any one of the Big Three can veto anything the United Nations may decree. What would you think of our law if the three richest men in our country, or the three biggest corporations, had the right to annul any law that did not suit them?

"It is reported that Stalin at Yalta said he did not see why Honduras should have the right to decide what the Soviet Union should or should not do. The proposal sounds funny when you put it that way. But suppose we had a world court with a judge from each of five small nations, say Honduras and Iceland and Switzerland and Ceylon and New Zealand; and now ask Stalin, 'Which do you think would offer the better chance of justice, a decision of that court, or two atomic bombs dropped, one on Moscow and one on Leningrad?'

"Do not think for a moment that Stalin is alone to blame for the veto. Our own government has made it plain that we are no more willing than Stalin to give Honduras a voice as to what we shall do. No one of the Big Three is ready to submit to a world government— and that is why we do not have a world government, but only a place to argue in. I am glad to have that place, a sounding board to carry voices all over the world, for it is only by discussion that we can find out who is to blame and what is needed in our desperate situation. It is only by the trial and error of parliament plus veto that we can convince ourselves of the need of a real world authority, with a world police force to back up what it says. We all have to watch our United Nations, criticize it, and find out how to improve it, or else to put the real authority in its place."

IV

They had agreed that in this opening program they would say nothing to alarm the most timid member of their audience. There wasn't time to get down to cases; they would be satisfied if they could cause their hearers to tell their friends about it, and to come back a week later. So now this earnest lady made a moral appeal to the public. So many people complained of the triviality and cheapness of radio programs, and here was a test of the public's desire for real intellectual food.

"We do not believe," said Laurel, "that the American people wish to drift blindfolded into a war of atomic bombs. We have gone to the trouble and expense of setting up a publishing plant and a radio program because of our faith that there are people all over this broad land who want to be able to live at peace and who will be concerned to discover why they cannot. We do not come as dogmatists, with ready-made solutions to force into your minds, but to give a hearing to various types of thinkers who know the subject and have something vital to say.

"Our program is dedicated to the American way. We believe in freedom of discussion and in government by popular consent. We subscribe to Jefferson's motto, that truth has nothing to fear from error where reason is left free to combat it. That does not mean that we grant the use of our platform to those whose purpose it is to undermine freedom of discussion. We grant them the right to try their undermining, but we let them do it in their own papers and at their own expense.

"And the same thing applies to those who are satisfied with the world as it is, and who value their dividend checks more than a just and ordered human society. They too have their organs of opinion and make use of them. The Peace Program is intended for those men and women who consider that world wars are monstrous and horrible things, and that the coming of two of them only twenty-one years apart indicates something vitally and fundamentally wrong with our society. If you agree with this statement, stay with us, and let us have peace."

Billy Burns the announcer was standing in front of the speaker with his watch in hand. Thirty seconds before her time would be up he signaled by raising his arm, and she began her peroration. When he dropped his arm she finished, and he began:

"Ladies and gentlemen, you have been listening to Mary Morrow, novelist and magazine writer, speaking on the opening quarter-hour of the Peace Program. This program has been set up by a group of friends who believe that world wars have their causes and that these causes can be discovered and remedied. The program will be heard over Station WYZ, New York, at seven every Thursday evening. It may also be heard over other stations which consent to carry it.

"Next Thursday's speaker will be Sir Eric Pomeroy-Nielson, English baronet, now visiting this country. Sir Eric was a flyer in World War I, and was severely wounded. Two of his sons were flyers in the recent war, both wounded, so you may believe that he knows about war. He is well known as a playwright and journalist, and will report to you on the English attitude to the hoped-for peace and the feared next war. The following week the eminent violinist, Hansi Robin, will play for you, and will answer questions on the subject of war and peace. Other programs of equal interest are being planned.

"We wish to inform you also that the Peace Group has arranged for the publication of a small weekly paper, to carry these broadcasts and make it possible for you to pass them on to your friends. This is to be a small four-page paper, devoted to the subject of world peace. We have put the price so low that no one who wants it will have to do without it. The price is fifty cents per year, which means that each copy will cost slightly less than one cent. Since fifty cents is inconvenient to send in the mail, we suggest that you send a dollar and list one friend as well as yourself. Or you may send five dollars and list ten persons. You may order it in bundles, one hundred for one dollar, and distribute it in your club, your school, your labor union or place of business. If you want to be munificent, you may send us your local telephone book and put everybody in your town on our mailing list.

"This paper, which is called *Peace*, is now in type, all but the broadcast of Mary Morrow, which has just been taken down by a stenographer. Tomorrow morning the printer will put it into type and the paper will go to press. We hope to start mailing tomorrow night. The address is easy to remember: Box One Thousand, Edgemere, New Jersey. You don't have to put anything else on the envelope; just Box One Thousand, Edgemere, New Jersey.

"And now our time is up. We thank you for listening and hope that you found it worth while. Let us have peace."

V

Well, they had got through alive, and they were all smiles and congratulations. They had put their hearts into it, and things began to happen right off the bat. The phone rang; it was Mr. Archibald, congratulating them on the broadcast; it was good, and they were proud of it. And then another jingle; it was a Mrs. Meyer Herzkowitz in New York; she wanted them to print a thousand copies of the paper for her, and she would mail them a check in the morning. So it went; they had only two telephones and these weren't enough, but it was almost impossible to get more on account of postwar shortages. The ladies would have to go, one after another, and exercise their charms upon the telephone company manager. This was a public service, something different from the usual appeals to such officials.

They had brought a basket with a picnic meal, and they took turns eating and answering phone calls. It was most exhilarating; no fewer than three persons were sending telephone books of small towns, and the group began to doubt if the ten thousand copies of the paper they had planned to print would suffice. The printer had known where he could get newsprint, provided they would put up the money; that being what their million dollars was for, they had put up for all the paper he could find, and it was stored in a warehouse in the town. In the morning they would tell him to run the press day and night.

Then they all had a good laugh. There was a telephone call for Miss Morrow, and Freddi, who answered, reported it was a man with a voice like a bassoon. Said the bassoon, "Is this Miss Morrow? My name is Harold Partridge and I wrote making you an honorable proposal of marriage, and you didn't answer." Said Laurel, "I am truly sorry, sir, but I am already married and have a son more than two years old. The thing for you to do is to help circulate our paper." Mr. Partridge was profuse in his apologies and promised to send in an order. "Nobody can say I am not a salesman," said Mary Morrow to Billy Burns.

Their minds were full of images of men and women for hundreds of miles around hastening to put folding money into envelopes and taking them out to the mailbox at the corner. A marvelous system in Megalopolis, the mail was collected every hour or so and taken to a substation, where it was put into a projectile and shot through a tube, reaching the main post office in a few seconds. As it happened, that main post office was right across the street from the Pennsylvania Railroad Station, and it had words graven upon its front, telling the world that not rain nor snow nor hail should stay these carriers from the swift completion of their appointed rounds. This meant that letters for Box 1000, Edgemere, would come out on an early morning train. The postmaster of the town had been notified of the storm that was going to hit him and had promised to have a couple of assistants on hand. The peace lovers, for their part, had half a dozen girls pledged to welcome the expected mail, and others were awaiting a possible call; most of them were middle-aged women, but they would all be "the girls," and no middle-aged woman had ever been known to object to that.

VI

Everything went according to schedule. Freddi went to the post office in the morning and came back exultant with two sacks full of mail. Yes, the American people didn't want another war! The sacks were emptied onto the tables, and all the group would have liked to pick up a few letters and tear them open; but there were rules that must never be broken. No letter must be read until it had been through the mill! The girls must take them and slit them with a sharp paper cutter and arrange them in long rows, then open them one at a time, set the money in the center of the table, mark the amount on the letter with a blue pencil, then fasten letter and envelope together with a clip—for someone, especially a foreigner, might have put the address on the envelope and failed to put it on the letter.

The bundles of letters must be taken to the stencil cutter, and only after that might even one of the "Big Four" be permitted to handle them. Every word had to be read by some qualified person, for in addition to an order it might contain advice, suggestions, questions, or further offers. Perhaps somebody might be offering to put up another million dollars—who could guess? The final authority, and the one to answer important questions, would be Lady Nielson, for the radio had been her idea, and it would remain her darling and her pet. It might run away with the whole show—again, who could guess?

The letters were ample reward for a year's thinking and planning. They were full of enthusiasm, and only a very few were hostile.

People wanted to help—all kinds of people, old and young, rich and poor. There weren't many business letters that first day, for they had been mailed at night, from people's homes. There were letters on fashionable stationery, in the tall handwriting which is esteemed by the rich because it uses up a lot of paper; there were letters in the trembling handwriting of the aged, and others from working people who hadn't mastered the problem of whether the "e" comes before the "i" or after it. People liked the program, and some of them liked the broadcasters; several marked their letters "personal," but it had been agreed that all letters that came to Box 1000 would go through the mill. Even the letters from young ladies who wanted to meet Billy Burns and enclosed their photographs to show what nice-looking young ladies they were!

VII

The mill began to grind. It ground out stencils, and these were put in long rows in boxes and carried to the stamping machines. Meantime, at the printshop, the press was turning out papers, and a boy was bringing loads of them. Papers and stencils were fed into the stamping machine—Sam de Witt had also procured this machine, and had done it at cost. The machine stamped each paper in the corner which had been left blank for that purpose, and presently there was a bundle of them, to be tied up and dumped into the same mail pouches in which the letters had been brought from the post office.

Four times that day sacks of letters were dumped out on the tables. Because papers were bigger than letters, more empty sacks had to be brought; presently the post office had no more, and the bundles had to be piled up in a car, and then the postmaster had to cry for mercy. He was going to need more help, more room, more everything; this business would mean that his office would acquire a higher classification and he would receive a higher salary, so it was a great day for him too.

All Edgemere had listened to the broadcast, the first that had ever come from this town, and the first time it had been mentioned on the air since the big fire several years ago. All Edgemere liked what it had heard, or so the Tipton family reported. More girls were needed, and Mrs. Tipton produced them; before long the workroom of the Peace office might have been the sewing circle of the First Methodist Church. But one big difference, no conversation!

A very strict rule, you had to have your mind on those letters and what they contained. You got a dollar and a half an hour out of it, and then when you got home you could tell family and friends all about it, and soon all the town would know that those people were taking in money by the basketful, so much that they had a hard time counting it. Two men went with it to the bank—one of them that tall, thin, young Jewish fellow, and he had a permit to carry the Luger pistol he had brought back from Germany. That was against the Army rules, but the way the GIs got round it, they took the thing apart and mailed each part separately to somebody at home.

That is the sort of talk you hear in small towns. Everybody knows everybody else, and what everybody is doing and saying and thinking. Everybody keeps careful watch over the conduct of the others, especially if they belong to the churches—which is, in effect, asking for it. So the church girls all knew that Billy Burns' real name was Budd, and that he was married to Mary Morrow, so it didn't seem quite decent to go on calling her "Miss." They had a little boy who was soon to be brought to The Willows. Miss Morrow must be the one who was putting up all the money, for she signed all the checks, but with another name. They had been spending money like water, and now they were taking it in as if it grew on trees.

They had employed a bookkeeper from New York, and he was boarding with one of the church members, so it wouldn't be long before the town knew whether it was true what they said, that they weren't going to make any profit out of this business. Sir Eric and Lady Nielson were each being paid a salary of three hundred dollars a month, and surely anybody ought to be able to live like a lord and lady on that. Lawyer Pegram said they really were what they claimed to be, he had read about them in the papers; he said that a baronet wasn't as high as a lord or a duke, but still he was pretty high, and it didn't make any difference if they were Socialists, and if their son was a Labour member of Parliament. Socialists were not as bad as Communists, or so Mrs. Tipton insisted, and she believed in God.

VIII

All this the newcomers learned through their laundryman, who called once a week for the wash, and delivered it three days later. He would stop in the kitchen, the weather being cold, and unless Laurel was very busy she would come and chat with him. She found him what is called a "character," and insiders know that to a novelist such a find may be as valuable as a gold mine. Nina, who lived on the ground floor, would stroll in too, because she wanted to understand America. They had agreed to live in this town for five years, and must keep on good terms with the population. Also, they were both women and liked to hear what was doing.

Comrade Tipton—they didn't learn his first name—had traveled widely and knew human nature from selling it patent medicines. He had read many books, and now he lived among people most of whom confined their reading to the sports pages and comic strips. He was a philosopher and looked with amused tolerance upon the delusions of his fellow townsmen. There were a few intellectuals in the place, he reported—an elderly lawyer, the young chap who kept the stationery shop, and an Italian refugee who blacked shoes at one of the barber shops. But mostly the townsmen were conventional people, against whom their laundryman carried on a secret, underground war, putting dangerous ideas into their heads without their realizing what was happening to them.

He was ready to do the same thing with half a dozen innocents who had been dropped, as it were, by parachute into his neighborhood. He regarded them as innocents because they were not "libertarians" like himself; they believed in governments, and expected to achieve reforms through governments, not realizing that governments were themselves the evil. Governments were the cause of wars; governments had authority to conscript men and order them to kill one another; therefore, trying to abolish war through governments was like trying to ward off the effects of arsenic by taking more of the same.

This he told them casually, and with a smile; he never tried to convert anyone, he said, because people resent conversion. "I'm just sorry to see you waste your time," he said. "If you believe in government, sooner or later you will be drawn into politics; you will help to elect somebody to an office, and then you will see him serving the little group that put up his campaign funds."

"What would you have us do?" inquired Laurel.

"If you really want the people to acquire power, you must organize them for independent action."

"You mean for revolution?"

"Oh, no, for that is just more government, more authority. What counts is economic power, and the way to it is by free associations, such as consumers' co-operatives. When co-operators have reached the goal of producing and distributing all their necessities they are on the road, and the only road, to pure democracy."

"Yes, Comrade Tipton, but don't they have to protect themselves politically? You must know that the people of Italy had a marvelous system of co-ops, but when Mussolini took power he wiped it all out overnight."

"When the people are so ignorant that they can be fooled by a Mussolini, there is no hope for them by any route. Mussolini would have overridden a vote just as well as he overrode the co-ops."

So there they had material for a hot argument. Comrade Tipton would have stayed all afternoon, forgetting his dingy white delivery wagon and its engine growing cold. But Laurel had a hundred letters to read and had to excuse herself. "Someday a little later," she promised, "after our work is organized."

The old gentleman with the white mustaches apologized. As he was going out he said, "I meant to tell you, your two gentlemen are going to be invited by the Kiwanis."

When Nina heard about this she asked, "What is a Kiwani?"

IX

Saturday's mail was bigger than Friday's, and Monday's promised to be bigger yet; the little office was in danger of being swamped. They were saved by a peculiarity of the religious life of this small town. The Methodists wouldn't work on Sunday, and neither would the "Christians," known as "Campbellites" to the rival sects. But one of the girls who had been hired was a Seventh Day Adventist; she was expecting the imminent Second Coming of the Lord and took literally the injunction to keep holy the seventh day. So she wouldn't work on Saturday but would work on Sunday, and indeed was pleased to do so, because it rebuked the unbelievers, the erring souls. Members of her Church were usually out of work on Sunday because of the evil practices of a world which knew not the true Gospel. The Adventists were honest folk, and once they had been taught the job they were helpful to a radio enterprise which made its appeal on Thursdays and therefore would have busy Sundays. The Sunday workers coming wouldn't meet the Saturday workers going, so there would be no chance for controversy.

The flood of mail continued through the week. They were getting New England now, and the Middle Atlantic states, and as far west as Chicago. The reason was that three other stations had used the program—for a price, of course. That was a way to get rid of money quickly, and it was what they were in business for. They got up a circular describing what they were doing and mailed it to every radio station in the country, with a letter inviting them to tune in on the program and see what they thought of it. This brought another lot of mail and a stack of rate cards.

They saw that they had a business on their hands, and it was more than Nina could handle. They must have a business manager, and the elegant Mr. Archibald made them a present of a young gentleman who was just out of Harvard and whose mother was in the New York Social Register. He was impeccable in speech and costume—and he wasn't anything else that you would have expected from such an introduction. He wasn't blasé but, on the contrary, full of eagerness; he had what he called "the social-justice bug," and had been unhappy because his mother insisted that he was not to sit around reading books all day but must go to selling bonds, a most odious business. Here was a magical way by which he could earn his keep and at the same time think about the things that interested him.

Gerald de Groot was his name—he was from one of those old Dutch families. He went to live, of all places, with a former patent-medicine vendor turned laundryman. The Tiptons had a spare bedroom because their daughter had gone to teach school in New York. Gerald liked bean suppers, and he liked to sit up half the night arguing with genuine members of the working class. He and Comrade Tipton never got tired of talk; "bull sessions," they called them, and one of the bulls had white whiskers and the other had smooth-shaven cheeks of a lovely rose-pink. Apparently the human spirit gets its stimulation from something new and different; Australia was as different from Harvard as Harvard was from Australia.

X

The syndicate business was booming too. Rick had engaged a competent middle-aged secretary to attend to his large correspondence, and another woman who would look after the files. He had Philip Edgerton as an assistant, and two youngsters just out of college as manuscript readers—recommended by a professor of literature in Alston's college. There was a flood of mail coming in; it appeared that the woods were full of people who wanted to write, and especially on the subject of what was wrong with the world. Authors told their friends, and these in turn told other friends, and so ad infinitum. Rick wrote a letter to the Authors' League of America, telling them about the enterprise, and after investigation they published the letter in their *Bulletin.* He wrote to his friends in England and to the P.E.N. clubs all over the world. He had a circular telling the story, which saved a lot of time. He sent it to professors of literature in hundreds of colleges, and also to college publications; here were the young writers, the writers of the future, and he wanted to get hold of them first. He would get an awful lot of trash, but the preliminary readers would weed that out.

They didn't dare to hope for genius, they would be satisfied if they could find real talent, a spark of any sort of life embodied in words, melody or feeling in verse, laughter or satire, anything alive; anything in story form that showed knowledge of some part of an infinitely varied world; an insight into the character, or understanding of the social process, of the class struggle, of politics or industry, of war or peace; anything new, odd, strange, touched with that mysterious thing called personality. Mostly, of course, you were disappointed; you got the commonplace, the dull; you got writers imitating other writers; you got people trying to earn a living the easy way—pitiful people whose lives were narrow and who dreamed of escape by this literary route. There were some whose visions were grandiose and exciting, but who had no trace of skill to put them into words; they used shop-worn symbols, stirring to them, but which left the experienced reader cold.

The printed word had been Rick's delight all his life, so he loved this job. For the first time he was entirely on his own; no editor, no publisher, no stage producer or man of money to tell him what the public wanted. Rick could choose what he thought was good, and he had the power to get it before the public in one form or another. He pretty well lost himself in the work. He would get up late, have his coffee, glance through the morning paper, and then go at his mail. In midmorning the secretary would come for dictation, and bring a load of stuff to be signed. After lunch he would read the immediate things, and later in the afternoon he would walk to the office, his only form of exercise. He would see what was going on there, consult with Philip and the others, and sign important letters. At dinner there might be an author or two, and talk about the various enterprises and how they were going; in the evening, unless there was somebody very important, Rick would excuse himself, put on his pajamas and dressing gown, stretch himself out on the bed with his head propped on a pillow, and read, read, read.

When he found something good he would call his wife or Laurel or Lanny. He was extremely conscientious and worried over things that were good and yet not quite good enough. He was haunted by the possibility that he might overlook some spark of talent; that he might be repelled by crudity and miss the first signs of originality. A great chance might come only once or twice in a year's work; if somebody else got the prize, the editor who had passed it up would put on sackcloth and ashes and go to the Wailing Wall.

XI

Philip was a treasure; he and Rick fitted like hand and glove. Philip loved books just as Rick loved them; he delighted in the hunt for good literature as other men delight in the hunt for gold, for buried treasure, for the secrets of the stars or of the atom. If he found something especially good he would call Rick on the telephone or come running over to the house to get Rick and the others to read it. He never wearied of talking shop—which meant to him the business of finding words that had life in them, and then getting them before the public and getting the public's reaction.

But you can't have everything in this world; and when you employ a man you have to take his family too—especially when you are living out in the country, a group set apart. Philip Edgerton had a wife— and oh, how the other ladies didn't like Alma Edgerton! Alma hadn't the slightest interest in what her husband was doing, and hadn't the brains to be interested even if she had had the desire. What Alma wanted was to be the most beautiful, the most statuesque, and the most socially elegant person in her ken. She wished to move only in the highest circles, and had been pained at the prospect of living in a "dump" like Edgemere, N. J. They had found an apartment in which they could manage to exist; but who was there to know, and where were they to go? Manifestly, no place but The Willows; and at that place they talked nothing but the bureau, the paper, and the radio programs. Alma was like the Englishmen in Bernard Shaw's *Man and Superman* who were bored to death in heaven but insisted on staying there because they thought they owed it to their social position.

No one ever saw Alma that her blond hair hadn't been adjusted to the last strand, her complexion tinted, and her lips smeared with all they could carry. She would sit and pose, turning her head sideways so that you could see her elegant profile; she would move with stately grace across the room. She didn't say much, because she knew that her remarks wouldn't make a good impression; but she would watch, and when anyone was looking she would put on her show.

Whom was she trying to fascinate? Was it Rick? Was it Lanny? Or was it some distinguished visitor? Gradually the suspicious ladies made up their minds that it wasn't sexual at all; it didn't matter whether it was a man or a woman, an old one or a young one; what Alma Edgerton wanted was to be gazed at. She wanted to imagine someone asking, "Who is that lovely creature?" Then she would be in heaven—and not bored.

How had Philip come to marry such a woman? Well, how could one ever know what any man would marry? Presumably he had been young and had thought her as wonderful as she thought herself. They had two boys, and Alma was sure they were wonderful because they were hers. She had taught them the same idea, and so they were two spoiled brats. Fortunately they had no social ambitions and did not want to come to The Willows.

What did Philip make of such a marriage, and what was his home-life? He was proud and never said a word about it. Presumably he shut himself up in his room and read. His friends were polite to his wife, and that was all he could ask. He seldom spent any money on himself; Alma spent it. He was getting three hundred and fifty a month, about the same as he had got in New York, and living was much cheaper here. He was getting more than his boss got; but then Nina was working too, so they had a double salary. Did that irk Alma, and would she have liked to have a job too? She had a Negro maid in to do the dirty work, while she rested in bed or attended to her beauty. She listened to the radio a lot, especially the soap operas. In the afternoons she put on her best and went shopping—and the towns-people did not fail to look at her, especially the men. She got what satisfaction she could from this and possibly managed to forget how far below her they all were in social station.

"Poor Philip!" said Laurel and Nina, those superior intellectual ladies. They wanted to change the whole world, but they had no idea how to change one marriage!

25

Breathing of the Common Wind

I

THEY were getting ready the next broadcast and the next paper. It was a lesson they learned right away, that when you had a weekly printing job there was never any respite. The week sped by, and a new Thursday came treading on the heels of the old. You couldn't enjoy the fan mail because you had to be thinking about keeping up to the standard, and applying the various criticisms and suggestions to the next issue. Even a small four-page paper was a task if you tried to have it good; you worried about whether it would be good enough, and which was the best among the assortment of articles. Was this too radical, was that too obvious? The printer became an enemy, calling you on the phone and saying he must have copy.

Rick took things as hard as if he hadn't been a veteran journalist. Hitherto the editors had had the final say, but now the responsibility was his alone. Now it was his turn on the radio—and dammit, what was an Englishman allowed to say over an American radio? Hitherto he had always said what he jolly well pleased; but now there were a thousand traps in his path, and one misstep might stymie the whole enterprise. When you spoke to Americans you were speaking to foreigners, and don't be fooled because they used a language resembling your own. You were speaking to Irish, and Germans, and fifty other nationalities and tribes, and to schoolchildren who had read about Valley Forge and Benedict Arnold, and how the redcoats had burned the village called Washington and no doubt had eaten the pigs that scavenged its muddy lanes.

Rick was to have more time than Laurel had had, for the reason that Billy Burns wouldn't be giving so long a spiel. It had been decided that the best way would be for Billy to ask questions; Billy had a proper American accent, and if he asked a question, that would take some of the curse off an Englishman's answers. The Big Four held a consultation and framed questions with the same care they would have given to framing the Charter of the United Nations.

The baronet's subject was going to be the attitude of Britain toward world peace. He was going to say that the attitude would of necessity be determined by America, for Britain was a poor country now, and it was an old British saying that he who pays the piper calls the tune. ("Surely they won't object to my saying that, will they?") Then he was going to be asked about the attitude of British Labour to the problem; and immediately there arose the question of how they were to spell the name. Over the radio it didn't matter, but it would go into the paper, and would the Americans grant the British Labour party the right to spell it in its own way, or would they think it was an affectation, or perhaps a misprint? And were you going to say British Labour and American Labor, and would you labour or labor to get your broadcast right?

II

Thursday came, as Thursdays have been doing since the days of the god Thor for whom they were named. Extra chairs were crowded into the studio for the friends who wanted to see as well as hear. Sir Eric arrived—a tallish, slender, dark-haired man, distinguished looking and dressed for the occasion; his wife had pinned a pink carnation in his buttonhole—and was that politically significant? He took his seat before the microphone and sat as still as death while the amiable Billy Burns once more told the public what the Peace Program was, and why a British baronet who had had to get along for almost thirty years with a crippled knee didn't want war for his grandchildren.

Then began the questions. "Sir Eric, will you tell us what is the attitude of the British government toward the problem of world peace?" And then, "Sir Eric, will you tell about the attitude of the British Labour party toward the problem?" Sir Eric answered that he thought the attitude of all Labor parties throughout the world was much the same; all of them hated war and were seeking ways to prevent it. Wherever Labor ruled, there would be agreements for reduction of armaments and for settlements through the United Nations. But unfortunately, in the totalitarian countries, Labor had nothing to say about its own affairs; strikes were forbidden, freedom of discussion was unknown, and the question you had to consider was not

what Labor wanted, but what thirteen men in the Kremlin wanted.
And then, "You think that those men in the Kremlin may want
war?"

"I don't know what they want and I have no way of finding out.
Even if they would tell me I wouldn't know whether to believe
them, and I wouldn't know whether they might change their minds
tomorrow. That is the difference between a totalitarian and a free
country; we in Britain and you in America have a public opinion, and
nobody has to be in any doubt as to what we think and want. But
totalitarian countries operate in the dark, and we can only guess about
them. I am guessing that the Politburo wants things that it cannot get
without war, and we have the task of convincing them that they cannot get it any other way. That makes a tragic situation for us Britons.
We are right between what will be the firing lines if war starts, and it
means that we shall have to spend on weapons what we had hoped to
spend on making our people comfortable and well."

"You think then that the question of war or peace depends entirely
upon Russia?"

"I wouldn't put it that way. I think the Russian leaders are moved
by fear as much as by hate. They are afraid of a revival of Fascism;
and I think that to the extent that we nationalize our industries and
bring real democracy to our country—democracy in industry as well
as in politics—we may be able to convince the Russians that we are
not out to unseat them. It is contrary to their dogmas to believe this,
but facts are stubborn things and may convince even the Politburo."

"Do you think this same method of nationalization should be tried
by America?"

"I am not here to advise Americans. I am a visitor and I do not
know your country very well. I can speak with authority concerning
British Labour and what is in their minds, because I have been a part
of that movement since my youth. I know that our people passion-
ately want peace. I believe that is the case wherever the working
people are free and can discuss public issues and educate their fellows.
The economic factors determine that. A publicly owned economy is
a public servant; it produces for the people's own use and its principles are those of co-operation. An economy that is privately owned
and is operated for profit is unable to pay its people enough to buy
its total product; so it is forced to find foreign markets and is the
victim of crises and slumps as soon as it fails to do so. That makes it
a genuine danger to peace."

III

This last sounded pretty much like telling Americans, and so Billy Burns made a joke of it, and Sir Eric shied away. He came back to British Labour, and explained the psychological problem that now confronted the British movement. The workers had hated and distrusted the bosses and had followed their program of "ca' canny," or taking things easy. But now the coal industry was being nationalized and others would follow quickly, and the workers would have to change their minds and realize that they were toiling for themselves and not for masters.

"That is something worth watching by the rest of the world," said the speaker—he didn't say "by Americans." He explained that the future of the workers' movement depended upon it; the advantage of co-operation over competition lay precisely in that mental change. Peace depended upon it, for peace was international co-operation replacing international competition. Peace depended upon the nations learning to trust and help one another, instead of trying to exploit and plunder one another. Peace meant willingness to work and produce wealth instead of trying to get it away from somebody else. The hope of peace lay in the mood of Labor rather than in the mood of speculators, profiteers, and collectors of rent and interest.

"Then you think, Sir Eric, that world peace depends upon the awakening Labor movement?"

"I wouldn't confine it to one class. We in Britain set out upon a definite program to win over the middle classes; to convince them that they would have more happiness and security in a co-operative world. We have also won over members of the upper class, so-called. It happens that I myself, through no merit of my own, am a member of that class. The title means nothing to me, and the only reason I use it is because I have sadly learned that the people in my homeland will pay more attention to what Sir Eric says than to any possible wisdom from plain Rick, which is what my friends call me. I hope the same thing is not true in democratic America." There might have been a tiny bit of irony in that, but Sir Eric tried not to show it in his tone.

It was the announcer's turn, and he told about the Peace Program, and named Hansi Robin as the guest for the following week. He told about the paper, and how it was booming; they had managed to get all the copies into the mail but had pretty nearly broken their backs.

He told about the encouraging mail and thanked all the writers. It was much more effective to refer to triumphs than it was to beg or even to hint. They had engaged additional help, being sure that people would be eager to have Sir Eric's instructive talk in print. "Remember the address: Box One Thousand, Edgemere, New Jersey."

They weren't really so sure, by any means. Rick himself was afraid of a bad reaction, for he had got the impression that America was very conservative-minded since the end of the war. He had avoided using the word Socialism in his talk, and he thought they ought to leave it out of the paper, at least until they had taught their readers what the word meant. He was even dubious about the suggestion Lanny had made, that they should follow the printed version of his talk with a poem which had been a part of the British Labour movement since its earliest days. It had been written by a humble poet named Ebenezer Elliott, called "the Corn-Law Rhymer." It had been sung at tens of thousands of meetings during more than a hundred years. It was called "The People's Anthem," and these timid friends of peace debated anxiously and finally compromised by printing no more than the first stanza:

> When wilt Thou save the people?
> O God of mercy! when?
> Not kings and lords, but nations!
> Not thrones and crowns, but men!
> Flowers of thy heart, O God, are they!
> Let them not pass, like weeds, away!
> Their heritage a sunless day!
> God save the people!

IV

Rick's fears were not justified; the flood of orders continued. Apparently Americans approved of an Englishman, provided he was modest and recognized the social position of America. They knew that England was their "unsinkable aircraft carrier," and they surely wanted to keep it afloat. They were troubled by the experiment in Socialism which the British were making, thought it was a dangerous precedent, and were sure it couldn't succeed; but meantime they couldn't let staunch allies starve. Nobody objected to the first stanza of "The People's Anthem," because it was against kings and thrones, and that was according to American traditions; the school books taught how we had got rid of them. If the anthem had said landlords and capitalists, that would have been something else again.

One immediate result of the broadcast was the coming of that invitation which Comrade Tipton had foretold. It was brought by a rotund gentleman, Mr. Puckett, who kept one of the town's two hardware stores. He was secretary of the Kiwanis, a "service club," and they wanted the honor of having Sir Eric and Mr. Burns as guests at their weekly luncheon; Sir Eric was to be the speaker. Rick, forewarned, accepted the invitation for both; it was indeed important to be on friendly terms with the people in their new place of residence, and this was a quick and easy way. Also, it was a way to learn about America, one of Rick's principal aims.

"You will find them a bunch of Babbitts," said Philip Edgerton, and that sounded forbidding. But really it wasn't so; they were very nice fellows, and put on an air of elaborate good fellowship which served all purposes for a couple of hours. The weekly luncheon was held in the banquet room of the town's best hotel, and they assembled in the lobby, each man with a round cardboard disk on which his first name was printed; it was etiquette to call him by that name. There was Edgemere's druggist, its department-store manager, its dentist, its town clerk; a garage proprietor, a doctor, the Methodist minister, and so on, some thirty men, all of the white-collar class. The main purpose was intergroup business—you scratch my back and I'll scratch yours; but incidentally they appointed committees and chipped in money and looked after small local improvements. Good fellowship was the motto, and of course they did everything to make a guest feel at home.

The meal was very American: chicken, mashed potatoes, peas, apple pie, and coffee. As he ate, Lanny couldn't help recalling that it was the same meal the American Army had served to Hermann Göring on the day he had surrendered. The menu had been published and had caused something of a flurry; people had said we were pampering that gross creature. The Army's answer had been that that was what the quartermaster had provided for that day, and you ate that or you ate nothing. It was the same here at Switzer's Inn—you weren't asked what you wanted, your plate was put before you.

Very probably they had never had a baronet before, and perhaps had never seen one. They were curious about him but wouldn't show it; they were playing the game of democracy, American style. His card read "Rick," and no "sir," no sir! They patted him on the back and told him he was welcome to the town. They gave him a slip with a printed version of the songs they would sing, so that he could join in. When he got up to speak they gave him a good round of applause, and they listened attentively to what he had to say.

He didn't mention his business here; he would have thought that bad taste. They would want to know about England; what was the meaning of the Labour victory, why had the British people kicked out Churchill, and what were they going to do now. He spoke briefly, and then they plied him with questions; they all seemed to be informed and were not blind to the meaning of British precedents for America. If a nationalized coal industry could be made to work, how long would it be before the United Mine Workers would be demanding the same thing? At present the British project didn't seem to be working very well; the young miners wouldn't go back into the pits. But Rick said that was a temporary phase, the British people were known for their common sense. He told what the Labour party was doing to keep the whole working class informed as to their position and their needs.

Altogether it was a pleasant occasion, a part of that "hands across the seas" movement which had been cultivated for half a century. They would have liked to stay all afternoon and ask questions, first about Britain, then about Russia, France, Germany, and the rest of Europe. But their rule was an hour and a half; they were businessmen and had to get back to work, and the same thing must be true of a guest. They shook hands all round, and the baronet and his unassuming friend Billy were assured that Edgemere was proud of having been put on the radio map.

V

Having accepted the invitation of the white-collar class, of course they couldn't turn down the working class; they came to one of Mrs. Tipton's bean suppers. This was America too; it was democratic, and couldn't have been anything else if it had wanted to. Also it was bisexual, and couldn't have been anything else, since it was a woman who cooked the beans. There was a steaming bowl of them, ladled out on paper plates, and there were sandwiches made of whole wheat bread, peanut butter, and leaves of lettuce. Also, something out of the ordinary, there was grape juice served in paper cups, because Lanny had remembered to send round a case.

All these supplies had been ordered from the People's Co-operative of Edgemere, an institution which the Tiptons had founded several years ago, and which they ran as a sort of adjunct to the Socialist party, and of the Methodist Church and the Model Laundry. Needless to say, the town grocers didn't like this and had complained to the proprietor of the laundry, who hadn't dared to fire Tipton for fear that he might take the business to a rival.

All that was a part of the class struggle, which you could read about in any Socialist textbook or copy of the *Call*. You could hear innumerable stories about it at the bean supper—indeed, the only way you could avoid hearing was not to come. The Tiptons knew this town inside out and washed its dirty linen in more than one sense of the words. They had constituted themselves a center of disaffection and preached the gospel of social change day and night, wherever they went. The coming of the Peace Program and its adjuncts was the most exciting event of their lives, and a large stout grandmotherly laundrywoman welcomed it quite literally with open arms. She was a somewhat unusual laundrywoman, in that she belonged to the Daughters of the American Revolution and spoke her mind even in that ultraconservative atmosphere. That revolution, a hundred and seventy years old, was respectable.

Present were the town's three intellectuals, previously mentioned by Tipton; the elderly lawyer, the stationer, and the refugee bootblack. There was a Swedish carpenter who had worked fixing up the Peace office; there was a history teacher from the local high school, and there were half a dozen students, one of them a daughter of Mr. Puckett, the Kiwanis hardware merchant. So it is that ideas get spread in a town. You can never be sure who will be the one to take them up; it can be the town's garbage collector, or it can be a son of the town's leading banker. There was a rich lady in Edgemere who sometimes came and ate beans when she might have been eating caviar; the wife of Philip Edgerton would come and eat beans because she was hoping to meet this elegant Mrs. Parmenter—the department-store Parmenters, you must understand.

VI

It was on this occasion that Comrade Tipton had his promised argument with Mary Morrow. You couldn't keep them apart, for the laundryman had been saving up ammunition for weeks, and an author of *Tendenz* novels wasn't the one to dodge a clash of opinion. Most of the company were with her, for this was a gathering of the Socialist local; Tipton was the lone individualist, or "libertarian," as he called himself, but that didn't worry him in the least. He distrusted politics because it used compulsion; he glorified the co-op because it was an exemplar of free association, the way to end the profit system without risk of setting up a police state.

He told the company about a recent experience of the co-ops in Kansas. The business crowd had proposed a law providing for the taxation of undistributed savings held by the co-operative wholesales. The individual co-operator would have been taxed again on these savings when they were added to his income. This law would have spelled the ruin of all the co-ops in Kansas and was designed for that purpose. The proposal raised a storm of protest from both the co-ops and their individual members, and the law did not pass. Said Tipton, "When one-third of all the people are banded together in co-operative enterprises they hold the balance of power in any state, and they can have their demands granted without dirtying themselves in political campaigns, where they are sold down the river by politicians they helped to elect."

To which Laurel replied very mildly, "Suppose, Comrade Tipton, that the state legislature had passed that bill in spite of all protest, what would the co-ops have done?"

"Since they had the balance of power they could have voted those legislators out of office."

"But just how do you vote a legislator out of office, Comrade Tipton? You don't find any place on the ballot where you vote against a man, do you?"

"No, you vote for some other man for that job."

"But suppose the other man was also in favor of the bill?"

"He wouldn't be; he would want to get elected."

"But how would he know, unless the co-ops made it clear to him? He would have to have an understanding with them; and even then he might turn out to be a crook."

"Indeed he might—he probably would."

"Then it seems to me the proper recourse of the co-ops would be to put up a man of their own, one whom they knew and could trust. I don't know the details about Kansas, but I'd venture the guess that the co-ops did just that, or threatened to do it, and that was why the legislators were afraid of them. If they had announced your program of refusing to soil their hands with politics, they would have been in effect disfranchising themselves; the legislators and other politicians wouldn't have paid the slightest attention to them, knowing that they had thrown away their one powerful weapon."

Lanny, watching closely, imagined that he saw the trace of a smile on the face of Mother Tipton. He could guess that she, a Socialist party worker, agreed with Laurel; but being a wise wife, she would let some other woman do the arguing.

VII

When you visited that pathetic little grocery store, situated in the poorest quarter of the town, its shelves only half full because it lacked working capital, you might form no high opinion of this form of working-class activity. But that was the way co-ops had begun, all over the world—ever since the time a hundred and two years ago when twenty-eight half-starved weavers in the old English town of Rochdale had put in a few shillings each to establish a business enterprise owned and operated by the people it served. They too had been unable to fill their shelves, but they had stuck to it because they had a principle. Anyone could join, and every member had one vote, regardless of how much money he had put in; the profits of the enterprise were returned to the members in proportion to the amount of each one's patronage. The business was done at prevailing market prices, and for cash only. The co-ops themselves did not go into politics, but their members were free to do so, and generally they did, for the reason revealed in the argument at the Tiptons'. The business groups resented the co-ops as a menace to what they were pleased to call "the American way," and presently their lobbyists would show up at the various state capitals with ingenious taxation measures designed to drive the newcomers onto the rocks.

The business-for-profit men had reason to worry, for the movement in America, slow to start, was now growing fast; it had more than five thousand units, with close to two million member families. In the Middle West it was creeping into one industry after another; the co-operative groceries had established a co-operative wholesale, for greater economy in buying; from there they had gone to producing and processing. A network of service stations had established a refinery, and then had purchased and were operating more than a hundred oil wells. There were rural electric co-ops, telephone co-ops, credit unions, and insurance associations. Comrade Tipton, a mine of information on the subject, would reel off the list: creameries, poultry raisers, fruit and grain marketers, medical and funeral associations, housing associations, campus co-ops, college bookstores—and so on and on. Altogether the amount of such business in the United States was almost a billion dollars a year.

Rick could tell them about the movement in England, for he had grown up with it; his father, considered an eccentric, had been an enthusiast for the system and had insisted upon buying all the family supplies from the nearest co-op, even though it was not very near. In

Britain the co-op wholesale was an enormous institution and had gone in for a great variety of manufactures, from shoes to the catching and canning of fish. The co-ops had nearly ten million members, which was, in proportion to population, as if America had forty million.

"An interesting thing to notice," the baronet told this little company, "how you Americans follow about a generation behind us in social change. You older people will remember Samuel Gompers and his slogan 'No politics in the unions.' Your CIO gave that up, since they backed the New Deal. But it appears that your co-ops are still officially clinging to the old English program of political neutrality, which we gave up a generation ago, for the same reason that the people in Kansas did—we had to defend ourselves against the Big Business crowd. We set up a Co-op party and elected members to Parliament. The recent victory was just as much a victory of the co-ops as it was of Labour; the two parties combined on both program and tactics and fought the campaign together."

The Swedish carpenter, Comrade Hanson, spoke up. "The change will come fast in this country. Both the CIO and the AFL are setting up co-ops for their members, and you can be sure they aren't going to be non-political. In my old country one in five of the population is a co-op member, and it would never cross the mind of anybody that the co-ops and the Social-Democratic party were anything but the same movement, one in the economic and the other in the political sphere."

After that elementary lesson the Peace people all joined the co-op grocery. They put in some working capital, so that the store could order half a dozen cases of grape juice and as many of pineapple juice for a household which intended to have denatured cocktail parties now and then. There were no dissenting votes, but there was one silent rebel, Alma Edgerton. Catch her ever being seen in that dingy little shop! Of course her defection would soon be noticed—and how Mrs. Tipton would despise that vain and empty-headed woman!

VIII

Don't think for a moment that the unassuming Billy Burns wasn't a busy gentleman these days. He had, among a score of jobs, that of answering the fan mail; he kept a stenographer busy all day long, thanking people for their praise, answering their objections, telling them what to do. He had another job, getting the names and addresses of key persons whom they would put on the free list of the paper. How did you get such names? He had to turn himself into a sales promoter and ask the advice of others in the business; he had to go to the library and look up reference books, then buy copies and bring them to the office and put a girl to work cutting stencils. In the *World Almanac* is a list of a thousand or so organizations, scattered all over America, and he had the idea of asking for the names and addresses of their members. The Authors' League of America sounded good, but unfortunately they would not give him the list. The American Peace Society sounded promising, and so, perhaps, the Anti-Saloon League; but there wouldn't be much use circularizing the American Bankers' Association.

It was necessary to use care in sending out free copies. If you sent too many, you might be classified by the Post Office Department as an "advertising medium." It was hard to see how such a judgment could be passed on *Peace*, which so far had carried no advertising at all; but you never could tell how the bureaucrats in Washington might view it. *Peace* was paying one and a half cents a copy on every single paper it mailed; when second-class entry was granted, most of this would be refunded; but the entry was slow in coming. They carefully saved the original of every subscription order; there were boxes and boxes of them piled up in a shed in back, and if an inspector came around they would take him there and let him dig to his heart's content.

Lanny got lists of foreign papers and of key persons abroad. He put two more girls at work cutting stencils all day long, putting such people on the mailing list. At the same time he would answer the fan mail, inviting likely prospects to put up part of the cost of this operation. He was becoming stingy with Emily's million. Five years mightn't be time enough to win the goal; it might take another five—and if the paper had to stop too soon there might be another war!

Now and then he would go into New York on the train—no use driving a car if your destination was the Wall Street district. He would visit the great bank where his own account, and his mother's and Marceline's, had been kept for a quarter of a century. Here also was the account of the American Peace Foundation, and an officer of the bank would take him down into the enormous vault, several stories below ground and guarded like nothing else in the world except a store of atomic bombs. The officer would stand by and watch while he opened a large safe-deposit box and took out a handful of gilt-edge securities —not without qualms as to which was the least likely to increase in value during the five-year period. He would button these in an inside pocket and take them down the street to a broker's office and order them sold "at the market." The money would be put to the account of "Laurel Creston, Treasurer," and the receipts would be duly filed and the accounts kept up to the close of each day's business. So if ever any agent of the Bureau of Internal Revenue or some other snooper came asking questions, he would find everything exactly as the law required.

IX

The group prepared a set of questions for Hansi Robin to answer in his radio interview, and Lanny made an appointment to meet Hansi in the city, to go over the questions and his proposed answers. Lanny arranged it so in order to give Bess an excuse to keep out of it gracefully. But when he arrived at the hotel where they were to meet, he discovered that his half-sister had failed to take the hint. She had come along, and she didn't make any bones about the reason. "I want to know if the Soviet Union is to be brought into this broadcast, and I want to say that if it is I shall consider it an act of great unkindness, not to say betrayal."

"Betrayal, Bess?" said Lanny. "Of what?"

"Of me and my rights in this matter. You know perfectly well what it means to me to have my husband seduced into taking a public stand on the matter."

Lanny had been trying his best to keep out of this quarrel, but he saw that he had got himself into the middle of it. Apparently there was no keeping out, for himself or anybody else; it was a world quarrel! "Hansi is forty years old," he replied as mildly as he could, "and surely it is time for him to make up his own mind what he believes."

"Hansi and I have been making a career together for twenty years, and I don't think he will deny that we have always regarded it as community property. It is true that he might have found other accompanists just as good or better, but he chose to blend our music with our marriage. He certainly knows that I have helped him, not merely with faith and enthusiasm, but with social influence and business judgment. Is that true, Hansi?"

"Yes, of course, Bess." The husband might have said more, but he didn't, and Lanny also kept silent for the same reason—that nothing he could say would help.

"All the world believes that we are at one in the cause of working-class emancipation; and now the question is, shall Hansi make a public announcement that this harmony no longer exists? So far we have managed to keep our disagreement a private matter. If it is to be dragged into the open, naturally I am concerned to know it, and I don't intend to let it happen without stating that I consider it a personal attack."

Lanny wanted to say, "You feel yourself free to voice your own opinions, Bess." But he saw the look of misery on his brother-in-law's face, and he decided that it was no third person's business to take up the gage. They were sitting in the lounge of a fashionable hotel, and even though they were well-bred persons who would never raise their voices it was no place for an argument.

X

Hansi kept silent, and Bess waited, implacable. At last Lanny took from his pocket the list of questions he had brought and quietly drew his pen through a couple of them. "Let us see if you cannot answer these others without troubling Bess," he said, and read the first one. "What do you believe to be the most important cause of war in the modern world, Mr. Robin?"

Poor Hansi knew exactly what he was allowed to say; he had been drilled in a hundred lessons at home and knew every word that would please his wife and every word that would move her to anger. He didn't want a row—how could any sensitive artist want a row with anybody, and especially with the woman he loved? Said he, "I believe there are many causes, but I am inclined to think the principal one is the fact that present-day governments are driven by economic compulsion to serve the interest of powerful groups seeking raw materials, foreign markets, and other advantages throughout the world."

"Will you give us an illustration of what you mean, Mr. Robin?"

"Well, for example, the pool of oil which I am told is the greatest in the world, situated in Arabia. Obviously all the great powers need that oil, and they are all intriguing and taking every measure short of actual war to get it for themselves. The oil belongs, or ought to belong, to the people of Arabia, and should be sold for their benefit. But there you have a feudal society, with corrupt and ignorant men holding power, and whatever money they get for the oil is spent upon luxury and display."

"And the remedy for this?"

"Manifestly some international authority, to see that the oil is made available on equal terms to all the world, and that the money is spent upon education and public improvements."

So far, so good. But presently Hansi began to hesitate and to have difficulty finding words. What could he say about any threat of war that he saw on the world's horizon now? Such a threat there surely was, and every Communist would give one answer about it and every non-Communist would give a contrary answer.

The violinist said lamely, "I think perhaps I had better write out the answers, Lanny." And Lanny knew what he meant. Hansi would write, and Bess would censor, and they might have the worst quarrel yet. It had been a mistake to invite this public statement; but Lanny hadn't realized it until it was too late.

XI

Lanny and Laurel took a trip, not a very long one, down to Princeton. Dear, kind, gentle Albert Einstein was the target for all the idealists and promoters of causes in the world. It was hard for him to say no to anybody, so he made speeches and signed manifestoes when he ought to have had his unique brain concentrated upon his unified field theory. Of course every propagandist thinks his own cause is of especial importance, and this married pair could make out a perfect case; for what good would it do to find a mathematical formula that would cover gravitation and magnetism, if all the world's great centers of civilization were going to be wiped out by atomic bombs and humanity forced to join the moles and the gophers underground?

This time Laurel didn't have to sit outside in the car. Nuclear fission was no longer the world's most closely guarded secret but had become the world's most notorious reality. Something just had to be done, and the physicists had formed themselves into an association to try to make an impression upon the public mind; the discoverer of the special and the general theory of relativity held himself the most responsible of all men, and was signing appeals to selected persons of means, trying to persuade them to put up two hundred thousand dollars to be used in awakening the civilized world to its peril.

And here came a man and a woman who had a whole million. What were they going to use it for? The great thinker sat in the elegant study which Jewish philanthropy had provided for him and for other top minds of all races and tribes. Laurel asked him, "Why are you a Zionist, Dr. Einstein?" And he answered, "I am a Zionist because I am a Jew." He told her that he had shipped all his belongings from Naziland to Palestine, hoping to go there; but now he wasn't sure whether he would ever be able to live there. Palestine had oil pipe-lines running through it, and that made it an epicenter of political earthquakes.

This elderly cherub with the halo of rebellious silver hair spoke like one of the Jewish prophets of old; but, unlike them, he was speaking to all mankind. He said that no nation and no race and no creed dared to think about itself in this crisis; this one concerned the whole of mankind, and no group could be left out. The atomic bomb had changed world unity from a poet's dream into a statesman's duty; it made international government an inescapable necessity. This new power released by modern science could transform the world into a garden of peace and plenty, or it could hurl mankind back into primitive savagery. "Choose well; your choice is brief, and yet endless!"

He plied the couple with questions as to what they were doing. He agreed with their ideas and was impressed by the practical judgment they had displayed. Of course he would come; they might set the date —and they set it right away for several weeks hence. They would go back home and engage time on as many stations as possible, and let him have ten minutes to tell the American people how they were sleep-walking on the edge of an abyss. Lanny would come for the learned elder in the car, bundle him up, and drive him to Edgemere, and when he was through they would feed him *smörgåsbord*, invite him to play a couple of Mozart sonatas, and then bundle him up again and drive him back to Number 14 Mercer Street, Princeton.

XII

Hansi Robin made his appearance and read his written answers in his usual quiet, unassuming manner. Bess didn't come—but you may be sure she was listening at home, to make certain that Lanny didn't tempt him to break faith. The answers were what Bess would call "wishy-washy," but then she would have said that about any statement that failed to proclaim the Soviet Union the champion and only hope of the workers of the world. There was just no compromising that issue; either you believed that the workers had to set themselves free by seizing the powers of government, or you didn't believe it—in which case the believers would call you names, of which "wishy-washy" was the very mildest. Much more likely they would call you a Red-baiter and a Social Fascist.

Hansi played a sad little "Lament" of his own composition, and if you knew the facts about his situation it would bring tears to your eyes. His marriage was drifting onto the rocks, and he knew it and suffered the pangs of parting in his imagination. Every day he bit his tongue off, as the saying goes. He was ashamed of his talk that evening, yet he really didn't need to be, as both Lanny and Laurel assured him. True, he dealt in generalities, peace and brotherhood and world unity;

but then, is it the business of a musical artist to be an economist and political scientist? Let him lift the standard for the wise and brave to repair to, and leave it for men of tougher fiber to carry that standard into action.

26

Mills of the Gods

I

NOT long after Pearl Harbor, President Roosevelt had proposed to the various Allied nations the forming of a War Crimes Commission, to collect evidence and provide for the trial and punishment of the guilty men. All through the rest of the war this body had been working, and in October of 1945, two months after the Japanese surrender, an International Military Tribunal brought indictments against twenty-two of the leading military and civilian officials of Germany, charging them with war crimes, crimes against humanity, and conspiracy to commit such crimes. Nürnberg was selected as the scene of the trial, and there in the Palace of Justice, one of the few buildings not destroyed in that ancient city, the most elaborate judicial procedure in all history was going on.

Captain Jerry Pendleton wrote Lanny about it. The twenty-two had been selected from among the fifty-two whom Jerry had been helping to guard at Mondorf, and he had helped bring them to Nürnberg and lodge them in the city's jail, adjoining the Palace. The purpose of the trial was to establish the guilt of Nazidom to the entire world, so there was every provision for publicity; a couple of hundred newspapermen were in attendance, and a swarm of photographers. A fascinating thing to the Peace conspirators of Edgemere, who had lived through the rise and fall of Nazism and had had it in their thoughts over a period of two decades, to read the accounts and see the faces of these men of blood and terror, who had risen so high and now had sunk so low. Had there ever been in human records such a turn of the wheel of fortune?

Lanny Budd was content to follow the events from afar. He had seen enough of these hate-filled creatures, and now he had found a labor of love, among people of love. He read the news accounts day by day and saw that the mills of the gods were grinding; he was pleased that they should grind exceeding small. How he wished that F. D. R. might have lived to watch the process; also Harry the Hop—that long-suffering man had passed from the scene of his success early in the new year. He had once told Lanny of a scene with the Boss, who had been in favor of the Army's plan of taking the war criminals out and shooting them as they were captured; it was Hopkins and Judge Rosenman who persuaded him that the wiser course would be to make a world show of it and put the record of Nazism formally and officially on the pages of history.

II

Lanny had told his father of his radio alias, and the father had been duly grateful. Now when he called on the telephone he asked for "Mr. Burns," and told the secretary, "It's his father." Robbie always asked first about the three-year-old junior Lanny, who had been brought to The Willows. Then he asked about the parents, and reported that his own family was well. Only after that would he mention business matters.

He called one afternoon while Lanny was sitting in his little cubicle in the onetime fuse factory, dictating letters in celebration of the weekly paper's passing the hundred thousand circulation mark. He told Robbie of this triumph, and Robbie in reply told of a businessman who had set his son up in charge of a brush factory and left him alone for a year; then he looked over the books and remarked, "It appears to me that you have been selling brushes at a loss." "Yes," replied the son, "but see what a big business we have done!"

After getting that off his chest, the father reported, "There is a call for you from Washington. You are to call the War Crimes Branch, Civil Affairs Division of the War Department General Staff. Ask for Colonel Josephus."

Lanny put in the Washington call, curious to know what the Army could want with him now. The voice at the other end of the wire did not explain but asked, "Could you make it convenient to come to Washington at once?" Lanny replied, "I am afraid that by the time I can get to an airport and get a plane the workday will be over." The voice replied, "Tomorrow morning will do."

Lanny glanced out of the window and saw that the weather was good; he said, "I will drive tonight. Can you make a hotel reservation for me?" He was told, "Come to the Mayflower. Your expense account will be honored."

He needed no clairvoyance to guess that they wanted information bearing on the trial, and he began searching his memory. It was hard to imagine that the Army, which had taken so many top-rank prisoners and collected so many hundreds of tons of Nazi documents, could need anything from a humble interrogation officer. They might, of course, have learned that he had been a presidential agent; but it seemed more likely that they had got word of his interrogations of General Emil Meissner and General-Major Furtwängler. He wondered, could Furt-wängler have turned against Göring, his chief?

The ex-P.A. told his wife about the call and suggested that she drive with him; she hadn't had a holiday in a long time. They both had competent secretaries and could keep in touch with the office by telephone. She said all right, so they told Nina and Rick, and then drove to the house and packed their bags. There were warm robes in the car and they would enjoy the snowy scenery, have dinner in Baltimore, and get into Washington in midevening, and perhaps take in a movie before they went to bed.

III

At nine next morning Lanny took a taxi to the Pentagon, that marvelous five-sided, five-storied building the Army had completed during the war. He didn't drive himself because he had been told about the complicated set of roads that led up to it and away from it. When you got inside there was a new labyrinth; the wits of Washington never tired of telling stories about people who had got in and never been heard from since—they were still following arrows and trying to follow directions in the four million square feet of enclosure.

But Lanny had good luck and presently was seated in the office in the War Crimes Branch, listening to the voice he had heard over the phone. It belonged to a slender young Jewish officer of the intellectual type, wearing those little rainbow cross-sections indicating that he had seen service in the ETO. It was a safe guess that he had not suffered over an assignment to collect evidence against the inventors of the crime called "genocide."

"It was good of you to come, Mr. Budd," he said; and then, with no more preliminaries, "As you doubtless know, the prosecution is closing its case against the Nürnberg war criminals, and it will then be the turn of the defense. The accused have the right to summon witnesses, and it appears that Göring has the idea that you will be in a position to testify as to his opposition to the war. Is there any truth in that?"

"There is some truth in it," replied the ex-P.A. after he had got over his surprise. "I know that Göring thought the invasion of Poland a mistake. But he refused to do anything about it; he told me that he had stuck his neck out once before, in the seizure of Prague, and had been proved wrong, so he wouldn't jeopardize his position a second time."

"It is rather difficult to see how that could help him, wouldn't you say?"

"Quite so. I am guessing that what he has in mind is a later stage, his efforts to dissuade Hitler from attacking Russia, and again his pleading for a settlement with the Allies when he saw that the war had reached a stalemate."

"You know that he did that?"

"He talked to me at length about it, and later Hitler himself confirmed it. Göring had gradually fallen out of favor with the Führer, largely because of this attitude, but also, of course, because of his failure to prevent the bombing of German cities."

"May I say, Mr. Budd, it is a little hard for us to understand how you could have been conversing with Göring and Hitler at those stages of the war?"

"Certainly, Colonel. I will tell you in confidence that in the summer of 1937 Roosevelt appointed me a presidential agent. I had for some time been posing as a Nazi sympathizer, getting information for two journalist friends, one in England and one in France. For eight years I served Roosevelt in the strictest secrecy, up to the day of his death."

"That explains the mystery. I have your record in the Army before me, but I forgot to inquire at the White House."

"I doubt if they could have told you anything, except that I had once had dinner there. At all other times I was taken into the White House by what is called the social door, and always at night. The President's man Baker attended to it."

"I see. Do you think that your testimony concerning Göring would be of any help to him?"

"I don't see how it could be. His judgment was better than Hitler's because he had a better brain, but his advice was on a purely military basis. He saw that Germany had lost the war, and he wanted to get out on the best terms possible. He wasn't thinking about justice or mercy or the saving of human lives, for such considerations did not enter into his mental make-up."

"You understand, Mr. Budd, he has no power to subpoena you. If you gave testimony, it would be because you wished to; presumably because you felt that he was entitled to have the benefit of your knowledge."

"I don't feel that way about him, Colonel Josephus. All I could testify about him is that he was a good companion and host. He has a first-rate mind and wide information. He would be pleased to hear me say all that on the witness stand, but I don't see that I owe it to him, and neither do I see how it could help to save his life."

IV

So much for that. The young officer thought it over and then started on a different line. "We have a mass of documents concerning Göring, but we haven't many eyewitnesses against him. Let me ask whether you have any knowledge that might be of use to the prosecution."

"I have been thinking about that on the way down here. I made a total of eleven trips into Germany as a presidential agent, and I met Göring on practically every trip. He seemed to enjoy my company and in some ways I enjoyed his. I have spent as much as a week at a time at Karinhall. So you see I would have a lot to recall. He is a free-spoken person and reveals himself with pride. He has a great respect for wealth and power, of the sort my father possesses; so I stood high with him from the beginning. When the Nazis took power, one of their shining marks was the Jewish financier, Johannes Robin, who had been my father's associate from the end of World War I. The Nazi who grabbed him was the Minister of Labor, Ley—as you know, he committed suicide in the Nürnberg jail just after the indictment had been read to him."

"I had accumulated a large dossier on Ley, but I didn't know about the Robin matter."

"The reason was, no doubt, that Göring got wind of it and grabbed Johannes. I went to see him and negotiated the deal whereby Johannes got out of the old prison on the Alexanderplatz by turning his entire fortune in Germany over to Göring. On the night of the Blood Purge —that was a year or so later—I was driving my car in Munich and met an SA man whom I knew. I stopped to speak to him, and at that moment three SS men leaped out of a car and shot him in the face. They took me to Stadelheim prison, where they were shooting men wholesale in the courtyard; I was sure my time had come. But apparently I must have made some impression by my insistence that I was a friend of Göring and the Führer; they kept me three days and four nights in solitary, and then took me to the city jail and kept me there for ten more. I was able to pick up news about what was going on outside—those days and nights when the Hitler gang shot some twelve hundred of their party dissidents."

"That is one crime for which we have not indicted them," remarked the official with the trace of a smile.

"I knew it was a civil war," Lanny continued, "but I had no way to know which side was coming out ahead. After the ten days they put me in a car and drove me to Berlin and put me in a prison there—I never found out the name of it. They took me down into a dungeon where they were beating and torturing people, and once more I thought my hour had struck. With an SS man on each side of me I stood and watched while they brought in an elderly fat Jew who looked like Napoleon the Third, and whom I had met socially—it was Solomon Hellstein, the Berlin representative of the great banking family. He was begging and pleading, but they stripped him naked and flung him onto a bench, and then four Nazi torturers whipped him with thin steel rods until his back was a bloody mess. I lost my head and shrieked at them that they were a disgrace to the human race. Then I was sure I had cooked my goose and would be next; but to my surprise they took me away back to my cell and left me there. Not long afterward there came Oberleutnant Furtwängler of Göring's staff—a man who rose to become general-major and was captured by our Seventh Army last year. I was surely glad to see him; he pretended to have come as a rescuer, it was all a mistake, and so on, but when he took me to Göring, that fat monster roared with laughter, and presently I realized that he had ordered me to be taken to see the beating. At first I took it for his idea of a joke, but then I decided that he had a purpose and had ordered the beating to be done so that I might witness it."

"What could that purpose have been, Mr. Budd?"

"It had to do with the younger son of Johannes Robin, whom the Nazis had grabbed and shut up in Dachau. I was trying to get him free and had appealed to Göring. Now I learned that Freddi was to be a pawn in the fat Nazi's game. Göring would free him, on condition that I would return to Paris and tell the members of the Hellstein family in that city what I had seen with my own eyes."

"Tell them! For what reason?"

"Göring believed that "the *Itzig*," as he called Solomon, had smuggled a great quantity of gold out of Germany, and he wanted to make the family return it. He knew that if I told them what I had seen they would believe me and would put up the ransom—and they did. I got

Freddi back according to promise, but they had tortured him so that he died not long afterward."

V

That was Lanny's story; he didn't tell it often, for it still gave him what people call "the creeps," even after almost twelve years. He had told it to Rick, and to his father, but never to Laurel. He could guess that Colonel Josephus would take a professional attitude toward it; he had been compiling dossiers wholesale and must have records of thousands of such crimes against humanity. He did not shudder or have to wipe any perspiration from his forehead; he said, "This strikes me as a possibly valid item of evidence, Mr. Budd. May I submit you to some cross-examination?"

"As much as you wish, Colonel."

"You can state that Göring told you he personally ordered this torturing?"

"No, I wouldn't quite say that; his phrase, as I recollect it, was that I had had an opportunity to study their penal institutions at first hand."

"But he admitted that he knew about the torturing?"

"Oh, certainly. He said I had seen their methods of dealing with a Jew *Schieber;* also he said, 'You can testify that they are effective.' "

"That, I should think, would rather bar him from any complaint if you should tell the story now?"

"I would so consider. He commented that when I told the Hellsteins in Paris, the story would be all over the city in a few hours, and his agents in Paris would know it."

"He told you that his purpose was to get the gold from the Paris family?"

"He said that explicitly—that he intended to get every mark of Solomon's money even if he had to flay him alive."

"And you told that to the Hellsteins in Paris?"

"As soon as I got there. It happened that I knew Olivie Hellstein, Madame de Brousailles, rather well; I believe she is still living in Paris, and I am sure she will confirm the story. Present, also, were her father and mother; I am not sure if they are still living. It was a painful scene. I don't know what they paid Göring, but Olivie will know. I read that poor old Solomon died in Paris not long afterward."

"Here is the situation, Mr. Budd. As a lawyer, I would call this a crime against humanity—several crimes, in fact: kidnaping, assault with deadly weapons, and extortion. It was also a conspiracy to commit those crimes. The question is, would you be willing to tell that story before the court?"

"I have been thinking about it ever since you phoned. As a result of so many years of secret work I have developed a sort of pathological attitude to publicity. It would mean unveiling my role to the public, and I shrink from that."

"Do you expect to do any more such work?"

"I hope very much that I never have to. Suppose I put it this way, Colonel: I don't *want* to tell the story, but if I am told that it is my duty to tell it, I will do so. I too have been in the Army, even though it was only with an assimilated rank."

"My own judgment is that the story should be told, and I think when I report to my superiors they will say the same."

"All right; then I will tell it."

"It would be my idea that you should accept Göring's invitation to appear as a witness for him. Tell frankly what you know about his attitude; tell anything in his favor that you wish—it can't do any harm. Then let the story of Solomon Hellstein be brought out under cross-examination. Its impact will be greatly increased that way, and since you are their witness, Göring's lawyers will not be permitted to try to impeach your testimony."

"I would much rather they were permitted, Colonel. The story is true, and I have nothing to fear from cross-examination. How soon would I be called?"

"The prosecution is closing, and Göring will be the first of the defendants to present his case. We should have to fly you to Nürnberg."

"How soon would I know your decision?"

"I am quite sure I can give it to you in the next day or two. Can you remain in Washington?" Lanny said that he could and would.

VI

The ex-P.A. reported to his wife, who had been out for a stroll, to renew her impressions of the capital of her native land: buildings with rows of white marble columns, parks with trees waiting for spring, shop windows as full of luxury goods as Fifth Avenue or the Rue de Rivoli, traffic as crowded as anywhere in the world—and behind the façade of splendor, in the center of city blocks, ramshackle, rat-infested slums set apart for Negro workers. Washington was unchanged, except for the number of men and women wearing uniforms and the number of foreign voices you heard.

Lanny told his story, including his prison misadventure. He expected Laurel to be shocked, and she was; but there was the other half of her, for which he had not made allowance—she too took a professional attitude. "Lanny, if you come out of hiding, you can tell your whole story! You can tell it over the radio!"

"Oh, good Lord!" he exclaimed.

"I have been thinking about it for some time. You have wonderful stories, and it's a shame not to make use of them. We could expand our program to a half hour and let you tell a presidential-agent story in the first part, as bait for the serious matters in the second half."

"So that's what you've been cooking up!"

"The whole bunch has talked about it, but nobody said anything because they knew you wouldn't do it. But if you once are out into the open, there'd be no reason for not doing it."

He didn't know what to say. He had been a publicity man of a sort for the past year, and he couldn't help realizing that people would like to hear behind-the-scenes accounts of F. D. R. and Harry the Hop and the rest of them; and about a P.A. who had made eleven trips into Naziland at the risk of his life; about the Berghof, and Karinhall, and the New Chancellery, Hitler and Göring and the little lame Doktor, and Hess who had flown to Scotland, and Strasser who had been shot in the Blood Purge, and Kurt Meissner who had been caught as a spy, and all the others who had risen to heaven and then sunk to hell.

"Think what it would mean to Robbie!" exclaimed the woman writer, hot on the scent of an "exclusive." When he asked what she meant she explained, "Don't you know that deep in his heart Robbie must be troubled about the reports that his son was a Nazi sympathizer and perhaps a paid agent of the enemy? Such whispers must be all over Newcastle."

"They saw me come home in uniform, didn't they?"

"Yes, but how can they know you didn't fool the Army? Rumors like that are hard to kill. If it definitely comes out that you were Roosevelt's agent, everything will be cleared up and Robbie will just about burst with pride."

"Robbie hated Roosevelt—I think as much as he did Hitler."

"Almost as much; and for you to be a New Dealer wouldn't please him at all. But this is a foreign matter and entirely different. You have been on the inside helping to win the war—he'd never get through bragging about it. If you don't believe it, call him up and ask."

VII

Lanny couldn't bring himself to talk about such a subject over the telephone. Instead, he took his wife to look at old masters in the National Gallery; and after that he had a bright idea—he called up the Shoreham and asked for Jim Stotzlmann.

Sure enough, Jim was in town. It was a matter of luck where you found him, for he spent his time between Washington and New York and Reno and Hollywood and Mexico City and Paris and the next place that happened to come into his head. He would cross the continent, dragging a fancy custom-built trailer behind him and taking little more than four days for the trip—seven or eight hundred miles a day was his stint. He had friends in every city, and made more at filling stations and "eats" joints on the way; everybody would open up to him because they liked the idea of being written about in his column that was published in several hundred newspapers. The poet Wordsworth had written that his heart leaped up when he beheld a rainbow in the sky, and here in this land of the free, people's hearts leaped up when they beheld a celebrity in a drawing-room, or driving a long aluminum house-on-wheels across the prairies and over the Rockies at a mile a minute.

The last time Lanny and Laurel had run into this scion of the great Chicago family in Washington he had said, "Oh, good!" and had taken them to Mrs. McLean's weekly shindig. That lady whose father had struck it rich was still in the ring, but on her way to death by an overdose of sleeping pills. Now Jim said, "Oh, good! You must come to Mrs. Mesta's party!" There was a new social queen, it appeared, and a much better one from Jim's point of view, for Evalyn Walsh McLean was a near-Fascist, whereas Perle Mesta came from Oklahoma City and had been converted to the Democratic party. Her money came from oil, and it came in gushes; she was the supreme provider of what Jim called "the hot-diggity hoopla."

Taught by previous experience, Lanny and Laurel had brought along their party clothes. Laurel would wear the same costume she had bought for Evalyn's party three years ago—one good thing you could say about the war, it had stopped the changes of fashion for a while. Jim came for them in his Cadillac, his secretary acting as chauffeur; when they got near the mansion—a rented one, said Jim—they found such a jam of cars that they had to get out and walk several blocks, fortunately on a mild spring night.

On the way their sponsor talked about Washington society, how it had been changing since the war, surely not for the better. New mobs were pouring in, seeking their fortunes—muleskinners from Missouri and carpetbaggers from the South, as Jim described them. "Not that I'm being snobbish," he added; "my great-grandfather was a canal boatman, and I guess as tough as they came. But this crowd is frantic to break in anywhere, anyhow. Gate-crashing has become such a nuisance that people issue cards and won't let even their best friends in without them; the cards specify the number to be admitted." He added that he had sent his secretary to have his card fixed up for three.

So they got in; and there was the oil lady from Oklahoma, short, plump, brunette; she wore black silk lace and open-work black gloves coming halfway up her arms, and she shone like a lighthouse with diamonds. She was pretty—but don't mistake the determination in those dark eyes. She was a fighting lady, fighting for prestige, for glory. To come to Washington with a name like Perle Mesta, née Skirvin, and make your way to the top of the social heap—that took the determination of a Napoleon and the strategy of a general staff. To have a Democratic President to dinner one evening and the Republican leader of the House the next evening; to have the Chief Justice and three other justices of the Supreme Court, seventeen senators, and a dozen diplomatic stars at the same reception—that was fame, that was something to which a woman would devote her life and upon which she would spend a fortune.

How did she manage it? Not by money alone; there were many other mansions where champagne flowed out of fountains and where fifty turkeys and as many hams were cooked and carved for a single social event. No, it took brains; you had to know how to flatter and please people, and how to make them talk about your doings. At one of her parties you might hear General Ike sing "Drink to me only with thine eyes," or Senator Pat Hurley, ex-muleskinner from New Mexico, give his famed Indian warwhoop. At the party attended by Lanny and Laurel was an enormous sturgeon which had been flown from the Black Sea, cooked in the biggest oven in Washington, and served whole on a silver platter which it took four men to carry. A hundred and seventy guests dug into this carcass and helped themselves, and went away and talked about it for days. So long as oil flowed, and sturgeons swam, and refrigerators froze, the world would welcome Perle Mesta's hospitality. "Two-party Perle," they called her, because she had shifted sides and still had Republican friends.

VIII

"Don't forget that you are a novelist," Lanny had said to his wife with a grin; so she left him to his own devices and let herself be squired by America's one and only millionaire newspaper columnist, who knew everybody. He made a lioness of her. "This is Miss Morrow, Mary Morrow, you know, author of an anti-Nazi novel." It was the first time Laurel had ever been so introduced, and she watched with her shrewd, darting eyes. Everybody pretended—oh, yes, of course, how interesting!—but she doubted if a single one of them had read her book. Eminent statesmen whose pictures she had seen in the papers would beam upon her, bend over her small figure and ask her opinion of the present policy toward conquered Germany and what she thought of the possibility of Nazism surviving underground.

It wasn't all pretense; it was the busy gentlemen's way of sounding out public opinion and getting ideas. Washington's political pot boiled all day and most of the night; the city had become the capital of the world, and these black-clad legislators and officials carried the world's fate in their pockets. Half a dozen would get off in a corner and hold an informal committee meeting while chewing up Mrs. Mesta's sturgeon and washing it down with her California champagne. Several diplomats would huddle in another room, and try to figure out how to improve their chances of a loan from the alphabetical agencies that ruled their future. "Why don't you take up a collection in this room?" inquired a lady who had had enough champagne to make her witty.

The ladies were here, one to each gentleman. Mostly they were wives, for political parties have to be decorous. Laurel reported that the wives looked as if they had been married when the statesmen were young; many of them had not kept up with the intellectual progress of their lords and masters. But they could all put on the clothes, and Laurel, who had been wandering about in the shops that morning, knew what it cost to put such items on display. She had been telling her husband about the wickedness of it: $975 for a scarf, plus $195 tax; a flexible bracelet with clasp, $4400, plus $880 tax; dainty sunburst earrings, $5500, plus $1100 tax; a natural Russian sable wrap, custom-made, $50,000, plus $10,000 tax; you could even have a fashionable mink coat for your dog, $246 plus $49.20 tax. You didn't bring your dog to a reception, but you would walk him in the park and meet other ladies, who would judge your social position by your dog's clothing as well as your own.

All Washington went by what was called protocol. New statesmen, new officials, new diplomats came, and their rank was predetermined. Every hostess had to know about this, and there were authorities who would furnish her the "dope" for a fee. There was a story of an ambassador who gave a dinner in honor of Toscanini, and invited so many high-ranking persons that he had to put the maestro at the bottom of the table. There was a story of a hostess who made a dreadful faux pas at an afternoon affair, setting one great lady to pouring tea and a lady of lower rank to pouring coffee. Too late it was explained to her, "Coffee outranks tea."

IX

It was the job of a woman novelist to observe all this and store it in her memory so that someday it might become "local color." It was not her business to preach. She wouldn't remind the gross feeders that millions were starving in Europe. She wouldn't show disgust at the swilling of liquor, but enjoy the jest about the three major parties in Washington—the Republican party, the Democratic party, and the Cocktail party. She would observe the large powdered bosoms, and if some of the powder had got onto a black velvet costume she would pretend not to see it. She would accept her role as literary lioness and not pin anybody down as to the names of her books. She would note the variety of perfumes, and recall the labels she had seen in the luxury stores, and wonder which was which—Frenzy, Menace, Innuendo, Whirlwind, Intoxication, Tailspin, Tigress, My Sin. A hundred-million-dollar industry had been built in America on the basis of titles such as these, and here you got the end products through your nose. No lady of refinement would mention the fact—if she knew it—that the smells were manufactured from a substance called ambergris, the result of indigestion suffered by whales.

Some of these powdered and perfumed ladies were kindly, and several had ideas. Laurel met one who actually had read her novel satirizing the Nazis; this lady was the tall and gray-haired wife of a senator from New England, and she said, "My dear, you take life too seriously. Believe me, the world isn't worth it. People won't do anything for you, and they won't appreciate what you do for them. You will only get wrinkles in your face, like me, and then men won't look at you any more."

Laurel would have liked to say that she had caught one man and that was enough; but she was guarding her tongue. "Come and see me some time," said the lady, and Laurel promised to do so, and moved on to another group. There was the wife of another senator, this time from the Rocky Mountains, and she looked as if she had walked all the way alongside a pack mule. She was expressing her opinion of men, in the presence of several of them. "Trust a man? I wouldn't trust one as far as I could th'ow a bull by the horns." The abbreviated word intrigued a novelist, and she would have liked to learn where the lady had been raised; but she had no chance to ask.

Lanny too was collecting impressions. In this crowd were fashionable people whom he had met in Irma's Long Island fox-hunting set, and in New York society, and in the playgrounds of Florida and Hollywood. Also he knew some of the foreigners, and they gathered about him; he spoke fluent French and German, some Spanish and Italian, and even knew a few words of Swedish and Dutch, not to mention Provençal and Ligurian. An unusual American, rich yet not cynical; these worried gentlemen, who had populations at home living on half rations, begged him for advice. What was going to happen to them, and how could the American people be brought to realize the situation and send help out of their abundance?

X

It was two o'clock in the morning when the trio took their departure from this super-party, and they sat in the hotel lobby for another hour discussing the people they had met. Jim was like a Russian, he would have talked all night. Lanny and Laurel slept late the next morning, and then the frugal novelist spent a couple of hours making notes, her own and her husband's. He telephoned the office to see what had come in the mail and to give orders; then they went for a stroll, to see what the art dealers in the city were offering.

Jim came to dine, bringing with him a newspaper friend, and the four of them sat before a radio set furnished by the hotel. It was Thursday, and at seven they listened to a station in Baltimore which carried the Peace Program. A novel experience for the Budd couple, to hear their product from outside. Gerald de Groot was taking the place of "Billy Burns" and doing it well; the program wouldn't suffer if Lanny went away.

The guest of the evening was Professor Alston, and he was questioned about his work with F. D. R. as a "fixer" and inside man. Roosevelt, a man of peace, had been forced to become a man of war. That had happened to George Washington, to Lincoln, and to Woodrow

Wilson—four times in our history; evidently there must be forces operating in our society, more powerful than the will or disposition of any statesman, driving our nation into war. It was the fashion to blame other nations; but the other nations blamed us, and blaming got us nowhere. Alston endorsed the effort of the Peace Program to try to find out what those forces were, and he agreed that they must be overwhelmingly economic. Let America apply its collective intelligence to finding out how we could so distribute the world's natural resources and trade that all the peoples could obtain the means of life and be secure against the assaults of dictators and despots.

A good talk, the other two men agreed. The newspaperman, a Washington correspondent, knew all the dirt, and during dinner he dished it out. If you were going to change the world, Washington was the place to begin, and the first task was to find a way to get the truth to the people, the facts about their government that the newspapers would never print. The town was fairly crawling with lobbyists and lawyers representing every form of wholesale greed, and the most elegant and perfectly legal forms of bribery existed wherever business touched government or government touched business. The American way of life, as it was called, consisted of the hand-in-glove operation of these two forces, and never since the beginning of the world had private interests collected such sums of money from public bodies. Every newspaperman knew what was going on, but few had any idea what to do about it, and most of them took it as a matter of course. "You reformers have whole mountain ranges to move," said this correspondent of a conservative and complacent newspaper.

XI

The expected call from Colonel Josephus came next morning. The War Crimes prosecution formally requested Mr. Budd to let himself be flown to Nürnberg at the government's expense, and there to give his testimony. Mr. Budd said, "OK." He wanted a couple of days to arrange his affairs, and then he would board a plane and be flown by the southern route. Arrangements could be made by phone, and his ticket, passport, and credentials would be brought to him by a messenger.

He drove his wife back to Edgemere and explained matters to Rick and Nina; he gave orders to his subordinates, dictated a stack of letters, and packed for both hot and cold weather. It was an old story to him: the big airport, the Constellation plane, silver now that the war was over, the blue-uniformed attendants, including the pretty stewardess, the packages of magazines and books to read, and the itinerary—Key West, Belém, Cape Verde Islands, Casablanca, Naples, Rome, Munich. Everything comfortable and safe—how pleasant it is to have money! Or prestige and political preferment will do as well.

BOOK NINE

Truth Crushed to Earth Shall Rise

27

Shame Cometh After

I

IN THE romantic medieval city of Nürnberg—Nuremberg to Americans—Lanny Budd had been a guest of Reichsminister Rudolf Hess at the *Parteitag*, in September of the fateful year of 1938. This was the great Nazi festival, held at the same date every year; they called it their Party Day, but it was eight days and nights of uproarious excitement, parading, shouting, singing and listening to propaganda bellowed from loudspeakers. The issue of war or peace with Britain and France had been hanging in the balance; the settlement known to history as "Munich" was in the making, and Lanny was sick with anxiety. But he had to march and sing and, above all, listen with the rest of them; he had been treated with high honor by the young Nazi fanatics because he was known to be the Führer's one American friend, and believed to be chosen *Gauleiter* of the North American continent. Their favorite song declared, "Today Germany belongs to us, tomorrow the whole world."

Everything had been done with that thoroughness which promised so much for the Fatherland and so little for her foes. A million or two party leaders and followers had poured into the city of half a million, and enormous tent encampments had been set up in all the suburbs, with Army cooking outfits serving millions of hot meals every day. The flags in the streets had been like the leaves of a forest, and everywhere you went were bands of men marching with banners and standards. The streets of the nine-hundred-year-old city were narrow and crooked, and made an American think of Grimm's fairy tales read in his childhood; the houses had high-pitched roofs, peaked gables, and innumerable chimney pots; the churches had tall spires and every sort of Gothic exuberance. And out on the enormous Zeppelin Field was a colossal spectacle, on which Adolf Hitler, man of imagination, had been working for some fifteen years; he had devised it, and year by year had improved it; in 1938 it was, quite literally, the *Parteitag* to end all Party Days—or, in German, *Parteitage*.

Indelibly stamped upon Lanny's memory was the Wagnerian scenery, combined with the solemnity of a Catholic High Mass; all the primitive sentiments that had been born in the hearts of the Germans in those dark forests where they had lived through centuries while getting ready for the conquest of the Roman Empire. Hitler had devised the ceremony of calling the roll of the Nazi martyrs, and to Hess had been assigned the calling. Hitler had devised the ceremony of the dedication of the flags, and had performed that himself, solemnly marching down the row of flags and touching each one with the sacred *Blutfahne*, which had been carried in the Beerhall Putsch and had been stained with the blood of those who had died or been wounded in that street riot.

Memories, memories! This very old city, home of the Meistersinger and Albrecht Dürer, lived in Lanny's mind as swarming with red-faced, sweating male creatures, fanaticism in their faces and rage in their hearts, that ancient *furor teutonicus* which the ancient Romans had known and dreaded. "Varus, Varus, give me back my legions!" The American art lover had hated hatred, but these men had been brought up on it, they had been taught it from childhood. Adolf Hitler had a favorite word, fanaticism, which was hardly ever omitted from any of his speeches, and he had put skilled psychologists and advertising men at work to make certain that the new generations of Germans would never know anything else.

Nineteen centuries had passed since the Emperor Augustus had sent his legions into these dark northern forests and the *furor teutonicus* had destroyed them. Since then the world had thought that Germany had become a civilized nation. But the Führer had come, and had revived the ancient *furor*, until the British and Americans had come and destroyed both Führer and *furor*. Here now was Nürnberg, a pitiful, a ghastly, sight; whole blocks of the medieval houses were nothing but wreckage, most of it burned as well as blasted; skeleton walls sticking up, and here and there a brick chimney with its pot still on top. It was the most completely smashed city the ex-P.A. had seen; the Americans, coming by day, had pinpointed the great factories and the railroad yards, and the British had come by night, doing their area bombing on the inner, walled portion—just what the Germans had done to London and a score of other cities, feeling so sure of victory. Now the sweating, khaki-clad hordes were gone, and from the city of the *Parteitag* all you saw were a few shivering women and children, hollow-cheeked and hollow-eyed, crawling into the caves they had dug for themselves in the rubble of their former homes.

II

Lanny hadn't had time to get word to Captain Jerry Pendleton that he was coming; he telephoned from the Grand Hotel, and Jerry drove in for him. Those two fellows were so happy. They exchanged bear hugs, and if they had been real citizens of the Riviera instead of just foreigners who resided there they would have kissed each other on both cheeks. Twelve years had crawled by since good old Jerry had come to Munich to try to help Lanny smuggle Freddi Robin out of the Dachau hell; he had failed, but it hadn't been his fault. Later, as an OSS agent, he had helped Lanny in Morocco and in Spain, and while Lanny had never mentioned being a presidential agent, Jerry had been a competent guesser. Now the struggle was over, and all there was left of the sacred city of Nürnberg was a hungry population having to be fed—and twenty-one miserable, cowed, and broken men, a few of them middle-aged but most of them old, prisoners in the same jail to which in their days of glory they had blithely consigned their political opponents.

Jerry wanted nothing so much as to sit down and tell about the things he had seen and done. But first the new arrival had to report himself to the U.S. Chief of Counsel and his staff. The chief himself was an Associate Justice of the Supreme Court, Robert H. Jackson, whom President Roosevelt had detailed to this special assignment. He was taking it with great seriousness, establishing what all Americans hoped would be a world precedent, so that any dictators contemplating another assault on the freedom of nations would know in advance what they would bring down upon their heads.

Lanny was turned over to a couple of the assistant counsel, and he told them his story. They thought it would be a charming bit of strategy to let Göring's counsel put an American on the stand as their witness, and then discover under cross-examination that he had something to say for the other side too. The only difficulty was the Germans weren't altogether fools and might be suspicious of the fact that the Americans were presenting them with a witness free of charge. They would be likely to ask if he knew anything to Göring's discredit —and how would Lanny answer?

He had given some thought to the question and had developed a peculiar point of view. He had lied to the Nazis wholesale, over a period of a decade and a half; but that had been because it was a matter of life and death for his country. This trial would be a matter of life and death for only one individual, and Lanny didn't think he wanted to lie in such a case. If the counsel asked him the question outright he would tell them the truth and then they probably wouldn't use him. The American prosecutors accepted his decision and said that if it happened that way they would call him as their witness.

III

The trial was going on every day, and the lawyers gave him a pass to the visitors' gallery, from which he could look down upon the scene. The spacious room was on an upper floor of the rambling old Palace of Justice—courthouse to an American. It was quite elegant and had been refitted in a way that had never before been known in any courthouse of the Old World or the New. In glass-enclosed booths sat four expert translators, wearing telephone headsets and having microphones in front of their lips. No matter in what language the testimony was given, it was at once repeated in the four languages of the trial: English, German, French, and Russian. Wires carried it to the judges, counsel, defendants, and even correspondents for the big news agencies. All that anyone had to do was to press one of four buttons, and he would hear the proceedings in the language of his choice. Testimony was limited to "dictation speed," and was taken down by stenographers in the four languages, so that errors in translation could be revised later. Before this ten-month trial would come to its end two hundred witnesses would have been heard and more than five million words have been taken down and printed.

Along one wall, in front of the windows, was a high platform with a long desk for the eight judges, two from each of the Big Four nations. The Russians wore military uniforms, the others wore judicial robes, and all had the flags of their countries behind them. In the main part of the room, in front of the judges' bench, were recorders and clerks. At one side, behind a barrier, sat representatives of the world press. Along the wall opposite the judges was the prisoners' dock, on which the twenty-one accused men were seated in two rows. In front of them, on the main floor level, were their attorneys, who were permitted to communicate with them—but if they wished to pass them anything they had to hand it to one of the American military police. A row of these, with white helmets, white buttons, and white belts, stood behind the defendants. All were clean-cut young soldiers, picked and trained, and each watched his assigned man with the eyes of a hawk. Since Ley had fooled them by hanging himself in the toilet with strips torn from a towel, they were doing their best to make sure there wasn't another "escape" via that route.

IV

To the son of Budd-Erling the most interesting sight in the room was the prisoners. For nearly a quarter of a century he had watched them on the stage of history, and many of them he had met in their homes or their offices, on political platforms or in military headquarters. Hitler wasn't here, nor Goebbels, nor Bormann, who was being tried in absentia; but all the other "greats" were in these two rows.

Der Dicke was now reduced in weight by about seventy pounds, but not improved by it, because where there had been bulges in his face and neck there now were many wrinkles; he wore an air officer's gray uniform without any decorations or insignia, and to anyone who knew him that made him look almost naked. He had been gradually disaccustomed to his drugs, so he looked alert and watched the proceedings intently. He occupied the number-one seat, the front row at the right, nearest to the press and the visitors' gallery, and it was evident that he was doing his best to keep in the limelight. He made faces by way of silent comment on the scene, tried always to catch the eye of any judge, and braced up and looked impressive whenever a camera was turned upon him. There were no flash bulbs, for the scene was periodically illuminated by floodlights, and photographers hovered behind glass windows, like ghosts that nobody saw. Posterity would have pictures as well as text!

Göring had been the Number Two Nazi; Number Three had been Rudolf Hess, so he had the next seat. Poor Rudi, who Lanny had fooled with fake spiritualist mediums and other devices! The P.A. had last seen him in a military hospital at Abergavenny, near the Welsh border, and Lanny had pretended to have bribed the guard, thus gaining Hess's confidence. Later the Number Three had had his own turn at fooling; he had pretended to have lost his memory but had succeeded only with himself. He had developed a case of genuine recurrent amnesia; it was off again, on again with his memory, and he seemed to be back and forth across the borderline of insanity.

Unhappy, distracted wretch, who had soared to such glory, and who had pulled off what was perhaps the most sensational individual stunt of the war, his flight to Scotland. He had really thought he could carry on negotiations with the heads of the British government and persuade them to make a deal with Adi Schicklgruber—who had never kept faith with any man an hour longer than it suited his purposes. Hess had helped him write and had edited a book defending that sort of tactics; and here he sat in the prisoners' dock, with only a little hair on his head and a little flesh on his features, and dark eyes that seemed to be peering out from two caves.

V

Lanny's eyes moved on down the row. At the *Nummer Zwei's* left who should it be but Joachim von Ribbentrop, champagne salesman who had bought his title from a distant aunt. Now he bore more resemblance to a pack peddler in the slums. The brashness was gone out of him, he was cowed and wilted, forgot to comb his hair or adjust his tie; his counsel worried because his story kept changing from day to day. Lanny Budd had never known him well, for he had been far too important a personage to bother with the playboy son of an American millionaire.

Next to him was Kaltenbrunner, head of the Security Police, the man who had carried out the extermination of the Jews; tall, thin, pale —never had there been a more mild-looking murderer of millions. Then came Rosenberg, the party philosopher, who had made a religion out of racial superiority; nervous and commonplace, he might have been a bookkeeper sitting on a high stool in the back part of your office. And next to him Frank, the butcher-governor of Poland. This bloody-handed one had recanted his Nazi creed; he had become a Catholic convert and was having "apocalyptic visions"; he repented his sins and made voluble expressions of penitence. Who but God could know if he meant it?

Next in that front row sat the vilest, so vile that none of the others would have anything to do with him: Streicher, the party's number-one Jew-baiter, who had turned his own obscene imaginings into tales about the hated helpless race. Lanny had seen him stride about the streets at the Parteitag, carrying a riding whip in imitation of his adored Führer. Now he was dirty and greasy, and his cruel face sweated freely when he was afraid—which was often. Placed next to him was Funk, president of the Reichsbank, a fawning little man who was sober now but had rarely been so in the happy old days. He protested to everybody who came near him that he had never known that among the treasures brought to his vaults were bushels of gold teeth knocked from the mouths of Jewish and Polish victims of the gas chambers.

Finally, at the end of the row, that tall turkey cock in trousers, the onetime president of the Reichsbank, who had never spoken to Dr. Funk in the ten years since Funk had taken his place. Dr. Hjalmar Horace Greeley Schacht had been born in Brooklyn and named for a great American; he had come back to tell the land of his birth the wonders of Nazism, trying to raise money for Hitler as he had so triumphantly done after World War I. Always he sat aloof and haughtily erect; he was a businessman, a financier, and expressed amazement and incredulity that he should be herded here with criminals. Lanny Budd could have testified that he had become completely disgusted with Hitler—after he had been fired; in Lanny's presence he had besought Robbie Budd to help him get the presidency of one of the great New York banks, to which his genius undoubtedly entitled him. He still had the red face, knobby forehead, and disagreeably wide mouth; but he looked queer without the five-inch stiff white collar he had affected in the days of his glory.

The second row included two Wehrmacht officers, Field Marshal Keitel and Colonel-General Jodl, who had been the Führer's house pets, to to speak, his personal generals who always said yes to everything. They paid for that glory now by being held responsible for his military crimes. Lanny had met and cultivated them at Berchtesgaden, and he saw that they were among the few prisoners who were dignified. Junker tradition sustained them; they were sure that nobody had the right to assume authority over them and they looked with contempt upon anything an enemy could do. Victors always did what they pleased, and to call it justice was mere Anglo-Saxon hypocrisy. Of the same opinion was Grand Admiral Raeder, also Grand Admiral Doenitz, who had taken Raeder's place in command of the Navy. The admirals wore plain dark-blue suits, and a correspondent remarked, "They look like discharged streetcar conductors."

Here in this aristocratic row belonged also Franz von Papen, "Satan in Top Hat" he had been called. He had helped Hitler to power, and later on Lanny had met him in Austria, where he had been intriguing and bullying, preparing the way for the Anschluss. Lanny had a vivid memory of how he bared his teeth and twisted his eyebrows when he was angry. He, like Schacht and the generals and admirals, was astounded to find himself in a prisoners' dock. He would know how to look elegant in his double-breasted pin-stripe suit, and he would assure his judges that love of country was the only motive that had ever animated him. Only the Russians would fail to be persuaded.

VI

Soon after Lanny's arrival Göring's defense began. This had been entrusted to Dr. Stahmer, a well-known lawyer of Berlin, soft spoken and shrewd, with close-cut white hair, a prominent nose, and rather thick lips. He took a fatherly attitude toward his rambunctious client. He was allowed four thousand marks for his services, this being put up by the eighteen prosecuting governments; but Lanny knew that Göring had large sums abroad, including New York and Buenos Aires, and he wondered if arrangements had been privately made. While the lawyer was outlining his client's case Lanny kept his eyes on the client and saw that he was almost beside himself with nervousness. He would fold his arms but could not keep the pose for as much as a minute; he would try to write notes, but his hands trembled. He kept pulling at the cord of his earphones—such an odd thing, to see everybody in the room looking like a telephone operator!

The first witness was Göring's adjutant, Bodenschatz, who testified that the Luftwaffe hadn't been ready in 1939, and how Göring had tried to carry on negotiations with England behind the backs of Hitler and Ribbentrop to avoid war. He told also how Göring had managed to have several of his friends released from concentration camps—but he didn't mention a young Jew named Freddi Robin. He drew a fancy picture of his chief as a man of humanity, a lover of peace; it was amusing to see the beaming smile on the face of the tiger.

But not so when Justice Jackson started his cross-examination. Apparently the Germans had not been used to American methods, and never could get used to them. The Chief Counsel had buried himself in this cause and knew every detail of it; he rarely had to consult his notes, except when he had a document to quote. Apparently the witness had never considered the possibility that an air force commander who knew that his force was not ready might have some other motive than love of humanity for trying to postpone a war. The witness was forced to admit that Göring's preparations were all meant for war and that Göring's speeches had admitted the fact.

Before the ordeal was over the witness had involved himself in a series of contradictions and misstatements, shown by documents which the Allies had captured and which the witness hadn't known about.

His face was red, and the perspiration stood out on his forehead. The same was true of his chief—he pulled at the earphones so hard that his MP had to intervene and tell him to behave himself.

That was the way this trial had been going for months. The prosecution had documents by the ton, for the Germans were the most meticulous makers and keepers of records. Every subordinate wanted written instructions as to everything he had to do; that went into his file, and thereafter it was sacred—he had seldom been able to bring himself to the point of burning anything, even when the enemy was in the streets outside the office building. So, when some office drudge would blandly assert that his chief was a man of love and mercy and had never had knowledge of any suffering inflicted upon the innocent, Jackson would produce an interoffice memorandum ordering that no more children should be sent to the crematoria because the labor shortage was acute and it had been found that children made very docile workers. "How about that, *Herr Dreckschnautze?*"

VII

There was a week-end adjournment, so Lanny had time to take a long walk with his ex-tutor, out of the sight of ruins and into the lovely countryside of Bavaria. Once you got away from towns little had been touched by war, and the peasants were all prosperous, selling food to the occupation forces at good prices and to the black marketeers at double prices. Some of the women still had the silk stockings their sons had sent them from Paris, and the *objets d'art* they had got from the well-to-do of Nürnberg and near-by Fürth, site of the great Messerschmitt airplane plant, now bombed completely flat. If you won the peasants' confidence they would tell you that things had been very good under Hitler. Some of the young men would add, defiantly, that the Führer's only mistake was that he didn't win the war. Others would curry favor with any Americans they met, saying that the Nazi swine in Nürnberg jail ought to be drawn and quartered, every one.

Jerry told about his job; a strange one, and certainly one that he had never dreamed of when he had been playing around on the Riviera thirty years ago and had met the charming Mrs. Budd and been engaged to give her son a respectable pretense of education. An interesting job, the one here in Nürnberg, but tedious too; you got tired of these deflated wretches with their unresting egotism and unceasing complaints. You looked forward to the day when you would see a row of them dangling by ropes and could be sure that a lesson had been taught that the next bunch of bandits would remember.

Lanny said, "I wonder! Perhaps the next bunch will be sure they are going to win, just as this bunch were." He went on to tell Jerry what his bunch of anti-bandits in New Jersey were doing, staking their hopes upon an effort to get the nations together and form a government which would have a police force and would put an end to world banditry forever. Professor Urey had been scheduled to talk about it the day that Lanny had left; next week it would be Einstein, and the week after that Stuart Chase, and after that the bunch would be on their own until Lanny got back.

He listened while Jerry described the routine of the prison and the trial. The accused were kept in solitary, each in a single cell with a small opening in the door through which a guard watched him day and night. They talked with their lawyers whenever the lawyers requested it, but always through a close-meshed wire screen and with a guard standing behind the prisoner. Because Göring had dominated all the other prisoners, trying to keep them from making admissions damaging to the regime, he had been relegated to a room by himself at meals—something he took as a terrible indignity. The other twenty were divided into five groups, carefully chosen so that the weak were kept from the influence of the strong. The arrangement had been worked out by Dr. Gilbert, the prison psychologist, on the basis of his knowledge of the evil crew. To hear him tell about the various personalities and the effect of each upon the others in his group was an experience absorbing to the son of Budd-Erling.

The work of guarding the outside of the Palace and the prison was shared in daily turns by the Big Four nations, but inside the buildings everything was American, and the routine had been studied and rehearsed to the last detail. The two buildings were joined by a viaduct walk, and while the prisoners were being marched across some unknown person had thrown a knife at them from a window, so now the viaduct was covered. On the other side was a court, and when the prisoners were getting their exercise there a warning bell rang and no office worker was permitted to appear at a window; soldiers with tommy guns stood below, keeping watch, with orders to shoot to kill.

When they went up to the courtroom each prisoner was accompanied by an armed guard, walking behind him. When they entered the Palace they went up in an elevator which the thoughtful Germans had provided long ago; each prisoner entered a little steel cabinet, just big enough, and having a window through which the guard watched him as the elevator carried them to the floor where the trial was being held. The elevator opened directly into the prisoners' box, and the guard came out first and then let the prisoner out.

"It's costing a lot of money," said Captain Pendleton, "but not so much as another war."

VIII

Lanny was invited to dinner at the prison officers' mess on the outskirts of town, and there he met Dr. Gilbert, the prison psychologist, a Columbia Ph.D who had been doing Intelligence work during the war. Gilbert was a pleasant-faced man in his early thirties; he knew German thoroughly and had the run of the prison. He would visit the prisoners at lunch, in the courtroom during intermissions, and in their cells after each day's ordeal. Then he would return to his office and make detailed notes for the future study of Nazi behavior. He was interested in meeting an American who had known Numbers Two and Three in the days of their glory, and he and Lanny spent much time comparing notes. His diary was being kept in secret, but he let Lanny see parts of it. An amazing thing to hear the secrets of the Nazis unveiled and to learn one by one the names of the men who had been plotting against Hitler in Hitler's own fortress; persons who might have been Lanny's friends and helpers, if only he had had a hint of their true attitude! Early in this trial the prosecution had put on the stand a high officer of the Abwehr, the Reichswehr's Counter-Intelligence Service, whose special duty it had been to uncover and arrest enemy agents such as Lanny. To his amazement he learned that not merely the witness, General Lahousen, but also his chief, the head of the Abwehr, Admiral Canaris, had been in the officers' conspiracy against the *Regierung*. Canaris, a man of Greek descent, hated and dreaded by all Allied agents, had been secretly suppressing information against the men he was supposed to destroy. He had been aware of widespread officer plots against the Führer!

Lahousen, on the witness stand, told how this conspiracy had been formed before the war, in an effort to prevent that war. He put into the record that Göring, Keitel, and Jodl had planned the bombarding of Warsaw and the extermination of the Polish intelligentsia, nobility, clergy, and Jews. Himmler, the arch-villain who had come so near to getting Lanny in his net, had actually got Polish uniforms, dressed up Polish concentration-camp inmates in them, and had them shot in front of the Gleiwitz radio station, in order to justify the charge that the Poles had committed "aggression" on this station.

Under cross-examination this highly placed witness told how, during the Russian campaign, orders had been given for the mass murder of Communists and Jews—this involving execution of both prisoners of war and civilians. After the escape of the French General Giraud from a German fortress, General Keitel had issued an order, at Hitler's wish, that Giraud should be assassinated; but Canaris and Lahousen had managed to sabotage this order. And so on and on! Ribbentrop gave his attorney some questions to be asked of this witness, but the attorney said it was no use. "He only throws them back in our faces with more damaging information."

This appearance of one of their high generals had taken the prisoners completely by surprise, and it was a fascinating thing to read Dr. Gilbert's account of Göring's fuming at his lunch hour. "That traitor! That's one we forgot on the 20th of July!"—meaning the thousand or more persons who were shot in 1944 after a bomb had come near to killing the Führer. "Hitler was right—the Abwehr was a traitors' organization! How do you like that! No wonder we lost the war—our own Intelligence Service was sold out to the enemy! Now I know why I never could depend on him for accurate information!"

Himmler had got onto Lanny's trail in Berlin, and Lanny had had to escape. He had perforce chosen the proletarian way, with the help of an old Social Democratic watchmaker, and it had proved hard and exhausting, as most proletarian ways are. Now what a sensation to discover that he might have called upon General Erwin von Lahousen at the War Ministry and been fitted out with proper papers and sent out as a German businessman to Sweden!

IX

One bit of melodrama after another in that slow-moving, solemn trial! Next had come Hess's sensational declaration that he was perfectly sane and that his amnesia had been faked. He couldn't bear to miss the excitement of the trial, and the pleasure of hearing himself talked about—even if it meant hanging! But Dr. Gilbert assured Lanny that poor Rudi's amnesia came and went and was perfectly genuine when it came—the doctor had made sure by a number of psychological traps. Lanny, watching the scarecrow figure in the courtroom, could readily credit this. He might have been taken to Rudi's cell if he had so requested, but he didn't. He had nothing to give to any of these tormented men, and nothing to get from them. The circumstances were too serious for mere curiosity.

It was in Dr. Gilbert's diary that Lanny read about Ohlendorf, a Nazi who had been jailed and had turned against the gang. He had been chief of the SD, the Security Service, and he told how Himmler, on behalf of the Führer, had given him orders for mass murder, and how he had been given command of an action group for the extermination of ninety thousand Jews. He went into the grisly details of the wholesale shooting of men and the gas-wagon extermination of women and children. While Ohlendorf testified Göring fumed, "*Ach*, there goes another one selling his soul to the enemy! What does the swine expect to gain by it? He'll hang anyway."

It was during cross-examination of this witness that Speer, one of the accused, took occasion to reveal that near the end of the war he had attempted to have Hitler assassinated and Himmler delivered to the enemy to be punished for his crimes. This was a bombshell to the rest of the group, and during the intermission Göring rushed to Speer, demanding to know how he dared to disrupt their "united front." Speer had been Reichsminister for Armaments and Munitions and had been responsible for foreign slave labor. Near the end he had had the courage to tell Hitler that the war was lost, and the revelation he now made was an effort to save his life—which it did. Göring's uncontrolled fury was one of the factors which had brought about the decision to keep the defendants in solitary and to divide them into groups at the lunch hour.

A curious phenomenon, the dominating will of this man, and the power he exerted over the others, even in jail. In Dr. Gilbert's diary Lanny read about Hermann's boyhood, about which he had previously known nothing. The *Nummer Zwei's* earliest recollection was of bashing his mother in the face with his two fists at the age of three. He had defied all authority, and even beatings by his cavalry-officer father had not subdued him. He had dominated his schoolmates, organized them for military exploits in the old castle which had been his home, and mocked and defied his teachers except those of military rank. He had been happy only in a school where he was being trained for battle and glory. He had found his destiny in World War I, flying alone in the air, defying danger and death, and shooting down twenty-eight enemy planes. Dr. Gilbert wrote, "Like the typical psychopath, Göring never outgrew the uninhibited acting-out of these infantile ego-drives."

28

Vengeance Is Mine

I

THE outside world went on about its affairs, not giving too much attention to these Nürnberg proceedings. Winston Churchill made a long trip to speak at a place called Fulton, in Missouri. After President Truman introduced him—which was as much as to say "I approve"—the retired Prime Minister told the world over the radio that it was in a dangerous situation. Said he, "No one knows what Soviet Russia and its Communist international organization intend to do in the immediate future, or what are the limits, if any, to its expansive and proselytizing tendencies." He said that what went on behind and in front of the iron curtain across Europe from Stettin to Trieste was "certainly not the liberated Europe we fought to build up." He advocated a fraternal association between Britain and the United States to retard the U.S.S.R.

This let loose a tremendous torrent of discussion—in the Nürnberg jail and Palace of Justice as everywhere else. The prisoners were allowed to have newspapers, and Papen read the story aloud to the other three in their lunch room—the group called "the Elders" by Dr. Gilbert. "*Donnerwetter nochmal!*" exclaimed the onetime vicechancellor. "He is outspoken, isn't he!" Admiral Doenitz remarked, "He's going back to his old line!" Neurath, former Minister of Foreign Affairs, commented, "It is still the British Empire first and last."

The most excited was Göring, for trouble between Britain and Russia had been his dream from the first. Make a deal with the Tories, he had urged Hitler, and get their consent to put Bolshevism out of business! "Naturally; I told you so!" he exclaimed to the doctor. "It has always been that way. You will see—I was right—it is the old balance of power again. . . . They could never make up their minds whether to balance us off against the East or the West. Now Russia is too strong for them, and they've got to counterbalance her again."

Three or four days later came the Russian reaction. The newspaper headline read, "MOSCOW CALLS CHURCHILL 'WARMONGER,' SAYS HE SEEKS TO SABOTAGE UNO." At which Göring rubbed his hands and chuckled, "The only Allies who are still allied are the four prosecutors, and they are allied only against the twenty-one defendants!" Doenitz's remark was, "Churchill was always anti-Russian—that is what I have always said."

II

There was the son of Budd-Erling, once more in the midst of that world situation—only now it was history. How many arguments he had heard about it, in Berlin and Vienna and Rome, Paris and Madrid and London, Washington, New York, and Newcastle, Connecticut! The basis of the deal called "Munich" had been that Britain should give Hitler some reasonable concession and win and keep his friendship, so that he would form a bulwark against the East. But Hitler had refused to be reasonable, Hitler wouldn't keep any promises, Hitler wouldn't stay put. The British statesmen had had the nightmare to contemplate that if Hitler could add the Russian resources to his own, he would be in position to go south through the Balkans and Turkey to the oil of the Near East, and through Iraq and Iran to India. So they had made a deal of mutual defense with Poland; and so, in less than a year, World War II was on.

And now another nightmare, even worse! Operating under her camouflage of Communism, Russia had got the Balkans and was threatening Turkey and Iran! Russia had got the eastern half of Germany, the whole of Poland, and the Baltic States. She had penetrated into China and wasn't getting out of Port Arthur and Dairen as she had agreed. She had got the northern half of Korea—and where was she going to stop? America was the only power in the world that might be able to stop her, and what was America going to do? So Britain's elder statesman had dropped his painting of landscapes and building of brick walls and had jumped into a plane and flown all the way to a town in the corn-and-hog country to sound the alarm and plead for help.

To be sure he was no longer Prime Minister, only Prime Orator. Britain had a Labour government—but what difference would that make in the outcome? How much attention would the chiefs in the Politburo pay to a government which called itself Socialist, when they were busy ousting and jailing the very same sort of persons in Estonia, Latvia, Lithuania, East Prussia, Poland, Eastern Germany, Rumania, Hungary, Yugoslavia, Bulgaria, Manchuria, and Northern Korea?

"Liquidating" them—most odious word when applied to human beings! You put them under the ground and left them for the worms, and they could no longer lift their voices against whatever party line the thirteen men in the Politburo saw fit to ordain.

III

These discussions coincided with Göring's testimony in his own defense. For three days he sat in the witness box and talked about himself—than which nothing pleased him more. He had been a prisoner for almost a year, he had sat through four months of this trial without being permitted to answer back, and now at last his days in court had come! He told about his background and his many decorations, his meeting with Hitler, his conviction that this was the great man Germany needed, his labors to help build up the party and his motives for doing it. He had taken charge of the SA—the Storm Troopers—and trained them. He had taken part in the so-called Beer-hall Putsch and had been wounded. He had become a member of the Reichstag in 1928, president of the Reichstag in 1933, and had helped Hitler to become chancellor in that year. He had set up concentration camps in Prussia to intern Communists.

After his session on the stand he sat on the cot in his cell, smoking his big Bavarian pipe and talking with Dr. Gilbert. "Well, how did I do? I showed them, didn't I? See my hand, how steady it is. I'm not nervous."

Praise was necessary to his ego, and the psychologist gave him some, to encourage him to talk. "Your story was clear, and the court was interested."

Der Dicke, fighting for his life, was in a serious mood, serious-cynical. "*Der Mann ist das grösste Raubtier*," he declared—the greatest beast of prey. "He is that because he has brains, he does not kill just to eat. Wars will become more and more destructive. It is fate. There is no way to prevent it."

Next morning he related the story of the Röhm Blood Purge, defending it as having been the necessary disciplining of disorderly and destructive elements in the party. Lanny Budd, sitting in the visitors' gallery, watching and listening attentively, thought of Gregor Strasser, of Hugo Behr shot in the face, of the captives in Stadelheim Prison whose fate he would never know. A strange whim of what Göring called fate—it was Göring who was the captive now, trying to guess what was coming to *him*.

Der Dicke sought to justify the anti-Semitic laws on the basis of the hostility of the Jews to the Nazi program and to all good things German. Some of his fellow defendants in the prisoners' dock hung their heads, for they thought this was bad tactics; Dr. Funk, the pudgy little coward, had tears running down his cheeks. Göring went on to tell how the regime had abolished unemployment—failing to mention how easy it is to put everybody at work if you don't mind printing unlimited paper money and are manufacturing not for a market but for war. He praised the annexation of Austria and claimed a great share of the credit.

And then, at his solitary lunch hour, to Dr. Gilbert, "You cannot say I was cowardly, can you?"

"No," replied the doctor, "you took the responsibility. But how about when you come to aggressive war?"

"Oh, I'll have plenty to say about that too."

"And about atrocities?"

He lowered his eyes; it was hard to face that question. "Only insofar as I didn't take the rumors seriously enough to investigate them—" His voice died away. How would he get away with that when the cross-examination began? He stood at the window, looking at the ruins of Nürnberg, plainly visible. Was he recalling the days when these streets had been bedecked with flags and he had ridden though them, covered with medals and greeted by cheering throngs?

At the afternoon session he dealt with the Czechoslovak affair, then with Poland, then with Norway. His defense was that independence of opinion among military leaders was unthinkable; you had orders and you had to obey them. "Perhaps this is the way to avoid wars in the future, if you ask every general and every soldier whether he wants to go home or not."

In his cell he boasted, "And all out of my memory! You would be surprised how few cue words I have jotted down to guide me. I am not like poor Hess. God, what a farce it is going to be when *he* gets up to testify!"

Next day he told about the attack on Yugoslavia and attempted to justify what his Luftwaffe had done at Warsaw, Rotterdam, Coventry. He admitted that he had discussed the plan to attack Russia a year after the starting of the war, but had advised Hitler to postpone it until they had taken Gibraltar, and then to try to bring in Russia against England. This was the part of his story that Lanny Budd knew best and could corroborate. The ex-Reichsmarschall was adhering to the facts most of the time; he had been listening to the cross-examination

of other witnesses and knew the risks of lying when the enemy has
in its hands tons of your records!

IV

Before Göring's cross-examination the defense put on another witness in his behalf, a Swedish engineer named Dahlerus. He had been
acting as a mediator for Göring, trying to persuade the British to let
Hitler have a part of his demands on Poland, so as to avoid the war.
This had been going on during the summer of 1939, and among the
English active in the affair had been the so-called "Wickthorpe set,"
Ceddy and Irma and their friends. Lanny had heard of this Swede
being in London and had got hints of what was going on. *Der Dicke*
had been acting on his own, confusedly trying to get more *Lebensraum* for Germany without taking quite so many risks as Hitler was
ready to take.

That was brought out in the cross-examination of Dahlerus, conducted by Sir David Maxwell Fyfe—it being a British affair. In the
end the witness admitted the insincerity of the whole "mediation"
effort. Göring had warned him that Ribbentrop was sabotaging the
negotiations and had even planned to have Dahlerus's plane crash on
the journey to England. (Amusing to see Ribbentrop blow up over
that; Göring had predicted to Dr. Gilbert that the ex-champagne
salesman would split a gut.) Dahlerus stated the impression he had
got out of the whole matter: that the Führer was abnormal, that
Göring was in a crazy state of intoxication, and that Ribbentrop was
a would-be murderer. Göring had no serious intention of avoiding
war but was merely trying to get Britain to give way and acquiesce
in the rape of Poland. There wasn't much comfort for the fat man in
that testimony, and there was despair among his fellow defendants.

The ex-P.A. went off and thought it over hard. He had waited, to
see how matters would shape up; and now the time had come for him
to be introduced to the defense counsel and offer his testimony. He
had to make up his mind what attitude to take. He had guessed that
they wouldn't be fools, but here it appeared that they were! They
had put this Swedish engineer on the stand when they knew that he
had written a book and told his whole story—and Göring had read
that book in his cell! The truth was, they were desperate for somebody to say a good word for this man of blood and terror; they wanted
it so badly that they might even take an American secret agent!

What did Lanny Budd owe to Hermann Wilhelm Göring? Not a

thing in the world. He had been fed some good meals, but he had paid amply with conversation, with jokes and stories, the coin in which men of wealth desire to be paid. But did he owe any loyalty, any truth? To the murderer of Freddi Robin, the plunderer of Johannes! The question answered itself. In deceiving Göring he would not merely be punishing one individual, he would be doing his part to deflate the Nazi ideology, the Nazi dream; he would be helping the German people recover from the effects of those poison gases they had been breathing for a quarter of a century.

So Lanny went to the American counsel and reported that after watching the trial for a couple of weeks he had changed his mind; he was willing to do what he could to keep the German counsel from guessing that he had anything to say against their client. Thereupon the American counsel informed the German that the *Nummer Zwei's* old friend was willing to testify on his behalf and had been flown here for that purpose.

Lanny was turned over to Dr. Stahmer and his assistants, and he told them the same story he had been telling Hitler and Göring for so many years: that he was a lover of peace who had been trying in his feeble way, first to prevent World War II, then to mitigate its fury and to end it as quickly as possible. Owing to his wealthy father's influence, he had been able to travel in wartime, and secretly to enter Sweden and Switzerland and from there go into Germany. He had paid many visits to both Göring and the Führer and had carried messages for them to influential persons who, like himself, considered the war to be madness and a crime against humanity.

Did the shrewd German lawyers swallow all that? Lanny would never know. Dr. Stahmer's conferences with his client were supposed to be secret, and no doubt he asked Göring what were the chances of this American's being sincere. The determining factor must have been the fat man's desperate need, but perhaps his vanity played a part also; he liked Lanny, and it would be hard for him to believe that Lanny didn't really like him. As for the matter of Solomon Hellstein and what Lanny had seen in the Berlin prison—that, he could guess, wouldn't come into Göring's mind. *Der Dicke* had done so much blackmailing and robbing, he had ordered so much plundering and killing, that the details couldn't all find room in his memory. If he recalled the episode, it would be as a joke; he had taken it that way, and Lanny had pretended to take it the same way. What, between two aristocratic Aryans, was a little whipping administered to the backside of a fat old *jüdischer Schweinehund*?

V

So a surprise witness was called: Mr. Lanning Prescott Budd took the stand and the oath. He gave his residence as Edgemere, N. J., his occupation as art expert. He told how this occupation had carried him all over Europe, and how he had purchased a number of paintings from Göring, and others for the Führer, prior to the war. He had used what influence he possessed to prevent the war, and he testified how Göring had tried successfully to prevent it in the autumn of 1938, and had expressed regret in 1939. He told how, visiting his old friends in the spring of 1941, Göring had confided to him how distressed he was over this long-drawn-out war. Göring had begged Lanny to intercede and try to prevent it, and Lanny had talked to the Führer about it.

Herrlich! Wunderschön! The two rows of prisoners beamed on this elegant, smooth-spoken gentleman, the friend of their cause; all but poor Rudi, who stared perplexed, as if trying to recall where and when he had seen that face. Foxy Grandpa Schacht spread his mouth in a wide smile; the last time he had seen Lanny he had blown the son of Budd-Erling to an elegant luncheon at the Herrenklub in Berlin, including *Kiebitzeier*—plovers' eggs—and had smoothly tried to engage him in the program to have the Allies go easy on the western front and let Hitler put the Russians out of business. Franz von Papen also beamed, remembering Lanny from Vienna—he never forgot anybody, or any of the million details of his long life of intrigue. Keitel and Jodl beamed; they hadn't liked seeing an American in the Berghof, but now his testimony suited them.

Dr. Stahmer had agreed not to ask any questions beyond the time of America's entry into the war. To have brought it out that an American had been dealing with the enemy would have been distressing to the American's important father, and moreover would have discredited him with the judges. So the defense rested, and one of the junior American counsel took over the witness, the one to whom Lanny had told his whole story and who had an elaborate set of typewritten questions in his hand.

VI

"Mr. Budd, will you tell the court when you last had a talk with Hermann Göring?"

"Yes, sir. I was permitted to interview him at Kitzbühel the day after his surrender, last May."

"I mean your last talk with him prior to his surrender."

"That was in the autumn of 1943 at his Karinhall estate."

"You were there as a guest?"

"I was."

"Will you explain to the court how an American citizen could be in Germany after your country was at war with Germany?"

"Yes, sir. For many years I had been posing as a Nazi sympathizer, and I had convinced Göring and Hitler and others of that."

"But it was not true?"

"No, sir. In reality I was a confidential agent of President Roosevelt, traveling into Europe and getting information for him." You could feel the rustle of excitement in the courtroom at that statement. Lanny's eyes moved down the double line of the prisoners, noting the expressions of consternation and dismay. The blood began to rush into Göring's usually pasty face, until it was a dangerous purple—dangerous to the fat man. Their eyes met, and Lanny did not turn his away.

"What, precisely, was your status?" continued the questioner.

"I was known as Presidential Agent 103. I was also known to several of the top men in the OSS, including General Donovan."

"For how long did you have that status?"

"From the summer of 1937 until the day of the President's death."

"And you made reports to him during that entire period?"

"Yes, sir. My last report was numbered seventy-one. I made a total of eleven trips into Germany for him—some of them long stays. I also made trips to North Africa, Italy, and Palestine, and I traveled with him to Yalta."

"You were paid for your services?"

"I was supposed to be a dollar-a-year man, but I never saw the dollar. The President entrusted large sums to me, to be used for secret work, and what I had left I turned over to the OSS after the President's death."

"How did you explain to Göring and Hitler your ability to travel to Europe in war time?"

"I told them that I was using my father's influence. My father is Robert Budd of Budd-Erling Aircraft."

"But that statement was not true?"

"No, sir. My father did not know what I was doing."

"Did Göring and Hitler pay you money?"

"They offered to, several times; but I told them I did not want money, I was doing what I did for love of the National Socialist cause."

"And they accepted that?"

"I tried my best to make it plausible, and so far as I could judge I was successful until the very last, when apparently Himmler got some information about me. I was warned and got out of Germany by way of Italy. The OSS had a naval seaplane pick me up from a fishing boat in the Adriatic Sea."

VII

This was a story—and a sensation. You could see the correspondents bent over their scratch paper, busily taking notes. If you had a reasonably good imagination you could see the headlines in the afternoon newspapers all over two American continents: MILLIONAIRE'S SON TRICKS HITLER AND GÖRING: ROOSEVELT AGENT GETS SECRETS, REJECTS BRIBE—this because the next question concerned what Göring had offered him. Lanny's reply was, "The choice of any of his paintings up to a value of a million dollars, provided that I would get him the blueprints of the new Budd-Erling jet fighter."

The cross-examination continued, and the witness told what Göring had said about his reasons for not desiring war in 1938 and 1939, the fact that his Luftwaffe wasn't ready; also why he had opposed the attack upon Russia, because one enemy at a time was enough, and by taking Gibraltar and crossing to North Africa the British could have been shut out of the Mediterranean. "Then it wasn't any motive of humanitarianism?" asked the lawyer, and Lanny replied, "In the years that I knew Göring, from 1933 to 1943, I never heard him mention any such consideration, except to jeer at it as delusion and fraud." Poor old fat man, they could see him pulling furiously at the telephone cord—as if he were pulling out the tongue of the witness.

"Just what did Göring tell you about his ideas of international morality, Mr. Budd?"

"He told me many times that there could be no such thing and it was nonsense—Quatsch—to talk about it. Dog would eat dog, and there was no way to prevent it. Economic forces were entirely beyond human control, and nations would fight whenever they thought they were strong enough to win. He talked a great deal about 'fate,' and he meant by it this inability of an individual to control his own desires and of a nation to control its politics. He was certain that the

German people were incapable of democracy, and that if National Socialism were ever destroyed some other form of military government would take its place almost at once."

"When did you first meet Göring, Mr. Budd?"

"I met him very soon after the Nazis came into power. I happened to know the family of Johannes Robin, the Jewish financier. My sister married his elder son, Hansi Robin, the well-known violinist. I had frequently been a guest on Johannes's yacht, and when I learned that the Nazis had seized him I went to Berlin to try to intercede. I appealed to Goebbels in the matter, and to my surprise I received a call from Oberleutnant Furtwängler—he has since become General-Major. He was a member of Göring's staff and requested me to call on the *Hauptmann*, as Göring then was, at the official Residenz. I did so, and Göring told me that Johannes was accused of having plotted to take money out of Germany. I pointed out to him that Johannes was about to take a yachting trip—I had been invited to go along—and a man could not travel in a yacht without cash.

"And what was Göring's response?"

"He called Johannes many foul names, based on his Jewishness, and declared his intention to strip him of every dollar he had in Germany and outside. The proposition I was to take to him in prison was that he was to make over his property in Germany to Göring for the price of one mark for each piece of property, and that he was to be allowed to keep those marks. He was to write checks for every dollar he had abroad, and when these checks had been cashed Johannes and his family would be released. Göring's phrase was, 'Naked came he into Germany, and naked will he go out.' I pointed out to him that Johannes had been a rich man when he had moved into Germany from Holland— I knew, because he had been my father's business associate. But that didn't do any good."

"Did Göring say what he would do if his terms were rejected?"

"He mentioned the tortures to which Johannes would be subjected. Furthermore, he put me under pledge that I would never tell anyone about this matter, and he said that if either I or Johannes violated the pledge, he, Göring, would compile a list of a hundred of his Jewish relatives and friends and make them pay the price. The point was, he was not going to have the good name of Germany slandered in the foreign press; he was going to get the money, but do it secretly."

"You took that proposition to Johannes Robin?"

"Oberleutnant Furtwängler escorted me to the city prison on the Alexanderplatz, and there in the presence of Furtwängler and two SS men I put the proposal to Johannes. I advised him to accept it, and he did so. The agreement was kept, except that Freddi, the younger son of Johannes, was arrested in Berlin—at least he disappeared, and when I appealed to Furtwängler he pretended not to be able to find out about him; and when I appealed to Göring he made the same pretense. That went on for a long time. I received a letter which Freddi had managed to smuggle out, telling me that he was a prisoner being tortured in Dachau. I tried other methods of getting him out without success. Finally Göring pretended to me that he had learned that my *Itzig*-friend, as he called him, was in Dachau, and offered me another bargain to get him out."

"Will you tell us what that bargain was, Mr. Budd?"

So Lanny told the long story of how he had happened to be in Munich, trying to find a way to buy or steal Freddi out of Dachau concentration camp, when the Blood Purge had fallen upon him. He had seen his SA friend Hugo Behr shot, and he himself had been taken to prison. He had spent a couple of weeks in three different prisons; at the end Göring had sent Furtwängler to get him out and had made a hilarious joke of it. "I give him credit for having a sense of humor," the witness said.

But nobody would have thought it, watching the face of that deflated wretch sitting in the prisoners' dock and staring at this false friend. Humiliation, anger, and fear were written there for all the world to read, and mixed emotions in all the other faces. Speer and Schacht were glad to see the fat man suffer. Poor Rudi, who was having one of his bad periods, was trying hard to remember where he had seen Lanny before, but he couldn't even remember what had been said to him the day before. Hans Frank, the murderer of three million Polish Jews, had turned religious, and couldn't make up his mind whether he was sorry for Göring, or pleased to see him punished for his spurning of repentance.

VIII

Lanny's story was a terrible blow for the ex-Reichsmarschall, as Colonel Josephus in Washington had said it would be. It was an accusation of extortion and kidnaping, even of murder, since both Freddi Robin and Solomon Hellstein had died as result of their mistreatment. The prosecuting attorney plied Lanny with questions and made him recall everything Göring had said and every detail of the dreadful scene in the torture chamber. Men were whipped there until they were bloody messes, and then they were dumped into another room and left lying there to live or die. Four men stripped to the waist laid on the lashes, and the room stank of dried blood and sweat. For almost twelve years the witness had kept silence, but now he spoke, and to the accused man it must have been like the ghost of Hamlet's father, or that of Banquo, coming back to demand vengeance.

A historian might question whether there had ever been in the world a man who bore the weight of more crimes than Hermann Wilhelm Göring—unless it was Hitler, or Himmler, or Streicher. It would have been hard to choose among them, and together they had brought more misery to mankind than any other set of humans you could name. There had been wholesale killers since the dawn of history, and doubtless also in its black midnight, but they hadn't had such vast populations to work on, or such vast amounts of treasure to destroy, or such wholesale means of destruction at their command. These top Nazis had lived at the apex of human civilization, and they had done the most to hurl it back into chaos and night; and here sat this shivering wretch, this poor hulk of fat and misery, trying to bluff it out, trying to keep up his courage, his pose before both friends and enemies, while forced to sit for ten months alternately listening to the story of the horrors he had wrought and then retiring to a lonely cell to contemplate what he had heard.

Also what he had seen! Early during the trial he had come into the courtroom and been told that movies were to be shown. "*Ach, Kino!*" he had exclaimed. He had rubbed his hands with pleasure, and even confused Rudi Hess had understood and exclaimed with the pleasure of a child, "Movies, movies!" They had put up a screen and proceeded to show the horrors of the concentration camps and the extermination factories—human bodies, almost skeletons, stacked in great piles, and shoved about by bulldozers; frozen corpses in the freight cars; prisoners being shot wholesale on the edge of trenches.

And then later, more movies, this time furnished by the Russians, whose sufferings had been the worst of all. The acres of corpses of prisoners left to starve in the stockades; the torture instruments, the mutilated bodies, the raped women and children, the guillotines and baskets of heads, the bodies hanging from lamp posts, the crematoria and gas chambers, the bales of women's hair, and other sights too horrid to be written about. Some had averted their eyes and taken off their headphones; some had wept, some had fallen ill and had had to be drugged in order to sleep. Dr. Gilbert's diary recorded Göring as complaining that the *Kino* had spoiled his show for that day; concerning Lanny Budd's testimony he remarked that he feared it had spoiled his show for good and all.

For the answer to that all three of them—prisoner, psychiatrist, and witness—had to wait nearly seven months longer, until that monster judicial procedure had ground to its end. When the verdicts came in, Schacht, Papen, and Fritzsche were found not guilty of the crimes charged. All the others were found guilty. Hess, Admiral Raeder, and Funk, head of the Reichsbank, got life imprisonment. Schirach and Speer got twenty years, Neurath fifteen, and Admiral Doenitz ten. The others were sentenced to death by hanging: Göring, Ribbentrop, Keitel, Kaltenbrunner, Rosenberg, Frank, Frick, Streicher, Saukel, Jodl, and Seiss-Inquart—this last the intriguer who had prepared for the seizure of Austria and later had been the tyrant of the Netherlands. Eleven most wicked men, each of whom deserved a thousand deaths if such a thing were possible.

When Dr. Gilbert returned to Princeton University at the conclusion of the executions, Lanny heard the story of their last days. Göring had lost his cockiness and accepted defeat. Said he to Gilbert, "You don't have to worry about the Hitler legend any more. When the German people learn all that has been revealed at this trial, it won't be necessary to condemn him: he has condemned himself." *Der Dicke* had the satisfaction of cheating the gallows; he had managed to conceal a cyanide capsule, and swallowed it, thus joining Hitler, Himmler, Goebbels, and Ley. The other ten were hanged, very early on a rainy morning, the 16th day of October of that year 1946, on three black scaffolds in the gymnasium of the prison courtyard.

29

Vae Victis!

I

LANNY had been getting airmail letters from home. Professor Einstein had proved a tremendous drawing card; a dozen extra stations had carried his question-and-answer program, some of them without pay. The flood of mail had grown, and two more Methodist and two more Seventh Day Adventists were working. Next week Robert Oppenheimer was to appear, to discuss the world implications of the atomic bomb. The Peace Program was booming.

How was it with peace? Not so good, if you could believe Bernhardt Monck. He was still in Berlin and could not be spared from his duties to come to Nürnberg; he begged Lanny to visit him before returning home. Things were going from bad to worse, he wrote; he was becoming a chronic worrier. For a man who had been facing persecution and death in many forms since before World War I, this was hardly surprising, but he gave such cogent reasons that Lanny decided to take the trip. Surely the capital of Germany was going to be a part of the world's future problem, and Lanny would get a briefing on the subject by the best-informed German he knew.

He applied to the military authorities, and he discovered that his testimony before the court had made him a personality in his own right. Hitherto he had been, first the grandson of Budd Gunmakers, then the son of Budd-Erling; later all wires had been pulled for him by the hidden hand of F. D. R. Now for a few days, perhaps even a few weeks, he was the man who had dealt Hermann Göring a swift kick in the pants and had put the zip into that ponderous international trial that had become something of a bore. "Why, certainly, Mr. Budd, if you want to go back by way of Berlin and London, we can fix it up."

Lanny had a seat in a plane—they were flying all over this conquered land, and only the conquerors rode in them. The conquerors commandeered whatever they wanted—hotels, apartments, offices, furniture, food—paying for it with paper money which they printed for the purpose. The Germans had done the same thing; indeed, it had become the custom all over the world. The ancient Romans had two words for it: *Vae victis!* Woe to the conquered!

II

The ex-P.A. was put up in a hotel in Grosser Wannsee and bummed a ride with some of the obliging officers whenever he wanted to get to the center of the city. Almost a year had passed since the war's end, and all the streets had been cleared of rubble; but oh, the spaces between the streets! Lanny had got used to the sight of ruins by now, but the center of Berlin was in a class by itself. There had been so much here to destroy that the sheer mass of destruction overpowered the senses. All these colossal buildings that had been meant to last a thousand years; these structures of granite and marble and sandstone that had embodied the glories not merely of Adolf Hitler but of Frederick the Great and Bismarck and the Kaisers—all, all heaps of wreckage, with hardly one stone standing straight upon another!

And the beautiful Tiergarten, the park where lovers had strolled, and conspirators too—anybody who wanted to be sure that no spy could overhear his words! It had all been turned into tiny plots for growing vegetables, and these had long since been eaten. The trees that should by now have been showing signs of buds were stumps cut low by people seeking firewood. The huge white marble statues of the Hohenzollern ancestors were mostly lying in the mud.

Lanny went walking in this ruined *Hauptstadt*. The Kaiser's Palace was smashed; the opera house was boarded up, and so was the Eden Hotel. The rounded roof of the Friedrichstrasse railroad station was a skeleton of black steel girders. He walked down famed Unter den Linden, as familiar to him as Fifth Avenue in New York. East from the damaged Brandenburger Gate, the American Embassy was only a shell, filled with bricks and girders up to the second story. Next was the Adlon, which had once been Lanny's home for months at a time; it was smashed halfway down and its front boarded up; you could go in by a rear door, as into a coal mine; about fifty rooms were still in use. There was gap after gap in that great thoroughfare; the Russian Embassy, the Bristol Hotel—and Lanny, who had been in Hilde Donnerstein's palace when it was hit, kept wondering how many persons of his acquaintance had perished in these various structures?

Spring had been on the way in Nürnberg, but here it was still cold; wind and rain came down from the North Sea, and people walked with their shoulders hunched and their coat collars turned up. You wouldn't have thought it possible that anyone could be living in these ruins, but every now and then you would see a man or a woman disappear into them, and you would discover that they had dug down into the cellars and devised ways to keep themselves warm. They dug everywhere, and whenever they came upon something of value, be it only a broken doorknob, they would take it to the black market and exchange it for three American cigarettes or a quarter of a pound of bootleg coffee. To that had come these proud, tough Berliners, who had been so full of sophistication, thinking themselves several notches above the rest of Germany. They had marched so gaily into Hitler's Third Reich, accepting *Unser Hermann's* assurance that no enemy bomb would ever fall on German soil.

Lanny had been coming to this city since boyhood. He had been impressed by its splendor and had seen only the good side of the German people, their kindness and hospitality, their cleanness and love of order. The officers in their bright uniforms had been picturesque, and he had been amused by their mustaches, twisted up at the ends in imitation of their Kaiser. World War I had taught him what lay behind that façade, and from that time on he had feared Germany and the German dream which had arrived in the world too late. The Weimar Republic had filled him with naïve hopes; he had longed so for a Socialist world, and he had discovered to his grief that the victorious Allied world didn't want anything of the sort, and for that matter neither did the Germans. Apparently the tough, grim Bolsheviks were the only kind of reformers who knew how to survive in such a world.

III

As Trudi Schultz had said to Lanny, they had been born at a bad time. They had had to watch the rise of that terrible Fascism, which took the worst pages out of Lenin's book and used them against Lenin's movement. Lanny's art business had brought him into Germany again and again, and he had heard the Nazi rowdies singing their songs about world conquest and had been in position to know just which of the great industrialists were putting up the money to buy uniforms and rubber truncheons and revolvers for the gang. The rich men were so afraid of Bolshevism that they couldn't imagine anything worse. That old turkey cock, Dr. Schacht, had been helping from the beginning, raising money for the militarists, and raising it for Hitler in Hitler's turn. Always for Germany, he would say; always for finance capital—and for whoever had it!

Was it fate, as Göring insisted? Was modern civilization always going to be at the mercy of one or another kind of wholesale exploitation and its military agents? All the Big Business people Lanny had ever known had insisted that they were men of peace; Lanny had met hundreds of them in the course of his life with Robbie and Johannes and Irma and her friends, and he couldn't recall one who hadn't been sure he was a man of peace. Zaharoff, the munitions king of Europe, had been horrified by both World Wars, and had naïvely expected that he could go on manufacturing munitions and selling them to governments and never see them used, except in small wars, like the putting down of savages. Eugene Schneider of Schneider-Creusot, Zaharoff's royal successor, had expressed the same idea to Lanny. Even Robbie, who considered wars inevitable, put the blame for them on other kinds of men than himself. Robbie was a man of peace, and if only the world would trust him and the rest of the businessmen, the competent, trained executives, the men of experience in affairs—if they could get together and run things they would quickly put the world in order.

What these efficient gentlemen had done was to devise an arrangement whereby the profits of the world's industry flowed to them, automatically and inevitably; and what they meant by peace was that this system was to continue and that nobody should ever challenge or disturb it. What Robbie meant by order was that the exploiters of the different nations should confer and work out a fair division of the spoils. Flaws in the system, doubts of its permanence, never disturbed Robbie's mind. American capitalism had provided the world with more plenty than the world had ever known before, and it was a model the other nations would follow as soon as they had arrived at the stage of intelligence in which they understood what was good for them.

IV

Such were Lanny Budd's reflections, walking among the awful wreckage of Adolf Hitler's Third Reich. He had managed to get Monck on the telephone—the Americans had restored parts of the system. The two men had made a date for dinner, and then Lanny strolled into the Russian sector—there were no restrictions as yet. He presented his credentials and asked for a permit to visit the ruins of the New Chancellery. Most of the old sights of Berlin were gone forever, but the one that he wanted to see was indestructible.

A little more than two years and a half had passed since he had last been in this enormous granite barracks—at least it had that shape. It represented Adi Schicklgruber's idea of architecture, very big, very costly, and perdurable, a monument that could be used and admired simultaneously. Then the stern, handsome young Aryans of the Leibstandarte had stood at every door, demanding passes and scrutinizing them carefully, accompanying you inside if you were a stranger. There was an enormous long corridor paved with red marble, and by and by you came to large doors with the bronze initials "AH" on them. Here you were questioned some more, then taken inside and thoroughly searched, whoever you might be.

Now the great ugly building was a corpse, sinking into slow decay. Bombed walls and ceilings had fallen, so that you could not get from the great entrance hall to the greater hall beyond. Rain had poured in through all the gaping windows and roof holes, and frost had broken up the panelings and the mosaic floors. The precious marble had been taken by the Russians to build a memorial, and the Soviet sentries at the entrances appeared indifferent and did not even bother to look at the American's pass.

But the entrance to the garden had been cleared, and here Lanny presented his pass to a Russian officer who knew a little English and who warned him to keep to the paths, because of buried mines. In that part of the garden upon which the Führer's private offices had looked out there stood an enormous block of concrete, as big as an ordinary cottage. It had one small but heavy steel door, which now had been cut open with a welding torch. Lanny went into a narrow passage which led to a flight of stairs going down into the earth. Overhead in that passage was eighteen feet of solid concrete, and the Führer's skilled engineers had assured him that would be enough to resist the impact of a direct hit by the biggest bomb ever made. Apparently they had been right, for the block stood intact.

V

Using a torch borrowed from the guard—with three cigarettes by way of thanks—Lanny descended several flights of steps, thirty-five or forty in all, deep under the earth. Two years and a half ago when he had trod them, Hitler had led the way, followed by his Bavarian damsel, Eva Braun; then had come his American friend, then Heinrich Jung, and last of all the Führer's steward, Arthur Kannenberg, who had been entertaining them with his accordion and the singing of *G'stanzln,* the folksongs which carried Adi back into his childhood. The sirens had been screaming, and presently the ground had quivered from the impact of bombs. Down there you couldn't hear them, you felt them in your bones.

Now storms had driven in through the open doorway and the stairs were wet; there was a smell of dampness, burned stuff, and decay. Below was that elaborate place of refuge which had so astonished Lanny; a central hall, which had evidently become a guardroom, for double-decker metal bunks had been installed, and the floor was littered with smashed rifles, cartridges and empty shells, bloody bandages and moldering German uniforms. The steel door leading to the private apartments moved stiffly on its hinges, and Lanny went into the drawing-room where he had sat the air raid through. There was water on the floor, and the deep-pile carpets behaved like sponges under his feet. Apparently an attempt had been made to burn the place by piling the furniture against the paneled walls; the paintings on the walls were charred and blackened, and the overstuffed sofa on which Lanny had sat was turned to charred lumps floating on water.

VI

Lanny explored this place thoroughly, for even at the price of wet feet and dirty clothes he wanted to assure himself as to the truth of the stories he had read about the Führer's death. Several of the rooms had been burned out, but not Hitler's bedroom. Here were his plain bed and his desk, and beyond was his bathroom, the door open. He had brought Lanny to the bedroom to show him a lovely painting he had brought from the Bechstein Haus; but that place on the wall was empty now. Under it was another overstuffed sofa, made of some light-colored, highly polished wood, and according to the accounts Lanny had received from the American Intelligence officers at Berchtesgaden, it was on this sofa that Hitler and Eva had shot themselves. Eva had sat at the right end and had shot herself through the heart; her master, now her husband, had sat beside her and had shot himself through the temple, slumping forward.

Lanny looked, and there was the story written in blood on the brocaded upholstery, on the wooden arm of the sofa, and on the floor beside it and in front of it; bloodspots dried and hard but unmistakable. Ten months had passed, but nobody had been interested in scrubbing them away. Lanny took his pocketknife and cut out a section of the stained upholstery and put it into his pocket; he had the idea that he would frame it, mark it "Blood from the brain of Adolf Hitler," and present it to some museum in America. It might serve as a warning to some ambitious politician of the future who might be tempted to seize power over the sweet land of liberty.

According to the story of Kempke, the chauffeur, he had helped to carry the body of Eva Braun up the stairs, wrapped in a blanket. The two bodies had been laid in a depression of the ground in the garden, left by some construction work. Many cans of gasoline had been poured over them, and when the flames had died down more gasoline had been thrown on, until the bodies had been entirely consumed.

Lanny inspected the rest of that elaborate Führerbunker—dining-room, kitchen, storerooms, generator plant, engine room, refrigeration room, telephone and telegraph rooms, hospital and operating room, and accommodations for a dozen persons who worked at these various services. The place had been looted and smashed, and the floor was covered with litter of every sort; but one souvenir was enough.

The visitor climbed back to the fresh air and inspected the garden. It had been ripped up by shells—the Russian shelling had been going on while the funeral pyre was blazing. Lanny saw the depression in the ground, the blackened earth, and the charred stuff not yet entirely washed away; there were large gasoline tins, shot through with bullet holes, doubtless after they had been thrown into the flames. At one corner of the garden was an armored concrete watchtower, from which, according to the recorded accounts, a sentry of the SD—Sicherheitsdienst—had stood and watched the cremation. There was no longer any doubt in the ex-P.A.'s mind that the story of the Führer's death was true in all details.

The *Amerikansi* returned to the Russian guard post, thanked the officer, and asked permission to dry his shoes and socks by the warm woodstove. They carried on a laborious conversation, while common soldiers stood by, grinning with pleasure over Lanny's efforts at Russian and expressing wonder over the fine pair of American shoes. They were friendly when you got them alone and they were sure that no MVD man was within hearing. They were happy when an *Amerikansi* pointed to himself and said "*Tovarish.*" When he asked if they were sure that Adolf Hitler was dead they all nodded their heads and said, "Da! Da!" He made a sensation when he said that he had known President Roosevelt. When he said that he had visited Kuibyshev four years ago and had talked with Stalin they were too polite to say they didn't believe him.

VII

Berlin had been divided into four sectors. The Russians had the largest, to the east; it contained most of the industries, and they had been busily carting off the machinery. They had plenty of justification, since the Germans had looted and wrecked the greater part of Russia and all of Poland; but much of the machinery was rusting because they had no place to store it and lacked the skill to put it to use. The Americans had the southwestern part, mostly residential, and the part which had been least destroyed. The British had the west-central, full of lakes and woods, and villas where they could be quite comfortable. The French had the smallest part, to the northwest; that was fair, since they had done by far the smallest part of the fighting.

In course of ten months all four of the groups had made the discovery that it is a complicated matter to govern three million people, most of whom do not understand your language. You couldn't very well kill them, and you had to give them something to eat; you had to maintain public services, and let the workers have jobs to keep them out of mischief. So the Big Four were discussing the project of holding elections in the autumn and letting the Germans take over the operation of a central government under Allied control. A difficult situation, for even the conquerors didn't understand one another's languages, and still less did they understand one another's ideas and purposes. They all wanted to keep Germany down and make sure that she would never again try to conquer Europe; they faced the embarrassing fact that the essentials of modern industry, steel and coal and chemicals, including synthetic oil, are also the essentials of war, and plants can be quickly converted.

President Roosevelt had apparently been persuaded to the so-called "Morgenthau plan," by which Germany was to be turned into an agricultural country. But in modern times the land had never been able to produce enough food for all its population; and who was going to make up the surplus? The Allies were up against the situation which had troubled old Clemenceau, the tiger of France; there were just twenty million too many Germans! They could perhaps be taught to limit their population, but who was going to see to that? They could perhaps be forced to emigrate, but what country would take them and who would pay the cost of transportation?

Or could they be tamed and taught to love democracy and drop their habit of putting on uniforms and marching and shouting *Sieg Heil*? Apparently that was what the Allies were deciding upon; but how were they to agree on the method? The Russians all wanted to make them into Marxist-Leninist Stalinists. Some British wanted to make them into Clement-Attlee Socialists and others into Winston-Churchill Tories. Some Americans wanted to make them into New Deal Democrats, and others into McKinley Republicans. The French, so far as Lanny was able to ascertain, wanted to make them into Frenchmen, at least those who lived anywhere near the River Rhine, and let the devil take the rest.

VIII

All this was what Bernhardt Monck wanted to talk to Lanny about. This onetime sailor, labor leader, *capitán*, and OSS agent had been taken on as a personnel adviser to the AMG. He kept track of Germans, looked up their records, and helped to sort out the liberal and democratic sheep from the Nazi goats. Lanny went to his apartment and had dinner with his little family, whom he had heard much about but had never met. Those two children had lived in Germany, France, and the Argentine and knew all three languages and some English besides. The war had paid no heed to children but had scattered them like seeds over the earth; however, this pair hadn't suffered, because their father had earned money from Lanny and his father and had used the Americans as a bank, much safer than anything in Adolf Hitler's realm or his French satrapy.

Monck poured out his heart to this trusted friend. He had had so many disappointments in his life—one long struggle for social justice which he had never seen. He had felt so confident that with the overthrow of Nazism there would be peace and a measure of security for this tormented old continent; but now his mind was full of doubts and tempted to despair. Were the Americans going to be equal to the job which had been thrust upon them? Did they even have any comprehension of the nature of that job? The Humpty-Dumpty of capitalism had fallen off the European wall and been smashed into a thousand pieces; and apparently all the President's horses and the President's men had no idea in their minds but to put Humpty-Dumpty together again.

The Big Four governments had agreed upon an elaborate program of denazification, and it read very well on paper; the trouble was with its application. It was Monck's business to investigate the record of this individual and that, and he would do so and make a report; but then he would find that the American authorities would make excuses for not acting. Yes, the individual may have been a Nazi; but then most Germans had been Nazis, or had had to pretend to be. What was needed right now was efficiency, and this individual had had experience and was willing to do what he was told. Monck would say to his American boss, "Yes, Major Porter, but doing what you are told isn't democracy. Doing what you are told is supposed to be the principal German vice and was what brought Hitler into power." That would be taken as arguing, and what Monck was supposed to do was to do what he was told.

It was one consequence of government by an Army, and it couldn't very well be ended until there was a civil administration in Germany, so Monck thought; and Lanny answered that it was more than that, it was a difference in national point of view. To an American, democracy meant political rights and civil liberties but had nothing to do with business. "In business we have private enterprise, which is autocracy undisguised. The boss owns the plant, and if the worker doesn't like it he can go elsewhere."

"Exactly," agreed the German; "and that means that I get nothing but blank looks when I try to explain to an American Army officer that the Social Democrats are the only people in this country who really believe in democracy and can be depended upon to oppose the return of some new and more subtly disguised form of Nazism. What the American is thinking about are property rights and efficiency in administration. The result is that while they are prosecuting Dr. Schacht for crimes against humanity they are appointing thousands of little Schachts to positions of authority all over Germany. When they get through, the country will be in the hands of the very same men who financed Hitler and who will have no idea in the world but to finance some new 'strong' government to keep the Socialists from winning an election."

IX

That was one of Monck's troubles; the other was at the opposite end of the social scale—the Communists. They were making all the difficulties they could for Socialists, as well as for Americans; they wanted everything to fail, not merely with capitalism, but also with Social Democracy, in order that the workers might be driven to Communism. Monck was of the opinion that the Western powers had made a grave error in consenting to four separate regimes for Germany; it was the one sure way to promote dissension and conflict. "They should have argued it out at the beginning and worked out an arrangement for one government; it was either then or never. As it is, they have established perpetual argument, and if it doesn't lead to war it will be a miracle."

A grave problem indeed for a German Social Democrat, for he was caught between the two firing lines, and neither side was his friend. The Americans dealt with the Socialists only because they had to, and forbade them to take any steps toward carrying out their program; as for the Russians, what they wanted was to shoot the Socialist leaders and throw their followers into concentration camps. They were doing that in their own zone of Germany; they had got up a so-called "Socialist Unity Party," to be run by the Communists, and if the Socialist leaders joined that they were all right, but if they didn't, they disappeared and nobody knew what had become of them. Kidnapings across the line were common, and Monck said that he would never go any-where near the line at night. It was quite like the old Nazi days.

Yes, the world was certainly in a mess! Americans had thought the world war was won and that the Allies were going to stand together and bring order and peace to Europe; but there they were, splitting apart—exactly as Hitler and Göring and the rest had foreseen. American boys in the Armed Forces were holding mass meetings, crying, "We wanna go home," and this movement was spreading to India, Korea, Japan, Italy, and France. There were places where officers didn't dare give orders to the men for fear they wouldn't be obeyed. Naturally, it looked to the Communists like the coming of world revolution, their newer world in birth.

"I don't need to tell you about the Russians," said the ex-*capitán*. "Your armies are going to pieces, but theirs stay put, and the same applies to the air forces. They are probing for weak spots all over the world, and wherever they find one they will move in. Their propaganda war has never been so active."

Yes, Lanny knew. Russia was still refusing to carry out her agreement that Dairen and Port Arthur were to be free ports. Russia was backing Yugoslavia's demand for Trieste. Russia was demanding a trusteeship over Tripolitania in North Africa. Russia was refusing to take her troops out of Northern Iran, and when Iran appealed to the Security Council of the United Nations, Russia denied the right of the UN to consider the matter. When the UN acted, Gromyko, the Russian representative, took a walk. A sensation throughout the world, caused by this young man with the dead-pan face. Was he going to stay out? He didn't say. Was Russia going to withdraw from the UN? Russia didn't say.

What was America going to do? Monck asked, and Lanny didn't have much to tell him. Lanny didn't know America's new President and couldn't guess how rapidly or slowly he was learning his job. His Secretary of State was an amiable, old-fashioned Southern gentleman, from the most old-fashioned state in the Union, South Carolina. James F. Byrnes was the only man in the country who could say that he had been representative, senator, justice of the Supreme Court, and secretary of state. He was an elderly politician, trained in the arts of compromise and reconcilement. For more than a year he had been traveling from one conference to the next, encountering for the first time in his life a force that would not compromise and would not be reconciled. Jimmie looked into the dead-pan face of Gromyko and the deader-pan face of Molotov and tried to guess what was going on behind those masks; it was something new in his experience, a trained and indoctrinated, silent and implacable, cold and deadly hatred.

X

Lanny explained, "We Americans are busy putting our Fleet and our Air Force up in mothballs, as we call it, and it will seem to us perfectly awful to have to start taking them out again. We hate war and everything about it. We want to bring the boys home and give them jobs making motorcars and electric refrigerators and other such useful articles. We want to use our spare money keeping the people of Europe alive and helping them to build a union of free nations. But I don't think we'll let ourselves be squeezed out of Germany, or even out of Berlin, and I think if we see that we have to, we'll start rearming all over again and getting ready to defend our position. We think that Roosevelt was very generous at Yalta and Teheran; indeed, our conscience troubles us a little because we gave away things that were perhaps not ours to give. You can be certain we won't give any more, and if we have to get tough, we will."

"You must understand," said Monck, "it's a matter of importance to me and mine, not to mention my comrades and my party. If we stick here and try to help you Americans, and then you back down and leave us, it would be certain death for me and probably for my family. You can't imagine how the Communists hate us, or the frenzy they will be in if they see their plans being balked. They are absolutely certain that they are going to be able to take Germany and make it into a Communist satellite. They have been training a hundred thousand German prisoners in Russia—men who have been indoctrinated and have become Communists, or have pretended to. You know about General Paulus, their commander."

"I have read about this army," Lanny replied. "Will the rank and file stay put?"

"The Russians are bringing them into Eastern Germany now, and a number of them have deserted and come over to our side of the line. They have dreadful stories to tell of the millions who have died in slave camps. They themselves are well fed, better than they will be on our side, but they prefer freedom."

"How much do they realize about what is going on?"

"Those I have talked to are in a state of bewilderment and don't know whom to trust. Nobody ever loved an occupation army, but after they have been here a while they know that they prefer Americans and American ways. All Germans, you know, look upon the Russians as a barbarous people who are dirty and don't know how to use a bathroom. What they did in the way of rape and looting in Eastern Germany would suffice to make it impossible to win us to their ideology. The Russians themselves are confused—they have a hard time making up their minds whether they are conquerors or comrades, and they try to be both, and it doesn't work."

XI

Stalin had delivered a speech in the month of February, in which he had said that the Soviet Union must have more heavy industry, to be prepared for any contingency. It was notice to the Russian people that they must face more years of deprivation, and it was notice to the outside world to do the same. This applied especially to America, the only nation which had the means to save Europe from starvation—and from Communist revolts which would follow in its wake.

"What can we do?" Lanny asked, and his friend replied with one word, three times repeated, "Propaganda! Propaganda! Propaganda! You must set up the most powerful radio stations in the world and answer the Communists in every language. You must employ the best writers and the best speakers you have, every skill of every sort, and meet the falsehoods and smash them. You must print cheap newspapers and leaflets in every language and flood every country with them. You must smuggle them into Russia by every device you can think of. It's a war—they have declared it, and you have to pitch in and win. If you spend one per cent of what you'll have to spend in a fighting war, you may save the other ninety-nine per cent. I can't imagine why your leaders don't see that."

"There are several reasons," the other explained. "Our people are afraid of government propaganda. They are afraid to give too much power to politicians—it might be turned against the people."

"But you did it during the war!"

"We did it, but we hated it, and we stopped it as soon as we could. The Office of War Information was abolished almost at once. When we have won a war we think everything is settled, and we hurry home to our private affairs."

"Including the private publishing of newspapers and the broadcasting of radio commercials!"

"That's a big factor in the matter. Our publishers and radio owners are scared of the very shadow of government competition. They'd rather risk going to hell than see it get a foothold. Their congressmen agree with them, and it will be like pulling teeth to get any appropriation out of them."

XII

This situation was made worse by the fact that a congressional election was due in November, and by all the signs there would be a Republican Congress to confront President Truman during his second two years. It had been that way after World War I, and the pattern appeared to be repeating itself; the people were tired, they were disillusioned, and wanted a change. The effect would be to make every decision harder; every measure would be judged by its political results, in keeping patronage and power away from the administration. A cheerless prospect indeed, and the best Lanny could do to relieve his friend's depression was to tell him about the Peace Program and promise to use its power to persuade the American people to prepare for ideological war.

Monck laid down the law. "America won't get anywhere unless it makes plain to the people of Europe that it is not trying to block progress along Socialist lines. The future of Europe rests between the Communists and the Socialists, and if you try to stop Socialism you will drive the workers straight into the Communist camp. Socialization of basic industry and free co-operatives in small manufacturing and retail trade—that is the only program that has any chance of winning Western Europe and keeping it."

Lanny answered, "That is our group's program, and we are doing our best to explain it." But somehow he couldn't work up much hope of making it go with Senator Taft of Ohio or Senator Wherry of Nebraska, not to mention the stone-age Democrats from the South such as Senator McKellar of Tennessee or Senator George of Georgia.

The two friends discussed the problem until so late that Monck wasn't willing for Lanny to go home; many crimes were committed on dark, rainy nights, in spite of the military patrols. Lanny slept on the sofa in the little living-room, and guessed that one of the children was sleeping on the floor. The family had a food allowance, and the visitor had not failed to bring them a package from the PX. Wonderful people, the Americans! They had cigarettes and chocolates and canned foods and razor blades and matches and soap without limit and could play Santa Claus wherever they went.

For the most part these superior beings lived lives quite separate from the Germans. The Americans rode in cars, while the Germans rode bicycles, and generally took them inside wherever they arrived, for fear of thieves. You couldn't buy a bicycle for any amount of German money; the standard price was six hundred cigarettes, or three cartons. When a German boy saw an American smoking, he would follow right at his heels, ready to pounce upon the butt. A butt is a *Stummel*, and the Americans called the pursuit of them "stummeling." Porters and others who cleaned offices made a good thing of it; they took the butts home and took out the tobacco and made new cigarettes. You could get a pound of potatoes for a single one.

Also, you might get a girl! The GIs called the girls "furlines," that being easier to say than *Fräuleins*, even when you mispronounced it, as most Americans did. Also they were called "fraternazis," and when a GI was going out with one of them he told his buddies he was going "fratting." As a result of this "buyers' market," the Army had a problem expressed by the letters VD. As a result of the food scarcity, the Germans had one expressed by the letters TB. War may be ever so glorious and ennobling at a distance, but it loses some of its glamour when you get too close.

XIII

Lanny had a debt to pay in Berlin, and next morning he and Monck walked to the Moabit district. This is one of the working-class quarters; having small factories scattered throughout, it had been well pasted with bombs. Whole blocks were smashed, and now women sat, even on this Sunday morning, digging out the bricks, scraping them clean, and piling them in neat rows; for this they got ten cents an hour, American money.

The tenement home of Johann Seidl, elderly watchmaker, had been hit, but not hard enough to wreck it entirely; the three upper stories were broken beams and plaster, but the two lower stories were intact, and the surviving families had moved down to the lower floors, presumably dividing the rent. Lanny found three families, eleven persons in all, occupying an apartment consisting of a medium-size kitchen and two small bedrooms. How they made out he didn't ask. When it rained hard the unplastered ceiling leaked badly, but they caught the water in pans, and fortunately the drain was in order.

Genosse Seidl was the Social-Democratic old-timer who had hidden Lanny from the human bloodhounds of Heinrich Himmler and had got him started by way of the underground to Italy. Monck had told him that the fugitive had got out safely but hadn't told him that he was now in town; the arrival created a sensation, especially when the American produced a package of goods such as Germans had not seen in several years—goods much too valuable for them to consume but which could be exchanged for quantities of potatoes and lard.

The visitor was introduced and shook hands all round; he found that he had become a legend, for the newspaper *Socialdemokrat* had published his testimony at Nürnberg, and Monck had told Johann that this Herr Budd was the "Comrade Thirty" he had saved two and a half years ago. *Wundervoll, unerhört,* a man who had fooled Hitler and Göring, and whose picture had been in the paper, and now here he was right in our kitchen!

Johann produced a treasure which he had managed to keep hidden through the bombing and other dangers—Lanny's watch. All the rest of his possessions had been burned, but you can't burn a watch, and if the Nazis had caught Johann with it they would have put him to the torture. Lanny had a new watch, so he told Monck to sell the old one and divide the proceeds between Johann and the family of Genossin Anna Pfister. That was the woman who had hidden Lanny for ten days in the cellar of her leather-working shop; the Nazis had seized her, nobody knew why or how, and had sent her to the Buchenwald concentration camp, which, of course, had been the end of her.

They had two chairs, and the guests sat on them; they talked and the others listened. There were no longer any secrets, for everybody had undergone a magical sea change, and there were no longer any Nazis. To have been a genuine anti-Nazi was an honor and source of preferment; to have been an anti-Nazi posing as a Nazi, as Johann Seidl had done, was to be in a trying situation; but Monck had known the truth and had testified, and now came the son of Budd-Erling to confirm it in a most dramatic way. Johann would almost certainly get a job now.

The visitor didn't ask these people about their lives, for what could they tell save of a dreadful winter, and hunger and cold, sickness and death? They wanted to hear about America and what the land of unlimited possibilities was going to do with them and their lives. Lanny told only the hopeful things—he couldn't bear to voice a fear or even a doubt. To him these people were the comrades of his youth, and there were millions of them, all over Europe, still clinging pathetically to the dream of a world of peace and order in which men built houses and inhabited them, planted vineyards and reaped the fruit of them;

they did not build and another inhabit, they did not sow and another reap! That was the Socialist world—but, oh, what a long time it took coming!

XIV

Lanny bade farewell to his proletarian friends and climbed from the bottom to the top of the social ladder. Ambassador Robert Murphy, career man of the State Department, had become political adviser to AMG in Berlin, and he and the son of Budd-Erling had become good friends while working together to win the French in North Africa from the Vichy side to the American. That had been only four years ago, but what an age it seemed, and what a cycle of history had happened since! The men in the prisoners' dock at Nürnberg had then been at the apex of their glory, and the American diplomatic representative, officially known as "Counselor to the Embassy at Vichy stationed in Algiers," had been a pygmy among many giants; a worried and unhappy pygmy, fearing not for himself but for his country and the free world.

Now he was in a new position of danger but wasn't supposed to think about it or to be afraid of the new set of giants he confronted. General Clay, the American commander, had only a few thousand troops in Berlin, while the Russians had an army just across the street from him. Moreover, the Russians had all the territory surrounding Berlin, and the Americans had only a narrow corridor through which to come and go. What would happen if the Russians should ever decide to close that corridor was something that nobody liked to think about. What you did was to be as friendly with them as they would let you; always smile, be patient, and try in every way to abate their suspicions.

That came naturally to Robert Murphy, for he was a genial person. His voice showed his pleasure when he heard Lanny's over the telephone. "Oh, good! Won't you come to lunch? Or to dinner? How long are you going to be here?" And so on, the way one talks to a man with whom one has been through dangers and with whom one has shared precious secrets.

The Ambassador's car came and brought the visitor to his residence. They had a quiet dinner and a long talk. So many things that Lanny could tell about: Roosevelt and his death, Los Alamos and Alamogordo, and the work of the Alsos mission. "You do get around, don't you!" said Murphy. He wanted to know for whom Lanny was working now,

and why he was in Berlin. Being a diplomat, he avoided a direct inquiry; but Lanny, understanding diplomacy, hastened to give assurance that he was on his own and not reporting on anybody. He didn't
mention the Peace Program because that might have made his friend
more cautious in his talk.

The impression Lanny got was that this blond, handsome gentleman
was so much concerned with the trees that he overlooked the forest.
He was trying to get things done in Germany, and sometimes it was
the British or the French who wouldn't let him, but most of the time
it was the Russians. The Russians objected to the forming of baseball
clubs for German boys and pointed to the agreement of the Big Four
that no political organizations were to be permitted. Under the Nazis
all sport clubs had been political, and the same was true in other countries, including the Soviet Union. There were endless problems connected with the schools—getting teachers who weren't Nazis and books
written and printed that contained no open or secret propaganda for
Nazism, Pan-Germanism, or other poisonous theories.

And so it went. There were six and a half million displaced persons
in Germany, and most of them couldn't be sent back to their homes
because their political coloration was wrong and they would be thrown
into jail or shipped to a slave-labor camp. That applied all the way
from the Baltic states to the Balkans, and to tens of thousands of Russians. There was nothing to do with them but keep them in refugee
camps, which could be nothing but the former German *Lagern*. They
were horribly crowded and miserably unhappy; they all wanted to go
to America, or, barring that, to the Argentine, or Palestine, or Australia, or wherever. Impossible to persuade them that there weren't
ships enough in the world to take them. The GIs were still being
shipped home, and surely they had precedence.

A sensitive-minded official was on the defensive about these conditions. He worried about opinion at home, where nobody could form
any notion of the problems of a four-power government whose members were often occupied in keeping one another from doing anything.
He pointed out that America had got much the worst of the Germany
partition; we had got the scenery, and there was no tourist trade.
Lanny pointed out what Monck had mentioned, that in our sector a
great part of the land belonged to feudal aristocrats, absentee noblemen
who did little or nothing with their estates. Why not put the DPs to
producing on them? The Ambassador looked uncomfortable; he had
always known that this agreeable, rich fellow countryman was a "Pinko."

XV

The ex-P.A. discovered that he was in a position to become something of a social lion if he so desired. His story had appeared in the Berlin papers, together with his picture, and a lot of people wanted to meet him and hostesses wanted to show him off. He stayed a few days and went about meeting the American officers of the governing staff, an immense bureaucracy with directors and deputy directors of this and that: staff sections for economic affairs, educational affairs, religious, fiscal, property control, information, public health, public welfare. All wanted to tell their stories to a traveling celebrity—even if he was that for only a week or two.

There was a world relief organization, UNRRA—United Nations Relief and Rehabilitation Administration—and there were complaints about its operations in Germany. Its head was a British general who lived in a ducal palace a long way from the wretched DPs whom he was supposed to be aiding. He was a charming, fashionable gentleman and would give you a royal good time if you went to see him; but you wouldn't hear much about the millions of victims of the war—Jews and Poles and such like. British officers looked out for the British Empire, as of old, and were wholly unsatisfactory to ardent young idealists who had got jobs because they were recommended by Professor Frankfurter.

Just now the papers reported that a new general director of UNRRA had been appointed. Ex-Mayor La Guardia of New York was promising to stir things up; did Mr. Budd know him? Lanny had never met him but had heard him over the radio, speaking in a high-pitched, excited voice. He was a squat little man, a comical figure of tireless energy; half Italian and one-quarter Jewish, yet four full quarters American. He was the friend of oppressed persons all over the world, and some of the Americans were hoping to see him give Lieutenant General Sir Freddie Morgan a chance to return to his native land. The General was quoted as saying that we were on the way to war with Russia and that our one duty was to build up Germany to be on our side. Lanny, who had heard of him at Wickthorpe Castle, was only too familiar with this point of view. He was shocked to discover that the American General Clay apparently had it also.

The Russians also were familiar with it, and it didn't help Americans to win their confidence. There were the so-called "Anders' Poles," anti-Soviet refugees who had been formed into an army to fight the

Germans and were now being subsidized by reactionary Polish groups in London. If the Russians had an army of anti-British Germans, that was tit for tat, and you might argue till the coming of the next war which side had started it and which carried the greater share of blame.

The point was to get both sides to stop at the same time; and to do that you had to listen to those who wanted peace and not to those who were sure that war was inevitable. It was necessary to make plain to the members of the Politburo that they were not going to be permitted to take the rest of Europe by force; but it was also necessary to make plain that the governments of the Western world were in the hands of men who had no will to resist social change by force, but rather to guide it by wisdom and understanding.

XVI

Lanny had one more project in Berlin. The idea had occurred to him that it would be fun to see himself as the Germans had seen him; it would rest his mind to know the answer to some of the riddles that had puzzled him over the years. What had Heinrich Himmler actually got on the Führer's American friend? What had he got on Oskar von Herzenberg and on Marceline? How had he found out that Monck was spying on Professor Plötzen, and had it ever been discovered that Lanny had helped Monck escape to Sweden? It would all be set down to the smallest detail with German *Gründlichkeit* in the voluminous files of the Gestapo.

Lanny had himself transported to Number 1 Wasserkafersteig, headquarters of the Berlin Document Center, Office of U. S. Military Government for Germany. He presented his credentials to the officer in charge and explained his purpose. The necessary clearance was granted, and he was taken to a room with a long table. GIs brought him folders, one after another as they were dug out.

The most fascinating experience that any war spy could imagine. It was like Judgment Day, when the books of the Recording Angel are supposed to be opened and all secrets revealed. It was as if the dream, or the nightmare, of Dr. Rhine had suddenly come true, and someone was able to read the minds of any and everybody else in the world. Here were practically all the persons the son of Budd-Erling had known in Germany, and some also in France, telling what they knew about his life and what they thought about his character: neatly typed documents in stilted official German, dated, and initialed by this and that official, often with comments. Many of the documents were duplicated in different files, having been accumulated by organizations or departments which had exchanged carbon copies.

The Gestapo had been watching Lanny from the first time that Göring had sent for him, in April of 1933. Lanny had known that they would be bound to do this and had guided himself accordingly. He was, they recorded, a Jew-lover, a sentimental idler, a spoiled, rich man's son. Kurt Meissner had said he was a weakling but harmless, which was about what the great *Komponist* had told Lanny to his face. Heinrich Jung had claimed credit for having converted him to National Socialism and certified to the fact that he was an ardent admirer of the Führer. *Seine Hochgeboren,* Graf Stubendorf, had condescended to testify that Herr Budd was a highly regarded *Kunstsachverständiger* and undoubtedly a friend of the German people—here was his letter, duly signed.

So it went, down through ten years. Various members of the Führer's household, also of Göring's, had been interviewed and had expressed opinions of this easy-going, self-satisfied American dilettante; they didn't trust him or like him, but the Führer was determined to use him, and so was the Reichsmarschall. He was reported as being the lover of Hilde, Fürstin Donnerstein—which wasn't true but might have been if he had wanted it that way. In 1940, before the invasion of France, Himmler had personally ordered a complete new investigation of him, and there were reports from New York and even from Newcastle, but they hadn't found out about his being married to Mary Morrow! There had come a favorable report about Robbie, who was a genuine Roosevelt hater and was using his son to get information to be used against the administration.

Then in 1943, with America in the war up to its eyes, this international playboy had come into Germany from Italy, escorted under the Führer's personal orders; that was when the Gestapo had really gone to work. But they hadn't got anything about his connections with Monck, either in Switzerland or in Sweden. Himmler had personally warned the Führer against him, but the Führer had insisted that he was an old friend—Hitler believed in everybody who had known and admired him prior to his taking power. The Abwehr, the Counter-Intelligence of the Army, had also done some research, interviewing everybody in Nazi Europe who had done art business with the American visitor; there was nothing wrong about him except that he had been a Social Democrat when he was young—something he had told the Führer about. *"Nicht mehr gehelligen,"* Adi had written on one report—don't bother me any more! That was one of the documents

Lanny held out to have a photostat made; he would have it framed and put on his wall.

The bust-up had come only when the Gestapo arrested Oskar von Herzenberg; under torture he had confessed and had named Lanny as having known about the plot on the Führer's life. Marceline had stood firm and had insisted that she had no idea where Lanny was. A general alarm had been sent out for him, and there was a huge dossier about the efforts to find him. One curious thing he made note of: the Gestapo files showed that they had notified Abwehr and that Abwehr had acknowledged the order and promised to take all possible measures; but when Lanny searched the Abwehr files he could not find a scrap about the matter. Apparently they had done nothing. He was left to speculate about two Abwehr officials who had testified against the Nazis at Nürnberg—they having been secretly working for the Allies all through the war and before. Dahlerus and Gisevius had known and protected various Allied agents in Germany, and it could be guessed that they had sidetracked the orders concerning Lanny Budd. Even Admiral Canaris, "the little Greek" who headed this important agency, might have been helping to protect an American spy. Canaris had been discovered and shot.

XVII

Having finished with his own career, Lanny turned to his wife's. She had been living in a pension in Berlin in the year of 1939, and suspicion had fallen upon her because she locked her manuscript up in her trunk so carefully and tore her spoiled pages into small pieces. Some of these pieces had been saved, and here they were, a set of jigsaw puzzles put together and pasted on sheets. Her room had been raided, but she had escaped and not been heard from again. Her clothing and books had been sold at auction, and the Gestapo had realized a total of marks 1927.53 therefrom. Her mss., which she had thought lost forever, were all here. The Army wouldn't part with the originals but for a small fee would make photostat copies of every page.

And then Miss Elvirita Jones—the name Lanny had invented on the spur of the moment, at his wit's end to get his fugitive out of Germany. He had taken her to the Berghof and introduced her to Hitler and Hess as a wonderful spiritualist medium; and of course the Gestapo had heard about that event. After she had been let out by way of Switzerland they had tried to track down Fräulein Jones; not even the excitement of the war's outbreak had caused them to forget her;

they had made inquiries among spiritualists in Paris, London, and New York, but no one there had ever heard of such a medium. Lanny wondered if this had been the work of Heinrich Himmler, hoping to get something on Lanny himself. Oddly enough, there was no record of the Elvirita Jones matter in any of the files on Lanny Budd. Apparently even German *Gründlichkeit* slipped up now and then!

they had made inquiries among spiritualists in Paris, London, and New York, but no one there had ever heard of such a medium. Lanny wondered if this had been the work of Heinrich Himmler, hoping to get something on Lanny himself. Oddly enough, there was no record of the Elvirita Jones matter in any of the files on Lanny Budd. Apparently even Gorman Grindlebach slipped up now and then.

BOOK TEN

He Shall Stand before Kings

30

Come You Home a Hero

I

THE Ambassador's car took Lanny to the British sector of Berlin, and from there he had a seat in a plane to London—the two armies did favors for each other in such matters. When he arrived he phoned Irma, to arrange to see Frances, and as always Irma invited him to the Castle.

An odd and rather amusing situation with his ex-wife now. The story of his testimony at Nürnberg had been in the London papers of course, and several of the baser sort which went in for gossip had mentioned that the self-confessed agent was the former husband of the Countess of Wickthorpe. And what were Irma and Ceddy going to make of that? The collapse of Nazism had been too complete for this noble pair to admit any trace of their old-time attitude; but what would be the case inside their hearts? The presidential agent had been deceiving not merely Hitler and Göring, but also Irma and Ceddy and all their friends; he had been a snake in the grass, slithering into their historic home, and no doubt laughing in his heart at them.

They knew it, and their friends must know it, yet there wasn't a thing they could do about it. Lanny was, indubitably, the father of Frances and had a legal right to half her time until she was of age and could make her own choice. If he couldn't come to the Castle he would take her elsewhere and might not bring her back. So everything must be as if nothing had happened; the host and hostess must be polite, even cordial; they must tell him to stay as long as he pleased and to come again whenever he pleased. It is well known that in the great world people frequently practice such arts of masquerade; they maintain a surface of friendship while in their hearts are raging storms of hatred, contempt, jealousy, spite. Civilized life could hardly exist if everybody spoke his real thoughts.

Few persons had had more practice in superficial courtesy than this ex-P.A. He didn't let himself worry because he had wounded the

vanity of these two persons who thought themselves so important—
Ceddy because he had inherited a title and a castle, and Irma because
she was the daughter of Chicago's onetime traction king. Lanny forbore to mention the Nürnberg trial, which was a world demonstration
of their lack of judgment; instead he told about the situation in Berlin,
a more agreeable topic, because it enabled them to imply that they
had been right all along. Hadn't they done their best to warn the world
against the dangers of Bolshevism? Hadn't they foretold how the
Soviet revolution was bound to turn into Russian imperialism of the
old type? The bear that walked like a man was now walking like a
proletarian, but he was the same bear and was walking to the very
same goals—warm-water ports on the Baltic and the Pacific, and control of the Balkans, the Dardanelles, the oil fields of Mesopotamia and
Persia, and, of course, the treasures of India and China!

II

Frances was sixteen and had magically become a young woman.
She had her mother's well-developed figure and dark brown hair
and eyes. From her father she had got a lively disposition and an inquiring mind. She was back on the regime of tutors and didn't find it
nearly so much fun as going to school in Connecticut; a castle and a
great estate couldn't take the place of the world. Irma's possessiveness
had something pathological about it, so it seemed to Lanny; Frances
to her was not merely a daughter but also an heiress. The fortune had
been growing like Jonah's gourd all through the war—the lawyers
had found some way to turn it into a "foundation" and have it settled in Canada, so that it didn't have to pay the awful income taxes
of Irma's native land. Such a fortune—Lanny hadn't been told the
figure—dominates the life of its possessor; impossible not to think of
such a person as something beyond the human.

Lanny took the valuable possession for a long walk, through lanes
and paths where English poets had composed their verses and English
gamekeepers had kept watch for poachers through several centuries.
There they could talk frankly, away from an observant large household. Frances said that she hoped to spend the summer in Newcastle,
and was her father going to be there, and would she see much of him?
She laughed as she said, "What mother is afraid of, I might fall in
love with an American."

..."*She* did," replied Lanny, "and so did her mother."

"But she thinks I'm too emotional and don't appreciate the importance of her money. She has never told me how much of it I am to have, and I think I'm to understand that it depends upon the sort of marriage I make."

"It is something you will observe," said the unorthodox father. "The more money people have, the more they want."

He didn't need to question either mother or daughter; he could understand that Irma wouldn't think any American good enough for Frances. What could you do with money in America? In England you could marry into a great family and have real distinction for the rest of your days. Irma and Ceddy would have been canvassing the dukedoms to pick out the most eligible heir; and if the man had been living with chorus girls for ten or twenty years that wouldn't trouble them in the least. The thing was to have entree to the Court.

There had been no way to keep Frances from knowing the part her father had played in Nürnberg, and there was no way to keep her from being excited over the idea of a presidential agent. She plied him with questions about what he had done and then about what he was going to do. When he told her about the Peace Program she was thrilled; and little by little he realized that that truce which had been declared with Irma when they had parted company—on the platform of a railroad station in Austria in the year 1937—that truce was about to come to an end. Frances Barnes Budd had come of age mentally and was getting ready to make her own choices.

He couldn't help being thrilled by the discovery that she was going to choose his side. She would come to Newcastle this summer—being well able to travel in a plane by herself, she insisted. Then she would want to visit Lanny and Laurel. She would see that exciting work going on, the weekly radio session, the famous guests coming to speak, and all the fun of getting out a paper. And then the syndicate, and the authors who came to dinner; she would read the articles that went the rounds and listen to the talk.

"Couldn't I have a recording of some of the broadcasts?" she inquired; and of course she could. He had some in a suitcase and was going to discuss them with the BBC. If the BBC would put them on, Frances would hear them, and it would be a sort of crucifixion for the daughter and heiress of J. Paramount Barnes. She wouldn't approve of a single word; they were the ideas that were ruining Britain and that she had been striving so earnestly to keep out of her little one's mind. But the little one would soon be as big as herself and would repeat the ancient and bitter pattern of the young who refuse to think as their elders do.

If Irma had been legally able to say no she would have said it; but she couldn't. She had to assent to the second visit to Newcastle; and in her mind would be the horrid idea that her precious daughter would meet a lot of Reds and Pinks and miscellaneous rabble—her father was just as bad as he had been the day that Irma had left him! He had been lying to her all the time since, and keeping the very worst company, having the most dangerous thoughts in his mind. Frances would meet some long-haired poet, a free lover, no doubt, and be seduced by him, and Irma would have to cut her off with a few thousand a month and leave the bulk of her fortune to her two sons, who, thank God, had the right sort of father and would never be exposed to contamination.

III

Lanny telephoned and made an engagement with Captain Alfred Pomeroy-Nielson, M. P., and went up to town and met him. The American was taken into the gallery of the House; the chamber of the Commons had been smashed by a bomb, and its members had taken over the chamber of the Lords. Lanny listened to a debate on the conduct of the coal industry; the arguments of His Majesty's Loyal Opposition made him mad, but he couldn't say a word. The British had their ancient ways of doing things, and no matter how much they changed they never admitted the change but went on pretending that it was exactly as it had been for several centuries. The speaker wore a heavy wig and embroidered robes, which meant pretending that it was at least five hundred years ago, and in front of him lay the five-foot mace which symbolized his authority and which had been made and decorated with regal symbols some three hundred years ago.

Alfy told his old friend everything he needed to know in order to go back and report the new British government to an American radio audience. He went with his friend to the offices of the British Broadcasting Corporation, a big eight-story structure built on a rounded point, so that it looked like an enormous barge forcing its way through the city. Alfy's purpose, he had told Lanny, was to remind those gentlemen, youngish in years but elderly in mind, that there really had been a change in Britain. They took Lanny's platters and promised to consider them for presentation to the British people; when Alfy, decorated flying officer and heir to a baronetcy, reminded them that Mr. Budd of Budd-Erling was that presidential agent who had just come back from testifying at Nürnberg, the BBC interrupted its printed schedule and invited him to tell his story to a British audience the following evening. So it came about that Lanny Budd's debut as a radio performer in his own name took place in England, and his little daughter in Wickthorpe Castle, Buckinghamshire, was so proud of him that it made her mother and her grandmother two very unhappy great ladies.

There was even worse to come. Alfy's younger brother, Scrubbie, returned from the wars; he was still in uniform, with his decorations on. He came to the studio, heard the broadcast, and exclaimed, "Oh, wizard!" When he heard about the recordings from America he wanted the worst way to hear them. "Oh, I've got to hear the Pater!" And how could the gentlemen of the BBC refuse such a request from a war hero? They said "Righto!" and they all sat and listened to the Pater; and of course what he had said about England was right, and they said "Righto!" again. One of the platters had come by airmail to Lanny in care of Alfy and contained Professor Einstein's talk; Scrubbie exclaimed, "Oh, Einstein! Wizard!" He wanted to hear that, and then he said, "Wizard!" And what could the BBC gentlemen do but agree?

Neither Alfy or Scrubbie was the least bit naïve, they both knew that Lanny wanted these voices heard by the British people and by Britons who listened all over Europe; they also knew that many of these gentlemen in authority were of the old, the Conservative, way of thinking. The two brothers knew that uniforms counted, and titles, and that praise in British accents would count where a polite suggestion in an American accent wouldn't. They kept on until the BBC had agreed to broadcast several of the talks. Alfy undertook to call the attention of the House of Commons to the broadcasts and to help in getting publicity from the press. Rick had been doing that sort of thing for more than a quarter of a century and hadn't failed to teach the tricks to his sons.

IV

It didn't take Lanny long to get his wife on the transatlantic telephone and tell her all that good news. Then he had another bright idea; he couldn't have been Beauty Budd's son without being something of a matchmaker, and he called the Castle and arranged for Frances to come to town by a certain train. He would meet her at the station and take her to a hotel where she could dress for the evening; he would take her to dinner, and then to a theater, and perhaps to supper; she would have a time and see a little more of her father, and he would put her on the train in the latter part of the next afternoon.

There was no objection that Irma could make; and Scrubbie was there, tall and thin, with wavy dark hair, pink cheeks, and an amiable naïve expression; his uniform spick and span and his decorations in plain view. Such objects were no more than a shilling a dozen in London just then, but this was a special young captain, from a family that Frances had heard her father talk about, an old family that lived not far from the Castle and had been friendly until the issue of Nazi-Fascism had arisen to divide them. Scrubbie had been in one of the big shows of the war, the bombing of the Ploesti oil fields in Rumania; he had helped to drive Rommel all the way back from Alamein to Tunis, and had made his limit of flights when he was nineteen. The stories he had to tell were wonderful, and he didn't mind telling them; he wasn't the old-style reserved Englishman, but enthusiastic and explosive, and hadn't been repressed by his parents the way Frances had been. She, for her part, was fascinated by his airman's language. How could there be a more delightful way to express pleasure or approval or indeed anything whatever than to exclaim, "Wizard!"

These two could hardly take their eyes off each other, and there was no reason why they should. When that delightful evening was over Scrubbie asked if he might be allowed to take Frances to the Zoo in the morning, and the permission was granted. When he and Lanny were alone the older man said, "You may have her if you can win her." The other blushed and said, "Oh, thank you, sir!"

That meant that he would call at the Castle, and they couldn't very well turn him away. Younger sons have always had a low rating in England, but still they rate, and when they have done their military duty you at least have to be polite to them. Scrubbie had already indicated to Lanny his interest in the Peace Program and asked if he might come and work for it for his keep. Lanny had said, "Sure." So the boy would be there when Frances arrived; he would be welcomed at Robbie's home, and now and then Frances would come to visit Edgemere. Altogether, Lanny could guess, there wouldn't be much left of Irma's dream of a dukedom. It might even come about that a good part of the Chicago traction king's fortune would be spent for the cause of world peace and co-operation!

V

The traveler was flown to Lisbon, white city on the River Tagus. It had been one of the world's spy centers all through the war, and he had come to know it well; but this time the plane stopped only for fuel, and then flew on to Bermuda, now a great American air and naval base. "The still-vexed Bermoothes," Shakespeare had called them, but this day the wind was quiet, and Lanny looked down on white-and pink-dotted rocky islands, surrounded by a sea that was indigo in the depths and emerald in the shallows. More fuel, and they rose magically into the air again and sped on for three or four hours, and were set gently down at the great Bolling Field, near Washington.

There Lanny got one of the shocks of his life; the press was waiting. He learned afterward that Laurel had arranged it, not asking his permission for fear he might worry about it too much; it would be better if he showed his surprise. If he was going on the radio for his cause he would have to grit his teeth and bear it. Returning from his mission made him important and provided an occasion for publicity. So here were half a dozen eager young men with pencil in one hand and a wad of copy paper in the other, and here were photographers telling him to turn this way and that and to "hold it." That is the way you get things done in the modern world, for you can't expect people to be interested in your work unless they know what you look like.

The son of Budd-Erling always looked right, having been brought up that way. The public would see a middle-aged gentleman stepping off the plane with his overcoat over his arm; he looked the way people imagine a diplomat ought to look, and he had not let himself develop a paunch. They would read his admission: Yes, he had been President Roosevelt's secret agent for a matter of eight years, and he had managed to fool Hitler and Göring and the other Nazis, with the possible exception of Himmler. He had had an uncomfortable time getting out of Germany late in the year 1943, traveling with false papers, playing the role of an office clerk searching for his bombed-out family; he had had to walk a good part of the way. Previously he had traveled over Europe incessantly and had helped to prepare for the landing in North Africa and then for Normandy. Now he was interested in the Peace Program; he told about it, and most of the papers printed what he said. They had ignored it so far, but now it was a story; it was what you had to have in order to make the headlines in America.

VI

The traveler went to Edgemere, and of course they were glad to see him; they would have been glad anyhow, but since he was a celebrity they were more so. All the girls in the office beamed and went home and told their families about him, and when he walked down the street people turned to look. The son of Budd-Erling! The man who fooled the Nazis! The man who told on Göring—the dirty dog— I hope they hang him! The day was Monday, and there was time to arrange for double time on Thursday. They would put off another speaker until the following week, and the man who had fooled the Nazis would tell all that he had seen at the Nürnberg trial, and how he thought it was going to turn out, and what he thought of our policy toward Germany, and of the chances for permanent peace.

Lanny was surprised by his wife and his English friends. They had been reserved and rather fastidious persons; radical in ideas but aristocratic in their personal attitudes. But now they were as excited as the girls and busily figuring out how to make the most of the opportunity. Lanny took it as a confirmation of the Marxist formula that economic forces mold character and opinions and determine political events. The Peace Group had staked their labors and their hopes upon this new kind of activity, and now it had taken control of them; they wanted to succeed—and this publicity was success. A new flood of letters poured in, and they had to get several more girls and arrange to enlarge their office. Laurel said, "We're almost meeting expenses, Lanny. We may be able to keep going for more than five years."

He answered, "I doubt if we have more than five years to decide the issue of peace or war for our time. What we had better do is to get more radio stations and make the half-hour period permanent."

Expand! Expand! That was the voice of America. Spend more money, hire more help, build more rooms—and get more publicity, attract more attention! Work harder, carry more responsibilities, and increase your blood pressure! Subject your mind and character more and more to the influence of these terrific economic forces! Don't have time to play the piano, or to read poetry, but occupy your mind with the hourly problems of your business—who is coming next on your program, what he or she is going to say, what his or her pulling power will be! What is going into the paper, and what was the subscription total last week, and so on and on—the world will see to it that you never have any rest, that you have too many visitors, too much fan mail, too many problems to solve! Unless you are very wise and careful you will be chain-smoking, taking a nip now and then, and developing that most fashionable of complaints, a stomach ulcer.

VII

Lanny had to take a walk and think about what he was going to say on his first appearance on the air at home. No doubt many of the fans would recognize the voice of Billy Burns, but that wouldn't do any harm; it would bring more mail, and lovelorn ladies would transfer their affections and imagine themselves with a new name, not so different. Lanny must remember that the listeners would want, above all else, a story; they would want to see Göring, that terrible creature, mad with greed, yet at the same time human, with impulses of friendship, of humor; in short, a child, untrained, able to take a kingdom but not to rule his spirit. They would want to see him in his magnificent palace, planned to become an art museum for all time; they would want a picture of him dressing up in stage costumes, running his elaborate toy trains, and worshiping at the shrine of his former wife, the Swedish countess.

And then his downfall, his surrender, his dream of seeing General Eisenhower, and the problem of whether or not he should carry his jeweled baton! His arrival at Mondorf, his knees shaking so that he could hardly walk, certain that he was going to be shot in the courtyard, as he had caused so many thousands of other men to be shot. And then, at the last, in the prisoners' dock, wearing his faded gray uniform, many sizes too big for him now, and without any of its decorations. And what was in his face when he sat there, and heard Lanny tell about his monstrous crimes, and realized that he had been made a fool of, not once, not twice, but continuously from 1933 to 1945? A strange thing when their eyes met, and Lanny saw the horror and the hate. He couldn't help feeling bad, because friendship is something important between men, and Göring had really had impulses of friendship toward Lanny even when he was trying to make use of him for nefarious purposes.

Also Lanny must say something about Dachau so that his listeners might not become sentimental about the mighty fallen. He must say something definite about the confusion of mind in the State Department and in American policy for Europe. Were we going to denazify or were we going to get efficiency at any cost? Was our Army going to prepare for the next war, or were our statesmen going to work for peace in spite of all obstacles? At present our official policy was the breaking up of the German cartels, those great industrial combines which had dominated the life of Europe, upsetting governments and determining peace or war for more than half a century. But General Clay was improvising a policy, he was following his own theory, or that of Wall Street, that German industrial power must be restored and built into a bulwark against Soviet Communism.

Great statesmanship was needed here, and care in every word that one spoke over the radio; not giving in to Russia, yet not challenging her, but trying to abate her fears and persuade her to a settlement that would leave her to work out her own problems in her own way, and leave the free peoples of the West to find their own methods of social change. That couldn't be done by the Army, nor yet by Wall Street; it had to be done by civilians who understood the real heart of America, the sweet land of liberty, and America's dream of the common man.

VIII

During Lanny's absence Gerald de Groot had been doing the introducing, and he now introduced Mr. Lanning Prescott Budd. Gerald had prepared his script, and the rest of the group had edited it. They didn't want it to sound like a radio commercial; they didn't want to say that Mr. Budd's experience had been extraordinary, for so many things had been extraordinary in this war. Hundreds of secret agents had gone into the enemy lands, and no doubt some of them had fooled the higher-ups. As for presidential agents, there were supposed to have been at least a hundred and three, though Lanny had his doubts and wondered if the figures might have begun at one hundred. Anyhow, don't brag; leave out the adjectives and say that he is the son of Robert Budd of Budd-Erling and was President Roosevelt's agent and managed to fool Hitler, Göring, and Hess. Also, that this was his first appearance on the radio since his return from the Nürnberg trial.

Lanny wasn't nervous, for this had been his life for many years and he knew it by heart. He told how he had first met the Führer of the Nazis, and how, using his father's prestige—be sure to listen, Robbie!— he had won the favor of the Führer's most capable assistant, that gross and greedy person whom the Germans had called "*Unser Hermann.*" He told a few of the terrible sights he had witnessed in Naziland, and the dismay that had seized him as he watched it proceeding step by step to take over the continent of Europe.

The speaker proceeded to preach his brief sermon. He didn't have to pull the tremolo stop, for his feelings were intense and revealed themselves without effort. He said that this generation had to decide whether civilization was to go on to new heights or to destroy itself in a series of blind and furious wars. He said that the decision was being made day by day, by the opinions the people held and expressed, by the votes they cast, by the actions they permitted their government to take. He identified himself with his friends of this Peace Group, who were convinced that, modern communications and modern weapons being what they were, there could be no permanent peace on this earth so long as competitive commercialism continued to dominate the lives of men. Free, democratic co-operation, plus birth control for all the races of mankind—these were the conditions upon which the progress of civilization could go on; the alternative being the swift destruction of all the treasures, material, moral, and intellectual, mankind had so far accumulated.

That was the peroration and led up to the announcer's closing remarks that hereafter the Peace Program was to be extended to a full half-hour, the first quarter-hour being given to a narration by Mr. Budd of one of his adventures in Europe or elsewhere. The second half would be a talk on the subject of world peace by a new guest speaker each week, the wisest and best they could find. Mr. Budd's remarks of this evening had been taken down by a stenographer and would go to press tomorrow morning in the little four-page paper called *Peace*, which was mailed to subscribers at the price of fifty cents a year.

Finally came the usual collection talk, to persuade people to send in money for subscriptions to their friends and others who might profit from the paper and the broadcast. Gerald read the honor roll—every week there were several new towns from which somebody had sent in a telephone book, with money to pay for sending the paper to everyone listed. Labor unions and lodges and other groups had subscribed for their members—and so on. "Remember the address, Box One Thousand, Edgemere, New Jersey."

IX

Laurel, the storyteller, had been right; people liked a story. They liked to imagine a hero, elegant, well dressed, suave, and able to travel over the earth and see the interesting places which so few of them would ever visit; someone who had access to the great ones of the earth, those whose pictures were printed everywhere but whom few would ever see in person. This favorite of fortune satisfied them, and people by the

tens of thousands decided that they wanted to hear his adventures and
to have their friends hear. The flood of mail swelled to a torrent, and
it became necessary to hire more girls, and to rent a room in the parish
house of the Methodist Church, and set up a double row of tables at
which the girls could sit and open envelopes and take out money and
mark the amounts on the letters.

Also, a team of union carpenters—time and a half for overtime—went
to work building a new long room at the back of the onetime fuse factory. Sam de Witt had to find another stencil-cutting machine. The machine that stamped the labels on the papers had to be worked twenty-four
hours a day—more time and a half. The same thing applied to the printing press; they had found that they could get the job done more cheaply
in the great metropolis, but they desired to keep the favor of their fellow
townsmen by patronizing home industry. It saved telephone bills and
time running back and forth with proofs; more important yet, they
would have the whole thing under their own control. They gave their
printer a guarantee, and he started adding a workroom and a larger
storeroom in back of his place; all in a tremendous rush, otherwise the
wrappers of bundles would have been working out in the backyard.

More important yet, Lady Nielson got to work on the telephone. She,
the Mother Superior of this radio project, had leaped to the decision
that Lanny Budd's adventures offered the opportunity for getting the
nation-wide circulation she craved. There are agencies which will arrange such things for you, and they are ready to go into action at the
drop of a hat. Nina put that hat on her head, and the rest of the insignia
of worldly importance on her person, and went into town and signed
a contract for the expansion of the Peace Program to include stations
covering the entire country. It would cost something like ten thousand
dollars a shot—but was there any way of spending Emily Chattersworth's
money that would have pleased the donor more?

Even that wasn't the limit of Nina's ambition. There were agencies
that had the magic power to cause advertisements to appear on a certain
morning or evening on the radio page of hundreds of different newspapers all over the three million square miles of the U.S.A. All you had
to do was to present the agency with proper credentials, or, better still,
a check on account, duly certified by a bank. This wins you respect and
will provide the services of a psychological wizard who has spent half
a lifetime studying the mentality of the American public and can tell
you exactly what words to use in order to have them rush to the radio
and afterward sit down and write a check, or go to the post office next
day and get a money order, or take a chance and stick a one- or five-

or ten-dollar bill in an envelope and mail it. When you go in for something on that scale you have to forget that you are a member of the British aristocracy and have spent a lifetime learning dignity and restraint; you have to use circus-poster words, motion-picture words—stunning, gripping, sensational, epoch-making, unprecedented, even supercolossal.

X

Get ready for the earthquake, the avalanche, the supercolossal cyclone! This time you will learn that America really is a big country; this time you will learn that it really has the oddly named places you've heard of, Podunk and Hoboken, Kalamazoo and Kissimmee and Tallahassee, Dead Man's Gulch and Deaf Smith County, not to mention two Faiths, fourteen Hopes, and one Charity. You will discover that there are even more queer people than there are queerly named towns; and also that there are, all over the land, tens of thousands of earnest, devoted people ready to respond to a call of idealism and get into motion the moment they are shown a goal. You will find that you have to sit up most of the night if you wish even to glance over their letters, and that you will need a corps of typists if you wish to answer. You will find that you have to have an expert receptionist to deal with the many who will wear a path to your door—including the gentlemen who want to propose to Miss Mary Morrow and the ladies with soulful eyes who just want to gaze into the brown eyes of Mr. Lanny Budd.

The ex-P.A. would never fail to go over with his friends every detail of what he expected to say; he would have headings on a little typewritten list, but would not write out his talk. When the next Thursday came round, the first of their double programs, he told in a quiet voice how as a boy he had spent Christmas at the home of a German friend named Kurt Meissner, who had grown up to be a famous pianist and composer. Said Lanny, "I never had any special talent myself, but I had the good fortune to have several friends who did." He told how through this boyhood friend he had come to know about a German political movement called National Socialism, and had been taken to meet its leader. Thus he had followed its growth year after year and understood how cleverly it had been contrived to play upon the weaknesses of the thwarted and embittered German people.

Lanny's story of Johannes and Freddi Robin had been told at Nürnberg, but the accounts that had got into the American papers were sketchy; so now he repeated it, not shrinking from the horror he had witnessed in the torture dungeon of the Berlin prison or the anguish he had felt when the broken body of a young Jewish idealist had been turned over to him by the Nazi gangsters on the bridge across the Rhine at Strasbourg. "You can imagine," he said, "how I swore a vow of resistance to that hateful system, and was moved to use my acquaintance with Göring and Hitler to gain their secrets, and pass them on to friends in Britain and America who would help awaken the public to the danger which Nazi-Fascism represented."

Then, through Professor Charles T. Alston, he had met President Roosevelt and become his secret agent. This had been in the summer of 1937 while the Spanish civil war was raging, a model of all the other wars that would rage if the three dictators, German, Italian, and Spanish, could have their way. The visitor had sought to persuade the Governor that they meant war and could mean nothing else; and in this he had been tragically vindicated.

XI

Such was the first half of the program, and immediately afterward the voice of Gerald de Groot informed the audience that next week they would hear the first of Mr. Budd's adventures in the service of our late great President. He hoped they would advise their friends to listen and would not fail to put their names on the subscription list of the little peace paper, in which they would find the printed text of the broadcast they had just heard. Then he introduced the second speaker, Professor Alston, who had been one of President Roosevelt's closest advisers, first while he was Governor of New York State and then while he was President of the United States, a period of sixteen years. They were bringing Alston on for a second time in order that he might vouch for the truth of Lanny's story.

The mild-voiced little gentleman, now in his seventies, possessed no oratorical arts; but as a geographer he had learned to know the physical world, and as an adviser to President Wilson at the Paris Peace Conference he had learned to know political Europe. He had helped to shape Roosevelt's plans for that unhappy war-torn continent; what Americans could and should do to help it back to sanity and health—always provided that the European peoples would do their part. There must be political unity and, no less important, economic unity; thereafter the whole world must unite to make certain that no more dictators arose to impose their will upon free peoples.

That led to the subject of the Soviet Union, now locked in a duel with the Western world in the Security Council of the United Nations.

Alston told what Roosevelt's mind had been on the subject of this emerging force of proletarian revolt; the President had hoped it might be guided into channels of co-operation and peace. He had said playfully that he had a Fifty-Year Plan for making friends with the Soviet Union. He was determined to trust Stalin, in the hope of winning Stalin's trust in return. In any case, it was a choice of the lesser of two evils, for Hitler had given abundant proof that nobody could trust *him;* and one or the other of these two had to win the war.

Yalta had been the last of Roosevelt's conferences with the Soviet chief; just two months later Roosevelt was dead. And what had happened in those sixty days? Enough to convince Roosevelt that the agreements were not going to be kept; the war was almost won, and friendship was no longer needed. The anxiety over this must have helped to break his heart.

And what was to be done now? What would Roosevelt himself have done if he had still been here? Surely he would have used the weapon of pitiless publicity; he would have brought the recalcitrant government before the bar of public opinion and kept it there. Mr. Gromyko might walk out of the Security Council as often as he pleased and stay out as long as he pleased, but he could not keep the world from being reminded, over and over again, of agreements that had been signed and published and then disregarded. Both the United Nations and the United States must go in for an educational campaign—propaganda, if you chose so to call it—on a scale never known so far; they must beat the Russians at their favorite game.

At the same time, said Alston, the American people must never for a moment fail to push their economic reforms, in order to avoid the next panic; they must remove their many social abuses, in order to deprive the Communists of their talking points. Said this onetime New Deal "fixer," "All our efforts will be vain unless we can show that our democratic system works, and that its end product is justice and opportunity for the common man."

XII

When that program was over they had supper and a long talk. It was an anxious time, and none of these amateur publicists tried to minimize the danger. The UN appeared to be going on the rocks. The world was splitting into two hostile parts, East versus West, one half behind the iron curtain and the other in front. It looked like an inevitable drift toward war; and did Russia mean war or was she just trying a bluff, getting everything that she could without war? Most of the Peace Group preferred the latter guess, but it was only a guess, and very trying on the nerves.

Alston said, "Something must have put Foreign Minister Molotov into a bad frame of mind, for he went out to San Francisco and almost kept the UN from getting started because he wouldn't agree to a voting procedure. That made it necessary for Harry Hopkins to fly to Moscow to try to patch things up with Stalin; it just about used up the last ounce of strength that poor fellow had."

"And yet you were foolish enough to disband your Army and Air Force!" exclaimed Rick.

"We so ardently wanted peace," replied the "fixer." "Truman went to Potsdam and met Stalin and I suppose believed what he was told. Truman himself is a rigidly honest man, and it was hard for him to realize that statesmen would pledge their country's good faith and mean to keep it only so long as it suited their purposes."

They talked about Vyacheslav Molotov, that strange person with the dead-pan face; his name meant "the Hammer"—but he was more like the anvil, Alston said, for you could pound upon him until you were exhausted and never make the slightest impression. Apparently Stalin used him as a sort of pillbox, a fortification into which he could retire. Stalin would come out, all geniality and obligingness, and tell you what you wanted to hear; then he would retire behind the pillbox, and you would find yourself confronting its blank face. Molotov, the Foreign Minister, the diplomatic agent, was the one you had to complain to when Stalin's agreements were not kept; and Molotov was the one who was capable of looking straight into your eyes and telling you things which he not merely knew were not true, but which he knew that you knew were not true. A bitter lesson you had to learn, soon or late, that truth had no meaning to any Communist; the only question that concerned him was the advancement of his cause.

"If you have any doubt of that," put in Rick, "all you have to do is to go to the writings of Lenin, and you will find it plainly stated."

"Just as plainly as in *Mein Kampf*," added Rick's wife.

XIII

Such was the state of the world in which the Peace Group had to operate; and what were they going to do about it? Much as they hated the idea, it was impossible to disarm in the face of Communist imperialism. America had to be able at all times to convince the Soviet leaders that they could not win a war. Molotov had discussed that with bitterness, saying that we were dangling an atomic bomb over his head. That at least was a truth that he recognized; nobody had ever heard him say that the bomb wasn't there.

But how would it be when he too had this deadliest of weapons? His foreign slaves were working day and night getting out the ore in Czechoslovakia—that was the reason that unhappy democratic land had been seized. Somewhere deep in Russia the scientists and the technicians, many of them German, were working to solve the problems of the bomb. Someday he would announce that he had it—and you wouldn't have the least idea whether to believe him or not.

From then on we too would live with the bomb dangling over our heads; the situation would be that we must have more bombs and better bombs, and the world's only hope of peace would rest on the fact that while the Russians could wipe out New York and Washington, they would know that they couldn't keep us from wiping out Moscow and Leningrad. The result would be that both sides would start putting their great factories and cities under ground. The human race would convert itself into moles, living and working by artificial light, and arresting and executing everybody who expressed an idea different from Lenin and Stalin on the one side and from Coolidge and Hoover on the other.

This prospect did not please the Peace Group; indeed, it seemed very much like being in jail, and their minds behaved like restless prisoners, trying every possible device to break out. Alston, who had known F. D. R. longer and even better than Lanny, told how the Governor had been worried by this problem. Lanny had talked with him the night before his death, Alston a couple of weeks earlier, just before his leaving Washington for Warm Springs. The Governor had begun to realize that his idea of a Fifty-Year Plan for making friends with the Soviet Union had been a sorry jest indeed; he had been played for a sucker—or whatever might be the Russian equivalent for that slang. The Communists meant to impose their system upon the world, and it was a fundamental dogma with them that this system was bound to triumph; it was something automatic, materialistically predetermined, and whoever stood in its way must be liquidated.

Lanny remarked, "I wonder if Truman has begun to realize it."

"I should think that Molotov would have convinced him," replied the ex-geographer. After a moment he added, "Why don't you go and see him and tell him all this?"

"*I?*" exclaimed Lanny. "He wouldn't know me from any other time-waster."

"I'm not so sure. He must have learned of your testimony in Nürnberg."

"Why don't you talk to him, Professor? He surely knows about you."

"Yes, but he knows the wrong things. Apparently he has made up his mind not to try to work with the old Roosevelt crowd. They think they know more than he does—and maybe they are right." Alston thought for a moment, then continued, "I'll tell you what: I'll go to Washington and suggest that he meet you. He'll be interested in knowing about Roosevelt's plan to send you to Stalin, and he might be moved to take it up for himself. It couldn't do any harm to give him the chance."

Lanny couldn't say no to this. He glanced at Laurel and saw the pain in her face. Another long journey for her husband—ten thousand miles or so! But she couldn't say no either.

31

Architects of Fate

I

So FAR the press had had little to say about the Peace Program. It was a maverick, a critter that bore none of the recognized brands; it was looked upon as something more adapted to Southern California than to an all-wise and distrustful metropolis. But when you started publishing advertisements in the papers—paying cash money to the business department—that put you in an altogether different class. When you advertise it must be that you have something. This program had a presidential agent, certified by the War Crimes Commission; also a presidential "fixer" who had been abused by the papers for eighteen years, long enough to make him a national institution.

So the revelations concerning Roosevelt's dissatisfaction with Russia were reported, and were cabled abroad, and in due course denounced by *Pravda*. On Thursday morning there appeared one of those fancy write-ups by which *Time* had managed to establish a new style and even a new vocabulary for the reporting of current events. The editors of this weekly sit "on the hills like gods together, careless of mankind." They are able to take the most tragic events in their stride, and if they were reporting the crucifixion of Jesus Christ they would not fail to make it picturesque and playful. It was a great event for the Peace Program when *Time* gave it the works; it let many thousands of serious-minded Americans know that there was a new development in the moral life of America.

But sailing is never smooth for any reformer in this tough period of history. This burst of success prepared the way for one of the Peace Group's great sorrows; Rick lost his chief assistant, the most valuable member of his staff. Philip Edgerton came to him with a hangdog look and stammered out his apologies—he was going to have to resign. His wife couldn't stand life in Edgemere, and no man can live and keep his mind on good literature while his wife is in a stew all day.

It was "that woman," of course. Laurel and Nina had distrusted her from the first hour, but they had always been polite, giving her no cause for complaint. But she wasn't like them, she couldn't interest herself in reading or in the idea of changing the world. There was nobody in this Godforsaken town whom she considered worth knowing or to whom it was worth while showing her clothes. She was frantic to get back to the city where she had friends of her own kind.

It was a serious matter to Rick, who had come to lean so heavily on Philip's excellent judgment. Again and again the younger man had brought him stuff by some new writer which the syndicate had taken and had sold. But Rick understood the situation, and that there could be no changing Alma. "Couldn't you do the work in the city and come out, say, two days a week?" he asked, and the answer was, "I've had a much better offer, one that I can't turn down."

So then, with a little pressure, Rick got the real facts: one of the big fellows was raiding them. One of the two-million-a-week boys! Their attention had been attracted by the sudden success of the new enterprise; there must be some brains behind it, and an editor whom Philip knew had called him up and questioned him about how the enterprise was run and then invited him to come in for a talk. The result had been an offer of a thousand dollars a month, instead of the three hundred and fifty the New Writers' Bureau was paying. And that wasn't all: there was the certainty of a raise—the top men on that magazine got from twenty-five to fifty thousand a year.

"You won't like the work nearly so well," pleaded Rick.

"I know, but Alma will be happier and will let me alone. I plan to do something for you folks; there'll be a lot of stuff that I'll recommend but that the magazine won't take, and there'll be no objection to my tipping you off to it."

"All right, old man," Rick said. "Good luck to you. And remember, the lamp will always hold out to burn, in case you can't stand the sort of stuff you have to read."

When he told the others about it Rick said, "I suppose that's to be our destiny—to train young fellows and let Big Business buy them up."

Laurel answered, "Next time, before we hire anybody, let's have a look at the wife."

II

During Lanny's absence in Germany, Laurel and Nina had been trying a few psychic experiments. No longer were there any war secrets which might leak out by this means; and Nina's curiosity had been aroused by some of the stories Laurel had told her, especially about how she had discovered this strange gift. There had been a night at the end of August 1939 when she and Lanny had been in Hitler's Berghof, trying to fool the Führer and his Number Three and postpone the dreaded coming of war. Laurel had pretended to be a medium and to fall into a trance; it had gone well, and perhaps she had fooled herself—nobody knows how these strange subconscious forces work. Laurel had actually fallen into a trance, and when she came out she was astonished to hear the story of a long dialogue, purporting to be a controversy between Zaharoff, the onetime munitions king, and Otto Kahn, the onetime New York banker and art patron. All that had come from Laurel's lips without her having had the slightest idea of it, or the slightest memory of it afterward.

People wouldn't believe such things, and there didn't seem to be much use trying to persuade them. Laurel had satisfied herself that the things happened and that she would never know how they happened, at any rate not in this life. She had come to be bored with both the old Greek rascal and the elegant international financier who talked perfectly in character but never said anything important. Madame Zyszynski, the old Polish woman who had taken the role of Laurel's control, seemed to be tired and discouraged, and Laurel was busy with the complex new life which she and her friends had created.

But Nina had reawakened her interest, and they had tried several séances. One result of this was that they had got to talking about Dr.

J. B. Rhine and the extraordinary experiments he had been carrying on for many years to test and prove the reality of what he called "parapsychology." They had his book, *New Frontiers of the Mind,* and Nina said, "Why don't we put him on a program?" No sooner said than done; she called him on the telephone at Duke University and told him what they were doing, and he said he would be pleased and honored to tell their large audience what parapsychology might do to improve the chances for world peace.

The other development was one for which Laurel had long been prepared in her talks with her husband. So many persons they had known in the past had come back or had purported to come back; and would it ever be Franklin Roosevelt? They were discussing him and thinking about him continually; at this juncture they all had their minds upon the mission which he had assigned to his P.A. Whether there was such a thing as a disembodied spirit, or whether it was all subconscious work of Lanny's mind, or of Laurel's, or of all their minds combined into some strange fantasy-making amalgamation—in any case, it was to be expected that he might present himself. Perhaps the very fact of their concentration upon him might bring him.

III

One evening, while Lanny was busy with his fan mail and Rick was in his study racing through manuscripts, hopeful as always of a find, Nina came to Laurel's room and said, "Let's have a try with Madame." It didn't take long and didn't tire Laurel, so she always assented; she lay down on her bed and closed her eyes, while Nina sat by, with a shaded light and a pad and pencil. That was the routine, and what would come out of it was a gamble, and afterward would be one of life's intriguing mysteries. Laurel began to breathe hard and moan slightly; then she was still. Nina said, "Is anybody present?" And a voice replied, "I am here. Madame."

It is one of the rules of this strange experiment that you must treat the voices as if you believed in them. It may be only a child's game, it may be a dip into an infinite mind, but whatever it is, one of the established rules is to treat the voices as if they came from another world. Nina asked, "Is anybody with you?" The reply was, "There is a gentleman here; he is tall and handsome and has a good smile."

"Will he tell us his name?"

"He says, call him 'Governor.' "

"Will you ask him what he wants?"

"He wants to know if Lanny is here."

"Tell him that Lanny is in the house."

"He wants to know if you will bring him."

"Yes, I will." Nina rose and ran quickly to Lanny's room and tapped on the door. "Come quickly! Roosevelt is here!"

A startling announcement, but Lanny, who had been making these experiments for years, could guess what it meant. He jumped up and went with long strides to his wife's room. He took the chair by her side, and Nina took another.

"Hello, Madame," said the ex-P.A. "How are you feeling tonight?" One must never fail in personal consideration for these mysterious entities.

"I am well, Lanny. There is a new gentleman here."

"I know him, Madame. Tell him I have been hoping to hear from him."

"He says you told him about me."

"Many times. I have been hoping he would find you."

"He says he is sorry that you missed the boat."

"Tell him I may take another. Does he think it will do any good?"

"He says, 'Nothing venture, nothing gain.'"

"Ask him if he can talk to me directly, Madame."

"He hears what you say but he cannot answer. He is new to our ways, he says. He thinks you made a mistake to return that money. You had earned it."

"Ask him how he knows I returned the money."

"He says that he still has his secret agents. He is laughing. He likes to make jokes."

"He always did. Ask him if he will come and talk to us now and then."

"He says he will try his best."

"Tell him that if I could depend on him, I would put him on the radio and let him give a fireside chat. It would get him many votes."

"He is laughing over that. He has a big laugh."

Laurel, lying on the bed, shuddered as if something were hurting her. Lanny waited a few moments, then went on, "Governor, make an effort, and see if you cannot speak to me."

A silence, followed by a startling thing—a voice that Lanny knew, and that all the world knew; a man's voice, deep and resonant. Coming from Laurel's mouth it was most uncanny. "I am going to be very busy, Lanny."

"What shall you be doing, Governor?"

"I am going to be haunting Molotov." And then another of those full-throated laughs that had greeted so many of Lanny's jokes, and his own. Lanny felt that he could see the fine head thrown back, that mouth open, and that large chest shaking. It shook Laurel, and she began to stir.

"Tell me, Governor," said the ex-P.A. when the storm had passed, "what shall we do about the Russians?"

The answer came promptly. "What can we do but what we have been doing? Offer friendship and be prepared for whatever comes. Be like the eagle on our dollar bill—an olive branch in one set of claws and a sheaf of arrows in the other."

"You still feel as you did when you talked with me?"

"The same, only more so. Stalin is not keeping his agreements, and I am being blamed for it."

"They say you gave him too much at Yalta."

"Of course, but what choice did I have? I had no means of knowing what the A-bomb would do. I had to get the Russians to join us; and they stated their terms. They are hard men, Lanny, and you and I are soft. Too soft, I fear."

"You are worried, Governor?"

The answering voice was grave. "There will come a man of the people for the people; and the people will know him."

A pause followed, and then Laurel began to moan. That always meant the end; no use trying to hold on. She opened her eyes and began to question Lanny. What had happened? When he told her, she was greatly moved. "The shepherd speaks!" she exclaimed.

They debated the problem that had been puzzling them for many years. Had it actually been Roosevelt? Had there been any part of Roosevelt in it? Or was it a construction of their own minds? Apart from the voice, there was nothing evidential about it; the voice had told them nothing they didn't already know. Lanny had told his wife about the check he had given to the OSS; he had told her every detail of his conference with the Chief on the night before his death. The representation had been extraordinarily vivid; but then, so were their impressions, their recollections of the great man. Quite possibly there might be a first-class actor in the subconscious mind of every human; certainly there was in Laurel's an entity, a being trained to imagine character and to set it forth in dialogue and actions.

They just didn't know; they possibly never would know in this life. When they died they would know—if they knew anything. If they didn't know anything, they wouldn't know that they didn't know.

"The days when thou wert not, did they trouble thee? The days when thou art not shall trouble thee as much."

IV

Dr. Rhine came on the night train from North Carolina, and Lanny and Laurel drove to meet him at the station in Newark. They told him about the séance while driving to Edgemere, and of course he wanted Laurel to promise him a try, which she did.

J. B. Rhine, trained as a biologist, had become convinced that the unexplored powers of the mind should no longer be left to the haphazard attention of amateurs and charlatans. He had become assistant to Dr. William McDougall, who had succeeded William James at Harvard University, and to the honorary title of dean of American psychology. Going to Duke University, McDougall had founded the Department of Parapsychology—the prefix "para" meaning "beyond," and applying to those powers of the mind which the conventional psychologist ignored because he couldn't explain them and didn't want to start his education all over again.

For the past fifteen years—all the time that Lanny had been fighting Hitler and Mussolini—the patient Dr. Rhine had been working to evolve a method for the mass production and testing of psychic phenomena. He and his assistants and students had been making tests, literally millions of them, to find out whether it was possible to read cards which were being turned up behind a screen or in another room—and then to read cards which weren't being turned up at all but were left face-down in a deck that had been freshly shuffled by the experimenter and never touched by the person being tested.

When it was shown that great numbers of persons could perform these feats, to such an extent that the odds against them were enormous, the conventional psychologists were left with the alternative of supposing that an entire department of a great American university was carrying on an elaborate hoax, or else of challenging those mathematical laws of probability which had been accepted by the scientific world for centuries. Some chose this latter course; others just wouldn't pay any attention—an ancient and long-established way of protecting your mind from disturbance. The consequences of believing what Dr. Rhine had proven were so devastating to the ordinarily received ideas about the mind, and indeed about all human affairs, that the average psychologist just couldn't face it, and the average college professor couldn't face the thought of what his dean would say and his prexy and his colleagues. It called for heroism, and the men who have that endowment usually choose livelier jobs than teaching in a classroom.

V

In the afternoon, when young Lanny had gone out to play in somebody else's garden, and after the telephone had been shut off and the front doorbell plugged, these half-dozen questioners of the infinity of mind sat waiting in a quiet room and met with one of those disappointments which become an old and sad story to every psychic researcher. "I can call spirits from the vasty deep."— "Why, so can I, and so can any man; but will they come when you do call for them?" They so seldom do that many questioners give up in disgust. And then, when you are unprepared and have no witnesses present, they come—or something that gives such a good imitation that your incredulity seems a grave discourtesy.

What came at Laurel's call were voices and seeming fragments of personality, mostly old people who seemed to have lost their memories; they gave names which no one present had ever heard, and they gave no reason for being there, or anywhere. When Laurel came out of the trance she was embarrassed; but Dr. Rhine said it was a common experience with him—for some reason he did not appear to be stimulating to the "spirits." Like Lanny, he hadn't been able to decide what they were; he was holding his mind open—something every scientist has to learn to do, in spite of the discomfort it involves. *Forse que si, forse que no,* as they sing in the opera.

But there were other things that the group at Duke had proved beyond any reasonable doubt. One was that some minds had the power to reach into other minds and take things out of them; distance made no difference whatever—one mind might be in North Carolina and the other in South Africa. Another was the power of some minds to see things that were hidden from the eyes—the gift called clairvoyance. Another was the power called psychometry, the power of some minds to get impressions of personality by touching objects which had belonged to that person. Yet another power Dr. Rhine had refrained from mentioning for a long time, because it was so difficult of belief and so likely to damage his credit—the power of foreseeing the future. But what could an honest scientist say when in his laboratory, not once but hundreds of thousands of times, men and women had shown that they could foretell what was going to be the order of a pack of cards which had yet to be shuffled? They couldn't get it all right, but they could get enough right to make the chances against its happening by accident millions and even billions to one.

So you went on in this unusual kind of laboratory, getting results that you hesitated for years to make known to your deans and prexies and academic colleagues. Could the human mind influence the motion of material objects without touching them? Could you, for example, cause dice to fall in a particular way that you desired? Try it and see; and, lo and behold, you could! The Negroes who had bent over crap games, whispering intensely, "Come seven, come eleven!"—they had been a joke to the educated world, but they had been right. Nor was it that the dice were loaded or that the Negroes were skilled in throwing them. Dr. Rhine's dice were shaken and thrown by a machine, hundreds at a time, and the man who did the willing never touched them; he called what he was "willing," and he got the results to such an extent that the chances against it were astronomical. Verily, as Hamlet had said, "There are more things in heaven and earth, Horatio, than are dreamt of in your philosophy."

VI

On that Thursday evening Lanny had promised to tell over the radio the story of how his second wife, Trudi, had been kidnaped by secret agents of the Nazis in Paris—this more than two years before the outbreak of the war. They had taken her to a château which was the home of a member of the German Embassy staff, Graf von Herzenberg, the father of Oskar. Lanny had managed to get access to the place and tried to save her, but in vain. This made an exciting story, and at the same time it threw a strong light on the problem of maintaining peace in a world where unscrupulous men could gain power by defying all those moral sentiments upon which our civilization has been based.

Then it was Dr. Rhine's turn, and he took his place at the microphone and told the Peace Program about the work of his laboratory. He had devised a deck of cards, "ESP cards," he called them, five each of five different kinds, a circle, a cross, a rectangle, a star, and three wavy lines. He told how he shuffled the cards and then set them face-down on a table before one of his students. Without touching the pack the student would undertake to call "down through," that is, to tell what the first card is, then the second, and so on. Rhine would write down the calls, and when all twenty-five had been made and recorded, the cards would be turned up and compared with the record.

The experimenter told an exciting story of a young divinity student who had come in by accident. Rhine had shuffled the cards and laid them face-down on the table; with the idea of discovering the effect of stimulation, he had offered to bet the student a hundred dollars that he couldn't call the top card. The student had called it correctly, and under the stimulation of repeated bets he had stood there, without stopping to take off his overcoat. This time Rhine had returned the card to the deck and shuffled again after each test, and the student had called twenty-five cards without a single error. "The chances against such a thing happening by accident," said Rhine, "are over two hundred ninety-eight quadrillions to one—that is, they require eighteen figures to express them. Yet the thing has happened five times under test conditions. When you have seen it once with your own eyes you can never thereafter doubt that the thing we call 'ESP,' extra-sensory perception, is a reality and a challenge to the thinking world. When the ancient Greeks observed that if you rubbed a piece of amber with a cloth it attracted light objects such as a feather, they were not especially interested; they didn't consider the possibility of an unknown natural force, and if you had told them that it was the same force that made the thunderbolts of Zeus, they would have accused you of impiety and made you drink hemlock. If you had told them that the dynamo and the radio were to come out of that force they would have been just as skeptical as the old-line psychologists are of our demonstrations."

VII

The speaker's subject was the possible effects of parapsychology upon world peace; and on that he said:

"If we can push our inquiries far enough to discover how to develop conscious control over ESP capacities we can take all the secrecy and surprise out of warfare and expose all plots and criminal schemes that are hatched by warmakers anywhere around the globe. Putting this on a scientific basis and broadcasting the information obtained back to a country would truly revolutionize internal as well as international relations. Every military man I have questioned on the matter has agreed that, given one hundred per cent intelligence on the one side, we could be practically certain of preventing a war; and, given one hundred per cent intelligence all around, the people of neither side would support a war if they had the choice. The best point of all would be that, given one hundred per cent intelligence of what its leaders are up to, no people would support a dictatorship.

"All this will seem fantastic without some preparatory factual matter, but those of us who have seen a subject call down through a deck of twenty-five cards that is completely screened from sensory range do not find it a big jump for the imagination to take. We know that distance and barriers and time do not block this strangely penetrating ability to perceive both events and thoughts without the senses. We also know that sometimes it breaks through into consciousness and tells us that conscious control is a possibility, though it still eludes us in the laboratory."

Dr. Rhine went on to discuss the impending war with Russia and the inevitable battle between democracy and the Communist dictatorship. Speaking as what he called a scientific idealist, he made an appeal that the democracies should put at least part of their weight behind an ideological war, a bloodless one, "which, by cutting the ideological ground from under the Communist state philosophy, would bring about progress and perhaps revolution from within."

Said he, "Russian state philosophy is materialistic in the extreme. Even Russian scientists have to hew to the line that makes man a machine and nothing but. This is the only philosophy suited to the ruthless dictatorship, the denial of civil rights, the ignoring of the freedom of the individual, and other characteristics of the Communist state. The answer to this is a new Renaissance. This materialism is supposedly based upon science. The answer to it is more science and better science. The best answer, if not the only one, is the investigations of the exceptional non-physical manifestations of the human mind that have come out of these parapsychological laboratories. It is true they are not yet widely recognized, but so is it always with new findings that contradict the current trend of thought. They are being fast confirmed and more widely recognized here and abroad. Given the means for more extensive researches and repetition of experiments, the evidence could be made compelling, even to the scientists behind the iron curtain. And what better antidote to give the intellectual leadership outside the iron curtain over whom so much anxiety has been exercised by editors, congressional committees, and the like? Kill materialism for a man and you can't make a Communist out of him, not of the Russian type."

The speaker apologized for all this as "a blunt and bare presentation." He was afraid that perhaps the subject was too abstract to handle; but he pointed out that the way you feel about a man depends upon what you think he is. "Emphasize the mere physical side of him as all that amounts to anything, and you have to take him on the basis of his color, his size, his physical appeal, which puts him in the cattle class. Emphasize, and enrich, and build up by discovery the side of the man concerned with his spiritual powers, his potentialities that still remain to be fully explored, and we get into things that command respect and interest, sympathy and fraternal feelings. Why not, then, put everything we have behind the search for these transcendent powers of the mind, these spiritual relationships man is capable of having with other men, transcending distance, and language, and color, and national boundaries? This kind of thinking it was that in our great religious leaders led us to the gospel of human brotherhood. Why not explore it, cultivate it, promote it if we like the product?"

That was the story; and how would it go with a radio audience? It was a religious appeal but without the label; and how many people were there in America willing or able to recognize religion when it came to them without clerical habiliments and symbols? The group sat in their small office and waited, as they always did after a broadcast; the telephones rang—they had been able to get eight of them now, in different parts of the building, and they had just enough people to answer: Lanny and Laurel, Rick and Nina, Freddi and Rahel, Gerald and the guest speaker.

They were kept there for an hour, for people who were told that the lines were busy tried again and again. Oh, yes, there were lots of people interested in the idea of a scientific religion; interested in trying to find out what made this strange universe work, and whether the soul of man was a bubble that could be burst, a candle that could be blown out—or did it have connection with an infinite Something that took an interest in it and could be appealed to, or at any rate submitted to? "O God, if there be a God, save my soul, if I have a soul!"

32

Ave atque Vale

I

ALSTON called Lanny on the phone. "I went to see the President," he said. "I told him all about you, and he was interested and promised to send for you. He said he hadn't known that anybody had been with the Governor the night before his death. The proposed mission to Russia was news to him too. I think he'll call you."

"How did you find him?" Lanny asked.

"Very friendly, and evidently keen for his job. I stayed only five minutes. I knew he had a string of appointments. He asked if I'd like to have a position, and I told him I had a nice quiet one; I thought that sixteen years of high politics were enough for an elderly man. He answered that one year had been almost too much for him. He said it with a twinkle; he has a good sense of humor."

"He'll need it," Lanny opined. "I'll await his call."

"I think he'll remember it, but of course his mind is under siege all the time. If he doesn't call in a week or two I'll remind him."

"Tell me what you told him about me."

"Mainly about your dealings with the old Boss." (A habit which had been deeply fixed in the mind of a "fixer," not to name names over the phone.) "He had heard about your testimony abroad, so that got me off to a good start. I told him about your program, and he promised to listen to it. Make the next one good!"

Lanny thanked his old friend and then told about the séance; he knew that Alston didn't take such matters seriously, but it would amuse him. What he said was, "If the Governor comes again, tell him we need him."

Lanny answered, "I'll ask him if *he* needs *you*. Maybe that will bring a reply that will convince you!"

II

Several days passed. The inevitable Thursday arrived, and the speaker was Dr. Goudsmit. He had taken up research duties in the

Brookhaven National Laboratory halfway out on Long Island, and all he had to do was to get on a train which took him under the East River, through the rock foundation of Manhattan Island, to the Pennsylvania Station; he would change to a train that went under the wide Hudson River to Jersey. What a surprise to the Indians to whom the twenty-four dollars' worth of trade goods had been paid, and also the Dutch payers, if anybody had told them by what route the tenth generation of their descendants would be traveling from Long Island to points west and south! Some of Goudsmit's forefathers might have been among them, for he was a Dutchman.

A genial person, full of humor and anecdotes, he told his friends of the Peace Program that he had been a Hollander, a Hollander of the Jewish faith, since he had grown up in a religious family. In the more than twenty years he had lived in America, he had discovered that the Jews were occasionally considered something apart. In Washington it had happened by accident that he had got a look at the dossier which had been accumulated on him when he was being considered to head the Alsos mission. Very tactfully it had been stated there that "the prospect has some valuable assets and some liabilities." There was a twinkle in the learned gentleman's eyes as he repeated that last word.

However, that was all water past the dam now; the mission had been completed, and the doctor was writing a book about it. This evening, he said, he would confine himself to the subject of world peace and the danger of letting Germany become a bone of contention between East and West. Lanny would introduce him by telling about their shared adventures on the Alsos mission. Everybody was amused by the tale of how Lanny had made a prisoner of that elderly magnifico of Nazi science, Lenard, and also how an American art expert had become *Bürgermeisterstellvertreter* of the town of Urach in the Swabian Alps. Also there was the story of Urfeld on the Walchensee, and how they had captured the great Professor Heisenberg, and had fled from having to capture six hundred SS troops.

"You can say that I am carrying on a slightly acidulous correspondence with that esteemed colleague," remarked Goudsmit. "He is back in Germany and has had time to revise his story. He has now decided that German physicists knew how to make a bomb and only lack of technical facilities defeated them. He also claims that they understood clearly the difference between a bomb and a chain-reaction pile. I have to state that he is mistaken, for I have inspected his own records and correspondence, and I know that his government gave him everything in the way of facilities that he asked for, but their scientists did not understand the bomb problems. They had made only a little progress toward building a chain-reacting uranium pile. They now admit they believed that it was such a difficult task that their American and British colleagues could not even venture to start on it during the war."

Lanny mentioned that during the broadcast, and the Nobel Prize winner went on to point to modern science as a model for the rest of the world in the advantages of co-operation and mutual aid. Progress had been made by scientists, not because they were better than other human beings; on the contrary, they possessed all the faults of common men and represented a wide variety of political opinions, temperaments, interests, and cultures. But each had learned that the success of his work depended heavily upon the work done by his colleagues elsewhere. Each knew that the pooling of knowledge was a necessity, and this state of affairs should serve as an example to the rest of the world. "If each of us could realize how his own life is affected by the fate of all other human beings, there could be a realistic approach to the problem of permanent world peace. That is a social lesson, fully as important as any other that scientists could ever have to teach."

III

Time passed, and a telephone call came for Mr. Lanning Prescott Budd; a voice said, "This is the President's secretary. Could you make it convenient to dine at the White House at seven tomorrow?" Lanny answered, "With pleasure," and the voice added, "Informal." Lanny asked, "I would appreciate it if you would arrange for a hotel room for me." The reply was, "You will be a guest at the White House overnight."

He told Laurel about it, and she elected to go along for the drive. "Someday I'd like to meet Truman," she said. "I like him because he is honest."

"And because he doesn't strut," added Lanny. "I wish I could take you this time, but it's his party."

He called the Mayflower Hotel, asked for the manager, and explained his situation; he couldn't ask the White House to arrange for his wife at the hotel, for it would appear that he was hinting for his wife to be invited to the White House. The manager said, "Certainly, Mr. Budd. We will have a room for her." In Washington, all you had to do was to speak the magic words, "White House," and they rolled out the red carpet for your feet.

The couple started early in the morning, so as to allow for flat tires. Highway 1 appeared to be as crowded as in wartime—the goods were still going to Europe and to the rest of the world; the people at home were clamoring for all the things they had done without for four or five years and wondering why they couldn't get them all at once. This was the route by which goods traveled from New England and New York and Pennsylvania, all the way to the South.

Full springtime had come; the fruit trees had put on their wedding garments and the other trees their liveliest green. A pleasant six-hour drive, and time for husband and wife to talk out the details of the growing enterprise they had taken upon their shoulders. They had lunch in Baltimore, and when they reached their destination they drove to the National Gallery and spent the rest of the afternoon. Lanny was known to the curators as an art expert. "Delighted to meet you, Mr. Budd"—and they took the couple down into their vaults where they had stored the priceless treasures which the couple had helped to rescue in Germany.

The Monuments people had been greatly troubled over this because some of them had given assurance to German museum curators that nothing would be taken from the country. But the government had quietly decided that the treasures from the Kaiser Friedrich Museum found in the Merkers mine in Thuringia should not be returned to Berlin until it was definitely known that they would be left to the Germans and not taken by the Russians. That was something you could only whisper. Meantime, works which had been damaged by dampness and salt were being repaired, and there were plans to let the American people see some of these treasures under Army guard.

IV

Promptly at five minutes to seven a taxicab turned into the White House drive and stopped at the sentry box inside the gate. The passenger gave his name to the young naval officer, who said "Proceed," and they drove up to the front of that historic building—which, though Lanny did not know it, was in a dangerous condition from the operation of termites and dry rot. Very soon the occupants would have to move across the street, while the nation spent several million dollars to keep its national home from collapsing. Tonight it was brightly lighted and looked dignified and elegant—something which is the case not merely with buildings but with empires just before they fall.

In front of the door two secret service men looked the visitor over without stopping him; but Lanny stopped because he had met one of them at Yalta, a long way off. In the spacious entrance hall a secretary received him and an elderly Negro took his hat and his bag. In the reception room he waited a minute or two, politely commenting to the secretary on the pleasant weather. Then he was led to the dining-room, and in the doorway stood his host, beaming expansively.

He was a man of medium height, perhaps a trifle less; stockily built, alert and quick in his manner and speech; smooth shaven and wearing spectacles. He was conspicuously neat in his attire; a gray suit, a gray-and-white striped tie to match, and the corner of a white handkerchief sticking out from his breast pocket. His hair matched his suit and was neatly cut. His voice had a slight twang, which was typical of the Middle West; he had been a farm boy and boasted of having plowed a straight furrow. His handshake was firm, and Lanny was careful to exert no pressure—knowing that the poor man must have shaken hands with a hundred people in the course of the day. He saw everybody who wanted to see him.

It was the smaller dining-room, and the table was set for five persons. There entered the matronly First Lady, quiet in manner but with alert eyes which took in everything. Long ago she had waited for her young Harry while he had gone to France to command a battery of artillery in World War I. When he came home she had taken him to Kansas City because she didn't want to live on a farm. It wasn't her fault or his that the haberdashery business had failed during the depression that had hit so soon after the war; Lanny thought it was a good thing, for Harry Truman might have to deal with another and worse depression before he got through with his present job, and the plain people might be glad that he had learned at first hand how it felt. He had stubbornly refused to go through bankruptcy and spent many years trying to pay off his debts.

The First Lady's name was Bess, and the daughter of the house was Margaret. She was a properly brought-up girl who was making a career for herself as a concert singer, giving pleasure to the public if not to sophisticated critics. The mother and daughter were Episcopalians, while the father was a Baptist; they were all devout and went alternately to one church and then the other. As a family they were as American as you could have found by a long search; Harry was a 33rd-degree Mason and a Shriner, a National Guardsman and a Legionnaire. He liked steak; he could, as the saying goes, "take his bourbon or leave it alone"; he liked to play low-stake poker, of the sort called "baseball" or "spit-in-the-ocean."

How much all that would fit him to deal with the problems confronting the modern world was something about which the elegant son of Budd-Erling had done a lot of worrying. Jackson County road overseer, district judge, freshman senator, and reluctant candidate for the vice-presidency—these things fitted a man to understand America and Americans but were hardly sufficient training to deal with the complications of European diplomacy, the age-old feuds and fears in the midst of which Lanny had been brought up. To say nothing of Japan and Korea, Manchuria, China, and the East Indies, Iran and Iraq, Turkey and Palestine, Arabia, Egypt, and Tripoli! Harry Truman would have to do his best and ask for the prayers of his Christian fellow countrymen.

V

The other guest was a friend of Margaret's, a student at the University of Virginia. You could see that he was awed by the company he was in, and he spoke only when spoken to; he listened with both his ears. The dinner was of the simplest: tomato soup, roast beef with potatoes and a couple of other vegetables, a green salad, and ice cream; about what they would have had in Independence, Missouri, if the haberdashery business hadn't failed—in which case Harry Truman would never have come to live in the White House.

It is bad form to talk about yourself at a dinner party—nothing is worse. More than once Lanny tried to stop, but they had read about him and wanted his story. From the President, it was a command; he wanted to know how one became a presidential agent. "I might want to have one or two myself," he said, that simple, straightforward man! A worldly minded one would have known how to extract the information while pretending to know it all; but not this ex-plowboy, ex-overseer of roads. He had never had a secret agent, and if he had ever heard of one it must have been in a mystery story or a movie.

Lanny told how he had been born and raised in Europe, and had lived among diplomats and munitions magnates and generals; had played tennis with two kings and many princes, and listened to "inside" conversation from earliest childhood. He had been his father's emergency assistant at the age of fourteen, a secretary at the Peace Conference at nineteen. When he had seen the horror of Fascism creeping over Europe he had pretended to outgrow his youthful radicalism, and to all his highly placed friends that had seemed quite in order; he had become a Fascist fellow traveler and watched the progress of that evil creed. He had made perilous trips into Germany for the President, staying sometimes for months; he had done secret work in Spain, Italy, Austria, and conquered France; he had been all over North Africa and had spent a couple of hours in the Kremlin with Stalin.

He told some of these adventures; and when the President did not ask for more, Margaret did. She remarked, "We listened to your program, Mr. Budd. We shall be among your audience from now on."

He answered, "You can do more than that. Come and sing for us, and our fortune will be made." She promised to consider it.

VI

The host took his guest into the beautiful oval room, his study. The night was warm, and they sat by an open window. Lanny underwent a cross-questioning that lasted three or four hours. Nothing interrupted them—the President must have so ordered. It was one of the most gratifying experiences of the caller's life, for he had been worrying and fearing about this new man, so obviously unprepared for his colossal task. Truman had been frank in voicing his dismay, and he had made many mistakes; he had found bad advisers among his old Missouri cronies, and when he had made decisions of his own he had revealed impulsiveness and painful lack of knowledge.

But he meant to learn. He wasn't going to be anybody's errand boy forever! He said so in tones that showed he meant it. "Mr. Budd, I have pledged myself to carry out Roosevelt's policies, and I mean that with all my heart. But events move so fast these days—we seem to be passing into a new era, and what Roosevelt would have done is something that no two of his friends agree about. I am blamed because I cannot work with the men whom he chose—but he knew those men and could control them; I don't know them, and they all want to control *me*. If they could get together, that might give me help, but they are split forty ways and squabble among themselves."

"Yes, Mr. President," replied the ex-P.A., "I have been watching. The best of them, Harry Hopkins, is gone."

"He did me a great service by going to Moscow. Stalin considered him an honest man—or at any rate he said he did and apparently trusted him. But it doesn't look as if he trusts *me*."

"Stalin is playing his cards close to his chest," commented Lanny, "and what he means can be learned better from what he does than from what he says. The Governor was greatly disturbed because their agreements were not being kept."

Truman wanted to know about that. He questioned his guest as to every word his predecessor had spoken on the subject. How sure could Mr. Budd be as to his recollection? Lanny said he had made notes that same night of everything important—it was all in the nature of instructions. He had brought the notes with him, and to Truman they were something like holy writ; he studied them, and Lanny deciphered this scribbled word and that, a sort of private shorthand in which a word might stand for a sentence.

What did the Communists really want? How far did they mean to go? It was like trying to understand the mentality of strange creatures that had suddenly alighted on the earth from another planet. Were they all blind fanatics and egotists or were there reasonable men among them? Lanny answered that there had been some, but many had been killed off. Litvinov had been a man who understood the West and how to get along with it, but he had been deposed, and you seldom heard his name.

"You must understand that to them capitalism is a form of corruption of the mind and spirit, and they defend themselves against it as you would defend yourself against a plague or against some religious idea that you considered impious. All their officials are watched and spied upon, and if they are too polite with foreigners, if they associate with foreigners unnecessarily, they are recalled. You see this young man Gromyko, who has walked out of the Security Council, and you think of him as grim and implacable; but I was told just the other day that he likes to stroll down Fifth Avenue and stop and gaze at the goods displayed. If he continues that practice you will see him go back home, and his place taken by someone less subject to bourgeois temptations."

Lanny's talk with Stalin—Truman wanted to know all about that. Lanny said he had made a formal report and it was in Roosevelt's files, but it was out of date. It represented what the Soviet leaders had wanted Roosevelt to believe four years ago, when the Germans had been close to Moscow and most of the government had fled to Kuibyshev. What had Lanny intended to say to Stalin a year ago? And would he say the same today? Evidently Truman was turning over the idea of asking the ex-P.A. to take up the role again; but Lanny gave no hint that he had thought of this.

He answered each question as clearly as he could. "You have to understand Communist doctrine, Mr. President, and also you have to have some idea of the factions that are pulling and hauling inside the party. They have a favorite word, 'monolithic'; they wish you to believe that the party is absolutely solid and rigid. But I suspect that the Politburo has its factions, and they dispute about what Marx taught and what Lenin would have done. Lenin himself had a fixed goal, but he was an opportunist when it came to tactics. I have some quotes that I use when I get into an argument with the comrades. One of them is from Lenin in 1905, the time of the first revolution: 'Whoever attempts to achieve Socialism by any other route than that of political democracy will inevitably arrive at the most absurd and reactionary results both political and economic.' Most Communists look blank when I read that to them."

"How, in the face of such a statement, can the Russians think they are followers of Lenin?"

"They do what so many of the religious sects have done—they give a different meaning to words. They call their regime 'democratic' because it is supposed to serve the interest of the proletariat; but they don't grant the proletariat the right to decide what its interests are."

"I suppose people quote the passages that suit them, just as they do with the Scriptures."

"Exactly. A hundred people read about Lenin for every one who reads him; and it's the same with Marx. I have argued with Russian Marxists but never met one who knew that Marx had admitted that the Anglo-Saxon countries might achieve the Socialist goal without violent overthrow of their governments."

"Did Marx really say that?"

"It's another quote that I carry in my mind. He said: 'We do not deny that there are countries like England and America, and, I might add, even Holland, where the worker may attain his object by peaceful means.'"

"I wish I had had those texts when I was in Potsdam," remarked the President wryly.

VII

One thing Lanny Budd got clear from this long interview, that here was a man who wanted to know facts and was not going to be permanently fooled. Never had a guest been put through such a grilling, not even by F. D. R. That man of many moods could be diverted, and would divert himself into the telling of jokes and stories; but this was a single-minded man, determined to improve his knowledge of world issues. He wanted to know everything that Lanny knew, not merely about Russia but about Europe as a whole, its principal countries and their leaders, and the economic conditions and states of mind of their people.

Germany, above all—a problem to tax the powers of any statesman. How could a proud people, beaten to the earth, be tempted or lured into adopting the philosophy of their conquerors and becoming democratic and peace-minded? Lanny had a full chance to set forth his own and Monck's idea that the giant steel and coal industries of the Ruhr, for a century a bone of contention between Germany and France, would have to be placed under international control and operated for the equal benefit of all the peoples of Europe. Harry Truman didn't say, "But that would be Socialism!" He said, "How would that work, Mr. Budd?" And he listened while Lanny pointed out that we had a post office and a forestry service and an atomic commission which gave equal service to all Americans, and no one found them menaces to freedom. There were many international commissions, and would have to be many more if the nations were to co-operate at keeping the peace.

The visitor had no idea how much or how little this man of the people had managed to learn about the Socialist movement, its ideas or its history. It was possible that he had never talked to a Socialist and had no notion that measures he himself was advocating were a series of steps toward a collectivist society. Lanny avoided the subject of prosperous America; let it wait until the next slump came! He talked about Europe, which was in the slump to end all slumps. The enlightened workers of Europe had learned who it was that had financed Nazi-Fascism and who would finance a resurgence of that hellish creed if they had a chance. The big industrial powers, the cartels, were the number-one enemy of democracy on that old continent, and the Social Democrats were the only group who had the political education and the moral force to carry out such a change and make it stick.

Lanny knew what his old Boss had said in answer to that statement, and he was not surprised when the new Boss said the same thing. "Suppose that I were to order the Army to carry out such a program, Mr. Budd, do you think the American public would back me or that Congress would vote me the funds? To get down to brass tacks, would the Democratic party be able to carry the election next November?"

"You are in better position to answer that than I," said the other. "I can only warn you that setting up the old owners in Europe means ordering another war. Also, I have to say that it means turning Europe over to the Commies in the end. It gives them all the arguments. They say to the workers, 'You see, America means capitalism; it means nothing else. The Americans care nothing about your rights or your interests.' And believe me, the Commies know how to say it; they are the world's best propagandists because they put their whole minds on it, they have no doubts or scruples, and there are no shades in their ideas —everything is either white or black. They have simplified the class struggle so that every child can understand it, and they see to it that every child does. I assure you, Mr. Truman, you have to choose between a Socialist Europe and a Communist Europe, and I think the same thing applies to Asia. If we try to impose 'private enterprise,' we shall have to do it with military forces, and do it over and over again, putting down one attempt at revolution after another. You have to ask yourself whether and for how long our Congress will support *that* program."

VIII

Lanny had been told that Harry Truman was an impulsive man; his enemies, who had broken the "honeymoon" with him, said so, and some of his friends admitted it. So the visitor wasn't surprised when, in the middle of the evening, his host suddenly demanded, "How would you like to go and have a talk with Stalin?"

Lanny wasn't impulsive but well prepared; he said at once, "If you ask what I would *like*, Mr. President, I answer that I am tired of traveling, and I have found work to do at home that interests me greatly. But if you should say that you *want* me to go, then, of course, I couldn't say no."

"What do you think would be Stalin's attitude to such a suggestion?"

"When I talked to him four years ago he invited me to come again, and he sounded as if he meant it. When I saw him at Yalta, a little more than a year ago, he asked me why I hadn't come; so I have reason to suppose that he would receive me. Would I make the application or would you?"

"I would prefer that you made it, because I would want it to be strictly between us. You would go for me and report to me and say nothing about it to anyone else unless I authorized you to."

"That part is all right; I dealt with the Governor for eight years on that basis. You would give me a letter to Stalin?"

"Surely. I would say that you are my friend and ask him to receive you as *his* friend. I could give you no definite proposal; I would just want you to talk to him as you have talked to me. Tell him my difficulties, as I have explained them; explain America to him—perhaps he doesn't always get the truth."

"That, I have no doubt, is the case."

"Very well then; talk to him heart to heart, if he will let you, and see if you cannot work out some suggestions as to how to arrest the growing hostility between our two countries."

"All I can answer," said Lanny, "is that if you ask me to carry out such a mission, I will do my best."

The President, having said that he could make no definite proposal, proceeded to suggest possible proposals and invited the son of Budd-Erling to do the same. Might it not somehow be possible that Stalin would content himself with developing the Communist society in those vast parts of the world which he now controlled, and leave the peoples of the rest of the world free to choose what form of government and economic system they wished to live under?

Lanny replied, "Shall I tell you what Stalin will answer to that proposal? He will say that capitalism does not leave the people free to make such a choice. He will point out that the reactionary Greek government is killing Communists rather freely. That is true; and what shall I answer?"

"Tell him that we might work out joint plans for a plebiscite in each country, and both sides agree to submit to a democratic decision."

Lanny couldn't help smiling. "You might have a hard time persuading the Greek government to accept that program."

"They want money from us," said Truman; "and it is for us to state the terms on which we are willing to put it up."

Still more complex was the problem of the atomic bomb that was hanging over Tovarish Molotov's head. The American government had proposed the so-called Baruch Plan, whereby all governments agreed to submit to international inspection as preliminary to the destruction of the American store of atomic bombs. Manifestly, that would be bad for any country which cherished ideas of ever again taking up arms; but what harm could it do to a country that had genuinely and sincerely given up the thought of resorting to military force?

Harry Truman asked that, and Lanny Budd answered, "You are dealing with the most suspicious and distrustful group of men in the world. All I can say is, I'll discuss it with their leader and bring you back an exact report of what he says. Shall I call on the Russian Ambassador and arrange for my application to Stalin?"

Said the President, "That might well cause a leak here in Washington. Why not make a try at sending a cablegram direct to Stalin himself? Remind him of his previous invitation and tell him you are ready to come now if he will receive you. Ask him to reply in care of Western Union and wait and see what happens."

"All right," said the P.A., no longer "ex."

IX

Lanny spent the night in solitary grandeur in one of the spacious bedrooms of the White House. He was free to imagine how many kings and princes, statesmen and other great, had preceded him; but no ghosts haunted him, and he lay for an hour or two fixing in his mind the instructions he had received. When he was awake and dressed, he went downstairs, and breakfast was served him alone; the President, he had read, kept a farm boy's hours and had been in his office long since. Lanny had the name of a secretary with whom he was to keep in touch, and now he asked for a taxi and had himself driven to the nearest telegraph office.

He wrote a message to Marshal Joseph Stalin, Kremlin, Moscow, reminding him of their previous meetings and saying that he had a communication of interest and would be glad to come if the invitation still stood. The girl who took this message gazed at the handsome gentleman with curiosity unconcealed; he wondered if she would consider it her duty to report him to the F.B.I., or possibly to the House Committee on Un-American Activities. He paid for the message, walked to the hotel where his wife was staying, and registered himself and reregistered her, "Mr. and Mrs." He told her that he had again been placed in the position of not talking about what he was doing.

X

The visiting couple entertained themselves in Washington. They called on Mrs. Perle Mesta and listened to that well-informed lady's opinion on the Democratic party's prospects in the coming congressional elections—not so good. Laurel called on the senator's wife whom she had met, and heard more of the same news. It appeared that after a war the people didn't find things as they wanted them and always insisted upon a change. The President's supporters were all making apologies for his boners.

Every day the Peace promoters called Edgemere, N. J., heard the news, and gave instructions. The second day was Thursday, and as they now had a Washington station on their chain the New York station arranged for Lanny to broadcast from where he was. He told about the secrets he had been digging out of the Gestapo files, and it made as good a story as anybody could want. Afterward the pair listened while John Haynes Holmes, in New York, gave an eloquent and moving statement of his belief that no political or economic movement, however soundly based, could bring permanent good to mankind unless it recognized the spiritual and moral nature of man and appealed to those forces in his heart. He talked about Gandhi and what this frail saint had to teach self-confident Americans.

Next morning came a telephone call from the Russian Embassy; the Ambassador, Mr. Novikov, desired to know if Mr. Budd would do him the honor to call. Mr. Budd would do so, and was informed that the Ambassador had received instructions from his government to provide Mr. Budd with a visa to enter the Soviet Union, and to advise them by what route he preferred to travel. Mr. Budd replied that he would fly by way of England and Sweden. He was told that if he would inform the Russian Embassy in Stockholm when he expected to reach that city, arrangements would be made there to fly him to Moscow. He could guess that the polite Mr. Novikov might have some curiosity concerning this trip, but if his own government hadn't seen fit to inform him, it wasn't Lanny's business to do so.

The P.A. phoned the White House secretary and was told to go to the State Department, now settled in its fancy new home in what is known as Washington's "Foggy Bottom." His passport was prepared in record time, and he took it to the Russian Embassy and had the visa stamped on it. He was to be flown next morning from La Guardia Field in an American commercial plane, his passage paid by the White House. From England he would be flown in a British commercial plane. From there on he would be the guest of the onetime secretary of the Bolsheviki. ("Majority" the word meant, but not a majority of the Russian people, only of the delegates to a revolutionary party conference, held near the beginning of the century.)

He went back to the hotel and packed his belongings and his wife's. A messenger came from the White House, bringing the letter to Stalin which President Truman had promised to write. So everything was ready, and when Laurel came in from a walk they had lunch and then stepped into their car. Secret diplomacy and matrimony do not go well together, for he couldn't discuss his plans and it left a gap in their conversation.

He was free to tell her about the plowboy who had risen so high; others had done so in the past. He was honest, and had come honestly by the many enemies he had made in the course of more than a year. That he was ignorant about many things was unfortunate, but what really mattered was that he said he was ignorant, and was determined not to remain so. He was a democrat both in the small-letter sense of that word and in the capital-letter sense; he believed in the plain people, liked them, trusted them, and meant to serve them. He had been a soldier and hated war—and that too was in the American tradition. There had been many soldier-Presidents, and one and all they had craved peace.

33

Peace in Thy Right Hand

I

HOME at Edgemere, Lanny reported to his friends. Gerald de Groot would continue the radio announcing. The revived P.A. spent a good part of the night reading and answering his mail, and early in the morning drove his wife across New York City to the airfield—she would drive the car back. The weather reports were favorable, and so was the season; he promised to cable her from London, and pretended not to notice when she wiped away tears. It would be that cold northern route on which he had so nearly lost his life.

The great silver bird rose into the sky, and he settled down to read a load of newspapers and magazines. Flying had become commonplace; one patch of sea and cloud looked exactly like the next, and what a civilized man wanted to know was what had been said in Congress and in Parliament, and what Jimmy Byrnes had been able to accomplish at the meeting of the Big Four foreign ministers in Paris. At the scheduled time they settled down on the immense airport in Newfoundland, which Lanny had seen at various stages of its growth throughout the war. Thousands upon thousands of great planes had been flying eastward— and fewer coming back!

They flew again. This time the sun was shining and the wind was light; they were flying straight to Scotland, not stopping at either Iceland or Greenland, as they did in bad weather. At the seaside town of Prestwick another of these great airports had been constructed; unlike most of the products of war, these could be used in peacetime. Since his plane for Stockholm did not fly until the next day, he phoned Wickthorpe and asked that Frances be sent in to his hotel. Irma was in a state of excitement because he had cabled that he wanted to take the child back to the States with him.

He was flown to London, and there he got in touch with Scrubbie, who had just got his discharge from the RAF. They would have another party, and it would be a case where three wouldn't be a crowd. He found that the friendship had been progressing normally, and of course both the young people were enraptured by the idea of flying back to America. When Frances was alone with her father she asked, "Don't you think he's a lovely person?" He told her that he didn't know anyone more so, and then added, "Don't fall in love too hard." She promised not to, but told him, "I think it's rather nice to have the idea."

The three went for a stroll in Hyde Park, to look at the tulips and other pleasant sights. "Oh, to be in England now that April's there!" So a homesick poet had written from Italy, and went on to say, "And after April, when May follows, and the white-throat builds, and all the swallows!" Many kinds of birds were here, enjoying the sunshine along with the elegant ladies and gentlemen, walking or riding. The war had been over nearly a year, and not a bomb had fallen in that time; all the creatures were glad to be alive, and Scrubbie, watching the swallows, said he was well satisfied to leave the air to them. No more darting and swooping—but walking on a smooth graveled path with the girl of his choice.

II

Again the much-traveled courier took off, northeastward across the North Sea and the tiny flat farms of Denmark. The last time he had made this trip the route had been indirect and top secret, but now it was one more milk run. They came to a beautiful clean city of small islands and large bridges and glided down to a rest. The last time, Lanny had been on his way to see Hitler, and this time it was another and different dictator. With all his heart he hoped that the differences were greater than the resemblances.

All he had to do now was to go to the Grand Hotel and from there telephone the Russian Embassy and announce his arrival. Not more than half an hour passed before an attaché brought the necessary papers and the information that his plane would fly next morning. From the extreme deference with which he was treated he could guess that this Embassy had information as to the reason for his trip. There was an evening for Lanny to spend with Eric Erickson, Swedish-American oil man who had been a secret agent of the OSS.

Once more into the air, this time in a Russian government plane—there was no other sort. The passengers, of whom there were a dozen, must have known that he was an American by his clothing and his bags; they bowed politely, but no one offered to chat. He read the latest issue of Dr. Rhine's *Journal of Parapsychology*—of which he could be sure they would not be permitted to approve.

Apparently the officers of the plane did not care how much of the city of Stockholm people saw or how much of the Baltic Sea; but when they neared the Russian coast, covers made of some composition board were put over all the windows, and there they stayed. Winston Churchill had talked about the iron curtain, and now Lanny discovered that there were plywood curtains also.

When the plane came down a couple of hours later and half the passengers got off, he was free to guess that it was Leningrad, but nobody told him and he did not ask. Other passengers came aboard, looked at him curiously and bowed, but left the seat beside him vacant. The plane rose again, and he was free to guess that Moscow would be next. He read awhile, then thought awhile, going over in his mind the things he wished to say to the Boss of the Soviet Union—an opportunity that few foreigners had and fewer had twice.

Was Stalin really the Boss? He denied it vigorously, but few paid attention to that denial. You could read that his power was still as great as ever; in other places you could read that he was old and tired and left decisions to the Politburo. Lanny couldn't expect to talk to the Politburo and had to assume that what he said to Stalin would count.

He could imagine the vast treeless spaces of this part of Russia, a year after the end of the most dreadful of wars. They were due to be green with grain—if the peasants had been able to get them plowed. All that the traveler saw was the long compartment of a plane, full of officers and civilians, some of them chatting, some dozing, some just sitting and staring ahead, as if they found life in the new world no different from the old.

III

The plane came down after another couple of hours, and there was Lanny's escort, a young Army officer, speaking precise copybook English. There were no customs formalities or other delays; the visitor was driven in a Lincoln car to the Metropole Hotel and told that his engagement with the Marshal would be at nine that evening. They served him one of those enormous Russian meals, several times as much as he could eat; he could only hope that the rest would not be wasted.

Captain Briansky offered to drive him to any of the sights he might like to see, but he chose to walk and stretch his legs. Since he knew few Russian words, the officer offered to act as his interpreter, and Lanny expressed himself as grateful. He was left to guess whether this was a courtesy or a precaution. He knew that the Russians were suspicious of foreigners, and naturally this made him suspicious of Russians.

Four years had passed since Lanny had strolled on the streets of Moscow. That had been the time of its greatest peril, with the German armies almost within artillery range and a spring offensive certain. There had been great bomb damage, and now it had mostly been repaired. Everybody was working—how efficiently was a matter of controversy, depending upon whether you read Russian or English. The people appeared tired and wore old clothing. This latter seemed more important to an American visitor than it did to the Russians, who for more than a generation had been living under war conditions, or war-preparation conditions, not so different.

It was a great and ancient city, with monuments and historical landmarks, most of which Lanny had seen. It was overcrowded, like all modern cities; people persist in moving into them in spite of discomforts. To a man fresh from Washington, with its shiny new marble buildings, and New York, with its Fifth-Avenue luxury shops and Park-Avenue elegance, Moscow seemed an enormous slum; but the people were working, and all were moving steadily. What was in their minds was something he had no chance to find out. He was trying to spare them the possibility of someday having an atomic bomb go off over their heads, and he could guess that if they had known about his effort they would have wished him luck.

IV

At a quarter to nine the car came to the hotel, and Lanny and his escort were driven to the near-by Kremlin, that ancient, high-walled fortress behind which the Tsars of old had kept themselves hidden from danger. In front of it is the immense Red Square, with the tomb of Lenin close against the wall. Lenin had won, and so he was a hero, a seer, a lay saint. Inside the walled enclosure were many buildings, and in one of them—only a chosen few knew which—Lenin's successor had his modest apartment.

Inside the gate the car halted and was searched by soldiers with flash-lights. Then it went on, winding here and there, and stopped in front of one of the old buildings in semi-darkness. Two soldiers stood on duty, and the captain spoke a few words and then led his visitor inside. There was an anteroom, and through an open door he entered the strange oval-shaped room in which four years ago he had had his conference. The ceiling was vaulted, and the walls paneled with white oak, alter-nating with surfaces of plaster. At one end was a flat-topped desk, with a chair in front of it and an armchair beside it. At the other side was a smaller chair in which sat a young man, slender and dark, the same who had served as interpreter on Lanny's previous visit. He rose but was not introduced.

Everything in that room was the same; Lanny could even imagine that the books on the desk were the same. There were several telephones, each of a different color to distinguish them. In the bookcase against the wall were the works of Lenin, and two encyclopedias, the Soviet one and the German Brockhaus. Near the entrance door was a glass case with a death mask of Lenin, and a grandfather's clock made of ebony. On the walls were portraits of Marx and Engels, with the heavy whisk-ers of our great-grandfathers' day. Nothing had changed in four years. Through an open door Lanny looked into a room containing a long table and maps on the walls; he could guess that it was the council room in which the defense of the Soviet Fatherland had been planned.

V

Captain Briansky tapped upon a closed door, and a few seconds later it was opened and the host came in. Lanny rose to greet him, thinking that he looked much more than four years older; his hair and mustache were of a lighter gray, and his pockmarked face was heavily lined. The war had taken its toll of him, as of F. D. R. Lanny had read that recently, for the first time, painters had been permitted to represent their leader as gray-haired, and this had given a shock to the people, who presumably had thought that he would last forever.

Joseph Vissarionovich Dzhugashvili was a small man, four or five inches shorter than Lanny, who was five feet ten. He was stockily built but not fat. He wore a dark blue Russian blouse and trousers tucked into boots. His head was large and his complexion somewhat sallow; his left arm was slightly shrunken. His life had been a hard one—he had a record of eight times imprisoned, seven times exiled, and six times escaped. He was the son of a drunken cobbler in the capital city of Soviet Georgia, in Transcaucasia. His devout mother had destined him for the priesthood and had sent him to a theological seminary, but he had come into contact with Socialist ideas and had set out to change this world instead of waiting for another.

He was a man of simple tastes and no formalities; when he liked a person he could be agreeable, and he had given every sign of liking the son of Budd-Erling. They shook hands, and Stalin said in English, "Welcome, Mr. Budd." He gave a nod to the captain, who excused himself and withdrew.

Lanny took out the letter Truman had given him and handed it to Stalin, who opened it, looked at it, then passed it to the interpreter. The letter had not been sealed, so Lanny knew what it said: that Mr. Lanning Prescott Budd had come at the President's request, after a conference with the President. He had the President's full confidence and would report faithfully what the Marshal had to say to him. He was not authorized to make specific proposals but to explain the President's point of view, which was an intense desire for friendship and understanding between the two countries.

The Boss listened attentively and then said something which must have meant "repeat," for the interpreter went through the letter a second time. Then he handed it back, and Stalin laid it on the desk. "Proceed, Mr. Budd," he said. "One sentence at a time, please." Lanny did not need this injunction; he was not one of those foolish persons who talk fast for a minute or two and expect an interpreter to cover it all in a sentence. He spoke slowly and carefully, weighing each word and waiting until each sentence had been translated.

"First," he said, "I wish you to know about my relations with President Roosevelt. I served him as a secret agent from 1937. I posed as a Nazi sympathizer and went into Germany eleven times, sometimes staying for months. I brought out secrets of a scientific character, including rocket bombs and atomic fission. I was with the President on the night before his death, and he then told me of his worry over the worsening of relations with the Soviet Union. He planned to send me secretly for a conference with you, and he briefed me thoroughly for this mission. I believe you would be interested in knowing exactly what he told me."

"By all means, Mr. Budd," said the Marshal promptly.

Lanny told the events of that never-to-be-forgotten night. He described the President's appearance and the conditions under which he was living. He impressed upon the Marshal the fact that he had made full and complete notes that same night, and he produced these notes, explaining that he had done the same for President Truman. Stalin took them and turned them over, page by page, while Lanny went on talking and the dark young man with eyeglasses went on repeating sentence by sentence. There was a prevalent idea that Stalin knew some English but preferred not to reveal the fact. Molotov knew the language well but rarely spoke it.

Lanny did not go into details concerning Roosevelt's dissatisfaction, for all these details were controversial; Stalin would have a different point of view, he would give an answer, and an argument might start. Lanny's strategy was to deal in generalities until he had made his main points. He said that Roosevelt had instructed him to express to the Soviet Marshal his profound distress over the decline of friendship between the two countries and to plead with him to accept the President's assurances and pledge himself to a renewal of the former cordial relationship. Just recently President Truman had learned of what Roosevelt had planned and had summoned Lanny and heard the story; he had asked the P.A. to take this trip and report to the Marshal that he shared President Roosevelt's fears, and also his desires; he wanted just as ardently as Roosevelt had done to get along with the Soviet Union on terms of friendship and mutual confidence, and to put an end to the continual bickering which had been going on during the thirteen months since Roosevelt's death. "My mission is confidential," added the P.A. "No one but President Truman knows that I have come, and no one but he will hear your reply."

VI

Such was the story; and the man who specialized in inscrutability sat as motionless as the Sphinx, listening to every word but giving no sign. Only his eyes moved—and these in the same peculiar way which Lanny had observed four years ago. While Lanny was speaking the eyes were upon his face, as if they were reading secrets inside his skull; when the interpreter started speaking the eyes dropped to the vicinity of Lanny's navel—though this was well covered by a well-knitted undersuit and an outer suit of brown English tweeds.

When the discourse came to an end the listener offered Lanny a cigarette; when the offer was declined he took up his pipe, filled and lit it, and thereafter puffed at intervals. "Mr. Budd," he said, "there is no one who desires good relations with your country more than I." He waited for that to be translated and then added another sentence, slowly and carefully. "But things which your country has done seem to us far from friendly, and we are unable to understand them. Do you wish me to go into those things?"

The envoy replied, "As you know, I am not authorized to make proposals, and with many of the details I am not as familiar as a negotiator would need to be. President Truman said to me, more than once, 'If the will to friendship can be established, if the determination for friendship exists' "—Lanny said each of these phrases separately, to let them register—" 'then negotiations can be carried on and just settlements can be reached.' One of the things that disturb the President most is the bitter hostility revealed by your press, and its continuing propaganda against our country."

The Red Marshal took a puff or two and then replied, "Has it escaped your notice that the greater part of your American press and radio reveals hostility to the Soviet Union and the ideas for which it stands?"

"Unfortunately, sir, that press is privately owned, and our government has no control over it. But you must know that it does not represent the feelings of either our people or our government. Seventy per cent of our press opposed President Roosevelt at one election after another, and four times the American people repudiated it."

"Yes, Mr. Budd; but don't you see the practical result of such a situation? The newspapers of your country are free to point out the faults and errors of my country, whereas you expect the newspapers of my country to remain silent concerning what we think are the faults and errors of yours. Where is the fairness in that?"

Lanny sat forward in his chair. "Mr. Stalin," he said, "I have been a Socialist since my boyhood—that is, more than thirty years. I distrust our capitalist press every bit as much as you do. I want to see Socialism come to America, and I am pleading with you from that point of view. We differ in our ideas of how to get it—that is all."

"Does President Truman share your ideas on that subject, Mr. Budd?"

"I did not ask him, but I doubt very much if he has ever read a book on theoretical Socialism. Like millions of other Americans, he will have to get his education as he goes along, from current events. One reason he asked me to come to see you is that I gave him a quotation from Karl Marx, to the effect that Marx did not deny that in countries like England and America, and even Holland, the worker might attain his objective by peaceful means. I am sure you must be familiar with that quotation."

"I am; but that was a long time ago, and I venture to doubt whether Marx would say the same thing today in the face of the enormous development of your trusts and the concentration of economic power in the hands of your capitalist class."

"I do not know your sources of information, Marshal Stalin. I beg you to believe that our labor unions are rapidly coming to political consciousness and that vast changes are impending in my capitalist country."

"Does your assurance include the ability of President Truman's party to retain the control of Congress next fall?"

"Alas, no. It is quite possible that we are in for a period of reaction, and that our workers will have to get their education in that painful way."

"And have you thought what is going to happen to the Soviet Union during that same period, Mr. Budd? What is going to happen to the friendship while the purse strings are controlled by men who carry out the will of Wall Street?"

"Let me tell you, sir, that the first or second time I met President Roosevelt he spoke these words: 'I cannot go any faster than the people will let me.' I assure you that if a Republican Congress should be elected, it would have the same check upon it. The people would not let it attack the Soviet Union, and if it attacked the new mass unions of labor, it would stir them to action and be kicked out of power again."

The reply to that statement was, "You are asking me to have much more faith in your country's institutions than seems reasonable to a foreigner."

VII

Lanny perceived that he wasn't getting where he wanted to get. He liked Senator Taft and Governor Dewey and the rest of the Republicans no more than Stalin did, and if there had been some way that Stalin could have made war on them and left the rest of America out of it Lanny would hardly have taken a ten-thousand-mile journey to make peace. He leaned toward his host and began very earnestly, "Marshal Stalin, I remind you once more that you are talking to a lifelong Socialist. I desire nothing on earth so much as a co-operative world, free from the exploitation of man by man. One of my reasons for coming here was the hope that you would permit me to tell you some of the things that I know about my own country and that you may not know."

"Certainly, Mr. Budd; I could desire no better source of information."

"First, our economic situation. Our history for a century and a half has been one unbroken cycle of boom and bust—that is, good times followed by bad. We both know the causes of this, and the one possible remedy. Our political history shows that every depression is followed by a burst of radicalism and social change. The last time our economy was saved by the New Deal's enormous spending program, begun in 1933. After four years the effects of this had begun to wear off, and the only thing that saved us from another collapse was the coming of war. Now we are in the midst of a boom because we are making up for the war destruction and shortages. When that task has been done we shall be on the verge of another smash."

"That is what our own economists tell us, Mr. Budd."

"The next will surely be the worst in our history. We are producing something like two hundred and fifty billion dollars' worth of goods, and our people do not receive money enough to purchase nearly that much. Our exports for the most part consist of gifts more or less disguised; that is, loans which can never be repaid, or lend-lease, or UNRRA. We shall be forced to devise other schemes to justify us in sending our goods to peoples that need them but have no dollars to buy them. This shrinking of markets will grow worse and worse, and in the end we shall be forced to socialize our basic industries and start producing for use instead of for profit."

"The usual answer to that, Mr. Budd, is another capitalist war."

"I know, Marshal, and that is the reason for my coming. I know that our people abhor war, and if we have no provocation our business masters will not be able to persuade us to rearm. I want to see the provocations removed."

"There will be none from us, Mr. Budd. Our attitude has been, and will remain, strictly defensive."

"You say that, sir, and I have no doubt that you mean it. What I am trying to do is to explain how matters look to Americans. Everywhere I turn I hear the statement that the aims of the Soviet Union appear to be identical with those of the old tsarist regime. They appear to threaten the democratic world; and, believing that, Americans will start to rearm, and they will be sure that their attitude is defensive. Two nations fear each other, they arm against each other, and never does either fail to be certain that its effort is defensive. The point I am trying to make is that to the extent that America rearms, the expected economic crash is postponed. We may spend ten billion a year, twenty billion, and it will constitute artificially created purchasing power. It may be just the amount that is needed to take up the slack, to keep down the inevitable glut, the overproduction of goods which is the cause of panics and hard times. Don't you think—looking at the matter from your own point of view—that it would be safer and wiser to make some sort of deal with us, abolish the threat of war, and let our ship of private enterprise drive full steam ahead onto the rocks toward which it is headed?"

Lanny waited, to see how that argument was taking effect. The Soviet master sat looking at him for as long as half a dozen puffs of his pipe. Could it be that there was a trace of a smile on that inscrutable face? Was he by any chance seeing in his mind's eye the pleasing vision of his dreaded foe dying in a self-induced convulsion? Lanny had no way to know.

VIII

When the host spoke again it was still soberly. "We have offered many times, Mr. Budd, to work out a program of general disarmament. Our offers have not been cordially received."

"That brings up the other matter about which I hope to talk to you —the atomic bomb. Mr. Molotov has complained that we dangle the bomb over his head, and I hope that you will not take such an attitude to what I say."

"I am not easily frightened, Mr. Budd." Now there was surely a smile. "Proceed."

"It happens that I learned a lot about the bomb. In preparation for my efforts as a presidential agent I was thoroughly briefed by Professor Einstein and an assistant, as early as the summer of 1941. Also I was present in New Mexico and witnessed the explosion of the first atomic bomb. I was ten miles away, lying flat on my stomach, with my eyes buried in the sleeve of my coat; even so I saw that terrifying light, and the shock would have knocked me off my feet if I had been standing. So I am afraid of that dreadful thing; and I am told that we have much worse ones now.

"I am not telling any secrets, Marshal, and am surely not asking for any of yours. I take it for granted that you are working to get the bomb, and that sooner or later you will succeed. I have tried to figure out what will be the situation then, and this is what I get: whichever side attacks first can destroy many of the other's cities, but they will not be able to destroy the other's supply of bombs, or fast planes to carry them. Common sense tells us that neither side will be keeping its store of bombs in great cities; they will be hidden in remote caves, in forests and other unlikely places, and they can be moved from time to time to balk the efforts of spies.

"So presently we have this situation: you have wiped out New York and Washington, Chicago and Detroit, and we in turn have wiped out Moscow and Leningrad, Magnitogorsk and other great industrial complexes. Meanwhile both sides are digging into caves and putting their industries under ground; it may go on until both sides are fighting with sticks and stones for lack of anything better. There may be revolutions of infuriated populations, but they may not be the social revolutions of which Marx and Lenin have written; they may be gangster revolutions—you may get another crop of Hitlers and Francos. I am sure that prospect will please you no more than it pleases me."

IX

Again Lanny waited, to let his voice sink and see what would be the reaction to this carefully thought-out discourse. "Puff, puff," said Stalin's pipe, and Stalin said nothing for a while. Then, "What you say is important, Mr. Budd, and I will tell President Truman that he has a persuasive messenger. What is your remedy for all this?"

"First, the settlement of the atomic question. The Atomic Energy Commission has, as you know, brought in a report, proposing effective international control of atomic fission, with the right of inspection and supervision by a UN authority."

"Unfortunately, Mr. Budd, we cannot have the same confidence in the UN that you have. We and our friends are a small minority in the organization."

"Yes, but you have the veto, and Mr. Gromyko is showing that you know how to use it. Let us be realistic, Marshal. You must know that, world antagonisms being what they are, no nation will surrender its weapons without being in a position to make certain that all other nations are doing the same. The memory of the last world disarmament program is too fresh in the minds of all statesmen."

"And what comes after the bombs are all destroyed?"

"If I could have my way, sir, you would come forward with your hands held out and say, 'We have had enough of this disputing. We have been allies in war and we mean to remain allies in peace. From now on we shall settle all our problems by impartial arbitration.'"

"Such a thing as impartiality is hard to find in this world, Mr. Budd. What, for example, would be your solution for the struggle of the Greek people for freedom?"

"President Truman referred explicitly to that. Let the UN order an armistice and supervise a free election in which the people shall choose what sort of government they desire. Our formula in America is ballots instead of bullets."

"And for Germany, what?"

"Obviously we must supervise Germany for a long time, to make sure that she does not rearm. We have to learn to do that together— or else we shall find ourselves competing for her support in another war. I am not saying that it will be easy to solve these problems; I am saying that we have to solve them or risk the loss of our civilization in the most awful holocaust of all time. Atomic power is an entirely new thing, Marshal Stalin, and we cannot go on as if it did not exist; we have to make the decision as to whether we shall use it to build up the world or to destroy it. I point out to you that it would be possible for the Soviet Union to get a large reconstruction loan from my country—provided only that we were assured it would be spent for civilian and not for military purposes. It is my hope to persuade you to carry on your warfare against capitalism by constructive methods. Prove to the world the truth of our Socialist theorem that the wastes of competition consume two-thirds of its product. Show the world how much more efficiently a co-operative economy can work. Give them an example of a nation without strikes and unemployment, panics and crises and fear. Surely we must not forget our old idealism, and let the capitalists drag us down to their level of thinking and doing!"

Lanny had been called a utopian and a dreamer by his father and many of his wealthy friends. He wondered, would the Red dictator hold the same opinion of him? Somewhere deep in Stalin's consciousness must be memories of his youth and the vision of a free and just world which had inspired him! Surely he could still recall the formula of Engels and Lenin that when the state was no longer an instrument of class repression it would fall into disuse and wither away! Having read literature and heard speeches like that since boyhood, Lanny knew all the phrases—and now was the time to bring them forth. He made it clear that he didn't want to compromise with capitalism or admit its right to dominate the world's economy. What he wanted was that the peoples who possessed democratic institutions and had learned to use them should find their own way of escape. Leave us alone, Marshal Stalin, and we'll know how to deal with our exploiters!

X

This interview continued until late into the night. The Red leader asked many questions, and some of them showed that he doubted the possibility of what Lanny wanted. At the end his statement was, "What you tell me is important, and I am obliged to you for coming. I promise you that I will think it over carefully and put it before my associates. There exists in your country the fixed notion that I rule Russia like a despot, but I assure you it is not so. We have a political party and we have a government, and I do not dictate, I advise."

The P.A. replied quietly, "I accept your assurance, sir. I would be very happy if I could know that you would advise in favor of a policy of live and let live in this crucial moment of our history."

This was a bid for Stalin to get down to cases, but he did not take it. Said he, "You may tell your President that I most earnestly desire and intend peace between our two countries. I can see no possibility of war, and we shall certainly not contemplate it or prepare for it. In the covenant of the UN we renounced force as a means of settling disputes, and we mean it and take it for granted that your country means it also."

When the interpreter had finished this last sentence the host pressed a button, and wine and cakes were brought in. While these were being consumed Stalin asked, "Is there anything I can do for you personally, to reward you for a long journey?"

Lanny had expected this and was prepared. "Yes, Marshal," he replied. "Let me explain that I have a half-sister, now living in France. She was involved in one of the conspiracies against Hitler and was shut up in Leipzig concentration camp and tortured cruelly. Now she is recovering, but she is still far from normal. She has an uncle of whom she was very fond and of whom she asks frequently. You know him, I believe—Jesse Blackless. He is old and can hardly be of service to you any longer. If I could take him out with me to join his niece, it would be a favor."

Thus the tactful diplomat; and the other's face clouded. "I am sorry to have to tell you, Blackless died of pneumonia about a year ago. I overlooked the fact that he was your uncle or I would have taken steps to inform you."

Lanny was shocked, and of course wondered if that story was exactly true or if his Red uncle had shared the fate of so many others of the Bolsheviks who had found themselves dissatisfied with a dictator's policies. Lanny would never know; and all he could say was, "I am saddened to hear that news. It was Jesse who first brought me into touch with Socialist ideas. It was because I had some of his literature in my pocket that I had my first brush with the police—that was in Paris, just after World War I. He and I had something to do with Lincoln Steffens being sent to Russia."

"Is there anything you would like to see in this country?" inquired Stalin, changing the subject; and Lanny said, "No, sir, it is my duty to take your message back to President Truman at once."

"I will arrange for you to be flown to Stockholm tomorrow," said the other, and they shook hands.

34

Hope to the End

I

LANNY'S plane did not fly until noon; meantime Captain Briansky inquired if he would like to visit the Ballet School. The Marshal himself had suggested this, because Harry Hopkins, on his visit a year ago, had expressed such interest in this world-famous institution. Hopkins had told the Marshal how much the visit had pleased him, and the Marshal had replied that he had been twenty-eight years in Moscow and had never seen the place. Later he had followed Mr. Hopkins' example and thought that Mr. Budd might like to do the same.

Such a message was a command, and Lanny was driven to the great institution, which had survived two wars and a revolution, and whose graduates had taught the world a fascinating variety of art. He was introduced to the instructors, and to the ballerinas en masse; they were all a-twitter with excitement over meeting an American who was a friend of both Marshal Stalin and President Roosevelt. He watched their training for an hour or two, and when he told them that in his boyhood he had studied at the Dalcroze School in Hellerau, they plied him with questions about this method. To an outsider there might have been something comical in the sight of a tall gentleman of forty-five, clad in tweeds, demonstrating gymnastics which were supposed to be executed by young people in scant, tight-fitting black bathing suits. But to these Russians dance techniques were the most serious things in the world, and when Lanny showed them by what motions a massed group of performers had manifested pity and terror, they felt themselves in hell with Orpheus and Eurydice.

Then back to the hotel, and after a generous lunch with the affable captain Lanny was driven to the airport and seated in a plane, again with blacked-out windows. A few hours later he was in Stockholm, where a reservation to London had been made for him. Early next morning he rose into a cloudless sky. He reached Croydon Airport well before dark, and his London hotel in time to do his telephoning, both to Irma at the Castle and to Laurel in New Jersey. Irma's protests had been feeble, and three seats had been engaged for the following afternoon. The American Embassy had ordered them, and it appeared that they had some influence with Pan-American Airways.

II

Next morning, Lanny read in *The Times* that this was the ninetieth birthday of George Bernard Shaw, and that in honor of the occasion his friends had assembled an exhibition of his books, manuscripts, playbills, and posters. The presidential agent had been thinking about Shaw, who had been at Hellerau, the object of eager if discreet curiosity to three musketeers of the arts, Lanny, Rick, and Kurt Meissner. Shaw had then been fifty-seven, and now he was ninety. What had those years done to him?

The showing was by invitation, and Lanny strolled to the new home of the National Book League in Albemarle Street. He introduced himself to the director as the secret agent who had testified against Göring at Nürnberg, and also as the friend and collaborator of the playwright, Sir Eric Vivian Pomeroy-Nielson. He received a card and joined a couple of hundred of the elect in letters, politics, and society assembled in the handsome eighteenth-century rooms. He listened attentively and applauded politely the addresses of John Masefield, president of the League, and Dean Inge, the speaker of the day, both of them witty and urbane.

Then the guests moved around to look at one famous name in several hundred different sizes and styles of type, framed and hanging on walls, or seen through the glass of showcases. First editions of everything from *An Unsocial Socialist* to *In Good King Charles's Golden*

Days, and the anniversary book prepared for this occasion, large, and labeled in large letters: *G.B.S. 90.* There were framed playbills and large posters of *Arms and the Man, Man and Superman, Back to Methuselah,* and the other great successes of stage and screen, some from performances given in France, Germany, and other European countries. The guests were amused by a framed letter dated 1875, from a firm of "estate agents" who testified in guarded terms that George B. Shaw who had been in their employ and who was now leaving was an earnest and diligent worker whom they could conscientiously recommend and for whose future they had good hopes.

The director came alongside Lanny and said in a low voice, "Don't leave yet, it's just possible that Shaw may come in." So the P.A. waited, and saw the tall, thin old gentleman with the famous white whiskers, the baby-pink skin, and bright blue eyes. He wore an inconspicuous business suit, a trifle shabby—since no one there had anything else in these days. He walked about, looking at the record of his life. He held himself proudly erect, but Lanny thought that he was a trifle tottery on his legs.

The art expert was introduced to the world's most famous writer, and found his manner as mild and benevolent as his pen was sharp. Lanny inquired whether he remembered the *Festspiel* in the year of 1913; when the playwright said that he did, Lanny remarked, "I was one of the small boys who danced in the chorus of the demons in Gluck's *Orpheus.* Outside, I had stood and looked at you for some time, but I was too shy to speak. I remember the wind blowing over the bright meadow—Hellerau—and there were lovely glints of gold in your beard."

"I much prefer it as it is," responded the nonagenarian. "It is a mark of experience."

"I was reminded of those days yesterday morning when I visited the Ballet School in Moscow. I found that the students there didn't know about Dalcroze, and they begged me to give a demonstration. I found it less easy at the age of forty-five than I had at thirteen."

"You will find it still less easy when you are twice forty-five," remarked the old gentleman with a touch of grimness. "Did I understand you to tell me that you were in Moscow *yesterday?*"

"I was flown here. And this afternoon I am to be flown to Washington. I have an appointment with President Truman, and it occurs to me that you might like to send him a message."

The playwright studied the face of the well-dressed American for a moment, then said, "Tell your President that I consider him the most unfortunate of men. In time he will find out why."

"I think he knows it already, sir. But you know, it is the role of the hero to turn misfortune into triumph. You may see it happen in the White House."

"Tell him to hurry," replied G.B.S. "I am not planning to stay much longer to watch the follies of this tormented human race."

"I have studied *Back to Methuselah*," said Lanny, "and I know how the elders are bored with the young. Thank you for your patience, sir." He moved on to give way to others who wished to speak to the great man. Before leaving, he thanked the friendly director and inquired, "How did you get him to come?" The reply was, "That was easy; we told him not to."

III

The three were to fly from Croydon Airport. Irma wouldn't come to town—she was so ill pleased with her ex-husband. His lordship drove his stepdaughter in and turned her over to her father. Scrubbie was in the hotel, but Lanny told him to keep out of sight—no point in mentioning that he was going along.

The route was by way of the Azores and Bermuda direct to Washington; pleasant weather and an uneventful trip. From Bolling Field Lanny phoned his wife to say that all were well and asked her to phone Robbie. Frances and the RAF captain would ride on what was called a "rubberneck wagon" and look at white marble buildings while Lanny attended to business. He called the White House and asked for the secretary; after some delay he was told that President Truman would receive him at nine that evening.

IV

It wasn't like going to F. D. R. and finding him in bed. Truman sat at his desk—he had to sign his name an average of six hundred times every twenty-four hours, he told Lanny, and constitutionally there was no way to escape it. He would sign some at night and get up at half-past five to finish; still he looked fresh—the Lord in whom he put his trust had endowed him with a tough constitution. He looked up at his agent, smiled, and held out a vigorous hand. "Well, Mr. Budd—you saw him?"

"I spent about three hours with him."

"And what did you accomplish?"

"I fear not much. I don't want to delude you or myself. I brought you some fine generalities, which may or may not preclude hostile actions. Only time can tell."

"Let me hear about it," commanded the other, and the P.A. told the long story. He was brief about what he himself had said, for Truman had already heard that. Following his notes point by point, he told everything that Stalin had said. The President interrupted only a few times, to make sure of some detail. When it was over he asked, "What do you make of it?"

"The longer I think it over," replied the messenger, "the less I know what to say. He made exactly the same protestations to me four years ago. Then he desperately needed help; now he has had the help, and his words are the same but his actions are different. I don't even know how much power he has or how much he uses. He didn't ask me to meet any of his associates, as he called them, and I don't know whether he will think it worth while to tell them what I said. I put a set of ideas into his mind, and we shall have to wait for his actions to find out if they had any effect. If you ask my advice, I'd give it in the maxim 'Trust in God, but keep your powder dry.'"

"That is a pretty depressing story," commented the President.

"As much so to me as to you," was the reply. "But we must never make the mistake of taking words for deeds. The words I spoke to him would have moved any true Socialist; if they fail to move Stalin it will be because the Soviet revolution has turned into Russian imperialism. It will mean that he respects only force, and we shall have to make it clear that we understand that language. I don't expect you to agree with me, Mr. President, that this country has got to have social ownership of its basic industries; but we can agree this far, that whatever we have, it will be what our people want and not what outsiders force upon us."

"You are right," exclaimed the ex-farm boy.

V

Laurel had stepped into the car and driven to Washington to meet the party. Three rooms in a hotel was a lot to ask, but the White House secretary arranged it. When Lanny and Laurel were alone in one of these rooms she came and sat beside him, saying with a happy smile, "I have written you a poem!"

He showed due husbandly interest, and she went on, "Not very much of a poem—only four lines! When you go on one of these long journeys I can never get away from the dreadful thought that you may never come back. I go to sleep asking myself, 'What would this world be like without him? Could I love life again, ever? Would I want to continue this struggle against evil?' Then I dream of you, and awaken in tears. All that set me to thinking about the strange thing we call memory—the reality of you in my mind. I tried to tell myself that if you were never to return"—her voice broke for a moment—"I should not have lost you; you would be with me still in the deeps of my own mind. So I comforted myself to sleep and dreamed of you, and when I came half awake, four little lines came singing themselves, and I called them 'Memory.'"

She put the paper into his hands, and he read:

> In my mind I see you yet,
> Great in dignity and grace;
> Never think I could forget
> The trusting sweetness of your face!

Lanny took her hands and held them. "Darling," he said, "you are a poet as well as a storywriter. Poets know secrets that ordinary people miss. You would always have me with you because you have created some of me in your own mind—much better than I am. Kiss me, and we'll have another pleasant memory!"

VI

In the morning they set out for Edgemere. It was Thursday, and Lanny hadn't missed a single one of the precious broadcasts. The guest of the evening was the editor of the *New Leader*, who was going to talk about the causes of depressions and by what signs you could recognize the coming of the next one in America. When they reached home Lanny would take a long walk and think up the story he wanted to tell on his part of the show.

Meantime he felt free to tell them where he had been and a little of what he had heard—under the seal of secrecy. He would tell Rick and Nina also, and Professor Alston and his father, but no one else. Frances listened, entranced; to her, Moscow was a legendary place, and Stalin a name of awe; but her wonderful father could go there and return, in less than one week! She listened to the discussions of what he had said and what the Red dictator had answered; she would listen to the radio talks, and the discussions of these—all those disturbing ideas which her mother and grandmother had tried so hard to keep from her. Being young and emotional, she would take fire and turn a violent Pink. Scrubbie, also, was of that hue, and she would fall head over heels in love with him, and marry him instead of a duke; she would agree with Lanny's ideas instead of her mother's, and so would be lost forever to Wickthorpe Castle. Who could tell, she might even get elected to Parliament some day, and rise up and answer Lady Astor— a Budd of Connecticut versus a Langhorne of Virginia!

When they reached home there were Rick and Nina, and the way they greeted their son showed the love they had in their hearts. A wonderful thing to have him here, safe and alive, after so many dangers, swooping and diving in the sky like a swallow, but many times faster, and pursued by deadly hawks! Being wise parents, they did not take long to realize what was going on in the heart of this lovely young girl. They were not worldly persons, but they were running an institution and could not be unaware of the existence of money. Having a sense of humor, they could not fail to smile over the idea of the Barnes fortune or any part of it joining the Peace Program. They would put their son to work and would take Lanny's daughter to their hearts and teach her all they could—and let Irma and Ceddy learn to like it.

VII

Here was a family group of eight persons, including Freddi Robin, and Gerald, who proceeded promptly to fall in love with Frances. She had no eyes for him, so he would have a broken heart; but he would be decent about it and drown his sorrows in work for the cause. The orders were pouring in, and the little paper was booming. After Frances had been taken up to Newcastle and had spent a few days there, meeting all her old friends and playing around—sailing boats, swimming, playing tennis, and motoring about the countryside—she suddenly decided that what she liked best was being with that exciting Peace Group, learning all about the radio business, and how to paste up the proofs of a newspaper; reading her father's fan mail and learning to answer it, and meeting all those intellectual people who came to dinner. Not forgetting, of course, that Scrubbie was there!

It made a happy family. There was Lanny Junior, going on five years, running about and getting into everything. All summer he would be in the garden, and in the winter he would be taken every morning to kindergarten. Laurel was going to have another baby, to provide a playmate for the first; also she was planning a book setting forth how democratic Socialism would work, in spite of all the hired writers who insisted it must lead to dictatorship. Free, voluntary, co-operative social ownership, such as Lanny had explained to Stalin—but, alas, Stalin hadn't seemed to learn. The Russians went right on with their tough program, their party line, called dictatorship of the proletariat, but really dictatorship *over* the proletariat.

However, somebody else had learned! That man of the people, that farm boy who had plowed a straight furrow, that prototype of all Middle Westerners—Harry S Truman had listened to what his P.A. had told him about the difference between public ownership under a dictatorship and the same under a genuine and alert democracy. The day came when the little family sat by the radio, listening to the President of the United States discussing the subject of atomic power and who was to own and control it. They heard him say, "This discovery was paid for with the people's money; it belongs to the people, and I intend to see that it is kept for the people."

When that speech was finished Laurel Creston had a light of glory in her eyes. She turned to Rick, exclaiming:

"*The shepherd speaks!*"

THE END

Appendix

Appendix A

World's End Impending

When the first volume of the Lanny Budd series, *World's End*, was accepted by the Literary Guild as its selected book for July 1940, the author was asked to prepare a statement for publication in the Guild's monthly bulletin, *Wings*. The statement is here reprinted, in this, the tenth and I hope final volume of the series. At that time the author had no idea that he had committed himself to nine additional years of hard labor; in fact, he thought that Volume One was the complete story. But the characters in it thought otherwise and insisted upon continuing.

FATE has put you and me upon the earth in one of the critical periods of human history; a dangerous time, but exciting—and certainly there has never been a time when it has been possible for the ordinary person to know so much about what is going on. The field is so enormous, the issues so crucial, that I, as a novelist, have for years been running away from them. I have said, "I am an American, and America is enough for me." So I wrote *Oil!*, dealing with one industry in my home neighborhood; and *Boston*, dealing with the Sacco-Vanzetti case; and *Co-op*, portraying the unemployed of my state and their efforts to establish self-help groups.

But all the time I was watching world events and hearing stories, and I suppose that whoever or whatever it is that works in the subconscious mind of a novelist was having his or her or its way with me; the big theme was stalking me and was bound to catch up. I saw the rise of Mussolini, and of Hitler, and of Franco; the dreadful agony of Spain wrung my heart; then I saw Munich, and said to myself, "This is the end; the end of our world."

I was walking up and down in my garden one night, and something happened; a spring was touched, a button pressed—anyhow, a novel came rolling into the field of my mental vision; a whole series of events, with the emotions that accompanied them, a string of characters, good and bad, old and young, rich and poor. I have had that happen to me before, but never with such force, such mass and persistence. There was no resisting it, and I didn't try. I spent the next thirty-six hours in a state of absorption. I slept little, but lay in bed and "saw" that theme; I ate little and talked little—I have a kind and long-suffering wife, and when I tell her what is happening to me she lets it happen. I trod the garden path hard under my feet, and filled sheets of paper with notes of characters, places, events—the whole panorama of *World's End*. Ultimately I had nearly a hundred typewritten pages of notes, a small book in themselves.

I am one of the fortunate ones in this land of ours. I live where the sun shines most all of most days, and in the morning I can take my typewriter out into the garden. I can wear a pair of bathing trunks and a white canvas hat while I walk up and down behind jasmine and rose hedges with the people of my books as they live their adventures and say their say. I suppose a psychologist would describe what goes on in the mind of a novelist as controlled multiple personality. These imaginary persons are more real to me than the people I meet in the outside world, for the latter keep me guessing, whereas the former are my grown-up children; they do what they please, and while they often take me by surprise, I am able to understand them instantly.

In a historical novel like *World's End* I cannot, of course, leave everything to my imaginary characters. I have to spend a part of my day reading books to refresh their memory as to places and events. In the evening, propped up in bed, I revise the morning's manuscript, or stroll in the garden and invite the next chapter to unroll itself. This, I take it, is the ideal life for the writer. Sticking to it, day in and day out, rarely seeing anybody or going anywhere, I can produce a thousand words a day, and at the end of a full year I have a thousand pages. It is the hardest kind of work, yet also the most delightful play. The end and goal of it all is you, the reader, and the day when you sit down and open the new book, my heart is in my mouth.

The scene of *World's End* is Europe, with a visit to New England and New York. The time is 1913 to 1919. I lived in England, Holland, Germany, France, and Italy during 1912 and 1913, and naturally my thoughts were there during the warmaking and the peacemaking. Also, the records are voluminous. For *World's End* I must have read a hundred books and consulted several times as many.

I could not write a novel about Europeans, except as subordinate characters. Most of the people in *World's End* are Americans living in Europe; I have known many of these, and new ones come calling and refresh my memory. If there was a place I wanted to know about, I could find someone who had been there; if there was an event I had to describe, I could find someone who had witnessed it. First and last I must have written several hundred letters and asked a thousand questions.

Of course there will be some slips, as I know from experience; but *World's End* is meant to be history as well as fiction, and I am sure there are no mistakes of importance. I have my own point of view, but I have tried to play fair in this book. There is a varied cast of characters and they say what they think.

Some of them are real persons, living or dead. George Bernard Shaw stood with me and my family on the "bright meadow," with the sunshine glinting in his whiskers as I have described him—or rather, to be exact, the description is my wife's. We were as happy as children at that "Dalcroze" festival—although I knew that the war was coming and took my son out of school in Germany for that reason. In the opening pages of *World's End* as I wrote them originally, there was more about the *Orpheus* dancing, but some of my friends persuaded me that a descent into hell was a misleading opening for a realistic novel. Whether they were right I shall never be sure.

Isadora Duncan I met in her prime, when she carried her magic with her into everyday life. Anatole France and Rodin I never met, but the records concerning them are detailed. Zaharoff was known to friends of mine, and the stories they tell about him are even stranger than the ones I have used in *World's End*. Woodrow Wilson I once watched in action. George D. Herron and Lincoln Steffens were among my oldest friends, and their widows have checked me on various details.

The Peace Conference of Paris, which is the scene of the last third of *World's End*, is of course one of the great events of all time. A friend of mine asked an authority on modern fiction the question: "Has anybody ever used the Peace Conference in a novel?" And the reply was: "Could anybody?" Well, I thought somebody could, and now I think somebody has. The reader will ask, and I state explicitly that so far as concerns historic characters and events my picture is correct in all details. This part of the manuscript, 374 pages, was read and checked by eight or ten gentlemen who were on the American staff at the Conference. Several of these now hold important positions in the world of troubled international affairs; others are college presidents and professors, and I promised them all that their letters would be confidential. Suffice it to say that the errors they pointed out were corrected, and where they disagreed, both sides have a word in the book.

The story of the German secret agent in Paris and the love story which is woven through these scenes are of course fictional. But I knew of a story not so different—*amor inter arma;* and it happens that an old friend of mine had much the same experience with the Paris police as befalls my hero. The glimpses of world revolution and its makers which I give you are from firsthand knowledge, for many of these men and women have been my friends since youth; they know that I respect their sincerity even when I do not agree with their tactics. This may sound suspicious to the House Committee on Un-American Activities, but it is useful to a novelist.

Now this offering of my spirit has been brought to maturity and goes out to you, my fellow citizens of a world on fire. John Milton wrote, with no false modesty: "A good book is the precious life-blood of a master-spirit, embalmed and treasured up on purpose to a life beyond life." I make no such claim for *World's End*, but I can say that I have put into it the best spirit I have; also whatever of knowledge of the human heart, of the world we live in, and of the future we are helping to make. Will it be the good life for which the saints have pleaded, or the "World's End," by fire and sword, which the prophet Isaiah predicted more than twenty-five centuries ago?

The above was written in 1940. Since then there have been nine years of continuous hard work, and nine more large volumes, which have been or are being translated and published in twenty-one foreign lands. They have received some adverse criticism, and cordial praise from such contemporaries as Gandhi, G. B. Shaw, H. G. Wells, Thomas Mann, Albert Einstein, and Theodore Dreiser. They have given pleasure and instruction to millions of people, and have brought thousands of letters of friendship and thanks. While these words are being typed, there comes a report from the small islands of Japan that the books are being advertised there on billboards and in streetcars, and that in three months the sales of *Dragon's Teeth* have almost equaled those in the United States in seven years. To some highbrow critics I repeat a challenge which I have issued several times before: name an American writer who achieved world fame during his lifetime and whose reputation has not held up since his death. That challenge has never been taken up.

The critics really do not matter; they are a small group which writes for a small audience. The reading masses have found interest plus information in the Lanny Budd books, and I tell them that they may trust the information, for I have done everything in my power to get the facts exactly right. A few errors of petty detail have been pointed out and corrected, but no critic or historian has ever pointed out a serious error in these books.

BOOKS BY UPTON SINCLAIR

ONE CLEAR CALL
PRESIDENTIAL MISSION
A WORLD TO WIN
DRAGON HARVEST
PRESIDENTIAL AGENT
WIDE IS THE GATE
DRAGON'S TEETH
BETWEEN TWO WORLDS
WORLD'S END
EXPECT NO PEACE
YOUR MILLION DOLLARS
LITTLE STEEL
OUR LADY
THE FLIVVER KING
NO PASARAN!
THE GNOMOBILE
CO-OP: A NOVEL OF LIVING TOGETHER
WHAT GOD MEANS TO ME: AN ATTEMPT AT A WORKING RELIGION
I, CANDIDATE FOR GOVERNOR AND HOW I GOT LICKED
THE EPIC PLAN FOR CALIFORNIA
I, GOVERNOR OF CALIFORNIA
THE WAY OUT: WHAT LIES AHEAD FOR AMERICA
UPTON SINCLAIR PRESENTS WILLIAM FOX
AMERICAN OUTPOST: AUTOBIOGRAPHY
THE WET PARADE
ROMAN HOLIDAY
MENTAL RADIO
MOUNTAIN CITY
BOSTON

MONEY WRITES!
OIL!
THE SPOKESMAN'S SECRETARY
LETTERS TO JUDD
MAMMONART
THE GOSLINGS—A STUDY OF AMERICAN SCHOOLS
THE GOOSE-STEP—A STUDY OF AMERICAN EDUCATION
THE BOOK OF LIFE
THEY CALL ME CARPENTER
100%—THE STORY OF A PATRIOT
THE BRASS CHECK
JIMMIE HIGGINS
KING COAL, A NOVEL OF THE COLORADO COAL STRIKE
THE PROFITS OF RELIGION
THE CRY FOR JUSTICE
DAMAGED GOODS
SYLVIA'S MARRIAGE
SYLVIA
LOVE'S PILGRIMAGE
THE FASTING CURE
SAMUEL, THE SEEKER
THE MONEYCHANGERS
THE METROPOLIS
THE MILLENNIUM
THE OVERMAN
THE JUNGLE
MANASSAS, A NOVEL OF THE CIVIL WAR
THE JOURNAL OF ARTHUR STIRLING

Plays

PRINCE HAGEN
THE NATUREWOMAN
THE SECOND STORY MAN
THE MACHINE
THE POT-BOILER
HELL

SINGING JAILBIRDS
BILL PORTER
OIL! (DRAMATIZATION)
DEPRESSION ISLAND
MARIE ANTOINETTE

CONCERNING THE CIRCULATION OF
THE *WORLD'S END* SERIES

In the following record the volumes of the series are indicated by their number in order of publication:

Vol. I	World's End	1940	Vol. VI	Dragon Harvest	1945
Vol. II	Between Two Worlds	1941	Vol. VII	A World to Win	1946
Vol. III	Dragon's Teeth	1942	Vol. VIII	Presidential Mission	1947
Vol. IV	Wide Is the Gate	1943	Vol. IX	One Clear Call	1948
Vol. V	Presidential Agent	1944	Vol. X	O Shepherd, Speak!	1949

In the United States the totals to April 30, 1949, including book-club editions, is as follows:

Vol. I, 180,349
Vol. II, 49,416
Vol. III, 56,732
Vol. IV, 54,155
Vol. V, 69,982

Vol. VI, 138,294
Vol. VII, 732,605
Vol. VIII, 39,242
Vol. IX, 29,308

In England the publishers, Werner Laurie, Ltd., report the following:

Vol. I, 33,490
Vol. II, 32,854
Vol. III, 46,304
Vol. IV, 39,260
Vol. V, 37,125

Vol. VI, 38,619
Vol. VII, 31,242
Vol. VIII, 18,512
Vol. IX, 30,000 (first printing)

All paper obtainable was used in printing these books, and editions were sold out in a month or so. Foyle's Book Club offered to take 140,000 copies of Vol. II, but paper was not obtainable.

Other countries are listed in alphabetical order:

ARGENTINA   Editorial Claridad, Buenos Aires. Vol. I, *El fin del mundo*, 6000; Vol. II, 3000; Vol. III, 3000; Vol. IV, 3000; Vol. V in preparation.

BELGIUM   Editions de la Paix, Brussels: entire series contracted for.
(*French language*)   Vol. I, *Fin d'un monde*, 11,187; Vol. II, *Entre deux mondes*, to be published in 1949.

BRAZIL   Cruzeiro, Rio de Janeiro. Vols. I to IV published; V and VI in preparation.

BULGARIA   "Haemus," Sofia: entire series contracted for.

CZECHOSLOVAKIA   Lincolns-Prager, London: entire series contracted for. Vol. I, *Konec Svĕta*, Part I, 13,000, Part II, 10,000; Vol. II, *Mezi dvĕma svĕty*, 10,000; Vol. III, *Dračí zuby*, 6964; Vol. IV, 10,000; Vol. V, 5000; Vols. VI and IX in preparation.

DENMARK   Thaning and Appel, Copenhagen: entire series contracted for. Vol. I, *En Verden gik under*, 8000; Vol. II, *Mellem to Verdener*, 5000; Vol. III, 5000.

FINLAND   Painopavelu, Helsingfors: entire series contracted for.

HOLLAND   N. V. Servire, The Hague: entire series contracted for. Vol. I, *Einde van een Wereld;* Vol. II, *Tussen Twee Werelden;* Vol. III, *Drakentanden;* Vol. IV in preparation.

HUNGARY   Lincolns-Prager, London: entire series contracted for. Vol. I, 1000 reissued; Vol. II, 1000 reissued; Vol. III, *A sárkány fogai,* 4800; Vol. IV, *Tág a kapu,* 1700; Vol. V, *Az Elnök ügynöke,* 1500; Vol. VI, 2100; Vol. VII in preparation.

INDIA
(*Tamil*)   S. Shanmugan, Terunelveli: entire series contracted for.
(*Hindi*)   B. K. Koul: entire series contracted for.
(*Bengali*)   Suddhodhan Sen, Calcutta. Vol. III.

ISRAEL   Ideal Publishing Co., Tel-Aviv: entire series contracted for.

ITALY   Mondadori, Milan: entire series contracted for. Vols. I and II to be published in 1949.

JAPAN   Ryo Namikawa, Tokyo: entire series contracted for, by permission of the U.S. Army. Vol. III, 45,000; Vol. VII, 30,000.

NORWAY   Aschehoug, Oslo: entire series contracted for. Vol. I, *En verden gar under,* 4000; Vol. II, *Mellom to verdener,* will be ready from printing office in May 1949; Vol. III, now translated into Norwegian.

POLAND   Roj Publishers, Warsaw: entire series contracted for. Vols. III and IV to be published at end of 1948.

RUMANIA   Cultura Nationala, Bucharest. Vol. VI, *Balaural;* Vol. VII in preparation.

SLOVAKIA   Pravda, Bratislava: entire series contracted for.

SWEDEN   Tiden, Stockholm. Vol. I, *De Sådde Vind;* Vol. II, *Mellan Twå Världar;* Vol. III, *Drakens Tänder;* Vol. IV, *Förtappelsens Väg;* Vol. V, *Presidentens Agent;* Vol. VI, *Drakskörd.* Vols. VII and VIII in preparation.

SWITZERLAND
(*German language*)   Alfred Scherz, Bern. Vol. I, *Welt-Ende,* 12,600; Vol. II, *Zwischen Zwei Welten,* 9000; Vol. III, *Drachenzähne,* 10,000; Vol. IV, *Weit ist das Tor,* 9000; Vol. V, *Agent des Präsidenten,* 4401 (sold in three months); Vol. VI, *Teufelsernte,* in preparation.

U.S.S.R.   Goslitisdat, Moscow: condensations of first five volumes published.

Index to the *World's End* Series

Index to the World's End *Series*

This index has been prepared to oblige readers who wish to look up particular characters or incidents in the Lanny Budd story. Casual mentions have not been listed. Episodes have been indicated only by the page on which they begin. Roman numerals indicate: I, *World's End;* II, *Between Two Worlds;* III, *Dragon's Teeth;* IV, *Wide Is the Gate;* V, *Presidential Agent;* VI, *Dragon Harvest;* VII, *A World to Win;* VIII, *Presidential Mission;* IX, *One Clear Call;* X, *O Shepherd, Speak.* Included are titles of chapters, set in capitals and small capitals, and of the various "books," set in capitals. The name of Lanny Budd has not been indexed.

The author hopes that nobody will read the index instead of reading the books.